COLLECTED
STORIES

COLLECTED STORIES

BY

LEWIS SHINER

SUBTERRANEAN PRESS 2009

Interior design by Lewis Shiner
Set in Bembo

First edition

ISBN 978-1-59606-252-8

Subterranean Press
P.O. Box 190106
Burton, MI 48519

www.subterraneanpress.com
www.lewisshiner.com

For Richard Butner

My first line of defense.

CONTENTS

INTRODUCTION

BY KAREN JOY FOWLER

I MEET A LOT of people these days who tell me they don't read fiction. Sometimes they don't read books at all, but more often they love books—they read history, adventure stories that really happened, political and economic works, biography, and memoir—but they don't want to waste their time on things someone has simply made up. They want, they tell me, to read about the real world.

The Bush administration is finally coming to its end. Among its many, many Orwellian contributions to the real world are:

- The Patriot Act, which has opened the possibility of American citizens arrested for violations of secret regulations whose content, even in court, they aren't permitted to know.
- The re-naming of suicide attempts while in US custody as "self-injurious behavior incidents," along with the re-classification of such attempts as an attack on the US military
- The argument that every inch of American soil is now a battlefield where courts should not second-guess the battlefield decisions of the president
- The re-naming of torture as "inhumane debriefings."

In the real world, as I write this, we are coming up on the 2008 US election. John McCain, the Republican Party candidate, has actually said that Sarah Palin, his pick for vice president, has foreign policy experience by virtue of living in Alaska, because Alaska is close to Russia on the map. I live by the ocean. It's almost like having gills.

In the real world, there is a puzzling array of things we all know to be true, but aren't supposed to say, or know to be false, but must pretend to believe.

We are not supposed to say that the ghastly attacks of 9/11 were in any way a response to our foreign policies. We are not supposed to say that our soldiers ever behave badly. Even those very soldiers, the ones who have behaved badly, are not supposed to come back home and tell us about it.

We must pretend to believe, as we rocket from war to war, that we are a peace-loving people. We live in the country God loves best above all countries. We must pretend to believe that we are hated for our freedoms.

In short, the real world is full of lies and doublespeak and it is making you crazy. We're all a bit crazy here. You will find more true things in the made-up stories of Lewis Shiner than you will in the real world of newspapers and newscasts.

IF I WERE ASKED what I admire most in this collection, if I had to choose only one word to describe this work, the word I would choose is honest. A Shiner protagonist is most often someone who is searching for the truth. A Shiner story will always insist on the hard truth over the comforting lie.

But fortunately, I get many more words here than just the one. Although I had read many of these stories in their earlier publications, I found enormous pleasure in reading them again. They are intimate stories, thoughtful, political, emotional, and imaginative. I myself have a fondness for historical pieces. When a collection of stories features Glenn Miller, Amadeus Mozart, Che Guevara, Nikola Tesla, and Jean Lafitte, you will hear no complaint from me.

I particularly admire the variety. Shiner is conversant with, comfortable in, and respectful of many traditions—included here are several stories that would be classified as realism. In addition, there are westerns like "The Long Ride Out," mysteries like "Deep Without Pity" and "The Killing Season," horror like "The Circle," and one piece, "Mark the Bunny," that would be socialist realism if Aesop had created the world. Most though are clearly or at least arguably science fiction. There are stories that work through cleverness and invention, like "The Lizard Men of Los Angeles" and "Sitcom." There are deceptively simple stories like the profoundly affecting "Flagstaff." Music is a recurring element and to see Shiner improvising, changing tone and tempo and generally mixing things up, is an additional pleasure.

There is a strong showing of Shiner's most famous stories—"The War at Home," "Love in Vain," "White City," "Jeff Beck," "Mozart in Mirrorshades," and "Perfidia." But the newest story in this collection, "The Death of Che Guevara" is already among my personal favorites.

With a few exceptions (see variety) Shiner doesn't work through dazzle, diversion, or sleight of hand. His prose is a model of clarity. When you come to the end of a story, you know what happened; you know how Shiner feels about it. The power seldom arises in trick and technique, but is located instead in voice and conviction. He is not the sort of writer who keeps an ironic distance. His work is more the heartfelt sort.

The gravitational center is a feeling of longing; no writer evokes this more or more powerfully. The Shiner protagonist is often a man for whom things have not panned out. This man longs for connection. He longs for a future he won't find, for a past he didn't have. For all of his science fictional roots, Shiner's gaze is usually to the past. But how he can create such a powerful nostalgia for a different time and place, while never once pretending that things went any better then and there than they are going here and now, is something I haven't yet figured out.

The Shiner protagonist most likely won't get what he wants. Or he will and it won't be what he wanted after all. The emotional world of these stories feels very like the real world to me.

BY THE TIME you read this collection, the election will be over. We are in a happier place! We don't even remember who Sarah Palin is. We associate her vaguely with machinations; we think maybe we saw her on one of the early seasons of *Survivor*.

Even here, though, even in this happier place, I know one thing for sure. Wherever we are, there is still reason for hope and there is still cause for despair. I am balanced pretty evenly just now between the two, but the hope is an amorphous, inarticulate sort while the despair is pretty specific. I'm afraid that I won't get what I hope for. Or that I will and it won't be what I wanted after all.

Reading these stories was good for me. The real world was driving me crazy with its degraded language of Orwellian dodge and all I wanted was something true. They will be good for you, too. Not good like cod-liver oil. These stories will be good for you like fresh air. Like music.

Karen Joy Fowler
October 16, 2008

PERFIDIA

"T HAT'S GLENN MILLER," my father said. "But it can't be."
He had the back of the hospital bed cranked upright, the lower
lid of his left eye creeping up in a warning signal I'd learned to recognize as a
child. My older sister Ann had settled deep in the recliner, and she glared at me
too, blaming me for winding him up. The jam box sat on the rolling tray table, and
my father was working the remote as he talked, backing up my newly burned CD
and letting it spin forward to play a few seconds of low fidelity trombone solo.

"You know the tune, of course," he said.

"'King Porter Stomp.'" Those childhood years of listening to him play
Glenn Miller on the console phonograph were finally paying off.

"He muffed the notes the same way on the Victor version."

"So why can't it be Miller?" I asked.

"He wouldn't have played with a rabble like that." The backup musicians
teetered on the edge of chaos, playing with an abandon somewhere between
Dixieland and bebop. "They sound drunk."

My father had a major emotional investment in Miller. He and my mother
had danced to the Miller band at Glen Island Casino on Long Island Sound in
the summer of 1942, when they were both 16. That signature sound of clarinet
and four saxes was forever tied up for him with first love and the early, idealis-
tic months of the war.

But there was a better reason why it couldn't have been Miller playing that
solo. If the date on the original recording was correct, he was supposed to have
died three days earlier.

THE DATE WAS in India ink on a piece of surgical tape, stuck to the top of a
spool of recording wire. The handwritten numerals had the hooks and day-
first order of Europe: 18/12/44. I'd won it on eBay the week before as part of
a lot that included a wire recorder and a stack of 78s by French pop stars like
Charles Trenent and Edith Piaf.

It had taken me two full days to transfer the contents of the spool to my
computer, and I'd brought the results to my father to confirm what I didn't
quite dare to hope—that I'd made a Big Score, the kind of find that becomes
legend in the world of collectors, like the first edition *Huck Finn* at the yard
sale, the Rembrandt under the nineteenth century landscape.

On my Web site I've got everything from an Apollo player piano to a 1930s Philco radio to an original Wurlitzer Model 1015 jukebox, all meticulously restored. During the Internet boom I was shipping my top dollar items to instant Silicon Valley millionaires as fast as I could find them and clean them up, with three full-time employees doing the refurbishing in a rented warehouse. For the last year I'd been back in my own garage, spending more time behind a browser than trolling the flea markets and thrift stores where the long shots lived, and I wanted to be back on top. It wasn't just the freedom and the financial security, it was the thrill of the chase and the sense of doing something important, rescuing valuable pieces of history.

Or, in this case, rewriting history.

ON THE CD, the song broke down. After some shifting of chairs and unintelligible bickering in what sounded like French, the band stumbled into a ragged version of "Perfidia," the great ballad of faithless love. It had been my mother's favorite song.

My father's eyes showed confusion and the beginnings of anger. "Where did you get this?"

"At an auction. What's wrong?"

"Everything." The stroke had left him with a slurping quality to his speech, and his right hand lay at what should have been an uncomfortable angle on the bedclothes. The world hadn't been making much sense for him for the last eight months, starting with the sudden onset of diabetes at age 76. With increasing helplessness and alarm, he'd watched his body forsake him at every turn: a broken hip, phlebitis, periodontal disease, and now the stroke, as if the warranty had run out and everything was breaking down at once. Things he'd done for himself for the five years since my mother's death suddenly seemed beyond him—washing dishes, changing the bed, even buying groceries. He could spend hours walking the aisles, reading the ingredients on a can of hominy, comparing the fractions of a pound that separated one package of ground meat from another, overwhelmed by details that had once meant something.

"Who are these people? Why are they playing this way?"

"I don't know," I told him. "But I intend to find out. Listen."

On the CD there was a shout from the audience and then something that could have been a crack from the snare drum or a gunshot. The band trailed off, and that was where it ended, with more shouts, the sound of furniture crashing and glass breaking, and then silence.

"Turn it off," my father said, though it was already over. I took the CD out and moved the boom box back to windowsill. "It's some kind of fake," he finally said, more to himself than me. "They could take his solo off another recording and put a new background to it."

"It came off a wire recorder. I didn't pay enough for it to justify that kind of trouble. Look, I'm going to track this down."

"You do that. I want to know what kind of psycho would concoct something like this." He waved his left hand vaguely. "I'm tired. You two go home." It was nine at night; I could see the lights of downtown Durham through the window. I'd been so focused on the recording that I'd lost all sense of time.

Ann bent down to kiss him and said, "I'll be right outside if you need me."

"I'll be fine. Go get something to eat. Or go to the motel and sleep, for God's sake." My father had come to North Carolina for the VA hospital at Duke, and Ann had flown in from Connecticut to be with him. I'd offered her my guest room, 25 miles away in Raleigh, but she'd insisted on being walking distance from the hospital.

In the hallway, her rage boiled over. "What was the point of that?" she hissed.

"That's the most involved I've seen him since the stroke. I think it was good for him."

"Well, I don't. And you could at least have consulted me first." Ann's height and big bones had opened her to ridicule in grade school, and for as long as I could remember she'd been contained, slightly hunched, given to whispers instead of shouts.

"Do you really need to control my conversations with him now?"

"Apparently. And don't make this about me. This is about him getting better."

"I want that too."

"But I'm the one who's here with him, day in and day out."

It was easy to see where this was headed, back to our mother again. "I've got to go," I said. She accepted my hug stiffly. "You should take his advice and get some rest."

"I'll think about it," she said, but as the elevator doors closed, I could see her in the lounge two doors down from his room, staring at the floor in front of her.

I HAD EMAIL from the seller waiting at home. Her initial response when I'd written her about the recorder had been wary. I'd labored hard over the next message, offering her ten percent of anything I made off the deal, up to a thousand dollars, at the same time lowballing the odds of actually selling it, and all the while working on her guilt—with no provenance, the items were virtually worthless to me.

She'd gone for it, admitting picking everything up together at one stall in the Marché Vernaison, part of the vast warren of flea markets at Saint-Ouen, on the northern edge of Paris. She wasn't sure which one, but she remembered an older man with long, graying hair, a worn carpet on a dirt floor, a lot of Mickey Mouse clocks.

I knew the Vernaison because one of my competitors operated a high-end stall there, a woman who called herself Madame B. The description of the old man's place didn't ring any bells for me, but the mere mention of that district of Paris made my palms sweat.

My business gave me an excuse to read up on music history. I already knew a fair amount about Miller's death, and I'd gone back to my bookshelves the night before. Miller allegedly took off from the Twinwood Farm airfield, north of London, on Friday, December 15, 1944. He was supposed to be en route to Paris to arrange a series of concerts by his Army Air Force Band, but the plane never arrived. Of the half dozen or more legends that dispute the official account, the most persistent has him flying over on the day before, and being fatally injured on the 18th in a brawl in the red light district of Pigalle. Pigalle was a short taxi ride from the Hotel des Olympiades, where the band had been scheduled to stay, and the Hotel des Olympiades was itself only a short walk from the Marché Vernaison.

I walked out to the garage and looked at the wire recorder where it sat on a bench, its case removed, its lovely oversized vacuum tubes visible from the side. I'd recognized it in the eBay photos as an Armour Model 50, manufactured by GE for the US Army and Navy, though I'd never seen one firsthand before. The face was smaller than an LP cover, tilted away to almost meet the line of the back. Two reels mounted toward the top each measured 4 inches in diameter and 1 inch thick, wound with steel wire the thickness of a human hair. More than anything else it reminded me of the Bell & Howell 8mm movie projector that my father had tortured us with as children, showing captive audiences of dinner guests his home movies featuring Ann and me as children and my mother in the radiant beauty of her thirties.

The wire recorder hadn't been working when it arrived, but I'd been lucky. Blowing a half century's worth of dust off the electronics with an air gun, I'd found the broken bit of wire that had fallen into the works and caused a short. That and replacing a burnt-out power tube from my extensive stock of spare parts was all it had taken—apart from cleaning the wire itself.

The trick was to remove the corrosion without affecting the magnetic properties of the metal. I'd spent eight hours running the wire through a folded nylon scrub pad soaked in WD40, letting the machine's bailers wind the wire evenly back on the reel, stopping now and then to confirm there was still something there. Then I'd jury-rigged a bypass from the built-in speaker, through a preamp and into an eighth-inch jack that I could plug into my laptop. With excruciating care, I'd played it into a .wav file and worked on the results with CoolEdit Pro for another hour, trying to control the trembling in my hands as I began to realize what I had.

WHEN I GOT to the hospital in the morning, my father was reading the newspaper. Ann was still in the same clothes I'd last seen her in; she'd already had circles under her eyes, so it was hard to say if they were deeper. "You're here early," she said, with a smile that failed to cover the implied criticism.

"I'm on a plane to Paris tonight."

"Oh really?"

"You going to find out about that tape?" my father asked.

"That's the idea. My travel agent found me a cheap cancellation."

"How lucky for you," Ann said.

"This is business, Ann." I stifled my reflex irritation. "That recording could be worth a fortune."

"Of course it could," she said.

"Don't give those French any more of your money than you have to," my father said.

"Oh, Pop," I said. "Don't start."

"We had to bail their sorry country out in World War II, and now—"

"No politics," Ann said. "I absolutely forbid it."

I sat on the edge of the bed next to him. "You're not going to die on me, are you, Pop? At least not until I get back?"

"What makes you so special that I should wait for you?"

"Because you want to see how this turns out."

"I already know it's a fake. But there is the pleasure of saying I told you so. You'd think I'd get tired of it after all these years, but it's like fine wine."

I leaned over to hug him, and his left arm went around my back with surprising power. He had two days' growth of beard and the starchy smell of hospital soap. "I'm serious," I said. "I want you to take care of yourself."

"Yeah, yeah. If you bag one of those French girls, ask if her mom remembers me."

"I thought you were only in Germany." His unit had liberated Dachau, but he never talked about it, or any other part of the war.

"I got around," he shrugged. His left arm relaxed, and I pulled away. "Don't take any wooden Euros."

Ann followed me out, as I knew she would. "He'll be dead by the time you get back. Just like—"

"I know, I know. Just like Mom. It's less than a week. He'll be all right."

"No, he won't." She was crying.

"Sleep, Ann. You really need to get some sleep."

I MYSELF SLEPT FITFULLY on the way over, too cramped to relax, too
tired to read, but my spirits lifted as soon as I was on the RER from DeGaulle
to the city. There was no mistaking the drizzly gray October world outside
the train for the US, despite billboards featuring Speedy Gonzales, Marilyn,
Disneyland, *Dawson's Creek*. The tiny hybrid cars, the flowerboxes in the
windows, even the boxy, Bauhaus-gone-wrong blocks of flats insisted that
excess was not the only way to live. It was a lesson that my country was not
interested in learning.

I'd been able to get a room at my usual hotel, a small family place in the
XVIIth Arrondisement, a short walk from the Metro hub at Place de Clichy
and a slightly longer one from Montmartre and Pigalle. I stopped at the
market across the street to pick up some fresh fruit and exchanged pleasantries with the clerk, who remembered me from my previous trip. The hotelier
remembered me as well, and found me a room that opened onto the airshaft
rather than the noise of the street.

The bed nearly filled the tiny room, and it called to me as soon as the door
closed. If I stayed awake until ten or eleven that night I knew my biological
clock would reset itself, so I forced myself to unpack, drink a little juice, and
wash my face.

"Hey, ho," I said to the mirror. "Let's go."

The number 4 Metro line ended at Porte de Clingancourt, the closest
stop to the markets. I walked up into a gentle rain and a crowd of foot traffic,
mostly male, mostly black and/or Middle Eastern, dressed in jeans, sneakers,
and leather jackets, all carrying cell phones, talking fast and walking hard.

I headed north on the Avenue de la Porte de Clingancourt, and the vendors
started within a couple of blocks. These were temporary stalls, made of canvas
and aluminum pipe, selling mostly new merchandise: Indian shawls, African
masks, tools, jeans, batteries, shoes. Still, it was like distant music, an invocation
of the possibilities ahead.

I passed under the Boulevard Peripherique, the highway that circles the entire city, and the small village of flea markets opened up on my left, surrounded by gridlocked cars and knots of pedestrians. The stalls here were permanent,
brick or cinderblock single-story buildings with roll-down metal garage doors
instead of front walls, and they were crammed with battered furniture, clothes,
books, and jewelry. Deeper inside, in the high-end markets like the Dauphine
and the Serpette, the stalls would have glass doors, oriental rugs, antique desks,
and chandeliers.

I walked north another block, then turned left into the Rue de Rossiers, the main street of the district. A discreet metal archway halfway down the block marked the entrance to the Marché Vernaison in white Deco letters against a blue background. Twisting lanes, open to the rain, wove through a couple of hundred stalls, some elaborate showplaces, like my friend Madame B's, some dusty, oversized closets piled with junk. As in any collector's market, the dealers were each other's best customers; I watched a man in a wide polyester tie and a bad toupee hurry past with a short wooden column in each hand and a look of poorly concealed triumph on his face.

Madame B's emporium was in the center of the market, a corner stall with sliding glass doors, pale walls, and a thick, sand-colored carpet to show off the filigreed wood cabinets of the Victrolas that were her specialty. She was talking to an official-looking man in a suit and black raincoat, so I stayed outside and admired a beautiful nineteenth century puppet theater until he was gone.

"*Bonjour,* François," she said, almost singing the words, and I looked up to see her in the doorway. She was somewhere in her 50s, a little older than me. She kept her black hair trimmed to shoulder length, with severe black bangs that matched her black-framed glasses, long black vintage dresses, and black cigarette holder.

"Problems?" I asked, nodding toward the man in the raincoat.

She shook her head and offered her hand, palm down. "What a lovely surprise to see you. You are buying today, or just looking?" She talked to me mostly in English, and I answered as best I could in French.

"Looking for a person." I showed her the photos of the wire recorder while we exchanged a few pleasantries. Her business was doing as badly as mine—no one had any money, and thanks to September 11 and the war in Iraq, US tourists had all but disappeared.

Eventually she pointed a long, red fingernail at one of the photos. "And this item," she said, falling into eBay slang like so many in the business, "it is not one of mine."

"They tell me it comes from somewhere in the Vernaison. An older man, perhaps, with long gray hair?"

"It is familiar, I think. When I see it I am interested, but it is maybe a little pricey. I go away for a day hoping the man will come to his senses, *et voilà,* the next day it is gone."

"You remember who it was?"

"I think maybe Philippe over in Row 9? Let us look."

She locked up and set a brisk pace through the rain, ignoring it, as most of the locals seemed to do. There were only nine rows in the market, running more or less north and south, but I still had trouble remembering where specific vendors were, and more than once had gotten badly turned around.

Row 9 was the slum of the Marché Vernaison, where old and broken things came to their last resting place before the landfill. I had to wonder how some of these vendors paid for their stalls, what pleasure they found in sitting all weekend amid a clutter of useless and ugly objects, their glazed eyes not even registering the few customers who hurried past.

At the bend where Row 9 curved east and emptied into the market's café, a man in his sixties sat with his eyes closed, listening to a scratchy LP on a portable phonograph much like the one I'd had in high school. He had long graying hair, aviator-style glasses, a checked flannel shirt, and an ascot. The booth matched the description the eBay seller had given me, down to the worn carpet and the Mickey Mouse memorabilia. There was some electronic gear as well: a cheap reel-to-reel deck from the early sixties, walkie-talkies, an analog oscilloscope, a pocket transistor radio.

"*Bonjour,* Philippe," Madame B sang again. He gave no indication that he'd heard. "This is my friend François," she said in French, "and he wants to know about something you might have sold."

"To a woman from the United States," I said, laying the photos out on his nearly empty desk.

Philippe seemed to live at a completely different pace from Madame B. He slowly picked up each photo and stared at it, as if searching for something in it that might cheer him up.

"It's a recording device," I said, hoping to hurry him. "It records on a spool of wire." I didn't know the French name for it.

"I must get back to my shop," Madame B said. "Good luck with your quest."

I kissed her on both cheeks, and as she rushed out she seemed to take the last of the room's energy with her. Philippe eventually sighed, set the last photo down, and gave an elaborate shrug.

"So," I said, struggling for patience, "this was perhaps yours?"

"Perhaps." His voice was barely audible over the music.

"I'm not with the authorities," I said, thinking of the man in the black raincoat. "I don't care whether you pay your taxes or how you do your accounts. I just want to know where this came from. I'm a dealer, like you, and it would help me very much to have the provenance. Is that the right word? *Provenance?*"

He nodded slowly. "Many things come and go from here. It is difficult to keep track of all of them."

"But this is very unusual, *non?* I think you have not had many like it."

He shrugged again. It felt like we'd come to a stalemate, and I looked around his stall for a couple of minutes, trying on a pair of sunglasses, paging through the postcards, trying to think of a way to reach him.

"You like Jacques Brel, yes?" I pointed to the record player.

"Of course. You know of him?"

"A little. I like that he quit performing when he got tired of it. And that he didn't want to play in the US because of Vietnam."

"You are American, or English?"

The implied compliment was that I hadn't immediately given myself away. "American," I said, "but not proud of it these days."

He nodded. "You have another Vietnam now, I think." He pointed to the record player. "You know this record?"

I'd recognized the voice, but nothing more, and risked the truth. "No," I said.

"You wouldn't. It was his first, only out in France."

"Do you have the radio broadcasts from 1953?"

"I have them. They are interesting, but they are on CD. The CDs are too cold, I think."

I myself didn't understand why having pops and hiss made a recording more desirable, but I also understood that plenty of others disagreed. "They are also on LP, a—what's the word?—'bootleg' in English."

"We say 'bootleg' too. You have this record? I have never heard of it."

"I have a friend who does. If you give me your address, it would be my pleasure to send it to you."

"Why?" The question wasn't hostile, but the skepticism surprised me. "Is it because of this information you want?"

"Because it would mean more to you than it does to the person who has it. And this person owes me a favor. It is a small thing."

He was quiet for a moment, and then he pointed to the record player and said, "Listen." On the record Brel was suddenly angry, spitting words in a theatrical fury. It didn't touch me, particularly, but I could see Philippe was moved.

When the song was over, he said, "I have been listening to this record for more than thirty-five years now. It is still incredible to me to hear a man be so ... plain and direct with his emotions."

"Yes," I said. "I know exactly what you mean."

He took a yellow wooden pencil from a can on his desk, looked it over, then used a thumb-sized sharpener to put an exact point on it. On a blank index card from a wooden box, he wrote his name and address in an ornate longhand, then tapped the card on its edge as if to get rid of any stray graphite before handing it to me.

"*Enchanté,*" I said, reading it, and offered my hand. "My name is Frank. Frank Delacorte."

He gave me a firm handshake. "Come back on Monday, in the afternoon. I will find out what I can."

IT WAS ALREADY getting dark when I came out of the Metro at Place de Clichy. I called the States on my cell and arranged to have the Jacques Brel bootleg expressed to Philippe. When I was done, a wave of fatigue hit me so hard I nearly passed out. I knew if I went back to the hotel I'd be asleep within minutes, so I walked down the Boulevard des Batignolles to Le Mont Leban, my favorite neighborhood restaurant. I'd never had the heart to tell them how wonderfully inept the English translations in their menu were: "Net of raw lamb, spied on," "Chicken liver fits in the lemon," and my favorite, "Girl pizza in meat, tomatoes."

They put me at a two-top in the window. I was thinking about a time right after college when I'd been working ridiculous hours at an electronics firm. I'd liked eating alone then, but now that I was pushing fifty, three years on from the breakup of a long marriage, it seemed more of a stigma. I liked my job, especially when I was busy enough to feel like I was reversing entropy in a substantial way. But I also knew I wasn't bringing anything new into the world. No new music, no kids, no world-changing inventions. A life like mine would have been plenty for my father; he'd been a soldier and then a salesman, paid his debts, and was going to leave the world a better place for who he'd been. And I was generally happy enough. What I missed was a sense of significance, which may have only been another way of saying I wished I had somebody to share it with.

I feasted on foul moudamas, moutabal, falafel, and moujaddara ("Puree of lens with the rice in the lebanese way") and thought about how much my father would have loved the place. We'd traveled to Europe twice when I was a teenager, and my father had attacked each native cuisine with curiosity and appreciation, while my mother had nibbled saltines and begged for a plain hamburger.

The memory made me impatient to talk to him, so I paid the bill and went out into the night. The locals were walking their dogs, or hurrying toward the Metro in evening clothes, or headed back to their apartments with a bottle of wine or a paper-wrapped baguette. The subtle differences from home—the melody of the barely audible voices in the background, the tint of the street-lights, the signs in the windows of the shops—were liberating, intoxicating.

I showered and got in bed and called the hospital. My father sounded weak but cheerful, and Ann tried very hard not to sound put upon. I was too tired to react, and I fell asleep within seconds of hanging up.

•

IT FELT ODD to have come so far and not be in pursuit of my mission on Sunday. My alarm woke me at 7:00, and I took the number 13 Metro line all the way across town to Porte de Vanves and spent the morning in the flea market there. I didn't find anything for myself, but picked up some wine labels for my father, who had been trying to develop pretensions in that direction ever since he retired.

By 1:00 PM the antique dealers were packing and the new clothing vendors were setting up. The sun had burned holes through the morning's ragged clouds, and I gave in to a sudden urge for the Seine and the Ile de la Cité.

Cynics say it's only a myth that Paris is full of lovers, but I saw them everywhere. A girl on the Metro to Saint-Michel had her arms around her boyfriend's neck and leaned forward to kiss him between every few words. I had to make myself look away, and when I did I saw a woman across from me watching them too. She was about forty, with very short blonde hair and a weathered, pretty face. She smiled at me in embarrassed acknowledgement and then looked down at her lap.

The sun was fully out on the Boulevard Saint-Michel, and locals had crammed in next to the tourists at the tiny café tables. I crossed over to the Ile de la Cité and saw more windblown couples holding hands in the gardens along the south side of Notre Dame, where the leaves were just starting to turn.

I wandered out onto the Pont Saint-Louis, which was closed to cars on Sundays, and stopped to hear a clarinetist and pianist who'd rolled a small upright piano out onto the bridge. The view was spectacular: the width of the Seine and the ancient Hotel de Ville to the north, the thrusting spires of Notre Dame behind me, the ancient, winding streets of the Latin Quarter on my right, the elegant 17th century mansions of the Ile Saint-Louis straight ahead.

A crowd of thirty or forty tourists listened from a discreet distance. I saw the blonde woman from the train there, closer to the musicians than the rest. She'd piled her coat and handbag at her feet; her short dress showed off a slim body and strong legs.

It was her feet that held my attention. She was moving them in an East Coast Swing pattern, rock-step triple-step triple-step, covering just enough ground to make her hips sway. I recognized it as a sort of international distress signal that meant, "Dance with me."

I was still deciding whether I should answer when the musicians wrapped up "New York, New York" and started the Benny Goodman classic "Don't Be That Way." It was more than I could stand. I walked up and offered her my left hand. She held up one finger, stashed her purse and coat next to the piano, then came back and took my hand and smiled, revealing a faint, ragged scar on one cheek. I turned her to face me, put my right hand on her back, and danced her out to the center of the bridge.

She was lively and responsive, picking up my leads but also feeling the music, shifting effortlessly between six-count and eight-count patterns, never losing her smile. It was one of my favorite songs, and the sun sparkled on the river and gulls circled the bridge, crying out in pleasure, and I recognized it as one of those rare moments that you know are perfect even as they're unfolding.

"I'm Frank," I said, when the song ended. "You're a great dancer." Then I caught myself and asked, *"Est-ce que tu parle anglais?"*

"Sandy," she said. "And I *am* English."

"Manchester?"

"Originally. London now. Good on you—most Americans can't tell Scots from Welsh. And you're a good dancer, too."

"Thanks." The band laid into "Moonglow." "You want to try again?"

After "Moonglow" they played "In the Mood," maybe the Miller band's most enduring hit.

"Why are you laughing?" Sandy asked.

"Glenn Miller," I said. "I'll tell you later."

Two other couples were dancing now, and the musicians hammed it up for us, the clarinetist pointing his instrument straight up at the sky, the pianist kicking away his stool to play standing up. They stretched the song for extra solos, but I still wanted more. When they finished I dipped Sandy low and held her there for a second or two, and then we were all applauding and I threw a five-Euro note in the clarinet case, and then they rolled the piano away and it was over.

"Wow," Sandy said. "That was fantastic. Do you fancy a coffee or a drink or something?"

We crossed over to Ile Saint-Louis, and I had to resist an impulse to take her hand. "What are you doing in Paris?" I asked.

"A week's holiday. Ending tomorrow, sad to say. Then it's the train and back to the Oxford Street Marks and Sparks." She looked over at me. "That's—"

"I know. Marks and Spencer. I've been in that very location."

"You're quite the world traveler, aren't you? Here on business?"

I told her about the wire recorder and Glenn Miller while we stood on line for takeaway hot chocolate at a hopelessly crowded café. I was still feeling the intimacy of the dance and saw no harm in talking about it. When I got to the part about the prostitutes and the drunkenness, I could see her expression change.

"But that's perfectly awful," she said. "What do you mean to do with this thing?"

"Auction it off, probably."

"Wouldn't there be a scandal? I mean, the man was a war hero."

My romantic fantasies were fishtailing away, and I was angry at myself for losing my head so easily, for assuming that moving well together meant anything more than that. "Our government lied about Glenn Miller, just like they lied about the weapons in Iraq."

She shook her head. "I can't abide hearing people talk about their leaders that way. It's so disrespectful."

I felt myself losing my temper. Political arguments always ended up reminding me of my own helplessness. What was my one vote compared to the power of PACs and big money special interest groups, to corporate campaign contributors and the media? I drank off my hot chocolate and threw the cup away.

"It was great dancing with you," I said, and meant it. "I've got to go."

I started to walk away, but she grabbed my arm, her fingers remarkably strong. "Wait."

I stood with my hands shoved in my pockets. She ignored my defensive posture and put her arms around my waist and buried her face in my chest. I could smell the sweet scent of her hair.

She said, "I've got to go back to my miserable, dull life tomorrow and I don't want this to be over yet. Please? Could we just go to dinner and pretend a little? Maybe go dancing? We don't have to talk about politics or Glenn Miller or anything important. We could be two different people entirely, just for tonight. Couldn't we?"

Without any conscious decision, my arms went around her. "Yes. Sure. Of course we can."

She looked up at me with eager gray eyes and a big smile and kissed me quickly, so sweetly and unexpectedly that it vaporized whatever will I might have had left.

SHE TOOK ME to the pet market at the entrance to the Cité Metro stop, where vendors were selling everything from hamsters and cockatiels to chinchillas and prairie dogs. True to the spirit of our bargain, I ignored any qualms I might have had about the cages and focused on her delight. From there, we crossed the Seine to the giant toy waterworks of the Pompidou Center where we watched a clown juggle fire on an enormous unicycle, then walked through the tiered gardens of Les Halles, holding hands as the sun set. We ate dinner at an Indian restaurant near my hotel, shying quickly away from topics that threatened to go sour, like our differing tastes in films, and struggling to stay with the ones that seemed harmless, like our distant pasts, or the places I'd been that she'd always wanted to go. The shared effort brought us closer, like a kind of training exercise.

When we stepped back into the street, the wind had picked up and the temperature had dropped. She nestled under my left arm for warmth and I opened my coat to bring her inside it, then turned her face up and kissed her. She tasted of cardamom and wine. Her lips were tense at first, then opened in surrender.

"Do you have someplace we can go?" she whispered.

"My hotel is just up the street."

"And do you have, you know—"

"Condoms? Yes. I didn't think I'd be using them, but—"

"But you never know."

Once in my room the mood turned awkward again. There was nothing there but the full-sized bed, two small end tables, and a half-size refrigerator. The TV hung from the ceiling and the closet was small and without doors. I went to shut the window to the airshaft and Sandy said, "It's freezing in here."

"I know," I said. "Sorry." I shed my coat and took hers. "Get your shoes off and get into bed. I'll warm you up."

The plastic mattress cover under the sheets made crinkling noises as we got in. I pulled the covers over us and held her for a minute or two, fully clothed, without saying anything. I listened to the rhythm of her breathing, both alien and comforting, and felt the muscles of her back slowly begin to relax. I buried my nose in her neck, inhaling the warmth of her skin, and then I was kissing her neck, her ear, her mouth. We slowly worked our way out of our clothes and pushed them out onto the floor, and then I had a condom on and was kissing her breasts and their small, clenched nipples, and moving down to taste between her legs. It had been so very long.

"Mmmmm," she said. "That feels wonderful, but if you're trying to make me come, I should warn you it's not going to happen."

"No?"

"Not with a man. Not even with a man present, if that was going to be your next question. I appreciate your thoughtfulness, but you should carry on and enjoy yourself."

"What's in it for you?"

"Don't fret, it feels lovely. Oh, don't let's talk. Just make love to me, will you?"

I had been seesawing between desire and irritation all night, but at that point I suspended all judgment and let my body have its way. As I entered her she said, "Yes. Oh, yes."

LATER, I ASKED her about the scar.

When she finally answered, it was in a firm, affectless voice. "I was coming home late from the clubs about four years ago and a man in a balaclava—what is it you call them?"

"Ski mask."

"Yes, one of those. He had a broken bottle and he dragged me into a car park. I was so startled at first I didn't think to scream until it was too late and he had the glass at my throat and was tearing my tights off. He never said a word, and when he was done he twisted the glass into my cheek, like he was disgusted with me."

"Christ. I'm so sorry."

"I had a mobile, and I called the police even as he was walking away. I was lucky—they caught him, and sent him up, though it was only for two years. That was when I left Manchester. I know the odds of it happening again were no worse there than in London, but I just couldn't feel safe there any more, you know?"

I didn't know what to do or say. We were both still naked and it seemed wrong to hug her, so I took her hand instead.

"It's easy to go from there to thinking men are just animals and all, but I didn't want to be like that. So I had to box it up and put it someplace, like it happened to somebody else. And in a way it did, you know, I mean, I wasn't part of it. And I know you're anti-authoritarian and that, but I will always be grateful there were authorities that night."

I resented her using her personal horror to score points in our ongoing hit and run political debate. She'd preemptively trumped anything I could say about the authorities having failed to prevent the assault in the first place, or their inability to keep her from living in fear afterwards. I hadn't been there, after all; I wasn't the one who suffered.

"And I don't blame men in general," she said. "There are nice things about them. Dancing. Sex, when it's sweet, like with you. You just can't trust them, that's all."

"What do you mean?"

"It's the sex thing. I mean, men cheat. It's the way they are."

"I don't," I said.

"Well. Perhaps you're the exception." She kissed my forehead in what seemed a very condescending way and turned her back to me.

I was still trying to find the words to answer her when she began to snore softly. I watched her for a while in the faint light from the airshaft and eventually I was able to work my way back to my first impression of her, one more lost and lonely traveler, not that different from me. I curled up against her back and felt her squirm slightly against me as she settled in, and then sleep took me too.

•

I WOKE AT 7 AM to Sandy sorting out her clothes in the half light. "You're not going?" I asked.

"I must. I have to pack and catch a train."

"Not just yet." I reached for her hand and showed her what I had in mind.

"Oh," she said. "Well..."

Afterwards, it felt as if we had wound the last eighteen hours back onto a reel and we were suddenly strangers again, with nothing to say to each other. She went to the bathroom, and then immediately began to dress.

"Can I come to the station with you?" I asked.

"I don't want you to even get out of bed." She bent to kiss my cheek and whispered, "Thank you. This was perfect."

"What about your address, or phone number? How can I get hold of you?"

She started to say something, then thought better of it. She wrote a phone number on a scrap of lined paper from her purse and handed it to me. "Bye now," she said, and slipped out the door.

I felt the way I did after a night of heavy drinking—back when I did that—minus the hangover. It was like I'd squandered something.

I tried to go back to sleep, but couldn't find a comfortable place for my mind or my body. The rain had returned, cold and steady, but I had warm boots and an umbrella, so I ate the hotel's continental breakfast and headed out to the Porte de Montreuil market, remembering to tuck a mini-cassette recorder in my pocket just in case.

The market was located in a faceless gray commercial neighborhood on the eastern edge of the city. It was mostly new clothing on Mondays, but deeper into the stalls there were always a few interesting antiques and collectables among the old tools and chipped plates. Nothing for me, though, not that morning.

I was nervous about going back to Vernaison. Philippe had meant well, I was sure, but too many times I'd come back to dealers like him and found only awkwardness and excuses. Once I'd turned around, though, I discovered I could hardly wait. I took the wet walk back to the Metro at nearly a run and hurried through two changes of trains.

When I finally got to Vernaison it was two in the afternoon and Philippe's booth was open, but deserted. I waited five minutes, pacing the narrow alley, and when I was about to give up, I noticed him coming from the front of the complex, head down, a FedEx package in his hands. My timing, I realized, could not have been better. He saw me, held up the package, and smiled.

I followed him into his stall. "You will forgive me," he said, and I waited while he carefully unwrapped the package, took out the record, and admired it. "Still sealed," he said. "Remarkable." He rubbed the edge of the album against the leg of his jeans with a practiced touch, parting the shrink wrap, and stopped to inhale the aroma of vinyl, cardboard, and glue before setting the record on the turntable and carefully cleaning it. I tried to picture him cooking a meal with the same deliberate speed, and imagined that he ate out a good deal.

The vinyl popped and hissed, an announcer made a brief introduction, and Brel began to sing, accompanying himself on guitar. *"Et voilà,"* Philippe said softly, then turned to me and said, in English, "I thank you so much for this gift."

"You're very welcome," I said.

He took another index card from his inside jacket pocket and handed it to me. I liked that he'd had it ready before the package came. "This is the man who sold me the recorder," he said in French. "Along with a lot of other things. He will see you this afternoon if you like."

"Thank you. This is very kind of you. If you don't mind, can you tell me what sort of other things you got from him?"

"They are mostly gone. A radio, a Victrola that our friend Madame B bought, some silverware. He had also some dishes and ladies' clothes that did not interest me. He is in the real estate business, he tells me. He comes across things from time to time in the houses he buys, and lets me know."

"He didn't say where he got the recorder?"

"I think from some old house. Maybe the owner died."

"Did you see the house?"

"The things were all in boxes, in the trunk of his car. I think maybe he lives in that car." He looked at me over the top of his glasses. "Seriously."

Just then a man in a black raincoat walked by. I didn't think it was the same man I'd seen at Madame B's on Saturday, but it made me unaccountably nervous. I thanked Philippe again and shook his hand, and as I left he was putting the needle back to the beginning of the album.

I CALLED THE NAME on the card, Vlad Dmitriev, from the street in front of the Vernaison. My nerves were still bad, and from the way I was looking around, people probably thought I was making a drug deal. I got a bad mobile connection, and it took me a while to convince him that I was an antique collector and not trying to trap him into admitting anything. He finally agreed to meet me at the edge of the markets, where the Avenue Michelet met the access road for the loop. I was to look for a cream-colored Mercedes.

Half an hour later the car pulled into the swarm of traffic at that corner—pedestrians, bicycles, motorcycles, vans—and parted them like a killer whale. Vlad had his window down, yelling and shaking his fist at a gang of kids that had tried to cross in front of him. He was a bit younger than me, with long hair slicked straight back, a short beard, and a black leather jacket over a dress shirt and new blue jeans. He reached across to open the door for me and beckoned me inside.

"Where you going?" he asked. "I'll drop you." His French was slangy and heavily accented, and I could barely understand him. As I settled in, I noticed an open shoebox on the back seat that seemed to be full of American passports, and I had to fight off a moment of panic.

"I don't know where I'm going next," I said. "I was hoping you could tell me."

"The stuff from that old house, it's worth a lot, is it?"

"Only to a collector," I said. He didn't seem threatening, but things were getting a little out of control for my comfort.

He nodded, pulled into traffic. "It's okay. I don't do the detail work. I leave that to guys like you and Philippe. I'm strictly wholesale where junk is concerned."

"This place, what was it?"

"Just an old apartment house in Montmartre. Place was a wreck. Crazy old lady ran the joint, couldn't keep up with it anymore. I'm going to knock all the walls out, put in some offices."

"The old lady, she's still alive?"

"She's alive, but I don't think she'll talk to you. She hates the whole world. Living in some crazy past that never really existed. Doesn't sound like it was so great back then, either."

"Have you talked to her much?"

"Not really. Business, mostly, you know. She says the place used to be a whorehouse during the war, and that she worked there. I think she's making it up."

"You're talking about the Second World War?" Vlad nodded as if it were obvious. "I really need to meet this woman. I could pay for her time."

"She doesn't give a crap for money. Not like me. You say this is worth a lot?"

"If you've got a card or something, I promise I'll send you some money if I get rich from it."

He thought about it, then said, "No, it's okay. I'll take you to see her. Maybe she'll talk. Who knows?"

We were headed south and west, toward the center of the city, winding our way uphill into the artsy Montmartre district, the highest point in Paris. Vlad slowed the car and leaned across me to point out a narrow red brick building sandwiched between two others just like it. "See that? That's one of mine. You're not looking for something like that, are you?"

"Sorry," I said. "Just visiting."

"Maybe when you sell your whatever-it-is and you're rich, eh?"

The steep, narrow streets, the walled-in gardens, the parks and streetlight-lined stairways seemed both welcoming and saturated with history. It was easy to picture myself living there, looking out one of those bay windows as I fixed dinner, Mingus on the stereo. Maybe when Pop finally goes, I told myself.

We turned down a cobbled alley and pulled into a narrow parking space. The building was plaster and wood, in poor condition, and Vlad led me up three flights of stairs to a peeling green door, one of three on the landing. He knocked, waited, knocked again. After a minute or so I assumed he would give up, but he said, "She's here, she's just making sure we're serious."

He kept knocking, and eventually I heard a faint *"je viens, je viens"* on the far side of the door. It opened on a chain, and the voice said, "Oh. Vlad," in vague disappointment.

She reopened the door without the chain, and while the door was closed I reached into my jacket pocket and turned on the minicassette recorder.

She wore a pink chenille bathrobe, which she held closed with one hand, and bunny slippers. Her face was striking—deeply lined, and yet with such clear skin that she didn't seem old enough to have been around for World War II. Her hair was white, with odd strands of gray and black, and came halfway down her back in a loose braid.

We followed her into the kitchen. "My good friend François has been begging me to introduce him to you. François, this is Madame Rochelle."

She took my hand and looked intently into my eyes. "So, you are a good friend of Vlad's? For this I am supposed to welcome you?"

I went with my instincts. "I just met Vlad a few minutes ago. I want to ask you about the wire recorder that he found in your house."

She pressed my hand and nodded. "Okay, Vlad, I will talk to François alone now."

Vlad hesitated, as if he didn't quite believe what he'd heard. Then he shrugged and took a business card from his jacket. "In case you are ever rich," he said. He squeezed the back of my neck in an oddly intimate gesture and let himself out.

"Come in," Madame Rochelle said. "If you insist on something to drink I expect I could find you some tea." Her French, like Madame B's, was musical, but in her case legato and husky. For my part, my own French was still ragged, but practice was bringing it back.

"I'm all right," I said.

She led me into the living room, which smelled damp and got a little second-hand light from the bedroom and a bit of filtered daylight through heavy orange drapes. She sat at one end of a faux Victorian couch with worn floral upholstery and I sat at the other.

"Talk," she said.

"I am here because Vlad found an old recorder in your house and took it to the flea market at Saint-Ouen, and eventually it ended up with me. There was a spool of wire with the machine that had a date of December 18, 1944. Do you have any idea what I'm talking about?"

"No, but I'm fascinated." She clearly wasn't. She lit up a cigarette and looked past me out the window.

"I think the recording contains the sound of someone being beaten to death. I think that person was Glenn Miller, the American musician."

"Not a very good musician, and he didn't die in my house. The military flew him back to the US, to Ohio, I think, and he died in a hospital there. This anyway is what a doctor friend told me."

The blood roared in my ears and I thought I might pass out.

"I forgot that my friend Louis had that machine going," she went on. "He wanted to record the great Glenn Miller playing with the band from the bar down the street. Everyone was much too drunk, especially Miller, and they sounded like a piano falling downstairs."

"Madame Rochelle, may I tape this conversation?"

"Why?"

"It is my only proof of what is on that recording wire. It makes it valuable."

"You are going to sell the recording wire?"

"I don't know yet."

"All right. You may tape."

I switched off the recorder surreptitiously as I took it out of my pocket, then set it on the coffee table and made a show of turning it on again. Madame Rochelle shot me a skeptical glance that told me I wasn't fooling her, but I felt better having it out in the open.

"How did the fight start?" I asked quickly. "Who was it that hit him?"

"That, my dear, is a much longer story. How much do you know about the black market here during the war?"

"Nothing, really."

"Okay. From the beginning, then." She took a deep drag on her cigarette and settled herself on the couch. "When the Germans came in 1940, they set our clocks ahead an hour, so we would be on the same time as Berlin. It brought darkness to our mornings and reminded us every day that we were defeated. That hour was the first thing they stole from us, but it was not the last.

"At first it did not seem so bad. We were already starving from the long siege, and when the first German tanks rolled into the city, the soldiers were tossing chocolate and cigarettes to us. Yes, like the way you Americans want to think of yourselves. We thought then the Germans would be bring order, but they only brought *papier timbré*—you know, bureaucracy—and long lines. They helped the black market with their own stupidity. They hired local men to provides all their supplies, so of course the local men stole everything they could. That was right where your flea market stands now, at the Port of Saint-Ouen."

"That's amazing."

"What you call coincidence? That is just fingers."

I wasn't sure I'd heard her right. "Excuse me?"

She wiggled her fingers at me. "You see this finger and this finger and you think they are different things, but there is one hand that moves them both. You understand? Anyway. You know the word *se débrouiller?* It means to get by, to make do. From this we had *le systéme D,* the way of getting by. Everyone did it. These days, you can't find anybody who was not in the Resistance, but then it was different. We did what we had to do. We stole, we dealt with *le milieu,* the criminals, we traded our heirlooms, we got drunk or high whenever we could so we didn't notice how hungry we were. Or we were one of the *collabos horizontales,* a whore, like me. We were most of us whores then.

"You Americans came, but there was still no food. Then the American deserters moved in and took over the black market, and it was bigger than ever. American soldiers were selling to them—that's how Louis got that wire recorder, from the American military. And Glenn Miller, he was friends with this Colonel Baessell, who was one of the worst. He would fly over from England with morphine he stole from the Army, hidden in cartons of cigarettes."

I knew the name Baessell, of course. He was the other passenger on the flight on which Miller allegedly disappeared. "Are you saying Miller was involved with smuggling morphine?"

"No. But everyone knew what this Baessell was doing, and Glenn probably knew too. He liked the things that Baessell could put his hands on. Booze and women. Glenn's appetites were enormous, and he was a very mean drunk. You know why? He was being eaten, from the inside out. Inside he was a great musician, but outside, his body could not play that well. He would have given everything he had if he could have been Jack Teagarden. You can't live like that, wishing you were somebody else."

My father loved Jack Teagarden, and used to lecture us on his awesome technique and control of the trombone. "So what happened on the night of the recording?"

"A man came in looking for Baessell, a boy, really, very young and nervous. He went right up to him at his table and pulled out a pistol and shot him, bang, in the face. Glenn came off the stage and knocked the gun out of his hand with his trombone, and they began to fight. People were running away now because of the gunshot. They knew the police would come and many of them should not have been there, deserters, black market traders like Louis. Still, someone could have stopped the fight. But there was no love here for Americans. They had not suffered the way we had."

I thought of the images I'd seen of the carnage at Omaha Beach and started to say something, but she cut me off.

"A few weeks of combat is not the same as years of hardship," she said. "And many of these men were like Glenn and Baessell, they had never seen combat. They came and took what they wanted—women, mostly, by force sometimes—and thought we should be grateful."

"What happened to Miller?"

"Like I say, he was a very mean drunk, and he was very drunk. Most fights I have seen have not lasted long, but this one—Glenn was crazy with anger and would not stop, and the boy, in the end, he was beating Glenn's head against the floor. I tried to stop it, finally, and then the Military Police came and took Glenn away. I was sure they would arrest us, but it seems they knew who the boy was who shot Baessell, and he left with them, and they said if we ever talked about it bad things would happen to us."

"Are you saying the US military was involved with Baessell's death?"

"Do I think it is possible that the US Army wanted to stop Baessell from stealing their morphine and didn't want the publicity of a trial? What do *you* think?"

"Have you ever told anyone else?"

"One time I told an American, after the war, and he was very angry with me and said I was lying. Then a few years ago a woman from England found me. She was doing a book about Miller, but then she went away and I never heard from her again or ever saw the book."

"Do you remember her name?"

"Sorry. I know these things are very important to all of you, but I don't care. They say life is short, but my life has been very long, and I am tired."

"You never thought of going to the newspapers when you saw the false reports of Miller's death?"

"Why? When your government decides to tell a lie, that is serious business. Like now, your President lies and nothing happens to him, but this man Wilson talks about the lies and the government sets his wife up to be killed."

I tried to find a polite way to ask if she could have been mistaken. "So you knew Miller well? He was a regular customer?"

"When I speak of his appetites, I do it from personal experience. He was not a bad person. He was not a wonderful trombone player, but he had a true gift as an arranger. He had a sense of humor. He was loyal to his friends, and he was brave enough to take on that boy with the gun. I don't understand your country. Your heroes cannot have appetites? You want to impeach Clinton for having sex, but you let Bush steal your election and carve up the country for his rich friends. All these soldiers who fought Hitler must be these brave idealists fighting the Good War. Well, the soldiers I saw, half of them had wine in their canteens and they wanted to know why they should be dying for stupid French people. But you never hear that now, just like you don't hear that Glenn Miller died drunk in a whorehouse. Your father, he was in the war?"

"The last part of it. He was very young."

"So many were at the end. Just children."

"He was with the group that found Dachau."

"Ah, yes, the camps. The Americans did many bad things at the camps."

"The *Americans* did?"

"Tortured and killed the guards. Shot German prisoners of war for revenge. Because they could not live with what they saw, and they were only human. Human like Glenn Miller." She looked at her watch. "I think you should go now."

And that was the end. Two minutes later I found myself on the street, dizzy from information overload, oblivious of the rain, clutching my recorder in one hand and my folded umbrella in the other. I sat on the steps of her building and rewound the tape for a few seconds to make sure I had her story. It was there, loud and clear.

"Holy Christ," I said.

I put the recorder back in my pocket and opened my umbrella and started walking. It was getting dark. At the end of the block I found myself on Rue Lamark, and followed it downhill past the stark white domes and towers of Sacré Coeur, then took the long flight of stairs down to Place Saint-Pierre.

It was the find of a lifetime, and now I had to decide what to do with it. My first instinct was to take it slow, send out a few emails to let key collectors know what I had, let word of mouth start the feeding frenzy that would doubtless ensue.

She'd stirred up a lot of different emotions, but most of what I felt was triumph. I'd waited a long time for this, and I was not going to screw it up.

MY FLIGHT WASN'T UNTIL Wednesday morning. I spent Tuesday at the Rodin Museum and the Gustave Moreau exhibit at the Musée de la Vie Romantique, then I picked up a few presents at the big Printemps department store, including a necklace with Russian-looking icons of the Virgin for Ann. I felt different, puffed up. No one was looking at me, but it was because they didn't know the secret I was carrying.

Afterwards, as evening fell, I walked around the Pigalle district. This was where Glenn Miller came to drink and let out his inner demons. It had changed, of course, since 1944. The Moulin Rouge now offered Vegas-style dinner-and-a-show, feathered-headdress nudity to busloads of tourists, and the shops were cluttered with sex toys and gag gifts—but there were still prostitutes and live sex shows and lonely men with their collars turned up against the night.

I dropped by the hotel around 7 PM to call and check on my father, and the night clerk stopped me in the lobby. "A man was here looking for you this afternoon, monsieur. He left this message."

It was a handwritten note, in English. "Urgent that I speak with you today. Please call me as soon as you get this, no matter how late." There was a local phone number and a name, David Smith.

I punched the number into my phone, nervousness edging toward fear. I had to remind myself that my passport was in order, my credit was solid, I'd done nothing wrong.

A woman's voice answered, and when I identified myself she switched to English with a colorless American accent. "Mr. Smith has been waiting for your call. Can you hold, please?"

When Smith came on, he too sounded like an American newscaster. "Mr. Delacorte. Thanks for calling back. If you can spare me half an hour tonight, I have some information I think will interest you."

"Are you trying to sell me something?"

"Quite the contrary. Do you know what a Missing AirCrew Report is? For example, if a military plane disappeared during World War II on a flight from a rural English airfield to Paris, there would have to be an MACR filed. Now do I have your attention, Mr. Delacorte?"

"Yes. Yes, I understand."

"I can be at your hotel in twenty minutes. Is that okay?"

"Yes, I guess so..."

"Great. See you then."

I dropped my packages in my room and washed up. Yes, I wanted to see a Missing AirCrew Report on Glenn Miller, but how would a stranger know that?

I was waiting in the lobby when he arrived, exactly twenty minutes from when I'd hung up the phone. He looked to be in his late thirties. He was wearing an expensively tailored gray suit, but his haircut and bearing both suggested the military. He had a quiet authority that went beyond self-confidence to intimidation.

He shook my hand firmly and said, "Is there someplace we can talk?"

"My room is a little small," I said. Ridiculous as it seemed, I didn't want to be alone with him.

He nodded toward a red vinyl-covered bench at the far end of the lobby. "Here is all right, I suppose. This won't take long."

We sat and he opened the manila envelope he was carrying and took out a single faxed page on plain copy paper. "You may read this here. I can't let you copy it or take any notes. When you're done I'll take it with me."

The form was crude, from a mimeographed original. At the top it said "R E S T R I C T E D" and beneath that "MACR NO. 10770." The heading was "WAR DEPARTMENT/HEADQUARTERS ARMY AIR FORCES/WASH-INGTON." I skimmed the report, which listed the command, squadron, departure, and destination points. The date was 15 Dec 44. Paragraph 10 listed the persons aboard the aircraft as John Morgan, the pilot, and passengers Lt. Col. Norman R. Baessell and Major Alton G. Miller.

The most interesting part was paragraph 5, "AIRCRAFT WAS LOST, OR IS BELIEVED TO HAVE BEEN LOST, AS A RESULT OF." There was an "x" next to "Other Circumstances as follows," and then the words: "Accidentally destroyed when aircraft strayed into Channel Bomb Jettison Area."

I read the whole thing again. "Are you serious?"

"The Norseman aircraft in which Major Miller was a passenger accidentally overflew an area in the English channel that was used for the disposal of bombs after aborted missions. Several observers on one of the bombers positively identified the Norseman."

"This is the Fred Shaw story that was in the tabloids in the eighties. There are a dozen holes in it. No one else ever came forward, there was no Mayday call, no wreckage—"

"And no MACR. Not available to the general public, anyway. It would have been a morale disaster if the truth had come out while our men were still in combat."

"I think this is a fake. For one thing, Baessell's middle initial was not 'R.'"

"No offense, Mr. Delacorte, but I think you're being a bit paranoid. The Army typist hit an 'R' instead of an 'F'. It's a simple typo."

"If this is the truth, why not admit it now?"

"If it were up to me, I would. But the military is a bit skittish about taking responsibility for past cover-ups at the moment."

Because of the current cover-ups, I thought. I didn't say it aloud because I was afraid of him.

"The important thing," he said, with what should have passed for a sympathetic smile, "is that anything else you may have heard is simply not true. There are rumors, for example, that he was murdered, or any number of other far-fetched scenarios. It was an accident, plain and simple. A piece of really lousy luck."

"You accuse me of being paranoid, but what am I supposed to think, with you showing up like this? Who are you? Who do you work for? How did you know I was investigating Miller's death? Who told you about me?"

"I'm sorry, Mr. Delacorte. I've told you all I can." He gently took the MACR from my hands and put it back in the envelope. "I will tell you that I have a legal background, and that both Major Miller and Colonel Baessell have living relatives. If you knowingly circulate libelous stories about either of them, you could find yourself—and your pertinent possessions—tied up in some very nasty litigation."

Smith, or whatever his name was, stood up. "I hope this was helpful to you," he said. "Enjoy the rest of your stay."

I COULDN'T EAT, couldn't sleep. I sat in my room in the half darkness and replayed everything that had happened since I'd come to Paris. Had I been followed? What about the men in the raincoats at the Marché Vernaison? No one connected with the wire recorder—not Philippe, Vlad, Madame B, nor Madame Rochelle—knew where I was staying. Was somebody reading my email?

And what was I to believe about Miller? Madame Rochelle had seemed completely convincing, but she had a political agenda and the only evidence to support her was a handwritten label on a spool of recording wire, currently in my safe deposit box in North Carolina. If the recording had been made by anyone other than Miller, or at some earlier time, her story was no more than that. As for "David Smith," assuming he was military, he also had a motive to lie. American officers involved in the drug trade, and the Army implicated in a black market coup d'état, was far worse than his friendly fire scenario.

But it was the betrayal that came back to me again and again. Somebody that I'd been with in the last four days was deceiving me.

I had to do something. I called my airline and took a financial beating to change my flight to a Friday departure—from London.

I ARRIVED AT Waterloo Station just after noon on the train from Paris, and used a pay phone to call the number Sandy gave me. I got an elderly woman at a florist's shop who'd never heard of Sandy or anyone answering her description. "Sorry, love," she said. "You'll find someone else, I'm sure."

I wasn't surprised as much as curious to see how far the deception went. I took the tube two stops north to Charing Cross Road and wheeled my suitcase down the crowded sidewalks of Oxford Street and into Marks and Spencer. I found the cosmetics counter and was about to ask a sales clerk for Sandy when I saw her.

She caught my glance and something like panic flashed across her face. I went up to her, saw the name "Margaret" on her nametag, and said, "Which is it, Sandy or Margaret?"

"Keep your voice down, please. Please. It's Margaret."

"What are you so afraid of?"

"Please, could you pretend to be buying something? Everyone here knows me. I don't want them asking questions."

I picked up a lipstick, took the cap off, drew a blood red line on a scrap of paper. "What kind of questions?"

She looked down and whispered, "I've got a fella. They all know him. If word gets back to him that some glamorous older bloke was coming round to see me, I'll be in it for sure."

I thought the "glamorous" was a nice touch. "We have to talk."

"Not here. I've got lunch in a quarter hour. I'll meet you just inside the main doors of the HMV across the street."

"You're not going to stand me up, are you? "

"I'll be there. Fifteen minutes, I promise. Just go now, okay?"

I lurked inside the main doors of the giant record store, checking my watch when I wasn't looking out at Oxford Street. I knew she could easily slip into the crowds and disappear if she had a mind to, and it was with vast relief that I finally saw her hurrying up the sidewalk.

I stepped out to meet her and she said, "Let's walk. I don't want anyone to see us here."

We headed west toward Tottenham Court Road. "So your boyfriend is the violent type, is he?"

She walked on in silence for a long time and then said, "Yes."

"Is he the one that gave you the scar?"

"No, that part was true."

"Were you ever working on a book about Glenn Miller? Interviewing people for it?"

She gave me a sidelong glance as if evaluating my sanity. "No."

That left the tough one. "Did you talk to anyone about me? In Paris, or here? I mean anybody, a girlfriend, a stranger, a cop?"

"No. It's my secret." She stopped and looked at me defiantly. "Everything I told you is true except my name and the phone number you made me give you."

"You didn't tell me about your 'fella.'"

"You didn't ask. You just assumed." She started walking again. "I needed what you gave me. Maybe it'll eventually give me the guts to change my life. But if I tell anyone, it won't be mine anymore. I don't want to share it."

The sound of her heels against the concrete was like the ticking of an enormous clock. "It's really arbitrary, isn't it?" I suddenly said. "Who we choose to believe? It's subject to coercion, or habit, or wishful thinking."

"You're saying you don't believe me? Not that I blame you."

"No. I'm saying I do. Believe you."

"I'm really sorry," she said. "I didn't think I'd ever see you again."

After a minute I said, "I lied to you, too. When I said I didn't cheat? I did cheat. I had an affair, toward the end of my marriage. I hated the deception, even though I couldn't resist the sex part, for a while anyway. But I broke it off and swore I wouldn't do it again, and I would either make my marriage work or get out. I ended up getting out."

"It doesn't matter. I mean, in the circumstances, I'd be pretty much of a hypocrite to complain, wouldn't I?" She reached out and ruffled my hair. "Is that why you came all this way? To confess?"

"Something weird happened last night in Paris. It's nothing I want to talk about, but I had to know you weren't involved in it. I had to see you, face to face, to know for sure."

"And now what?"

I hadn't even thought about it until that moment, but once I did it seemed inevitable. "I want you to do something for me. Can you call in sick tomorrow?"

"I just got back from holiday."

"Tell them you picked something up in Paris."

She laughed, then turned serious again. "Listen. What happened in Paris..."

"It's not like that. I need to go to an abandoned airfield about 50 miles north of here. It's called Twinwood Farm."

I CALLED MY FATHER and told him about my change of schedule, then I spent the rest of the day arranging a hired car, finding the cheapest hotel I could, and reading at the British Library. Margaret met me at my hotel the next morning wearing jeans and a sweater, and I felt a pang of desire for her that I couldn't seem to shake.

We took the M1 north out of London, then the M6 on to Bedford. My head was too full for me to feel like saying much. Margaret talked easily about her boyfriend, her job, how envious her friends had been of her trip to Paris, and I was happy enough for the distraction.

I stopped at the post office in the town of Oakley and asked a man in his sixties if he'd ever heard of Twinwood Farm. "You're joking, son," he said. "Everyone knows of it now, what with the Glenn Miller festival just there in August."

We followed his directions and drove due east, through the tiny village of
Oakley Hill and onto a well-kept tarmac road. We passed a sparse forest, then
restored hangars and outbuildings as we pulled up to the control tower itself,
a two story brick cube painted in broad vertical tan and olive camouflage
stripes. I parked in front and we got out into a cold wind. Margaret went
up to the building and looked in the windows. "It's some sort of museum,"
she called back. She read from a plaque: "'...opened on second June 2002 ...
contains a tribute to Major Alton Glenn Miller, who took his final flight from
here fifteen December 1944.'"

After a while she came back to where I stood by the car, hugging herself
against the cold. "Don't you want to look?"

"I thought there might be something left of him here," I said. "But I'm too
late. The myth has taken over."

"People need myths."

"We need the truth. But all we get is the amusement park version of it. And
nobody cares."

"You care," Margaret said. "Isn't that enough?"

I DROPPED MARGARET at a tube stop near the car hire agency. We had real
phone numbers for each other this time, but I doubted we would ever use
them. I slept poorly that night, and not at all on the long, long afternoon flight
back to the States.

I went straight to the hospital from the airport and found Ann and my
father watching the news. My father switched off the set as soon as he saw
me; Ann looked like she was going to protest and then thought better of it.
I hugged them both and handed out their presents and we made some small
talk about the flight, how my father was feeling, the tepid meal he'd just eaten.

"So," my father finally said. "How was the wild goose chase?"

I sat on the edge of the bed and took his hand. "I've got somebody who says
it was Miller on the tape. What you heard is the sound of him being murdered—
murdered by somebody working for the US Army." Apparently, somewhere over
the Atlantic, I'd made up my mind about who I was going to believe.

"You can't trust the French. They're all Communists." He smiled as if he
were joking.

"I want to ask you something, Pop. I want you to tell me about Dachau."

"It was horrible. You've seen the pictures. You don't need to hear it from me."

"I do need to hear it from you. I want you to tell me what you did there."

He saw then that I knew, and that I wasn't going to let him escape. "I don't
feel like talking about it," he said meekly.

"Francis?" Ann said.

I waved her off. "I learned some things in Paris, and then I read some more things in the library in London."

My father said, "I don't have to—"

"We have to stop pretending everything's simple, Pop. Black and white, Greatest Generation and Axis of Evil. We have to take responsibility for what we do, and tell the truth about it. We can start right now."

I kept staring until he looked away. "Ann," he said, "could you leave us alone for a minute?"

She started to get up and I said, "I'd like her to stay for this."

I could feel her glare on the back of my head. "Francis, what do you think you're doing?"

"Sit down," I told her, still looking at my father. "Pop, tell me what you did."

He was motionless for so long I was afraid I'd given him another stroke. Then the tears started to run down his cheeks. "I've never talked to anybody about this," he said. "Not ever."

"Go ahead," I said. "We love you. Nothing you can say is going to change that."

"It might. It very well might."

I waited.

He sighed and said, "It wasn't a death camp, not like Auschwitz. Those were all in Poland. Dachau was a work camp. Not that there was a lot of difference, except they kept the prisoners alive longer. More or less alive. You've seen the pictures, you two have known about it all your lives. We didn't. We were kids, most of us, and we'd grown up in a sane, reasonable world. Until we went in that camp we didn't know why we were fighting that war in the first place. We thought it was about cleaning up somebody else's mess. We knew the Germans were brutal, inhuman, but nothing prepared us for what we saw.

"We went crazy, all of us. You couldn't look at those starved, brutalized remnants of humanity and feel anything but rage and hatred. Blinding, murderous rage."

"You shot the guards," I said.

"Lined them up and shot them."

"With no trial," I said.

"No trial, no questions, nothing. But that wasn't the worst."

"Tell me the worst, Pop."

"We had to search all the buildings. I was paired up with a Jewish guy from Brooklyn, a big tough kid named Schlomo. We found one of the guards hiding out in a latrine. Schlomo told me to keep him there, and he went out, and he came back ... he came back with one of the prisoners. And we stripped the guard naked and..." He faltered.

"Go on," I said, and squeezed his hand.

"And we gave the prisoner a bayonet. I lost my nerve then, but Schlomo stayed and watched."

My father took a long breath and closed his eyes. "He told me later what happened. The prisoner ... first he castrated the guard. Then he gouged out his eyes, one at a time. And then he started stabbing him, faster and faster, over and over. It wasn't until then that the guard finally started to scream, and then they were both screaming, and then it was all three of them, and I could hear them from outside."

My father opened his eyes. "I don't care about the guard. There was no torture, no punishment horrible enough for what he did. But I can never forgive myself for letting that poor bastard prisoner become a murderer too. It's like I took the last decent thing away from him."

I held my father and let him cry for a while. "Did you ever tell Mom about this?"

"No," he said. "She would have..."

"Say it."

"Some day, years later, when I was least expecting it, she would have used it against me."

"Never," Ann said, a whisper with claws. "She would never have done that."

I slowly let go of my father, stroked his forehead a couple of times, and turned back to face Ann. "Yes, Ann. She would have." Her eyes burned into me, hating me. "For five years I've stood by and let you turn her into a plaster saint. Whenever Mom got scared—like after those huge, screaming fights she and Pop would have—remember?—she would turn cold and vicious and spiteful. You used to know that. Now it's like you're turning into her, and I hate it."

"Get out," Ann whispered. "Just get the hell out of here."

"Not this time. You ran me off from Mom's deathbed, and I'm not going to let you do it again."

"You don't know how to take care of people, Francis. You're too spoiled and too selfish. Mother and I made you that way, God help us, by giving you everything you ever wanted."

"I don't have everything I ever wanted," I said slowly. "I never did. Mom and Pop didn't have the perfect marriage. We're not the perfect kids. Neither of us."

I watched her anger overwhelm her, to the point that she could no longer speak. She jumped out of her chair and ran from the room.

"She's so angry," my father said. "I've never understood that."

"Mom's death hit her hard."

"Yeah. Me, too." We sat in silence for a while, and then he said, "What are you going to do with that recording?"

"I guess I'm going to play it for people. Starting with the *Washington Post*. If they don't want to write about it, I'll go to the *New York Times* and work my way down. I'll put it on the Internet and hand it out to strangers on the street. If I get sued, so much the better. The story has to get out. It's important."

"Okay," my father said.

It was after midnight in Paris and my body was aching for sleep. "You want the TV back on?" I asked him.

"That would be great."

I fell asleep in the chair almost immediately, and when I woke up the room was dark and silent. I went to the window and watched the stars for a while. My father made a noise and turned over. "Frank?" he said sleepily.

I sat down next to him and touched his shoulder. "I'm here," I said. "I'm here."

STUFF OF DREAMS

"If it gets to be too much," Matheson told me, "you can always bail out. Like this."

He clenched his fists and folded his arms in an X across his chest. With his white intern's smock and his unkempt wiry hair, he looked like he was getting ready to step out on the karate mat.

"You just cross your arms and duck your head and you'll come out of it. Sort of like a fetal position, only you're standing up. I don't know why it works, but it does."

"What do you mean," I asked, "'too much'?"

Matheson shrugged. "You've got to understand. This isn't just lights and colors we're talking about here. You're going across into a whole other world, even if it is inside your head. It gets more real every time you take the stuff. It's going to have its own people, own rules, everything. You may find yourself in a situation you want out of, that's all. Hell, didn't you ever wish you could just turn off an acid trip?"

I nodded, looking at the small plastic pouch he'd given me. It was like a Tubex system, with five small doses of the drug and a steel plunger unit. Adonine, he'd called it.

"And you don't know anything about it?"

Matheson shook his head impatiently. We were in the middle of the hallway, right by the nurses' station, and I could understand why he was uncomfortable. "I sent a sample to PharmChem last week," he said. "It was a stat order, so I should get the analysis in a couple more days. That should answer all your questions."

I was just making excuses and I knew it. It was time for my rounds, and I didn't want to get caught in the middle of a drug deal either. So I handed Matheson a twenty and put the package in my coat pocket.

Matheson winked as he tucked the bill away. "You won't be sorry," he promised. "It's a real trip."

THAT NIGHT I went across for the first time.

I closed the blinds on the gently falling snow outside and sat on the edge of my bed. Everything I needed was laid out on the night table beside me, but I still hadn't made up my mind whether I was going to go through with it or not.

It was one thing for Matheson and another for me. Matheson wasn't afraid of drugs, had even used heroin off and on for several years. I'd used the usual chemicals in undergraduate school, and when I'd gotten into med school I'd sometimes taken speed in the morning and Valium at night. But never to the point of dependence, and I'd never liked using needles on myself.

But Matheson said this was special, and since Sarah had moved out, it didn't make much difference anyway. I'd been losing interest in everything, and some kind of desperate measures were in order.

Even this.

The plunger assembly screwed together easily, and the plastic sheath popped off the needle with a little pressure from my thumbnail. I tied off with a piece of surgical tubing and made a fist with my left hand. When I patted the inside of my elbow, the vein rose up fat and blue.

I swabbed the vein, and the touch of the alcohol made my whole arm go cold. When I held the assembly up to the light, the silvery drug seemed to roll in the syringe like a glob of mercury. I squeezed out the bubble of gas and watched the first drop roll down the shaft of the needle.

My arm was starting to go numb. I had to make up my mind. Setting my teeth, I put the needle into my arm.

I eased the plunger back a fraction with my thumb and watched purple ribbons of blood swirl into the silvery liquid. The sight of it nearly made me sick, but I pushed the plunger in all the way, just the same.

THE CITY STRETCHED OUT in front of me like a deserted movie set. Low white buildings, some with short towers and domes, spread across a broad plain and ran halfway up a nearby hill. Everything had an unfinished look, as if it had been built from sketches or rough cardboard models.

I turned slowly around. Behind me a path led into a sparse forest and disappeared. To either side a broad, deserted highway ran unbroken to the horizon. I was standing at the head of a walled footbridge that crossed about twenty feet above the highway.

I sniffed the air and tasted freshness, a clean smell like sun-dried clothes. I felt slightly high, but my head was clear, and I knew I was having some kind of dream experience. It didn't seem important at the time.

Nothing else moved. The highway was unused, the sidewalks were empty, even the pale blue-white sky was completely clear. On second look, it was obvious that no one had ever lived in the city, not in its present condition, anyway. What had seemed to be doors and windows were only recesses in the solid walls and didn't open into anything.

I reached out and touched the wall that edged the overpass. It gave a little under my hand, like Styrofoam. I took a couple of tentative steps out onto the walkway, and it seemed to hold my weight well enough. On the other side, a narrow lane wandered down into the center of the city.

As I walked slowly down the street, I noticed how comfortable everything was. The feeling was like *déjà vu,* but without any of the frightening overtones. I felt pretty sure I had dreamed something similar before, possibly even lived in a city like it when I was growing up. Whatever the reason, I seemed to know my way around already and knew what I was going to see around every corner. I stumbled once, falling against the side of a building. The light cotton clothes I wore weren't even torn, but I did feel the impact in my shoulder. The vividness of it surprised me, and I stopped and pinched myself, the way you're supposed to do in dreams. It hurt, but nothing changed in the city around me. If the pain is real, I thought, maybe injury is real, too. Maybe that's what Matheson meant by "too much."

It seemed to me that I walked for at least three or four hours. Even though there wasn't anything to see, only the monotony of white buildings and narrow streets, I couldn't seem to get bored with it. I didn't get physically tired either, or hungry, or thirsty. My body seemed to run like a finely tuned machine.

Then, suddenly, it ended. A wave of dizziness hit me and I leaned against a wall to steady myself. While I watched, my hand turned transparent and I looked down to see my legs fading away. A moment later I was in my bed, exhausted and disoriented, but awake.

I lay there for a minute or two, eventually realizing that I was staring at my bedside clock. It took another little while for me to make sense of the hands and see that I'd only been across for an hour of objective time.

I got up for a glass of water, and after a couple of minutes I could tell that I wasn't about to go back to sleep. I took 30 mg of Dalmane, and after about half an hour I managed to drift off.

"FANTASTIC," I SAID to Matheson the next day. We were eating in the cafeteria, but I didn't have much appetite. The Dalmane, with its long half-life, was keeping me relaxed, but I could still feel the excitement of the night before. "I mean, nothing really happened, but the sensations ... just incredible."

Matheson's smile twitched. "Sure," he said. He was playing nervously with his silverware and his eyes were shot with red. "That's because this city of yours is like, well, a model of your subconscious. If you could take the inside of your head and build it in 3D, that's what it would look like. That's why you're so comfortable there."

"Where do you go? The same place?"

"No. For me it's something more ... primitive. Somebody else could be on a beach or in a little town in Ohio. Somehow the stuff is tapping into your memories or dream centers or something like that."

'Where did you get it?"

"You remember a guy named Davis, intern, just transferred down to St. Mary's? He turned me on to it."

"Where did he get it?"

Matheson smiled that nervous smile again. It was starting to make me uncomfortable. "I guess he wouldn't mind my telling you. Davis introduced me to him down at the Pub one night. Calls himself Smith. Weird little guy, short and pudgy, lots of fat around his neck, kind of gray-brown skin. I don't know where the hell he comes from."

"Does he cook it up himself?"

"Who knows? He's the ultimate source of all of it I've ever seen. Ask him about it yourself if you want to. He's there two or three times a week." Matheson's eyes were darting back and forth again, and the same piece of food had been pinned on his fork for two minutes.

"What about..." I struggled for the right word, "side effects?"

"Blake, you worry too much."

"That's not much of an answer."

"Okay, there's a little risk. There's a little risk in everything."

"What's the risk in this? Specifically."

Matheson shrugged, said, "Dependency," and looked at his food long enough to eat the bite on his fork. "But it's not the kind of big deal you want to make it out to be. If you want to stop, you can stop."

Right, I thought. How many junkies do I know who tell me they're not hooked?

"I had some trouble getting to sleep last night," I said. "You know, afterwards."

Matheson nodded. "Yeah, that happens. Just use some Valium or something. You'll be all right."

I couldn't place what it was about Matheson that was bothering me. But then I hadn't had enough sleep, and there was an edginess under the fatigue that might have been the Dalmane wearing off. It could have just been me.

THE DAMP HEAT from the radiators gave the hospital an ancient, sour smell. One of the fluorescent tubes over the nurses' station was flickering, so fast that the irritating effect was almost subliminal. When I got up to make my rounds that afternoon, the corridors seemed like narrow, dirty tunnels. Even the faces of the nurses were sliding into a dreary anonymity. I made it through the afternoon somehow and got Matheson to cover for me in case I was needed that night.

Once I was back in the apartment, the fatigue seemed to burn away. More sleep, I decided. If I took the drug earlier, I'd have more time to recover before going back to the hospital.

I ate a little, almost by reflex, and took a shower. Then I went to bed and put another dose of Adonine in my vein.

THE CITY WAS coming to life.

It hadn't made it all the way yet, but the buildings had grown real doors and windows, and I could sense movement behind them. The sky was a deeper blue, and for the first time I realized that there was no sun in it, just an unbroken dome of color.

There was a coolness in the air that I could taste but couldn't really feel, like springtime or early morning. Just outside the edge of my vision I could see blurs of motion, and I could hear the rippling of conversations without words.

I walked downhill, toward the center of town. None of the shadow people got within fifty feet of me, and the ones in the distance had the fuzziness of pictures taken with an unsteady hand. I could see they were wearing the same sort of loose clothes that I had on, but that was the only detail I could make out.

In the center of the valley the road split, one fork winding into the hills to my left and the other continuing straight ahead. A small, barren park had grown up in the center of the Y since the night before, complete with benches and leafless trees. The ground had the color of infield dirt on a baseball diamond, but was hard-packed and dry.

I sat down and closed my eyes, wondering what would happen if I fell asleep. A dream within a dream?

Sleep didn't come. So I experimented with controlling the dream itself. I tried to bring one of the people closer to me, just by concentrating, but it didn't work. Nothing happened when I tried to will changes in the buildings or the trees, either. The shape of the city was either coming right out of the drug, or from some unconscious level of my own mind.

My scientific curiosity didn't last long. Like anything else associated with the waking world, it seemed irrelevant in the city. I got up and started walking again, aware just below conscious thought that I was looking for something. I followed the branch of the road that led through the valley, looking at the buildings. I didn't pay much attention to the blur of people on the streets, even though there seemed to be more of them every minute.

Individual houses out of the jumbled architecture looked familiar. The land on either side of the street rose as I got farther from the center of the city, and it was on one of these low hills that I saw a house I was sure I knew. It was two stories high, white as all the others, but with a square ledge between floors that ran all the way around the building. The slope leading up to it appeared rocky from a distance, but close up turned out to be made of the same hard, uniform substance as the ground in the park.

I sat down and waited without being sure why. After what seemed like half an hour, a single figure detached itself from the crowd and climbed the long stairway up to the house.

It was a woman, and she was more nearly in focus than anyone I'd seen thus far. I'd never laid eyes on her before, but she was as familiar as my own reflection. Her hair and eyes were a dusty tan, the color of the slope behind her. Her body was wide in the shoulders and hips, but her waist was narrow and her breasts were small.

She turned at the top of the steps and looked at me just long enough to let me know she'd seen me. Then she turned and went into the building.

I waited for her outside. Without drifting clouds or a moving sun I had no idea of how much time passed. When she came out again, I followed.

She had the same elusive, flowing walk as the others in the city, and it was hard for me to keep up with her. More and more people were appearing on the sidewalk in ones and twos, and they were no longer staying out of my way. I had to weave around them, nearly breaking into a run to keep the woman in sight. Still she kept putting distance between us and finally disappeared when two people stepped out of a doorway as she passed.

She was gone without a trace, without an alley or a storefront to have ducked into. I circled the block twice, and when I was sure she was gone, I wandered back toward the park.

The sight of her had aroused something in me, something sexual. but also a deeper sort of longing that I couldn't really pin down. I sat on the bench, and before long things seemed to heel over sideways and I came back across.

AGAIN THE EXPERIENCE had only lasted an hour, even though the subjective time had been even longer than the night before. My body was limp with fatigue, and when I got up to take some Valium, the room did a slow roll.

I swallowed two 5-mg tablets and went back to bed, but an hour later I was still awake. Things seemed fuzzy and distant, and I felt cranky as an exhausted child. I took 500 mg of Placidyl and left the problem of waking up for the next morning.

SNOW HAD BEEN FALLING all night and the roads were buried in slush. Putting the chains on my tires turned into a contest of wills that I almost lost. I kept the heater of the little Volkswagen turned up all the way while I drove to the hospital, and I still couldn't get warm.

All through morning report I kept glancing over at Matheson. He was in bad shape, bleary-eyed and jittery, as if he'd been shooting amphetamine for a week. The chief of staff was presenting a case of tricyclic antidepressant overdose, and I was bored right through my exhaustion. My eyes kept wandering to Matheson, then to the yellowing walls, the scarred gray tile, and the peeling veneer of the conference table.

It was late afternoon before I found Matheson alone, and even then he was so distracted that I had to struggle to keep his attention. His behavior was irritating, but the residual Valium kept it from bothering me too badly. I finally got him to agree to slip away to the Pub for a few minutes. We got our coats, and both of us had them on and buttoned before the elevator stopped at the ground floor. I caught him looking at me.

"Hypothermia?" I asked.

He nodded. "I'm always running a fever when I come out of it. The next day I might get as low as 95."

The bar was on the other side of the street from the hospital, and we crossed in the middle of the block. Dark gray mounds of snow were clotted on the edges of the sidewalks.

"How long have you been taking it?" I asked him.

"Week and a half."

"Every night?"

He looked at me strangely, then glanced away. He nodded.

The Pub was already crowded. Everybody from premeds at the university to senior residents hung out there, and the tables were packed tighter than boats full of refugees. I stood with Matheson at the bar and tried to shut out the throbbing voices and burning cigarette smoke. I was feeling nauseated, but ordered a beer anyway. Matheson didn't want anything.

I stared into the foaming yellow fluid for a minute, then blurted out, "Are you feeling okay?"

"I suppose I'm a little edgy, I guess. Yeah, edgy, why?"

"You look lousy, man. I think that drug is tearing you up."

"Hey, it's nothing. It's nothing. There's some rebound excitability, that's all."

He looked down at the bar, at his hands pounding out some strange rhythm, as if they didn't even belong to him. "Besides," he said. "It's worth it."

Suddenly he turned and stared at something across the room. "That's him," he said quietly. "Smith."

I followed Matheson's eyes and saw him in one of the booths. There was no mistaking him. He was too dark for a Mediterranean, but he had a green-gray cast to his skin that I'd never seen in an African. His head was bullet-shaped, totally hairless, and his neck looked like an uneven stack of pancakes. His small, pudgy eyes seemed to roll back and forth between the people he was talking to, and there was something about him that I didn't like at all.

I turned back to Matheson. The noise and the damp smell of crowded humanity was getting to me. "I don't like this," I told him. "I'm getting out."

Matheson shrugged. "Do what you want."

I COULDN'T SLEEP.

I'd stayed at the hospital past midnight, determined to exhaust myself so I could sleep without using Adonine. One good night's sleep, I was sure, would take care of the physical problems I'd been having and would prove that I could do without the drug.

I choked down half a sandwich and went to bed, but it was no good. I took 50 mg of Seconal, and another 50 half an hour later. My spine was humming like a power line, and I had to pull extra blankets down from the closet in order to get warm. The small noises of the apartment—creaking floors, whistling in the water pipes—made me jump uncontrollably.

I'd been constipated for two days, but that night my bowels turned to water.

I was a walking textbook of withdrawal symptoms. After only two days on the drug. "Rebound excitability," Matheson had said. My ass.

The Seconal was making my stomach flutter, and the sheets felt like they were made out of sandpaper. I started telling myself all the things that people tell themselves in that kind of situation. Like how I was going to get myself some real help, that I was going to talk to Matheson and get off the stuff for good. First thing in the morning.

That was when I got the hypo kit out and loaded up another dose.

CARS HAD COME to the city. They were red and blue and bright green, and from where I stood on the footbridge they looked like the toy cars I'd had as a kid.

For the longest time I just stood there, watching the cars slowly slipping under me, unable to see anyone inside them. For the first time that day my body temperature felt normal, my bowels didn't hurt, and my hands were lying still.

It was an acute physical pleasure just to be alive. On this side of the drug, anyway. I wondered how sick and screwed up I would have to get on the other side before it started leaking through.

Eventually I walked downtown to the park. The trees had grown uniform light-green leaves, and a carpet of yellowish grass had spread over the ground. I sat on the same bench, searching each passing group of people for the woman but not finding her.

Everyone had faces this time, regular features that didn't belong to anyone

I knew in the waking world. I felt I knew something about each of them just from the way they looked, a sense of how they would react if I spoke to them. Occasionally their eyes would flicker in my direction, then pass on.

Two men sat on a bench across from me and started playing some sort of card game. Instead of a standard four-suit deck, they were using cards with stylized paintings on the faces–chickens, rabbits, bears. I couldn't make any sense of the game, even to the point of knowing who would play next.

For the first time I felt a loss of control, a sense that something was going on that I didn't understand. It suddenly became clear to me that the city was reality for the people who lived in it. They were self-conscious entities, not just Disney robots there to put on a show for me.

The thought made me distinctly uncomfortable.

I got up and walked past the card players. One of them glanced up at me quickly, then went back to the game. He turned up a card with a dog on its face, and the animal seemed to have a sinister significance.

I stayed on the low road, headed for the house where I'd seen the brown-haired woman. The streets were crowded, and this time the other people on the sidewalks were noticing me, stepping out of my way and changing directions to avoid me. It was as if I were becoming more real to them instead of the other way around.

There were no cars on the streets, and the entire level of technology in the city seemed lower than that of the highway that ran past it. I saw pushcarts, and even a sort of rickshaw, but no horses or mules. Or for that matter, birds, dogs, cats, or insects.

When I got to the woman's house, I sat and waited again, but it was only a few moments before I saw her standing in the doorway. Her mouth was moving, trying to form words or maybe just wavering in and out of a smile. She made a curious gesture with her hand, twisting her wrist as she raised it, then quickly dropped it again. I got the meaning, though, and began climbing the steps toward her. She waited until I reached the top, then turned and went into the house.

The front room looked like a modern museum before the art was moved in. The walls were white and the windows were simply openings to the outside, without glass or shutters. The furniture was like everything else in the city—white and squared off, without ornament. The chairs were cubes of some porous material, and what must have been a couch or bed was just an oblong of the same stuff.

The woman motioned toward the longer block and I sat down on it. It was softer than it looked, with a texture like very dense foam rubber. The woman sat at the other end of it, maybe two or three feet away. Her eyes were ringed in black, making them seem to leap out at me. Her nose was small and bent, like a tiny beak, and her lips were thin and sharply defined.

"Who are you?" I asked her. It was the first time I'd tried to say anything on the other side, and the words seemed to waver a little as they came out.

She shook her head at me, bouncing her short, tangled hair. Her mouth was working again, but she didn't smile. From somewhere out of sight she came up with a deck of the same cards that the men in the park had been using. She started to deal them out, and when I held up a hand to stop her, she ignored me.

"I don't understand this game," I told her. She shook her head again and finished dealing. The cards were laid out in the shape of a five-pointed star. She reached out and turned over the top card of one of the piles. The face of the card showed a snake's head.

She seemed to be waiting for something, and so I reached for one of the piles. She stopped my hand and held on to it. I felt a slow excitement building in my chest and thighs. I looked into her face and saw no resistance. Leaning across the cards, I took her face in my other hand and kissed her.

Her mouth moved under mine with a sort of abstracted passion. I got up and stood in front of her and tried to pull her into an embrace, but she rested her head against my chest. The feel of her was light and vaguely electric, as if a mild current were running across her skin.

I tried to turn her face toward me, but she pulled away and began gathering up the cards. When they were in one pile her hands seemed to swallow them. She touched my face and went back out the front door.

I lay down in the coolness of the room, remembering dark, snowy mornings, the grimness of the hospital, the squalor of my apartment, all with the detachment of someone looking at last night's dreams. When the images began, I was sure I was going back across to wake up again, but it didn't happen.

I lay there for what seemed like hours, then finally got up to walk the streets again. The subjective time I spent in the city was growing with every dose of the drug. When I finally did begin to fade, I felt like I'd spent a full day in the city. I didn't even sense the transition as I went back across. The Adonine had cleared up the withdrawal symptoms, and the Seconal I'd already taken dropped me into a dreamless sleep.

"I GOT THE ANALYSIS today," Matheson said. He didn't seem happy about it, but then he wasn't in any shape to be happy about anything. The orbits of his eyes looked bruised and the skin on his hands was translucent. If he'd come into Emergency looking that way, they would have started feeding him intravenously on the spot.

We went into the conference room and shut the door. He pulled an envelope from his pocket and tossed me a few sheets of paper. They were the standard charts and graphs that PharmChem always did—high pressure liquid chromatography, UV spectroscopy, and so on. I was shivering and depressed, and couldn't concentrate on the needle-like peaks on the paper.

"They separated out two fractions," Matheson said. "One proteinaceous, the other RNA."

"What does it all mean?" I asked.

"It's a virus," Matheson said.

"What?"

"A virus," he repeated. "A short-lived, non-contagious virus. The virions are small enough to cross the blood-brain barrier and hook on to some form of receptor in the brainstem. Then they shoot a load of RNA into the cells."

"Holy Christ," I said. I was picturing a drawing from one of my college textbooks, showing the virion crouched over a cell, long, spidery legs plugged into the receptor, its bulbous head bent down to the cell wall and its beak raping the cell, the coiled strands of RNA spurting out of it.

That was what I'd been doing to my brain.

"The narcotic effects," Matheson went on, "seem to come from the protein coat, which floats off into the cerebro-spinal fluid after the virus has shot its wad."

"What," I asked, fighting nausea, "does the RNA do when it gets in there?"

"They don't know. There was a note with the analysis, from the technician who ran the tests. He said they weren't set up to do any more, but he was interested and had kept out a sample to run some tests of his own."

"Something must have caught his attention."

"You're damn right it did. Thirty percent of the amino acids in the protein coat are optically backwards. On top of that, the nitrogens in what should have been the cytosine residues are in the wrong places. This shit is bizarre. It's like it came from another planet."

I had a sudden vision of Smith, his beady eyes and strange, oily skin. I was wearing long underwear and heavy clothes to fight the hypothermia, but I still felt a chill run straight through me.

"Matheson," I said. He had been about to walk away. "I—tried to do without it last night. I couldn't."

He nodded distractedly, "You've been across what, three times? It'll sort itself out. You'll get used to it. You want me to get you some more?"

His casual attitude put me off and I didn't answer him for a minute.

"Well?"

"All right," I said at last. "Get me some more."

•

I LEFT THE WARD at 10:30 that night. I was in no shape to deal with patients, but I'd muddled through the day somehow. I had only enough concentration to take care of what was directly in front of me, and the world
had closed down to the moment and the area of space I was occupying. The
feeling of dirtiness around me had gotten worse, and even while part of my
brain was trying to tell me it wasn't real, the rest of my mind was recoiling
from it. I could barely remember what happened when I took the drug; all
I had was the vague knowledge that when the day was over I would take
it again.

I'd left the heater blazing all day and the apartment was like a sauna. I didn't
even bother to eat anything since I would have lost it to the diarrhea anyway.
After showering I wiped the thick steam off the bathroom mirror and looked
at myself.

I was in nearly as bad a shape as Matheson. Loose skin hung off the wash-
board of my ribcage. My elbows and knees looked swollen compared to
the arms and legs they clung to. My face was as dull and expressionless as a
wooden mask.

I toweled off and got into bed. The empty syringe from the night before
was still lying on the bedside table. I stared at it for a long time before fitting
a new unit dose into the holder. Then I swallowed two of the 50-mg Seconals
so I wouldn't wake up when the drug wore off.

The red-brown beginnings of a bruise discolored the inside of my elbow
where I'd done a bad job the night before. I had to tie off my other arm and
give myself the shot left-handed.

Virus, I thought, as I watched the blood mixing with the thick, metallic
drug. A wave of nausea went over me, and my right hand clenched the sheets
up into a knot. I pushed the plunger home.

IT WAS LIKE waking up from a bout with the flu to find my fever broken
and the sun shining. I stood at the end of the footbridge and breathed the
sweet-smelling air that blew out of the trees. The miseries of the day seemed
to seep out of me and right on into space. I remembered everything that had
happened, right up to the needle sliding into my arm, and it all seemed clearer
to me than when it had actually been going on.

But that was another world. I couldn't even think of it as the real world, not
any more.

Instead of going into the city, I turned and followed the dirt road into
the trees. Dry, summery-looking leaves had sprung out everywhere. Once
it was out of sight of the city, the road turned parallel to the highway and
led downhill. A few hundred yards along it I came to a shallow, clear stream.

Trees ran along both banks, and rocks arched the river into spray and foam. It was right where I'd known it would be, and I got out of my clothes and waded into it.

The woman appeared from somewhere in the trees and sat on the bank watching me. I tried to get her to join me, but she didn't seem to understand what I wanted. Finally I got out of the water and lay on the bank beside her. She touched my stomach and her fingers gave me that strange, tingling sensation again. I pulled her down to kiss her, but after a moment she eased back and lay down a little farther away. An alienness about her kept me from pursuing her, even though I was aroused and wanted her.

"Can you understand me today?" I asked her. My voice sounded clearer to me, but still wasn't coming through for her. She shook her head.

It felt like a long summer afternoon that we spent there by the river. Sometimes she would sketch stylized figures in the dirt; sometimes I would go back in the water and swim. Then, without any kind of warning, she got to her feet and walked away. I dressed and followed her, but she was still faster than I was, and she had disappeared by the time I reached the overpass.

It didn't seem to matter. I went back to the park and sat for a while on the bench. As I sat there, relaxed, staring into the empty sky, I realized that the time I spent in the city was now the only time I had to think things out. If any intelligent decisions were to be made, it had to be then and there. The first decision I had to make was whether or not I was willing to give the stuff up.

After that came the question of whether or not I would be able to.

I was still trying to sort it all out when a sudden flash of movement caught my eye. Someone had just ducked into a side street, and the motion riveted my attention. City people didn't move that way.

I got up and ran to the alley for a look. The people I passed almost seemed to resent my moving so quickly, turning to stare at me with narrowed eyes. I ignored them and turned the corner just in time to see a heavyset figure disappearing around the next block.

I would have known him anywhere. It was the man Matheson called Smith.

I ran after him. When I rounded the comer I saw him knocking at one of the doors that faced the street. He was looking around anxiously, and I ducked back out of sight. When I leaned out for another look, he was gone.

I moved to the window of the building and peeked inside. Like all the windows in the city, it was just an open place in the wall, and I found myself staring right at Smith's back. In the shadows beyond him stood one of the city's people, dressed in the usual light pants and shirt. There was a look of eagerness on his face that I'd never seen in any of them before. He was concentrating on something in Smith's hand, and I craned my neck for a better view.

It was a plastic pouch of Adonine. At that instant the city man raised his eyes and saw me, and Smith followed the direction of his gaze. He turned his bulk around to face me and focused his flat, piggish stare on me.

I looked from Smith to the Adonine, my mind filling with questions. But it was too late for answers. I could already feel the tingling in my legs that meant the drug was wearing off. I tried to fight it, but the force pulling me back was too strong. In a moment I had faded completely away.

MATHESON DIDN'T SHOW UP for morning report. I was groggy from the Seconal, but I'd taken a Valium anyway to try and take the edge off my nerves. It had made me calmer, but it hadn't helped the fuzziness in my brain. I couldn't seem to shake the delusion that I was working in a decaying zoo, not a hospital. Why doesn't somebody clean the cages? I kept wondering.

If it kept up I was going to need something stronger than Valium. Thorazine, maybe.

No, I told myself. Not Thorazine. I'm not crazy.

Between the withdrawal symptoms and worry over Matheson I was a wreck by the end of morning report.

"Blake."

It was my name. The sound of it had startled me so badly my leg had jumped into the table. If it hadn't been for the Valium, I would probably have gone completely to pieces.

"Yes?" I said.

"Stay here a minute," the chief resident told me. "I want to talk to you."

Christ, I thought. He knows. They all must know.

"You look terrible, doctor," he said. "What's wrong with you?" He had a face like a kindly old GP, but it seemed to me like he was smiling with some sort of secret pleasure.

"Ocelots..." I said. It came out as a mumble, but I was terrified by the loss of control.

"What?"

I cleared my throat and tried again. "I'm not ... sleeping too well, that's all. Nothing else. Nothing wrong."

"I've heard you've had some personal problems lately," he said. Was he talking about Sarah? Or something else? What was he after?

"Some, sir," I said. "Nothing I can't handle."

"All right," he said. "I'll take your word for it. But we can't have our doctors running around here looking worse than the patients. Start taking care of yourself, will you?"

"Yes, sir."

"Oh, and Blake?"

"Yes, sir?" He had caught me just as I was turning and I had to casually reach for the table to steady myself.

"Do you know anything about Matheson? He's still not here, and no one's heard from him at the desk."

I tried to concentrate on his eyes, tried to keep the parts of my body still. "No, sir," I said. "I don't know anything about it."

He was wearing a strange look, and I knew he hadn't believed me. He was after something, I was sure of it, but I didn't know what it was.

"All right, Blake," he said. "That'll be all."

MATHESON DIDN'T ANSWER his phone when I tried his apartment. I kept at it all morning, and when lunch break came I went looking for him.

Driving was bad. My concentration was even worse than the day before. From second to second I had to fight to remember where I was, what I was doing. I had the car heater on full, and it still wasn't enough. I imagined I could feel tiny drafts blowing in from the edges of the windshield and doors. Traffic was heavy, and I might have made better time on foot, but I couldn't face leaving the warmth of the car. When gaps formed in front of me, I accelerated too hard, and twice I nearly went off onto the sidewalk.

I finally skidded into a parking place next to Matheson's car. Before I knew what I was doing, I had the door open and was searching the glove compartment for Adonine. I didn't find any. So I slammed the car door and ran up the stairs. The effort left me exhausted and shaking in front of his door. I pounded on it and rang the bell, and when nobody answered I pried the ancient lock open with my pocketknife.

Except for a few details I could have been looking at my own apartment. It seemed unbelievably filthy to me. A narrow bed sagged at one end of the room, and a hot plate sat on top of a small icebox at the other. The walls were covered by tilting bookshelves, and a closet was stuffed with dirty clothes. The area around the bed was littered with empty Adonine cartridges.

The covers were heaped on the mattress, and the refrigerator was full of food, but Matheson was gone. And if he had any Adonine in the apartment, it was gone too.

I went back for another look at the bed, pulling the blankets onto the floor. There, laid out between the sheets, was a pair of heavy wool pajamas, just as if the body that had been in them had vanished into the air. Tied loosely around one of the arms was a piece of surgical tubing.

•

NO ONE ON THE WARD had any idea where Matheson could be. I called St. Mary's long distance to find Davis, the only other user I knew. No one had heard of him.

With Matheson gone I had to stay on the ward all night. I never had a chance to get to the Pub and look for Smith, which meant no chance to get any more of the drug.

I was down to my last dose, and every time I thought about it, I started to panic all over again.

I CAME ACROSS that night gasping like a drowning man. I dropped to my knees and leaned my head against the cool stone of the overpass.

It was a relief to be able to think again. I remembered pieces of the day—Matheson's disappearance, the confrontation after morning report—and it seemed incredible to me that I'd managed to get through it at all. Then I dismissed it, the way I would a bad nightmare, and went on to other things.

What bothered me most was seeing Smith in the city. It was the first time I had seen anyone from the waking universe on this side. If it had been Matheson, or my parents, or Sarah, it might have made sense. But, seeing Smith, I had the eerie premonition that he wasn't there because of any associations I'd had with him in the other world. I was sure that he was somehow part of the drug, part of the information carried by the RNA.

I had to know for sure. I walked into town to look for him.

I could sense a new feeling on the streets. For no specific reason I felt like I had become the center of attention everywhere I went. People seemed to be talking behind me as I walked by, and there was a murmur following me that sounded openly hostile.

The house where I'd seen Smith my last time across was deserted. I cut through the center of town to the woman's house, but it was empty too. Even the furniture was gone.

Back in the park I stood under a tree and watched the people moving by me. The streets were crowded now, and I could hardly walk without running into people. Whenever I touched any of them I felt the mild charge of contact, the way I had with the woman. Anyone I touched pulled away from me and turned to whisper to someone else.

After a few minutes I got tired of waiting and went out on the streets again. I don't know how long I'd been walking when I saw Smith, but he almost seemed to have been waiting for me. He was lounging against the wall of a building, apparently alone, and when I got within a block of him, he began to walk away. He didn't make any sign that he'd seen me, but I was sure he had. He stayed a block in front of me, sometimes seeming to want to look back at me, but never quite going through with it. When I picked up the pace a little, so did he.

We'd been walking away from the center of town, at first, in the general direction of the woman's house. Then he'd turned right to return to the main avenue, and right again, taking us back the opposite way.

By the time we passed the park I sensed that something was happening. Fewer people were on the sidewalks ahead of us, and a constant murmur came from behind. I stopped, and ahead of me Smith leaned against a wall and waited. I started toward him, then turned in the middle of a step.

Thirty or forty of the citizens were following me. They all wore loose white clothing, all had fair hair and pale skin. An intensity about their faces frightened me. When I turned on them they stopped where they were, casually, and started talking among themselves. I couldn't hear their voices, but their eyes were still fixed on me. When I took a step toward them they held their ground, and when I backed away they moved slowly after me.

I turned and ran for Smith, but he was more agile than he looked and darted away down the block. I chased hard after him and heard the footsteps of the crowd following me.

We were almost to the footbridge over the highway. Smith stumbled with exhaustion and collapsed against a concrete retaining wall, his back to me. I slowed to a walk and stopped just behind him.

"Smith?" I said. "Turn around." He ignored me. I started to reach for him when something ominous in the noise of the crowd made me look back.

They were coming for me, like an army of zombies out of a horror film. Their flat, neutral eyes were locked on me, and they were shuffling forward with a deliberation that terrified me. I backed away from them instinctively, moving out onto the footbridge. They were only a few yards away when I heard another noise behind me and turned to see a second army of them coming out of the woods.

I suddenly knew what Matheson had been talking about. All my desire for answers went away, and the only thing I wanted was to be out of there.

I crossed my arms over my chest, ducked my chin, and squeezed my eyes shut.

When I opened them I was fading away and the crowd was dimming into blackness.

I came to in my bed, burning with fever. My skin was hot and tight, and my throat was cracking like a dry river bottom. I sat up, wanting to get up for water, but I never made it. Sleep fell on me like a warm avalanche.

THE DETAIL MAN from Sandoz had a card table set up outside the Emergency Room, giving away coffee and donuts. He was pushing Hydergine, which was supposed to help you if you were senile. That wasn't my problem. I asked him for some Mellaril samples, trying to keep my teeth from chattering. He got a narrow box out of his case and gave me a strip of ten unit doses.

The tablets were light green, 100 mg, intended for advanced psychotics. I wasn't crazy, I knew that, but the symptoms were similar. Only the Seconal that was still in my system kept me calm enough to deal with the razor-cut drug rep in his three-piece suit. As soon as I was out of his sight, I tore open one of the blister pacs and swallowed the pill dry.

By eight o'clock I was relaxed, and the visions of dirt and decay had started to recede. I managed a vaguely coherent presentation and even got through morning rounds without any real trouble.

I called Matheson's apartment twice during the morning, with no answer. I hadn't really expected any. I fought to keep myself from thinking about the fact that I was completely out of Adonine.

By lunchtime I couldn't think about anything else. I took another hundred milligrams of Mellaril and washed it down with hot coffee.

In the quiet hours of the afternoon I went through Matheson's locker in the conference room. When I didn't find anything I started pulling out his books and papers and dumping them on the floor, searching frantically for even a single dose of the drug.

"What are you doing?"

I whirled around to see a look of horror on the face of the charge nurse. I had a dreamlike vision of myself—red, swollen eyes, hollow cheeks, shaking hands and chattering teeth.

I ignored her, scooping the papers back into the locker and slamming the door on them. I pushed past her into the hallway and tried to keep from breaking into a run as I headed for the cafeteria. Sweat was running off of me, but I felt like there was ice in my stomach and I needed to pour something hot onto it.

THAT AFTERNOON I SAW a letter for Matheson in his box. It had a Pharm-Chem return address on it, and so I slipped it in my pocket. The first chance I had I took it into the men's room and tore it open.

It was from the chemist who had done the first analysis. He'd been feeding the rest of the Adonine to rats, and he hadn't been ready for the results he'd gotten.

"I'm certain," he wrote, "that this drug is forcing reticular formation cells to make a reverse transcriptase. The fraction of rat brain homogenate from the reticular activating system contained not only the viral RNA, but a large quantity of radically altered DNA."

RNA was supposed to make protein. But if what the chemist was saying was true, this RNA was turning around and building new, abnormal DNA, and God only knew what that new DNA was doing to the cells of my brain, or what effect it was having on my perceptions.

"It is recommended in the strongest possible terms that you *do not* administer this substance to human subjects. As well as taking control of cellular metabolism, the drug is found to have an *extremely high* addiction liability."

So what else is new? I thought. I crumpled the letter and flushed it away.

AT SIX O'CLOCK I was pushing my way through the happy hour crowd at the Pub, looking for Smith. I had to shout at the bartender to get him to hear me, and when I finished the description, he said he had no idea of who I was talking about. He gave me some coffee, but I couldn't swallow more than a sip of it. When I set the cup down on the bar, a kid was standing next to me.

"I've seen him," the kid said.

"Where?"

"In here sometimes. He was in here last night, talking to a friend of mine. I think he said he'd be back here tomorrow night."

"Tomorrow?" It was like a cold fist in the gut.

"That's what he said."

I walked away from him and went back out into the snow.

I kept it up as long as I could, working in a radius out from the hospital that took in every bar, restaurant and pizza joint in the circle. But before long the cold was just too much for me, leaving me shaking so badly I couldn't even walk. I drove back home through the thick, drifting flakes of snow, thinking about a city where there was no winter.

I took three more Mellarils and sat shivering under my blankets, waiting for them to work. The ticking of the snow against the windowpane took forever to fade, but sometime around dawn I finally dozed off.

I dreamed of the city, but I wasn't really there. It was like watching it through a glass-bottomed boat, or through a plastic bubble that I could press myself against and almost put my hand through, but not quite. It was as much comfort to me as a photograph of a lost girlfriend.

I called in sick the next morning and lay in bed, dazed from the drugs, shattered by a sense of emptiness and loss. Sometime in the afternoon I stumbled out of bed and dressed in the dim light reflected from the snow outside.

Even over long underwear and another layer of clothes, my shirt and pants hung loosely on me. My joints creaked when I moved, and my face belonged in Dachau.

I had to drive to the Pub; I couldn't walk it in that awful cold. I finally staggered in, sat in a back booth, and ordered coffee. I washed down a Mellaril with the first cup and sat back to wait.

I waited an endless time, a longer time than I was able to keep track of. When my cup was empty someone filled it, and I sipped at it again until it was dry.

With my coat and gloves on, sitting still, I was all right, but the world seemed to come and go. I couldn't remember the last time I'd eaten anything.

When Smith finally came in, I was nearly delirious, unable to tell if I was seeing him in a waking reality of in another drug-twisted dream. The place had somehow filled up around me, and Smith was about to disappear into the crowd.

I lurched to my feet and went after him.

"I need to talk to you," I whispered at him hoarsely.

He turned slowly, and those tiny, hot eyes went into me, burning me the way they had once before, somewhere else that I didn't quite remember.

"What?"

"I need to talk to you. Outside." I had to lean against the wall of a booth, but otherwise I was all right.

"What about?" His face had no expression, was as slick and hard as blue-black clay.

"Adonine," I said.

Smith turned to the two people he was with and muttered, "Excuse me. I'll be just a second."

I led the way to the back door. I could barely feel my feet and I had to move slowly to keep my balance. We went through the metal fire door, and the cold air poured over me like the water of a frozen lake.

"Now. What was it you wanted?" Smith's voice was hollow and soft, as if it wasn't really coming from his body.

"Adonine," I croaked. "I'm an addict. I need help."

He tilted his head. "I don't know what you're talking about."

"Adonine!" I shouted. "The drug! Like you gave Matheson! Like you gave Davis!"

"Matheson?" he said, with a gentle sort of curiosity. "Davis? Am I supposed to know these people?"

"Don't lie to me, you bastard!" I shouted, moving in on him. "You know what I'm talking about. Now give it to me!"

His eyes widened with fear. I grabbed the lapels of his coat and felt a sudden tingling. It was a sensation I'd had before, in a dream somewhere. He brushed my hands away.

"Get away from me," he hissed. Sweat started out across his bald, tapering head, and he backed away.

"No more crap, Smith!" I shouted. "Give me the drug!"

I lunged for him again and missed, falling into the snow against the side of the building. Smith was glancing nervously from side to side, but he had nowhere to run. I was blocking his only way out. He backed up until he was spread-eagled against the back wall of the alley.

I grabbed him again and started to shake him. "The drug, Smith! Give me the drug!"

He screamed, and with a sudden movement he threw me aside. My head went into the pavement, stunning me for an instant. But I got up on my hands and knees and started for him again.

And froze.

Smith's eyes were closing and he was drawing into himself like a trapped animal. Then, very slowly, he folded his arms and tucked his head to his chest.

His body seemed to sparkle for a moment in the gray light of evening, then he was gone.

THE WAR AT HOME

TEN OF US in the back of a Huey, assholes clenched like fists, C-rations turned to sno-cones in our bellies. Tracers float up at us, swollen, sizzling with orange light, like one dud firecracker after another. Ahead of us the gunships pound Landing Zone Dog with everything they have, flex guns, rockets, and 50-calibers, while the artillery screams overhead and the Air Force A-1Es strafe the clearing into kindling.

We hover over the LZ in the sudden phosphorus dawn of a flare, screaming, "Land, motherfucker, land!" while the tracers close in, the shell of the copter ticking like a clock as the thumb-sized rounds go through her, ripping the steel like paper, splattering somebody's brains across the aft bulkhead.

Then falling into knee-high grass, the air humming with bullets and stinking of swamp ooze and gasoline and human shit and blood. Spinning wildly, my finger jamming down the trigger of the M-16, not caring anymore where the bullets go.

And waking up in my own bed, Clare beside me, shaking me, hissing, "Wake up, wake up for Christ's sake."

I sat up, the taste of it still in my lungs, hands twitching with berserker frenzy. "'M okay," I said. "Nightmare. I was back in Nam."

"What?"

"Flashback," I said. "The war."

"What are you talking about? You weren't in the war."

I looked at my hands and remembered. It was true. I'd never been in the Army, never set foot in Vietnam.

THREE MONTHS EARLIER we'd shot an Eyewitness News series on Vietnamese refugees. His name was Nguyen Ky Duk, former ARVN colonel, now a fry cook at Jack in the Box. "You killed my country," he said. "All of you. Americans, French, Japanese. Like you would kill a dog because you thought it might have, you know, rabies. Just kill it and throw it in a ditch. It was a living thing and now it is dead."

THE AFTERNOON of the massacre, we got raw footage over the wire. About a dozen of us crowded the monitor and stared at the shattered windows of the Safeway, the mounds of cartridges, the bloodstains, the puddles of congealing food.

"What was it he said?"

"Something about 'gooks.' 'You're all fucking gooks, just like the others, and now I'll kill you too,' something like that."

"But he wasn't in Nam. They talked to his wife."

"So why'd he do it?"

"He was a gun nut. Black market stuff, like that M-16 he had. Camo clothes, the whole nine yards. A nut."

I walked down the hall, past the potted ferns and bamboo, and bought a Coke from the machine. I could still remember the dream, the feel of the M-16 in my hand. The rage. The fear.

"LIKE IT?" Clare asked. She turned slowly, the loose folds of her black cotton pyjamas fluttering, her face hidden by the conical straw hat.

"No," I said. "I don't know. It makes me feel weird."

"It's fashion. Fashion's supposed to make you feel weird."

I let myself through the sliding glass door into the back yard. The grass had grown a foot or more without my noticing, and strange plants had come up between the flowers, suffocating them in sharp fronds and broad green leaves.

"DID YOU GO?"

"No," I said. "I was 1-Y. Underweight, if you can believe it." In fact I was losing weight again, my muscles turning stringy under sallow skin.

"Me either. My dad got a shrink to write me a letter. I did the marches, Washington and all that. But you know something? I feel funny about not going. Kind of guilty, somehow. Even though we shouldn't ever have been there, even though we were burning villages and fragging our own guys. I feel like ... I don't know. Like I missed something. Something important."

"Maybe not," I said. Through cracked glass I could see the sunset thicken the trees.

"What do you mean?"

I shrugged. I wasn't sure myself. "Maybe it's not too late," I said.

I WALK THROUGH the haunted streets of my town, sweltering in the January heat. The jungle arches over me; children's voices in the distance chatter in their odd pidgin Vietnamese. The TV station is a crumbling ruin and none of us feels comfortable there any longer. We work now in a thatched hut with a mimeo machine.

The air is humid, fragrant with anticipation. Soon the planes will come and it will begin in earnest.

STRAWS

HE HAD APPARENTLY spaced out for a second or two. When he came to, a large, annoyed woman was leaning in toward him. "Mister? Mister, are you even listening to me?"

He looked at the receding rows of fluorescent lights on the struts of the cavernous ceiling, the gleaming linoleum floors, the pallets of sale-priced plastic coolers and Special K and motor oil, and then he looked at the rack of merchandise at his back and understood that he was in a Wal-Mart, behind the returns counter.

He heard his own voice saying, as if by reflex, "Do you have your receipt?"

AT THE FIRST OPPORTUNITY, he locked himself in a bathroom stall and dug out his wallet. His driver's license showed the right name, birthdate, and photo, but it had been issued by the State of North Carolina, and it listed an address he'd never heard of.

He scrubbed his face at the sink. It was him in the mirror, a tanned and healthy 56, hair mostly gray but still all there. He felt groggy, as if he'd woken prematurely. It was only the numbness, he thought, that kept the panic at bay.

If he didn't push, he found he knew the answers to some questions. He was due to clock out in an hour. When he left the parking lot he would go under the highway, turn left, and merge.

HE FOUND HIS WAY to a battered white Toyota pickup in the employee section. The key in his pocket started the engine. He forced himself not to think too hard as he drove, taking the turns that seemed to have a certain inevitability. He wound up on a dirt road near someplace called Pittsboro, in front of a small brick house surrounded by high yellow grass, pines, and live oaks.

He parked next to a purple Nissan Sentra in the driveway, and tried the front door of the house. Inside, a woman sat watching TV in the living room. She was in her mid-thirties, plump, blonde, and plain. Her black polo shirt had a monogrammed logo for something called Harris Teeter and a nametag that said JESS. She was young enough to be his daughter, but he didn't think she was. She smiled when she saw him, and it lit up her face in an attractive way.

"I brought some of that rotisserie chicken home," she said. "Is that okay? We had some of those little red potatoes like you like."

"Sure," he said.

"You hungry? I could put it on the table right now." She seemed a little nervous, a little eager to please.

"Sure," he said.

TEN MINUTES INTO DINNER, after she'd talked about a host of people he'd never heard of, she slowed to a halt. "You're having that memory problem again, aren't you?" She had an accent that mixed a hint of Canada with a Southern twang.

He wondered what she thought the problem was. "I guess maybe so," he shrugged. In fact his memories were quite vivid. They just didn't match anything in front of him.

"Aw." She came around the table and wrapped him in a hug. She smelled of cooking, but not unpleasantly. His body seemed to know her, to take comfort in the embrace. "It was that email from Murray, wasn't it?" she said. "I was afraid it was going to bring one of these on."

"Email?" he said.

"Aw, no. I hate this. I wish I hadn't said anything, 'cause now you're going to have to read it, and it'll hurt you all over again." She ran the back of her right hand over his cheek. "Could you at least eat a little more dinner before you go look?"

He shook his head, and she let him go.

The computer turned out to be in the front bedroom, which also seemed to be his studio. He was shocked to see his guitar there, the gold-top Les Paul he knew so well, perched on a guitar stand. Next to it he saw a Fender Precision bass, a keyboard, and a Tascam multi-track cassette recorder that had probably been state of the art in 1986.

He perched on the edge of a battered love seat and picked up the Les Paul. It fit into his arms like a lover, like a piece of a lost world.

He looked up to see Jess in the doorway.

"I wish there was something I could do," she said. "I hate to see you this way. If you want to play guitar, go on ahead. It seems to help sometimes. I'll put your dinner in the fridge."

He returned the guitar to its stand and gave her a hug and a kiss on the cheek. It seemed the polite thing to do.

The computer was already on. He powered up the monitor and it blinked and showed his email program. Halfway down the screen was a message labeled "Your cat is on the roof" from someone named Murray Black. It read:

> You will probably think me a coward for doing this in email. So I'm a coward already. The bad news is that Sugar Hill passed on PALOMITA.

Yeah, I know. Turns out they're closing down their North Carolina office and consolidating all the operations in Nashville. The guy you talked to after the Local 506 show is no longer with the company, and is in fact leaving the business entirely. (Can't say I blame him.) This will be all over the Internet tomorrow. Jeff, I don't know what else to do. I would love to be your manager but the sad truth at this moment is, there is nothing here for me to manage. I don't believe it's the record, it's just the business. I know that doesn't help a lot right now.

IT WAS THE THINGS he *did* remember that made him feel like he was in free fall. He knew *Palomita*. It had come out on Warner's, and had won a Grammy for Album of the Year.

He put his name into Google and came up with a home page. The site had his photo and a list of his homemade CDs for sale. They were the albums he knew. He clicked on the Bio link and read the three skimpy paragraphs there.

Nothing he read matched his own memories, which were vivid and detailed and indisputably authentic. Like his first night in LA in June of 1970, barely 20 years old and driving up into the foothills to pick out the letters of his name in the infinite recession of lights. Opening for Linda Ronstadt at the Troubadour in the summer of '71, retreating from the onslaught of celebrities and kingmakers to the bar, where he met an amiable kid from Texas named Don Henley. Then sitting on the balcony of his Laurel Canyon apartment that December afternoon in '75, watching the breeze stir the eucalyptus as Henley offered him the lead guitar slot that Bernie had just vacated.

There had been the craziness at the end of the seventies that had culminated in his hanging off the wrought iron grill of a hotel balcony by one hand, ten floors above the Champs-Elysées, scaring himself into changing his life. His first day back in the studio, two years sober, laying down the first tracks for the first solo record. The day he saw Kathleen for the first time, walking out of the surf at Laguna, August 22, 1990, orange hair, orange one-piece suit, the sunset exploding orange behind her, knowing that she was the one. Playing the final mix of *Palomita* for her in the front room of their house in San Miguel fifteen years later, the voices of the street kids and the smell of jacaranda floating in the windows.

He grabbed the phone and dialed his home number. On the third ring a man's voice answered in Spanish. Yes, this was the right number, yes, San Miguel de Allende. No, and he was truly sorry, but he'd never heard of a Jeff McCoy and knew no one named Kathleen.

•

THE WEBSITE HAD SAMPLES from *Palomita*. He was surprised by how similar they sounded, even with him playing all the instruments himself, to the studio versions he knew.

He pushed the chair back from the computer and looked around the room. It had a musty odor, the smell of mold growing in the back of a closet. The wooden floors were stained and dented, the rug worn through in the center. He let himself, carefully and tentatively, try to imagine what it must be like to live here.

There was a framed, autographed photo of Don Gibson on the wall, and just as he knew the way from Wal-Mart to this room, he knew why the photo was there. Gibson, after failing at three different record labels, had washed up in a trailer park north of Knoxville where, in a single afternoon, he'd written "Oh Lonesome Me" and "I Can't Stop Lovin' You" back to back, the songs that revived his career and went on to sell tens of millions of copies.

To cling to that dream of a Don Gibson moment, as each year the odds grew longer, seemed a nightmare beyond endurance.

Somebody had told him once that if you could see your hands in a dream, you could take control of it. He looked as his hands and whispered, "I'm ready to wake up now. I'll count to three. One. Two..."

JESS WAS ASLEEP when he finally came to bed. He'd played guitar for a while after all, and nodded out on the loveseat. But when he woke up he was still there, in a tiny house near a town called Pittsboro.

HE WAS ON REGISTER 3 in the morning. A young guy kept staring at him as he rang up three pairs of socks and two pairs of running shorts. "You know who you look like?" the guy said. "You look like this singer named Jeff Mc-Coy."

"Yeah," he said. "That's me."

"You're kidding! I can't believe it. You're working at Wal-Mart? I saw you at the Cradle last year. You were incredible. I thought you were, like, big time."

"Yeah," he said. "Me too."

SOMETIME AFTER LUNCH he felt the numbness begin to wear off. He hadn't realized how much it had been protecting him until it was gone. But now every minute, every second, was agony. Scanning candy bars and girdles and plastic leftover containers, feeding checks into the printer, cracking a roll of quarters over the drawer. Staring at the clock, willing the time to pass. What in God's name was he doing here?

How much longer could this go on?

NINE HARD QUESTIONS ABOUT THE NATURE OF THE UNIVERSE

1 ON A WEDNESDAY in November of 1957, nine-year-old Danny
Armbruster disappeared from a subdivision outside Mesa, Arizona. His
parents had expected him back since nightfall. Danny, meanwhile, had picked
up a bullhead in the front tire of his bike and was having to walk it home.

The sun had just gone down when Danny saw the light in the sky. For a
second he thought he'd gotten turned around and it was the moon. Only it
was the wrong shape for the moon, longer than it was tall. And the color was
an intense blue-white, like the glow of the welding torches at his father's plant.

The light continued to grow and began to wobble slightly. Danny caught a
glimpse of a deeper, reddish color on the underside. Suddenly he knew he was
looking at a flying saucer.

He could make out the shape of it now, like two dinner plates front to front.
A cone of light sprang out of the bottom and swept toward him over the
desert. His common sense told him to head for home, but he was afraid to run
under the ship. He thought of a kangaroo rat he'd seen once, paralyzed by the
lights of the car, going under the wheels despite his father swerving to miss it.
It was like it had lost control of its own desires.

This can't be happening, he thought. Can it?

The machine settled onto the desert. Bits of dirt and rock were sucked up
into the weird glow and pinged away into the darkness. Danny felt grains of
blowing sand nick his face and arms. For some reason he made no effort to
turn away or cover his eyes. He just stood in silence until three small men in
silver suits came to lead him onto the ship.

2 A MAN FROM Project Blue Book came to talk to Danny's parents.
Since the two Sputnik launches by the Soviets that fall, there had been
a massive "flap," or wave of sightings. He listened to Danny's mother describe

the eerie lights in the sky and took pictures of a charred mesquite bush near the road where Danny's bicycle had been found. The pictures were sent on to the Foreign Technology Division at Wright-Patterson AFB. Danny's mother never heard from the Air Force again.

The police found no fingerprints but Danny's on the bike, and the FBI declined to investigate when no ransom demands were made.

A year after the boy's disappearance, a middle-aged man in battered clothes came up to Danny's father in the parking lot of the plant where he worked. "Don't worry about your boy," the man said. "The space people have him. He's all right. Really. He's getting to see things ... things you could never imagine."

"Who are you?" Danny's father said. "What do you want?"

"I want you not to worry," the man said, backing away.

"Hey!" Danny's father shouted. "Come back!" He chased the man for a block or more, only to lose him in a crowd. Danny's father called the police, who were unable to locate the man.

Danny's father decided, after several sleepless nights, not to tell his wife about it. In the past year they had been harassed by dozens of letters and phone calls from "contactees" and they only seemed to prolong his wife's suffering. Eventually he forgot the entire incident.

3 THE ALIENS WERE about four feet tall, wore silvery uniforms, and had pale gray skin. Their foreheads were large, their noses little more than the sharp intersection of the planes of their cheeks. Their eyes were outsized, dark, and widely separated, and their lips were so thin that their mouths seemed to disappear when they were closed. At first Danny couldn't tell any of the aliens apart.

They took him into a room that was as shining and white as a new refrigerator and strapped him to a table that was not quite long enough for him. He didn't think to resist at first, but as the things they did to him got more and more unpleasant, he began to be afraid.

They filled his mouth with a gummy pink substance from something like a toothpaste tube. Danny choked on it. The alien ignored all his struggles and held Danny's mouth closed for several seconds. Then he pulled the wad out and dropped it into a slot on the wall.

The touch of the alien's hand was cold, damp, and scaly, and when it reached for Danny again, he tried to pull his head away. Another alien came forward and guided a metal skull cap onto Danny's head while the first one held him motionless. Danny felt a prickling in his scalp, then a wave of intense pleasure, like the last bell on the last day of school. It was followed just as suddenly by a feeling of weightlessness and nausea. Danny threw up and the aliens backed away, letting him turn his head so the stuff would run out of his mouth.

In a few seconds they had reduced him to the level of an animal, shivering, terrified, unable to speak or move. They put adhesive patches on the skin inside his elbows and behind his knees, rolling up his jacket sleeves and pants legs to do it, then tore the patches off and fed them into the wall. They took blood from his left ankle, then pulled his pants down and poked at his genitals with a metal rod.

When they finished, two of them carried him out of the laboratory and through a series of white-walled rooms. The numbness in Danny's brain had worn off. "What are doing?" he shouted. "Where are you taking me?" Their only answer was to put him in a tiny room and leave him alone there.

4 DANNY CRIED HIMSELF to sleep, lying on what seemed to be a padded shelf that grew out of the wall. It was the only thing in the room that was not hard, white, and shiny. In the morning they brought him into another part of the ship. One of the aliens handed him a cup with something in it that looked like a vanilla milkshake and smelled like Cream-of-Wheat. His stomach seemed to accept it, and it did clear the bad taste out of his mouth.

The room didn't have any chairs in it, so Danny stayed on his feet. He couldn't see any kind of controls or instruments, only a pedestal in the middle of the floor that held a fan-shaped sculpture. It looked like white plaster. The wide end of the fan merged with the ceiling.

"How long are you going to keep me here?" Danny asked. He was taller than any of the aliens, and now that he'd rested he wasn't quite as afraid. "My parents are going to be looking for me, you know. You can't just hide me here forever."

"You will not be going back," one of the aliens said. It wasn't speaking English, but the meaning of what it said seemed to come into Danny's head anyway. It was a little like a movie he'd seen once, where the people were speaking French, but the real words were written on the screen, and he almost felt like he understood what they were saying.

"Look," said another one of the aliens.

The wall in front of Danny darkened. In seconds it was black enough to show pinpoints of light. With a sudden spasm in his leg muscles, Danny realized he was looking out into empty space. In the distance the stars were smeared with an orange haze. It looked like a water-color painting, thickening to make dust-colored mountains and waves, then thinning away again to nothing. Several of the stars behind it shone with a fierce blue-white glow. In another part of the sky Danny saw an oval of light, its arms spiraling out into nothingness. The space between the stars was blacker than anything Danny had ever seen, and the bright colors of the stars took his breath away. The longer he looked, the more of them he could see.

He watched for a very long time, trying to get used to the idea of what they meant. Finally he turned back to the aliens and nodded to them. As they led him back to his cell, he was crying again.

In time he got used to the physical hardships—the ceramic-looking bucket instead of a toilet, the lack of baths or fresh clothing, the monotonous diet. By and large he had the run of the ship, though he never saw anything that looked like a control room.

The worst of it was the boredom. The aliens walked around him like he was a piece of furniture, and never talked to him unless they had to. There was nothing to read, nothing to watch except the nearly motionless expanse of stars.

One day he lost control, in the middle of the big room with the screen and the fan sculpture. "Damn you!" he said, screaming and crying all at once. "Goddamn you to hell!" It was the worst thing he knew to say. "Don't you care? What kind of people are you? Don't you have any feelings? Don't you care what happens to me?"

One of the aliens stopped. "We are not people," it said reasonably. "And no, we do not care."

Much later, long after he'd lost count of meals and naps, after he'd lost all sense of time whatsoever, something new appeared on the screen.

A planet.

Danny slept a half dozen times before the planet grew large enough to fill the screen. As the ship closed in, Danny kept expecting the green-gray blur of the surface to resolve into recognizable detail. Instead the alien ship simply dipped into the living soup of the planet's atmosphere.

In seconds he was unable to see anything but whirling yellow feathers and smaller green, furry seeds. They flew toward him at a fantastic rate of speed, hung motionless against the surface of the screen for a few seconds, then were whipped away by the turbulence. Slowly Danny made out a shadow in the background. He understood that the image he watched was like TV, that the things he saw there couldn't actually break through to reach him. All the same he found himself squirming in fear.

It looked a little like the giant insects he'd seen in dinosaur books, only much, much bigger. It was only when the thing stopped and hovered directly in front of the camera that Danny could see all the hideous differences. A huge, oval mouth, surrounded by loose flaps of skin, took up most of what seemed to be the head. The rest of its body was lopsided and covered with white dust or mold. It sucked puffballs and green seeds continuously into its mouth. Halfway down its belly something like an open sore dripped thick liquid into the air.

"What is it?" Danny asked one of the aliens.

"It is what it is."

"That's a stupid answer."

"What you are to your planet, it is here."

"You mean, that thing can think?"

"It has a language. It fights wars. It has a God."

The next time he slept, Danny had a nightmare about the monster's God. Ever since his parents had admitted that Santa Claus and the tooth fairy were not real, he'd wondered if God wasn't more of the same thing. He'd never had the nerve to ask his parents, and now it was too late.

5 SOMETHING ELSE HAD HAPPENED to Danny in the endless time since he'd been brought into the ship. Wispy, colorless hair had begun to grow on his face and body, and his voice had started to crack. The thing he still thought of as his weenie would sometimes swell up and become very sensitive, especially in the mornings. He found that by lying on his stomach and moving a certain way he could relieve the pressure, though he felt guilty afterwards about the mess.

He went through a period of severe disorientation. He spent hours touching the fine hairs on his face, longing for a mirror. It seemed to him that he spent more time sleeping than awake, but without a clock he couldn't be sure. He forgot his mother's middle name.

He worried about his teeth and gums until he developed sores inside his mouth. He showed them to one of the aliens and told it he was sick. The alien took him back to the hospital room and filled his mouth with the gummy pink stuff. "You are not sick," the alien said, after the stuff had been fed to the wall. "It is in your mind."

Danny went a little crazy. He lunged at the alien. Before he could do more than raise his arm to throw a punch, he felt a vibration go up his spine. He passed out and woke up in his cell. He beat on the walls and screamed until he was too exhausted to move.

In time they let him out again. He had learned not to assault them, but it hadn't made him less sullen and irritable. He was close to trying it again anyway when something more interesting came up.

It was another planet, blue-green, hazed with clouds. He refused to leave the area in front of the screen, staring endlessly for the first sight of something that would tell him he was home. Instead he finally woke from a doze to the sight of a single vast, unfamiliar continent below the ship. He went to his cell and cried helplessly from one meal to the next. When he came out again, it was to watch the ship descend over a city of cubical white buildings.

Three aliens led him from the ship to a maze of hallways. It ended in a room that had clearly been designed for him. It had a bed, even though the bedspread, pillows, and sheets were all part of the same molded piece. It had a desk with paper and pens, shelves with real books, and best of all, a bathroom with a toilet, a shower, and a toothbrush. Several sets of loose cotton pants and shirts were laid out on the bed. Two screens set into the wall showed an Earth-like field and a clear blue sky. When the overhead light was turned off the screens showed a moonlit version of the same scene. He had day and night again, even if he had to make them himself.

The door, of course, locked behind the aliens when they left.

He washed and put on new clothes and started on the books. Most of them had multiple copies, as if the aliens had hijacked a trainload of them and piled them on the shelves without thought. One group seemed to be a shipment of war novels, another was diet and exercise books. Other clusters were science fiction, Peterson field guides, and one entire shelf of paperbacks in French.

He went through the novels first, skimming, looking for the parts where men and women were together. He learned a little, only enough to make his curiosity worse.

He'd been there long enough to be tired of the books when the door opened and a girl walked in. Danny was sitting at his desk, writing a letter to his parents that he knew they would never see.

He was stunned by the sight of her. He thought at first that he had made her up. Then she combed through her dark, curly hair with one hand and pulled it back, kept pulling it back until he could see her entire hairline, and still she pulled on it, until tears came up in her eyes.

Danny knew he couldn't imagine anything that strange. "Hey," he said. "Are you okay?"

She was maybe a little older than Danny, her small breasts just showing under the long, shapeless dress that she wore. She did not seem to be all right at all. Her eyes were puzzled and her mouth was slack. Her body was thick with excess weight. Danny wondered how she could have gotten fat on the aliens' tasteless food.

He went over to her and gently worked her fingers loose from her hair. Her eyes followed him, but she didn't show any real interest until he started to back away. Then she made a bleating noise and threw her arms around him. She smelled clean and Danny found himself getting excited by the touch of her, even though the weird way she acted made him nervous.

"Can you talk?" he asked her. He worked her arms loose and sat her on the edge of the bed next to him. "Can you say anything at all?" Now that he was over the initial shock, he could see that she was not all that nice to look at. Her eyes were small and puffy, her nose flat and thick, and her skin was shiny with oil. "Can you tell me your name?"

"Muh-muh-rnuh..." the girl said.

In a moment of insight, Danny realized that she hadn't survived the things that he'd been through, the repeated shocks, the isolation, the horror of the aliens always around.

"Mary?" he asked. "Is that your name?" When she didn't answer, he tried to smile at her. "Well, that's what I'll call you, okay?"

She seemed calmed by the sound of his voice. When he stood up she let him go. He kept an eye on her as he walked to the door. "Hey," he said loudly. "What am I supposed to do? Can you hear me? There's something wrong with this one. You understand? She's broken. I can't fix her, if that's what you want."

He got no answer. He went back to his routine of reading and drawing and pacing the room. When he tried to talk to her, she simply stared at him.

Eventually he took a bath and went to bed, dressed for once because the girl was there. She had fallen asleep on the bed. He lay down carefully so he wouldn't wake her and turned off the light.

Sleep wouldn't come. Every time the girl shifted her weight, his eyes came open and his heart beat loudly. He felt like he'd been lying there for hours when he noticed that she wasn't asleep anymore. By the sound of her breathing, he could tell that she'd turned to face him.

Then she began to touch him. Danny was embarrassed at first, then a little frightened. But her hands were knowing and insistent, and he felt sick and feverish and could not make himself pull away. She took his trousers down and began to stroke his penis. He felt the pressure build up inside him but before it got messy she rolled onto her back and began to pull at him.

"What?" he whispered. "What do you want?"

She kept grabbing at his waist and his legs until he finally rolled on top of her. She took hold of his penis and began to pull at it. He started to lose his erection, not understanding what she wanted, ashamed because he didn't know what to do.

She took his right hand and placed it over her breast. He felt the end of her breast get hard, and it made the same thing happen to his penis. She pulled at him, and he felt his penis slide into something warm and wet. Her hips moved jerkily under him, and he exploded inside her.

Lights flashed in front of his eyes. He gasped for breath. He smelled something he'd never smelled before, an earthy, exciting odor that at the same time left him repelled and sad. The girl groaned and started to snore. Danny's head cleared. He was appalled at what he'd done. He had made sex with this ... this *thing,* that was ugly and brain damaged, little better than an animal.

He went to the bathroom and washed himself, then lay down on the part of the floor that was sculpted to look like a rug. To his own surprise he was asleep in seconds.

The shame was still with him when he woke up. He ignored the girl all day, and when he was ready for bed he turned out the lights and lay down nervously where one edge of the bed met the wall. She reached for him and he pushed her away. The second time she came for him he pushed her so hard she slid off the bed and sat on the floor, crying quietly. Danny stayed on the bed, arms folded, unable to sleep. After a while he turned the lights on and read. When he absolutely couldn't stay awake any longer, he put his head down and slept on the desk.

When he woke up she was gone.

6 AFTER THAT, whenever he found himself thinking about the girl, remembering the smell of what they'd done, or the feeling of her breast in his hand, Danny would exercise. One of the health books was about something called "yoga," and Danny found out the harder he practiced at it, the better he felt.

He began to build himself up. He knew he was getting taller by the way his clothes fit him, and before long he could see the shape of his body change, his stomach flattening and the muscles turning to hard outlines under his pale skin. He would cover the drain in the shower and look at himself in the pool of water there, sometimes until he forgot where he was. He was fit, he thought. Fit and ready. But for what?

He had nicknamed the alien who brought his food Fremount, after the character in *Pogo.* The little alien wouldn't reveal his real name and answered only the most direct questions. One day another alien brought the cup. This one had more wrinkles around its eyes and a forward tilt to its walk. Danny named him Howland Owl.

"Where's Fremount?" Danny asked.

"Drink this and come with me."

Danny swallowed the food in two gulps. The alien led Danny down a series of white corridors. At the end was a room divided in half by some kind of glass. On the other side was a dwarfish, naked creature with a face like a Neanderthal. Its entire body was covered with long, widely separated black hairs.

"You may talk," Howland said.

"Hello?" Danny said.

"He gives you greetings," Howland translated, looking at the dwarf. Danny guessed that the mind-talking worked the same for the dwarf as it did for Danny. Both of them could understand anything the aliens thought.

Howland turned back to Danny. "It asks you how you retain your water."

"What?"

Howland repeated the question.

"I don't understand," Danny said. "What does he mean?"

Howland made no response.

"Ask him..." Danny said, "...ask him if he has a family."

Howland relayed the question, then said, "It says it will have had. It asks if you are light."

"Light?"

Howland moved its hands as if it were stroking a large globe. "Light," it said.

Danny felt his eyes begin to sting. "Tell him to make sense. I can't understand what he's asking me. Can't you see that?" He wanted to hit something. Mostly he wanted to hit the hairy little dwarf. He would have taken a swing at Howland if he'd thought he could get away with it.

Howland brought him back to his room. His next meal was brought by Fremount, as usual.

7 DANNY MADE A CALENDAR. Every time he slept he marked off a day. He knew it wasn't accurate, but it helped tie him to the passing time. By his reckoning, the visit with the dwarfish alien was followed by nearly two years where nothing broke his routine. He exercised. He read. He sat in the lotus position, thinking about as little as it was possible for him to think. In the dark he dreamed about his parents, his best friend Tom, about pot roast and candy bars, about snow and forests and mountains, about dogs and fish, about school, about half-remembered girls and women he had known.

Waking up was always the hardest part.

He seemed to have stopped growing. His beard, when he didn't use the depilatory cream the aliens gave him, came in dark and full. Dark hair covered his legs and crotch. Whenever he asked them, the aliens cut the hair on his head with some kind of pistol that had no blades and made no noise. Lately one or two of the fallen hairs would be white.

He read and he exercised and he wrote letters and drew and he tried to keep the voices in his head quiet.

Until the woman came.

His first reaction, when she knocked on his door and simply walked in, was shyness. His brain was numb. Eventually he realized that she had been talking for some time and he hadn't heard a word she'd said, or even noticed what she really looked like.

She was at least pretty, by anyone's standards. Her hair was long and reddish brown, her eyes a clear gray. It seemed to Danny at first that she was younger than he was, but it turned out they had taken her in 1957 also, and she had been 12 at the time.

Her name was Autumn.

"That's a beautiful name," Danny told her.

"Yes," she said, "it is."

Danny couldn't think of anything worth saying. When his silence went on too long, Autumn stood up. "I'm just down the hall," she said. "Come and see me sometime." As if they were two people who'd met in a hotel somewhere.

"I can't," Danny said. "I'm locked in."

Autumn opened the door. "No you're not," she said, and left.

Danny stood where she'd been and sniffed the air. He believed he could detect a lingering sweetness there. He felt flushed and off-balance, and his heart beat so loudly and so strangely that he thought it might give out any second.

He sat in the lotus position and fought for control. He concentrated on not moving until enough time passed that it didn't seem so urgent any more. Then he waited a little longer. Then he got up and went to her.

Miraculously his door opened to his touch. The corridor had changed since the last time he'd seen it. Now there was only his door and one other, twenty yards away. He walked to the other door and knocked, and Autumn opened it.

Her room was identical to his, except that the books on the shelves were different. She sat on the bed and brushed her hair, over and over, while he looked through the books.

"You've been here a long time, haven't you?" she said.

"Yes."

"Long enough to read all those books of yours?"

"Three or four times."

After a while he sat on the bed and touched her hand. She didn't pull it away, but she didn't move closer to him either. She just sat there and smiled at him in a vague sort of way. He wanted to put his penis in her, but she was so self-possessed, so alien in her own way, that he didn't know if he should try. He didn't even know if he should ask her.

They talked about other things until they both were falling asleep between sentences. She told him how she'd been on a ship the entire time until she met Danny. That she had grown up in Chicago, that her parents were musicians, that she would have been a dancer but she'd grown too tall.

When Danny went back to his room he dreamed about the two of them in a huge house that had grass for carpets and slow, strange animals for furniture. He woke up refreshed and excited and went to her room, but he could see around the edges of the door that her lights were still off. He went back to his room and exercised until he was tired enough to sleep a little more. On top of all the other strangeness, it bothered Danny to see how different their rhythms of day and night were.

They spent another day talking, some of it reading quietly, and another long night apart. All the time a peculiar tension built in him, and on the third day it broke.

They were looking at his books together when her shoulder brushed his. He turned and put his hand around her elbow. She looked at him and smiled. He touched her breast, his fingers shaking, and she smiled again. He put his arms around her and kissed her clumsily, and she put her arms around his waist. He led her to the bed and took her clothes off. He almost wanted to cry when he saw how soft and smooth and tautly muscled her body was.

"Have you ... have you done this before?" he asked.

"No," she said. Her eyes were a little out of focus and her voice shook.

As he knelt between her legs, he was suddenly frightened. He turned off the lights, but it didn't help him get hard again. "I'm sorry," he whispered. "I don't really know what I'm doing either."

"It's okay," she said. She held him and he ran his hands through her hair, wondering at the way it smelled. Love, he thought. I'm in love. Is it really this easy? What happens now?

He never fell asleep, just seemed to float, and thoughts went spinning around in his head. After a long time he wasn't afraid any more. Autumn's place was tight and very dry and not at all the same as Mary's had been. Afterwards there was blood on the bed. Autumn said that was all right, that it was supposed to be that way.

For a long time Danny couldn't get to sleep. He wished he had somebody to talk to, somebody to explain the things he felt. If he was grown up now, why did he still feel like a little boy? If it was right for him to do what he did with Autumn, why did he feel so guilty?

In time the sex got better, and the guilt just went away.

He told Autumn that he loved her. He told himself it didn't matter that she didn't say it back to him.

It was about two of Danny's months later that Autumn told him she was pregnant. It had been a happy time for both of them, Danny teaching her yoga, Autumn teaching him to dance. They read together, slept together, even showered together, and now they were going to have a child together.

"Are you sure?" he asked her.

"Pretty sure. I didn't bleed last month and I feel sick when I wake up, and, well, I can just feel it."

"That's wonderful!"

"Is it?"

"Isn't it?"

"Look around you! Do you see any doctors? Anybody who knows anything about human medicine at all? And if the baby is born, *if*, then where is it going to grow up? In these two little rooms? And never see a real sky or trees or birds or other people?"

He held her until she cried herself out. "It'll make us a family," Danny said. "That's all that matters, that we're a family and that we love each other, right?"

Autumn didn't answer.

During the pregnancy they quarreled more and more often. Autumn would only make love after Danny sulked for days at a time. She was clearly frightened that something would go wrong, and any time the rhythms of her body changed she would panic.

When her labor began in earnest, she began to scream hysterically. Danny was in his own room, where he'd been spending most of his time lately, and he got to her about the same time the aliens did. One of them looked like Howland Owl, the one that had taken him to see the dwarf. They said nothing to Danny, just led Autumn away.

Time slowed. Danny waited uneasily in Autumn's room. Everything he tried—reading, meditation, sleeping—ended with him pacing the floor. When Autumn finally came back she was pale, exhausted, and no longer pregnant.

"The baby...?" Danny asked.

"They took her."

"Took her?"

"I heard her cry. She was alive, she was crying, and they took her away." Autumn lay down and went to sleep. Danny stretched out beside her and it seemed he'd just closed his eyes when Autumn's screams woke him.

The aliens came for her and they wouldn't let Danny go with them. He sat on the edge of the bed until Fremount brought his food.

"What have you done with her?"

"She is sick," Fremount said.

"And the baby?"

Fremount turned away.

"The baby!" Danny shouted. "What about our little girl?"

The door closed in his face.

They're going to keep the baby, he realized. If they had been humans, they would at least have had the decency to lie, to tell him she was dead. But they were aliens, and they didn't care. For the first time since the ship he hated them, blindly, savagely, and the hate kept him going until they brought Autumn back.

She was completely empty. She refused to eat, sitting all day in her room with her arms wrapped around her legs, staring into space. If he tried to comfort her, she jerked away at his touch, startled by it. She slept badly, moaning and thrashing herself awake. The only thing Danny could do for her was stay away.

Eventually she began to eat again. Her sleep became quieter. She slept most of the time. When she was awake she managed an occasional smile. She even let him make love to her, but only when she was bleeding. "No more babies," she whispered to him afterwards. "Not ever again. They won't take anything from me again."

8 IN AUTUMN'S ROOM was a shelf of physics books. After Danny had read everything else, he started on them. They were tough going at first, but he needed the challenge.

One day the alien called Howland Owl came for him again. He brought Danny into a long, narrow white room. Nine of the aliens sat along one side of it, like a jury.

"What do you see," one of them asked, "when you perform sex?"

"See?" Danny asked.

"Do you see God?" asked another one.

"I don't know what you're talking about."

"Last night," said yet another one, "you performed sex and the woman said, 'Oh God.' What did she mean?"

"You were *listening?*" Danny said. He was not very surprised, really.

"Answer the question," Howland said.

"You're crazy. God doesn't have anything to do with it. It's just something people say."

"Then when *do* you see your God?" another asked.

Danny hesitated, then said, "I don't have a God." He waited for lightening to strike. When it didn't he was almost disappointed. "If there was a God, I wouldn't be here. If there was a God, it wouldn't have let you take my daughter from me. God is just something they tell kids. It's supposed to make them think that things make sense. Just another fairy tale."

"Do many of you feel this way?"

"Many people? I don't know. Maybe they all do."

After a silence, Howland said, "Come. I will take you back to your room."

"Just a minute," Danny said. He picked one of the aliens to stare at. "I want to see my daughter."

The alien returned his stare. "The child does not belong to you."

"Like hell," Danny said. "What are you afraid of? Why won't you let me see her? For God's sake, she's my child!"

"Why," the alien said, "do you ask a favor in the name of a God you do not believe in?"

Danny charged the alien and woke up on the bed in his room.

He told Autumn about the interview. "I know," she said. "I went through most of that on the ship. That's what they do."

"Snoop? Steal babies?"

"Haven't they ever told you? They look for God. I don't think they mean it the way we do. I mean, they're not looking for a big old man with white hair. But that's their job."

"Their job?" Danny started to laugh. "All of them? All of those ships, those other planets, those other aliens? Their job?" Tears rolled down his face. "That's why they kidnapped us? To look for *God?*" He cried until his whole body felt dried out, then he slept, longer and deeper than he had for a long time.

A while after that he tried to talk to Fremount about their ships. "It says here," he said, pointing to the physics book, "that nothing can move faster than the speed of light. What about your ships? How do they do it?"

"I will ask," Fremount said.

Later an alien that Danny had never seen before came to the room. "I will help you with your questions," it said.

Danny named the alien P.T. Bridgeport. "Is it true your ships go faster than light?" he asked.

"Faster?" the alien said. "How do you mean faster?"

Danny had the same sinking feeling he'd gotten talking to the hairy dwarf. Very carefully he explained the speed of light, using Astronomical Units since the aliens would have to know the distance from the Earth to the Sun.

"Are you trying to tell me," Bridgeport said at last, "that light is either a particle or a wave?"

"Yes."

"But it isn't. Light is a state of the aether."

Danny went back to the book and showed the alien the Michelson-Morely experiment that disproved the existence of the aether. Bridgeport picked up the book and read several pages, its bulbous eyes flicking back and forth across the lines. "It says here that FitzGerald could explain those same results as compression of the aether."

A few meals later Danny asked to see Bridgeport again. He showed it something called the Double Slit Experiment, where, under certain conditions, a stream of photons would create an interference pattern. The results seems to vary depending on what the experimenters tried to prove.

"I don't understand," Danny said.

"Nor do I," Bridgeport said. "I have performed an experiment similar to this, and these are not the results I obtained. May I borrow this?"

Danny pointed to the duplicate copies on the shelf. "Be my guest. But haven't you read it already?"

"Why?" Bridgeport asked him. "What could we possibly learn from your primitive science?"

When Bridgeport returned, it seemed tired, or older. Danny had been around the aliens long enough to realize something had gone wrong with its body.

"Well?" Danny asked.

Bridgeport was quiet a long time before answering. "Now, when I run the experiment, I get an interference pattern, just like in your book. When I leave the room and my assistant runs the experiment ... there is no pattern."

"What are you trying to tell me?"

"In your book. The man Heisenberg. He says the outcome of an experiment is determined by the desired results. That is more or less what he says. It seems this is even more true than he realized."

"But ... which is the real answer?"

"Both. Either. Any answer you like."

"My God."

"No. There is no God in this. If there is today, maybe not tomorrow." Bridgeport started for the door.

"Wait," Danny said. "Come back. I want to ask you..."

The alien was gone.

Next mealtime, Danny asked Fremount for Bridgeport. "That one is dead," Fremount said.

Danny was stunned. "Dead? But how?"

"I am no longer allowed to talk to you," Fremount said.

Danny went to Autumn's room. They spent so little time together that their schedules had become out of synch. This time Danny found her awake.

"I think I killed one of them," he told her.

"How?"

"Physics," Danny said. "Or maybe religion. I'm not sure I know the difference anymore."

"Good," Autumn said, going back to her book. "Kill them all. All of them."

9 A FEW MEALS LATER they came for him. They led him out a new doorway into another maze of halls. The first he realized he was on a ship was when a wall near him turned dark and he saw the stars again. They hadn't warned him to pack anything or even let him say goodbye to Autumn.

After that first surge of anger, his heart pounded with new hope. He searched the ship, finally found an alien, and poured out his questions. Were they taking him home? Was Autumn on board? Was his daughter? How long would it take?

The alien ignored him.

He exercised and meditated and slept. He thought about Autumn more than he wanted to. He kept count of the number of times he slept, into the hundreds, then lost count. He started again, got into the hundreds again, then gave up for good.

He hung on.

When he finally saw a blue world in the viewscreen, he was afraid to hope. He sat cross legged on the floor, searching for a landmark, remembering the last blue world. And then the clouds broke and he saw the telltale shape of the Mediterranean and the long curve of Africa dropping away, and he cried for the last time in his life.

The saucer let him off in Texas, dressed in his loose white robes. They gave him a few hundred dollars in cash and some small disks of pure gold. He'd read about time dilation and the twin paradox and hoped the money would still be good.

"Aren't you going to say goodbye?" he asked one of the aliens as he stood in the open port of the ship.

"Goodbye," the alien said.

Danny walked over a hill and saw a ribbon of asphalt that led off into the distance. He sat in the hot sand at the top of the hill and smelled the sunlight.

He had spent long hours thinking about what he would do if he ever got home, how he would lie low, spend his time in the closest thing to a library he could find, learn enough to blend in. The one thing he was not prepared for was to find that the world had not changed.

He stood in a Greyhound station in Temple, Texas, looking at a newspaper dated June 6, 1958. He thought about Bridgeport's experiments. He wondered if it was 1958 only because Danny's imagination hadn't been strong enough to take him farther into the future.

He used some of the cash for a Salvation Army suit and a bus ticket to Arizona. He kept the gold in his boots and barricaded the door of the motel room where he spent his first night back on Earth.

He couldn't get over the richness of the smells in the air.

By Albuquerque he had the flu. He spent a week in a motel, convinced he was dying. In the delirium of his fever, objects lost their focus. Everything turned into random patterns of energy, mere conditions of the aether, and he felt himself sink into the bed. He was terrified. It had become a question of faith, not in God, but in something more basic, and his faith was slipping. Suddenly he knew how Bridgeport must have felt.

I am going to believe, he told himself. I believe in furniture and in floors. I believe in clothes and food and bodies with skins that keep them from sinking into mattresses. Whether they are real or not, I believe in them. My belief will make them real.

A few hours later his fever broke and he slept.

Back in Mesa, he watched his parents for several weeks. They were now much younger than he was. Finally, unable to resist, he tried to talk to his father. His father seemed frightened by him, so Danny left him alone.

He bought several books and magazines that promised to explain UFOs to him. He managed to read half of one of them before throwing them all away.

He took a job working for a landscape company in San Diego where he could work outdoors, within the sound and smell of the ocean. He was liked but never befriended by his fellow employees. The owners respected his good physical condition and his love for growing things and tolerated his occasional periods of dreaminess.

He spent his last years in a rest home in Scottsdale, Arizona, finally marrying another patient there. Until the week of his death he paid for an ad in the personal columns of newspapers in New York, Chicago, and Los Angeles. The ad read: "Autumn, please call me, Danny," followed by his address and phone number. None of the replies was genuine.

His funeral, in December of 1975, was small. His wife, and some of the other rest home patients, attended. After the service a strange light was seen in the sky. It hovered, then disappeared at a tremendous rate of speed. The Air Force declined to investigate.

WHITE CITY

ESLA LIFTS the piece of sirloin to his lips. Its volume is approximately .25 cubic inches, or .02777 of the entire steak. As he chews, he notices a water spot on the back of his fork. He takes a fresh napkin from the stack at his left elbow and scrubs the fork vigorously.

He is sitting at a private table in the refreshment stand at the west end of the Court of Honor. He looks out onto the Chicago World's Fair and Columbian Exposition. It is October of 1893. The sun is long gone and the reflections of Tesla's electric lights sparkle on the surface of the Main Basin, turning the spray from the fountain into glittering jewels. At the far end of the Basin stands the olive-wreathed Statue of the Republic in flowing robes. On all sides the White City lies in pristine elegance, testimony to the glorious architecture of ancient Greece and Rome. Its chilly streets are populated by mustached men in topcoats and sturdy women in woollen shawls.

The time is 9:45. At midnight Nikola Tesla will produce his greatest miracle. The number 12 seems auspicious. It is important to him, for reasons he cannot understand, that it is divisible by three.

Anne Morgan, daughter of financier J. Pierpoint Morgan, stands at a little distance from his table. Though still in finishing school she is tall, self-possessed, strikingly attractive. She is reluctant to disturb Tesla, knowing he prefers to dine alone. Still she is drawn to him irresistibly. He is rake thin and handsome as the devil himself, with steel gray eyes that pierce through to her soul.

"Mr. Tesla," she says, "I pray I am not disturbing you."

Tesla looks up, smiles gently. "Miss Morgan." He begins to rise.

"Please, do not get up. I was merely afraid I would miss you. I had hoped we might walk together after you finished here."

"I would be delighted."

"I shall await you there, by the Basin."

She withdraws. Trailing a gloved hand along the balustrade, she tries to avoid the drunken crowds which swarm the Exposition Grounds. Tomorrow the Fair will close and pass into history. Already there are arguments as to what is to become of these splendid buildings. There is neither money to maintain them nor desire to demolish them. Chicago's mayor, Carter Harrison, worries that they will end up filthy and vandalized, providing shelter for the hundreds of poor who will no longer have jobs when the Fair ends.

Her thoughts turn back to Tesla. She finds herself inordinately taken with him. At least part of the attraction is the mystery of his personal life. At age 37 he has never married nor been engaged. She has heard rumors that his tastes might be, to put it delicately, Greek in nature. There is no evidence to support this gossip, and she does not credit it. Rather it seems likely that no one has yet been willing to indulge the inventor's many idiosyncrasies.

She absently touches her bare left ear lobe. She no longer wears the pearl earrings that so offended him on their first meeting. She flushes at the memory, and at that point Tesla appears.

"Shall we walk?" he asks.

She nods and matches his stride, careful not to take his arm. Tesla is not comfortable with personal contact.

To their left is the Hall of Agriculture. She has heard that its most popular attraction is an 11-ton cheese from Ontario. Like so many other visitors to the Fair, she has not actually visited any of the exhibits. They seem dull and pedestrian compared to the purity and classical lines of the buildings that house them. The fragrance of fresh roses drifts out through the open doors, and for a moment she is lost in a reverie of New York in the spring.

As they pass the end of the hall, they are in darkness for a few moments. Tesla seems to shudder. He has been silent and intent, as if compulsively counting his steps. It would not surprise her if this were actually the case.

"Is anything wrong?" she asks.

"No," Tesla says. "It's nothing."

In fact the darkness is full of lurking nightmares for Tesla. Just now he was 5 years old again, watching his older brother Daniel fall to his death. Years of guilty self-examination have not made the scene clearer. They stood together at the top of the cellar stairs, and then Daniel fell into the darkness. Did he fall? Did Nikola, in a moment of childish rage, push him?

All his life he has feared the dark. His father took his candles away, so little Nikola made his own. Now the full-grown Tesla has brought electric light to the White City, carried by safe, inexpensive alternating current. It is only the beginning.

They round the east end of the Court of Honor. At the Music Hall, the Imperial Band of Austria plays melodies from Wagner. Anne Morgan shivers in the evening chill. "Look at the moon," she says. "Isn't it romantic?"

Tesla's smile seems condescending. "I have never understood the romantic impulse. We humans are meat machines, and nothing more."

"That is hardly a pleasant image."

"I do not mean to be offensive, only accurate. That is the aim of science, after all."

"Yes, of course," Anne Morgan says. "Science." There seems no way to reach him, no chink in his cool exterior. This is where the others gave up, she thinks. I will prove stronger than all of them. In her short, privileged existence, she has always obtained what she wants. "I wish I knew more about it."

"Science is a pure, white light," Tesla says. "It shines evenly on all things, and reveals their particular truths. It banishes uncertainty, and opinion, and contradiction. Through it we master the world."

They have circled back to the west, and to their right is the Liberal Arts Building. She has heard that it contains so much painting and sculpture that one can only wander helplessly among it. To attempt to seek out a single artist, or to look for the French Impressionists, of whom she has been hearing so much, would be sheer futility.

Under Tesla's electric lights, the polished façade of the building sparkles. For a moment, looking down the impossibly long line of perfect Corinthian columns, she feels what Tesla feels: the triumph of man over nature, the will to conquer and shape and control. Then the night breeze brings her the scent of roses from across the Basin, and the feeling passes.

THEY ENTER the Electricity Building together and stand in the center, underneath the great dome. This is the site of the Westinghouse exhibit, a huge curtained archway resting upon a metal platform. Beyond the arch are two huge Tesla coils, the largest ever built. At the peak of the arch is a tablet inscribed with the words: WESTINGHOUSE ELECTRIC & MANUFACTURING CO./TESLA POLYPHASE SYSTEM.

Tesla's mood is triumphant. Edison, his chief rival, has been proven wrong. Alternating current will be the choice of the future. The Westinghouse company has this week been awarded the contract to build the first two generators at Niagara Falls. Tesla cannot forgive Edison's hiring of Menlo Park street urchins to kidnap pets, which he then electrocuted with alternating current—"Westinghoused" them, as he called it. But Edison's petty, lunatic attempts to discredit the polyphase system have failed, and he stands revealed as an old, bitter, and unimaginative man.

Edison has lost, and history will soon forget him.

George Westinghouse himself, Tesla's patron, is here tonight. So are J.P. Morgan, Anne's father, and William K. Vanderbilt and Mayor Harrison. Here also are Tesla's friends Robert and Katharine Johnson, and Samuel Clemens, who insists everyone call him by his pen name.

It is nearly midnight.

Tesla steps lightly onto the platform. He snaps his fingers and gas-filled tubes burst into pure white light. Tesla has fashioned them to spell out the names of several of the celebrities present, as well as the names of his favorite Serbian poets. He holds up his hands to the awed and expectant crowd. "Gentlemen and Ladies. I have no wish to bore you with speeches. I have asked you here to witness a demonstration of the power of electricity."

He continues to talk, his voice rising to a high pitch in his excitement. He produces several wireless lamps and places them around the stage. He points out that their illumination is undiminished, despite their distance from the broadcast power source. "Note how the gas at low pressure exhibits extremely high conductivity. This gas is little different from that in the upper reaches of our atmosphere."

He concludes with a few fireballs and pinwheels of light. As the applause gradually subsides he holds up his hands once again. "These are little more than parlor tricks. Tonight I wish to say thank you, in a dramatic and visible way, to all of you who have supported me through your patronage, through your kindness, through your friendship. This is my gift to you, and to all of mankind."

He opens a panel in the front of the arch. A massive knife switch is revealed. Tesla makes a short bow and then throws the switch.

The air crackles with ozone. Electricity roars through Tesla's body. His hair stands on end and flames dance at the tips of his fingers. Electricity is his God, his best friend, his only lover. It is clean, pure, absolute. It arcs through him and invisibly into the sky. Tesla alone can see it. To him it is blinding white, the color he sees when inspiration, fear, or elation strikes him.

The coils draw colossal amounts of power. All across the great hall, all over the White City, lights flicker and dim. Anne Morgan cries out in shock and fear.

Through the vaulted windows overhead, the sky itself begins to glow.

Something sparks and hisses, and the machine winds down. The air reeks of melted copper and glass and rubber. It makes no difference. The miracle is complete.

Tesla steps down from the platform. His friends edge away from him, involuntarily. Tesla smiles like a wise father. "If you will follow me, I will show you what man has wrought."

Already there are screams from outside. Tesla walks quickly to the doors and throws them open.

Anne Morgan is one of the first to follow him out. She cannot help but fear him, despite her attraction, despite all her best intentions. All around her she sees fairgoers with their necks craned upward, or their eyes hidden in fear. She turns her own gaze to the heavens and lets out a short, startled cry.

The sky is on fire. Or rather, it burns the way the filaments burn in one of Tesla's electric lamps. It has become a sheet of glowing white. After a few seconds, the glare hurts her eyes, and she must look away.

It is midnight, and the Court of Honor is lit as if by the noonday sun. She is close enough to hear Tesla speak a single, whispered word: "Magnificent."

Westinghouse comes forward nervously. "This is quite spectacular," he says, "but hadn't you best, er, turn it off?"

Tesla shakes his head. Pride shines from his face. "You do not seem to understand. The atmosphere itself, some 35,000 feet up, has become an electrical conductor. I call it my 'terrestrial night light.' The charge is permanent. I have banished night from the world for all time."

"For all time?" Westinghouse stammers.

Anne Morgan slumps against a column, feels the cold marble against her back. Night, banished? The stars, gone forever? "You're mad," she says to Tesla. "What have you done?"

Tesla turns away. The reaction is not what he expected. Where is their gratitude? He has turned their entire world into a White City, a city in which crime and fear and nightmares are no longer possible. Yet men point at him, shouting curses, and women weep openly.

He pushes past them, toward the train station. Meat machines, he thinks. They are so used to their inefficient cycles of night and day. But they will learn.

He boards a train for New York and secures a private compartment. As he drives on into the white night, his window remains brilliantly lighted.

In the light there is truth. In the light there is peace. In the light he will be able, at last, to sleep.

PRIMES

1 FOR NEARLY AN HOUR Nick had been stuck on Interstate 40, surrounded by the worst traffic he'd ever seen. He'd watched the last heat of the sun set fire to the horizon and burn out, and now the first stars were tunneling through the haze. He had one arm out the open window in the unnatural 60-degree heat of the desiccated January evening. In the better parts of his brain, to keep himself amused, he was revising the code for his new graphics driver project.

Once past the Durham Freeway, I-40 had narrowed to a two-lane bottleneck. Traffic seemed to have doubled since that morning, with two cars trying to squeeze onto the road for every one that crawled off in defeat.

He was wearing a black T-shirt from the 544 club in New Orleans, where he and Angela had danced on their honeymoon two years before. A huge diesel rig inched past him on the right. The trailer was stark white except for the rear panel, where the number 544 stood out in stark black numerals. Nick glanced down at the dashboard clock. It was 5:44. For an instant he felt an abyss of inexplicability open under him, and then he shook it off. It was a bizarre coincidence, nothing more, something to tell Angela about, if he ever made it home.

By six he was close enough to the Lake Jordan exit that he could pull onto the shoulder and ease around the motionless right hand lane. It took fifteen minutes more to cover the remaining mile and a half to his driveway, and by then he was too tired to think much about the Cadillac parked where Angela's gold Acura should have been. Her battery had been acting up, he knew, and she'd probably gotten a ride home with somebody from Duke Hospital, where she was on the faculty.

In truth, for most of that particular day, Nick had been consciously happy. Despite the endless commute, despite approaching deadlines on his driver, the components of his life were laid out in what seemed a comfortable and sustainable order. He and Angela had no debts except the house, and they'd nearly paid that off. They'd both weathered the latest flu epidemic and were back to full health. And Thursday was Nick's night to cook. His attention was already shifting from traffic and programming to the free-range chicken and sour cream and tortillas waiting in the refrigerator to be transformed into *enchiladas suizas.*

The fear didn't fully hit him until he climbed out of the truck and saw the color of the door that he was about to slam shut.

His beautiful white pickup truck was bright red, red as a stoplight, red as blood.

He'd been driving that pickup for four years, from the time before he'd moved to North Carolina and met and married Angela. He'd bought it back in Austin, where a white paint job could make the difference of a few crucial degrees in the inside temperature under the Texas sun. It had been white when he'd gotten into it in the office parking lot at a quarter to five. He knew himself to be sober, drug-free, and possessed of a clean bill of psychiatric health. It was simply not possible that the truck was red.

He tried to remember if he'd noticed the hood of the truck while he was driving home. It had been dark, and he hadn't been paying attention. He looked at the key in his hand. It was the wrong size and shape and there were no other keys with it. His hand lunged reflexively for his pocket and found nothing there. All of his pockets were empty: no wallet, no checkbook, no change.

He searched the red truck. It too was empty except for a jack behind the seat and an owner's manual in the glove compartment. It could be a rental, he thought. Maybe he'd been in an accident that damaged his short term memory, and nobody had realized it. Maybe he'd absentmindedly left his wallet somewhere.

He started to run for the house, his shoes slapping awkwardly at the sidewalk. The front door was locked and he pounded on it with the flat of his hand until he heard the lock click and felt the door swing inward.

The man who opened it was in his thirties, tall and fit looking, with an angular face and fair receding hair. He wore a long-sleeved blue oxford-cloth shirt, crisply pressed khakis, tasseled loafers. He had a drink in his left hand. He looked Nick over and stepped aside to let him in. "Angela?" the man said, looking behind him, "I believe Nick has arrived."

The accent, as Nick knew it would be, was cultivated British. Nick had seen the man's photo in one of Angela's albums that dated back to before Nick's time with her. His name, Nick knew, was David. He was Angela's first husband, and he'd died in 1995.

2 "DAVID GRAHAM," David said, extending his hand. "I expect you're a little surprised to see me here."

"I thought you were dead," Nick told him, looking down to find he'd gripped David's hand by sheer reflex.

"Ah. Angela said much the same thing."

Nick backed into the living room and sat on the couch to ease the trembling in his legs. "What are you doing here?"

"I'm afraid I live here, actually."

Angela appeared in the doorway that led into the kitchen and leaned against the jamb, arms folded. She was still in her hospital scrubs and Nick couldn't help noticing, as he always did, how that shade of green set off the red-gold in her hair. A little mascara and eyebrow pencil would have made her conventionally beautiful, but she disdained makeup and so instead her appeal was more subtle. It had taken Nick all of a minute and a half—the interval between the first time he met her and the first time he managed to make her laugh—to be overwhelmed by it.

Nick tried and failed to read her mood through the barricade of her posture. David, on the other hand, was as transparent as glass. He looked at Angela with wonder, longing, and a fading glow of residual despair.

"Is anybody going to tell me what the hell is going on here?" Nick heard his voice go shrill in the particular way that inspired him to self-loathing.

"It's not just here," Angela said. "It's all over the news."

"So you just, what, came home, saw David, and turned on CNN for an explanation?" In fact it wouldn't have surprised him. She found her stability in the calm urgency of the newscasters, in the way they stood between mere mortals and the avalanche of information that threatened to bury all of civilization.

"I got home at four-thirty. About an hour later I went out to get something from my car and it was gone, and there was some strange car in the driveway instead. I got freaked and came in and tried to call the police, but all the lines were tied up. That's when David walked in on me." She stopped for a second, and Nick could see her fast-forward through her emotions. "At that point we knew something big was happening." She turned away. "Come on in and see."

Nick followed them meekly into the den and sat on the sofa between them. He was just in time for a recap of the day's top story.

Between five and six in the afternoon, Eastern Time, the population of the east coast of North America had doubled, as had the population of the western bulge of South America, which lay along the same longitude. The phenomenon seemed to be spreading westward at the same rate the Earth revolved.

Nick understood that what he was hearing was true, believed it on a cellular level, but he couldn't find a handle for his emotions. The scale of the disaster seemed to overshadow his own confusion and panic.

"I've checked the other stations," Angela said, answering a question he hadn't needed to ask. "If it's a hoax, they're all in on it."

"It's not a hoax," Nick said. He glanced at David. "You know it's not a hoax."

"With some significant exceptions," said CNN anchor Judy Woodruff, "every human being in the affected area—which now includes Chicago, Memphis, and the eastern edge of New Orleans—seems to have an exact double." The camera panned to a duplicate Judy Woodruff in a canvas chair at the edge of the set, patting nervously at her shoulder-length blonde hair.

The scene shifted to Bernard Shaw interviewing his double on a Washington DC street corner that was sliding into chaos. In the background, abandoned cars stood with their doors open as pedestrians swarmed without apparent purpose between them. Half of the people in the crowd had twins standing somewhere near them. What struck Nick was that not all the pairs wore the same clothes, and some had radically different outfits or hair styles. The picture jumped periodically as someone from the alarmed, but not yet hysterical, mob collided with the camera operator.

"So what are these 'significant exceptions' she was talking about?" Nick asked Angela. "Is that us? And where did David come from?"

"David lives here," David said.

"They don't know yet," Angela said. "Shhhhh."

The street scene ended abruptly, and during a second or so of on-screen darkness Nick heard the ambient noise of an impending press conference: chairs shifting, throats clearing. "We're live," somebody said, and then the screen cleared to show a generic wood-grain folding table under harsh fluorescent lights. Two identical men sat at the table, each with long dark hair and a single diamond stud in his left ear. A young woman reporter Nick didn't recognize said, "We're here at MIT with the Doctors Jason Berlin of the theoretical physics department. Gentlemen, I understand you have a theory to explain the bizarre events we've seen tonight."

"Merely a hypothesis," said the Dr. Berlin on Nick's left. "Have you ever heard of something called the 'Many Worlds' interpretation of quantum physics?"

"I'm not sure," the reporter said. "Was it ever on *Star Trek?*"

"Frequently, as a matter of fact," said the Dr. Berlin on the right. "It's a sort of thought experiment that postulates an infinite number of universes parallel to our own, in which all possibilities are real."

The other Dr. Berlin nodded. "Exactly. And every possibility splits off a new world. For instance, you might have a world where the Axis Powers won the Second World War. Or where Fidel Castro played major league baseball."

The reporter said, "What does that have to do with what we're seeing tonight?"

The first doctor leaned forward. "Picture our Earth, and then a second Earth that's almost identical, but not quite. Call it, I don't know, call it Earth Prime. In one of them Bill Clinton is President, in the other it's Dan Quayle."

"Dan Quayle?" Nick asked. "Is he kidding?"

Angela shushed him again.

"There'll be other differences," the second doctor said. "Some people will have died in one world and not in the other. Two otherwise identical people will have different jobs, different spouses. Now suppose these two universes, that had split off at some point in the past, merged together again."

"How could that happen?" the reporter asked.

"I have no idea. Maybe the universe is downsizing." The crowd, which had been buzzing with low conversation, now erupted in nervous laughter. "But you'd see what we're seeing—most people would be duplicated, though with all kinds of subtle variations."

"Why isn't it happening all at once?" the reporter asked. "Why only people? Why no trees or cats or skyscrapers?"

The first doctor shrugged and the second said, "Frankly, we're at a bit of a loss to explain that just yet."

"Back to you, Judy," the reporter said. "Or is that Judy Prime?"

Angela hit the mute button and sat for a moment, as if gathering herself. Then she looked past Nick to David and said, "Tell me. How did I die?"

3 DAVID GOT UP and refilled his glass from the liquor cabinet under the TV. Then he sat down again and said, "Car crash. The brakes were bad on the Mazda, and you insisted on going out in the rain to rent a film. We had a bit of a row about it, actually, and I only gave in because I felt like I was coming down with something and I wasn't up to getting wet. You ... you slid through a stop sign." He took a drink. "A sixteen-year-old girl hit you broad-side. They pronounced you dead at the scene."

"In my world," Angela said, "you went out for the movie. A movie you didn't even want."

The rising tide of emotion threatened to wash Nick out to sea. "Excuse me," he said, and went to the kitchen.

There he discovered that the refrigerator was wrong. No orange juice, no 7-Up, no raw materials for enchiladas. Instead he found two six packs of Heineken, a pizza box, some leftover Chinese takeout, a few half-pint bottles of Perrier. Over the hum of the refrigerator he heard David, his voice choked with emotion, say, "My life ended that night."

Nick closed the refrigerator and stared at his reflection in the window above the kitchen sink. "'My life ended that night,'" he mouthed, and watched himself mime putting a finger down his throat. Then he washed his face in the sink, trying to scrub away the fear and jealousy and despair.

As he turned from the sink, looking for someplace to throw his paper towels, he saw that morning's *News and Observer* on the butcher block table. The headline read, "Quayle apologizes for State of Union blunder."

"Oh my God," Nick said.

It was not, then, a merger of two worlds. It was a hostile takeover where one world vanished and one remained. The trees and cats and skyscrapers the reporter had been talking about belonged to someone other than Nick. David was not the intruder; like he'd been saying all along, David lived here.

Nick looked at Angela where she sat in highly-charged conversation with David on the couch and did the math. Angela was not an intruder here either, world of origin notwithstanding. There was only one person who didn't fit in the equation, and Nick had been staring at his reflection only moments before.

5 NICK HAD CAUGHT Angela on the rebound, and he knew he'd never have had a chance with her otherwise. He'd still been in Austin when David died, still been married to his first wife, still involved in an affair that was about to turn publicly sour in a narrow circle of acquaintance. He was writing code then for a small software house called Computics and thinking more and more about North Carolina.

Computics had a customer named Richard who sold medical information systems in the Raleigh area. On a business trip in 1995 Richard had shown Nick around the Triangle and Nick had been impressed with how green everything was, how it rained even in August. Summer rain in Texas was only a distant memory. When everything fell apart in Austin the next year—divorce, threats of more layoffs at Computics, another summer of rationed water and parched brown lawns—Nick packed it in and headed east. Richard helped him find a job and an apartment, and at his New Year's party four months later he introduced Nick to Angela.

Nick was graceful for a man his size, and he'd taken the trouble to dress well that night: charcoal suit, silk tie, cufflinks. Somehow he summoned the nerve to ask Angela to dance. She'd been drinking for the first time since David's funeral that June, and it was the champagne that said yes.

A year and a half into the marriage Nick insisted on therapy, where Angela complained that Nick was too much in control, that he wanted her but didn't need her, that he didn't truly need anyone. In the third week she admitted that she loved Nick, but not in the way she'd loved David. She was afraid to love anyone that much again.

Nick slept in the guest house for a month after that, wanting to leave but imprisoned by his desire for her. Finally that desire became stronger than his anger and they began to make love again. He moved back into the bedroom and their attempt at therapy became, like David, one more thing they didn't discuss. Life was good again, or at least comfortable, until one day he came home and his pickup was red and David was waiting for him in the living room.

7 DAVID FIXED mushroom omelets and they ate on TV trays in the den. Nick suppressed the thought that this was how the world ended, with neither bang nor whimper, but with CNN analyzing it to death.

After dinner Nick did the dishes and then took the portable phone into the darkened formal living room. The lines were jammed, but after half an hour he managed to reach his mother in San Antonio. She was fine, she said, but this duplicate version of herself kept following her around and talking incessantly. Nick nodded silently; his father was dead, then, in this world too. His mother supposed she would just have to put up with the inconvenience. Then the duplicate got on the phone and seemed unable to understand why he wasn't calling from Austin.

After he hung up he sat in the darkness for a long time. Eventually he switched the phone on again, and after a dozen attempts got through to directory assistance. He tried Raleigh, Durham, and Chapel Hill without finding a listing for his name. He tried again in Austin and this time the computer-generated voice recited a phone number—not his old one, but an exchange that Nick recognized as West Lake Hills, a big step up from his old neighborhood east of I-35.

That knowledge made it even harder to call. He could hear a voice saying, "I wondered when I'd hear from you," a tired and put-upon voice that Nick suddenly realized was that of his father, the fat, balding, sweaty and selfish man Nick had spent his whole life trying not to turn into.

If it had been the other way around, if Nick had been flush and his other self in Austin broke and desperate, Nick would have reached out to him in a heartbeat. But this way, to have to call from a position of weakness, even with no intent of asking for help, was more than he could bring himself to do.

He put the phone down, an immense sense of loss flowering slowly in his mind. He went out the sliding glass door at the back of the kitchen and crossed the patio to the guest apartment, a free-standing building that in Texas he would have called an *abuelita,* a grandmother's house. It was unlocked. He switched on the light to face what his logical mind had assured him he would find there: all of his books gone, all his vinyl albums and CDs, the bookshelves he'd put together and stained by hand, the Heathkit amp he'd built in college, his Math Cup from high school, all gone.

David's guest house instead contained a chair, a double bed with a white chambray spread and no headboard, a pair of framed Impressionist prints on the walls. A green banker's lamp bowed over the night stand, resting on top of a 1997 almanac and a John Grisham novel.

Nick sat on the bed and closed his eyes. When he opened them again, the room hadn't changed. It was full of absence. No favorite T-shirts, no photos of old girlfriends, no plastic model of the Space Shuttle from eighth grade. Every physical object that meant anything to him was gone.

11 BY THE TIME Nick got back to the den, the many-worlds theory of the Doctors Berlin had expanded to fill the gap left by any other rational explanation. CNN now referred to the crisis as the "Prime Event" and their art department had produced a graphic showing twin Earths just touching edges inside an infinity symbol.

At seven p.m. eastern time, CNN estimated the population of Mexico City at 60 million, a figure Nick could not meaningfully comprehend. Much of the city was on fire by 8:00 and the smoke, on top of the already lethal pollution, quickly sent population estimates downward. The sidewalks were choked with corpses of the very young and very old, and the reporters began to speak in hushed voices about typhus and cholera.

Despite warnings, LA drivers began to head out into the worst traffic jam in California history. Meanwhile, gang members cruised the fringes of enemy turf, waiting to mow down newly arrived doubles of rival gang members as they appeared. "Too many f*cking Crips already, man," a young Blood told reporters, his "fuck" censored by a faint beep. "I ain't sharing with no f*cking primes."

Airline traffic had come to a complete halt as nearly empty planes disappeared from airport gates and hangers, only to land minutes later fully laden with primes. There were no rental cars, hotel rooms, or clean public rest rooms to be found in North America. Restaurants were out of food, service stations out of gas, ATMs out of money.

Eight o'clock Thursday night in Durham was 3 AM Friday in Moscow and along the Palestinian border; 5 AM in Sarajevo; 10 in the morning in Beijing. Around the world everyone was poised for 5 PM ethnic cleansing time, taking an example from the LA gangs, or more likely not needing one.

At nine Angela switched to a local channel and learned that banks were limiting withdrawals to $100 per day per account, and holding all checks until the federal government told them exactly what their exposure was. Meanwhile local police departments asked all off-duty officers—prime or otherwise—to show up for night duty at banks, groceries, convenience stores, malls, and emergency rooms.

At ten o'clock Nick stood up. "Look, I can't just sit here and watch this anymore."

Angela stared at him as if he'd lost his mind. "This is only the most devastating event since, what, the extinction of the dinosaurs?"

"At least the dinosaurs didn't sit around watching comet reports on CNN," Nick said. "I can't do anything about what's happening, and I can't just sit here and passively soak up any more second-hand pain and suffering. I'm full up."

Nick saw he was keeping Angela from the next round of disasters. He turned to David and said, "I know I don't have any right to ask this..."

"Of course you'll stay here," David said. "Take the guest house for as long as you need. I should think you already know where everything is."

"Yes. Thank you." The less charitable part of Nick's personality knew David wouldn't think of turning them out, not while Angela was part of the equation.

He picked up a handful of newspapers and magazines in the living room and went back outside.

13 HE WAS EXHAUSTED, and he badly wanted Angela to find him asleep if she did happen to look in. Two troubled marriages had taught him that sleeping well could indeed be the best revenge, but that night his twitchy nerves made it hopeless. After half an hour of flinging himself from one side of the bed to the other he switched on the banker's lamp and reached for the almanac.

He verified that Dan Quayle was President, impossible as it had seemed at first. In this universe—David's World, as he'd come to think of it, not without bitterness—Clinton had been caught *en flagrante* two days before the 1992 election and the press had crucified him. Bush had not only won, but solidified a new era of conservatism. Quayle rode the rising backlash against affirmative action, foreigners, feminism, and welfare straight into the White House.

What surprised Nick was how little difference it had made in the end. *Time* magazine featured Saddam, Tony Blair, and Nelson Mandela cheek to jowl with faces Nick had never seen before: a Father Dominguez who was leading an armed insurrection in the Yucatan; Selma Jones, US ambassador to China, who was urging favored nation status for the totalitarian regime; Davy Davis, teen heartthrob, who had the Ricky Nelson role in the upcoming feature film version of *Ozzie and Harriet*. But for all he knew, Selma Jones had been ambassador to China in his world as well, and Nick had never kept up with matinee idols.

The thing that really seized his attention was a three-page spread on the man who'd just been anointed the richest in the world: Harvey Chambers, CEO of the Computics empire headquartered in Austin, Texas.

Nick, like everyone else in the business, had many times heard the story of the Xerox Palo Alto Research Center and the point-and-click interface they'd invented for one of their pipe-dream projects. In Nick's World, Steve Jobs saw a demo and went home to build the first Macintosh. Bill Gates saw the Mac, and then there was Windows.

In David's World, Harvey Chambers saw the demo first. He was a comics fan, so instead of windows his operating system had "panels," and instead of dialog boxes it had "captions" and "balloons." Parents didn't get it, but kids did, and the first computer-savvy generation grew up on Computics. Chambers avoided Apple's fatal error and licensed out his hardware designs to third party vendors, concentrating his own efforts on software—first games, then study aids, then office suites, growing up with his customers. Jobs and Gates never had a chance.

Like Gates in the world Nick came from, Chambers was locked in a battle with the Department of Justice. With a Republican that Chambers had helped elect in the White House, presiding over a Republican Congress, Justice never had a chance.

In Nick's World, Computics had never pioneered anything. Chambers had sold the struggling company in the late eighties and retired to Mexico to do some serious drinking. The people who'd known him said he'd had too much ambition and too little luck, a combination they thought would kill him in the end.

Nick's rich double in Austin no doubt worked for this gleaming, world-beating Computics, pickup long ago traded for a hunter green sport utility, the *Wall Street Journal* delivered every morning so he could check his stocks as he sat in his overstuffed leather armchair, careful to avoid wrinkling his Brooks Brothers suit. It was a scab Nick should have been able to pick at successfully for quite a while, but instead his attention kept drifting to more fundamental questions.

Like how he was going to live, for one. Angela would have work—it didn't take Nostradamus to predict a shortage of doctors. The computer industry, however, looked like it could be in a serious recession as people concentrated on the basics of food, shelter, and transportation. All the things Nick no longer had.

The thought of the Angela-shaped hole in this world brought him to the toughest question of all. He and Angela. Angela and David.

He woke at some point before dawn with Angela curled into his back, holding him. The knowledge of something terribly wrong nagged at his memory, just within reach, but he shied away from it and dove back into sleep.

17 DAVID WAS the perfect gentleman. He made breakfast for Nick in the morning while Angela slept in, and gave him a robe to put on after his shower. He even found a couple of old T-shirts and a pair of sweat pants that Nick was able to fit into. While Nick tried to wake up, David went about his business, making reassuring noises on the phone to his most important clients without communicating any real data. He seemed to function in some gray area between the law and finance, and Nick was content not to know any more than that. "It's too early to tell," David said into the phone, to one client after another. "We'll just have to see how this all falls out."

On the news that morning they had an explanation, of sorts, for the red pickup. The two Doctors Berlin, now instant celebrities, were explaining the situation in terms of conservation of angular momentum (the primes who appeared in cars or planes were already moving at a high rate of speed) and conservation of mass and energy in a closed system (twice as many people, but only the same number of cars, planes, bicycles, and so on). Anyone who'd been driving at the time of the Prime Event had ended up in a car from David's World that wasn't in use at the time. Cars had disappeared from dealerships and rental agencies and even locked garages, then turned up on the highway with people like Nick behind the wheel.

"Improbable as this sounds," one of the doctors said on the TV in the next room, "there's a precedent for matter relocating itself like this. All the way back in 1964, Bell's Theorem projected this kind of behavior from subatomic particles into the macrocosmic world."

Meanwhile, repo agents were already out in force, and the reporters expected steady growth in that sector of the economy for at least the next few weeks.

The news didn't help the clenched feeling in the pit of Nick's stomach. He watched Angela stumble in and sit at the kitchen table with a cup of coffee and knew he had to get moving. If he went back to bed and pulled the covers over his head like he wanted to, he might never come out. The next time David was between calls, Nick said, "I'm going in to work."

"Why?" Angela said.

"Because I have to at least try. I can't just keep sitting here."

"Be careful," David said. "They say traffic is even worse today than last night."

Nick bent over to kiss Angela goodbye, and she turned away at the last second, putting one arm around his neck and squeezing briefly. Her self-consciousness was palpable and Nick attributed it to David being there in the room, watching. Nothing had happened between Angela and David yet, Nick was sure, but he knew he was an idiot to walk out and leave them alone there together.

Nonetheless he turned away and started toward the door, and David followed him. "Listen," David said, and Nick turned to see him holding out two twenty-dollar bills. "Think of it as a loan, if you must. You can't go out there with empty pockets."

He was right, of course. Nick had no idea how much gas there was in the truck, and he had nothing to take for lunch. "Thanks," he said, the word leaving a numb spot on his tongue.

He turned the red pickup around and waited at the head of the driveway until, with a resigned nod and a flick of the hand, a middle-aged man finally let him join the slow parade of cars. On the commercial stations the drive-to-work crews hashed over the news with morbid humor, inviting people to call in with their most humiliating prime story. Nick escaped to a university station playing Mozart.

What most surprised him were the numbers of people on foot. Most were men, some with their thumbs out, some just walking with their heads down, postures closed against the morning chill. There was menace in the hard metal of the other cars, and Nick kept turning the radio down because he thought he heard something: a collision, a scream.

Just before the 54/55 exit, he saw a late model Honda and a Ford Explorer pulled over on the shoulder and two men, one black, one white, shoving and grabbing at each other beside the cars. As Nick slowly rolled past he could see the tight, weary expressions on their faces. Two miles later he saw a squad car stopped on the westbound side, and a cop forcing someone face down onto the hood.

For minutes at a time, one or another of the walking men would keep pace with Nick's truck as it inched forward. Once Nick turned his head and found one of the men staring in at him through the passenger window. The man's gaze was flat, empty of emotion. As if, Nick thought, the absence of hope had stranded him in an eternal present, without envy or expectation. Nick averted his eyes, his desire to offer a ride utterly quashed by the images of violence he'd seen throughout the long night on the television screen, and by the ugliness he'd already witnessed that morning through the windshield of his truck.

He made it to the office in just under two hours. The front desk was deserted when he first walked in, then John, the slight, middle-aged receptionist, ducked out of the conference room and looked at him blankly. "Can I ... help you with something?"

"Is Lisa in?" Lisa was the owner, and Richard had introduced her to Nick on his first trip to North Carolina. There was a chance she might remember him.

"Everyone's in a company meeting now," he said.

"Is this about the prime business? Because until yesterday I worked here. Your name is John Fanthorpe and your father was a logger in Oregon. Lisa's kids are named Spike and Janet. The alarm on the back door goes off every morning at 8:31 and nobody will drink the coffee when Dave Lee makes it."

John thought it over while Nick counted silently to five. "You might as well come in," he said at last.

Nick stood against one wall and scanned the room. He knew all but two of the fifty or so people there. Almost all of them were sitting in pairs, and some of the ones from Nick's world met his eyes and nodded. Both Dave Lees, Nick noticed, had on identical black jeans, black running shoes, and black 3dfx T-shirts.

One Lisa sat in the audience. The other Lisa stood at the front of the room and said, "You have to keep in mind that we're a small company, and a lot of federal guidelines don't apply here. Hell, you know as well as I do there aren't any federal regulations to cover this kind of mess. So what it comes down to is, I'm going to do whatever I think is best for the company, because in the long run that's going to do the most good for the greatest number of you all.

"I've got to sit down and crunch some numbers and make some decisions. So what I want everybody to do is to go on home." There were groans from the audience. "I know, it took you hours to get here. But you should all be home with your families right now. I will call each and every one of you before five o'clock today, Bell South and GTE willing, so that means any of you primes that aren't staying with your originals, come up here and give me a number where I can get hold of you."

Nick had heard the TV reporters distinguish between "primes" and "originals" but it sounded different when it was his job on the line. It sounded like there was no point in signing up.

"That's it," Lisa said. "Everybody go home, try and be cool, wait for this thing to shake itself out. I'm not even going to ask for questions because there aren't enough answers to go around right now."

Hands went up anyway and one or two people started sentences with "What about..."

Lisa shook her head decisively. "I'm serious, people. I'll talk to you all one-on-one later today." She held up one placating hand and left the room.

Nick forced himself to get in line and put his name and David's phone number on the legal pad. The Lisa who'd been sitting in the audience came up behind him. "Hey, Nick. I looked over the employee list and didn't see your name."

"Apparently I'm still in Texas," Nick told her. Lisa had been all right for an owner. She didn't pretend to be one of the gang, but she didn't distance herself either. Her office door was open most of the time, which meant on bad days Nick had been able to hear her yelling into the phone all the way back to his office. She was about fifty, with purplish-black skin and the first traces of gray in her short, stiff hair.

"Uh oh," she said sympathetically.

"Yeah. Kind of takes a bite out of my seniority."

"You want some coffee or anything? It's not bad, Dave Lee didn't make it."

"No thanks. I got a long drive coming up."

They sat on two of the folding chairs and Lisa said, "I'll tell you what. I don't think seniority or equal opportunity or even friendship is going to matter much. I know what I'd do in her place. If I could have two Dave Lees and lose a few entry-level programmers to do it, I wouldn't hesitate. Especially since I could probably get the second Dave dirt cheap."

"And let's face it, who would know better than you what she'd do?"

"Indeed."

"So what happens to you?"

"Lisa's putting me and the kids up for the time being. My guess is she's going to offer me some kind of a buyout. The thing is, the old definitions of wealth are probably going to cease to matter much. Don't get me wrong—I'm sure the same people are going to be on top, probably by a greater margin than ever, but the units of measure are going to change. Nobody knows yet what that measure is going to be, but the more liquid it is, the more likely it is to carry the day. So if she offers me a big wad of stock, it's probably not going to hurt her much to do it. She can salve her conscience on the cheap, and I'll have to take it, because what choice do I have? Which means I have to find a way to turn that stock into something to eat and a place to sleep." She drained her coffee cup, which featured Gary Larson cartoon dinosaurs. "What about you?"

"My situation is a bit complicated. Angela's dead husband is alive here and her double isn't. I think she's going to have to make a choice, and … let's just say my seniority isn't looking that good anywhere."

"Maybe seniority won't matter there, either."

"Yeah. We can always hope, right?"

And hope did, in fact, die hard, Nick realized, as he found himself headed toward his old office as if he would find some trace of himself there. Instead he found a fierce-looking young woman with black hair and a thin face, staring at the computer screen and typing with blinding speed. She had her own posters on the wall, no plants, no stereo. There would be no email for Nick on her machine, no code for his new graphics driver.

On the way out he ran into Tom, his project leader. Tom was heavy and graying, with a bristling white mustache. He and Nick had been friends, but never particularly close.

"Hey, Nick," he said.

"Thereby identifying yourself," Nick said, "as Tom Prime."

Tom nodded. "A bunch of us fifth wheels are talking about having a picnic tomorrow over at Lake Crabtree. Start around noon or so, go on all day. Everybody bring what they can. Maybe take our minds off things for a little while."

"I'll just have to see," Nick told him. "Tomorrow seems like a million years away right now."

19 IT TOOK NICK less than an hour and a half to get back to Hope Valley Road. As he idled past the bank which no longer held any of his money, he watched a National Guardsman in full riot gear turn people away from the cash machine, which bore a hand-lettered sign reading "Out of Service."

"It's a fucking lie!" a woman was screaming. Tears were running down her face and she was waving her ATM card in the Guardsman's face. "There's nothing wrong with that machine except the greedy bastards who shut it down!" The Guardsman was faceless behind his Plexiglas mask, but Nick could read the nervousness in his posture.

Nick looked away. The two twenties in his pants pockets had a palpable weight. The urge to drive to Food Lion and squander the entire forty dollars on candy bars and balloons and toys almost overwhelmed him. Being an adult was more of a burden than he could carry. He wanted someone to take him by the hand and either beat the hell out of him or tell him everything was going to be all right.

Instead he drove back to David's house and the chilly comfort of CNN.

On Headline News, the world's religious leaders stepped up for their share of the limelight. "If God had no hand in this," Pat Robertson asked, "then who put these drivers into automobiles to guard their safety? Who put these passengers into airplanes? Science can't explain what's happened to us in the last twenty-four hours. Life is a miracle, and we've just seen six billion miracles in a single day."

Anchor Lynne Russell noted, without comment, that the whereabouts of only one Pat Robertson was known. Whether the one who addressed the nation was original or prime was likewise a mystery.

Twin Dalai Lamas, from separate encampments, each declared the other to be but *maya,* illusion, a physical manifestation of earthly greed. The Pope, meanwhile, had gone into seclusion with his prime, intimating that they might be a while.

On the scientific side of the fence, the EPA issued a statement pointing out that the simple body heat of an additional six billion people, not to mention the carbon dioxide they exhaled, could escalate global warming catastrophically. One source speculated that the entire land surface of the planet could be desert within ten years.

The global population continued to drop rapidly, however. The combined overnight death toll from Bosnia, Khazakhstan, Jordan, Somalia, and Mexico was already estimated in the tens of millions, with no end in sight. Large portions of LA, London, and Moscow were on fire, while Mexico City had burned out from lack of oxygen. Australia and New Zealand had both closed their borders, turning back all incoming sea and air traffic while ferrying foreign tourists out of both countries on nationalized Qantas planes.

President Quayle, not knowing what else to do with him, had appointed the Bill Clinton from Nick's world as Special Advisor on Prime Affairs. The "Affairs" part had commentators sniggering. The two emerged at 5:00 eastern time to announce the formation of the US Peacekeeping Force, a new organization that would incorporate existing members of the Army, National Guard, and local police forces, plus anyone else who wanted to volunteer. The government promised all recruits three meals a day, a place to sleep, their nation's gratitude, and pay in the form of government scrip to be redeemed when the crisis was over.

"That's it," David said. "They just flushed the dollar down the loo."

At the inevitable press conference, with a freshly minted USPF logo on a banner behind him, Quayle said, "The mission of this force is to protect private property, safeguard human life, and provide an orderly." He squinted at his TelePrompTer. "Transition."

"Property first, of course," David said, and Nick felt a surge of warmth toward him.

"Transition to what?" Angela asked.

"Martial law," Nick said. "God help us all."

Helicopter footage showed an unbroken line of the desperate and homeless that stretched from Mexico City to the Texas border—cars, bicycles, pedestrians, wagons, horses. Somebody had blown up the International Bridge at Laredo in the early morning hours. The US Border Patrol blamed right-wing extremists and the Governor of Tamulipas blamed the US Border Patrol. The loss of the bridge made no perceptible difference. The tidal wave of humanity rolled across the Rio Grande like it was a mud puddle, and refugees simply swarmed over the few cops who were willing to open fire.

"In Austin, Texas," Russell said, "billionaire Harvey Chambers has become a one-man Works Progress Administration." Nick had been drifting into his own alarming fantasies of Quayle's personal New World Order, but the mention of Austin brought him back. The screen showed what seemed to be thousands of workers outside a huge complex of steel and glass towers. As one crew cleared live oaks and mesquite bushes in a long straight line, a second crew came behind them, digging a shallow trench. In the background still more workers unloaded massive blocks of stone from flatbed trucks.

In the foreground, a young male reporter in khakis and a polo shirt turned to the camera and said, "Offering good pay, hot food, and accommodations at a Tent City of his own creation, Chambers has commissioned a large-scale building project on his Computics campus. Though Chambers hasn't released any details of what he's up to, it doesn't take one of his resident geniuses to make an informed guess. It looks to be a very high, very thick wall, and with the visitors headed his way from south of the border, he may need it."

An hour later, as Nick was washing the dinner dishes, the phone rang. David didn't answer so Nick let the machine take it. "This is a message for Nick," Lisa's voice said. "I'm sorry, but we're not going to be able to find a place for you. I'm sure you appreciate the situation." Nick could hear her relief that she didn't have to break the news to him directly. "If you haven't heard, though, the government is going to have jobs for anybody who needs one."

23 NICK WOKE AT SEVEN the next morning, cranky and sullen. He'd been dreaming about deserts and sandstorms, and in the middle of it all a pyramid with Computics logos carved into its sides.

Angela murmured something unintelligible and turned her back to him as he got out of bed. He dressed and went over to the main house, shivering a little in the distinctly colder morning air. David was still not up, so Nick made coffee and brought in the paper. Enjoy this, he told himself. Solitude is now the most precious commodity on Earth.

The front page told him that the USPF was an instant hit. The government, cleverly anticipating that they wouldn't have enough guns or uniforms to go around, had declared that volunteers were to provide their own uniforms of blue jeans and white shirts. Their commanders would issue them red bandannas. They were encouraged to bring along their own personal weapons.

In separate, but nearly identical statements, two Ralph Naders warned that there was little difference between the USPF and licensed vigilantism. Any unstable person with a piece of red cloth and a gun could wreak unchallenged havoc. The reporter covering the story dismissed him with as a harmless crank.

Saturday had always been Nick's favorite day of the week. Just seven days ago he'd cooked his strawberry mint crepes in his special pan and sat on the patio in the sun to eat them. This Saturday he spread the classifieds—reduced to eight pages from the usual two dozen—across the dining room table and looked for work.

There were personal ads, mostly from primes looking for missing persons. Auto dealers were looking for temporary repossession specialists and drivers. And there was still plenty of work for telemarketers. The rest of world seemed to be holding its breath.

David eventually wandered in and logged on to his Internet provider so

Nick could check job listings on the Web. The Web seemed largely unfazed by the Prime Event. And why not? Nick thought. There was no shortage of room in cyberspace. Ads for electronic stock trading services still popped up everywhere. On ZDNet, Jesse Berst—now with two photos of himself at the head of his column—asked his readers if it was the end of life as they knew it or simply the biggest stunt yet by Harvey Chambers and Computics to stall the Justice Department. The AltaVista search engine invited Nick to ask a question like, "Where did all these people come from?"

He found half a dozen openings for C++ developers in the area, though he suspected most of them were no longer viable. He switched over to the Computics Writer program, figured out the slightly cheesy interface, and put together a quick resume. If he had to fill out a job application, he wondered, would there be a box to check if you were a prime?

By the time he'd emailed the copies of his resume, it was after noon. Angela, puffy and uncommunicative, was watching CNN with David. Special Presidential Advisor Bill Clinton was addressing protesters at the Washington Mall. "I'm a prime just as many of you are," he said. "I know your sense of dislocation and anxiety."

The crowd jeered and shouted insults.

Clinton raised his hands. "I urge you to return to your homes. This disruption is only delaying our efforts to bring help to those of you who need it the most." Clinton's words disappeared under a chorus of heckling, and finally he shrugged and walked away with his head down, surrounded by bodyguards in dark suits.

Voices began to chant, "No justice, no peace," over and over. Nick could hear growing alarm in the voices of the CNN reporters, and then, moments later, the crowd seemed to buck, like a single organism reacting to a shock. The camera swung wildly around to show a wedge of USPF recruits in white shirts and red bandannas, swinging clubs and baseball bats and firing something into the air. The screen filled with smoke from pepper spray and tear gas, leaving sound as the only evidence of what was happening: screams, grunts, the sound of wood impacting flesh, the muted thunder of running feet. Nick, horrified, covered his ears and went into the bathroom, running water in the sink to mask the noise of the TV.

When he came out he had decided to go to the picnic at Lake Crabtree. He had real friends there, and friendship seemed less contingent than everything else in his life at that moment. He got all the way to the hall closet, looking for his softball and glove, before he remembered that he wouldn't find them there.

He stuck his head back into the den, where CNN had moved on to the next atrocity and David and Angela were in the midst of a heated discussion. "...has

nothing of real value to back it up," David was saying. "There's no disincentive
to inflation."

"Where have you been for the last thirty years?" Angela was leaning forward
aggressively, but Nick could see she was enjoying herself. "Money isn't real.
It's a necessary fiction that everybody's bought into for the sake of the game.
There's nothing to back it up but good intentions anyway."

"There's your, what do you call it, Federal Reserve System."

"It's the Emperor's New Money, except the emperor is naked now. So
people will transfer all their leftover hope and need to this government scrip.
It's Tinkerbell money, but people will clap for it. Wait and see."

Why can't I look up from people being beaten and debate economic theory? Nick wondered. If I could have fought with her like that, over something
other than wounded feelings, then maybe she could have loved me too.

"Listen," he said. "There's a company picnic thing at work, and I think I
want to go." Too late, and with too little enthusiasm, he added, "You guys can
come along if you like."

David looked at Angela, who was already shaking her head. "I'll pass,"
she said.

"I think there's some veggie dogs in the freezer," David said, "if you don't
want to go empty handed."

29 THE CROWDING was less severe on I-40, but there was still in-
sufficient room for Nick to shake off the restlessness that gripped
him, to push the accelerator to the floor and watch the landscape come hur-
tling at him. He knew it was just another misguided impulse, like the one that
had sent him to the closet for his baseball glove.

He got to Lake Crabtree by two and parked at the edge of the entrance
road. Groups of families seemed to be living in the open-walled picnic structures and in camper trucks in the parking lots. Long lines waited outside both
restrooms. It took Nick twenty minutes to find Tom and the others where
they'd built a fire in the center of a soccer field and ringed it with Styrofoam
coolers. The wall reminded Nick of Harvey Chambers' macroengineering in
Austin, and that in turn reminded him of his dream.

Nick offered his veggie dogs and half a loaf of oat bread. "Is it okay to just
build a fire like this?"

"You're kidding, right?" Tom said. "What exactly are you worried about?
Pollution from the smoke? Using up precious natural resources? Park rangers
busting us for not having a permit?" He waved an arm at the crowds that surrounded them. "All that stuff is over. Moot. Finito."

They sat down together and roasted a couple of hot dogs while Tom told his story. Everybody had a story now, though Nick considered his own rather pedestrian.

"I was working late," Tom said, "so I wasn't on the highway when it happened. Sometime before six I got up and went to the bathroom, and when I came back this other guy who looked just like me was sitting in my chair, typing on my computer. It was the single weirdest moment of my entire life. That feeling, to be looking at something for which you know there cannot ever be a rational explanation. I just turned around and went back into the hall and pictured that kid in the *Little Nemo* comic strip. You're too young to know what I'm talking about. Anyway, he had this hat with a sign on it that said 'Wake Up!' Flip, his name was. I tried everything I could think of to wake up—looking at my hands, pinching myself, holding my breath.

"About that time the two Lisas came by and rounded everybody up who was still in the building and took us into the conference room. We borrowed John's boom box and listened to the news, and of course once we understood what was happening we all wanted to go home, make sure our wives and husbands and kids were okay.

"There was only one car between me and the other Tom, and by this point we'd figured out whose world this was. I mean, he had the keys and my pockets were empty. So he gave me a ride home and put me and my Suzie up in his and his Suzie's guest room. I guess I can't really complain, but ... you can't tell the difference between us by looking. Only I'm in the guest room and he's in the whole rest of the house. He drives and I have to ask if I can ride along. And he always makes me ask. He hasn't refused me anything, but he always makes me ask."

They both looked at the fire for a minute, and then Tom said, "Doesn't it bother you? Them calling us 'primes'?"

"What do you mean?"

"You're a math person, like me. What's the definition of a prime number?"

"Divisible only by one and itself."

"Doesn't that seem lonely to you? Do you remember what they call numbers that aren't 1 or a prime?"

Nick shrugged. "I forget."

"Composites. Because they're made up of other numbers. But the primes are all alone."

"Maybe they're just self-sufficient," Nick said, in an attempt to lighten him up.

"You think?" Tom asked, staring with an intensity that made Nick look away.

After another brief silence Tom said, "You know what's really weird? The other Tom, he doesn't have any trains." In Nick's world, Tom didn't actually have a guest room because it was completely given over to his model railroad.

"When I asked him about it, it was the first time he showed any real interest in me. 'I always thought about doing that,' he says. 'I had this Lionel set I really loved when I was kid.' And I go, 'Yeah, I know. I was there.'

"But they're all gone, all those trains I put together by hand. The Texas Eagle. Southern Pacific Number One. Wiped out." He snapped his fingers. "Just like that. I mean, you have to wonder what exactly is the point, when you can lose everything, just like that."

Although sympathetic, Nick hadn't lost sight of the fact that he'd come to the park to get cheered up. He ate two hot dogs and drank a Coke, then extricated himself to join the softball game starting nearby. Other than having to play barehanded, it was the best he'd felt in two days, running, chasing fly balls, swinging a big stick at something.

Darkness ended the game by 5:00, and even with the night turning rapidly cold, the beer started to flow. Nick was not much of a drinker, and without physical exertion to distract him his thoughts kept stumbling over Angela, Angela and David, alone together back at David's house.

"Hey," a voice yelled. "Anybody here speak Spanish?"

At the edge of the fire Nick saw John the receptionist next to a slight man in black jeans, denim jacket, and a battered straw cowboy hat.

Nick walked over. "A little," he told John, and nodded to the other man. *"Que tal?"*

"Es mi esposa," the stranger said. *"Ayúdame, por favor."*

"Okay," Nick said, and asked him what the trouble was with his wife.

"She's having a baby," the man said. "But it's too soon." His Spanish came fast and slurred, the way Nick was used to hearing it in Texas. "I need the hospital, but I can't take her because somebody stole my car."

Nick looked back at the fire, thought briefly about Angela again, and then remembered all the men he'd passed on the road in the last two days. Guilt welled up inside him.

"Okay," he said. "I'll take you."

"Gracias, muchas gracias. Dios te paje."

The man's gratitude made Nick even more uncomfortable. As they started across the field he said, "My name's Nick. Where are you from?"

"I'm Carlos." He shook Nick's hand. "I come from Veracruz, originally. Just now from San Antonio."

Nick said that he used to live in Austin.

"I know Austin," Carlos said. "There is supposed to be much work there." He was nervous and sweating, and it was getting very dark. Nick heard voices nearby and couldn't pinpoint where they came from. Suddenly he felt vulnerable and a little foolish.

"*Aqui es,*" Carlos said abruptly.

Someone shone a flashlight in Nick's eyes, and he had to fight the urge to turn and run. After a few seconds his eyes cleared enough to see a middle-aged woman in a black mantilla sitting on the grass. A girl who didn't seem older than her late teens had her head on the woman's lap. Two or three other men, one of them now holding the flashlight on the girl, stood in the shadows.

Nick asked if she could walk.

"I don't know," Carlos said.

They were only a hundred yards or so from one of the parking lots. "I'll go get my truck," Nick said, realizing, once the words were out, that they might think he was running away. "Carlos, you want to come with me?"

Nick half-ran, half-walked toward the spot where he'd left his truck. Carlos jogged beside him, thanking him again. "It's the red one, there," Nick said, then pulled up short. A man in jeans and a white sweatshirt was sliding a flat piece of metal into the window on the driver's side.

"Hey," Nick said in English. "Hey, what're you doing?"

The man glanced at Nick with apparent disinterest and went back to work. In the glow of a nearby streetlight Nick could see the man's dirty blond hair and narrow eyes.

"That's my truck!" Nick said, his voice cracking as the humiliations of the last two days reached critical mass. He ran at the man, grabbing for the hand with the jimmy. The man spun away, leaving the jimmy in the truck door and pulling something out of his waistband.

It was a .38 revolver. For a second, as the muzzle swung in front of his face and the hole in the barrel filled the world, Nick considered that he was about to die. He reacted to the thought with sadness and a flash of self-pity.

"Correction, mother*fucker,*" said the man with the gun. "According to the VIN, this here truck's the property of University Ford in Chapel Hill." There was something red around his neck. Nick realized that this was one of the new vigilantes, whatever it was they were calling themselves.

"Look," Nick said, "this man's wife is sick. We need to get her to the hospital."

"I don't see nobody." Nick looked back and saw that Carlos had disappeared. "Now," the man said, "you got the key to this thing?"

Nick could hear the pulse in his neck as his T-shirt scraped against it. It seemed oddly slow, but so was everything compared to the speed of his thoughts. He went through several possibilities before he finally said, "Yes."

"Hand that son of a bitch over."

Nick took the truck key out of his pocket. His hand trembled and he stood looking at it for what seemed like a long time.

"You scared, motherfucker? You got every reason to be."

In fact Nick felt enraged and helpless, which was something altogether different. It made him want to cry. As he held out the key it shook loose from his fingers and clanged on the asphalt.

"You clumsy piece of shit! God dammit!" The man took one step back and waved the pistol toward the weeds by the side of the road. "Get over there and get on your God damn knees."

"No," Nick said, listening to his voice squirm out of control again. Self-loathing washed over him. "You've got the key, you've got the truck, you probably just killed that poor guy's wife and child. If that's not enough, go ahead and kill me too."

"You prime fuck. You think if I did kill you, anybody would give a God damn?" Nick saw then that the man was more afraid than Nick was, that Nick had caught him off guard by showing up so unexpectedly, that the man had failed to think through what it would mean to point his gun at someone. Nick still wanted to smash his ugly head with a baseball bat, but he no longer believed the man was ready to shoot him.

"You've got the truck," Nick said again, to remind the man that he had, after all, won. Then he turned and walked away, wondering if he'd misjudged and if the man would shoot him after all.

He walked into a clump of trees and pissed against one of them. It wasn't as private as he would have liked, but at that point he was beyond caring. It felt like hot blood draining out of him, and he was weak and shaky when he finished.

Carlos and the others were gone. Nick made a half-hearted attempt to look for them, then went back to the company fire. He thrust his hands nearly into the flames and there still was not enough heat to warm him.

Tom and Lisa materialized on either side of him. "Are you okay?" Lisa asked. "What happened?"

Nick could only shake his head. "What's going to become of us?"

31 LISA GAVE HIM a ride home. "It's only a couple hours out of my way," she said.

"He had a Palm Pilot," Nick said. He couldn't seem to stop rehashing the incident in his head. "I didn't really register that until just now. It was in a little holster thing on his belt. He was using it to run the Vehicle ID Numbers. Crackers with guns and hand-held computers."

"Now that's really scary," Lisa agreed.

"He called me a 'fucking prime.' No, wait. He said, 'you prime fuck.' There was this absolute hatred in his voice."

Lisa glanced at him just long enough to make him wish he'd kept his childlike discoveries to himself. "Yeah, okay," he said. "Nice weather we're having."

Lisa laughed. "Not for long. They say it may freeze tonight."

She let him out in his driveway, and he walked around to the driver's side. "You want to come in or anything? David's being pretty accommodating, I'm sure he wouldn't mind my asking."

"It's late."

Nick nodded. "Thanks for the ride."

She put a hand lightly on his arm. "Take care of yourself, all right? Just take everything slow and easy. You'll be surprised what you can learn to live with."

She turned around in the driveway and Nick saw her hand come up over the roof of the car in a final salute before she pulled onto Hope Valley Road and was gone. Was that the goal, then? he wondered. To find out exactly how much he could in fact put up with? Until he too was shambling along the roadside on sheer inertia, eyes glazed, with nothing behind him and nothing in front of him?

The house was dark except for a single light over the kitchen counter. Nick stopped there to scrub his face with dishwashing liquid and water as hot as he could stand. His fingers still twitched slightly, as if he'd had too much coffee.

He went on through into the den. The TV was off for once and the house was deathly silent. Nick knew something was wrong, but he couldn't say what it was. The night's violence had left him thinking murder and mayhem, and that was the only reason he went into David's bedroom.

Before he could speak he heard the rustling of covers followed by Angela's voice saying, "Nick?"

He froze.

"Oh my God," she said. "Oh my God. We fell asleep."

Nick switched on the light. Angela was holding the sheet up over her bare breasts. David was blinking, pushing himself up on one elbow.

Nick turned the light off again.

"Nick?" Angela said. "Nick, wait. Oh, Christ, Nick, I'm so sorry..."

What Nick really wanted was a long, hot shower. He knew, though, that it would be some time before he got one. "When you're dressed, David," he said, "I need to talk to you for a minute." He went back to the den and sat on the couch.

The two of them came out together a few seconds later. David was in pants and shirt, Angela in a terrycloth robe. Angela was crying silently.

"Just David," Nick said.

She looked at David, then at Nick, and thought better of whatever she'd been about to say. She went through the kitchen and the sliding glass doors to the guest house.

"I'll need a few things," Nick said. "Some sweat clothes, or some drawstring pants, maybe a jacket. Whatever you have that might fit me. A sleeping bag if you've got one."

"Look here, I'm really sorry about this. We didn't either of us mean for it to happen—"

"I don't want to talk about it. Could you see if you could find those clothes?"

David nodded and left the room. Nick leaned his head back and closed his eyes. He couldn't remember ever being so exhausted. Part of it, he knew, was the anticipation of fatigue to come.

"Nick?"

He started awake, amazed to realize that he'd actually drifted off for a few seconds. David was holding out a soft-side flight bag. Inside Nick found clothes, a tightly rolled sleeping bag, a Swiss Army knife, a couple of towels, a first-aid kit, some toilet paper. At the bottom was something metallic that Nick fished out and set on the couch beside him. It was a .22 target pistol.

David laughed nervously. "I expect some might think me a bit mad to offer you that in the circumstances. But I thought you might—"

"No, thanks," Nick said. "Just put it away somewhere, will you?"

David stashed it in one of the built-in drawers next to the TV, and when he came back he had money in his hand. "I've only got a couple of hundred here at the house. If you want to wait till tomorrow I could sort you out some more."

"No," Nick said. "This will do." The money only made Nick more resentful. The business with Angela was a separate issue, something he'd known would happen sooner or later. At that moment he hated David because David had everything to give and because Nick had nothing to do but take it. It made Nick careless of what David thought of him, made him greedy and arrogant and willing to push for more.

Instead he zipped the bag and stood up. Then he followed David's gaze and saw Angela in the kitchen doorway. Her cheeks were still wet. "You're not going...?" she said. "Please, please don't go. Wait until morning. Let us talk about it, at least."

"I'm just going over to Richard's house." David didn't flinch, willingly complicit in the lie. Nick felt the chill he'd known once when he'd cut himself badly in the kitchen. The knife had gone much too deeply into his flesh, but there was no true sensation at first. "I'll call you," he said, in a hurry to get outside before the pain hit.

"Be careful," Angela said, with a catch in her voice that Nick knew he would remember later.

He hefted the bag and walked outside.

37 THE NIGHT WAS clear and cold, and he stopped to put on David's jacket. Once he got moving, he was actually making better time than the cars on Hope Valley, and there was satisfaction in that. It took him only half an hour to get to I-40, where he turned right and headed west along the access road.

Fragments of his dream flashed through his mind, overlaying the reality of the stalled and abandoned cars beside the road, the smell of exhaust fumes, the trash tangled in the thick, brown grass of the hillsides. It was easy to imagine the drought never ending, the trees withering, falling, decaying into dust, while the privileged few huddled in their pyramids. But who would actually choose the desert, given the choice? Who would not walk, head down, putting one foot in front of the other, for hundreds and hundreds of miles toward whatever hope was left?

He'd been walking for an hour when he heard voices speaking Spanish beside him. He looked up, in the space of a second imagining that it might be Carlos, somehow with his wife and a healthy, if slightly premature, baby, and that they would offer him a ride because he had at least tried to help.

Instead it was a battered pickup that coasted along beside him, three men in the cabin. They all wore baseball caps and work clothes. One of them saw Nick's searching look and nodded stiffly.

Nick nodded back and said, *"Buenas noches."*

"Buenas," the man said. *"A donde vas?"*

"Tejas," Nick said, giving it the Mexican pronunciation. "Austin."

"Us too," the man said in Spanish. "I hear there's much work there."

"It's true," Nick said, also in Spanish. "I saw it on the television."

Work, he thought, and more. For Nick it meant the only person in the world who would have to take him in, no matter what. Because how could you look into someone's face, knowing they were just the same as you, and turn them away?

The man smiled and jerked his head at the bed of the pickup truck, cluttered with tools and folded plastic and canvas tarps. "You want a ride?"

"Gracias," Nick said. *"Muchas gracias."*

The truck paused momentarily and Nick vaulted over the side. He propped his duffel against the back of the cab, and in minutes he was asleep.

THE LONG RIDE OUT

THE SWEET TASTE of cold and wood smoke hung in the air. Marlin rode low in the saddle, his shoulders curled against the hungry wind. His hat was pulled down tight, and his eyes didn't move as he passed the crude shacks at the edge of town.

He tied his horse in front of the saloon, unwinding his long body as if a sudden movement might snap it. He turned down the collar of his greatcoat and checked to make sure his big Army Colt was loose in its holster. The saloon door was a single chunk of white pine, still oozing sap, and he had to put his shoulder to it to force it open.

The long room inside was quiet, and not much warmer than the street. Clusters of people sat nursing coffee and drinks, talking quietly if they talked at all. Marlin spotted a few farmers the railroad had brought in from Europe: rounded hats, nervous eyes, skin as red as blood. At the far end of the room a half-dozen cowboys turned over cards with patient boredom.

Marlin walked up to the bar. "Whiskey," he said, and when the drink came he tossed it straight down and felt it pull his lips into a grimace. He nodded for a refill.

When he turned to face the room they were all watching him. "I'm looking for a man named Kraamer," Marlin said. "Anybody here know of him?"

One of the cowboys turned casually and rang the spittoon with a stream of tobacco juice. Marlin knew the long, thin face from somewhere, the blond hair that fell limply to his shoulders. He smiled at Marlin and showed his brown-stained teeth.

Marlin felt the lines in his own face, the gray in his hair, the chill in his bones. He was too old for this. He set a half dollar on the bar and started for the door.

"Don't get in a huff," the bartender said. Marlin looked back. "Kraamer lives about a mile west of town. Follow the railroad and take the first trail south."

Marlin touched his hat and went out into the cold.

LEAVING HIS HORSE to follow the tracks, Marlin pulled a grimy telegram from his coat pocket with one gloved hand. It was addressed to the Iron Horse Saloon in Dodge City, and it read: 100 DOLLARS TO ANY MAN WHO CAN FIND MY DAUGHTER. MUST BE HANDY WITH A GUN. ASK FOR KRAAMER, LINCOLN CITY.

The sun was nearly down when he reigned in beside a big sod house, fifty feet long and completely overground. Parched yellow grass grew out of the roof. There was flat prairie in all directions, without a sign that anybody had ever tried to farm it. As Marlin got down a tumbleweed rolled out of the desolate land behind him and hung onto his leg. He kicked it aside and led his horse to the corral.

"You must be the gunfighter," said a man from the door of the house. He was short and balding, maybe fifty years old. His new denim overalls were already stained and torn.

"That's right. You Kraamer?"

The old man nodded, his corncob pipe bobbing up and down. "Bit long in the tooth for this line of work, ain't you?"

"I made it this far. There's a lot can't say that."

The old man laughed once, like a cough. "Once you see to your horse, come in and get some supper."

The mud walls of the house gave off a damp smell, but at least it was warm inside. A fire snapped in the stove and Marlin stood in front of it to warm his hands. Two iron-frame beds stood at one end of the single room, and there was a cupboard and a table and chairs near the stove. The furniture was all store-bought, light and strong, obviously well-used. In contrast there was a brand-new steamer trunk in the corner.

"Going somewhere?" Marlin asked.

"Had an idea once to travel and see the world. That was before the present trouble, of course. Sit down, I'll find you a plate."

Kraamer talked while Marlin ate, pouring himself shots of whiskey out of a clay jug. "I'm a homesteader," he said. "I guess you already figured that. On the other side of my property is a rancher by the name of Britton. He's got about ten thousand acres, but he won't be happy if he gets a million. North of me is the railroad. Besides my homestead, the government says I can buy a hundred and sixty acres of railroad land too."

Marlin nodded; it was how the railroads turned their government-granted land into money. It was the reason they brought crowded boatloads of farmers over from Europe and dumped them in this God-forsaken wilderness.

"So I bought me my acres, five years ago. Only now the town's staring to grow up out here, and Britton's got his eye on them. I'm close to the river, and the land is good for this part of Kansas. It's gonna be worth a lot of money someday, someday soon.

"Now my daughter's gone. I know Britton's got her, even if he won't admit it. If I took the deed to my land over there tomorrow, I know I'd get her back."

"How old is she?" Marlin asked around a mouthful of beans.

"Twenty-six. I know what you're thinking. You're thinking she's gone off with some man. I'll tell you something for nothing. Eva loves this land, mister. She would never leave it on her own. Never."

"If Britton wants your land so bad, what's to stop him from taking it?"

"He'd have to kill me first, and that still wouldn't give him the deed. I got nearly a thousand acres, and that deed could be on any one of 'em. Only me and Eva know where it is, and both of us are on the stubborn side. The only thing I'm afraid of is he might hurt her before he finds out how stubborn she is."

Marlin nodded, started to push back his chair, then jumped away from the table. He clawed at his gun as he watched a six-foot diamond-back rattlesnake slither across the floor.

Kraamer ran toward him shouting, "Stop! Don't shoot!" Marlin hesitated, wondering if the old man had lost his mind. "It's just a bullsnake," Kraamer said. "Kills mice, even rattlers sometimes. He won't hurt you."

Marlin holstered his Colt, feeling the skin crawl in the middle of his back. "He's marked uncommon like a rattler."

"No poison," Kraamer said, letting the snake glide over one of his boots. "You could say this here snake's a friend of mine."

THE MORNING SKY looked like snow again as Marlin rode into Britton's ranch. Four cowboys drifted over from the breaking pens as he tied up in front of the house.

"He'p you?" one of them said.

Marlin got down. "I came to see Britton."

Another cowboy said, "Yesterday you was looking for Kraamer. You just like looking for people, or what?" He rubbed his gloved hands together and smiled.

The first cowboy said, "Kraamer, he ain't too pop'lar round here." They all nodded at that. All of them had pleasant expressions on their faces, and holstered guns at their sides.

The second one said, "We sure would hate to think you were working for him or anything." Somehow they had all gotten between him and the house.

"All right," said a voice from the doorway of the house. "Y'all boys get back to work. If you ain't got enough to keep you busy, you talk to the foreman."

The cowboys shuffled away and Marlin climbed the stone steps to the house. The man in the doorway was tall and thick, with white hair like a clump of brush on his head. He wore a clean white shirt and string tie and he didn't seem to notice the cold.

"You Britton?" Marlin asked.

The man nodded. "You from Kraamer?"

"That's right."

"Come on in."

Marlin's boots made a solid sound on the wooden floor. Some walls were rock and mortar, some adobe. A fireplace filled half of one wall and Indian rugs lay in front of it. Marlin sat in a heavy chair and accepted a cup of coffee from a black woman with stiff white hair.

Britton stood with his back to the fire. "What did Kraamer tell you?"

Marlin sipped at his coffee, then rubbed his lower lip. "He said you wanted his land."

"Did he tell you some hogwash about his daughter, too?" Marlin nodded. "I figured. That story of his is all over town. So what's your part in this?"

"I'm not working for anybody just yet," Marlin said. "Once I figure out what's going on, then I'll decide what I want to do about it."

"Fair enough. Here's my side of it." He brushed at the back of his trousers and sat down in a chair like Marlin's. "I've been here a long time. I came west on the Santa Fe Trail thirty years ago. That was back before the railroad, back before everybody went land crazy. My wagon broke down on this very spot and it seemed like a sign. I made it through a hard winter, and by the time spring came I didn't feel like moving on any more. I traded with the Comanche and the Sioux, and later on I fought 'em when I had to. I fought for Statehood too, even though I am a cattleman, because I believe in this country. I believe in railroads, despite the way some men are getting filthy rich off of them. I believe in cities and progress, and I believe only a damn fool would try to get in their way.

"When the railroad came through I had a small spread and I was doing all right. But I realized those railroad cars could be taking cattle to market, and I saw what a man with vision could do here. Land means cattle, cattle means money. Enough money means power, and a chance to make a mark. Lincoln City doesn't have to go the way of Dodge City and Abilene. It could have an opera house instead of a gallows, schools instead of bordellos." He looked hard at Marlin. "You have any children?"

"Never worked out that way for me," Marlin said.

Britton nodded. "My wife took sick carrying our first child. I lost them both. Never had the heart to marry again. But I could make this a town where people that do have families could live in peace." He waved one hand, as if to clear the air. "Enough of that. About the time I had my vision, Kraamer came along, full of bright ideas and a love of money. That was fifteen years ago.

"To make a long story short, we cut a deal. How much do you know about homestead law?"

Marlin shook his head. "Not much."

"Well, the law has got its weak spots, like any other. It says a man can stake a claim, wait five years, and sell it. Then he's free to move on and do the same thing again. Between homestead, preemption, timber grants and what have you, that comes to a lot of land. Which I have bought and Kraamer has gladly sold to me."

Marlin shifted in the chair, which seemed to be suffocating him. "Where is all this leading?"

"To this. The business I have with Kraamer is between us. He's no helpless sodbuster being crushed by big cattle interests. Ask anyone in town. The other homesteaders think Kraamer is worse than dirt.

"I don't have his daughter. He may know where she is, he may not. But she's just an excuse to bring you into this, to stir things up. All that can happen is that you'll get hurt or killed. Believe me, Kraamer is just not worth it."

THE BLOND COWBOY from the saloon was sitting on the fence by the front gate. Marlin reigned in and said, "I used to see you in Dodge. It's Wallace, isn't it?"

"That's right. I heard about you too." The man's smile had a greedy look to it.

"That's a difference between us, Wallace. I've always found enough trouble without having to go look for it."

"You won't have to look for me," Wallace said. "I'll be around."

THE TOWN OF Lincoln City was a street, a stable, and a few buildings on either side. Paint was apparently in short supply. A brand-new bank sat across from the saloon, and next to it was a diner and a rooming house. Marlin tied up his horse and went into the diner.

The place was empty except for a red-haired boy in his early twenties. Marlin sat at the table next to his and took off his hat. He could hear the wind whistle through cracks in the plank wall.

A waitress came out of the back and wiped her hands on her apron. Marlin pointed at the boy and said, "I'll have what he's having." She was pretty in a strong, capable way, with a thick waist, small breasts, and ribbons tied up in her yellow hair. She smelled pleasantly of scented soap.

When she went back to the kitchen the boy said, "I hear you're working for old man Kraamer." He didn't look up as he spoke.

"Haven't made up my mind yet," Marlin said.

The woman came back with a plate of roast beef and Marlin set to work on it.

"It's hard," the boy said, "to tell what's what sometimes. Being in a strange town and all."

Marlin sopped up some gravy with his cornbread. "That about says it, all right."

"Hell, a man might not know where to start."

"I'd be grateful," Marlin said, "for any help that might be offered."

"Of course, it's hard to help somebody when you don't know what he's looking for."

They ate in silence for another minute, then Marlin said, "This man Kraamer might just be trying to get his daughter back."

The boy nodded and pushed his plate away. "Then again, his daughter might not want to come back."

"That thought had crossed my mind," Marlin said. "It's a shame she's not around herself, to talk with."

The woman came back out of the kitchen with a basket of cornbread and set them on the kid's table. He winked at her as she ruffled up his hair. "This here gentleman," said the kid, "was wanting to talk to you, Eva."

"JOHN NASH," said the boy, and held out his hand. Marlin took it, half rising as Eva sat at his table. "Me and Eva are going to get married."

Eva didn't seem to have heard him. Her gaze was level and penetrating. "What did my father tell you about me?"

"Said you'd been kidnapped by Britton."

She leaned back and smiled. "Well, I wasn't."

"I guess things around here are a bit complicated for me. Your father wants me to find you, and here you are right under his nose. He says Britton's his enemy, and they're the next thing to business partners."

"It's true Daddy doesn't know where I am. But that's because he doesn't ever come to town, except to the general store. I'm afraid you've come all the way from Dodge for nothing. I'll take care of him myself."

"Well, that's fine. But I'd still like to know a couple of things before I go. If you're daddy's not afraid of Britton, why's he so concerned about you?"

"He needs my signature so he can sell off my claim."

"Your claim?"

"I claimed a quarter section next to Daddy's five years ago. It's legal, all right. Daddy put me up to filing the claim and now he thinks he can just sell it to Britton. Only I don't want to sell. That's why I left, came to town where he can't get at me. If I'd have stayed out there he would have made me give it up ... whether I wanted to or not."

"Your daddy hits you?" Marlin said.

"Only when he's drunk."

Marlin pushed back his plate and wiped his mouth. "I don't much care for a man beating up on a woman, family or no. But that ain't here nor there. If Britton's got no quarrel with your daddy, what's that gunslinger from Dodge doing here?"

"Wallace?" She was suddenly nervous. "There's ... some kind of bad blood between Mr. Britton and Daddy. I don't know what it's about." She wouldn't look at Marlin.

"Why don't you tell me the truth?" he asked gently.

She stood up and brushed at her apron. "People got limits, mister. Ain't it about time for you to move on?"

AT THE BANK next door, Marlin rapped on the teller's window. The building was as empty as the diner, with room enough for a big city's business. The one teller had his feet up on the counter and a green eyeshade pulled low. Marlin was becoming impatient for things to make sense.

"'Scuse me," Marlin said. "Who do I talk to about a loan?"

The teller, a thin man with a thin mustache, opened one eye and pointed toward a door.

The man in the back room had a well-fed look, garters on his sleeves, and a short haircut. He had a land map spread out on his desk, with law books holding down the corners. A stove in the corner gave off a cheerful heat.

Marlin said, "I'm just curious. I'm looking for a man who knows about money, somebody I could maybe put a couple of questions to."

The man looked flattered and said, "What sort of questions?"

"I wondered what land around here is going for. If I wanted to get me a spread here someday, how bad would it be likely to set me back?"

"Well," the banker said, "government land is a dollar and a quarter and acre, standard price. Then there's offered land, as they call it under homestead law, and that's yours for the taking. But I'll warn you, the last of the offered land went about five years ago. The government land is still around, but none of it close to town or the river. Good land could cost you up to five dollars an acre on the open market. There's a land office across the street, of course. They might be able to turn something up for you...?"

Marlin shook his head. "Sounds a bit out of my price range. Thank you just the same."

The banker stood up before Marlin got to the door. "There are, you know, other options..."

"How do you mean?"

"Well, you don't have to have cash, you see. The principals of the bank are quite willing to lend money with land as collateral."

"Really? Is that a common practice?"

"Of course. Just the other day ... well, I couldn't go into any details, you understand. But yes, it's not uncommon at all."

"How much per acre are we talking about?"

The banker shrugged modestly. "Perhaps as high as ... five dollars an acre? Maybe higher?"

"Even for land that didn't cost that much in the first place? You could still borrow as high as five an acre against it?"

"I don't quite see what you're driving at, but yes. The railroad has brought civilization to these parts, and civilization is the magic elixir that turns land into money. God's not going to be making much more land than we got, I figure, so this bank's willing to take a risk on the best of it."

MARLIN PULLED UP a few hundred yards from Kraamer's house. The front door was slightly ajar and only a thin line of smoke trickled out of the chimney, despite the cold. Marlin got down slowly and dragged his big Army Colt out of its holster.

He pushed the door open with one foot. The inside of the house was dark and musty and smelled of blood. Kraamer lay in the middle of the floor, flat on his back. His empty eyes stared up at the ceiling. There was a bullethole in his chest.

Wallace, Marlin thought. Not likely to be anybody else around that cool and that accurate. One shot, right through the center of the heart.

He put his gun away, turned, and saw the snake. Somebody—no doubt Wallace again—had put a bullet in its head. Half its length still lay in a hole in the wall, but the hole had been dug out and dirt lay all around it. A shovel and an empty metal box, smaller than the diameter of the hole, had been dropped next to the snake.

Marlin used the shovel to dig a shallow grave in the middle of the floor. The ground outside would be frozen solid for months yet. After a moment's hesitation he dragged the body of the snake out of the hole and threw it in the ground next to the old man. He piled dirt over both of them and rode back into Lincoln City.

HE SAT IN the saloon for an hour or so, his greatcoat piled on the chair next to him, blowing into his cupped hands to keep them warm. It was nearly dark when Wallace arrived.

Wallace stood at the bar and downed a shot of whiskey. Trying to look casual, most of the clientele began to move out into the street. "I'll buy you a drink before you leave town," Wallace said to Marlin.

Marlin stood up and walked over to the bar. They were about ten feet apart. "You're a little ahead of yourself. I got business to take care of before I go."

"What business is that?"

"Somebody shot an old man to death this afternoon, and stole the deed to his land. I mean to settle accounts."

"You're wrong, mister. That ain't your business at all."

"Old man Kraamer lied to me, and maybe he wasn't much of a neighbor. But I ate his cooking and slept under his roof, and that counts for something. It's not to do with money, and it's not to do with owning anything, so I guess folks around here might not understand it too well."

"You're about to have the opportunity to join the old man," Wallace said. "And his snake."

Marlin ignored him. "What bothers me, really, is that I misjudged Britton. He seemed a decent sort, too decent to hire scum like you."

"I fight my own fights," Wallace said. He seemed genuinely angry. "Britton's a coward. He never meant anything but talk, just like you. And I've had enough. Get out or shoot."

It had been leading to this, and Marlin had let it happen. Now he wondered if it had been a mistake. He was old. Still, at the sight of Wallace's grinning face, he felt the cold fire spread through his body. There was a tiny spasm in the ring finger of his right hand where it rested on the bar. This one last time, he told himself. If I live through this, I promise I'll never tempt fate again.

Then Wallace reached and so did Marlin. The air of the confined space exploded with the noise of guns and the stink of powder. Marlin was not a one-shot surgeon. He held the Army Colt straight out with both hands and emptied the cylinder.

When it was over he was alive. He looked down to see if he was all in one piece and saw no blood.

Wallace was dead.

People moved back into the bar, circling like vultures over the body. In the darkening street, Marlin could see the snow finally coming down. He pushed through the crowd and pulled a sheet of paper out of the dead man's shirt. He unfolded it, expecting to see the deed to Kraamer's farm. Instead it was a mortgage note from the bank. The bottom edge was damp with blood. "I'll be damned," Marlin said.

Suddenly Eva Kraamer was standing by Wallace's body. She put up her hands and screamed. Tears started in her eyes. Then she dropped to her knees and began to go through the dead man's pockets.

Marlin pulled her aside by one arm. "Here's your paper," he said, holding the mortgage note by one edge. She stared at him for a second or two, her jaw trembling, and then snatched it away.

"Your daddy got greedy, didn't he? Thought he could sell Britton land that had been mortgaged, and by the time Britton found out, he'd be long gone, packed up in his brand-new steamer trunk and riding the first train out."

It was a railroad age, Marlin thought. If you just moved fast enough, you wouldn't have to answer for anything. Rockefeller and Gould and Vanderbilt were proof of that. They were building a world that had no place for him.

He shook off the thought and said, "Then Britton got wise. He called Wallace in just to throw a scare into the old man, nothing worse than that. Of course your father didn't know that, and so he sent for me.

"Then you got involved. You figured your daddy was about to wind up dead. I don't think that bothered you too much, only what happens to the money if Wallace kills him? So you had a meeting with Wallace, and by the time it was over, you two had your own deal. Wallace brings the mortgage paper to you instead of Britton, and you cut him in."

Eva seemed to get calmer and calmer as Marlin talked. It told him he had the truth of it. "My only question is," he said, "what were you planning to do with Wallace when you finished with him? You didn't think your boyfriend Nash could handle him, did you? Or did you think he'd just go away once he'd run all your errands for you?"

Finally Eva smiled. "Nash is a sweet boy, but he don't know much about the real world. And neither do you, mister. I might sell my daddy's share, but not mine. I loved that land. Daddy was about to lose it all. Everything I did was just to keep the land that belonged to me.

"And I will keep it, too. You can't prove a thing against me."

Marlin realized he still had hold of her arm. He let it go and said, "Land. You people are crazy. You're all crazy."

He stopped at the bar to put on his greatcoat and take one last shot of whiskey. "You moving on?" the bartender asked.

"That's right," Marlin said. "Back to Dodge."

The man seemed satisfied. "That's a long ride," he said.

Marlin looked at the body on the floor. "Not as long as some," he said. He tossed a coin on the bar and walked out into the falling snow.

SITCOM

LET ME TELL YOU about a TV show. If you're under 35, it's probably a
major part of your life. If you're 42, like me, it probably doesn't mean
much to you, and you'll find it hard to understand how a simple situation
comedy could destroy my marriage and make me doubt my sanity. And you'd
never, ever believe the rest of it: that it got Richard Nixon elected president
and killed the sixties.

It did, though.

I'm talking about *The Harrigan House*. You know, the one *Time* magazine
called "America's favorite TV show." Only I'd never heard of it until last week.

My name is Larry Ryan, and I'm a freelance magazine writer. My wife—
we're still married, but that's just a matter of time at this point—is named
Linda, and she's nine years younger than me. At 33, she's a card-carrying member of the Harrigan Generation.

She sells hosiery at a boutique operation in Highland Mall, some nights
until after ten. It was just last week that she came into my study to give me a
peck on the cheek and ask me to tape a show for her. *"HarriganMania,"* she
said. "It's on ABC at eight."

"What mania?"

"Harrigan. You know, the Harrigans?" She let out a quick snatch of song.
"That's life at the Harrigan house."

"I have no earthly idea what you're talking about."

"I love it. You sound just like the professor. Except it's 'I haven't the foggiest
notion.'"

"What professor?"

"Professor *Harrigan*. Why are you being this way?" She wrote "8:00/
ABC/2 hrs" across my notes for the stock car racing piece I was writing and
walked out.

I TOOK A LUNCH BREAK at 2:00 and turned on MTV while I ate. I came in
on a Tabitha Soren interview with a blonde teenager named Denise O'Brien.
Under her name on the screen was "Janie Harrigan" in quotes.

"This is too weird," I said, probably out loud. The occasion was a live stage
show, off-Broadway, where a bunch of semi-professional actors like O'Brien
recreated *Harrigan House* episodes line-for-line on a minimal set. Tabitha

flagged down a passing boy in his twenties and asked him, "Do you know who this is?" The boy stared for a second and then yelled, "Janie Harrigan!"

When I went back to work, I couldn't concentrate. I admit I've never been a sitcom fan. Maybe they failed to get their hooks into me at an early enough age, since my father never permitted them in the house. He was full of rules like that, as if the fact that he taught at s m u law school gave him some kind of anointed knowledge of right and wrong for him to crack over my little brother Phil and me like a whip.

Even so, how could I miss something that's this much a part of the cultural gestalt? I'm in the entertainment business; I do profiles of musicians, actors, athletes. It didn't make sense.

It's hard to sit and stare at a computer screen when your mind is not on your work. I found myself up and searching the house for the t v section. If the show was such a big deal, it had to be in syndication—probably two or three times a day. But I couldn't find it anywhere in the schedule.

In my business, if you want answers you pick up the phone. I called Austin Cablevision and got a woman in the p r department.

"You wouldn't believe how many calls we get for that show," she told me. "We had it on up until, I don't know, a couple of years ago or so. t b s, I think it was. It seems like whoever it was that owned the rights pulled it off the market. I don't know if it was the studio or what. Maybe they're gearing up for a videotape release or something."

"The shows aren't on tape?"

"Never have been. I think the video rental places get as much grief over it as we do. Seems crazy, doesn't it? A show that popular and it's just not around any more?"

I HAD TO GO OUT that afternoon for the usual post office and Fed Ex drops, so I swung by the Bookstop in Lincoln Village. The woman who asked to help me was about my age, wearing a long dress and glasses.

It's one thing to sound like an idiot on the phone, and another to do it in person. I found myself suddenly embarrassed. "Do you, uh, have anything about a t v show called *Harrigan's House?*"

"*The Harrigan House?* Sure. You can take your pick."

She showed me to the section. There was an oversized paperback called *HarriganMania,* same as the special Linda wanted me to tape, and one called *That's Life at the Harrigan House.* Then there was *Harrigan House: The Compleat Episode Guide* and a smaller, brightly colored one called *The Ultimate Harrigan House Trivia Book.*

"Good lord," I said.

"I have a confession to make," the woman said. "Until these books started coming in, a couple of years ago? I'd never heard of the damned show."

I looked up at her from where I knelt by the row of books.

"Maybe," I said, "we're too old."

The girl who checked me out was in her late teens. "The Harrigans," she said. "Cool."

The guy at the next register, who was blond and not much older, looked over. "Oh yeah," he said. He turned *HarriganMania* over to check out the photos on the back. "Remember this one? The pie fight?"

"Yeah," the girl said. "It's like really sad about the professor, you know?"

"What do you mean?" I asked.

"You know. Dying and all."

"Oh," I said. "Yeah."

INSTEAD OF WORKING that afternoon I read *HarriganMania*. It was hard to understand what all the fuss was about—even Tina Storm, the author and self-proclaimed "number one Harrigan fan," admitted that the show's premise was "dumb," the episodes were "banal and formulaic," and the acting was "wooden at best." After reading a few of the episode synopses, I had to agree. I found myself skipping on to the next section.

The bare facts were these: The show premiered on ABC on Friday night, September 27, 1968, at 8:00 pm Eastern. It ran seven seasons, through 1975, 161 half-hour episodes in all. John "Prof" Harrigan was an English teacher at Ivyville College and "Mom" (Joan) was a widowed socialite; Nancy, their unflappable housekeeper, was from "back East" somewhere. The five kids were the show's gimmick, such as it was: Mom and the Prof each had one child from a previous marriage, Jeff and Janie respectively. They'd adopted one child together, Joey, plus taking in Nancy's daughter Judy to raise with their own.

The first episode took up shortly after the arrival of the fifth child, who was actually the Prof's little brother. He had obviously come very late in life to Prof's parents, since he was only five—younger than any of the other kids—when he arrived at the Harrigan house. The death of his (i.e. the Prof's) parents, and any possible associated traumas, were never alluded to.

In fact, the show didn't just avoid controversy, it completely obliterated it. There were no student protests at Ivyville College, not even in the wake of the Kent and Jackson State shootings of 1970. Adopted brother Joey was pure WASP, not Italian or Jewish, let alone black or Hispanic, let alone Vietnamese. How could he be, since the Vietnam War didn't seem to exist in the world of the Harrigans?

The episodes I was able to slog through dealt with such matters as the importance of investing your allowance wisely and strategies for being popular in school. The professor was a bit pompous, but always full of good, solid common sense at the end. Like when little Jimmy gave the other kids permission to misbehave because he was, after all, their uncle. The Prof straightened everything out at the end when he explained that it was a combination of age, experience, and position that made authority work, and it took all three.

It was that kind of attitude that doubtless attracted Richard Nixon and prompted him to declare, two weeks before his 1968 presidential victory: "It's my favorite show. Families like the Harrigans are what makes this country great." When they asked Hubert Humphrey about the Harrigans, he said, "Who?" At least that was how Tina Storm, who was a decade too young to vote at the time, remembered it. The next week, in mock elections in grade schools and junior highs across the country, Nixon won by a landslide.

Professor Harrigan reminded me uncomfortably of my own father, who was of course an avid Nixon supporter. He was so convinced of his own infallibility, so rigid, so heroic in his own eyes. The difference was that Prof Harrigan was able to tell his kids that he loved them, and in turn his kids thought he was a hero, too.

Harrigan catch phrases abounded. Prof's "I haven't the foggiest notion," of course, and his "Do you mind?" every time he found one of Mom's cats in his favorite armchair. Little Jimmy's cries of "Say uncle!" Janie's accidentally overheard remark, "Professor Arrogant you mean!" which was later picked up by the rest of the family—in a good-natured way, of course.

There weren't a lot of pictures in *HarriganMania*. Pub shots of the actresses, none of whom I recognized, and few posed studio stills. There was nothing from the actual episodes because Sheldon Browne, the show's creator and producer, had supposedly refused permission.

I had a tingling feeling that meant there was a story lurking somewhere. The feeling turned into certainty when I got to the chapter about The Song.

It was irresistible, Storm said, like the theme from *Gilligan's Island* or any of those other viral little tunes that hook into your brain and refuse to let to. In sixty seconds the theme covered the entire hare-brained setup, including the business with Prof's little brother "who was an uncle and a brother to them all."

The theme was performed by the 1910 Fruitgum Company, of "Simon Says" and "1 2 3 Red Light" fame. According to the book, an extended version of the song hit the top ten late in 1968.

That, I knew, was wrong, and I could prove it.

I had a lot of music reference books, including *Billboard's Top Ten Charts* and Norm N. Nite's *Rock On Volume II*. The 1910 Fruitgum Company was listed in both books, but not "Theme From *The Harrigan House*" or anything remotely like it, not by any artist. Okay, big deal, Storm had been sloppy in her research. Instead of a feeling of superiority, I got a chill.

THAT NIGHT I WATCHED the *HarriganMania* special while the VCR taped it. In typical network fashion it was all form and minimal content. Tina Storm was the host, and she spent most of the show interviewing celebrities about their favorite *Harrigan House* episodes, and what the Harrigans meant to them. "The Harrigan House," Jay Leno said, "was like an island of calm in troubled times. It was a place you could come to for milk and cookies while the rest of the world was full of riots and Vietnam and girls putting you down." Shannen Doherty, wearing a "Do You Mind?" T-shirt, said, "Prof Harrigan was the father everybody wants to have. He was just *so* cool." Arnold Schwarzenegger said, "The Harrigans were about family values. Why can't there be shows like that today?"

There was an overblown emotional farewell to the actor who played Prof, who had died a few months ago in a private plane crash while doing a dinner theater tour. Then more tears were shed over the kid who played Joey Harrigan, who'd died of an OD in 1980. The woman who played Mom was brought onstage for a standing ovation, then hustled off again because she hadn't aged well and was obviously drunk.

In one segment they read excerpts from the thousands of letters the show had received from kids who wanted to run away from their own families and come live in the Harrigan House. The studio had been forced to come up with a form letter explaining that the Harrigans were fictional, that the kids should stay with their own parents and make the best of it.

Sheldon Browne did not make an appearance; he had refused permission to use any clips from the show. So instead we got footage of *The Harrigan House Live Onstage,* and shots of the *Harrigan House* comic books and trading cards, dolls and board games.

At the end all the celebrity guests got onstage and sang The Song together.

AT TEN LINDA got home and we had sandwiches. I went on to bed while she stayed up to watch the tape. I read for a while and then tried to sleep. Linda's side of the bed was cold and empty, not that that was anything new. Most mornings I had to be up at eight to talk to editors in New York, while she slept in. More and more we seemed to live in separate worlds.

Maybe I could try harder. I thought I would go in and see if she wanted to talk, or maybe even fool around a little. I put on a robe and got far as the doorway into the living room. Linda sat on the couch, tears rolling down her face. I couldn't remember the last time I'd seen her cry. Her lips moved as she sang along softly with the tape:

> *And there they had their own little world*
> *Nancy and the kids, the professor and his spouse*
> *Laughter and love for each boy and every girl*
> *That's life in the Harrigan house.*

She didn't see me as I turned and went back to bed.

WHEN LINDA AND I first dated there was an awkwardness that I chalked up to her being only 20 years old, compared to my worldly 29. I thought it would pass in time, but it never did.

I went in the next morning, which was a Saturday, to talk to her. I found her curled up on the couch, watching a black-and-white movie from the forties and reading the morning paper.

"So," I said. "Did you like the special?"

"It was great."

"I watched it while it was taping." For just a second she looked at me with real curiosity and interest, the first time in longer than I could remember. The look went away when I said, "I have to admit I didn't get it."

She turned back to the movie. "Well, you don't like TV. You say so all the time. I wouldn't really expect you to 'get it.'"

"So maybe you could help me, here. What is it you like so much about the Harrigans?" She shrugged, and I could see her slipping into hurt and anger. I kept after her anyway, knowing I should stop, a little angry at her myself for liking something that seemed so awful to me. "I mean, it didn't seem to have much to do with the real world. It's like some fascist fantasy, where there aren't any black or poor people, women just stay home and have babies, there's no crime, no injustice..."

"And what's wrong with that?" She was actually angry and letting it show, something even rarer than her tears. "Does everything always have to mean something? Some of us are tired of real life. I have customers in my face all day and when I get home I just want to relax. I don't need to be challenged or stimulated, I want things to be nice. *The Harrigan House* was a nice show, okay? Is that so terrible?"

"I was just asking."

"Just asking. With that superior tone in your voice. Just because you went on a few protest marches in the sixties, that's supposed to make you some kind of holy person. Well, look at yourself. You used to talk about this Great

American Novel you were going to write, about how you were just doing journalism while you got your novel together. Now you don't even bother to talk about it anymore, let alone do anything. You don't even vote, for God's sake. Your talk and everybody else's holier-than-thou talk about changing the world is just bullshit. Talk is all it is. The rest of us want to keep our houses and cars and TV sets, thank you very much. *The Harrigan House* is shown all over the world. Eastern Europe, Somalia, Brazil. That's what everybody wants, everywhere. To be like the Harrigans."

"Linda, I—"

"You think I like my shitty job? You think I like it that we're too poor to have kids? You think I wouldn't trade my life for Mom Harrigan's in a second? Or for the life of any one of those kids?"

"I'm sorry." With a tinge of bitterness I added, "I guess I didn't know you were that unhappy."

"Surprise! I am! Are you going to tell me your life is that great?"

"It's not so bad that I want to live in a sitcom."

"Fine. Don't then." She turned away again and the conversation was over.

AFTER LINDA LEFT for work I called my brother, who lives on the other side of town. He's two years younger than me, but he's got a steady job at Community National Bank, a big house, kids, and a bass fishing boat. *"The Harrigan House?"* he said. "I don't think I ever watched it when it was first on. The kids watch the reruns."

"But you've heard of it."

"Hasn't everybody?"

"Put one of the kids on, will you?"

"Sure."

The phone clunked, and a second later a voice said, "Hi, Uncle Larry."

"Hi, Danny. Do you ever watch *The Harrigan House?*"

"We used to. It's not on any more."

"Did you like it?"

"I don't know. It was kind of dumb."

"But you watched it."

"Yeah."

We talked about baseball for a minute or two and then I got Phil back on the line. "Is this for a story or something?" he asked.

"Maybe. Just bear with me for a second, okay? Do you remember ever actually seeing this show, or is it just that you heard the kids talk about it?"

He thought it over. "I guess I never did actually watch it. It's just part of the culture, you know? Like how you can not watch TV or read the paper, but still know everything that's going on? It's like it's part of the air we breathe and the food we eat or something."

THE STOCK CAR racing piece was a loss, at least for the moment. I went downtown to the main library to put an end, once and for all, to the knot of dread at the bottom of my stomach.

The first place I checked was the *TV Guide* for the week ending September 27, 1968. The Friday night listings had ads from all three networks featuring their new shows. *The Harrigan House* was not among them. Eight o'clock Eastern was seven o'clock in Texas, and nothing started at that hour. The second half of *High Chaparral* was on NBC, the second half of *Wild Wild West* was on CBS, and the second half of *Operation Entertainment* was on ABC. I tried the rest of the night's schedule, then the rest of the week. I tried the next week's issue, and the week's after that. Then I moved on to the fall of 1969 and 1970.

No *Harrigan House.*

I got the *New York Times* and the *Austin American-Statesman* on microfilm and checked them as well. I looked up *Harrigan House* in the *Reader's Guide to Periodical Literature.* There were no entries until the mid-eighties, and then the articles were either of the where-are-they-now or the sitcom-that-defined-a-generation variety.

I double-checked the alleged date of the show's premiere in *People,* and xeroxed the incriminating page from *TV Guide.*

Back at home I called LA Directory assistance. Sheldon Browne's number was unlisted, of course. I dug out my research on an article I'd done the year before on telephone hackers—phone phreaks, they call themselves—and dialed the number of a kid in LA. He got me Browne's home number while I waited, and threw in his fax for good measure.

A personal secretary answered at Browne's house. I was sure she would hang up on me if I mentioned the Harrigans so I said, "My name is Larry Ryan. It's about an investment of his. It's rather urgent, I'm afraid."

"Please hold." There was faint classical music on the line for less than a minute. "Mr. Browne does not recognize your name. What company are you with, sir?"

"Uh, Merrill Lynch."

"Mr. Browne has no investments with Merrill Lynch." The line went dead.

In for a penny, I thought. I punched his fax number into my machine, scrawled my name and number at the bottom of the *TV Guide* page, and fed it through.

The phone rang approximately a minute and a half later.

•

"SO," THE VOICE SAID. "You've discovered the secret of *The Harrigan House.*"

"Is this Sheldon Browne?"

"I suppose it is." His voice sounded tired. "A journalist, are you?"

"Well ... yes."

"I don't care. If you're recording this, fine, you have my consent. None of it will do you any good."

In fact I hadn't thought to record it, but I turned the machine on as soon as he mentioned it. "I'm onto something," I said, "but I don't know what it is. All I have right now are questions."

"The answer to one of them, Mr. Ryan—that is your name?"

"Yes."

"The answer is, *Harrigan House* never existed. I never created it. There are no tape archives that I'm refusing to license to video or put in syndication to the cable stations. It's never, to my knowledge, actually appeared on a television screen anywhere."

"But ... that's impossible."

"I said that for years, to anyone who would listen. No one wanted to believe me."

"But the books, the trading cards, the TV special last night..."

"You're a journalist, Mr. Ryan, an educated man. I'm sure you're familiar with Voltaire? 'If God did not exist, it would be necessary to invent him?'"

I DIDN'T BELIEVE him at first. On Monday I made a few calls to editors I'd worked with for years. "Try the *Weekly World News,*" they said. "We don't do that kind of story, Larry, what the hell's wrong with you?"

At the end I even got desperate enough to think about the *Weekly World News.* But what was the point of burying the truth amid all those Elvis sightings, UFO encounters, and miracle cures?

Late at night I tried to make the pieces fit together. How long had this been going on? Did it go all the way back to the sixties? If the Harrigan audience wasn't old enough to vote, how could they have swung Nixon's election? The easy answer was that they had exerted some kind of influence on their parents, conscious or otherwise.

The other answer is much more frightening. What if the same elemental forces that had brought an entire TV show into existence had also created Nixon—five o'clock shadow, political history, Pat, Tricia, Julie, Checkers, and all? My mind shrank from the thought as violently as those of the Harrigan generation had fled from the tumult of the sixties.

•

IT WAS JUST yesterday morning that I came into the living room and found the morning paper in my chair at the breakfast table. Linda was in her place, head buried in the Lifestyle section.

"Do you mind?" I said, picking up the stack of papers. I hadn't thought of Prof Harrigan until the words were already out of my mouth. Obviously I had let myself get deeper into the Harrigan world than I realized.

Linda peered around at me, a big grin on her face. "'Do you mind?'" she said back to me.

I smiled. "Oh well," I said. "That's life—"

And suddenly I saw where I was headed. Linda's warmth and acceptance reached out to me like a roaring fire in a blizzard. It was the chance of a lifetime. I could be part of something larger than myself, an unconscious conspiracy of light and happiness that could shelter me from a world of fear and anger and despair.

All I had to do was finish the sentence.

THE DEATH OF CHE GUEVARA

Interview with Haydée Tamara Bunke Bider, January 7, 1988, for the Argentine newspaper Clarín. *Translated from the original Spanish.*

How did you come to take the name Tania?
When they recruited me for the mission in Bolivia, I asked if I could pick my own *nom de guerre.* I chose Tania in honor of Zoya Kosmodemyanskaya Anatolyevna, who used the name when she was a partisan in the Great Patriotic War. She was tortured and executed by the Nazis in 1941 in the German-occupied Soviet Union.

In those days, the early sixties, we were all in love with the Soviet Union and Mao, and maybe also a little in love with death. I think that was especially true of Che.

What made you become a revolutionary?
I came by it naturally. My parents are both Communists, and had to escape Hitler's Germany because of that, and because my mother is Jewish. Here in Buenos Aires they were both members of the Communist Party and actively supported the guerrillas. In 1952, when I was 14, we moved back to the German Democratic Republic, and I joined the socialist youth organization—the Free German Youth—and later I was allowed to join the Party.

I grew up accepting Marxist historical analysis as the natural order of things. As I learned how the poor are treated in imperialist countries, and saw more and more of that as I traveled, it reinforced all those ideas and hardened my determination to change things.

You have to understand how exciting the Cuban Revolution was to all of us when they won their first victories in 1957 and '58. There they were, only 90 miles from the US, defying the most powerful oppressor on Earth and getting away with it.

Then, in 1960, I met Che in Berlin. He had found his purpose in life, and he was radiant. After that I wanted nothing more than to go to Cuba. I used to sign all my letters with the slogans of the Revolution: *Patria o muerte* [homeland or death], and *Venceremos* [we shall overcome].

In May of 1961 my dream came true and I got to visit Cuba. That was all it took for me—Cuba became my home.

What kind of a man was Ernesto "Che" Guevara?
Magnetic. Everyone says this about him, and everyone is right. On the one hand, he was incredibly strong because of his will and his absolute devotion to the Revolution. On the other hand he was physically weak because of his asthma. The strength and weakness were forever at war inside him. You could see the pain of it in his eyes, and it made him sensitive to the pain of others, especially the helpless.

To the powerful, he was not so kind.

He did everything with intensity. He was like a crazy man in combat, but when he listened to you he was quiet and looked in your face and he was entirely yours. This was very attractive, to men and women alike. Those who were close to him were passionate about him.

What about the stories that the two of you were romantically involved?
I've seen the stories. Ridiculous, and full of errors. The writers clearly did not know what they were talking about.

You and Che both nearly died in Bolivia.
Bolivia was a mistake.

Che believed absolutely in exporting the Cuban Revolution throughout America. As soon as they consolidated their power in Cuba, Che began talking to Fonseca in Nicaragua and Ramirez in the Dominican Republic, and also to rebels in Paraguay and Haiti.

But Bolivia was his obsession. He'd been nursing it for years, all because of geography. He looked at the Bolivian *altiplano* and thought how a revolution there could spread in all directions—to Brazil, Peru, Chile, Paraguay, and most of all to his homeland in Argentina.

From the start there were problems. The Bolivian Communist Party wanted to pursue an electoral strategy and didn't want to support us. And the CIA was tracking us the entire time.

My mission was in the cities. I had been in Bolivia since November of 1964 under deep cover as an ethnologist, making contacts in the government and universities. Che arrived two years later, operating in the countryside. But they had one setback after another, and then in March of 1967 everything started to come apart.

Three *compañeros* arrived in La Paz with no one to take them into the jungle. So I did it, and once I got there I was delayed, and the result of that was that my cover was blown. So I stayed with the guerrillas. That was very exciting for me, to finally get my own M-1 rifle and be a part of the fighting. It was what I'd been waiting for all my life.

Then, in April, on a long march, another *compañero* and I got sick. We had high fevers, and Che made us stay behind with a second group. We were supposed to reconnect, but it was difficult—the radios never worked properly, new recruits deserted, and the peasants would constantly betray us.

For example, in August we met a man named Rojas who gave us food and put us up at his house and promised to guide us across the river the next day. But there was something about him I didn't like, and the more we questioned him, the more evasive he got, until he finally admitted that he had alerted the army about us and they were waiting in ambush for us. Without a doubt, if we had trusted him we would all have been slaughtered.

The very next day we finally met up with Che's group. We were badly shaken from our close call, and they were in terrible shape as well. Che was sick with asthma, everyone was hungry, exhausted, and in low spirits.

We argued for days after that. Che wanted to stay. He didn't care about the risk, he only wanted to finish what he'd started. It was one of his flaws— he could be fatally stubborn. We kept telling him, over and over, that he was endangering everything. If he died in Bolivia there would be no revolution in Argentina, and the struggle for the rest of Latin America would be set back years, maybe decades.

Finally he was so sick that he couldn't argue any more. We took him across the border into Argentina, where the *montoneros* [leftist rebels] met us with medicine and food and guns and many men. I think he saw then that we had made the right decision.

How was it when you and Che met with Perón?
The entire event was dreamlike. The *montoneros* first smuggled us into Cordoba, and we flew from there to Mexico DF, and from there to Spain. We were travelling for over 24 hours with little sleep. Che was in his "Ramón Benitez" disguise, where he shaved back his hairline and had gray at the temples and thick, black-rimmed glasses. I was "Marta Iriarte" with blonde hair and cat-eye sunglasses. Our own parents would not have known us.

One of Perón's associates, Ramón Landajo, brought us into his study. I was so nervous. I don't have to explain to you, you're Argentine, but it's hard for the rest of the world to understand the sheer force of gravity that man had. The poor of Argentina, his *descamisados* [shirtless ones], loved him with such intensity, and that love was the fuel that he burned. When I was a girl in Buenos Aires, every time it was a beautiful spring day, one of my friends would say, *"¡Qué día peronista!"* As if Juan Perón had made the day especially for her.

Now, let me say that my parents thought him a fascist. They would talk about how he learned his political philosophy from Mussolini, and how he never really cut his ties to the Army. Some of that is true enough, but why did the Army hate and fear him so much that his political party was outlawed, that during most of the time he was in exile it was dangerous to even speak his name in public?

Which is to say, I didn't come to the meeting as an acolyte of Perón. Still, Che and I both liked the fact that he always refused to deal with the Yanqui imperialists. It was only after he let the Army force him out in 1955 that the North American corporations began to siphon the wealth out of our country. *Privatization*—that is the English word for "looting."

He was quite old by this time, 72, and the years had been hard on him. He was still a very large man, but his strength was failing. He stood up when we came in the room, and you could see that even that effort cost him.

He was very cordial, very respectful, very gracious. We had coffee, exchanged a few pleasantries. He asked about the flight, we talked about the weather in Madrid, Che gave him a box of Montecristos. But there was still tension. Like so many, he had a hatred of Communism that went beyond the rational, as if it were some kind of contagious cancer.

It was Perón who made the first move. "You know," he said, "I am uncomfortable with what you are up to in Argentina. I have many questions."

"That's why we're here," Che told him. "Our hope is that we can answer all your questions and come away with your blessing and support."

"If you win your Revolution, what happens then?"

"The first order of business," Che said, "is to reverse the damage that Onganía did in 1966. Expel the imperialist corporations, starting with the oil companies. Nationalize the industries that the military auctioned off. Create jobs for the *descamisados.* Make Argentina truly independent of the US. These are all things that you would do yourself, are they not?"

And Che drew him out like that, got Perón to talk about his own dreams for Argentina. It was beautiful to watch. The subject got on to land reform, and Perón asked, "What of the land owners? What of the *estancias* in the countryside? Do you intend to confiscate all that land for the State?"

"Let me tell you something," Che said. "In Cuba, we left the small farmers alone. We didn't advertise the fact, but it's true. We only broke up the big plantations, starting with the ones owned by foreigners, like United Fruit. Again, our goals are no different than those of the left wing of the *peronsitas,* who operate under your name."

We talked then about life with the *montoneros,* and the news we had of *compañeros* that Perón knew. It was going really well, until finally—and we knew this had to happen—he said, "What about the firing squads?"

Even Fidel had been concerned about the number of men that Che sentenced to death, starting in the Sierra Maestra and continuing through the trials and mass executions after the Revolution. But Che was inflexible.

"I was in Guatemala in 1954 when the Arbenz government was brought down by United Fruit and the CIA. It would never have happened if Arbenz had been strong enough to eliminate the men who were his sworn enemies, the men who continued to plot against him, the men who betrayed him and tried to assassinate him. How do you think the Cuban Revolution survived when the US has overthrown every other popular government in America? You have to kill them before they kill you."

Perón was shaking his head. "You would make Argentina run with rivers of blood."

I could see Che getting worked up, and I didn't know how to stop him. "There are already rivers of blood in Argentina," he said. "And in Guatemala and Nicaragua and El Salvador. It's the blood of the poor. It's the blood of the innocent, who are kidnapped and tortured by government death squads paid in Yanqui dollars. That's what Arbenz gave Guatemala when he resigned. That is the legacy of cowardice."

He'd gone too far. I could see Perón's face go stiff. Because of course that's what Perón himself had done in 1955, resign rather than let Argentina be plunged into civil war. "You are a very unforgiving young man," Perón said. "I hope the years bring you more compassion."

And that was all. Perón said he had much work to do and Landajo took us back to our hotel.

Che was angry with himself for getting carried away, angry with me for not stopping him, and I was angry with him for blaming me for his own mistakes. Altogether it was a long, miserable night. Che, of course, had insisted on our staying in a cheap hotel and the beds had fleas—misery upon misery.

You can only imagine our amazement the next morning when there was Landajo again, arriving in the middle of breakfast, saying that Perón wanted to see us again.

"You do the talking this time," Che said to me as we were getting in the car. "I will keep my mouth shut."

In the end there was little for us to say. Perón had clearly had a bad night too. He seemed very frail.

"I don't have much longer," was nearly the first thing he said. "I want to go home."

"Join us," I said. "We can find you a cabinet position if you want, though that seems demeaning for a man of your stature. We could make you a Hero of the Revolution, with a generous pension, and of course you would be one of our trusted advisors, a full participant in the government."

He said, "I don't see how I could be a part of a Communist government."

"We don't have to use the word Communist," I told him. I could see Che straining not to cut me off, wishing he had never let me talk. "We will call it a socialist government."

And that was how it went. Point by point we hammered out a compromise that Perón could live with.

How did Argentina react to the news?
The people were overjoyed. Che and Perón together? The only thing we lacked was bringing Evita back from the dead. Everyone wanted to join us— grandmothers, little kids, middle class shop owners.

For three months we built our strength, moving slowly down from the mountains. There was little resistance from the government—I think they knew they were doomed. On March 19, 1968, just as the first leaves were starting to turn with the fall, we marched into Buenos Aires and took the Casa Rosada without firing a shot. Perón flew in the next day from Madrid.

Shots were fired later, however.
There were executions. The Argentine military had allowed themselves to get in the habit of taking over the government every few years. It was a bad habit, and Che intended to break them of it.

What was Perón's role in the new government?
To be honest, it was very small. He did convince Che to hold elections, which Che was not keen on doing. And he suggested we run John William Cooke for President, which was quite a brilliant idea. Cooke was Argentine-born, Perón's handpicked representative during the exile, yet he had been in Cuba since 1960 and was close to both Che and Fidel. He was the perfect blend of socialism and *peronismo*.

We were surprised how conservative Perón had become in his old age. He worried that business would suffer under Che's direction, he worried about the US invading us—

Quite rightly, as it turned out.
True, but that was no reason to appease them. It was a full time job, keeping Perón on our side. If he'd lived longer he would probably have

started his own faction and started a long and bitter power struggle. I don't mean to sound callous, but it's just as well he only lasted a year after he came home.

How did you feel when the US invaded that July?
We had already lived through one US invasion back in Cuba, so we were not intimidated. If anything, the invasion at La Plata was even more pathetic than the Bay of Pigs fiasco.

The US was in the middle of the Tet Offensive at the same time, and already sending their young men to Vietnam as fast as they could draft them, so they had no reserves available. They ended up with a few hundred mercenaries from Tachito Samoza in Nicaragua and Stroessner in Paraguay, a collection of poorly trained rejects that hated each other more than they hated us. The US military was in a hurry, you see, because it was an election year and Eugene McCarthy had come out in support of the Revolution. They wanted to knock McCarthy out of contention with a quick victory.

And they underestimated us. The CIA knew that Che had disbanded the army and executed the top generals. They didn't seem to understand that Che had also created a citizen's militia, like we had in Cuba, consisting of a hundred thousand armed men and women who were completely loyal to Che and Perón and who passionately hated the US.

Also, as crazy as it sounds, I don't think the US officers in charge fully understood that it gets very, very cold in Buenos Aires in July.

The invasion was good for us in the end, because when it failed, it got McCarthy elected. That ended the imperialist invasion of Vietnam and kept the US mostly out of Latin America for a few years.

Mostly?
Well, the CIA simply hid what they were doing from McCarthy and continued to raise money for their favorite dictators any way they could—selling drugs and weapons, getting contributions from imperialist corporations like Ford, Bank of America, ITT.

What was your role after the Revolution?
I had developed a taste for combat. By 1969 things were stable at home and we decided on Paraguay for our next focal point. Stroessner was one of the worst dictators on the continent, with a laundry list of human rights violations: kidnapping, torture, murder, corruption, on and on. He was of course one of the favorites of the US. And we wanted to pay him back a little for sending his soldiers against us.

Those were very happy days for me. To see the first light of hope in the face of a peasant who has been held down his entire life. To see his pride and gratitude when you put a gun in his hands and suddenly freedom becomes something real and attainable.

It took two years to bring Stroessner down, and in that time the entire balance of power shifted. Allende won a free election in Chile, and suddenly there were four socialist countries in America.

It's funny, because the US used to threaten people with their so-called domino theory, the idea that if they let Vietnam fall to Communism, the rest of the countries in Southeast Asia would topple one by one. The left made cruel fun of this idea, and yet it came to pass here. We had barely finished celebrating in Paraguay when the Sandanistas won in Nicaragua.

Honestly, it blurs a little for me after that. Was Duarte in El Salvador next, or was it the Bandera Roja in Peru? Then Bolivia, at last, and Guatemala.

Where were you when McCarthy was assassinated?
That was December of 1972, after he'd just won his second term. I was in Chiapas, in Mexico. As in so many of our campaigns, all the money had been spent on guns and we were left with a miserable radio that never worked properly. We were deep in the jungle, trying to get news of what was happening in the US, and all we could get were bits and pieces, then everything would turn to static. The Mexican soldiers were terrified when they heard that there was martial law in the US and the military had taken over the White House. They thought it was going to be the end of everything.

In fact, it was not so bad for us. The US had to bring all of their troops home just to stop the rioting, and when the news came out that it was the CIA who shot McCarthy, they really had their hands full.

Plus, it was a moral victory for us, in a way. It was the US being forced to admit what we had always known, that pure, free-market capitalism is not compatible with democracy. Chicago School Economics really needs a dictator, and now the US had its own in General Westmoreland.

People in Latin America had seen enough dictators. It brought many of them over to our side.

What was your reaction to the Southern Wall?
Well, the irony, of course, is that same year, 1975, the Berlin Wall finally came down. I flew home to be a part of it, and I got to be with my parents in the crowd that welcomed West Berlin and West Germany to the Eastern Bloc. Everyone was holding candles and singing the "Internationale," chorus after chorus, in one language after another—Russian, German, French, Spanish.

Grown men wept. Mothers told children who couldn't even read yet to always remember that day.

Meanwhile, Westmoreland was using enslaved dissidents to build his own Wall, that ten-foot high monstrosity along the Mexican border. The US never admitted it, but more than ten thousand of those young people escaped into Mexico in the process, many of whom joined the rebel army. I don't know how many died, or how many more died later, trying to get over the Wall and into Mexico.

You asked me earlier why I became a revolutionary. Really, the answer is a single word: justice. And I have to say I felt a powerful sense of justice when the US was reduced to one more third world country, crushed by their own military coup.

When did you first meet the woman who called herself Agochar Kaur?
Ah, so we come to Veronique, already.

I met her at the same time that Che did. September of 1979, early spring in Buenos Aires.

Let me try to explain to you what it was like. Our dreams had come true. Every country in Latin America had either a socialist or a left-leaning government. Even Canada had the Labour Party in power, and the only reason they closed their border was that they simply could not handle the flood of immigrants from the US with no skills and no money. Though in private it's said that there were jokes about building their own Wall to, quote, finish the job Westmoreland started, unquote.

We were completely independent of the Yanqui imperialists. The poor people of America—except the ones in the US—were better off than they ever had been. There was still much work to do, but we were building schools and factories and hospitals and dams, we were educating children and training adults. There were people who had never had anything at all who now had at least a little land under their control and a future to look forward to.

At the same time it took constant, constant vigilance. For every hundred *descamisados* who worshipped Che, there was one bitter former bank manager or *estancia* owner who hated him with a desperate, suicidal fury. There were lots of guns around because of the militias. So it was not safe for Che, or even for me, to walk the streets.

Che was a gregarious, social person, and living in that kind of isolation was poisonous to him. Back in Cuba, he would go out every Sunday morning to participate in the voluntary labor crews and work beside the people—cutting sugar cane, loading trucks.

It was hard for me, too. I love music and dancing, especially the Argentine folk dances, the *zamba* and the *chacarera*. These are dances you do in the square at the Feria de Mataderos, with dozens of other couples and hundreds of people watching and clapping along. It's not the same when you're locked away in the Casa Rosada.

So, from time to time, we would disguise ourselves and go out in the streets with one or two bodyguards. Yes, it was dangerous, but without being able to do that, our lives would not have been worth much.

It was a Sunday, and we were in Plaza Dorrego, in the old San Telmo neighborhood. You know the flea market there, with vendors in the streets, tango *orquestas* and tango dancers, marionettes, painters, mimes, thousands of people all enjoying themselves, locals and tourists alike.

And there, down Calle Defensa, sitting against a corrugated steel shopfront, was this one waiflike girl, wearing a turban and playing a steel bowl. She was unearthly, pale, all in white, with a beautiful elfin face and an immensely long scarf. The bowl had indentations in it, like steel drum, and she ran her fingers over it to make it vibrate in these different pitches while she sang in a language I couldn't understand. A dozen people sat cross-legged on the cobblestones, watching her. The music was very quiet, and it seemed to make a zone of silence around her. You could hear every sound she made over the crowd and the bandoneons and the touts.

She paid no attention to any of us. After singing and playing for another five minutes, she put the bowl aside, set the cushion she'd been sitting on next to the wall, and stood on her head, facing out to the street.

Che was captivated. He crouched next to her and tried to talk to her. Very quickly he saw that she didn't have much Spanish, so he changed to French.

"What language were you singing in?" Che asked her.

"Gurmukhi."

"Gurmukhi? What kind of language is that? Did you make it up?"

"It's from India."

"And your instrument? Is that from India too?"

"Switzerland."

She seemed to know how absurd it was for Che to be squatting there and talking to an upside-down woman, but didn't seem to care—as if she had nothing better to do at the moment. As for me, I was terribly uncomfortable, as you can imagine. It's difficult to stand by and watch a man you admire make a fool of himself over a woman. It's something better done in private.

"Where did you learn to stand on your head like that?"

"From Yogi Bhajan."

"And who is that?"

"My teacher."

Che was not one to give up easily. "What is your name?" he asked her.
"Agochar."

"Is that really the name you were born with?"

"It's the name I use."

"And are you not going to ask me my name?"

"I know who you are."

This snapped me to attention.

"You can't possibly know who I am," Che said.

The girl said, "Shall I call you Ernesto? Or shall I call you—"

"Stop," Che said.

Both bodyguards and I, at the same time, had put our hands inside our jackets.

"How do you know this?" Che asked her.

"By the stink of death on you." She never stopped smiling.

Che pretended to smell his armpit. "This shirt was clean only last week."

"It's not in your clothes. It's not on your body."

"Where is it, then?"

She didn't answer him, she simply went away. Her expression barely changed, her body didn't move at all, but her focus was gone and she was inside herself.

Che was not used to being ignored by women. "If you know who I am, come to dinner with us. You can bring your pillow and your ... thing."

"Ramón," I said. Che always used his cover name on our excursions. "Don't be a fool."

He gave me a look meant to push me away. "Tell me how I can find you again," he said to the girl. "Do you have an address? A phone number?"

After a long time, as if from a great distance, she said, "I will find you."

"Will you? When?"

But that was clearly all she was going to say. I took his arm and told him, "Ramón, come away. Now. You're putting all of us in danger."

He let me pull him away, but it was clear he was completely smitten. He talked about little else the rest of the night.

He was still married to Aleida at that time. The marriage was not doing so well. Aleida didn't like Buenos Aires and missed Cuba. She was busy with the children and had withdrawn from public life. And Che, well, Che always needed a lot of attention.

He ordered his chief of security to find this Agochar. I didn't interfere, because I was curious about her too. I wanted to know if she was a threat, if she was working for someone.

My own sources learned she was French, that her real name was Veronique Jarry, that she had lived in the United States from 1970 through 1976, studying with this Yogi Bhajan. At some point during that time she converted to the Sikh religion. After that she lived in India, Nepal, Rhodesia, and Mexico, apparently supporting herself by teaching yoga. She had only been in Argentina for a few days. I decided that she was probably crazy but harmless.

For four days Che's people looked for her, and then on the fifth day, as Che became more and more obsessed, she arrived out of nowhere at the Casa Rosada, asking for him.

I had instructed the staff downstairs to call me if a woman matching her description showed up. Unfortunately, they feared Che more than me, so they called him first. He refused to consider my advice, which was that we arrest her, fingerprint her, and interrogate her until we knew exactly who she was and what she wanted. Instead he took her into his office and locked the door.

There was nothing I could do. I put half a dozen armed guards outside his door and told them to break it down if they heard anything they didn't like.

That was the beginning.

How did Agochar change Che?
She broke him. She destroyed him utterly.

Some called her a female Rasputin.
It was not like that. Che had always been strongly influenced by women. It was part of his charm. Growing up, he doted on his mother and ignored his father. Then there was the failed love affair that set him off traveling all over South and Central America. He didn't really become a Marxist until Hilda [his first wife] converted him in Mexico. And as any Jesuit can tell you, there is no believer as fierce and intolerant as a new convert.

By the time Agochar came along, he was ready for a change.

It wasn't just sex, he could have sex anytime he wanted. He liked powerful women, and she was very much that. She knew magical and spiritual systems, history, current events—and then there were the things she could do with her body. I think Che saw that as an expression of will, that she could turn herself into a human pretzel.

Did Che learn yoga from her?
He was never good at it, but he tried. He claimed it helped his asthma.

Did you ever talk to Agochar yourself?
Yes, several times. It was unavoidable.

But I remember early on she had some kind of impulse to win me over.

Che had installed her in an apartment with a huge courtyard, and she was growing vegetables there in enormous red clay pots. She asked me to tea and we sat outside, talking in French, there among all those plants propped up with stakes and covered by chicken wire to protect them from the birds.

"There must be many things you want to ask me," she said.

I asked why she had come to Argentina.

She said, "It was time to leave Mexico, and I saw a poster of Che, and I knew I had to come here. I knew he needed me."

"He needed *you?*"

"He has so much energy, as much as anyone I have ever known. But it was clearly not flowing properly. For whatever reason—moving around too much as a child, his troubles with his father—he is badly blocked in his first *chakra*. Are you familiar with the *chakras?*"

I told her that I was because I did not want to hear her explain them to me.

"Well," she said, "then you know that makes him rootless, and very rigid."

"A certain rigidity is not a bad thing in a soldier," I said.

"He can be so much more than that. He could change the world."

"He *has* changed the world," I said.

"I don't mean in the old ways. He could change the world the way Ghandi did. All the killings, all the executions, do you understand why he had to do that?"

"Of course. To prevent a counterrevolution."

"I don't mean the excuses he made. I mean the real reason, the psychological reason. When he kills a man who has betrayed the cause, or a man whose faith is weak, he is trying to kill those doubts in himself. That weakness in himself. He needed me to teach him to seek out his doubts and his weaknesses and listen to them. His strength is his weakness and his weakness is his strength."

I saw then that we would never agree, that we could not even talk to each other.

Did Agochar influence national policy?

Yes, of course she did. Or rather she influenced Che, and he began to dismantle the Revolution, piece by piece.

It started with Bolivia. You can't have all these separate socialist nations living cheek by jowl without some squabbling. Bolivia was trying to "adjust" their border with us—in their favor, of course. Che wanted simply to capitulate. "If all men are brothers," he said, "what difference does it make?"

This was early 1980, still in the heat of summer. Che was openly living with Agochar, though he had not divorced Aleida. He was making no attempt to hide his transformation. Here was Che, who had never worn anything but military fatigues, not even when he went to the OAS conference, not even when he met Chairman Mao, here he is on national TV in blue jeans, holding up his fingers in a peace sign. Or he would come to a cabinet meeting wearing sweat pants and sit cross-legged on the floor.

What I began to realize was that Agochar was right. Che was full of doubts and questions, always had been. Until she came along he had held his doubts in check with his iron will. He was very childlike, and like many children he loved to shock people. Communism had been one way to shock the adults of the world, the rich Yanqui imperialists. But Communism was no longer so shocking, and he had found a new way to upset people, even those closest to him.

Don't get me wrong. Other things about him didn't change. He never gave up his compassion for the poor and the helpless. But as Agochar said, compassion can be as much a weakness as a strength.

As it proved to be in the case of Bolivia. We argued long into the night over the situation, and before we could come to any kind of agreement, the thing was done, the Bolivians had gotten away with it.

Next Che began to insist on amnesty for the former members of the Argentine armed forces still in prison. This from Che, the king of the firing squads. I refused, of course, but he went behind my back and announced it to the press. We were forced to either go along or admit to the disunity that Che had created in the government.

This man, who used to lecture anyone within hearing distance about Marx and Lenin, was now lecturing about Ghandi and Martin Luther King.

"Where is Ghandi now?" I asked him once. "Dead. King? Dead. King's Civil Rights Movement? Dead. John Kennedy, Bobby Kennedy, Gene McCarthy? Dead, dead, dead. Assassinated, every one. When you put violence against non-violence, violence always wins. Have you forgotten who our enemy is? The United States does not believe in peace. The United Fruit Company, or United Brands, or Chiquita, or whatever they're calling themselves this week, does not believe in peace. The CIA does not believe in peace."

We were at a state dinner, and I'm sure I was embarrassing the others at our table. Everyone was in formal wear except for the three of us: Agochar in her white robes and turban, Che in a tie-died T-shirt, me in uniform. Agochar didn't say a word, just smiled her little inward smile. She didn't have to speak, because her words were now coming out of Che's mouth.

"Ghandi freed India," he said. "King won support for Civil Rights that violence never would have. Sometimes you have to give your life for your ideals. You used to know that, Tania."

"Sometimes you have to do the harder thing," I said, "and keep on living. What if you'd died in Bolivia in 1967, would there even be a Revolution in Latin America? Who will take your place when the CIA sees this weakness in you and shoots you down?"

"King came forward to carry on Ghandi's work. I have now come forward to carry on King's work. When they kill me, someone else will come along to shoulder the burden. Because the cause is just."

Wasn't he also planning to disarm the militias?
That was the last straw. Without the militias we would have been defenseless against a US invasion. Che claimed we could stop them through non-violence. At this point it was clear that he was insane.

Can you talk about the night of his death?
I went to see him in his apartment. I persuaded him to send Agochar away. I spent half an hour trying once again to change his mind about disarming the militias, but it was clear that nothing would convince him.

When I took out my pistol, he merely nodded. "You have come to kill me, then."

I could not meet his eyes.

"What did the others say?" he asked me.

"They know nothing of this," I told him. "I'm doing this entirely on my own."

He didn't fight or try to run. There was even a kind of eagerness about him. He sat up straight and said, "Be calm, and aim well. You are going to kill a man."

You must know that it was Agochar's arguments at your trial that helped give you a life sentence rather than the death penalty.
I am aware of the many ironies of the situation. Be assured that she did me no favor.

Had you anticipated that the power vacuum left by Che's death would lead to a second invasion by the US?
I had considered it, yes. But if Che had had his way, the US would have invaded anyway. And the reason they were successful this time is that they were able to make use of those ex-Army officers that Che set free.

The hold the US has now is tenuous, and I don't believe they will prevail. Because of me, Che lives on in the minds of the people as a martyr, and not as the traitor he had become.

For that reason, if no other, it was necessary for me to execute him.

At your trial, Agochar said, "The problem with capital punishment is not the harm it does to the one executed; it is the harm it does to those who pass and carry out the sentence."
Obviously I do not agree.

There is only one judge of a person's actions, and that judge is history. History will deliver my final verdict, and I am content with that. *¡Patria o muerte! ¡Venceremos!*

HIS GIRLFRIEND'S DOG

ONE DAY he saw himself the way his girlfriend's dog saw him. Huge, slow, precariously built, insensitive to moods and hungers and smells, overly fastidious about privates and dung. Soon he found his girlfriend incomprehensible, perhaps even cruel. Her actions seemed deliberately meant to puzzle him. His sense of play offended her.

After they broke up she would call him. "Ernie misses you," she would say. "What about you?"

"Of course not," she would say, confusing him yet again. "He sees me every day."

DEEP WITHOUT PITY

His eyes were open and his head bobbed around at an impossible angle. He was sitting in about forty feet of water, stone dead, one arm pinned between the rocks. As best I could tell, he had been dead when he landed there. The mud and ooze around him were as serene and smooth as he was.

The cop who was assisting me swam over and made a palms up gesture. I shrugged back at him and began to work the body loose. The corpse had only one leg, and as I worked I wondered what he had been doing in the lake. I got the arm free and kicked toward the quicksilver surface above me. The body turned bloated and heavy when I broke water with it, and it took three of us to load it into the police launch.

I dried off and got a Coke out of the cooler. It was getting to be another Texas scorcher, and the sunlight bouncing off the surface of the lake felt like it had needles in it. My mouth was dry from breathing canned air, and the carbonation burned like fire. Winslow, from the sheriff's office, sat down next to me. "I appreciate this, Dan," he said.

"No problem." Sam Winslow and I had grown up together about twenty miles outside Austin in a little town called Coupland. We'd fought a lot as kids, and there were still plenty of differences in our politics and educations. But being on the police and fire rescue squad had brought me closer to him again, and I was glad of it. A private detective needs all the friends he can get. "What do you make of it?" I asked him.

"Accidental drowning, looks like." I raised an eyebrow but didn't say anything. "He's got a bump on the head that could have come off a rock. We'll see what the coroner says."

"Any idea who he is?"

Winslow shook his head. He'd gained weight in his face recently and his jowls vibrated with the gesture. "No one-legged men on the missing persons list. Looks like it could be a war wound, maybe. Worth a try sending the prints to Washington."

Sailboats like scraps of paper blew across the lake. Winslow turned to the driver of the boat. "Let's get the meat to the freezer."

A burst of static and a chattering voice made me jump. Winslow went to answer the call, and I leaned over the rail and looked at the water. My reflection came back at me—stocky, tan, with a head of short sandy hair that had receded half way up my skull. I looked my age, and it was getting to where that was no bargain any more. A few gulls darted over me, complaining in harsh, strident voices. "You're a long way from the ocean," I said, looking up at them. "You better take what you can get."

Winslow came back, not bothering to hide his excitement. "You can forget nature boy over there," he said, nodding to the corpse. "We got real news on our hands. I hope you didn't have anything planned for the rest of the afternoon."

Winslow was my ride back to Austin, which meant I was along for the duration of whatever emergency had come up. "You know I don't. C'mon, spill it."

"They just found Jason King," Winslow said, and his eyes shifted to a big house above us, over the lake. "He's been murdered."

THE CURRENT FAD was for sex scandals, so Austin had found Jason King. His story was the usual thing—a not-too-competent secretary who claimed she was kept on for immoral reasons. King was a county commissioner, which in Texas is a big legislative job, so the papers had been getting all the mileage they could out of it for the last week. Now it looked like it had caught up with King in a very big way.

Ed McCarthy had been waiting for us in the squad car while the boat was out. His baby blue uniform was drenched with sweat, and his dark glasses glinted at me evilly. "How was the swim, gumshoe?" he said.

"Not bad, flatfoot," I answered. Ed grinned and I grinned and we all got in the car.

Winslow leaned back and said, "That's the trouble with you guys. You watch too much TV."

The car took off with a huge billow of dust, and we shot down the gravel roads with the siren cranking. Winslow had gone quiet, and I knew he was thinking about the case. Jason King was a hot item, and Winslow was just starting to realize how carefully he was going to have to watch his step. One mistake and he was a scapegoat, both for the sheriff and the people at the capitol. The smile slid quietly off his face and the burned-in wrinkles came back.

McCarthy pulled up in front of a big two-story house. Ahead of us the road ended in a white painted barricade, then fell off a cliff into the lake. There were three or four cars already at the house, including a brown sheriff's car and an ambulance, its multicolored lights still turning silently. We walked up the flagstones to the house, and it seemed to lean out over us. The upper story sat on a row of colonial-type columns, and the contrast they made with the ranch styling of the rest of the house set my teeth on edge.

The ambulance attendants passed us with a stretcher, and Winslow lifted the sheet for a quick look. The bullet had come through the back of the head, at close range. The face was almost completely gone. Winslow dropped the sheet and nodded, and they carried the body away.

The sound of voices led us upstairs. Inside, the house seemed to be trying to live down its nouveau-riche exterior. The carpets were thick, running to subdued colors and patterns. The upstairs hall was hardwood paneled, with brass light fixtures and framed lithographs on the walls. I recognized a Matisse and a Picasso.

When we got to the door of the study everyone looked up for a minute, then went back to popping flashbulbs, dusting prints and taking measurements. Chalk marks near the door showed where King had fallen, and a rusty stain disfigured the carpet. In the background I could see an English-style library arrangement with leatherbound books and heavy furniture.

A middle-aged cop in uniform who I knew by sight but not by name made his way over to us. He pointed out a heavy set Chicano in white ducks who was wandering around with a look of profound misery. "That's the houseboy," he said. "Name's Chico. He found the body. Yesterday was his day off, so he can't pin down a specific time for the killing."

"How did he find it?" Winslow asked.

"Came up to see if King wanted dinner, and saw him. He's only been here about an hour."

"Did you find the gun?" I asked.

He showed us a Colt long barrel .38, and the spot near the body where it had been found. "Houseboy positively identifies it as King's own gun."

I stepped over a small grey man with a magnifying glass and looked at King's desk. In the center of it was a big loose-leaf scrapbook, the kind that ties together with a silken cord. It was open to an article on the Korean War. I flipped through it casually, recognizing photographs of King, his wife, and various others at various ages. Beside it was a desk pad, and the words "Green Chevy" and a phone number were written on it, surrounded by the short crisp lines of a compulsive doodler. I memorized the number, just to have something to do.

On the corner of the desk, as if it had been put aside, was a steel construction handbook. I looked through it, too, but failed to make any sense of it. A few pages were marked, but it would have taken an expert to tell me what that meant. Under it was a mimeo sheet with the heading "County Bond Proposal." The only other object was a cigarette lighter which I was afraid to touch because of fingerprints. It was standing on end, and from behind the desk I could make out an insignia of some sort, a lightning bolt and the word "Thundermugs."

I looked up to see Winslow at the door. "They've got Mrs. King downstairs," he said to me. "I'll be with her for a while." I nodded and went to the window.

Filmy curtains fluttered in the wind, and it seemed cooler to be up above the lake. I was only in the way in the study, and I had no professional interest in the case. So I fought my way back to the door and went downstairs and into the back yard.

The lawn gave out at a six-foot hurricane fence that surrounded the house. I walked down to the gate and let myself out onto the top of the cliff.

I had started sweating as soon as I stepped outside, and the water looked cool and inviting below me. It looked to be about a fifty-foot drop, almost perfectly straight down to the water. I followed the line of the cliff for a while, and found a path that wound its way down to a shelf just above the water. It was covered with a coarse river gravel that was too uncomfortable to sit on, so I crouched for a while and watched the sailboats. They were a symbol to me of the kind of people, like the Kings, who had everything I never would have—money, prestige, a sense of time. But the sense of time was a lie, and even people like Jason King could die, suddenly, in a brief flash of mortality. I climbed back up the path.

"IT'S OPEN AND SHUT," Winslow confided to me on the way back to town. "Marion King has a motive, what with all this mistress business, and she can't account for herself at the time of the murder."

"Why wasn't she staying at the house last night?" I asked.

"She was at her sister's. She says her sister was sick. I say like hell. Here's how it was.

"Marion King quarrels with her husband over the mistress and moves out. She thinks it over, decides she wants a divorce, say. Then she tells her sister she's going to a movie. She doesn't want her sister to know she's even seeing her husband again. She goes to the house, tells him she's leaving him for good. He pulls a gun, threatens her. That's the last straw, he says, I'd be ruined. They struggle over the gun, it goes off."

"King was shot through the back of the head," I said.

"Okay, she pulls the gun and threatens him. He tries to walk out on her, and bang, it goes off. Maybe she didn't mean for it to."

The road heaved and dipped over countless hills between the lake and the outskirts of the city. The swaying car and white heat were numbing me. I considered asking Winslow what he made of the scrapbook and lighter, but changed my mind. It wasn't my case, and there was no point in stirring things up.

They dropped me at my house, and I waved as they pulled away. Two bills sat waiting for me in the mailbox, and a jug of milk had gone sour overnight. I cooked a couple of hamburgers and took a shower, then went outside with a beer. I sat in the front lawn and drank the beer and pulled Johnson grass.

Johnson grass is a vicious, predatory plant that can take over a lawn in a matter of weeks. All its leaves come out of a central root system, and to pull it up you have to track down all the runners and separate leaves and pull them back to the center. Pulling Johnson grass is just the job for an out-of-work detective. I stayed at it until it got too dark to see what I was doing.

My employment status changed at ten o'clock the next morning. I heard a tapping at the door and dropped my book into the center drawer of my desk. Before I could say anything, a husky blond kid with short hair and bangs came in. He introduced himself as Jeffrey King, the dead man's son.

I offered him a chair, noticing a gold cross at his throat and a strong smell of aftershave at the same moment. I guessed him to be about eighteen.

"I assume you know what happened to my mother," he said. I nodded, and he went on. "She didn't kill him, Mr. Sloane. If you knew her, you would know she couldn't have done it." He had a clear, ringing voice, with a taste of the deep south—Alabama or Georgia—in his accent. He was calm, direct, painfully sincere.

"I know the man who's handling the investigation," I said. "He's a friend, and he's an honest man. You can trust him to see that justice is done."

"The Lord said, 'Woe to you lawyers also, for you load men with burdens hard to bear, and you yourselves do not touch the burdens with one of your fingers.' It doesn't matter to Mr. Winslow whether my mother did it or not. I'd prefer to have someone working with her interest in mind."

His mannerisms and voice were those of a mature public speaker. I had to keep blinking my eyes to be sure he was the same person who'd come in the door.

"Let's hear your side of it," I said.

He paused, collected himself, seemed to be waiting for the right beat to come in on. "I can't claim my mother and father had a perfect marriage. They've been rather ... distant from each other for some time. It was perfectly natural for her to leave the house in which my father had committed adultery. 'Do not look back or stop ... lest you be consumed.' But that hardly means she would kill. The thought would not even occur to her."

"Do you live with your parents?"

"No. I'm in a dormitory at school, Texas Seminary."

I nodded, made a nonsense note on my blotter. I printed the letters slowly, paying no real attention to them. "Did you get along with your father?"

"I hardly see what that has to do it."

"Look, Mr. King—"

"Jeffrey."

"All right, Jeffrey, if we're going to work together you're going to have to trust me. If I ask a question, it's probably for a good reason."

He blinked his eyes down, then back up to mine. "My father was a difficult man. I respected him, and I honored him, as I was taught to do."

I decided I was not going to be able to crack Jeffrey King, and that it probably wasn't worth my effort anyway. "All right, Jeffrey," I said, "I'm interested." I recited my rates, adding, "Plus a bonus if I get her off. A hundred will do for a retainer."

"Will a check be all right?"

I nodded, and while he started writing I asked him, "Who do you think did it?"

He finished making out the check, tore it out with a long, backhanded rip. Then he looked at me with smoldering eyes. "The whore," he said. "Charlene Desmond."

"Have you met her?"

"No. But I've read what she said in the newspapers. She's evil, Mr. Sloane. A desperate, misguided woman." He was sounding twice his age again, and I wondered just how much he knew about desperate, misguided women.

"What's her motive?"

He shrugged. "Who knows? But she must have known Chico was off on Thursdays. That would be the day when she was used to visiting my father. So when she wanted something from him, she knew when he would be alone. He refused her, probably refused to continue his relationship with her, and she shot him."

"Um hmm," I said, and picked up the check. "Can I reach you at this number?" He nodded. "All right. I'll get on it right away. If there's anything else I need, I'll call you."

He left and I threw open a window. The smell of baking asphalt wafted in from Congress Avenue, but it was an improvement. I called the sheriff's office and asked for Winslow.

"Hello, Sam. This is Dan. Looks like we're going to be working together."

"How's that?" His voice had a tentative sound to it, a little frayed at the edges.

"On the King case. His son hired me."

"Oh really."

"What's wrong? You and Jeannie slug it out again?"

"No. No ... just can't see why you'd want to bother with the King case. It's all over but the trial."

"Well, maybe so. But I still got to make a living. Listen, can you give me some info? I need to know where the King woman stands."

"Like what?"

"Like did you get prints on the gun?"

"Yeah. They were smeared, but we got two good sets. One hers, one his."

"Do you have an address for Charlene Desmond?" He gave it to me and I wrote it on the blotter.

"One more thing," I said. "What about traffic up at the King house Thursday night. Did you find out anything?"

"The cab companies say none of their people went up there. Neighbors don't remember much." He found a quieter, apologetic tone. "Say, Dan, I have to go."

"Yeah. I understand. See you, Sam." I did understand. I'd been around long enough to know the sound of pressure coming down.

IN 1959 I gave up my DA haircut and sold my Chevy and joined the Marines. My girlfriend was very proud of me for about two weeks, then she found somebody who was still in the neighborhood, and that was that. When Kennedy sent the "advisors" to Vietnam in '61 I was along for the ride, and I was flying choppers by '62. Then my hitch was up, and I was ready to go home. So my sergeant got me drunk and got me to sign a blank piece of paper and I was suddenly in for three more years. They hadn't been able to make their idea of a man out of me, and they wanted another chance.

I didn't want to give it to them. I'd been rooked and they knew it, but the pressure was on. I tried to raise a stink, but it was hopeless, and finally the word came down: if I wanted out badly enough I could have a Dishonorable Discharge. I walked out of the Commandant's Office in Saigon and watched a Buddhist monk pour gasoline on himself and set himself on fire. I went back into the Commandant's office and talked some more. I finished my hitch at a desk in Germany.

I took my hand-to-hand combat training to Pinkerton while I was at Berkeley on the GI Bill. They used me for muscle while I finished my college, and let me do my required two years of investigating when I got out. With my license in hand I proceeded to starve for a year in a Northern California full of private eyes and impoverished kids. It was 1971 and the magic that was Berkeley was dead, along with the magic of most everything else.

I moved back to Austin and found some of it again. The kids were here, and it was a wide-open, all-night sort of town. The work wasn't much better, but I made do with odd jobs here and there. I made friends, and I found out that I'd been under pressure for a lot more years than I'd known. And now it was all coming back.

I drove down 11th to the Courthouse Annex where the commissioners had their offices. I had nothing particular in mind by visiting the place, but it was close enough to be worth the effort. I found a tree to park under and went inside. The withered smell of the place wrinkled my nose.

King's office was locked with an air of permanence. I tried the door and it echoed hollowly down the hall. The next one over was open, though, and said Hoyt Crabtree, County Commissioner, so I went in. A drab, middle-aged woman looked up from her typing and gave me an encouraging smile.

"Do you have a key to next door by any chance?" I asked her. "I'm working for Jeff King..." I let the sentence hang as if it explained everything.

"Oh yes. Jeff was such a nice boy. How is he?"

"Fine," I assured her. I sat on the edge of a table and tried to look cheerful and harmless.

"I'm afraid I don't have a key," she said. "Was it important? I could call the janitor..."

I waved my hand. The janitor would doubtless want more credentials than I could offer him. "Not really. Did you know Jason King very well?"

"Oh yes, both him and that dreadful secretary."

"Dreadful?"

"Yes. I can't understand why someone would tell lies like that just to get a fine man like Mr. King in trouble."

"You think she was lying, then?"

She wrinkled her nose. "Pshaw. I'm sure of it. He hadn't the slightest interest in her. I don't think she would have lasted another week, even if that awful scandal business hadn't come up. He was forever having to ask me to help out in getting his work done. I swear he only kept her on as long as he did out of pity."

A huge man stuck his head out of the back office, then lumbered into view. He must have been six foot six and weighed over two fifty. "Oh, Mr. Crabtree," she piped, "this nice young man is a friend of Jeff King's." I didn't try to correct her.

"Daniel Sloane," I said as he shook my hand, a broad smile on his face and his eyes utterly vacant. He had graying hair that looked like a stack of hay, and when he spoke he sounded like the pedal notes on a pipe organ.

"Pleased to meet you," he boomed, his eyes already wandering around the room. "Terrible thing about Jason, I could hardly believe it." He was headed out the door and hardly seemed conscious of the fact that I was in front of him. He shuffled forward and I backed out of the way, but then he was coming at me again. "Knew him for years," he said, and I found myself standing outside his office. He shook my hand again, and said, "Give my sympathies to the family if you see them, pleasure meeting you." The door closed gently in my face.

It took me a minute, but I calmed down enough to shrug and walk away. I imagined that Crabtree had been having a lot of trouble with reporters and rubbernecks. I sympathized with his position. I still wanted to drop a grenade down his shirt.

CHARLENE DESMOND'S HOUSE sat up on a hill overlooking Pease Park and Shoal Creek. It had been a luxury neighborhood years ago, and now was full of college students, like everywhere else in Austin. The place looked deserted, but I knocked anyway. After two or three tries, the door opened back on the chain and a woman's voice said, "What do you want?"

I showed her my license and said, "I'm looking for Charlene Desmond." I could see just a little of her face, wrinkled, wearing too much makeup, topped off by salt and pepper hair.

"She's not in."

"Are you a relative?"

"I'm her mother."

"I'd like to ask you a few questions, if I may."

One finger came out from behind the door and pointed at the wallet still in my hand. "Does that mean I have to let you in?"

"No, ma'am. It just means—"

"Oh, Mother," came a friendly voice from inside. "Let him in." She shut the door and I heard the rattle of the chain being let off.

The inside of the house smelled faintly of incense. Furniture was sparse, consisting mainly of throw pillows, low tables, and those bedspreads from India that everyone used to have. Sitting on a divan, legs tucked up under her, was a small blonde who I took at first glance to be a little girl. Her eyes had too much makeup, though, and her body was too clearly developed. She was wearing blue jeans and something I think they call a tube top, that had no other means of support than what she provided herself. She gave me a broad, slightly coy smile. "I'm Charlene Desmond."

"Daniel Sloane. May I sit down?"

"Sure."

I took off my coat and sat in the only real chair in the room. She turned and stared at her mother until the older woman left. "Mother has been such a help this last week I can hardly believe it. But she does go too far sometimes. Drink?"

"No thanks," I said. It was too early for me by about five hours. There was a table to my right, by the front window, and she stood at it and poured coke over some bourbon. Light from the drawn Venetian blinds made intense stripes across her hands.

"I expect you've had a good share of visitors lately," I said.

"Yes," she said, and took a big slug of the drink. If it weren't for the violence of her makeup and the lines it didn't quite hide around her eyes, I could have taken her for a teenager. "It's pretty exciting, really. I'm used to attention—" here a not-quite-shy smile—"you know ... but not anything like this."

"Do you mind if I ask you some questions?"

"That's what I figured you were here for. What sort of questions?"

"I'm a private investigator. I'm trying to clear Mrs. King."

"Oh." She looked down at her glass and shook the ice cubes around in it. She seemed almost embarrassed that I had brought up the idea of the murder.

"How did you get drawn into all this?" I asked.

She shrugged, still looking down. "The usual way, I suppose. I came in from the pool when his regular secretary got married, and I just stayed on." She stubbed out the remains of one cigarette and lit another with a lighter sitting on the table. It was a standard Zippo, with a lightning bolt insignia on it. It was an exact duplicate of the one on Jason King's desk. "Then he asked me out—I guess I'd been there about a week—and I knew better than to say no. I'd had enough trouble getting on there in the first place."

"What sort of trouble?"

"Well, my typing's not very good." She showed me her dimples. "But I have a nice telephone voice and a good memory."

Her flirting was irritating, not so much on a personal level, but because she didn't seem to be able to turn it off. "How did you finally get hired?" I asked, leaning back and propping my head up with one arm.

"Mr. Crabtree needed somebody one day while I was there trying to get in, and took me. He didn't even know I wasn't in the pool. Then they sort of had to let me in. It's complicated. Like a union, sort of." She finished her drink and went over to get another one. "Sure you won't join me?" she asked.

I shook my head. The inertia was starting to get to me, and I felt like I was wasting my time. The woman was shallow and a little on the cheap side, but she didn't strike me as a killer. She lit another cigarette and I asked her about the lighter.

"Did that belong to Jason?"

She looked down at it as if she'd never seen it before. "I suppose so," she said. The whiskey seemed to be affecting her. "The Thundermugs ... must have been his outfit, huh?"

She reminded me of a high-school kid just out for the summer. She seemed disjointed, adrift in the moment. It was all a big vacation, and Jason King had paid the bill, first in publicity and now with his life.

By the third drink she was talking about King without being prompted. She had the conversation under her arm and was running with it.

"He was a nice man. Not a big spender, but not a tightwad. He'd take me out sometimes. Sometimes we'd go to his house. He lives out by the lake. Once we went down to the beach by his house, it was late at night, and we made love right there, in front of God and everybody."

I'd had enough. I stood up and looked around for my coat.

"You can knock it off now, Ms. Desmond," I said. "You were no more Jason King's mistress than I was. You don't know enough about him to talk for a full minute without repeating yourself. There's no beach by King's house. There's a rocky ledge, but believe me, lady, I wouldn't try it. The reporter that bought your story should be kicked out on his ass."

She sat up, stunned. She looked as though I'd hit her. "Now look here," she said, her words a little slurred. "I don't want that kind of language in this house."

"Did you come up with this little scheme on your own or did somebody put you up to it?" I walked over to her, but not close enough to have to smell the whiskey.

"I think you should get out," she snarled. "Mother!" Her voice got shrill and I put my coat on.

"Call me if you change your mind," I said, and stalked out of the house.

Driving back to the office, I made a quick recap. If the Desmond woman was out, that left me high and dry. I had two suspects left, the kid who'd hired me and the woman I was supposed to clear. I'd scored one point though, since Marion King's motive *was* pretty well shot. Charlene Desmond's story couldn't have held water at the bottom of the ocean, and I doubted that Mrs. King would have fallen for it.

I parked around the corner from my office and went into the GM Steakhouse. After a $2.07 sirloin and a large milk I was in a better mood. After all, I had a client and a hundred dollars. What could go wrong?

The phone was ringing when I got back to the office. I caught it in time, and heard Winslow's voice.

"Found out who our bathing beauty was," he said. "His name was Ernie Singleton. He was a grunt in Korea, lost the leg there. Last residence was Dayton, Ohio. No relatives, no friends, no nothin'."

"So why did he come here?" I asked.

"To drown, looks like."

"Ha ha, I got a hot one for *you,* now. The King sex scandal was a put-up job."

"That's not too funny. You got proof?"

"I don't need it. The chick is as phony as a three-dollar bill. She'd never wash in court."

"Well, maybe the wife believed her."

"Hey, look," I said, "I've heard of blind justice, but don't you think you're carrying this a bit too far? Don't you even want to check this out?"

I listened to a long silence on the other end of the wire, then Winslow said, "Uh, something's come up. I'll get back to you, okay?" and he was gone.

I held the dead receiver in my hand for a minute, then hung up and dialed the *Austin American-Statesman*. "City desk, please."

I had time to tap my fingers on the desk a couple of times and scratch my nose, then a voice said, "Hello?"

"Bennie? This is Dan."

"Let's see ... Dan ... Dan..."

"Don't rub it in, I'm sorry. I've just been out of circulation for a while."

"I'll say. Did you marry her?"

"No. I got out at the last minute. It was close, though. Listen, I may have a story for you in a bit. I need some information first, though. Like who would a county commissioner have for an enemy?"

"A bad enough enemy to bump him off, you mean? I thought the wife did it."

"Maybe not that bad. Maybe just bad enough to throw a little dirt on him."

Bennie whistled. "That way, huh? Okay, I can give you a list. How long you got?"

"Just hit the high points."

"A county commissioner wears a lot of hats, friend. To start with, of course, it could be somebody who lost an election to him, or thinks he could take over the job. Or one of the other commissioners. But what you're after probably has to do with county contracts."

"Whoa. What sort of contracts?"

"Mainly roads, but all the contracts are let through Commissioner's Court. That includes libraries, parks, hospitals, you name it."

"Good. What else?"

"Commissioners appoint county officials, run the welfare department, handle the budget and all that. Each commissioner is responsible for the roads in his precinct, and since King used to be in construction, you've got a tie-in there. He could have brought along some old enemies when he moved up. Let's see, there's a bond issue coming up, but the contracts on that haven't been given out yet, so I'm afraid that's no help."

"It's help," I said, "but I wish you could have narrowed it down a bit more."

"That's the breaks, kid. Now what about that scoop?"

"I'll let you know. 'Bye."

So there I sat. Not at a dead end, but facing an endless field of possibility. The bond issue may or may not have been important; it had been on his desk when he was killed, but I had no way of knowing what it meant.

I looked at my cards, and I was holding no suspects, no clues, and didn't even have a long suit. It was time to get some help.

I STILL HAD FRIENDS at the county jail, and they hustled Marion King into a visitor's booth for me in no time at all. I could tell from her bearing that she was merely allowing the guard to lead her. She had a lot of dignity and authority in her walk. They were obviously treating her with respect; she was still in her street clothes and her long brown hair was neatly brushed out. Her eyes looked dull and resigned, but she gave me a weary smile anyway. "My guard thinks pretty highly of you," she said. She was naturally gracious, had an instinctive ability to put people at their ease.

"I try to get along," I smiled. She was a handsome woman, with a sort of strength that denied the years that were visible in her face. She settled herself in the chair beyond the glass and waited.

"I'm not sure where to start," I said, "but if it means anything to you, I know your husband was not involved with Charlene Desmond."

Her mouth made an ugly line across her face. "Tell me something new. Jason would no more have had that tramp for a mistress than he would have robbed a bank. He just didn't have it in him."

"Just how do you mean that?" I asked, intrigued by the hint of resentment in her tone.

She sighed. "You've met Jeff, so I think you can understand. Jason was very much like Jeff, without the religious mania. That's why they didn't get along—they were so similar. Both of them were so demanding, so harsh, even toward themselves. There were times when I wished Jason would have taken a mistress, anything, just to get him out of his shell. But I'm sure you didn't come here to listen to my discontents." She was the hostess again, detached from her surroundings.

"On the contrary. I'll take any information I can get right now. Do you have any idea who might have killed your husband?"

"I'm sorry, Mr. Sloane, but I never kept up with my husband's business."

"Couldn't it have been somebody from his personal life?"

"What personal life? If he had someone over to the house it was either in connection with the county or with his construction work."

"He was still active in construction, then?"

"Only as a consultant. Anything else would have constituted conflict of interest. Not that he couldn't have gotten away with it, of course—this is Texas—but my husband was a very scrupulous man."

"Why did you move out on him, then, if you'll pardon my asking?"

"I didn't move out. I went to stay with my sister because she was ill. Jason hardly cared whether I was there or not, and both of us knew the scandal was nonsense. I saw no reason to stay around simply to avoid gossip."

"I'd like to talk with your sister. Where does she live?"

"Off Cameron Road, north of the airport." She gave me the address. "Her name is Jenny Shaw. She lives alone. That's why she needed me."

I was silent for a moment, looking at the sunlight through the intersecting lines of the barred window.

"Do you—" Her voice caught and she cleared her throat. "Do you think they'll convict me?"

I shrugged. "It would help if you'd tell me what you know."

She looked me in the eyes and said, "I already have." It was not too bad, but she shouldn't have pulled her eyes away at the end. I stared at her for a minute, but it was no use. I wasn't going to get anything more out of her.

"If you think of anything else that might help at all, tell your guard. She'll get word to me somehow." I couldn't shake the feeling that she was hiding something, but I had no clue as to how to get at it.

The sergeant at the desk let me use the phone. "Jeffrey? This is Dan Sloane."

"How are you? Any news?" He didn't sound particularly concerned.

He and Winslow had both given me scenarios of the murder, and now a third one was taking shape in my mind. It was ugly, and I wanted to get rid of it. It started with Jeff waiting till the house was empty on Thursday night to confront his father. They quarreled, Jason walked away, and Jeff reached for the gun. The he stopped and wrapped his hand in a handkerchief so he wouldn't leave any prints...

No. No soap. People who shoot in anger worry about prints afterward, not before. Still, he seemed to have a real martyrdom compulsion, and people have been known to hire detectives to punish themselves. In more ways than one.

"Your friend the scarlet woman didn't do it," I said. "Your father never gave her anything but letters to type. And not many of those, from what I hear."

"It seems I've made a serious mistake. And it's too late to rectify it."

"What's that supposed to mean?" I had an awful, sinking feeling that the kid was about to confess. I held on tight to the receiver,

"He has cursed his father ... his blood is upon him."

"Jeffrey, have you got an alibi?"

"I beg your pardon?" He sounded like I'd just woken him up.

"Where were you when your father was killed?"

"With a Bible study group."

"Can you prove it?"

"Yes. Why?"

"Nothing," I said. "Never mind. " I sighed, a little, and began to understand what Marion King had been talking about. If his quotations didn't get me, his self-righteousness would. I decided to give him written reports from that point on. I said goodbye and drove out to Cameron Road.

The house was mass produced, built to last three years and now in its fourth. I parked at the curb, and a herd of little kids rattled past me on plastic tricycles with huge front wheels. I noticed that the lawn had lost its battle with Johnson grass.

Jenny Shaw answered the front door with a wary smile. "I'm Daniel Sloane," I said. "I'm a private investigator." In all the years I'd been doing it, I'd yet to find a positive name for it. When I introduced myself I had to be ready to face hostility and distrust. The private detective had lost all his glamour, was back to being the dirty little peeper at the window. Sometimes I felt that way about myself.

"Come in," she said, and held the door open. She was cast out of the same mold as her sister, with the same rich brown hair and the same large but attractive features. Her hair was cut shorter, though, and fell in a more relaxed way. Her eyes were brighter, less strained. She was perhaps five years younger, but looked more like ten. She was one of the more attractive women I'd seen in a while, and washed Charlene Desmond from my memory like a long drink of water.

"Could I get you a cup of coffee?" she asked. "Or something stronger?"

"Coffee would be fine. Please."

I sat on the edge of a chair and looked at the prints on the walls. Her taste ran to symbolists and expressionists. She came back with two cups of coffee and handed me one. "There's cream and sugar on the table," she said, pointing.

"Black is fine."

She sat on the sofa and examined me. "You're working for my sister?"

"Your nephew, actually," I said, "but it comes to the same thing."

"How can I help you?"

"I'm not sure. I seem to be losing ground faster than I'm gaining. All I know at this point is that someone set Jason King up for that scandal. Maybe the secretary, maybe someone behind her. It might even be a reverse blackmail scheme, where they would have dropped the charges if King paid them. Whoever set it up probably killed him, or is at least involved in the murder somehow. But I don't have any clue as to who it is. I think your sister does, but she won't tell me."

There was a long silence. I could tell she was thinking something over, and I didn't want to give her an opportunity to let it go. At last she said, "Can I trust you?"

I shrugged. "That's a pretty vague term. If you mean will I lie, cheat and steal to protect a client, no. If you mean do I have a conscience, yes, but I put caution and common sense above it."

"That's a fair answer," she said. "You see there's ... something I didn't tell the police. I may have been wrong, but then again they never asked the right questions, either. They seemed to have their minds made up, and I saw no need to bring something up that might look, well, compromising for my sister."

"The police have a little trouble thinking along more than one track at once," I agreed, thinking with regret of Winslow.

"The day of the murder—that is, the afternoon before it—Marion got a call here. I answered it and it was a man's voice, a soft, gentle voice. He asked for her by her first name, so I didn't think it was a reporter or anything. It even sounded sort of familiar somehow. Anyway, I let her talk to him. I went in the next room, and I only heard bits and pieces of her side of the conversation. "

"Can you remember anything, anything at all?"

"Well, at first she sounded really shocked, stunned, to hear the voice. She sounded as if she didn't believe it. Then she got very quiet. I had to come back in the room for something and I heard the tail end of it. She said something like 'all right, eight o'clock at Jason's' or something like that. I know she was making a date to meet him there. Does that make sense to you?"

"It makes a lot of sense. Whoever that was could be our blackmailer. Did he happen to say where he got your number?"

"No, but it would have to be from Chico or Jason, wouldn't it?"

I agreed that it would. "One more question. This could be a hard one. Do you think your sister was having an affair?"

"No. Not that she wasn't capable of it. She certainly didn't have enough feeling for Jason to stop her. It's just that I suppose she hadn't had a good enough offer. That's usually the case, isn't it?" Her smile was enigmatic, and too sad to be threatening.

"Would there be anybody else she might be trying to protect?"

"Not that I know of. *Cherchez l'homme*, is that it?"

"Right. Just find a man with a gentle, soft-spoken voice. No problem."

I got ready to leave. She took my hand at the door. "I think you're a good person, Mr. Sloane. I'm glad you're on our side."

I didn't know what to say. It was too sudden, after having had doors slammed in my face all day. I muttered a thank you and walked out to the car.

So now I had a suspect again. A man with a voice. Marion had set up an appointment with him, possibly to pay the blackmail. But what was her relationship to him? Was she involved in the setup? Was she the killer herself?

The warm openness of the afternoon was telling me to call it a day. My eyes burned and I felt heavy and sour with sweat. The air was just right for a swim, or at least a sunbath. And part of me wanted to go back to the little peeling house and ask Jenny Shaw to dinner.

I fought off all the evil impulses. The devil, as I was sure Jeff King would have told me, was finding work for my idle hands. I had plenty of time still to go out to the house on the lake. So I slammed my car into gear and rattled off toward Lake Travis.

"No, sir, I don't know." A trace of accent still touched Chico's voice, but it was barely noticeable. He had lines of sorrow etched in his face, and I saw Jason King in the new light of the respect, perhaps even friendship, he had earned from this man. "I hadn't heard the voice before. But I trusted him, somehow. He said he was an old, old friend of Mrs. King's, and I believed him."

I paced up and down the kitchen, unable to put my finger on what was bothering me. It had started when I walked in the house, and wouldn't let me go.

"Did Mr. King leave the house much at night? To go out to a nightclub or eat or anything?"

"No sir. Particularly not lately, since his car has been in the shop."

I turned to him. He looked like an old man in the steeply filtered light of the afternoon. "You mean he had no car the night of the murder?"

A look of anguish came over the man's face. "No sir. I wanted to stay with him, but he said he would be all right. I wish I had stayed anyway. I feel as if..."

"Don't blame yourself," I said. "There's nothing you could have done." Suddenly I wanted to go to the study. I couldn't explain it, but the hunch was strong, and was reason enough in itself "I need to go upstairs. Is that all right?"

Chico nodded. "Of course. You are a friend of Mr. Winslow's. Please make yourself at home."

Everything was just the same as it had been the day before. The chalk outline of the body stared up at me from the carpet. I walked around the room, reading the titles of books off the shelves, then came back to the desk. I opened the book of photos and paged through them from the beginning. There were school pictures, through high school, and in several of these and later ones I saw a younger version of Marion King. In two of them there was another man. Once picture didn't have Jason in it at all.

Marion and the man were posed in front of a fountain. They had their arms around each other, laughing. I felt instinctively that Jason had taken the picture himself, and they were laughing at something he'd said. I stared at the man's face. I tried to visualize it older, with wrinkles. Then I tried to see it with various combinations of facial hair. Finally I tried to see it heavier, with jowls, or bloated with fat.

Then I had it.

I called the sheriff's department. A voice told me Winslow was out, but I didn't try to force the issue. I asked for McCarthy and got him.

"I understand I'm not too popular down there," I said.

"Not very, but you didn't hear that from me."

"Thanks, Ed. Listen, you got a teletype from Washington with the file on a GI named Singleton, Ernie Singleton. You think you could find it for me? It just came in today."

"I'll check. Hold on."

After a moment I heard a sound of pages rustling on McCarthy's end. "Got it." he said.

"I need his war record. See if it lists who his commanding officer was at the time he was wounded." There was more rattling of paper. Then the sound stopped and there was a long pause.

"Did Sam see this?" McCarthy asked.

"I don't think he paid much attention to it. C'mon, let's have it."

"I think you know."

"Tell me anyway."

"Wounded May thirteenth, 1953. Commanding officer Lt. J. King."

THE JAIL WAS twilight dark, dismal, eternal. The kind of light that things and people disappear in. A ragged light came on in the ceiling as they let me into her cell.

I didn't waste my time. If Marion King had murdered her husband, I had spent a long day for nothing. I had to find out.

"Ernie's dead, Mrs. King. You can stop covering up for him now."

She whirled on me with fiery eyes. "How do you know about that?"

"I fished him out of Lake Travis yesterday. It looked to me like he'd been murdered, but it was none of my business at the time. As to your relationship to him, what I know is just from legwork. I want you to tell me the rest of it. I don't want to threaten you, but if the DA finds out about Ernie it could be bad for you."

I'd pumped the anger right out of her. She sat down on the hard cot. "How far back?"

"All the way. If you tell me something I already know, I can stand it."

"All right." She took a breath. "Ernie and Jason and I were a threesome. Jason and Ernie were best friends. They both loved me. This was in the early fifties. Jason was in ROTC in high school, and he went to Korea when he graduated. So did Ernie, as a private. When they got back, I was to have decided who I was going to marry. I don't know which I would have chosen, but I didn't have to decide. Ernie didn't come back." Her voice stayed level, but the tears were starting in her eyes. I didn't interrupt her.

"The first I knew he was alive was when he called me two days ago. I nearly fainted. He told me he had something important to tell Jason and me, and he sounded like he was in trouble. We set up a time to meet at Jason's house. He didn't show up."

"Ernie was missing a leg, Mrs. King. He lost it in Korea, under your husband's command. Given the circumstances, I think he might have been bitter toward your husband, even blamed him for the injury."

She was hiding her face, and her shoulders trembled a little. "Jason confessed to me that night, before he was killed. He left Ernie to die. It was the only evil thing he ever did in his life, and he's suffered for it ever since, inside.

"I don't know why Ernie waited so long to come back, but yes, Ernie had plenty of cause to hate my husband. Do you think he killed Jason?"

I shook my head. "It just doesn't work out. If it was murder and suicide, how did Ernie get to the house? The police checked the cab companies, and they were all negative. He couldn't have gotten very far without a crutch, but none was found anywhere near the body." I shook my head again. "You don't get a lump like that falling through thirty feet of water. You're just not moving fast enough. Unless he hit himself over the head, he was murdered."

"By my husband?"

"No. Same reasons. How would your husband have brought him there? His car is in the shop. Likewise Ernie's crutch, his clothes, any other personal effects. Your husband had no way to get rid of them. And it doesn't make sense that he'd kill Ernie at the foot of his own driveway. It's too obvious."

"So who killed my husband? Who killed Ernie?"

"I don't know. I just don't know."

IT HAD BECOME time for a drink, a little past it, in fact. I sat in a rocking chair on my front porch with a glass of straight rye and thought about luck. Some people had it, some didn't. I had gotten close, built up a good, solid case. But unless I could produce the real killer or killers, I had wasted my time. The State could turn Ernie Singleton into a whole new motive and put Marion King away despite all my beautiful logic.

The only clues I had left might not have been clues at all. The bond election, which might or might not have made an enemy for Jason King. The steel book which might or might not have been used to discover a piece of shaky engineering. The words "Green Chevy" and a phone number, which might refer to a new car to replace the one in the shop.

Frustration was eating up my gut. I could say goodbye to a night's sleep unless I did something.

I went into the living room and got out a piece of paper. I sat by the phone and wrote out two numbers. One of them belonged to Jenny Shaw. The other I had memorized from the pad on the dead man's desk. I tore the sheet in half and folded the numbers, then mixed them up on the desk.

If Jenny Shaw's number came up, I was going to take her out and buy her a drink, or maybe several, if she would have me. If the other number came up I would at least exhaust my remaining clue. I closed my eyes and picked one.

It was the number from King's desk. My stomach was heaving worse, now, and I wondered if I weren't making a mistake. Almost certainly there would be no answer at all, at worst an irate stranger that I'd pulled away from his TV. But that was not what I was afraid of. I was afraid that a murderer would answer the phone, and I had no idea what I was going to say to him.

I dialed the number. My hand shook and I loused it up the first time. So I dialed it again.

The phone rang once, twice, three times. It took an eternity. I was starting to breathe easier when I heard a sharp click.

"Hello," said a deep, booming voice. My stomach lurched and my mouth dried up. I recognized the voice, and I started adding things up that should have been obvious long before.

"Is this Hoyt Crabtree?" I said, forcing my voice low.

"Of course it is. What do you want?"

I took a shot at it. "Bonds. I want to talk to you about some county bonds." My brain spun while I waited for his answer. If he bit, then Crabtree was in it up to his gills. If not, then I was at another dead end.

"Maybe you'd better come over here," he said at last. "I think we need to talk."

"Maybe I'd better. What's the address?" I wrote it down, my pulse hammering in my ears. "I'll be right over," I said.

HE LIVED OVER the river, west of town. I parked in his driveway, behind a green Chevy, and walked up to his door. For a moment I wished for a gun, but I knew it wouldn't do me any good. In any situation where I needed it, I probably wouldn't get the chance.

I was right. A big cowboy answered the door, let me in, then threw me at a wall. I leaned against it, stunned, and fought back the reaction that started to come over me. I concentrated on the man's hands as he searched me in the clumsy, embarrassed manner that country people have when they have to touch another man. When he was done I turned and looked at him, seeing limp blonde hair, a western shirt, jeans. I might have hit him, but at that moment I noticed Crabtree.

He sat casually in an armchair, and there was another big cowboy to his right. There was a dull look to Crabtree's face, and a big .38 in his hand. "Sit down," he said, and I sat on the couch behind me. My head felt soft and pulpy.

"So you're the private eye. Yes, I know who you are. I checked you out after you came snooping around the office. I'm amazed at your persistence." There was malice in his eyes and the shaggy white hair brought out the red in them.

"While you were checking that out," I asked, "you didn't happen to mention anything to the sheriff about a nice quick conviction for Mrs. King, did you?" The man by the door reacted to Crabtree's expression and slapped me across the face. He carried a lot of weight, and my head almost went into the wall again.

Crabtree's gun barrel came to rest in line with my stomach. "You won't need to hit him again," he said. "He's going to tell us all he knows."

I didn't like his attitude. "I know a lot of things," I said. "Two and two are four, Lincoln is the capital of Nebraska..."

The hammer of the gun clicked back. It was cheap drama, but effective.

"You may have to help me a little," I said slowly. "But I think I have most of it now. Jason King caught you taking kickbacks on road contracts. He knew enough about the business to know your contractors were cutting corners. So you scared up a sex scandal to get him out of the way.

"Then he got something on you. Not the scandal, obviously. You wouldn't kill somebody as important as King over a little thing like that. But you would kill somebody you thought might not be missed. Like Ernie Singleton. That's what Jason King found out, and that's why you had to kill him."

Crabtree laughed. "Who's Ernie Singleton?"

"He's the boy who really had the goods on King. He showed up at Charlene's, for some reason, and offered to throw in with her. He left a lighter behind that had an insignia of the outfit that he and King were in. I don't know what he offered her, but she was afraid to handle it herself. That was when she made her mistake and called you in.

"That tipped Ernie off that something was phony, and I'm sure it didn't take him long to find out what it was. But he knew about your connection, so he had to go. You dumped him in the lake because it was as good a place as any, and because if the body did show up it would only be something else for Jason King to explain. Only our local sheriff didn't make the connection, and by then it was too late anyway.

"Because Jason King had been watching for Ernie, and he saw your car. A green Chevy. I saw it just now, outside. He recognized it and called you up."

"I like your imagination," Crabtree said.

"Not imagination. King doodled while he talked on the phone, and it's all on paper. When you came over, he pulled a gun and threatened to call the police. But he didn't have the heart to use it, and you took it away from him, shot him carefully in the back of the head, and ran. What could you lose? Mrs. King was perfect to take the rap."

I noticed that I was trembling, and the adrenalin in my system was reaching a critical level. Crabtree said, "I don't think anybody will believe that."

"Sure they will." My voice sounded like it was coming from the other side of a waterfall. "Not the murders alone, or the scandal. But throw in the bond deals, the pressure on the sheriff's office—it's clear as a bell. Your name is the one thing that ties everything together."

Crabtree seemed to think it over. "Maybe you're right," he said. "Let's go for a ride."

I got to my feet. I could feel the oppressive heat in the room as if it were a jungle, and my nose was full of that sickly sweet Asian smell that I'd never been able to wash away. I was shaking with the tension of it.

Charlene Desmond burst into the room. Her face was puffy and red, and she was staggering. "Hoyt, you lied to me," she shrilled. "You killed that soldier, and you promised there wouldn't be anything like that! And Mr. King! You..." I saw her move through the air at him, fists bunched up in little girl style.

"Look out, you idiot!" Crabtree yelled, but he was too late .

She had deflected the gun, and I had lost control.

I had gone icy cold and everything was moving in slow motion. I hadn't wanted it to happen, but the Marine Corps' instincts had taken over and there was nothing I could do to stop it. My stiffened hand took Crabtree's wrist, and I felt the bones shatter under it. I kicked the gun in the corner and planted my foot in the closest of the cowboys. He went down and the other one swung at me. I slipped under his arm easily and started punching, short hard throws of the fists with snap at the end. He sank to the floor.

I turned to Crabtree, breathing hard and looking for something to kill. I stood in front of him, blood lust racking my body and my hands shaking with it. I fought for control, got it back, lost it, got it back again. My eyes cleared and my head pounded like a jackhammer. Then my knees got soft and I was all right again.

"Call the police," I said to Charlene, and watched her until she did it. The room was quiet, and Crabtree's eyes, full of hatred, followed me as I sat in a chair. I remembered the pistol, finally, and picked it up out of the corner.

When she finished on the phone Charlene sat on the couch across from me. "He still loved her," she said, her voice drunkenly sentimental. "He stayed away because he loved her. He only came back because he thought her husband had betrayed her."

I realized she was talking about Ernie Singleton. "He didn't want to hurt Mr. King, I know he didn't. He was just angry. I don't think he would have done it. He just loved her, that was all. Isn't it sweet?" She looked up at me with wet red eyes. "Isn't it just too sweet?"

Eventually the police arrived.

AT SIX IN THE MORNING Winslow let me go. Crabtree was behind bars and Marion King was out. It was over.

"You've still got your license," Winslow had said to me, "but then it wasn't my decision." I looked for a trace of the friendship that we'd still had only two days before, but it was gone. A hundred things came to mind, but none of them would have made any difference if I'd said them. I'd made everybody look bad, and stepped out of line time after time. People didn't forget things like that easily. Maybe after a few months we'd all be friends again. I'd go back to Winslow's house for dinner, and we'd get drunk on beer and laugh it all off. But I thought not. We'd learned too much about each other in the last two days for things to ever be the same again.

Jeff King was waiting for me when I came down the steps. He must have been there for hours, He gave me a check for five hundred dollars and an anemic smile. "God bless you," he said to me. I shook his hand and drove away.

I was too full of coffee, too hypertense, too frightened by the Vietnam flashback to get any sleep. So I drove out to Lake Travis and watched the sun come up over the water. I changed into a bathing suit and swam out into the chilly waters of the lake. It was going to be another beautiful, clear, broiling hot day. There would be more days like it, and suddenly it was going to be fall, and Austin would have tricked us out of another year.

That was when I hated the city, the times when it fooled you into thinking the days would never end, that time itself did not exist. It had fooled Jason King, and he had let that ugly part of his past slide away, and believed it could not touch him. But time was there, deep as a lake, without pity or sorrow or love. A man could drown in it.

I swam back to the shore and fell asleep under the neutral, staring eye of the sun.

THE CIRCLE

For six years they'd been meeting on Halloween night, here at Walter's cabin, and reading ghost stories to each other. Some of the faces varied from year to year, but Lesley had never missed one of the readings.

She'd come alone this year, and as she parked her Datsun at the edge of the graveled road she couldn't help but think of Rob. She'd brought him to the reading the year before, and that night they'd slept together for the first time. It had been nearly two months now since she'd heard from him, and the thought of him left her wavering between guilt and sadness.

Her shoes crunched on pine needles as she dodged the water droplets dripping from the trees overhead. The night was colder than she had expected, the chill seeping quickly through her light jacket.

She hopped onto the porch of the cabin and rapped on the door. Walter's wife, Susan, answered it. "Come in," she said. "You're the first one."

"It's cold out there," Lesley said.

"Isn't it? Tea's ready. Sit down and I'll bring you a cup."

Lesley had barely settled by the fireplace when the others began to trickle in. Some of them had books, others had manuscripts, most of them also had wine or beer. All of them wrote, several of them professionally, and about half the stories each year had been written for the occasion.

Lesley hadn't felt up to writing one herself this year. In fact she hadn't felt up to much of anything since she and Rob had broken up. His bitterness had hurt her badly, and she was hoping that something would happen tonight to pull her back out of herself.

She hoped it would be the way it used to, when the stories had been chilling and the nights had been damp and eerie, and they'd gotten themselves so scared sometimes that they hadn't gone home until daylight.

They'd been younger, then, of course. Now that they were all closing in on thirty they seemed to be more afraid of election results and property taxes than they were of vampires and werewolves.

Around nine-thirty, Walter stood up and ceremonially lighted the candelabra over the fireplace. The other lamps were turned off, and Walter stood for a moment in the flickering candlelight. He looked a bit like an accountant in his sweater and slacks, with his horn-rimmed glasses and his neatly trimmed mustache.

"Well," he said, clearing his throat, "I think we're all here. Before we get started, we've got something unusual I wanted to tell you about. I got this in the mail last week." He held up a large manila envelope. "It's from Rob Tranchin, in Mexico."

Lesley felt a pang again. "Did he..." she blurted out. "Did he say how he is?"

She felt all the eyes in the room turning on her. The others had never liked Rob all that well, had only put up with him for her sake. While all of them dabbled in the occult, Rob was the only one who had ever taken it seriously, and on more than one occasion he'd had shouted arguments with some of them on the subject.

"I, uh, can't really tell," Walter said. "There was a note inside, but it didn't say much. Just said that he'd written a story for us and that he wanted somebody to read it at tonight's, uh, gathering. It's not very long, I took a quick glance at it, so if nobody minds I'll just draw a card for Rob and one of us can read it when that turn comes around."

Behind Lesley, Brian muttered, "I hope it's not some more of that occult shit of his," but there was no formal objection.

Walter took the ace through eight from a deck of cards and shuffled them, then let each of the others draw for a turn. Brian had the ace and read "Heavy Set" by Bradbury. Walter followed with a new story that he'd just sold, another Halloween story, and the chill seemed to creep in through the windows. Lesley read a piece from Beaumont and even gave herself shudders.

Then Susan took a turn, her straight blonde hair and pale skin looking cold and waxen in the candles' flicker. Everyone shifted nervously as she finished, and Lesley thought happily that it was really happening again. We've done it, she thought. We've gotten ourselves so worked up that we're ready to believe anything.

"It's Rob's turn," Walter said quietly. "Anyone want to do the honors?"

When no one else spoke up, Lesley said, "I will."

I'M STILL CARRYING HIM, she thought as she took the envelope from Walter. Without wanting to, she finished the thought: Someone has to. Poor childish Rob, with his tantrums and his grandiose dreams. How long would he keep haunting them?

She took the manuscript out of the envelope. It was handwritten on some kind of ragged paper that looked like parchment. She recognized the scrawled printing, despite the peculiar brownish ink he'd used.

She glanced at her watch, then went back to the manuscript. "It's called 'The Circle,'" she said.

•

SHE BEGAN TO READ.

"'For six years they'd been meeting on Halloween night, here at the cabin by the lake, and reading ghost stories to each other.'"

Lesley looked up. Something about the story was making her nervous, and she could see that same unease on the shadowy faces around her.

"'Some of the faces varied from year to year, but a central group remained the same. They had a lot in common—they played their games with each other, went to movies together, and sometimes they went to bed with each other.'"

Lesley felt a blush starting up her neck. She might have known he would do something like this to embarrass her. He'd been so jealous of the few stories she'd sold, and when she'd tried to offer him some advice he'd blown up. That had been the first quarrel, and he'd come back to it again and again, more bitter each time, until finally he'd left for Mexico.

Well, I'm the one reading this thing, she thought. If it gets any more personal, I'll just stop.

"'Together,'" she read, "'they'd decided that the supernatural was fit material for stories on Halloween, and not much else. Thus they, in their infinite wisdom, were not prepared for what happened to them that Halloween night.

"'The leader of the circle got a story in the mail that week. It was written by someone he had known, but never really considered a friend. Because of his beliefs, he didn't recognize the power that lay in the pages and in the ink that the story was written on. And so he accepted the challenge to read the story aloud that Halloween.

"'They met at the cabin and read their stories, and then they began to read the story by the man who was not with them anymore. And as soon as they began to read it, a heavy mist settled down around the cabin.

"'It was like a fog, but so thick you could almost feel it squeeze between your fingers. It carried the salt smell of an ocean that shouldn't have been there, and everywhere it touched, the world ceased to exist.'"

Lesley's mouth had gone dry. She was leaning forward to pick up her teacup when she saw the window.

"Oh my God..." she whispered.

Beyond the window was a solid mass of white.

THEY ALL STARED at the fog outside the window. Guy and his new girlfriend Dana had been sitting under the window, and they moved into the center of the room. "What is it?" Dana asked. Her voice had a tremor in it that made Lesley even more frightened than before.

"It's called fog," Brian sneered. "Haven't you ever seen fog before?" He started for the door. "Look, I'll show it to you."

"Don't—" Lesley started, but her throat caught before she could finish the sentence.

The candlelight glinted off Brian's moist lips and oily hair. "What's the matter with you guys? What are you afraid of?"

He jerked the door open.

The fog lay outside like a wall of cotton wool. The edge of it, where the door had been, was as smooth as if it had been cut with a razor. Not even the thinnest wisp tried to reach through the doorway.

"See?" Brian said, sticking his arm into it. "Fog." Lesley saw his nose wrinkle, and then she smelled it herself. It was a salty, low-tide odor like dead fish.

"Yuck," Brian said. He took a step toward the porch of the cabin, lost his balance, and caught himself by gripping the molding on either side of the door. "What the hell?"

He extended one leg as far as it would go, then lay down and reached out into the fog. "There's nothing there."

"I don't like this," Susan said, but no one was listening to her.

"No porch," Brian said, "no ground, nothing." Almost imperceptibly they all began to move closer to the fireplace.

"Close the door," Walter said calmly, and Brian did as he was told. "Lesley, what's the next line of the story?"

"'With the fog came the sound of the wind. It howled and it screamed, but the air never moved and the fog lay heavy over the cabin.'"

The noise began.

It started as a low whistle, then built into a moaning, shrieking crescendo. It sounded less like a wind than a chorus of human voices, frightened and tortured out of their minds.

"Stop it!" Susan screamed. "Stop it, please make it stop!" Walter put his arms around her and held her head to his chest. She began to sob quietly.

They were now a circle in fact, a tight circle on the floor in front of the fireplace, knees touching, eyes searching each other's faces for some sign of understanding.

"What is it?" Dana cried. She was nearly shouting in order to be heard. "Where's it coming from?"

Lesley and Walter looked at each other, then Lesley's gaze dropped to the floor.

"It's that story, isn't it?" Dana said, her voice so high it was starting to crack. "Isn't it?"

"It must be," Walter said. His voice was so low that Lesley could barely hear it over the howling outside. "Rob must have found something in Mexico. A way to get back at us."

"This isn't happening," Brian said. "It's not. It can't be."

"It is," Walter said, raising his voice over the wind. "Pretending it isn't real is not going to help." Susan whimpered, and he held her tighter to his chest. "Look, we've all read stories like this. Some of us have written them. We all get irritated when people refuse to accept what's happening to them. How long is it going to take for us to admit what's happening here?"

"All right," Brian said. "It's real. What do we do?"

Lesley said, "The paper and ink. Rob said they were special. In the story."

"Why don't we just burn the damned thing?" Brian said. "We should have done that in the first place." As if in answer, the wind roared up to a deafening volume.

"No," said Walter. He waited until the noise subsided again and added, "What if we burn it and trap ourselves here? If only we knew how it ends."

"That's easy enough," Brian said. He reached across and took the papers from Lesley's unresisting fingers.

"No!" Walter shouted, lunging at him, but Brian had already flipped over to the last page.

"We all die," he said, handing the story back to Lesley. "Not very well written, but pretty gruesome." His levity failed completely. The wind was so loud it seemed to Lesley that the walls should have been shaken to pieces.

"Ideas?" Walter said. "Anybody?"

"I say burn it," Brian said again. "What can happen?"

"Rewrite it," Lesley said.

"What?" Walter asked. Lesley realized that the awful noise had swallowed her words.

"Rewrite it!" she repeated. "Change the ending!"

"I like it," Walter said. "Guy?"

He shrugged. "Worth a try. Anybody got a pen?"

"No," Lesley said. "I don't think that'll work."

"Why not?"

"I think," she said, "it's written in blood."

SHE KNEW IT was up to her. It was like belling the cat—her idea, her responsibility. Before any of the others could stop her, she got a safety pin out of her purse and jabbed it into the index finger of her left hand.

She rolled the point of the pin in the droplet of blood, then tried to draw an X across the bottom of the page she'd been reading from. The point of the pin just wouldn't hold enough. Finally she just wiped her finger across it, and then did the same thing on the last two pages.

"Now," she said. "What do I write?"

They all sat and looked at each other while the ghost wind shrieked at them.

"How about, 'Everything returned to normal,'" Guy said.

"What's normal?" Brian asked.

"He's got a point," Walter admitted. "We may need to be more specific."

"Not too specific," Lesley said. "I've only got so much blood."

No one laughed.

"Okay," Walter said. "Does anybody know what time Lesley started reading?"

"I checked," Lesley said. "It was 11:18."

"All right. How about, 'Everything returned to the way it had been at 11:18 that night?'"

There were nods all around. "Go for it," Guy said.

This time Lesley had to use the pin. It was slow going, but she finally got the words scrawled across the bottom of the page.

The wind continued to scream.

"Read it," Walter said.

Lesley's hands were shaking. Come on, she told herself, you didn't lose that much blood. But she knew it wasn't that. What if she read it and it didn't work? She couldn't stand that horrible, shrill noise much longer.

From the back of her mind a grim thought began to nag at her. What were the gruesome things the story said happened to them?

Let it work, she prayed. Let everything be the way it had been. Just exactly the way it had been.

"'Everything,'" she read, her shaking voice barely topping the roar of the wind, "'returned to the way it had been at 11:18 that night.'"

IT WAS QUIET.

The night was clear and cold, and water dripped from the trees to the layer of pine needles on the ground.

Lesley looked at her watch. It was 11:18. "It's called 'The Circle,'" she said. She began to read.

TWILIGHT TIME

THE PART OF the machine they strapped me to looked too much like an electric chair. A sudden, violent urge to resist came over me as the two proctors buckled me down and fastened the electrodes to my scalp. Not that it would have done me much good. The machine and I were in a steel cage and the cage was in the middle of a maximum security prison.

"Okay?" Thornberg asked me. His thinning hair was damp with sweat and a patch of it glistened on his forehead.

"Sure," I said. "Why not?"

He turned some switches. I couldn't hear anything happen, but this wasn't *I Was a Teenage Frankenstein* and sparks weren't supposed to be climbing the bars of the cage.

Then a jolt of power hit me, and I couldn't open my mouth to tell Thornberg to cut the thing off. My eyes filmed over and I started to see images in the mist. A distant, calmer part of my brain realized that Thornberg had cut in the encephalograph tapes.

We'd been working on them for weeks, refining the images detail by detail, and now all the pieces came together. Not just the steep hills and narrow streets of the town, not just the gym and the crepe-paper streamers and Buddy Holly singing, but the whole era: the flying saucer movies, the cars like rocket ships, rolled-up blue jeans and flannel shirts and PF Flyer tennis shoes, yo-yos, the candy wagon at noon recess, William Lundigan and Tom Corbett and Johnny Horton. They all melted together, the world events and the TV shows, the facts and the fiction and the imaginings, and for just one second they made a coherent, tangible universe.

And then I kicked and threw out my arms because I was falling.

I FELL THE WAY I did in dreams, trying to jerk myself awake, but the fall went on and on. I opened my eyes and saw a quiet blue, as if the sky had turned to water and I was drifting down through it. I hit on my hands and knees and felt the dirt under my fingers turn hard and grainy, felt the sun burn into my back.

Off to the left sat a line of low, gray-green hills. The ground where I crouched was covered with tough bullhead weeds and the sky overhead was the clear, hot blue of an Arizona summer.

The San Carlos Mountains, I thought. He did it. I'm back.

From the angle of the sun it looked to be late afternoon. I'd landed outside the city to avoid materializing inside a crowd or a solid wall. I sucked the good clean air into my lungs and danced a couple of steps across the sand. All I wanted was to get into town and make sure the rest of it was there, that it was all really happening.

I found the highway a few hundred yards to the south. LeeAnn was a tight feeling in my chest as I headed for town at a fast walk. My eyes were so full of the mountains and the open sky that I didn't notice the thing in the road until I was almost on top of it.

The pavement was not just broken, but scarred, cut by a huge, melted trench. Something had boiled the asphalt up in two knee-high waves and left it frozen in mid-air. The sand around it looked like a giant tire track in icy mud, a jagged surface of glassy whites and browns.

The strangest part was that for a couple of seconds I didn't realize that anything was wrong. My memories had become such a hash that the San Carlos Reservation had turned into a desert from a Sunday afternoon *Science Fiction Theater* and any minute I expected to see Caltiki or a giant scorpion come over the next rise.

I knelt to touch the asphalt ridge. Nothing in the real 1961, the one in the history books, could do this to a road.

A distant rumbling made me look up. A truck was coming out of the east, and it was swollen with the outlandish bumps and curves of the middle fifties. I jogged toward it, waving one arm, and it pulled up beside me.

The driver was an aging Apache in faded jeans and a T-shirt. "*Ya-ta-hey,* friend," he said. "Goin' to Globe?"

"Yeah," I said, out of breath. "But I need to tell you. The road's ... torn up, just ahead."

"Got the road again, did they? Damn gover'ment. Always got to do their tests on Indian land. You want a lift?"

"Yeah," I said, "Yeah, I do. Thanks."

I got in and he threw the truck in gear with a sound like a bag of cans rolling downhill. I tried to remember the last time I'd seen a gearshift on the steering column.

"My name's Big Charlie," he said.

"Travis," I said. The cab of the truck smelled like Wildroot Creme Oil, and a magazine photo of Marilyn Monroe stared at me from the open glove compartment. A rabbit's foot hung off the keys in the ignition and I had to remind myself that life was cheap in the sixties, even the lives of seals and leopards and rabbits.

A hysterical DJ on the radio shouted, "K-Z-O-W, kay-ZOW! Rockin' and rollin' Gila County with Ozzie and Harriet's favorite son..." The voice drowned in an ocean of reverb and out of it swam the sweet tenor of Ricky Nelson, singing "Travelin' Man."

Somehow the music made it all real and I had to look into the wind to keep the water out of my eyes. Up ahead of us in Globe was a 15-year-old kid listening to the same song, starting to get ready for his end-of-the-school-year dance. At that dance he was going to meet a girl named LeeAnn Patterson and fall in love with her. And he was never going to get over her.

Never.

Big Charlie eased the pickup off the road and found a place to cross the strip of melted glass. When the song finished, the radio erupted in a flare of trumpets. "This is Saturday, May the twenty-seventh, and this is Kay-Zowzow-zow NEWS!" Big Charlie turned the volume down with an automatic flip of the wrist, but I didn't care. The date was right, and I could have rattled off the headlines as well as the DJ could. Thornberg had made me do my homework.

Khrushchev and Kennedy were headed for test-ban talks in Vienna. Freedom Riders were being jailed in Mississippi, and the Communists were stepping up their assault on Laos. Eichmann was on trial in Jerusalem, and Alan Shepard was still being honored for his space flight of three weeks before.

On the local scene, six teenagers were dead over in Stafford, part of the rising Memorial Day Death Toll. Rumors were going around about a strike against Kennicot Copper, whose strip mines employed about half of Globe's work force.

Eddie Sachs was going to be in the pole position when they ran the 500 on Tuesday. The Angels had taken the Tigers, and the Giants had edged the Cubs in 13.

A decade of peace and quiet and short hair was winding down; a time when people knew their place and stayed in it. For ten years nobody had wanted anything but a new car and a bigger TV set. Now all that was about to change. In a little over a year the Cuban missile crisis would send thousands of people into their back yards to dig bomb shelters, and "advisors" would start pouring into Southeast Asia. In another year the president would be dead.

All that I knew. What I didn't know was why there was a huge melted scar across the desert.

Suddenly the truck's brakes squealed and I jerked back to attention. My eyes focused on the road ahead and saw a little boy straddling the white line, waving frantically.

The truck slewed to the left and stopped dead. A girl of 12 or 13 stood up from a patch of mesquite and stared at us like she wanted to run away. She had a good six years on the boy, but when he ran back to her it seemed to calm her down.

"Hey," Big Charlie shouted, leaning out his window. "What do you kids think you're doing?"

The boy was tugging on the girl's arm, saying, "It's okay! They're both okay, I'm sure, I'm really sure!"

The boy pulled her gently toward the driver's window of the truck. "Can you help us, mister?"

"What's wrong? What's the big idea of standing out there in the middle of the road like that? You could have got killed."

The boy backed away and the girl stepped in.

"We ... we were running away from home." She looked down at the boy as if she needed confirmation, and if I hadn't known before that she was lying, I knew it then. "We ... changed our minds. Can you take us back, mister? Just as far as town? Please?"

Big Charlie thought it over for a minute and seemed to come up with the same answer as me. Whatever they'd done probably wasn't that serious, and they were bound to be better off in town than hitchhiking in the middle of the desert.

"In the back," he said. "And watch what you're doing!"

They scrambled over the side of the pickup, their sneakers banging on the side walls. I turned to look at them as we pulled away, and they were huddled by the tailgate, arms around each other, their eyes squeezed shut.

I wondered what they were running from. They looked like they hadn't eaten in a couple of days, and their clothes were torn and dirty. And what in God's name had the boy meant when he said we were "okay?"

Don't worry about it, I told myself. Don't get involved. You haven't got time to get mixed up in somebody else's problems. You're not going to be here that long.

We passed Glen's Market at the foot of Skyline Drive, the one with the heavy wooden screen door that said "Rainbo is good bread" and the rich smells of doughnuts and bubble gum and citrus fruit.

"Where do you want to get off?" Big Charlie asked me.

"Downtown, anywhere." The highway had curved past Globe's three motels and now the grade school was coming up on the right. The Toastmaster Cafe, and its big Wurlitzer jukebox with the colored tube of bubbles around the side, was just across the street. Overhead was the concrete walkway that led from one to the other. It seemed a lot closer to the ground than it used to, even though I'd tried to prepare myself for things being smaller than I remembered.

Number 207 on the Toastmaster's Wurlitzer was "True Love Ways" by Buddy

Holly. I could almost hear those thick, syrupy violins and the hollow moan of King Curtis' saxophone as we turned the corner and pulled up in front of Upton's.

"This okay?" Big Charlie asked.

"Fine." I was thinking about the smell of pencil shavings and the one piece of gum that was always stuck. in the drain of the water fountain at the high school across the street. I got out of the truck. "I really appreciate it."

"Not to worry," Big Charlie said, and the pickup rattled away down Main.

The counter inside Upton's swung out in a wide U, dotted with red plastic-covered stools. The chrome and the white linoleum made it look more like an operating room than a place to eat, but it passed for atmosphere at the time.

"Help you?" said the kid behind the counter.

His name was Curtis and he lived up the street from my parents' house. He was a lot younger than I remembered him, and he could have done with a shampoo. It was all I could do not to call him by name and order a Suicide. The Suicide was Curtis' own invention, and he made it by playing the chrome spigots behind the counter like they were piano keys.

"Just coffee," I said.

Five of the tables along the south wall were occupied, two of them by clean-cut families at dinner. Dinner tonight was a hamburger or the 89 cent Daily Special: fried chicken, three vegetables, tea or coffee. The women's dresses hung to mid-calf and most of the male children had flat-top haircuts that showed a strip of close-shaven skull in the middle. Everybody seemed to be smoking. A woman around the corner from me had bought the Jackie Kennedy look all the way, down to the red pillbox hat and the upswept hair. Two seats away from her a kid in a T-shirt and a leather jacket was flipping noisily through the metal-edged pages in the jukebox console.

When I looked up, the two kids from the highway were sitting next to me. The girl was getting some stares. Her face was streaked with dirt and her shirt was thin enough to make it obvious that she should have been wearing a training bra under it.

"My name's Carolyn," she said. "This is Jeremy."

She put her arm around the boy, who smiled and picked at his fingernails.

"I'm Travis. Is he your brother?"

"Yes," the girl said, at the same time that the boy said, "No."

I shook my head. "This isn't going to get us anywhere."

"What do you want to know for, anyway?" the girl asked.

"I don't really care. You're following me, remember?"

Curtis was standing by the brand-new Seeburg box in the corner. He must have gotten tired of waiting for the kid in the motorcycle jacket to make up his mind. He pushed some buttons, a record dropped, and the room filled with violins. The bass thumped, a stick touched a cymbal, and Ray Charles started singing "Georgia."

"Why do you keep doing that?"

"Doing what?"

"Rubbing your hair that way. Like it feels funny."

I jerked my hands away from my ragged prison haircut. Ray was singing about his dreams. "The road," he sang, "leads back to you..."

I knew that he was talking to me. My road had brought me back here, to see Curtis standing in front of the jukebox, to the music hanging changeless in the air, to LeeAnn. Even if Brother Ray and Hoagy Carmichael had never imagined a road made of Thornberg's anti-particles.

"Stop that," the girl said, and for a second I thought she was talking to me. Then I saw that Jeremy was staring down at the countertop, chewing on the ridge of flesh between his thumb and forefinger. Blood started to trickle out of the front of his mouth. The sight of it put the music out of my head and left me scared and confused.

I hadn't looked at him closely before, but now that I did I saw scabs all over his arms and spots of dried, chocolate-colored blood on his T-shirt. His eyes were rolling back in his head and he looked like he was going to go backwards off the stool.

Carolyn slapped him across the mouth, knocking his hand away. He started to moan, louder than the jukebox, loud enough to turn heads across the room.

"I have to get him out of here," the girl said, pulling him to his feet.

"He needs a doctor," I said. "Let me..."

"No," she said. "Stay out of it."

I flinched and she ran for the door, tugging Jeremy after her. They were halfway across the floor when the door swung open.

A man in loose slacks and a sport shirt stood in the doorway, staring at them. The little boy looked like he'd just seen the giant wasp in *The Monster from Green Hell*. His jaw dropped open, and he started to shake. I could see the scream building from all the way across the room.

Before he could cut loose with it, Carolyn dragged him past the man and out into the street. The man stood there for a second with a puzzled half-smile on his face, then shrugged and looked around for a seat.

When my stomach started jumping I thought at first that I was just reacting to all the confusion. Then I remembered what Thornberg had said about phase shifting, and I knew I only had about a minute before the charge that had sent me back wore off.

I left a quarter on the counter and went to the men's room in back. The smell of the deodorant cake in the urinal almost made me sick as I leaned against the wall. I felt drunk and dizzy and there seemed to be two of everything. Then the floor went out from under me and I was falling again.

I sailed back up toward the future like a fish on the end of a line.

I SPENT TWO DAYS in debriefing. Thornberg got to ask the questions, but there was always a proctor or two around, videotaping everything.

From Thornberg's end everything had looked fine. One second I'd been there, the next I'd just winked out. I was gone a little over an hour, then I popped back in, dizzy but conscious, and all my vital signs had been good.

Thornberg's excitement showed me for the first time how personally he was involved. He seemed frankly envious, and I suddenly realized that he didn't just want the experiment to work, he wanted to be able to go back himself.

I was too caught up in my own questions to worry very long about Thornberg. My common sense told me everything that had happened to me had been real, but my rational mind was still having trouble. Who were those two kids, and what were they running from? What could have torn up the highway that way?

The proctors liked it a lot less than I did. "We've been through the government files," one of them said on the second day. "No experiments on the San Carlos Reservation. Nothing even in development that could have caused it."

"So how do you explain it?" Thornberg asked.

"Hallucination," the proctor said. "The whole experience was completely subjective and internal."

"No," Thornberg said. "Out of the question. We saw his body disappear."

The proctor stood up. "I think we'd better suspend this whole thing until this is cleared up."

"No!" Thornberg got between the proctor and the door. "We've got to have more data. We have to send him back again."

The proctor shook his head. The gesture didn't put the slightest wrinkle in his maroon double knit uniform.

"You can't stop me, you know," Thornberg said. "You'll have to get an executive order."

"I'll get it," the proctor said, and stepped around him.

When the door was closed Thornberg turned to me. "Then we send you back first. Now."

I LANDED BACK where I'd come from, leaning against the dingy walls of the rest room for support. My head cleared, and the last two days could have been no more than a fever dream caused by bad coffee on an empty stomach.

I started back into the restaurant. The jukebox was playing "Sink the Bismarck" by Johnny Horton. Horton was a big local favorite, and he'd died just a few months before in a car crash in Texas.

The man in the sport shirt, the one that had scared Jeremy so badly, was sitting in a booth with a cheeseburger. I stood for a second in the shadows of the hallway and watched him. He looked ordinary to me—short, curly hair, no sideburns, no facial hair. His shirt was one of those short-sleeved African prints in muted oranges and blues that wanted to be loud but couldn't quite bring it off. Sunglasses peeked out of the shirt pocket.

He looked like a tourist. But why would there be any tourists in Globe, Arizona, in 1961?

And then I saw his fingers.

His right hand was tucked under his left elbow and the fingers were moving in short, precise gestures against his side. I'd seen hands move like that before, keying data into a computer by touch.

Cut it out, I told myself. So the guy's got a nervous habit. It's none of your business.

I picked up my copy of the newspaper from the counter and tore off the masthead, including the date. If the proctors wanted some proof, I'd try to oblige. I folded the strip of newsprint and put it in my back pocket, dropping the rest of the paper in the trash.

Once on the street I saw men all around me in short-sleeved shirts buttoned to the neck. Long, rectangular cars covered with chrome and sharp angles cruised the streets like patient sharks. TV sets blinked at me from the window of the furniture store, their screens cramped and nearly circular. I stopped and watched a toothpaste ad with an invisible shield in it and remembered the craze for secret ingredients.

That 15-year-old kid across town had a theory about secret ingredients. He believed they were codes, and that aliens from space were using them to take over the Earth. GL 70: Town Secure. AT-7: Send More Saucers. He dreamed at night about great domed ships gliding over the desert.

I thought about the scar in the highway and the man in the restaurant and got another chill. This one turned my whole body cold.

My feet carried me down the street and stopped in front of the National News Stand. The door was locked, but through the window I could see the line of comics: *Sea Devils* and *Showcase* and *Rip Hunter, Time Master*. My father made me stop buying *Rip Hunter* because it was ruining my sense of reality; every time Rip and his crew went back in time they found aliens there, tampering with human history.

Aliens.

A spin rack by the door was full of science-fiction paperbacks. The short, fat
Ace Doubles were crammed in next to the taller Ballantines with the weird,
abstract covers. Right at the top, in a pocket all to itself, was Ruppelt's *Report
on Unidentified Flying Objects.*

Flying saucers.

Further back, where I could barely see it in the dimness of the store, was
the rack of men's magazines. When the old man with the cigar that ran the
place wasn't paying attention I used to go back and thumb through them, but
I never found quite what I was looking for.

The store was like an unassembled Revell model kit of my childhood. All the
pieces were there, the superheroes and the aliens and the unobtainable women,
and if I could just fit them together the right way I might be able to make
sense of it. In a lifetime I might have done it, but I only had another hour.

I felt too much like an aging delinquent in the T-shirt I was wearing, so
I bought a fresh shirt at the dimestore across the street and changed in their
rest room. I thought for a second about time paradoxes as I threw the old one
away, then decided to hell with it.

The dime store clock said seven-thirty and the dance should have started at
seven. Enough of a crowd should have accumulated for me to become another
faceless parent in the background. I started uphill toward the high school and
was sweating by the time I got there. But that was okay. You could still sweat
in 1961, and your clothes could still wrinkle.

All the doors to the gym were open and Japanese lanterns hung inside the
doors. From across the asphalt playground I could hear the heavy, thumping
bass of "Little Darlin'" by the Diamonds.

I went inside. A banner across the far end of the gym read "Look for a Star"
in crude, glittering letters. Across thirty years I remembered the sappy lyrics to
the song that had been forced on us as our theme. Four-pointed stars, sprayed
with gold paint, dangled from the girders, and the lanterns over the punch
bowls had Saturn rings stapled to them.

Most of the teachers stood in a clump. I recognized Mrs. Smith's hooked
nose and long jaw; she'd cried when she found the drawing of her as a witch.
Mr. Miller, next to her, was still wearing the goatee that he would be forced to
shave off the next fall because it made him look "like a beatnik."

About half the kids in my class were already there.

Bobby Arias, class president, and Myron Cessarini, track star and sex symbol,
were quietly breaking hearts at their own end of the gym. Over by the opposite wall was Marsha Something-or-other, the one that threw up all over the
floor in sixth grade, with the wings on her glasses and waxen skin.

But no sign of LeeAnn or the 15-year-old Travis. I went outside to get away from the heat and the close, sweat-sock smell of the place. Coals of cigarettes glowed where a few of the adults were taking advantage of the growing darkness. I sniffed the clean air and tried to think of reasons why I didn't want to stay right where I was for the rest of my life.

Lots of reasons. Racism. Sexism. People throwing trash on highways and dumping sewage in the creeks and not even knowing it was wrong. No sex. Not on TV, not in the movies, especially not in real life. Nice girls didn't. Curfews. Dress codes. Gas-guzzling cars.

Still, I thought. Still...

Somebody was tugging at my sleeve.

"Hey, mister," said a little boy's voice. "Hey."

I winced at the sound of it. "What are you following me for? What do you want from me?"

"We need help," Carolyn said. "If they catch us they'll kill us."

"Who will?"

"Them," Jeremy said.

He wasn't pointing at anybody. Giant ants? I wondered. "I don't understand. What is it you want me to do?"

The girl shrugged and turned her face away from me. I could see tears glistening in her eyes. Jeremy sat crosslegged on the asphalt in front of me and reached out to hold onto one of Carolyn's ankles. With my back to the wall of the gym I felt hemmed in by them, emotionally and physically.

Some obscure sense of guilt kept me asking questions. "What's wrong with Jeremy? What happened in that restaurant?"

"My father says he has some kind of eppa ... eppa..."

"Epilepsy?"

"Yeah. And he gets it whenever he gets too close to them."

"Was that one of them in the restaurant?"

"Yes."

Fingers moving against his side, empty-eyed, sunglasses. Reporting on me? "Who are they?"

The girl shook her head. For a second I saw past her hollow eyes and dirty brown hair, had just a glimpse of the woman she might be if she hung on long enough. "You won't believe me," she said. "You'll think I'm crazy. "

"I'm starting to think that anyway."

"What if I said they were from space? What would you say then?" In the last of the light her eyes had a hard gray sheen.

Oh God, I thought. *Invaders from Mars.* What's happening to my past?

"See?" she said. "I warned you."

"What about your parents? Can't they help you?"

"My father..." She stopped, swallowed, started again. "My father was all I had. They killed him. Jeremy's parents too. He's from California, and they had him in one of their ships, but he got away. That's where he got the ... epilepsy. From what they did to him. My father ... my father and me found him wandering around San Carlos and brought him back to the store."

That told me where I'd seen her before. Her father ran a rock shop out on the edge of the Apache reservation. My folks had taken me out there once to see the peridots, the green crystals that only turn up in extinct volcanic craters around San Carlos and somewhere in South America. I'd noticed her because I'd just gotten to the age where I was noticing girls, but we had shied away from actually speaking to each other.

She was wearing a big peridot ring, probably her father's, on the index finger of her right hand. "If they killed your father," I said, "why didn't you call the police?"

"I did. But when the policeman came, he was ... one of them. Jeremy ran off into the desert, and I ran after him. Now they're looking for both of us."

No matter how uncomfortable I felt, I had to believe that her story was just a fantasy. I had to make myself believe it. But even if I'd been sure she was hallucinating, what could I do for her? She needed a family and a psychiatrist and I couldn't be either one in the time I had left. I took some money out of my wallet.

"Look," I said. "Here's twenty bucks. Go take a bus to Phoenix or somewhere. Call an aunt or a grandfather or somebody you know you can trust and get them to help you out. Okay?"

She knew she'd lost me. I could see it in her eyes.

She wadded up the bill and held it in her fist. "They know who you are," she said.

"What?"

"They saw us with you. They'll be looking for you, now, too."

My heart slowed back to something like normal.

"That's okay. I'll risk it."

I watched them until they faded into the darkness.

"In the Still of the Night" by the Five Satins was playing in the gym and I wanted to go in and listen to it. I wanted to forget what the girl had told me and see what I'd come to see and get out of there.

I took about two steps before my stomach cramped, driving me back against the wall of the gym.

"No," I whispered, "Not yet. Not now. Please."

I was wasting my breath. In less than a minute the dizziness came over me and everything fell away.

•

THE PROCTORS WEREN'T too happy about my coming back in a different shirt. They didn't care too much for the newspaper masthead either, but they had their executive order and they decided it was all academic anyhow.

They threw me in my cell and refused to let me talk to Thornberg. This time the proctors debriefed me, and I told them as little as I thought I could get away with. One of them might have been the one that had threatened me after the last trip, but I couldn't be sure. Between the uniforms and the dark glasses they had an unnerving similarity.

Dark glasses, I thought. Sunglasses. I remembered fingers moving against a bright sport shirt.

Cut it out, I thought. You're letting your imagination go crazy. Don't get sucked into somebody else's fantasy.

Finally they left me alone and I wondered if the experiment was really over. Thornberg would probably not live through the disappointment. To have worked so hard and then lose it all, to never get to use his own machine...

And what about me? I thought. To have gotten so close to seeing LeeAnn only to miss her by a few seconds?

Memories came rushing back, out of control. The first time we'd made love, in the back of my parents' Chevy II station wagon with the seat folded down. Our first winter at Arizona State, LeeAnn in a miniskirt and rag coat that hung to her ankles, wrapped in yards of fake fur. Politics and marches, graduation and marriage, the underground newspaper in Phoenix in the late sixties. Our first house, LeeAnn's thirtieth birthday, the flowers and the cheap red wine...

And then the day the Proctors' Amendment passed the House. Politics and marches again, me reluctant at first, but LeeAnn outraged and dedicated, young again in the space of a few days. The first victories, Colorado voting against ratification, Texas leaning our way. People starting to wonder if the proctors really would be better than their local police, even in Houston.

And then one by one we were getting killed or crippled or lost in the basements of jails. They told me the day they arrested me that LeeAnn had died trying to construct a bomb, for God's sake, when she had never even touched any kind of weapon.

I never got a trial, because the proctors were now the Law. No charges, no lawyers, just a cell and a lot of memories.

Time moved on.

As much as I hated the proctors, I knew better than to blame them. They hadn't elected themselves; the citizens of the United States had listened to their televisions and voted them in, so it was their fault too. But mostly it was time's fault. Time had passed. Times had changed. So I sat in a jail cell and thought about what it had been like to be 15 years old, before I had any idea of what time could do.

That was where Thornberg found me. He needed somebody with a memory of a specific time and place that was so strong that his machines could focus on it and follow the time lines back to it. Because it was dangerous, his funding agency had sent him to the prisons to look for volunteers, and when he saw how I tested out, he wanted me. I don't think the proctors had taken him seriously until the first test had worked, and once it did they seemed to panic.

What were they afraid of? What did they have to lose? Were they afraid I was going to escape through a hole in time?

Or were they afraid I was going to learn something they didn't want anybody to know?

I was still thinking about it late that night when I heard my cell door open. It was Thornberg.

"How did you get in here?" I whispered.

"Never mind. The question is, do you want to go again? Tonight? Right now?"

We headed straight for the lab, and I changed into my traveling clothes. Thornberg was nervous, talking the whole time he strapped me in.

"What I don't understand," he said, "is how you can have a past that's not the same as my past. Why does yours have tracks in the desert and flying saucers?"

"How should I know?" I said. "Maybe everybody's past is different. People never remember things the same way as anybody else. Maybe they are different. What are those waves your machine uses?"

"Retrograde probability waves."

"Retrograde because they move backwards in time, right? But couldn't they branch off, just like regular probability waves? Your machine uses my brain waves to sort through all those probabilities, so it would have to take me to whatever I thought the past was, right?"

Thornberg was interested. He'd gone back to his console, but he wasn't reaching for the controls. "If that's true, why is there no record of your melted track in the desert?"

"The different pasts all lead to the same place, the present. I guess there could be other pasts that lead to other presents, that 'Many Worlds' theory you were telling me about. In my past the proctors don't want any record of the mess their spaceships made, so they just covered it up. In yours, you never knew of any spaceships. But they lead to the same thing, with the proctors in power."

"You have a lot of imagination."

"Yeah. I do. Imagine this, then. Suppose I change something? Made it so my past hooked onto a different future? Just like switching a train onto another track. You said every decision we make creates a whole new universe."

"No," Thornberg said. "Out of the question. Do you have any idea of the risk? At the end of the hour you'd be pulled back here anyway."

Or into another future, I thought, but I didn't say it. "All right. Calm down. If we're going to do this, we'd better get started."

Thornberg just stared at me for a few seconds, and I could see how frightened he was. My only question was whether he was afraid for me or afraid I'd go off into some other future and leave him stuck in this one.

I never got the answer because his hand snaked out and started pushing the buttons.

SEEING MYSELF WALK into the gym was as immediate as a glance in the mirror and as distant as looking at an old photograph. I wanted to go over to myself and say, straighten up for God's sake, and turn your collar down. But even so I could see myself through my 15-year-old eyes and know that the slouch and the clothes and the haircut were the only ways I could say the things I didn't have words for then.

The kid had three-inch cuffs in his blue jeans, and the light jacket he wore over his T-shirt wasn't red, like James Dean's jacket in *Rebel Without a Cause,* but only because a red jacket would have been somebody else's uniform and not his own. His hair was too long for a flat top and not long enough for a DA, but five minutes didn't go by without him running a comb through it at least a couple of times.

Somebody put "Twilight Time" by the Platters on the record player. The overhead lights went out and two deep blue spots swept over the dancers. Martin and Dickie, the kid's best friends, were off to his left, talking behind their hands and bumping each other with their shoulders. The kid just stood there and stared into the crowd around the bleachers, and at the few daring couples out on the gym floor, intently, like he was trying to find somebody.

So was I.

Tony Williams sang about falling in love all over again, "as I did then."

And she walked in.

For thirty years I'd been haunted by this memory. It was strong enough to get me out of prison, to send me back in Thornberg's machine, and now I was standing just across a high school gym from her.

And she was just a girl. Just a 15-year-old girl.

Skinny and shy and awkward, her first night in a new town, talked into coming to this dance by her mother and the principal of the school, both of them afraid she would go all summer without making any friends.

And then her mother said something to her that made her laugh and her head dropped down and the long red hair fell over her face and it wasn't just a girl anymore, it was LeeAnn, and I felt like somebody had just put a fist into my throat.

I turned my back on her and stood in the doorway, letting the hot night air work on my eyes until I could see again.

Something moved, just out of the range of the lanterns. Carolyn and the boy again, I thought. I didn't want to see them, didn't even want to think about them anymore. Hadn't I done enough? What more did they want from me?

I was turning back to look at LeeAnn when a flash of color across the gym distracted me. The man from Upton's, the one in the sport shirt, darted through the crowd, fingers working against his left side.

A voice behind me said, "Come outside and we'll talk." The delivery was as deep and smooth as a T V announcer's.

I turned. Two of them filled the doorway, tall, non-descript, their eyes and mouths so hard it looked like their facial nerves had been cut. They would have made terrific proctors.

Admit it, I told myself. You want to believe it. If the proctors come from out there somewhere, that lets you off the hook. It lets everybody off. Sure T V rots people's brains and fast food makes people fat and gives them heart attacks, but it's not our fault. We're just being manipulated by creatures of vastly superior technology.

"Outside," one of them said. "Let's go."

But suppose you really did want to take over the world. Where would you start? Level Washington with your laser cannons? Why not just take over a few ad agencies? Tell people they want to buy lots of polyester, throw your weight behind mindless situation comedies. In a few years people don't care what they watch, or what they eat, or what they wear, and after a while they don't care about anything else either. You've got everything, without having to fire a shot.

Except maybe a few in the desert, just to keep in practice.

"What do you want from me?" I asked, letting them maneuver me out onto the playground. "What's going on?'"

The one in the lead showed me a pistol. It looked a lot like a squirt gun I used to have except that the end of the barrel was hollow and the thing had a heavy, chromed sense of menace about it. "The Others want to talk to you. "

"Others? What Others?"

"They're waiting in the ship. Outside town." Either this is real, I thought, or it isn't. If I could bring back a shirt and a piece of newspaper then it was probably real, or at least real enough to get me killed.

I decided to be scared.

"Fine," I said. "Let's talk. What do you want to talk about?"

"Over there," said the one with the gun.

I had just looked to see where he was pointing when a wail came out of the darkness. It sounded like it had been building up inside of something that wasn't strong enough to hold it, and it had just blown its way free.

Jeremy.

"What's that?" whispered the one with the pistol.

"It's that kid, I think," said the other one.

"Well, shut him up, for God's sake."

The second alien disappeared into the shadows just as Jeremy screamed. The one with the gun looked around involuntarily, and I went for him.

We hit the asphalt and rolled. I felt one knee tear out of my pants, just like in the old days. The alien was bigger and stronger than I was and he came out on top. He was pounding at me with his left hand, trying to get the gun around to use it on me. I grabbed his right wrist with both hands and yanked his elbow down into the pavement. The gun rattled in his grip, and I slammed the elbow again. This time the gun came loose and skittered away into the darkness.

With both hands free, he really opened up on me. I tried to cover up, but I didn't have enough hands, and he got a good one into my ribs. Everything turned white for a second, and he started on my face and head.

I thought maybe I should have let him keep the gun. That way it would at least have been quick. In a few more seconds he was going to kill me with his bare hands anyway.

Just like they'd killed LeeAnn.

I went a little berserk, but all it got me was a knee in the gut. I was finished.

A sound whipped through the air above me. I saw a flash of pink light and then the alien fell off of me.

I rolled onto my side and pulled my knees up to my chest. I was still fighting for breath when my eyes cleared enough to see Carolyn a few feet away, still holding the gun straight out in front of her, a stunned look on her face. Jeremy sounded like pieces of his throat were coming loose, and a shadow flashed in the corner of my vision.

"Carolyn," I said, and she came unstuck, firing the pistol again. I saw the second alien fall as Jeremy's scream cut off in mid-air,

I got onto my hands and knees. In the distance, like some kind of cosmic soundtrack, I could hear Brenda Lee singing "I'm Sorry" in the gym. The music echoed flatly off the asphalt.

"You okay, mister?" Carolyn asked.

"Yeah," I said. "Okay." For once I was glad to see her.

A hand laser, I thought. A junior version of the thing on their ship that had cut that line through the desert. Like it or not, the aliens were as real as anything else in this version of 1961. Whether this was really my past or just some kind of metaphor, the aliens were a part of it.

Jeremy staggered over and threw his arms around Carolyn's waist. Even in the dimness of the playground I could see that her eyes were dry and clear. She looked at the gun in her hand. "This changes things," she said. "This changes everything."

The words echoed in my mind. I thought of Thornberg and his Many Worlds. The smallest thing, he'd said, can change the entire universe. In time.

"Back at the dance," I said. "There's more of ... them." I couldn't bring myself to say "aliens."

"That's okay," she said. "We'll take care of it."

"Take care of it? But you're just..." I tried to stand up and didn't make it.

Gently she pushed Jeremy aside and knelt down next to me. "You're hurt," she said. "There's nothing you can do to help anyway." She took the peridot ring off her index finger and slipped it onto the little finger of my left hand. "Here," she said. "This is for the twenty dollars you gave me. We'll use it to find some people to help us. To fight. To change things. They're just getting started, and it's not too late. We can change things."

She stood up, started to walk away, and then looked back over her shoulder. "You'll see," she said. She was gone.

I lay there a while and looked at the stars. I hadn't seen that many stars in the night sky in a long time. When I tried to stand up again I made it, and got to the drinking fountain behind the baseball diamond.

The same piece of gum was in the drain. I smiled and cleaned myself up as best I could.

I stayed in the shadows just outside the door of the gym and watched for a while. I couldn't see the third alien.

She did it, I thought. She did it, and she's going to keep on doing it. And if she's very lucky and very strong, maybe...

No, I told myself. Don't even think about it. Don't get your hopes up. She's just a girl and this may turn out to only be a dream.

LeeAnn stood at the punchbowl, talking to a kid in rolled-up jeans and a tan jacket. The record player hissed and then Buddy Holly started "True Love Ways." The strings answered him, high and rich, infinitely sad.

The kid shuffled his feet and jerked his head at the dance floor. LeeAnn nodded and they walked into the crowd. He took her awkwardly in his arms and they slowly moved away until I couldn't see them anymore.

I CAME BACK to some kind of deserted warehouse. The cage was gone. So was the jail and so were the proctors.

After the first couple of days I didn't have much trouble finding my way around. Most of my friends were still the same, and they told me they were used to my being a little quiet and disoriented. They told me I'd been that way off and on since my wife LeeAnn died in a car wreck two years before.

Thirty years were missing out of my new life, and I spent a lot of time at my computer, calling up history texts and old magazines and doing a little detective work on the side. I learned about a scientist named Thornberg at NASA, but he never answered the letter I wrote him.

The past and the future invent each other; Thornberg taught me that, and the past I invented has given me a future without LeeAnn. But somewhere in this new future of mine there should be a woman named Carolyn, born in Arizona in the late forties, maybe a year or two younger than me. I don't know exactly what I'm going to say to her when I find her, or whether she'll even believe me, but I think she'll recognize her ring.

LeeAnn is dead and Buddy Holly is dead, but people are walking the streets, free to make their own mistakes again. The sky overhead is filled with ships building a strange and wonderful future, and, in time, anything seems possible.

JEFF BECK

FELIX WAS 34. He worked four ten-hour days a week at Allied Sheet
Metal, running an Amada CNC turret punch press. At night he made
cassettes with his twin TEAC dbx machines. He'd recorded over a thousand of
them so far, over 160 miles of tape, and he'd carefully hand lettered the labels
for each one.

He'd taped everything Jeff Beck had ever done, from the Yardbirds' *For Your
Love* through all the Jeff Beck Groups and the solo albums; he had the English
singles of "Hi Ho Silver Lining" and "Tally Man"; he had all the session work,
from Donovan to Stevie Wonder to Tina Turner.

In the shop he wore a Walkman and listened to his tapes. Nothing seemed
to cut the sound of tortured metal like the diamond-edged perfection of
Beck's guitar. It kept him light on his feet, dancing in place at the machine,
and sometimes the sheer beauty of it made tears come up in his eyes.

On Fridays he dropped Karen at her job at *Pipeline Digest* and drove
around to thrift shops and used book stores looking for records. After he'd
cleaned them up and put them on tape he didn't care about them anymore;
he sold them back to collectors and made enough profit to keep himself in
blank XLIIs.

Occasionally he would stop at a pawn shop or music store and look at the
guitars. Lightning Music on 183 had a Charvel/Jackson soloist, exactly like
the one Beck played on *Flash,* except for the hideous lilac-purple finish.
Felix yearned to pick it up but was afraid of making a fool out of himself.
He had an old Sears Silvertone at home and two or three times a year he
took it out and tried to play it, but he could never even manage to get it
properly in tune.

Sometimes Felix spent his Friday afternoons in a dingy bar down the street
from *Pipeline Digest,* alone in a back booth with a pitcher of Budweiser and
an anonymous brown sack of records. On those afternoons Karen would
find him in the office parking lot, already asleep in the passenger seat, and she
would drive home. He knew she worried about him, but it never happened
more than once or twice a month. The rest of the time he hardly drank at all,
and he never hit her or chased other women. Whatever it was that ate at him
was so deeply buried it seemed easier to leave well enough alone.

•

One Thursday afternoon a friend at work took him aside.

"Listen," Manuel said, "are you feeling okay? I mean you seem real down lately."

"I don't know," Felix told him. "I don't know what it is."

"Everything okay with Karen?"

"Yeah, it's fine. Work is okay. I'm happy and everything. I just ... I don't know. Feel like something's missing."

Manuel took something out of his pocket. "A guy gave me this. You know I don't do this kind of shit no more, but the guy said it was killer stuff."

It looked like a Contac capsule, complete with the little foil blister pack. But when Felix looked closer the tiny colored spheres inside the gelatin seemed to sparkle in rainbow colors.

"What is it?"

"I don't know. He wouldn't say exactly. When I asked him what it did all he said was, 'Anything you want.'"

He dropped Karen at work the next morning and drove aimlessly down Lamar for a while. Even though he hadn't hit Half Price Books in a couple of months, his heart wasn't in it. He drove home and got the capsule off the top of his dresser where he'd left it.

Felix hadn't done acid in years, hadn't taken anything other than beer and an occasional joint in longer than he could remember. Maybe it was time for a change.

He swallowed the capsule, put Jeff Beck's *Wired* on the stereo, and switched the speakers into the den. He stretched out on the couch and looked at his watch. It was ten o'clock.

He closed his eyes and thought about what Manuel had said. It would do anything he wanted. So what did he want?

This was a drug for Karen, Felix thought. She talked all the time about what she would do if she could have any one thing in the world. She called it the Magic Wish game, though it wasn't really a game and nobody ever won.

What the guy meant, Felix told himself, was it would make me see anything I wanted to. Like a mild hit of psilocybin. A light show and a bit of rush.

But he couldn't get away from the idea. What would he wish for if he could have anything? He had an answer ready; he supposed everybody did. He framed the words very carefully in his mind.

I want to play guitar like Jeff Beck, he thought.

He sat up. He had the feeling that he'd dropped off to sleep and lost a couple of hours, but when he looked at his watch it was only 10:05. The tape was still playing "Come Dancing." His head was clear, and he couldn't feel any effects from the drug.

But then he'd only taken it five minutes ago. It wouldn't have had a chance to do anything yet.

He felt different though, sort of sideways, and something was wrong with his hands. They ached and tingled at the same time, and felt like they could crush rocks.

And the music. Somehow he was hearing the notes differently than he'd ever heard them before, hearing them with a certain knowledge of how they'd been made, the way he could look at a piece of sheet metal and see how it had been sheared and ground and polished into shape.

Anything you want, Manuel had said.

His newly powerful hands began to shake.

He went into his studio, a converted storeroom off the den. One wall was lined with tapes; across from it were shelves for the stereo, a few albums, and a window with heavy black drapes. The ceiling and the end walls were covered with gray paper egg cartons, making it nearly soundproof.

He took out the old Silvertone and it felt different in his hands, smaller, lighter, infinitely malleable. He switched off the Beck tape, patched the guitar into the stereo and tried tuning it up.

He couldn't understand why it had been so difficult before. When he hit harmonics, he could hear the notes beat against each other with perfect clarity. He kept his left hand on the neck and reached across it with his right to turn the machines, a clean, precise gesture he'd never made before.

For an instant he felt a breathless wonder come over him. The drug had worked, had changed him. He tried to hang on to the strangeness but it slipped away. He was tuning a guitar. It was something he knew how to do.

He played "Freeway Jam," one of Max Middleton's tunes from *Blow By Blow.* Again, for just a few seconds, he felt weightless, ecstatic. Then the guitar brought him back down. He'd never noticed what a pig the Silvertone was, how high the strings sat over the fretboard, how the frets buzzed and the machines slipped. When he couldn't remember the exact notes on the record he tried to jam around them, but the guitar fought him at every step.

It was no good. He had to have a guitar. He could hear the music in his head but there was no way he could wring it out of the Silvertone.

His heart began to hammer and his throat closed up tight. He knew what he needed, what he would have to do to get it. He and Karen had over $1300 in a savings account. It would be enough.

•

HE WAS HOME AGAIN by three o'clock with the purple Jackson soloist and a Fender Princeton amp. The purple finish wasn't nearly as ugly as he remembered it, and the guitar fit into his hands like an old lover. He set up in the living room and shut all the windows and played, eyes closed, swaying a little from side to side, bringing his right hand all the way up over his head on the long trills.

Just like Jeff Beck.

He had no idea how long he'd been at it when he heard the phone. He lunged for it, the phone cord bouncing noisily off the strings.

It was Karen. "Is something wrong?" she asked.

"Uh, no," Felix said. "What time is it?"

"Five-thirty." She sounded close to tears.

"Oh shit. I'll be right there."

He hid the guitar and amp in his studio. She would understand, he told himself. He just wasn't ready to break it to her quite yet.

In the car, she seemed afraid to talk to him, even to ask why he'd been late. Felix could only think about the purple Jackson waiting for him at home.

He sat through a dinner of Chef Boyardee Pizza, using three beers to wash it down, and after he'd done the dishes he shut himself in his studio.

For four hours he played everything that came into his head, from blues to free jazz to "Over Under Sideways Down" to things he'd never heard before, things so alien and illogical that he couldn't translate the sounds he heard. When he finally stopped, Karen had gone to bed. He undressed and crawled in beside her, his brain reeling.

HE WOKE UP to the sound of the vacuum cleaner. He remembered everything, but in the bright morning light it all seemed like a weirdly vivid hallucination, especially the part where he'd emptied the savings account.

Saturday was his morning for yard work, but first he had to deal with the drug business, to prove to himself that he'd only imagined it. He went into the studio and lifted the lid of the guitar case and then sat down across from it in his battered blue-green lounge chair.

As he stared at it he felt his love and terror of the guitar swell in his chest like cancer.

He picked it up and played the solo from "Got the Feelin'" and then looked up. Karen was standing in the open door.

"Oh my God," she said. "Oh my God. What have you done?"

Felix hugged the guitar to his chest. He couldn't think of anything to say to her.

"How long have you had this? Oh. You bought it yesterday, didn't you?

That's why you couldn't even remember to pick me up." She slumped against the door frame. "I don't believe it. I don't *even* believe it."

Felix looked at the floor.

"The bedroom air conditioner is broken," Karen said. Her voice sounded like she was squeezing it with both hands; if she let it go it would turn into hysteria. "The car's running on four bald tires. The TV looks like shit. I can't remember the last time we went out to dinner or a movie." She pushed both hands into the sides of her face, twisting it into a mask of anguish.

"How much did it cost?" When Felix didn't answer she said, "It cost everything, didn't it? *Everything.* Oh God, I just can't believe it."

She closed the door on him and he started playing again, frantic scraps and tatters, a few bars from "Situation," a chorus of "You Shook Me," anything to drown out the memory of Karen's voice.

It took him an hour to wind down, and at the end of it he had nothing left to play. He put the guitar down and got in the car and drove around to the music stores.

On the bulletin board at Ray Hennig's he found an ad for a guitarist and called the number from a pay phone in the strip center outside. He talked to somebody named Sid and set up an audition for the next afternoon.

When he got home Karen was waiting in the living room. "You want anything from Safeway?" she asked. Felix shook his head and she walked out. He heard the car door slam and the engine shriek to life.

He spent the rest of the afternoon in the studio with the door shut, just looking at the guitar. He didn't need to practice; his hands already knew what to do.

The guitar was almost unearthly in its beauty and perfection. It was the single most expensive thing he'd ever bought for his own pleasure, but he couldn't look at it without being twisted up inside by guilt. And yet at the same time he lusted for it passionately, wanted to run his hands endlessly over the hard, slick finish, bury his head in the plush case and inhale the musky aroma of guitar polish, feel the strings pulse under the tips of his fingers.

Looking back, he couldn't see anything he could have done differently. Why wasn't he happy?

When he came out, the living room was dark. He could see a strip of light under the bedroom door, hear the snarling hiss of the TV. He felt like he was watching it all from the deck of a passing ship; he could stretch out his arms but it would still drift out of his reach.

He realized he hadn't eaten since breakfast. He made himself a sandwich and drank an iced tea glass full of whiskey and fell asleep on the couch.

•

A LITTLE AFTER NOON on Sunday, he staggered into the bathroom. His back ached and his fingers throbbed and his mouth tasted like a kitchen drain. He showered and brushed his teeth and put on a clean T-shirt and jeans. Through the bedroom window he could see Karen lying out on the lawn chair with the Sunday paper. The pages were pulled so tight that her fingers made ridges across them. She was trying not to look back at the house.

He made some toast and instant coffee and went to browse through his tapes. He felt like he ought to try to learn some songs, but nothing seemed worth the trouble. Finally he played a Mozart symphony that he'd taped for Karen, jealous of the sound of the orchestra, wanting to be able to make it with his hands.

The band practiced in a run-down neighborhood off Rundberg and I-35. All the houses had large dogs behind chain link fences and plastic Big Wheels in the driveways. Sid met him at the door and took him back to a garage hung with army blankets and littered with empty beer cans.

Sid was tall and thin and wore a black Def Leppard T-shirt. He had acne and blond hair in a shag to his shoulders. The drummer and bass player had already set up; none of them looked older than 22 or 23. Felix wanted to leave but he had noplace else to go.

"Want a brew?" Sid asked, and Felix nodded. He took the Jackson out of its case and Sid, coming back with the beer, stopped in his tracks. "Wow," he said. "Is that your ax?" Felix nodded again. "Righteous," Sid said.

"You know any Van Halen?" the drummer asked. Felix couldn't see anything but a zebra-striped headband and a patch of black hair behind the two bass drums and the double row of toms.

"Sure," Felix lied. "Just run over the chords for me, it's been a while." Sid walked him through the progression for "Dance the Night Away" on his 3/4 sized Melody Maker and the drummer counted it off. Sid and the bass player both had Marshall amps and Felix's little Princeton, even on ten, got lost in the wash of noise.

In less than a minute Felix got tired of the droning power chords and started toying with them, adding a ninth, playing a modal run against them. Finally Sid stopped and said, "No, man, it's like this," and patiently went through the chords again, A, B, E, with a C# minor on the chorus.

"Yeah, okay," Felix said and drank some more beer.

They played "Beer Drinkers and Hell Raisers" by ZZ Top and "Rock and Roll" by Led Zeppelin. Felix tried to stay interested, but every time he played something different from the record Sid would stop and correct him.

"Man, you're a hell of a guitar player, but I can't believe you're as good as you are and you don't know any of these solos."

"You guys do any Jeff Beck?" Felix asked.

Sid looked at the others. "I guess we could do 'Shapes of Things,' right? Like on that Gary Moore album?"

"I can fake it, I guess," the drummer said.

"And could you maybe turn down a little?" Felix said.

"Uh, yeah, sure," Sid said, and adjusted the knob on his guitar a quarter turn.

Felix leaned into the opening chords, pounding the Jackson, thinking about nothing but the music, putting a depth of rage and frustration into it he never knew he had. But he couldn't sustain it; the drummer was pounding out 2 and 4, oblivious to what Felix was playing, and Sid had cranked up again and was whaling away on his Gibson with the flat of his hand.

Felix jerked his strap loose and set the guitar back in its case.

"What's the matter?" Sid asked, the band grinding to a halt behind him.

"I just haven't got it today," Felix said. He wanted to break that pissant little toy Gibson across Sid's nose, and the strength of his hatred scared him. "I'm sorry," he said, clenching his teeth. "Maybe some other time."

"Sure," Sid said. "Listen, you're really good, but you need to learn some solos, you know?"

Felix burned rubber as he pulled away, skidding through a U-turn at the end of the street. He couldn't slow down. The car fishtailed when he rocketed out onto Rundberg, and he nearly went into a light pole. Pounding the wheel with his fists, hot tears running down his face, he pushed the accelerator to the floor.

KAREN WAS GONE when Felix got home. He found a note on the refrigerator: "Sherry picked me up. Will call in a couple of days. Have a lot to think about. K."

He set up the Princeton and tried to play what he was feeling and it came out bullshit, a jerkoff reflex blues progression that didn't mean a thing. He leaned the guitar against the wall and went into his studio, shoving one tape after another into the decks, and every one of them sounded the same, another tired, simpleminded rehash of the obvious.

"I didn't ask for this!" he shouted at the empty house. "You hear me? This isn't what I asked for!"

But it was, and as soon as the words were out he knew he was lying to himself. Faster hands and a better ear weren't enough to make him play like Beck. He had to change inside to play that way, and he wasn't strong enough to handle it, to have every piece of music he'd ever loved turn sour, to need perfection so badly that it was easier to give it up than learn to live with the flaws.

He sat on the couch for a long time and then, finally, he picked up the guitar again. He found a clean rag and polished the body and neck and wiped each individual string. Then, when he had wiped all his fingerprints away, he put it back into the case, still holding it with the rag. He closed the latches and set it next to the amp, by the front door.

For the first time in two days he felt like he could breathe again. He turned out all the lights and opened the windows and sat down on the couch with his eyes closed. Gradually his hands became still and he could hear, very faintly, the fading music of the traffic and the crickets and the wind.

WILD FOR YOU

IT WAS A PONTIAC FIREBIRD with a custom paint job, a metal-flake candy-apple red. The personalized plates said WILD4U.

I was right behind her on that big clover-leaf that slopes down off Woodall Rogers onto I-35. The wind caught a hank of her long blonde hair and set it to fluttering outside her window. I saw her face in her own rear-view as she threw her head back. Laughing, or singing along with the radio, or maybe just feeling the pull as she put the pedal down and scooted into the southbound lane.

She was a beauty, all right. Just a kid, but with a crazy smile that made my heart spin.

I whipped my pickup into fourth but I couldn't get past this big white Caddy coming up on me from behind. The two lanes for Austin were fixing to split off in half a mile. An 18-wheeler filled up one of them and the Caddy had the other. I eased off the gas and watched her disappear over the horizon, a bright red promise of something beyond my wildest dreams.

It was mid-afternoon, sunny with a few clouds. The weather couldn't decide if it was summer or winter, which is what passes for fall in Texas. I wasn't but a kid myself, with my whole life in front of me. I put Rosanne Cash on the tape deck and my arm out the window and let those white lines fly by.

I WAS AT the Fourth Street Shell station in Waco, halfway home, when I saw that little red car again. I'd just handed my credit card to the lady when the squeal of brakes made me look up. There it was, shiny and red, rocking back and forth by the Super Unleaded.

I kept one eye on it while I signed the receipt. The driver door opened and this guy got out. He was in jeans and a pearl button shirt and a black cap. I can't say I liked the looks of him. She got out the passenger side and leaned across the top of the car, watching the traffic. I couldn't hardly see her because of the pump. I hung around the ice cream freezer, hoping she'd come inside. Instead the guy came in to pay cash for five dollars' worth.

I followed him out. She turned to get back in the car and I felt a chill. Her hair was shorter than it had been, just barely past her collar. And her face looked older too.

I couldn't figure what the hell. Maybe she'd got her hair cut? She'd had time, as fast as she'd been driving, and as long as we'd been out. I felt like I'd already spent half my life on the road. Or maybe this was her older sister had borrowed the car somehow.

Weird, is what it was. I got back in the truck and hit it on down the highway. About two miles on they came up behind me to pass, and that's when I saw the license had changed. Now it said MR & MRS.

Right as they pulled up next to me, I looked over at her. She was staring out the window, right at me. She pointed a finger, like kids do when they're making a pretend pistol. And smiled, that same crooked smile.

For some reason that really got to me. I don't think I'll ever forget it.

SOME THINGS ARE just Mysteries, and you don't expect to understand them. When I passed that car south of Belton, there were different people in it. The woman driving looked like the blonde girl, but was old enough to be her mother. There was a dark-haired girl in the passenger seat, maybe thirty years old, and two little kids in back. The dark-haired girl was turned around to yell at them. The speed limit had gone back up to 65, but they chugged along at 60. The plates were standard Texas issue and there was bumper sticker that said ASK ME ABOUT MY GRANDBABY.

Tell the truth, I was too tired to think much of it anymore. The sun had started to set, and I had this pinched kind of pain between my shoulders. About thirty miles on I saw a roadside rest stop and pulled in.

I might have slept a quarter of an hour. The sky had clouded over and the sunset lit everything up pretty spectacular. It was being thirsty woke me, and I gimped over to the water fountain on stiff legs.

Luck or something made me look back at the highway. That metal-flake red Firebird pulled off at about thirty miles an hour, just barely rolling. The old lady was by herself again. While I watched, she hung a left turn under the interstate and disappeared.

I had my drink of water, remembering that pointing finger and crooked smile. I got back in the pickup and followed. When I came out on the northbound access, I saw the car pulled over in the Johnson grass at the side of the road. I parked behind it and eased out of the truck.

There was nobody inside. Up ahead an ambulance screamed onto the northbound entrance ramp, siren going and lights flashing. After a few seconds the lights went out and it crested a hill, headed back the way we'd come.

TILL HUMAN VOICES
WAKE US

THEY WERE at 40 feet, in darkness. Inside the narrow circle of his dive light, Campbell could see coral polyps feeding, their ragged edges transformed into predatory flowers.

If anything could have saved us, he thought, this week should have been it.

Beth's lantern wobbled as she flailed herself away from the white-petaled spines of a sea urchin. She wore nothing but a white T-shirt over her bikini, despite Campbell's warnings, and he could see gooseflesh on her thighs. Which is as much of her body, he thought, as I've seen in ... how long? Five weeks? Six? He couldn't remember the last time they'd made love.

As he moved his light away, he thought he saw a shape in the darkness. Shark, he thought, and felt his throat tighten. He swung the lamp back again.

That was when he saw her.

She was frozen by the glare, like any wild animal. Her long straight hair floated up from her shoulders and blended into the darkness. The nipples of her bare breasts were elliptical and purple in the night water.

Her legs merged into a green, scaly tail.

Campbell listened to his breath rasp into the regulator. He could see the width of her cheekbones, the paleness of her eyes, the frightened tremor of the gills around her neck.

Then reflex took over and he brought up his Nikonos and fired. The flare of the strobe shocked her to life. She shuddered, flicked her crescent tail toward him, and disappeared.

A sudden, inexplicable longing overwhelmed him. He dropped the camera and swam after her, legs pumping, pulling with both arms. As he reached the edge of a hundred-foot drop-off, he swept the light in an arc that picked up a final glimpse of her, heading down and to the west. Then she was gone.

HE FOUND BETH on the surface, shivering and enraged. "What the hell was the idea of leaving me alone like that? I was scared to death. You heard what that guy said about sharks—"

"I saw something," Campbell said.

"Fan-fucking-tastic." She rode low in the water, and Campbell watched her catch a wave in her open mouth. She spat it out and said, "Were you taking a look or just running away?"

"Blow up your vest," Campbell said, feeling numb, desolate, "before you drown yourself." He turned his back to her and swam for the boat.

SHOWERED, SITTING OUTSIDE his cabin in the moonlight, Campbell began to doubt himself.

Beth was already cocooned in a flannel nightgown near her edge of the bed. She would lie there, Campbell knew, sometimes not even bothering to close her eyes, until he was asleep.

His recurring, obsessive daydreams were what had brought him here to the island. How could he be sure he hadn't hallucinated that creature out on the reef?

He'd told Beth that they'd been lucky to be picked for the vacation, that he'd applied for it months before. In fact, his fantasies had so utterly destroyed his concentration at work that the company had ordered him to come to the island or submit to a complete course of psych testing.

He'd been more frightened than he was willing to admit. The fantasies had progressed from the mild violence of smashing his CRT screen to a bizarre, sinister image of himself floating outside his shattered office windows, not falling the 40 stories to the street, just drifting there in the whitish smog.

High above him, Campbell could see the company bar, glittering like a chrome-and-steel monster just hatched from its larval stage. He shook his head. Obviously he needed sleep. Just one good night's rest and things would get back to normal.

IN THE MORNING Campbell went out on the dive boat while Beth slept in. He was distracted, clumsy, bothered by shadows in his peripheral vision.

The dive master wandered over while they were changing tanks and asked him, "You nervous about something!"

"No," Campbell said. "I'm fine."

"There's no sharks on this part of the reef, you know."

"It's not that," Campbell said. "There's no problem. Really."

He read the look in the dive master's eyes: another case of shell shock. The company must turn them out by the dozens, Campbell thought. The stressed-out executives and the boardroom victims, all with the same glazed expressions.

That afternoon they dove a small wreck at the east end of the island. Beth paired off with another woman, so Campbell stayed with his partner from the morning, a balding pilot from the Cincinnati office.

The wreck was no more than a husk, an empty shell, and Campbell floated to one side as the others crawled over the rotting wood. His sense of purpose had disappeared, left him wanting only the weightlessness and lack of color of the deep water.

AFTER DINNER he followed Beth out onto the patio. He'd lost track of how long he'd been watching the clouds over the dark water when she said, "I don't like this place."

Campbell looked back at her. She was sleek and pristine in her white linen jacket, the sleeves pushed up to her elbows, her still-damp hair twisted into a chignon and spiked with an orchid. She'd been sulking into her brandy since they'd finished dinner, and once again she'd astonished him with her ability to exist in a completely separate mental universe from his own.

"Why not?"

"It's fake. Unreal. This whole island." She swirled the brandy but didn't drink any of it. "What business does an American company have owning an entire island? What happened to the people who used to live here?"

"In the first place," Campbell said, "it's a multinational company, not just American. And the people are still living here, only now they've got jobs instead of starving to death." As usual, Beth had him on the defensive. In fact he wasn't all that thrilled with the Americanization of the island. He'd imagined natives with guitars and congas, not portable stereos that blasted electronic reggae and neo-funk. The hut where he and Beth slept was some kind of geodesic dome, air-conditioned and comfortable, but he missed the sound of the ocean.

"I just don't like it," Beth said. "I don't like top secret projects that have to be kept behind electric fences. I don't like the company flying people out here for vacations the way they'd throw a bone to a dog."

Or a straw to a drowning man, Campbell thought. He was as curious as anybody about the installations at the west end of the island, but of course that wasn't the point. He and Beth were walking through the steps of a dance that Campbell now saw would inevitably end in divorce. Their friends had all been divorced at least once, and an 18-year marriage probably seemed as anachronistic to them as a 1957 Chevy.

"Why don't you just admit it?" Campbell said. "The only thing you really don't like about the island is the fact that you're stuck here with me."

She stood up, and Campbell felt, with numbing jealousy, the stares of men all around them focus on her. "I'll see you later," she said, and heads turned to follow the clatter of her sandals.

Campbell ordered another Salva Vida and watched her walk downhill. The stairs were lit with Japanese lanterns and surrounded by wild purple and orange flowers. By the time she reached the sandbar and the line of cabins, she was no more than a shadow, and Campbell had finished most of the beer.

Now that she was gone, he felt drained and a little dizzy. He looked at his hands, still puckered from the long hours in the water, at the cuts and bruises of three days of physical activity. Soft hands, the hands of a company man, a desk man. Hands that would push a pencil or type on a CRT for another twenty years, then retire to the remote control of a big-screen TV.

The thick, caramel-tasting beer was starting to catch up to him. He shook his head and got up to find the bathroom. His reflection shimmered and melted in the warped mirror over the bathroom sink. He realized he was stalling, staying away from the chill, sterile air of the cabin as long as he could.

And then there were the dreams. They'd gotten worse since he'd come to the island, more vivid and disturbing every night. He couldn't remember details, only slow, erotic sensations along his skin, a sense of floating in thin, crystalline water, of rolling in frictionless sheets. He'd awaken from them gasping for air like a drowning fish, his penis swollen and throbbing.

He brought another beer back to his table, not really wanting it, just needing to hold it in his hands. His attention kept wandering to a table on a lower level, where a rather plain young woman sat talking with two men in glasses and dress shirts. He couldn't understand what was so familiar about her until she tilted her head in a puzzled gesture and he recognized her. The broad cheekbones, the pale eyes.

He could hear the sound of his own heart. Was it just some kind of prank, then? A woman in a costume? But what about the gill lines he'd seen on her neck? How in God's name had she moved so quickly?

She stood up, made apologetic gestures to her friends. Campbell's table was near the stairs, and he saw she would have to pass him on her way out. Before he could stop to think about it, he stood up, blocking her exit, and said, "Excuse me?"

"Yes?" She was not that physically attractive, he thought, but he was drawn to her anyway, in spite of the heaviness of her waist, her solid, shortish legs. Her face was older, more tired than the one he'd seen out on the reef. But similar, too close for coincidence. "I wanted to ... could I buy you a drink?" Maybe, he thought, I'm just losing my mind.

She smiled, and her eyes crinkled warmly. "I'm sorry. It's really very late, and I have to be at work in the morning."

"Please," Campbell said. "Just for a minute or two." He could see her suspicion, and behind that a faint glow of flattered ego. She wasn't used to being approached by men, he realized. "I just want to talk with you."

"You're not a reporter, are you?"

"No, nothing like that." He searched for something reassuring. "I'm with the company. The Houston office."

The magic words, Campbell thought. She sat down in Beth's chair and said, "I don't know if I should have any more. I'm about half looped as it is."

Campbell nodded, said, "You work here, then."

"That's right."

"Secretary?"

"Biologist," she said, a little sharply. "I'm Dr. Kimberly." When he didn't react to the name, she softened it by adding, "Joan Kimberly."

"I'm sorry," Campbell said. "I always thought biologists were supposed to be homely." The flirtation came easily. She had the same beauty as the creature on the reef, a sort of fierce shyness and alien sensuality, but in the woman they were more deeply buried.

My God, Campbell thought, I'm actually doing this, actually trying to seduce this woman. He glanced at the swelling of her breasts, knowing what they would look like without the blue oxford shirt she wore, and the knowledge became a warmth in his groin.

"Maybe I'd better have that drink," she said. Campbell signaled the waiter.

"I can't imagine what it would be like to live here," he said. "To see this every day."

"You get used to it," she said. "I mean, it's still unbearably beautiful sometimes, but you have your work, and your life goes on. You know?"

"Yes," Campbell said. "I know exactly what you mean."

SHE LET CAMPBELL walk her home. Her loneliness and vulnerability were like a heavy perfume, so strong it repelled him at the same time that it pulled him irresistibly toward her.

She stopped at the doorway of her cabin, another geodesic. This one sat high on the hill, buried in a grove of palms and bougainvilleas. The sexual tension was so strong that Campbell could feel his shirtfront trembling.

"Thank you," she said, her voice rough. "You're very easy to talk to."

He could have turned away then, but he couldn't seem to unravel himself. He put his arms around her, and her mouth bumped against his, awkwardly. Then her lips began to move and her tongue flicked out eagerly. She got the door open without moving away from him, and they nearly fell into the house.

HE PUSHED HIMSELF UP on extended arms and watched her moving beneath him. The moonlight through the trees was green and watery, falling in slow waves across the bed. Her breasts swayed heavily as she arched and twisted her back, the breath bubbling in her throat. Her eyes were clenched tight, and her legs wrapped around his and held them, like a long forked tail.

•

BEFORE DAWN he slid out from under her limp right arm and got into his clothes. She was still asleep as he let himself out.

He'd meant to go back to his cabin, but instead he found himself climbing to the top of the island's rocky spine to wait for the sun to come up.

He hadn't even showered. Kimberly's perfume and musk clung to his hands and crotch like sexual stigmata. It was Campbell's first infidelity in 18 years of marriage, a final, irreversible act.

He knew most of the jargon. Mid-life crisis and all that. He'd probably seen Kimberly at the bar some other night and not consciously remembered her, projected her face onto a fantasy with obvious Freudian water/rebirth connotations.

In the dim, fractionated light of the sunrise, the lagoon was gray, the line of the barrier reef a darker smudge broken by whitecaps that curved like scales on the skin of the ocean. Dry palm fronds rustled in the breeze, and the island birds began to chirp and stutter themselves awake. A shadow broke from one of the huts on the beach below and climbed toward the road, weighted down with a large suitcase and a flight bag. Above her, in the asphalt lot at the top of the stairs, a taxi coasted silently to a stop and doused its lights.

If he had run, he could have reached her and maybe could even have stopped her, but the hazy impulse never became strong enough to reach his legs. Instead, he sat until the sun was hot on his neck and his eyes were dazzled into blindness by the white sand and water.

On the north side of the island, facing the mainland, the village of Espejo sprawled in the mud for the use of the resort and the company. A dirt track ran down the middle of it, oily water standing in the ruts. The cinder-block houses on concrete piers and the Fords rusting in the yards reminded Campbell of an American suburb in the fifties, warped by nightmare.

The locals who worked in the company's kitchens and swept the company's floors lived here, and their kids scuffled in alleys that smelled of rotting fish or lay in the shade and threw rocks at three-legged dogs. An old woman sold Saint Francis flour-sack shirts from ropes tied between pilings of her house. Under an awning of corrugated green plastic, bananas lay in heaps and flies swarmed over haunches of beef. At the end of the main street was a *farmacia* with a faded yellow Kodak sign that promised One Day Service.

Campbell blinked and found his way to the back, where a ten-year-old boy was reading *La Novela Policiaca*. The boy set the comic on the counter and said, "Yes, sir?"

"How soon can you develop these?" Campbell shoved the cartridge toward him.

"*¿Mande?*"

Campbell gripped the edge of the counter. "Ready today?" he asked slowly. "Tomorrow. This time."

Campbell took a twenty out of his wallet and held it face down on the scarred wood. "This afternoon?"

"Momentito." The boy tapped something out on a computer terminal at his right hand. The dry clatter of the keys filled Campbell with distaste. "Tonight, okay?" the boy said. *"A las seis."* He touched the dial of his watch and said, "Six."

"All right," Campbell said. For another five dollars he bought a pint of Canadian Club, and then he went back onto the street. He felt like a sheet of weakly colored glass, as if the sun shone clear through him. He was a fool, of course, to be taking this kind of chance with the film, but he needed that picture. He had to know.

HE ANCHORED THE BOAT as close as possible to where it had been the night before. He had two fresh tanks and about half the bottle of whiskey left. It was barely noon, the sun a white ball of fire in the sky.

Diving drunk and alone was against every rule anyone had ever tried to teach him, but the idea of a simple, clean death by drowning seemed ludicrous to Campbell, not even worth consideration. Fate obviously had something more convoluted in mind for him.

His diving jeans and sweatshirt, still damp and salty from the night before, were suffocating him. He got into his tank as quickly as he could and rolled over the side.

The cool water revived him, washed him clean. He purged the air from his vest and dropped straight to the bottom. Dulled by whiskey and lack of sleep, he floundered for a moment in the sand before he could get his buoyancy neutral.

At the edge of the drop-off he hesitated, then swam to his right, following the edge of the cliff. His physical condition made him burn air faster than he wanted to; going deeper would only make it worse.

The bright red of a Coke can winked at him from a coral head. He crushed it and stuck it in his belt, suddenly furious with the company and its casual rape of the island, with himself for letting them manipulate him, with Beth for leaving him, with the entire world and the human race. He kicked hard, driving himself through swarms of jack and blue tang, hardly noticing the twisted, brilliantly colored landscape that moved beneath him.

Some of the drunkenness burned off in his first burst of energy, and he gradually slowed, wondering what he possibly could hope to accomplish. It was useless, he thought. He was chasing a phantom. But he didn't turn back.

He was still swimming when he hit the net.

It was nearly invisible, a web of monofilament in one-foot squares, strong enough to hold a shark or a school of porpoises. He tested it with the serrated edge of his diver's knife, with no luck. He was close to the west end of the island, where the company kept their research facility. The net followed the line of the reef as far down as he could see and extended out into the open water.

She was real, he thought. They built this to keep her in. But how did she get past it?

When he'd last seen her she'd been heading down. Campbell checked his seaview gauge, saw that he had less than five hundred pounds of air left. Enough to take him down to a hundred feet or so and right back up. The sensible thing to do was to return to the boat and bring a fresh tank back with him.

He went down anyway.

He could see the fine wires glinting as he swam past them. They seemed bonded to the coral itself, by some process he could not even imagine. He kept his eyes moving between the depth gauge and the edge of the net. Much deeper than a hundred feet and he would have to worry about decompression as well as an empty tank.

At 100 feet he tripped his reserve lever. Three hundred pounds and counting. All the reds had disappeared from the coral, leaving only blues and purples. The water was noticeably darker, colder, and each breath seemed to roar into his lungs like a geyser. Ten more feet, he told himself, and at 125 he saw the rip in the net.

He snagged his backpack on the monofilament and had to back off and try again, fighting panic. He could already feel the constriction in his lungs again, as if he were trying to breathe with a sheet of plastic over his mouth. He'd seen tanks that had been sucked so dry that the sides caved in. They found them on divers trapped in rockslides and tangled in fishing line.

His tank slipped free, and he was through, following his bubbles upward. The tiny knot of air in his lungs expanded as the pressure around him let up, but not enough to kill his need to breathe. He pulled the last of the air out of the tank and forced himself to keep exhaling, forcing the nitrogen out of his tissues.

At 50 feet he slowed and angled toward a wall of coral, turned the comer, and swam into a sheltered lagoon.

For a few endless seconds he forgot that he had no air.

The entire floor of the lagoon was laid out in squares of greenery: kelp, mosses, and something that looked like giant cabbage. A school of red snapper circled past him, herded by a metal box with a blinking light on the end of one long antenna. Submarines with spindly mechanical arms worked on the ocean floor, thinning the vegetation and darkening the water with chemicals. Two or three dolphins were swimming side by side with human divers, and they seemed to be talking to each other.

His lungs straining, Campbell turned his back on them and kicked for the surface, trying to stay as close to the rocks as he could. He wanted to stop for a minute at ten feet, to give at least a nod to decompression, but it wasn't possible. His air was gone.

He broke the surface less than a hundred feet from a concrete dock. Behind him was a row of marker buoys that traced the line of the net all the way out to sea and around the far side of the lagoon.

The dock lay deserted and steaming in the sun. Without a fresh tank, Campbell had no chance of getting out the way he'd come in. If he swam out on the surface, he'd be as conspicuous as a drowning man. He had to find another tank or another way out.

Hiding his gear under a sheet of plastic, he crossed the hot concrete slab to the building behind it, a wide, low warehouse full of wooden crates. A rack of diving gear was built into the left-hand wall. Campbell was starting for it when he heard a voice behind him.

"Hey, you! Hold it!"

Campbell ducked behind a wall of crates, saw a tiled hallway opening into the back of the building, and ran for it. He didn't get more than three or four steps before a uniformed guard stepped out and pointed a .38 at his chest.

"YOU CAN LEAVE him with me."

"Are you sure, Dr. Kimberly?"

"I'll be all right," she said. "I'll call you if there's any trouble."

Campbell collapsed in a plastic chair across from her desk. The office was strictly functional—waterproof and mildew-resistant. A long window behind Kimberly's head showed the lagoon and the row of marker buoys.

"How much did you see?" she asked.

"I don't know. I saw what looked like farms. Some machinery."

She slid a photograph across the desk to him. It showed a creature with a woman's breasts and the tail of a fish. The face was close enough to Kimberly's to be her sister.

Or her clone's.

Campbell suddenly realized the amount of trouble he was in.

"The boy at the *farmacia* works for us," Kimberly said.

Campbell nodded. Of course he did. Where else would he get a computer? "You can have the picture," Campbell said, blinking the sweat out of his eyes. "And the negative."

"Let's be realistic," she said, tapping the keys of her CRT and studying the screen. "Even if we let you keep your job, I don't see how we could hold your marriage together. And then you have two kids to put through college..." She shook her head. "Your brain is full of hot information. There are too many people who would pay to have it, and there are just too many ways you can be manipulated. You're not much of a risk, Mister Campbell." She radiated hurt and betrayal, and he wanted to slink away from her in shame.

She got up and looked out the window. "We're building the future here," she said. "A future we couldn't even imagine fifteen years ago. And that's just too valuable to let one person screw up. Plentiful food, cheap energy, access to a computer net for the price of a TV set, a whole new form of government—"

"I've seen your future," Campbell said. "Your boats have killed the reef for over a mile around the hotel. Your Coke cans are lying all over the coral bed. Your marriages don't last and your kids are on drugs and your TV is garbage. I'll pass."

"Did you see that boy in the drugstore? He's learning calculus on that computer, and his parents can't even read and write. We're testing a vaccine on human subjects that will probably prevent leukemia. We've got laser surgery and transplant techniques that are revolutionary. Literally."

"Is that where she came from?" Campbell asked, pointing to the photograph.

Kimberly's voice dropped. "It's synergistic, don't you see? To do the transplants we had to be able to clone cells from the donor. To clone cells we had to have laser manipulation of the genes..."

"They cloned your cells? Just for practice?"

She nodded slowly. "Something happened. She grew, but she stopped developing, kept her embryonic form from the waist down. There was nothing we could do except ... make the best of it."

Campbell took a longer look at the picture. No, not the romantic myth he had first imagined. The tail was waxy looking in the harsh light of the strobe, the fins more clearly undeveloped legs. He stared at the photo in queasy fascination. "You could have let her die."

"No. She was mine. I don't have much, and I wouldn't give her up." Kimberly's fists clenched at her sides. "She's not unhappy, she knows who I am. In her own way I suppose she cares for me." She paused, looking at the floor. "I'm a lonely woman, Campbell. But of course you know that."

Campbell's throat was dry. "What about me?" he rasped, and managed to swallow. "Am I going to die?"

"No," she said. "Not you either...."

CAMPBELL SWAM for the fence. His memories were cloudy and he had trouble focusing his thoughts, but he could visualize the gap in the net and the open ocean beyond it. He kicked down easily to 120 feet, the water cool and comforting on his naked skin. Then he was through, drifting gently away from the noise and stink of the island, toward some primal vision of peace and timelessness.

His gills rippled smoothly as he swam.

FLAGSTAFF

I T WAS NOT yet noon when they pulled into the motel. Rain in the early morning had rinsed the air and left it fresh and cool, tasting of the fall to come. Lee's father set the handbrake but left the engine running as he got out, boots crunching in the gravel.

Lee crawled halfway over the front seat to look at the dashboard clock. He crossed the fingers on both hands, daring to hope that the day's driving was already over, that they would not have to try motel after motel. Lee had a good feeling about this one. Its wooden siding was the color of milk chocolate, and the air through his open window tickled his nose with the green scent of pines and junipers. There was even a pool, though in truth it was too cold to think about swimming.

A white-haired lady opened cabin seven for Lee's father, and a few seconds later Lee heard a toilet flush, followed by a repeated clacking as his father tested the lock on the front door. Finally he came out nodding and then stood for a moment in the watery sunshine, long-sleeved khaki shirt buttoned to the throat, hands in the pockets of his pleated trousers, looking into the distance.

Lee tried to smile at his mother, who seemed oblivious.

They locked their suitcases in the room and drove back into town. Lee's father was whistling now, his right arm up on the seat back, his left elbow propped in the window, as if he were another man entirely from the one who'd been driving with fierce concentration since dawn. "So," he said to Lee's mother, "what do you think? Nice place, huh?"

She smiled bravely. "Very nice."

"There's a Rexall," Lee said. "With a fountain. Can we? Can we?"

His father sighed. "I suppose so."

They parked and Lee ran ahead. Hand-lettered signs in the drug store window advertised typing paper, Alka-Seltzer, cold cream. The sweet smell of frying meat hung in the air inside. Lee spun himself around and around on his chrome and red vinyl stool while his father read the menu. "Stop that," his father said, and Lee faced the counter, sitting on his hands to help himself keep still. When it was his turn Lee ordered a hamburger and a chocolate milkshake and then asked, "Can I look around?"

His father seemed to be studying himself in the long mirror behind the fountain. "Go," he said.

On a wire spin rack Lee found a Jules Verne he'd never seen before, a movie tie-in edition of *Master of the World* with Vincent Price on the cover. He stashed the book behind a stack of *Moonrakers* and moved on to the toy aisle. The cramped space was filled with Duncan yo-yos, Whammo Slip'N'Slides, and Mattel cap pistols. On the bottom shelf Lee found a Wiffle Ball and orange plastic bat that filled him with a longing he thought might overwhelm him.

He went back to the lunch counter and wolfed his food, then sat with his arms wrapped around his narrow chest, trying to gauge his father's mood while struggling with his own impatience, hope, and fear. His father ate slowly, drank a second cup of coffee, and smoked a cigarette while Lee's mother applied a fresh coat of lipstick. Finally Lee's father stood up with the check and started for the register by the front door. Lee tugged at his father's pants leg and showed him the book. His father glanced at it and nodded. "Okay."

He seemed distracted in a mild, pleasant way, so Lee pressed his advantage. "Look," he said, and showed his father the bat and ball.

"I thought you wanted the book."

He didn't seem angry so Lee said, "Can I have this and the book too?"

"What would you do with it? If I get this job, I'm not going to have time to play with you." Lee knew his father wouldn't have time to play with him in any case, but he was caught by something in his father's voice. His father was thinking about the job in the same way that Lee was thinking about the bat and ball. And though Lee knew, even at ten years old, that the job would not work out, the hope itself was contagious.

"Please?" he said.

In the car Lee's father said, "Roger Maris back there is going to teach himself baseball and become a sports hero and the envy of all his friends. If he had any."

The bat and ball were attached with wire to a long red piece of cardboard that read "Junior Slugger." It made Lee happy to just to hold it in his lap—the newness of it, the hard perfection of the plastic. The possibilities.

They got back to the motel with the entire afternoon still in front of them. Lee begged his father to play with him and eventually his father relented. They stood under the sharp-smelling trees and Lee swung at three pitches and missed them all, having to chase the ball after each one. "Not so hard!" he said.

His father, cigarette in the corner of his mouth, grunted and tossed him an easy, underhanded pitch. Lee connected and the ball sailed past his father's outstretched hand, through the trees, to land near the swimming pool.

"Don't look at *me*," his father said.

Lee ran after it, and by the time he got back his father was gone.

Lee tried to toss the ball up with one hand and hit it as it dropped. It was harder than it looked, and after a while he went back inside.

His father was teaching his mother a game he'd just learned. He had five small dice that he kept in a prescription vial. It was like poker, he told her, and he showed her how to draw up a score sheet on a piece of scratch paper.

Lee's bed smelled like clean ironing, and he made a pile of pillows to lean against while he read. His new book was about a man named Robur who was brilliant but had no use for the world. He built a flying platform and circled the earth in it, refusing to come down. As he read, Lee was distantly aware of the patter of the dice and his mother's nervous laughter.

Finally Lee's father said to him, "Why don't you get your nose out of that goddamned book and go outside for a while?"

As Lee closed the door, carrying his new bat and ball, he heard the lock turn behind him. Ahead of him was the new city and the rest of the world.

He sat for a while in a green wooden chair at the edge of the swimming pool. The water had the pale color of a hot summer day, while the sky was a deep, artificial blue, the color of swimming pools and plastic cars. It was like the world was upside down.

Nearly four decades later, with a happy marriage, an elegant North Carolina home, a secure job, Lee has everything his father always dreamed of. But somehow one day has become like the next. That afternoon in Flagstaff haunts him, and the thing he least understands is how his memory of it could be suffused with such a quiet glow of happiness.

And in 1961 Lee raises the plastic bat to his shoulder, tosses the ball high above his head once more, and swings.

TOMMY AND THE
TALKING DOG

"**I**F YOU CAN answer three questions," the dog said, "you can wear the magic shoes."

Tommy looked up and down the deserted street. "Did you ... say something?"

"That's right. Didn't you hear me?" It was a gruff voice, with just a trace of an English accent, and it was definitely coming out of the dog.

"You're a dog." In fact it was a huge, fat bulldog, with big flaps of skin hanging off the sides of its face. From where it sat, on the front steps of the abandoned motel, it looked Tommy straight in the eye.

"That's correct," the dog said.

Tommy stared hard at the dusty windows of the motel office. "This is a trick, right? There's a TV camera back there, and you want to make me look stupid."

"No tricks, Tommy. Just three questions."

"C'mon," Tommy said. He deepened his voice. "Sit up." The dog stared at him. "Roll over. Play dead."

"Cut the crap, Tommy. Do you want the shoes or not?"

"Let me see them."

The dog shifted its weight to one side, revealing a battered pair of red Converse All-Stars. "Yuck," Tommy said. "Those are gross."

"Maybe," the dog said, "but they're magic."

"What are the questions?"

"Which of the following presidents died in office? Lincoln, McKinley, F.D.R.?"

"C'mon. They all did. That's the same dumb question they use when they're trying to sell you a free portrait on the telephone."

"Which weighs more, a pound of feathers or a pound of lead?"

"They both weigh a pound. This is stupid. Next you're going to ask me who's buried in Grant's Tomb."

The dog narrowed its eyes. "Have you done this before?"

"Ulysses S. Grant," Tommy said. "Lemme see the shoes."

They were just his size and felt pretty good, even though they were scuffed up and the metal things were gone out of the side vents. "I don't feel any different," Tommy said.

"You need the shoes to look for the treasure," the dog said.

"What treasure?"

"When you're wearing the shoes, you can open the doors of the motel rooms."

"Uh uh. No, sir. My parents told me not to go in there. Besides, they're all empty anyway."

The dog shrugged. Tommy had never seen a dog shrug before. "Suit yourself," the dog said.

"Hey, wait a minute. Tell me about this treasure."

"You have to find that for yourself." The dog started to walk away.

"Hey!" Tommy said. "Come back here!"

The dog kept on walking.

Tommy flexed his toes inside the shoes. Magic. He looked at the row of motel rooms, their dusty tan walls almost golden in the late May afternoon. He would already be in trouble if his folks knew he was hanging around the place.

He went to the first door and opened it.

Inside a woman sat in a chair, watching TV. Tommy felt a hot flush go up his face. "Jeez, I'm sorry," he said. "I didn't think there was anybody here."

"It's okay, Tommy," the woman said. "Come on in."

Tommy took another step into the room. "You know me?"

"Sure," the woman said. "You're wearing the shoes." She was a little older than his mother, and very fat. An open Whitman Sampler box sat by her thick right arm.

"Who are you?" Tommy asked.

"Nobody. Just a mother." The room was bigger inside than out and didn't look like a motel. There was a playpen in one dark corner with two kids in it. One of them hit the other with a plastic rattle. A third kid crawled around on the floor, dragging a blanket. The place smelled bad, like sour milk and old coffee and the bathroom at school.

A man's voice on the TV said, "Susan's going to have my baby."

"What are you watching?" Tommy asked politely.

"Nothing. Just a show."

The kid who was getting hit started to whimper. The woman put a chocolate into her mouth with a quick, almost guilty snap of the wrist.

"Well," Tommy said. He felt the way he did when he'd been looking forward to going swimming and it rained. "I have to go."

"Shhh," the woman said. "This is the good part." Tommy went out quietly and closed the door. He wondered what the dog had expected him to find. He went to the next room and knocked gently.

"Come on," said a big male voice.

Tommy opened the door and found himself in front of a long wooden desk. Behind the man at the desk was a window with narrow blinds, slanted to let the sun in. It made it hard to see the man's face.

"Tommy!" the man said. "Come right on in!" He stood up and held out his hand. Tommy shook it and backed away. "How in the world are you?"

"Fine," Tommy said. "How come you know who I am?"

"The shoes, son, the shoes! Now what can I do for you?"

Tommy hoisted himself up into a chair that was too big for him. He noticed a funny smell and sneaked a quick sniff at his hand. The man had left some kind of aftershave on it. It was so strong it made Tommy's eyes water. He rubbed the hand on his jeans.

"Do you know anything about a treasure?" he asked.

"A treasure," the man said, sitting back down. Tommy could now see his mustache and the way he'd combed his hair over the bald spot on top of his head. He wasn't that old, but he had circles under his eyes, and his smile wiggled like it wanted to come off. "Well, I may not know where to find a chest of gold doubloons, but I can tell you how to get rich." He leaned across the desk and whispered, "Superconductors."

Tommy pictured a man in red-and-blue tights taking tickets on a train. "What?"

"Superconductors," the man said. "They're like metal, you know, how it carries electricity? But they do it better and they're very, very cold ... well, hell. I don't know that much about how they work. But I'll tell you, there's a fortune there!" He slapped the desk. "A fortune!"

A little box on the desk buzzed. He punched a button and said, "Yes?"

A woman's voice said, "Mr. Connell for you on line seven, sir." She sounded like she was trying to whisper and sing at the same time.

"Stall the old fart, would you honey? And say, don't forget our *business* meeting tonight. I got us a room over at the motel." The man winked at Tommy, using his whole face, and punched another button on the box.

A picture frame on the desk showed a woman and two boys. The woman didn't look as though she belonged to the voice in the little box. "Not a word to my wife, now, Tommy," the man said. "You know how it is."

"No," Tommy said. "How is it?"

Before the man could answer, the box buzzed again.

"I'm sorry, sir, Mr. Connell says it's urgent."

The man grabbed the telephone and punched at a blinking light. "Goddammit, J.C., what the hell is eating your ass now? ... You what? ... You *what?* All of them?" The man put the phone back and fumbled at the drawer of his desk. His face was the color of cement. "Superconductors," he whispered, and started putting tiny white pills under his tongue.

"I ... I better go now," Tommy said. The man didn't answer, and Tommy hurried outside.

The sun was setting. The world looked very tired and dusty. "Hey, dog?" Tommy called. There was no sign of it. Slowly Tommy went to the next door and opened it.

A woman lay on the bed. She was dressed kind of like the cheerleaders on the football games his father watched on Sunday afternoons. She had shorts made out of silver material and a thin red shirt tied above her stomach. When she sat up, Tommy could see her breasts wobble under the thin cloth. They were very big, and drooped when she leaned forward.

"Hi, Tommy," she said. "Find the treasure yet?" She lit a cigarette from the butt of one that was in the ashtray.

"No," Tommy said. She had a dry, scratchy voice that was very sad. "Who are you?"

"Me? I'm a hooker, Tommy."

"A hooker? What's a hooker?"

The woman shook her head. Her hair was glued in place with too much hairspray, and she wore more makeup than Tommy had ever seen on one person before. "A hooker is a woman who ... well, she tries to cheer up men that aren't very happy at home."

"Could you cheer *me* up?"

"You're a little young, Tommy. It usually doesn't work anyway. See, grown-ups aren't very happy people a lot of the time. They look for power or money or sex, and when that doesn't work, they usually just sit around and watch TV."

"There isn't any treasure, is there?"

"I don't know, Tommy. I didn't find it."

"What's that?"

The woman had tied a belt around her arm, and was filling a hypodermic needle. "It's like medicine, Tommy. I think you'd better go now."

"Yeah," Tommy said.

It was almost dark outside. Tommy sat on the curb and took off the red All-Stars and put his own shoes back on. "Hey, dog!" he shouted. "Hey! You can have your stupid shoes back!" There was no answer. Tommy threw the shoes toward the motel as hard as he could. They broke the window of the first room, where the fat woman had been watching TV, and through the broken glass Tommy could see the room was empty.

•

WHEN HE GOT HOME, his parents asked him what was wrong. He told them he was just tired. He took a bath and went to bed and stared at the wall for a long time. Eventually he fell asleep.

School was almost out for the summer. With the windows open and the hot, dusty smell of the outdoors in all the rooms, it was almost pointless to continue. Teachers struggled on anyway, to the accompaniment of shuffling feet and shifting bodies and stampedes at recess.

For Tommy it didn't matter anymore. He looked at Mrs. Aiello and thought about the fat woman in the motel room, and the woman whose picture had been on the businessman's desk. When he looked at Susie Bishop, the prettiest girl in class, he saw her in tight shorts and too much makeup. When Bobby Cubitto called out an answer in class, Tommy thought of him shouting into a phone.

He went by the old motel on the way home every day. There was never a sign of the dog. He even looked in the room with the broken window, but the shoes were gone. His parents knew something was bothering him, and his father tried to talk to him.

"Do you believe in magic, Dad?" Tommy asked. "Talking animals, stuff like that?"

"Well, Tommy," he said, and cleared his throat. Tommy noticed that his father had started parting his hair on the other side and combing it up to cover a thin place on top. "Things like that are called allegories. That means they aren't real themselves, but they stand for something real. Do you see? So if an animal in a story tells you something, it may just mean that you're getting a message from your conscience or something like that."

"But it's not real."

"Not really."

ON THE LAST DAY of school they got out at noon. Tommy wandered the streets aimlessly, not wanting to go home. He found himself in a subdivision he didn't know very well. He walked with his head down, kicking a small black rock ahead of him as he went.

Something moved in the corner of his vision. It was a big bulldog.

Tommy ran after it. The dog saw him and cut through somebody's yard. Tommy didn't slow down. He ducked under a clothesline and chased the dog down an alley. It veered again and Tommy stayed right behind and suddenly it skidded into a flower bed, cornered by a chain link fence. Tommy jumped on it and forced it to the ground.

"Talk to me!" Tommy said. He remembered what the man had shouted into the phone. "Talk to me, goddammit!"

A screen door banged behind them. "Hey, you!" said a woman's voice. "Get out of those flowers! What are you doing?"

"I'm sorry," Tommy said, grabbing a fistful of the dog's fur. "My dog ran away. I'll pay you for the flowers. I'm sorry, I really am."

"That's okay," the woman said. "Just be more careful." She looked him up and down. "How are you going to get him home? He doesn't even have a collar."

Tommy shrugged.

"I'll get you a piece of rope," the woman said. She went into the house and came back with a piece of scratchy cord. "Here."

"Thank you," Tommy said. "I'm sorry about the flowers."

He dragged the dog out to the street. He hoped the woman hadn't seen him yelling at it. He would have looked really stupid, yelling at a dog to talk to him. He sat down on a curb. It *was* stupid. The dog was just a dog, and didn't deserve to be treated this way.

"Hey," the dog said. "This rope really itches."

"You *can* talk."

"Of course."

"Why did you give me those shoes? Why did you send me into those motel rooms with all those miserable people? What was the big idea?"

"No big idea. You're a special kid. Special things happen to special people. You don't ask for explanations."

"What about the treasure?"

The dog licked its chops noisily. "Take off the rope first, how about?"

"Tell me about the treasure."

"I don't feel much like talking with this rope around my neck."

The dog and the boy stared at each other, and then Tommy took off the rope.

"There isn't any treasure, is there?" Tommy asked.

"Not in that motel, no."

"Then you lied to me."

"Look, kid, I didn't say it was *in* there, I said you had to *look* for it there. See, sometimes you already have something and you don't know it. So you still have to look for it, even though you already have it."

"Have what?"

"A way of looking at things. Of finding people in empty motels or finding words in the mouth of a dog."

"Then I just made you up. You're not even real."

"Reality is whatever you decide it's going to be. You can have a reality where there are talking dogs and magic shoes, or you can be like the people in that motel. Like your parents. It's up to you."

"That's the treasure?"

"That's it." The dog got up and snuffled away down the street. It stopped in front of a big new car, lifted its leg, and peed on the tire. The drops spattered onto the dusty street like little gold coins.

"See you around, kid," the dog said over its shoulder.

"Will I?" Tommy said. "Will I see you again?"

"Sure," the dog said. "Life is full of surprises."

Tommy put the rope in somebody's trash can and started home. What do you know? he thought. After a while he started to whistle.

O Z

They fucking ripped the joint. Ozzie bit the head off a white lab rat during "CIA Killers" and Toad threw a 16-inch floor tom into the audience. Three girls rushed Ozzie during "Bay of Piggies," one of them with no shirt on. The cops had to empty the place with tear gas.

The goddamn reporters were mobbed outside. "Twenty-five years," one of them shouted. "How does it feel?"

"Piss off," Ozzie said. He was pushing fifty, still skinny and barely strong enough to last through a two-hour set. How the hell was he supposed to feel? "I was acquitted, remember? You know who did it. They all went to jail. All hundred and fifty of them. So leave me the fuck alone."

"But why rock and roll?" another one shouted.

Because I was going nuts. Framed, beaten, tried, but never forgiven. Fuck you all, he thought. You got the greatest era of peace in the history of the world. No more assassinations, America out of Vietnam before it even got ugly, manned colonies on Mars. All because one reporter stumbled on the biggest conspiracy in history, with agents everywhere from the Mafia to the CIA to the Birchers to the goddamn Rosicrucians. All of them in Attica now, the ones that had lived.

But what about me?

"Why not?" Ozzie said.

"Lee!" another one shouted. "Lee, over here!"

"It's not Lee anymore," Ozzie snarled. "It's Ozzie Oswald, nice and legal, got it?"

Then he was into the limousine, soundproof, bulletproof, the kind Kennedy should have had. He laughed at the crowd and held up his middle fingers. If I had it to do over, he thought, I *would* have killed him myself. What do you think about that?

The limo took him off, laughing, into the night.

LOVE IN VAIN

THE ROOM HAD whitewashed walls, no windows, and a map of the US on my left as I came in. There must have been a hundred pins with little colored heads stuck along the interstates. By the other door was a wooden table, the top full of scratches and coffee rings. Charlie was already sitting on the far side of it.

They called it Charlie's "office" and a Texas Ranger named Gonzales had brought me back there to meet him. "Charlie?" Gonzales said. "This here's Dave McKenna. He's an Assistant DA up in Dallas?"

"Morning," Charlie said. His left eye, the glass one, drooped a little, and his teeth were brown and ragged. He had on jeans and a plaid short-sleeved shirt and he was shaved clean. His hair was damp and combed straight back. His sideburns had gray in them and came to the bottom of his ears.

I had files and a notebook in my right hand so I wouldn't have to shake with him. He didn't offer. "You looking to close you up some cases?" he said.

I had to clear my throat. "Well, we thought we might give it a try." I sat down in the other chair.

He nodded and looked at Gonzales. "Ernie? You don't suppose I could have a little more coffee?"

Gonzales had been leaning against the wall by the map, but he straightened right up and said, "Sure thing, Charlie." He brought in a full pot from the other room and set it on the table. Charlie had a Styrofoam cup that held about a quart. He filled it up and then added three packets of sugar and some powdered creamer.

"How about you?" Charlie said.

"No," I said. "Thanks."

"You don't need to be nervous," Charlie said. His breath smelled of coffee and cigarettes. When he wasn't talking his mouth relaxed into an easy smile. You didn't have to see anything menacing in it. It was the kind of smile you could see from any highway in Texas, looking out at you from a porch or behind a gas pump, waiting for you to drive on through.

I took out a pocket-sized cassette recorder. "Would it be okay if I taped this?"

"Sure, go ahead."

I pushed the little orange button on top. "March twenty-seventh, Williamson County Jail. Present are Sergeant Ernesto Gonzales and Charles Dean Harris."

"Charlie," he said.

"Pardon?"

"Nobody ever calls me Charles."

"Right," I said. "Okay."

"I guess maybe my mother did sometimes. Always sounded wrong some-how." He tilted his chair back against the wall. "You don't suppose you could back that up and do it over?"

"Yeah, okay, fine." I rewound the tape and went through the introduction again. This time I called him Charlie.

Twenty-five years ago, he'd stabbed his mother to death. She'd been his first.

IT HAD TAKEN ME three hours to drive from Dallas to the Williamson County Jail in Georgetown, a straight shot down Interstate 35. I'd left a little before eight that morning. Alice was already at work and I had to get Jeffrey off to school. The hardest part was getting him away from the television.

He was watching MTV. They were playing the Heart video where the blonde guitar player wears the low-cut golden prom dress. Every time she moved, her magnificent breasts seemed to hesitate before they went along, like they were proud, willful animals, just barely under her control.

I turned the TV off and swung Jeffrey around a couple of times and sent him out for the bus. I got together the files I needed and went into the bedroom to make the bed. The covers were turned back on both sides, but the middle was undisturbed. Alice and I hadn't made love in six weeks. And counting.

I walked through the house, picking up Jeffrey's Masters of the Universe toys. I saw that Alice had loaded up the mantel again with framed pictures of her brothers and parents and the dog she'd had as a little girl. For a second it seemed like the entire house was buried in objects that had nothing to do with me—dolls and vases and doilies and candles and baskets on every inch of every flat surface she could reach. You couldn't walk from one end of a room to the other without running into a Victorian chair or secretary or umbrella stand, couldn't see the floors for the flowered rugs.

I locked up and got in the car and took the LBJ loop all the way around town. The idea was to avoid traffic. I was kidding myself. Driving in Dallas is a matter of manly pride: if somebody manages to pull in front of you he's clearly got a bigger dick than you do. Rather than let this happen, it's better that one of you die.

I was in traffic the whole way down, through a hundred and seventy miles of Charlie Dean Harris country: flat, desolate grasslands with an occasional bridge or culvert where you could dump a body. Charlie had wandered and murdered all over the south, but once he found I-35, he was home to stay.

•

I OPENED ONE OF the folders and rested it against the edge of the table so Charlie wouldn't see my hand tremble. "I've got a case here from 1974. A Dallas girl on her way home from Austin for spring break. Her name was Carol, uh, Fairchild. Black hair, blue eyes. Eighteen years old."

Charlie was nodding. "She had braces on her teeth. Would have been real pretty without 'em."

I looked at the sheet of paper in the folder. Braces, it said. The plain white walls seemed to wobble a little. "Then you remember her."

"Yessir, I suppose I do. I killed her." He smiled. It looked like a reflex, something he didn't even know he was doing. "I killed her to have sex with her."

"Can you remember anything else?"

He shrugged. "It was just to have sex, that's all. I remember when she got in the car. She was wearing a T-shirt, one of them man's T-shirts, with the straps and all." He dropped the chair back down and put his elbows on the table. "You could see her titties," he explained.

I wanted to pull away but I didn't. "Where was this?"

He thought for a minute. "Between here and Round Rock, right there off the interstate."

I looked down at my folder again. Last seen wearing navy tank top, blue jeans. "What color was the T-shirt?"

"Red," he said. "She would have been strangled. With a piece of electrical wire I had there in the car. I had supposed she was a prostitute, dressed the way she was and all. I asked her to have sex, and she said she would, so I got off the highway, and then she didn't want to. So I killed her, and I had sex with her."

Nobody said anything for what must have been at least a minute. I could hear a little scratching noise as the tape moved inside the recorder. Charlie was looking straight at me with his good eye. "I wasn't satisfied," he said.

"What?"

"I wasn't satisfied. I had sex with her, but I wasn't satisfied."

"Listen, you don't have to tell me..."

"I got to tell it all," he said.

"I don't want to hear it," I said. My voice came out too high, too loud. But Charlie kept staring at me.

"It don't matter," he said. "I still got to tell it. I got to tell it all. I can't live with the terrible things I did. Jesus says that if I tell everything, I can be with Betsy when this is all over." Betsy was his common law wife. He'd killed her too, after living with her since she was nine. The words sounded like he'd practiced them, over and over.

"I'll take you to her if you want," he said.

"Betsy...?"

"No, your girl there. Carol Fairchild. I'll take you where I buried her." He wasn't smiling any more. He had the sad, earnest look of a laundromat bum telling you how he'd lost his oil fortune up in Oklahoma.

I looked at Gonzales. "We can set it up for you if you want," he said. "Sheriff'll have to okay it and all, but we could prob'ly do it first thing tomorrow."

"Okay," I said. "That'd be good."

Charlie nodded, drank some coffee, lit a cigarette. "Well, fine," he said. "You want to try another?"

"No," I said. "Not just yet."

"Whatever," Charlie said. "You just let me know."

Later, walking me out, Gonzales said, "Don't let Charlie get to you. He wants people to like him, you know? So he figures out what you want him to be, and he tries to be that for you."

I knew he was trying to cheer me up. I thanked him and told him I'd be back in the morning.

I CALLED ALICE from my friend Jack's office in Austin, 30 miles farther down I-35. "It's me," I said.

"Oh," she said. She sounded tired. "How's it going?"

I didn't know what to tell her. "Fine," I said. "I need to stay over another day or so."

"Okay," she said.

"Are you okay?"

"Fine," she said.

"Jeffrey?"

"He's fine."

I watched 30 seconds tick by on Jack's wall clock. "Anything else?" she said.

"I guess not." My eyes stung, and I reflexively shaded them with my free hand. "I'll be at Jack's if you need me."

"Okay," she said. I waited a while longer and then put the phone back on the hook.

Jack had just come out of his office. "Oh oh," he said.

It took a couple of breaths to get my throat to unclench. "Yeah," I said.

"Bad?"

"Bad as it could be, I guess. It's over, probably. I mean, I think it's over, but how do you know?"

"You don't," Jack said. His secretary, a good-looking Chicana named Liz, typed away on her word processor and tried to act like she wasn't having to listen to us. "You just after a while get fed up and you say fuck it. You want to get a burger or what?"

JACK AND I went to UT law school together. He'd lost a lot of hair and put on some weight but he wouldn't do anything about it. Jogging was for assholes. He would rather die fat and keep his self-respect.

He'd been divorced two years now and was always glad to fold out the couch for me. It had been a while. After Jeffrey was born, Alice and I had somehow lost touch with everything except work and TV. "I've missed this," I said.

"Missed what?"

"Friends," I said. We were in a big prairie-style house north of campus that had been fixed up with a kitchen and bar and hanging plants. I was full, but still working on the last of the batter-dipped French fries.

"Not my fault, you prick. You're the one dropped down to Christmas cards."

"Yeah, well..."

"Forget it. How'd it go with Charlie Dean?"

"Unbelievable," I said. "I mean, really. He confessed to everything. Had details. Even had a couple wrong, enough to look good. But the major stuff was right on."

"So that's great. Isn't it?"

"It was a setup. The name I gave him was a fake. No such person, no such case."

"I don't get it."

"Jack, the son of a bitch has confessed to something like three thousand murders. It ain't possible. So they wanted to catch him lying."

"With his pants down, so to speak."

"Same old Jack."

"You said he had details."

"That's the creepy part. He knew she was supposed to have braces. I had it in the phony case file, but he brought it up before I did."

"Lucky guess."

"No. It was too creepy. And there's all this shit he keeps telling you. Things you wish you'd never heard, you know what I mean?"

"I know exactly what you mean," Jack said. "When I was in junior high I saw a bum go in the men's room at the bus station with a loaf of bread. I told this friend of mine about it and he says the bum was going in there to wipe all the dried piss off the toilets with the bread and then eat it. For the protein. Said it happens all the time."

"Jesus Christ, Jack."

"See? I know what you're talking about. There's things you don't want in your head. Once they get in there, you're not the same any more. I can't eat white bread to this day. Twenty years, and I still can't touch it."

"You asshole." I pushed my plate away and finished my Corona. "Christ, now the beer tastes like piss."

Jack pointed his index finger at me. "You will never be the same," he said.

YOU COULD NEVER TELL how much Jack had been drinking. He said it was because he was careful not to let on if he was ever sober. I always thought it was because there was something in him that was meaner than the booze and together they left him just about even.

It was a lot of beers later that Jack said, "What was the name of that bimbo in high school you used to talk about? Your first great love or some shit? Except she never put out for you?"

"Kristi," I said. "Kristi Spector."

"Right!" Jack got up and started to walk around the apartment. It wasn't too long of a walk. "A name like that, how could I forget? I got her off a soliciting rap two months ago."

"Soliciting?"

"There's a law in Texas against selling your pussy. Maybe you didn't know that."

"Kristi Spector, my God. Tell me about it."

"She's a stripper, son. Works over at the Yellow Rose. This guy figured if she'd show her tits in public, he could have the rest in his car. She didn't, he called the pigs. Said she made lewd advances. Crock of shit, got thrown out of court."

"How's she look?"

"Not too goddamn bad. I wouldn't have minded taking my fee in trade, but she didn't seem to get the hint." He stopped. "I got a better idea. Let's go have a look for ourselves."

"Oh no," I said.

"Oh yes. She remembers you, man. She says you were 'sweet.' Come on, get up. We're going to go look at some tits."

THE PLACE WAS BIGGER inside than I expected, the ceilings higher. There were two stages and a runway behind the second one. There were stools right up by the stages for the guys that wanted to stick dollar bills in the dancers' G-strings and four-top tables everywhere else.

I should have felt guilty but I wasn't thinking about Alice at all. The issue here was sex, and Alice had written herself out of that part of my life. Instead I was thinking about the last time I'd seen Kristi.

It was senior year in high school. The director of the drama club, who was from New York, had invited some of us to a "wild" party. It was the first time I'd seen men in dresses. I'd locked myself in the bathroom with Kristi to help her take her bra off. I hadn't seen her in six months. She'd just had an abortion; the father could have been one of a couple of guys. Not me. She didn't want to spoil what we had. It was starting to look to me like there wasn't much left to spoil. That had been 18 years ago.

The DJ played something by Pat Benatar. The music was loud enough to give you a kind of mental privacy. You didn't really have to pay attention to anything but the dancers. At the moment it seemed like just the thing. It had been an ugly day and there was something in me that was comforted by the sight of young, good looking women with their clothes off.

"College town," Jack said, leaning toward me so I could hear him. "Lots of local talent."

A tall blonde on the north stage unbuttoned her long-sleeved white shirt and let it hang open. Her breasts were smooth and firm and pale. Like the others she had something on the point of her nipples that made a small, golden flash every time one caught the light.

"See anybody you know?"

"Give me a break," I shouted over the music. "You saw her a couple months ago. It's been almost twenty years for me. I may not even recognize her." A waitress came by, wearing black leather jeans and a red tank top. For a second I could hear Charlie's voice telling me about her titties. I rubbed the sides of my head and the voice went away. We ordered beers, but when they came my stomach was wrapped around itself, and I had to let mine sit.

"It's got to be weird to do this for a living," I said in Jack's ear.

"Bullshit," Jack said. "You think they're not getting off on it?"

He pointed to the south stage. A brunette in high heels had let an overweight man in sideburns and a western shirt tuck a dollar into the side of her bikini bottoms. He talked earnestly to her with just the start of an embarrassed smile. She had to keep leaning closer to hear him. Finally she nodded and turned around. She bent over and grabbed her ankles. His face was about the height of the backs of her knees. She was smiling like she'd just seen somebody else's baby do something cute. After a few seconds she stood up again, and the man went back to his table.

"What was that about?" I asked Jack.

"Power, man," he said. "God, I love women. I just love 'em."

"Your problem is you don't know the difference between love and sex."

"Yeah? What is it? Come on, I want to know." The music was too loud to argue with him. I shook my head. "See? You don't know either."

The brunette pushed her hair back with both hands, chin up, fingers spread wide, and it reminded me of Kristi. The theatricality of it. She'd played one of Tennessee Williams' affected Southern bitches once, and it had been almost too painful to watch. Almost.

"Come on," I said, grabbing Jack's sleeve. "It's been swell, but let's get out of here. I don't need to see her. I'm better off with the fantasy."

Jack didn't say anything. He just pointed with his chin to the stage behind me.

She had on a leopard skin leotard. She had been a dark blonde in high school but now her hair was brown and short. She'd put on a little weight, not much. She stretched in front of the mirrored wall, and the DJ played the Pretenders.

I felt this weird, possessive kind of pride, watching her. That and lust. I'd been married for eight years and the worst thing I'd ever done was kiss an old girl friend on New Year's Eve and stare longingly at the pictures in *Playboy*. But this was real, this was happening.

The song finished and another one started and she pulled one strap down on the leotard. I remembered the first time I'd seen her breasts. I was 15. I'd joined the Liberal Religious Youth at the Unitarian Church because she went there Sunday afternoons. Sometimes we would skip the program and sneak off into the deserted Sunday school classrooms and there, in the twilight, surrounded by crayon drawings on manila paper, she would stretch out on the linoleum and let me lie on top of her and feel the maddening pressure of her pelvis and smell the faint, clinically erotic odor of peroxide in her hair.

She showed me her breasts on the golf course next door. We had jumped the fence, and we lay in a sandtrap so no one would see us. There was a little light from the street, but not enough for real color. It was like a black and white movie when I played it back in my mind.

They were fuller now, hung a little lower and flatter, but I remembered the small, pale nipples. She pulled the other strap down, turned her back, rotating her hips as she stripped down to a red G-string. Somebody held a dollar out to her. I wanted to go over there and tell him that I knew her.

Jack kept poking me in the ribs. "Well? Well?"

"Be cool," I said. I had been watching the traffic pattern and I knew that after the song, she would take a break and then get up on the other stage. It took a long time, but I wasn't tense about it. I'm just going to say hi, I thought. And that's it.

The song was over and she walked down the stairs at the end of the stage, throwing the leotard around her shoulders. I got up, having a little trouble with the chair, and walked over to her.

"Kristi," I said. "It's Dave McKenna."

"Oh my *God!*" She was in my arms. Her skin was hot from the lights and

I could smell her deodorant. I was suddenly dizzy, aware of every square inch where our bodies touched. "Do you still hate me?" she said as she pulled away.

"What?" There was so much I'd forgotten. The twang in her voice. The milk chocolate color of her eyes. The beauty mark over her right cheekbone. The flirtatious look up through the lashes that now had a desperate edge to it.

"The last time I saw you, you called me a bitch. It was after that party at your teacher's house."

"No, I ... believe me, it wasn't like..."

"Listen, I'm on again," she said. "Where are you?"

"We're right over there."

"Oh Christ, you didn't bring your wife with you? I heard you were married."

"No, it's..."

"I got to run, sugar, wait for me."

I went back to the table.

"You rascal," Jack said. "Why didn't you just slip it to her on the spot?"

"Shut up, Jack, will you?"

"Ooooh, touchy."

I watched her dance. She was no movie star. Her face was a little hard, and even the heavy makeup didn't hide all the lines. But none of that mattered. What mattered was the way she moved, the kind of puckered smile that said yes, I want it too.

SHE SAT DOWN with us when she was finished. She seemed to be all hands, touching me on the arm, biting on a fingernail, gesturing in front of her face.

She was dancing three times a week, which was all they would schedule her for any more. The money was good, and she didn't mind the work, especially here where it wasn't too rowdy. Jack raised his eyebrows at me to say, see? She got by with some modeling and some "scuffling" which I assumed meant turning tricks. Her mother was still in Dallas and had sent Kristi clippings the couple of times I got my name in the paper.

"She always liked me," I said.

"She liked you the best of all of them. You were a gentleman."

"Maybe too much of one."

"It was why I loved you." She was wearing the leotard again but she might as well have been naked. I was beginning to be afraid of her, so I reminded myself that nothing had happened yet, nothing *had* to happen, that I wasn't committed to anything. I pushed my beer over to her and she drank about half of it. "It gets hot up there," she said. "You wouldn't believe. Sometimes you think you're going to pass out, but you got to keep smiling."

"Are you married?" I asked her. "Were you ever?"

"Once. It lasted two whole months. The shitheel knocked me up and then split."

"What happened?"

"I kept the kid. He's four now."

"What's his name?"

"Stoney. He's a cute little bastard. I got a neighbor watches him when I'm out, and I do the same for hers. He keeps me going sometimes." She drank the rest of the beer. "What about you?"

"I got a little boy too. Jeffrey. He's seven."

"Just the one?"

"I don't think the marriage could handle more than one kid," I said.

"It's an old story," Jack said. "If your wife puts you through law school, the marriage breaks up. It just took Dave a little longer than most."

"You're getting divorced?" she asked.

"I don't know. Maybe." She nodded. I guess she didn't need to ask for details. Marriages come apart every day.

"I'm on again in a little," she said. "Will you still be here when I get back?" She did what she could to make it sound casual.

"I got an early day tomorrow," I said.

"Sure. It was good to see you. Real good."

The easiest thing seemed to be to get out a pen and an old business card. "Give me your phone number. Maybe I can get loose another night."

She took the pen, but she kept looking at me. "Sure," she said.

"YOU'RE AN IDIOT," Jack said. "Why didn't you go home with her?"

I watched the streetlights. My jacket smelled like cigarettes, and my head had started to hurt.

"That gorgeous piece of ass says to you, 'Ecstasy?' and Dave says, 'No thanks.' What the hell's the matter with you? Alice make you leave your dick in the safe deposit box?"

"Jack," I said, "will you shut the fuck up?" The card with her number on it was in the inside pocket of the jacket. I could feel it there, like a cool fingernail against my flesh.

JACK WENT BACK to his room to crash a little after midnight. I couldn't sleep. I put on the headphones and listened to Robert Johnson, "King of the Delta Blues Singers." There was something about his voice. He had this deadpan tone that sat down and told you what was wrong like it was no big deal. Then the voice would crack, and you could tell it was a hell of a lot worse than he was letting on.

They said the devil himself had tuned Johnson's guitar. He died in 1938, poisoned by a jealous husband. He'd made his first recordings in a hotel room in San Antonio, just another 70 miles on down I-35.

CHARLIE AND GONZALES and I took my car out to what Gonzales called the "site." The sheriff and a deputy were in a brown county station wagon behind us. Charlie sat on the passenger side and Gonzales was in the back. Charlie could have opened the door at a stoplight and been gone. He wasn't even in handcuffs. Nobody said anything about it.

We got on I-35 and Charlie said, "Go on south to the second exit after the caves." The Inner Space Caverns were just south of Georgetown, basically a single long, unspectacular tunnel that ran for miles under the highway. "I killed a girl there once. When they turned off the lights."

I nodded but I didn't say anything. That morning, before I went in to the "office," Gonzales had told me that it made Charlie angry if you let on that you didn't believe him. I was tired, and hung over from watching Jack drink, and I didn't really give a damn about Charlie's feelings.

I got off at the exit and followed the access road for a while. Charlie had his eyes closed and seemed to be thinking hard.

"Having trouble?" I asked him.

"Nah," he said. "Just didn't want to take you to the wrong one." I looked at him, and he started laughing. It was a joke. Gonzales chuckled in the back seat, and there was this cheerful kind of feeling in the car that made me want to pull over and run away.

"Nosir," Charlie said, "I sure don't suppose I'd want to do that." He grinned at me, and he knew what I was thinking, he could see the horror right there on my face. He just kept smiling. Come on, I could hear him say. Loosen up. Be one of the guys.

I wiped the sweat from my hands onto my pant legs. Finally he said, "There's a dirt road a ways ahead. Turn off on it. It'll go over a hill and then across a cattle grating. After the grating is a stand of trees to the left. You'll want to park up under 'em."

How can he do this? I thought. He's got to know there's nothing there. Or does he? When we don't turn anything up, what's he going to do? Are they going to wish they'd cuffed him after all? The sheriff knew what I was up to, but none of the others did. Would Gonzales turn on me for betraying Charlie?

The road did just what Charlie said it would. We parked the cars under the trees and the deputy and I got shovels out of the sheriff's trunk. The trees were oaks, and their leaves were tiny and very pale green.

"It would be over here," Charlie said. He stood on a patch of low ground, covered with clumps of Johnson grass. "Not too deep."

He was right. She was only about six or eight inches down. The deputy had a body bag, and he tried to move her into it, but she kept coming apart. There wasn't much left but a skeleton and a few rags.

And the braces. Still shining, clinging to the teeth of the skull like a metal smile.

On the way back to Georgetown, we passed a woman on the side of the road. She was staring into the hood of her car. She looked like she was about to cry. Charlie turned all the way around in his seat to watch her as we drove by.

"There's just victims ever'where," Charlie said. There was a sadness in his voice I didn't believe. "The highway's full of 'em. Kids, hitchhikers, waitresses ... You ever pick one up?"

"No," I said, but it wasn't true. It was in Dallas. I was home for spring break. It was the end of the sixties. She had on a green dress. Nothing happened. But she had smiled at me and put one arm up on the back of the seat. I was on the way to my girlfriend's house, and I let her off a few blocks away. And that night, when I was inside her, I imagined my girlfriend with the hitchhiker's face, with her blonde hair and freckles, her slightly coarse features, the dots of sweat on her upper lip.

"But you thought about it," Charlie said. "Didn't you?"

"Listen," I said. "I've got a job to do. I just want to do it and get out of here, okay?"

"I know what you're saying," Charlie said. "Jesus forgives me, but I can't ask that of nobody else. I was just trying to get along, that's all. That's all any of us is ever trying to do."

I called Dallas collect from the sheriff's phone. He gave me a private room where I could shout if I had to. The switchboard put me through to Ricky Slatkin, Senior Assistant DA for Homicide.

"Dave, will you for Chrissake calm down. It's a coincidence. That's all. Forensics will figure out who this girl is and we'll put another 70 or 80 years on Charlie's sentence. Maybe give him another death penalty. What the hell, right? Meanwhile we'll give him another ringer."

"You give him one. I want out of this. I am fucking terrified."

"I, uh, understand you're under some stress at home these days."

"I am not at home. I'm in Georgetown, in the Williamson County Jail, and I am under some fucking stress right here. Don't you understand? He *thought* this dead girl into existence."

"What, Charlie Dean Harris is God now, is that it? Come on, Dave. Go out and have a few beers and by tomorrow it'll all make sense to you."

"HE'S EVIL, JACK," I said. We were back at his place after a pizza at Conan's. Jack had ordered a pitcher of beer and drunk it all himself. "I didn't use to believe in it, but that was before I met Charlie."

He had a women's basketball game on TV, the sound turned down to a low hum. "That's horseshit," he said. His voice was too loud. "Horseshit, Christian horseshit. They want you to believe that Evil has got a capital E, and it's sitting over there in the corner, see it? Horseshit. Evil isn't a thing. It's something that's *not* there. It's an absence. The lack of the thing that stops you from doing whatever you damn well please."

He chugged half a beer. "Your pal Charlie ain't evil. He's just damaged goods. He's just like you or me, but something died in him. You know what I'm talking about. You've felt it. First it goes to sleep, and then it dies. Like when you stand up in court and try to get a rapist off when you know he did it. You tell yourself that it's part of the game, you try to give the asshole the benefit of the doubt, hell, somebody's got to do it, right? You try to believe the girl is just some slut that changed her mind, but you can smell it. Something inside you starting to rot."

He finished the beer and threw it at a paper sack in the corner. It hit another bottle inside the sack and shattered. "Then you go home and your wife's got a goddamn headache or her period or she's asleep in front of the TV or she's not in the goddamn mood and you just want to beat the..." His right fist was clenched up so tight the knuckles were a shiny yellow. His eyes looked like open sores. He got up for another beer, and he was in the kitchen for a long time.

When he came back I said, "I'm going out." I said it without giving myself a chance to think about it.

"Kristi," Jack said. He had a fresh beer and was all right again.

"Yeah."

"You bastard! Can I smell your fingers when you get back?"

"Fuck you, Jack."

"Oh no, save it for her. She's going to use you up, you lucky bastard."

I CALLED HER from a pay phone, and she gave me directions. She was at the Royal Palms Trailer Park, near Bergstrom Air Force Base on the south end of town. It wasn't hard to find. They even had a few palm trees. There were rural-type galvanized mailboxes on posts by the gravel driveways. I found the one that said Spector and parked behind a white Dodge with six-figure mileage.

The temperature was in the sixties, but I was shaking. My shoulders kept trying to crawl up around my neck. I got out of the car. I couldn't feel my feet. Asshole, I told myself. I don't want to hear about your personal problems. You better enjoy this, or I'll fucking kill you.

I knocked on the door, and it made a kind of mute rattling sound. Kristi opened it. She was wearing a plaid bathrobe, so old I couldn't tell what the colors used to be. She stood back to let me in and said, "I didn't think you'd call."

"But I did," I said. The trailer was tiny—a living room with a green sofa and a 13-inch color TV, a kitchen the size of a short hall, a single bedroom behind it, the door open, the bed unmade. A blond-haired boy was asleep on the sofa, wrapped in an army blanket. The shelf above him was full of plays—Albee, Ionesco, Tennessee Williams. The walls were covered with photographs in dime-store frames.

A couple of them were from the drama club; one even had me in it. I was sixteen and looked maybe nine. My hair was too long in front, my chest was sucked in, and I had a stupid smirk on my face. I was looking at Kristi. Who would want to look at anything else? She had on cutoffs that had frayed up past the crease of her thighs. Her shirt was unbuttoned and tied under her breasts. Her head was back, and she was laughing. I'd always been able to make her laugh.

"You want a drink?" she whispered.

"No," I said. I turned to look at her. We weren't either of us laughing now. I reached for her, and she glanced over at the boy and shook her head. She grabbed the cuff of my shirt and pulled me gently back toward the bedroom.

It smelled of perfume and hand lotion and a little of mildew. The only light trickled in through heavy, old-fashioned Venetian blinds. She untied the bathrobe and let it fall. I kissed her, and her arms went around my neck. I touched her shoulder blades and her hair and her buttocks, and then I got out of my clothes and left them in a pile on the floor. She ran on tiptoes back to the front of the trailer and locked and chained the door. Then she came back and shut the bedroom door and lay down on the bed.

I lay down next to her. The smell and feel of her was wonderful, and at the same time it was not quite real. There were too many unfamiliar things, and it was hard to connect to the rest of my life.

Then I was on my knees between her legs, gently touching her. Her arms were spread out beside her, tangled in the sheets, her hips moving with pleasure. Only once, in high school, had she let me touch her there, in the back seat of a friend's car, her skirt up around her hips, panties to her knees, and before I had recovered from the wonder of it, she had pulled away.

But that was 18 years ago and this was now. A lot of men had touched her since then. But that was all right. She took a condom out of the nightstand and I put it on and she guided me inside her. She tried to say something, maybe it was only my name, but I put my mouth over hers to shut her up. I put both my arms around her and closed my eyes and let the heat and pleasure run up through me.

When I finished and we rolled apart she lay on top of me, pinning me to the bed. "That was real sweet," she said.

I kissed her and hugged her because I couldn't say what I was thinking. I was thinking about Charlie, remembering the earnest look on his face when he said, "It was just to have sex, that's all."

SHE WAS WIDE AWAKE and I was exhausted. She complained about the state cutting back on aid to single parents. She told me about the tiny pieces of tape she had to wear on the ends of her nipples when she danced, a weird Health Department regulation. I remembered the tiny golden flashes and fell asleep to the memory of her dancing.

Screaming woke me up. Kristi was already out of bed and headed for the living room. "It's just Stoney," she said, and I lay back down.

I woke up again a little before dawn. There was an arm around my waist, but it seemed much too small. I rolled over and saw that the little boy had crawled into bed between us.

I got up without moving him and went to the bathroom. There was no water in the toilet; when I pushed the handle a trap opened in the bottom of the bowl and a fine spray washed the sides. I got dressed, trying not to bump into anything. Kristi was asleep on the side of the bed closest to the door, her mouth open a little. Stoney had burrowed into the middle of her back.

I was going to turn around and go when a voyeuristic impulse made me open the drawer of her nightstand. Or maybe I subconsciously knew what I'd find. There was a Beeline book called *Molly's Sexual Follies,* a tube of K Y, a box of Ramses lubricated condoms, a few used Kleenex. An emery board, a finger puppet, one hoop earring. A short-barreled Colt .32 revolver.

I GOT TO THE JAIL at nine in the morning. The woman at the visitor's window recognized me and buzzed me back. Gonzales was at his desk. He looked up when I walked in and said, "I didn't know you was coming in today."

"I just had a couple of quick questions for Charlie," I said. "Only take a second."

"Did you want to use the office…?"

"No, no point. If I could just talk to him in his cell for a couple of minutes, that would be great."

Gonzales got the keys. Charlie had a cell to himself, five by ten feet, white-painted bars on the long wall facing the corridor. There were Bibles and religious tracts on his cot, a few paintings hanging on the wall. "Maybe you can get Charlie to show you his pictures," Gonzales said. A stool in the corner had brushes and tubes of paint on the top.

"You painted these?" I asked Charlie. My voice sounded fairly normal, all things considered.

"Yessir, I did."

"They're pretty good." They were landscapes with trees and horses, but no people.

"Thank you kindly."

"You can just call for me when you're ready," Gonzales said. He went out and locked the door.

"I thought you'd be back," Charlie said. "Was there something else you wanted to ask me?" He sat on the edge of the cot, forearms on his knees.

I didn't say anything. I took the Colt out of the waistband of my pants and pointed it at him. I'd already looked it over on the drive up and there were bullets in all six cylinders. My hand was shaking so I steadied it with my left and fired all six rounds into his head and chest.

I hadn't noticed all the background noises until they stopped, the typewriters and the birds and somebody singing upstairs. Charlie stood up and walked over to where I was standing. The revolver clicked on an empty shell.

"You can't kill me," Charlie said with his droopy-eyed smile. "You can't never kill me." The door banged open at the end of the hall. "You can't kill me because I'm inside you."

I dropped the gun and locked my hands behind my head. Gonzales stuck his head around the corner. He was squinting. He had his gun out and he looked terrified. Charlie and I stared back at him calmly.

"It's okay, Ernie," Charlie said. "No harm done. Mr. McKenna was just having him a little joke."

CHARLIE TOLD GONZALES the gun was loaded with blanks. They had to believe him because there weren't any bulletholes in the cell. I told them I'd bought the gun off a defendant years ago, that I'd had it in the car.

They called Dallas and Ricky asked to talk to me. "There's going to be an inquiry," he said. "No way around it."

"Sure there is," I said. "I quit. I'll send it to you in writing. I'll put it in the mail today. Express."

"You need some help, Dave. You understand what I'm saying to you here? *Professional* help. Think about it. Just tell me you'll think about it."

Gonzales was scared and angry and wanted me charged with smuggling weapons into the jail. The sheriff knew it wasn't worth the headlines, and by suppertime I was out.

Jack had already heard about it through some kind of legal grapevine. He thought it was funny. We skipped dinner and went down to the bars on Sixth Street. I couldn't drink anything. I was afraid of going numb, or letting down my guard. But Jack made up for me. As usual.

"Kristi called me today," Jack said. "I told her I didn't know but what you might be going back to Dallas today. Just a kind of feeling I had."

"I'm not going back," I said. "But it was the right thing to tell her."

"Not what it was cracked up to be, huh?"

"Oh yeah," I said. "That and much, much more."

For once he let it go. "You mean you're not going back tonight or not going back period?"

"Period," I said. "My job's gone, I pissed that away this morning. I'll get something down here. I don't care what. I'll pump gas. I'll fucking wait tables. You can draw up the divorce papers, and I'll sign them."

"Just like that?"

"Just like that."

"What's Alice going to say?"

"I don't know if she'll even notice. She can have the goddamn house and her car and the savings. All of it. All I want is some time with Jeffrey. As much as I can get. Every week if I can."

"Good luck."

"I've got to have it. I don't want him growing up screwed up like the rest of us. I've got stuff I've got to tell him. He's going to need help. All of us are. Jack, goddamn it, are you listening to me?"

He wasn't. He was staring at the Heart video on the bar's big screen TV, at the blonde guitarist. "Look at that," Jack said. "Sweet suffering Jesus. Couldn't you just fuck that to death?"

STEAM ENGINE TIME

T HE KID TURNED UP the gaslight in his room. The pink linen wallpaper still looked a little dingy. Ever since J. L. Driskill had opened his
new place in December of '86, the Avenue Hotel had been going downhill.

There was a framed picture on the wall and the Kid had been staring at it
for an hour. It was an engraving of a Pawnee Indian. The Indian's head was
shaved except for a strip of hair down the middle. There were feathers in what
hair he had, and it hung down over his forehead.

He compared it to what he saw in the mirror. He was pretty badly hung over
from jimson weed and unlabeled whiskey the night before. His fine yellow hair
went every which way, and his eyes were mostly red. He got out his straight
razor, stropped it a couple of times on his boot, and grabbed a hank of hair.

What the hell, he thought.

It was harder to do than he thought it would be, and he ended up with a lot
of tiny cuts all over his head. When he was done, he took the razor and used it
to cut the bottom off his black leather duster coat. He hacked it off just below
the waist. For a couple of seconds he wondered why in hell he was doing it,
wondered if he'd lost his mind. Then he put it on and looked in the mirror
again, and this time he liked what he saw.

It was just right.

THERE'D BEEN A SALOON at the corner of Congress Avenue and Pecan
Street pretty much from the time Austin changed its name from Waterloo
and became the capital of Texas. These days it was called the Crystal Bar.
There was an overhang right the way round the building, with an advertise-
ment for Tom Moore's 10 cent cigars painted on the bricks on the Pecan
Street side. The fabric of the carriages at the curb puffed out in the mild
autumn breeze.

The mule cars were gone and the street cars were electric now, thanks to
the dam that opened in May of the year before. They were calling Austin "the
coming great manufacturing center of the Southwest." It was the Kid's first big
city. The electric and telegraph wires strung all over downtown looked like the
history of the future, block-printed across the sky.

The Kid was a half-hour late for a two-o'clock appointment with the
Crystal's manager. The manager's name was Matthews, and he wore a bow tie

and a starched collar and a tailormade suit. "Do you know 'Grand-Father's Clock is Too Tall for the Shelf?'" Matthews asked the Kid.

The Kid had kept his hat on. "Why sure I do." He took his steel-string Martin guitar out of the case and played it quiet with his fingers.

> *It was bought on the morn*
> *Of the day he was born*
> *And was always his treasure and pride*
> *But it stopped—short—*
> *Never to go again*
> *When the old man died*

I'm going to God-damned puke, the Kid thought.

"Not much of a voice," Matthews said.

"All I want is to pass the hat," the Kid said. "Sir."

"Not much of a hat, either. All right, son, you can try it. But if the crowd don't like it, you're out. Understand?"

"Yes sir," the Kid said. "I understand."

THE KID CAME BACK at nine that night. He'd bought some hemp leaves from a Mexican boy and smoked them, but they didn't seem to help his nerves. It felt like Gentleman Jim Corbett was trying to punch his way out of the Kid's chest.

The ceiling must have been thirty feet high. The top half of the room was white with cigar smoke and the bottom half smelled like farts and spilled beer. Over half the tables and all but a couple of seats at the bar were full. The customers were all men, of course. All white men. They said ladies dared not walk on the east side of the Avenue.

Nobody paid him much attention, least of all the waitresses. The Kid counted three of them. One of them was not all that old or used-up looking.

Some fat bastard in sleeve garters pounded out "The Little Old Cabin in the Lane" on a piano with a busted soundboard. The Kid knew the words. They talked about the days when "de darkies used to gather round de door/When dey used to dance an sing at night." If there was anything going to keep him from turning yellow and going back to the hotel, that had to be it.

There was a wooden stage about three feet wide and four feet high that ran across the back of the room. Just big enough for some fat tart to strut out on and hike up the back of her skirts. The Kid set the last vacant bar stool up on the stage with his guitar case. He climbed up and sat on the stool. It put him just high enough up to strangle on the cloud of smoke.

The piano player finished or gave up. Anyway, he quit playing and went over to the bar. The Kid took out his guitar. He had a cord with a hook on the end that came up under the back and let him carry the weight of it on his neck. It was what they called a parlor guitar, the biggest one C. F. Martin and Sons made. With his copper plectrum and those steel strings it was loud as Jesus coming back. Still the Kid would have liked a bigger sound box. It would have made it even louder.

Somebody at the bar said, "Do you know 'Grand-Father's Clock'?"

"How about 'Ta-ra-ra-boom-de-ay'?" said somebody further down. The man was drunk and started singing it himself.

"No, 'Grand-Father's Clock!'" said another one. "'Grand-Father's Clock!'"

The Kid took his hat off.

Maybe the whole bar didn't go quiet, but there was a circle of it for thirty or forty feet. The Kid looked at their faces and saw that he had made a mistake. It was the kind of mistake he might not live through.

There were upwards of fifty men looking at him. They all wore narrow brim hats and dark suits and the kind of thick mustaches that seemed to be meant to hide their mouths in case they ever accidentally smiled.

They were none of them smiling now.

The Kid didn't see any guns. But then none of them looked like they needed a gun.

The Kid played a run down the bass strings and hit an E7 as hard as he could with his copper pick. "'Rolled and I tumbled,'" he sang, "'cried the whole night long.'" He was so scared his throat was swollen shut and his voice came out a croak. But his hand moved, slapping the rhythm out of the guitar. The craziness came up in him at the sound of it, to be playing that music here, in front of these people, rubbing their faces in it, like it or not.

"'Rolled and I tumbled, lord,'" he sang, "'cried the whole night long.'" He jumped off the stool and stomped the downbeat with his bootheel. "'Woke up this morning, did not know right from wrong.'"

He pounded through the chords again twice. He couldn't hold still. He'd seen music do that to folks, lived with it all his life, sharecropping in a black county with the families just one generation out of slavery, seeing them around their bonfires on Saturday nights and in their churches Sunday mornings, but this was the first time it had ever happened to him.

It was time for a verse and he was so far gone all he could sing was "Na na na na" to the melody line. When it came around again he sang,

Well the engine whistlin'
Callin' Judgment Day

I hear that train a whistlin'
Callin' Judgment Day
When that train be pass by
Take all I have away

Through the chords again. It was play or die or maybe both. The song roared off the tracks and blew up on B9. The last notes hung in the air for a long time. It was so quiet the Kid could hear the wooden sidewalk creak as somebody walked by outside.

"Thank you," the Kid said.

One at a time they turned away and started talking to each other again. A man in a plaid suit with watery blue eyes stared at him for another few seconds and then hawked and spat on the floor.

"Thank you," the Kid said. "I'd now like to do one I wrote myself. It's called 'Twentieth Century Man.' It's about how we got to change with the times and not just let time get past us. It goes a little like this here." He started to hit the first chord but his right hand wouldn't move. He looked down. Matthews had a hold of it.

"Out," Matthews said.

"I was just getting 'em warmed up," the Kid said.

"Get the hell out," Matthews said, "or by thunder if they don't kill you I'll do it myself."

"I guess this means I don't pass the hat," the Kid said.

HE SAT ON the board sidewalk and wiped the sweat off the guitar strings. When he looked up the not-so-old waitress was leaning on the batwings, watching him.

"Was it supposed to be some kind of minstrel song?" she asked. "Like the Ethiopian Serenaders?"

"No," the Kid said. "It wasn't no minstrel song."

"Ain't heard nothin' like it before."

"Not supposed to have. Things everybody heard before is for shit. 'The Little Old Cabin in the Lane.' Songs like that make people the way they are."

"What way is that?"

"Ignorant."

"What happened to your hair?"

"Cut it."

"Why?"

"So it'd be different."

"Same with your coat?"

"That's right."

"You sure like things different."

"I guess I do."

"Where'd your song come from?"

"Back home."

"Where's that?"

"Mississippi."

"Well," she said. "I sort of liked it."

The Kid put the guitar back in the case. He shut the lid and closed the latches. "Thanks," he said. "You want to fuck?"

She looked at him like he was a dog just tried to pee on her shoe. She made the batwings bang together as she spun away hard and clomped across the saloon.

THEY'D LAID AUSTIN OUT in a square. Streets named after Texas rivers went north and south, trees went east and west. The south side of the square lay along the Colorado River so they called it Water Avenue. There was West Avenue and North Avenue and East Avenue.

East of East Avenue was colored town. The Kid carried his guitar east down Bois d'Arc Street, pronounced BO-dark in Texas. Past East Avenue there weren't street lights any more. Babies sat barefoot in the street and there was music but it didn't seem to be coming from anywhere in particular. The air smelled like burned fat.

The Kid finally saw a bar and went inside. This time it got quiet for him right away. "Son," the man behind the bar said, "I think you in the wrong part of town."

"I want to play some music," the Kid said.

"Ain't no music here."

"They call it 'blue music.' You ever hear of it?"

The man smiled. "Didn't know music came in no colors. Now you run along, before you make a mistake and hurt you self."

HE WENT BACK to his hotel long enough to pack his bag and then he went down to the train station. He sat on a bench there and read a paper somebody had left behind. It was called *The Rolling Stone.* It seemed to be a lot of smart aleck articles about books and artists. There was a story by somebody called himself O. Henry. The Kid didn't find anything in there about music.

But then, what would you write about a song like "Grand-Father's Clock" or "The Little Old Cabin in the Lane"?

An old colored man pushed a broom back and forth, looking over at the Kid every once in a while. "Waitin' for a train?" the old man finally asked.

"That's right."

"Ain't no train for two hour."

"I know that."

He pushed his broom some more. "That your git-tar?" he asked after while.

"It is," the Kid said.

"Mind if I have me a look?"

The Kid took it out of the case and handed it to him. The old man sat next to the Kid on the bench. "Pretty thing, ain't it?"

"You play?" the Kid asked him.

"Naw," the old man said. He held the guitar like it was made out of soap and might squirt out of his hands if he squeezed down. "Well. Maybe I used to. Just a little. Ain't touched one in years, now."

"Go ahead," the Kid said. The old man shook his head and tried to hand the guitar back. The Kid wouldn't go for it. "I think maybe you could still play some."

"Think so?" the old man said. "Well, maybe."

He put his right thumb on the low E string and just let it sit there. After a while he fitted his left hand around the neck and pushed at the strings a little. "Oooo wee," he said. "*Steel* strings."

"That's right," the Kid said.

The old man closed his eyes. His head started to go back and for a second the Kid thought maybe the old man was drunk and fixing to pass out. Then the old man took a jack knife out of his pocket and set it on the knee of his jeans.

It made the Kid uncomfortable. He didn't think the old man was actually going to knife him over the guitar. But he couldn't see any other reason for the thing to be out.

The old man didn't open the blade. Instead he fitted the handle between the ring finger and little finger of his left hand. Then he ran it up and down the strings. It made an eerie sound, like a dying animal or a train whistle gone crazy.

Then the old man started to play.

The Kid had never heard anything like it. The notes howled and screamed and cried out bloody murder. The old man played till his fingers bled and the high E string broke in two.

When it was over, the old man sat for a second, breathing heavy. Then he handed the guitar back. "Sorry about that string, son."

"Got me another one." Tears ran down the Kid's face. He didn't want to wipe them off. He thought maybe if he just left them alone, the old man might not notice. "Where ... where did you learn to do that?"

"Just somethin' I figured out for my own self. Don't mean nothin'."

"Don't mean nothin'? Why, that was the most beautiful thing I ever heard in my life."

"You know anything about steam engines?"

The Kid stared at him. A couple of seconds went by. "What?"

"Steam engines. Like on that locomotive you gonna be ridin'."

The Kid just shook his head.

"Well, they had all the pieces of that steam engine lyin' around for hundreds of years. Wasn't nobody knew what to do with 'em. Then one day five, six people up and invent a steam engine, all at the same time. Ain't no explanation for it. It was just steam engine time."

"I don't get it," the Kid said. "What are you tryin' to say?"

The old man stood up and pointed at the guitar. "Just that you lookin' for a life of misery, boy. Because the time for that thing ain't here yet."

JUST BEFORE DAWN, as the train headed west toward New Mexico, it started to rain. The Kid woke up to lightning stitched across the sky. It made him think about electric streetcars and electric lights. If electricity could make a light brighter, why couldn't it make a guitar louder? Then they'd have to listen.

He drifted back to sleep and dreamed of electric guitars.

KINGS OF THE AFTERNOON

FROM SOMEWHERE BEYOND the ragged palm trees came the scream-ing of sea birds. He lay with his head in Kristen's lap, watching the lines around her mouth. Her voice, with its rounded European vowels, seemed to mingle with the hissing of the sea.

"...I had crawled to the top of the hill," she said, "and the water was close behind me. All I could smell was the burning of the bodies, and I knew that all of California was finished. They found me there, not conscious, and I was in a dream."

Landon closed his eyes.

"In the dream I was sleeping," she said, "and I was wrapped in a sort of blanket, soft, silver colored. From a distance I seemed to be watching, and the sun was up but making no shadows, and nothing seemed to be lighted, you know, but sort of glowed. Someone was carrying me, I could feel the hands, and they took me to the edge of a water. I remember the dark of it, and a mountain out in the middle. There was waiting a boat, and other hands reach-ing up for me. The hands, you know, were not human, but like fingers made out of rocks, and the body too was rough and lumpy. I had not then even seen the men inside the saucers, but I knew what they looked like.

"A big sail the boat had, black and stretching, but there was no wind. The hands took me and the boat moved away from the land.

"The sea was thick and clinging and full of odd lights."

Landon stirred. A seagull stumbled across the beach toward them, its body coated with dark, glistening oil. The bird rattled its wings with a noise like gunfire. Landon sat up, watched the bird stagger and fall into the sand, one dark, empty eye fixed on him. Landon pulled his Colt and fired. The impact flung the bird into a ditch beside the highway.

He lit a cigarette, the match trembling in his hand. The smoke hurt his lungs and he coughed as he stood up.

"Let's go," he said.

ALONG THE SIDES of the highway, abandoned cars lay rusting in the sun. The sky was free of saucers, and the wind carried the smells of the sea.

Landon drifted into a doze, waking as Kristen pulled into a weathered café beside the road. The big Pontiac convertible skidded on the gravel and jerked to a stop between two plastic execucars.

"Where are we?" he asked through a yawn. The heat had glued his black sport jacket to his shoulders.

Kristen shrugged. "Here." A hand-painted sign over the door read DON's CALIFORNIA STYLE DINER and a card in the window added "Yes We're OPEN."

The smells of grease and cigarettes drifted through the screen door. Landon opened it and stood for a moment framed by the doorway, leaving his sunglasses on, making no effort to hide the holstered Colt at his side.

A few executives lingered in back, sketching on their napkins. Kristen led the way to a booth, and Landon sat down, his sweat-damp trousers squealing against the red vinyl. A boy in a soiled apron took their order, then went back to a row of beer mugs on the bar.

"Your eyes," Kristen said, "they still hurt...?"

He nodded. A close call with a saucer the day before had nearly blinded him, the road melting into a steaming gash in front of him. He had fought the car off the road, tears streaming down his face, as the saucer whipped away, leaving a mile-wide path of fire behind it.

Kristen, sitting with her legs stretched out on the seat, touched his arm. She pointed toward the kid at the bar, who had started to juggle the glasses he was supposed to be polishing. Landon took off his sunglasses. The kid was no more than five-eight, wearing boots, a T-shirt, and dirty jeans. His hair was shaggy and stood up like a brush on top, tapering into long sideburns. Light flashed off tortoise shell glasses that hid his eyes. A cigarette hung from his mouth.

The act was meant to be casual, but Landon sensed a desperation behind it, a hunger for attention and for something else as well. The executives had gone quiet, and there was a thump as one of the glasses hit the table on its way back up. Kristen suddenly caught her breath and then Landon saw it too, fragments of the shattered glass hanging above the kid's head.

The kid stepped aside, catching the other two glasses, and the fragments pinged harmlessly on the linoleum. The kid casually dried his hands and reached for a broom to sweep up the mess. Landon noticed the red stain on the towel, the trembling in the kid's fingers, the odd sensuality of his gestures.

The kid brought their hamburgers, puncturing the beer cans with sharp, graceful stabs of the opener. Landon couldn't help but notice the way Kristen watched the kid. He put his sunglasses back on.

"Bring one for yourself if you like," Kristen said. The boy nodded. He was older than Landon had thought at first, maybe early twenties.

"You have a name?" Landon asked.

"Byron," the kid said. He ate a potato chip off Landon's plate, then spun away.

"Hey," one of the executives said as he passed. "Bring me a beer, will you?"

Byron smiled at him. "Fuck off," he said casually. He brought a beer back to Landon's table as the executives lined up meekly at the counter, perspiring in their dark grey suits. A small man with sores on his face came out of the kitchen and accepted their plastic cards with a conciliatory smile.

"Assholes never tip anyway," Byron said. He turned a chair around and sat with his head resting on his folded arms. The executives filed out and Landon caught the odor of hot plastic as they started their electric cars.

"So," Byron said. "You cats are like ... outlaws?" He kept looking back at Kristen's face, again and again. He rubbed the back of his thumb under his nose and said, "I seen your car."

"That's right," Landon said.

"I mean," the boy said, a sudden urgency screwing up his face, "it's like ... if I ... I mean..." Then he spun out of the chair and out the front door.

"He's insane," Landon said.

"He is beautiful. Can we keep him?"

Landon shrugged and finished his beer. "If you want him badly enough."

As they started for the door the man with the sores said, "Ain't y'all planning to pay for that food?"

Landon turned so the light from the doorway glinted on his Colt. "Just put it on our bill."

"I never seen you before," the man whined. "I got to make a living too. I'm on *your* side."

"Tell it to Robin Hood," Landon said. "I'm only in it for the money."

They found Byron leaning against the front of the building, one foot planted into the wall. He'd taken off his apron and had a red zip jacket over one shoulder. He lit a cigarette and said, "Where you headed?"

Landon pointed north. "New Elay."

The kid took the cigarette out of his mouth and said something to it, too quietly for Landon to hear.

"What?"

"Take me with you."

Landon didn't like the edge of hysteria in the kid's voice. Before he could say anything, Kristen stepped in front of him and got behind the wheel. "Get in," she said to both of them.

THE LAND WAS GUTTED and torn for miles in all directions, rolling down to the oily Arizona coastline. Stucco crumbled from the walls of the shattered building, and vines tore the red tiles from the roof.

Behind a growth of acacias lay a burned-out neon sign that read MOTEL CALIFORNIA. Landon leaned against the sign, watching Byron. The kid walked in circles around the parking lot, sniffing the dusty air and squinting up at the sky. He squatted at the edge of the moss-filled swimming pool and tossed pebbles into the murky green water. The boy had been with them for two days now and hardly said a word.

"Come on," Landon said. "Let's see if we can find you a room."

They worked down the row of cabins until they found one with most of the furniture still intact. Landon kicked idly at a pile of rat droppings and poked into the corners with a broken chair leg. The air held the tang of mold, urine, sour linen. He wound a window open and let in the gritty ocean breeze. A cough gently shook his chest.

Byron stretched out across the bare mattress and locked his hands behind his head. A smile stretched his cheek muscles into tight cords. "Now what?" he asked.

ON THE HORIZON were the executive office towers, massive, opaque, impenetrable. They'd passed the residence blocks on their way into New Elay, equally fortified and remote. The buildings in between, Landon saw, had taken their share of punishment from the saucers. Shattered glass and collapsed walls littered the sidewalks; glittering trenches of fused concrete cut the streets.

Kristen drove at high speed, weaving through the lines of plastic cars and fuming executives. Pedestrians, most of them in rags, stared at Landon with blank acceptance. A pack of children chased a dog with a mixture of malice and desperation. An old woman squatted to urinate outside an abandoned storefront.

Landon took a Peacemaker in a worn leather holster out of the glove compartment. Turning sideways in the car seat he showed Byron how to load and fire it. The kid wound his fingers slowly around the grip, his eyebrows contorted in an agony of concentration. Landon watched as the gun seemed to be absorbed into the boy's hand.

Byron stood up on the back seat of the convertible and took aim at one of the execucars. The driver turned pale and swerved across the road, glancing off the cars on either side of him. Byron rolled his head back and laughed at the sky.

They pulled up in front of a heavily barred store window. A pair of steer's horns were mounted above it. "A meat market?" Byron asked.

"Lots of cash, pal," Landon said. "The liquor stores are too dangerous anymore." He got out and looked back at the kid. Byron had taken his glasses off and was carefully putting them into the pocket of his red windbreaker. Without the glasses, the kid's moist, deepset eyes gave him an unearthly beauty. He vaulted over the side of the car, holding the pistol as if he'd been born with it.

"Just stay out of the way," Landon said. "No grandstanding. Point the gun but don't shoot it, all right?"

Kristen led the way in, carrying a Luger and a cloth sack. Standing in the doorway, Landon kept his own gun in casual view. He could smell the raw meat, his stomach reacting with reluctant hunger. The customers shifted quietly out of the way as Kristen emptied the cash box. Byron stood in the center of the room, radiating quiet menace.

Kristen signaled, and Landon went back out to the car. The crowd had more than doubled in size in the minute or so they'd been there. Up and down the block Landon saw people moving toward him. He started the car and began inching forward. Kristen pushed through the crowd and got in the passenger seat, holding the sack of coins in her left hand. Then she looked back and shouted, "Hurry up! What are you doing?"

Byron was halfway up the metal grille that covered the front window. "He's taking his trophy," Landon said. The kid swung onto a metal bracket and began to tug at the huge pair of horns.

"Son of a bitch!" he yelled, the horns giving way under him. He dropped ten feet to the sidewalk, landing in a crouch, one hand slapping the cement. The other still held the horns.

He vaulted into the back of the car, holding the horns over his head. Landon was astonished to see a few smiles and raised arms in the crowd. He leaned on the car horn, pumping the clutch, moving forward a foot at a time. The crowd stared at Byron.

Just as he began to make some headway a frail blonde teenager stepped directly in front of the car. She looked hypnotized. Landon swerved, brushing her aside with the hood of the Pontiac. "Idiots," he said. "It's their money we just stole."

He could see Byron, framed in the rear view mirror, holding the horns over his head.

FROM THE DOOR of the cabin Landon could see Byron slumped in a corner, mumbling and nodding rapidly. A bottle of pills was open by his foot, and his hands played nervously over a pair of bongos. A girl was stretched out on the mattress, writhing slowly with some internal pain or pleasure. The sight of her soft breasts and rumpled brassiere, her long legs tangled in the sheets, gave Landon a pang of formless longing.

"So fucking high, man," Byron mumbled, eyes swollen nearly shut. "This shit, this shit ... so goddamned high..." His fingers twitched and fluttered over the surface of the drums, coaxing out a shallow, frantic rhythm. "Spinning ... falling ... crashing ... saucers crashing, and like..."

Landon turned away. "Where is she?" the kid screamed. Landon walked to the beach, the hot sand working in between his toes, foam spattering his black coat and trousers. Behind him he could still hear Byron railing against the saucers and screaming for his mother.

The day was clear enough that Landon could see shadowy mountains across Mojave Bay. Among the litter of plastic and rubber on the beach he found a bleached skull and the bones of a single grasping hand. A fit of coughing took him and he crouched in the sand until it passed.

From the distance came a low vibration, like pedal notes on an organ. The flat disk of a saucer dipped into the horizon and disappeared.

THE MOTEL DRIVEWAY was crisscrossed with tire tracks. The smell of gasoline hung in the air. Byron's motorcycle was gone and Landon had a sense of foreboding as he pulled up in front of Kristen's room.

"Where is he?" he asked, not getting out of the car.

She looked worn, the lines of her face all pointing downward. "Gone," she said. "With four, five others. On motorbikes. They are after the saucer, I think."

"What saucer?"

"On the radio, it was. They say one low along the coast was flying, maybe in trouble."

"Christ," Landon said.

The tracks turned south along the coast road. Landon swung the Pontiac around after them. Unless they stayed on the highway, there was no chance of catching them. Landon let the landscape on either side of the road melt into a yellow blur.

Eventually he realized that he'd been hearing a low screaming noise for some time. It seemed to be coming from ahead of him. Finally he saw a faint glow off to the east and pulled over. He got out and slammed the door, the noise inaudible over the throbbing whine.

The source of light lay over the next dune. Landon put on his sunglasses and drew his Colt. The sound carried a pulsing resonance that he could feel in his belly. He went over the top of the dune, his left hand pressed against the side of his head.

A saucer perched on narrow stilts over the sand. Landon had never been so close to one before. Its sheer size was overwhelming, at least a hundred feet in diameter. The entire surface glowed with a milky light.

Five men on motorcycles circled the saucer. They wore long hair and sleeveless denim jackets, their faces sunburned and expressionless. As Landon watched they wrestled their machines over the same rutted circles in the sand, again and again.

The riders ignored Landon as he walked toward the single abandoned motorcycle parked under the edge of the saucer. He climbed a flight of stairs into
the underside of the ship, holding his gun like a talisman in front of him. The
ladder opened into a small corridor, and Landon found himself in a curving
passageway that followed the outside wall. The roar of the motorcycles and
the high-pitched whine had both faded once he was inside, and now he could
hear the muffled tones of a human voice.

The luminous wall to his left suddenly gave out and Landon looked into
the control room of the saucer. The walls were covered with cryptic designs,
and the air smelled like mushrooms. In the center of the floor was a raised
platform; two figures were struggling behind it. Landon ran around the
platform and pulled Byron off the alien creature, pinning his arms behind his
back. Byron fought him for a full two minutes, the power of his anger seemingly endless. At last his strength gave out, and Landon tied the kid's arms with
his own jacket.

The gnarled alien watched the process with black, expressionless eyes. Landon
caught himself staring at the creature, reminded of a crumbling sandstone sculpture. He forced himself to look away and wrestled Byron out of the saucer.

The other riders were still circling. The pitch of the saucer's whine climbed
threateningly and Landon sensed it was about to explode. Byron struggled free,
shrugged out of the jacket, and ran for his motorcycle.

"Leave it," Landon shouted, unable even to hear himself. It was hopeless.
He ran for the shelter of the nearest dune. He got over it and slid down the
far side on hands and knees. He burrowed into the loose sand and faced away
from the saucer, coughing and gasping for air. In the last moment before the
explosion, he saw Byron's motorcycle silhouetted against the sky. It shot over
the crest of the dune and tumbled gently into the sand at Landon's feet, throwing the kid harmlessly to one side.

Another motorcycle followed, and was caught in midair by the full force
of the blast. There was an instant of total light, then absolute darkness. When
Landon was able to open his eyes again, there was no trace of the machine or
the rider.

He pulled Byron into a fireman's carry, wondering if they had been hopelessly irradiated. It made little difference. The boy made a few weak gestures of
resistance, then collapsed across Landon's shoulders.

"WHY?" BYRON SHOUTED, slamming a beer bottle into the wall. "What's
stopping me? Who makes these rules that I'm breaking? The saucer men, that
can't even talk? The police, that are too scared shitless to do anything? The
fucking executives in their little toy cars? *Tell me!*"

The kid's anger seemed to have been building over the months, steadily, inexorably, since they'd first found him in the decaying café.

Three sullen girls sat on the floor near him, paying no attention to Landon at all. One chewed gum, another patiently put her hair in a high pony tail. "It's me," Landon said. "You're putting my life on the line when you push things so hard. Mine and Kristen's both."

"If you can't take the pressure," Byron said, his voice suddenly quiet, "maybe you're just too old."

LANDON GOT UP from the bed and pulled on his trousers. Kristen dozed in a narrow band of sunlight, relaxed now, an arm behind her head, displaying the muscles of her ribcage.

Landon slipped on his stained white shirt, combed through his thinning hair with water from a pan in the bathroom. Then, almost as an afterthought, he buckled on his holstered gun.

The fading sunlight drew him outside. A mosquito sang past his ear, and he idly waved it away. He took a pint of whiskey out of the car and stretched out on a lounge chair by the pool. Strange columnar mosses grew in the dark water, the beginnings of a new evolutionary cycle. Landon drank, shifting as one of the frayed vinyl straps gave way under his weight. The warmth of the whiskey met the heat of the sun somewhere in his abdomen and radiated away into space. A single bird whistled in the distance.

Gradually he became aware of a new sound, close to the scream of a saucer, but more prolonged. It grew into a siren, and Landon turned his head to see a police car moving toward him from the north.

He capped the bottle of whiskey and sat up, thinking of Kristen, vulnerable in the motel room. As he got to his feet, he saw Byron leaning against the door to his cabin. He wore a black T-shirt, leather jacket, and jeans, his glasses hanging from one hand. A huge reefer dangled from his lips. He wore the Peacemaker strapped low on his leg, and his eyes were wary and exhausted.

Landon felt the pull of destiny, a movement of forces in planes perpendicular to his own. The approaching car, the tense, expectant figure of Byron, the murky pool at his feet, all seemed part of a ritual, a tension in the universe that had to be worked out.

The lower limb of the sun touched the ocean and the world turned red. Light from the police car streaked the evening as two men got out, carrying lever action rifles. Their khaki uniforms glowed ruddy gold in the dying sunlight.

Finally one of the cops said, "Put your guns in the dirt." Landon held himself perfectly still.

Suddenly one of Byron's girls walked out the motel room. The contours of her body were clearly visible through her sweatshirt, contemptuous of the law, threatening civilization.

"Hold it," one of the cops said.

The girl knelt by the pool, dipping one hand in the fecund water. "Fuck you," she said, not looking up.

The cop raised his rifle, working the lever in short, nervous spasms. "Halt, I said!" His anguished voice reminded Landon of Byron. The girl ignored him, watching the spreading ripples.

The bullet took her in the head, scattering fragments of her skull and whitish brain tissue over the pool. Landon, only a few feet away, stared at her gushing blood in horrid fascination. He pulled out his pistol in a kind of daze and turned to see Byron with his Peacemaker already out. The kid opened up, cocking the pistol with the flat of his left hand as fast as he fired. The two cops seemed to wait for the shots to tear into them, spinning with the heavy impacts, dust splashing up over them as they hit the ground.

Kristen stood in the open door of her room, wearing a threadbare white cotton shift, still unbuttoned. Her lips formed an unspoken question, then she went back inside. Landon heard the sound of drawers opening and shutting, the rustle of clothes.

Byron spat the stub of his reefer into the dirt and picked up his glasses from where he'd let them fall. He turned the collar of his jacket up, rolling his shoulders in a protective gesture. As he got into his sports car, he held Landon's eyes for a long moment. Then he roared off onto the highway, his tires grazing the head of one of the dead policemen.

Landon left the girl's body by the pool and began loading his things into the Pontiac.

A FEW DAYS LATER, swinging south toward Yuma, they passed by the old motel. Hundreds of people, most in their early teens, wandered through the ruins, their faces full of confusion and the gathering darkness.

ON THE LAST DAY of September, Landon rode into town with Kristen for supplies. He waited in the car as the daylight faded, his feet propped up on the dashboard. Coughing gently, he closed his eyes and listened to the crickets and the evening breeze in the palms. The crunch of gravel startled him and he looked up to see what must have been fifty grey-suited executives surrounding him.

The fear that finally came over him was the result of the failure of his imagination. It had not begun to prepare him for what he saw. The men stood with easy authority, their meekness and submission gone without a trace. They carried heavy weapons that Landon had never seen before, intricate masses of tubing and plastic that conjured death and burning.

One of them stepped forward. He was empty handed, authoritative. "Where's the kid?" he said.

Landon shrugged. "We haven't seen him for a week." Kristen came out onto the sidewalk and Landon watched the fear and puzzlement spread over her face.

Another gray-suited figure pushed his way through the crowd and addressed the empty-handed man. "We've searched the town, J.L. He's not here."

J.L. nodded and looked at Landon. "Where would he have gone?"

"Anywhere," Landon said, struggling for equilibrium. "No place."

The man turned to Kristen, still standing in the doorway. "What about you?"

Kristen stared back, wordless, hostile.

Another man pushed through. "They've located him, J.L. He's driving a sports car up the coast, towards New Elay. Some foreign job, silver, with numbers on the side."

"Green's outfit is up there. Have them take him before he gets to town. It shouldn't be hard, in this light. And tell him to make it look like an accident. It'll save trouble in the long run."

"The saucers," Landon said.

"What?" J.L. said.

Landon pointed to the weapons, the communicators. "You made a deal. You sold out the rest of the human race so you could keep on going the way you were. That's why your buildings and your cars never get hit by the saucers. Because you sold the rest of us out and now they let you run things. What did you give them? Women and young boys? Gasoline? Grey flannel suits?"

One of the junior executives reached over and slapped Landon across the mouth. J.L. shook his head and the man stepped back. "Get out of here," J.L. said. "We're through with you."

Kristen said, "You're letting us go?"

"Do you think," J.L. said, "that we couldn't have taken you any time we wanted? That if we want you again we won't be able to find you? We don't care about you. It's the kid that's dangerous. You're just a part of the scenery. Just part of California."

"California's gone," Landon said, tasting blood. "It's on the bottom of the ocean."

For the first time Landon saw a hint of emotion in the man. "No," he said. "Not as long as we have a use for it. As long as there's a coast, there'll be a California."

"The king is dead," Landon said. "Long live the king."

He was talking to the sunset. The men were gone, and Kristen sat on the hood of the car, smoking and looking out to sea.

From somewhere beyond the ragged palm trees came the screaming of sea birds.

STICKS

HE HAD A 12-inch Sony black-and-white, tuned to MTV, that sat on a chair at the end of the bed. He could barely hear it over the fan in the window. He sat in the middle of the bed because of the sag, drumming along absently to Steve Winwood's "Higher Love."

The sticks were Regal Tip 5Bs. They were thinner than 2Bs—marching band sticks—but almost as long. Over the years Stan had moved farther out over the ends. Now the butts of the sticks fit into the heels of his palms, about an inch up from the wrist. He flipped the right stick away when the phone rang.

"Stan, dude!" a voice said. "You want to work tomorrow?"

"Yeah, probably. What have you got, Darryl? You don't sound right."

"Does the name Keven Stacey mean anything to you?"

"Wait a minute." Stan switched the phone to his other ear. "Did you say Keven *Stacey?* As in Foolsgold, Keven Stacey? She's going to record at CSR?"

"You heard me." Stan could see Darryl sitting in the control room, feet up on the console, wearing double-knit slacks and a T-shirt, sweat coming up on his balding forehead.

"This is some kind of bullshit, right? She's coming in for a jingle or a PSA."

"No bullshit, Stanley. She's cutting a track for a solo album she's going to pitch to Warner's. Not a demo, but a real, honest-to-Christ track. Probably a single. Now if you're not interested, there's plenty of other drummers in LA..."

"I'm interested. I just don't understand why she wants to fuck with a rinky-dink studio like yours. No offense."

"Don't harsh me, bud. She's hot. She's got a song and she wants to put it in the can. Everybody else is booked. You try to get into Record One or Sunset Sound. Not for six months you won't get in. Even if you're Keven Stacey. You listening, Stan?" He heard Darryl hitting the phone on the edge of the console. "That's the Big Time, dude. Knocking on your door."

JUST THE NIGHT BEFORE, Stan had watched Foolsgold in concert on HBO. Everybody knew the story. Keven used to fuck the guitar player and they broke up. It was ugly and they spread it all over the *Goldrush* album. It was soap opera on vinyl, and the public ate it up.

Stan too.

The stage was blue-lit and smoky, so hot that the drummer looked like he'd

263

been watered down with a garden hose. Every time the lead player snapped his head back, the sweat flew off like spray from a breaking wave.

Keven stood in the middle of the stage, holding a thin white jacket around her shoulders like there was a chill in the air. When she sang she held on to the mike stand with both hands, swaying a little as the music thundered over her. Her eyes didn't go with the rest of her face, the teased yellow hair, fine as fiberglass, the thin model's nose, the carefully painted mouth. The eyes were murky and brown and looked like they were connected to brains and a sense of humor. And something else, passion and something more. A kind of conviction. It made Stan believe every word she sang.

STAN FINISHED HIS Dr. Pepper and went into Studio B. The rest of Darryl's first-string house band was already there, working out their nerves in a quiet, strangely frenzied jam. Stan had turned over his drums to Dr. Jackson Sax, one of the more underrated reed players in the city and a decent amateur on a trap set. Jackson's trademark was a dark suit and a pork-pie hat that made him look like a cross between a preacher and a plain-clothes cop. Stan was one of the few people he ever talked to. Nobody knew if he was crazy or just cultivating an image.

Stan himself liked to keep it simple. He was wearing a new pair of Lee Riders and a long-sleeved white shirt. The shirt set off the dark skin and straight black hair he'd inherited from his half-breed Comanche father. He had two new pairs of Regal Tip 5Bs in his back pocket and white Converse All-Stars on his feet, the better to grip the pedals.

The drums were set up in a kind of elevated garden gazebo against one wall. There were boom mikes on all sides and a wooden rail across the front. If they had to, they could move in wheeled walls of acoustical tile and isolate him completely from the mix. Stan leaned with his right foot up against the back wall.

There was some action in the control booth and the music staggered and died. Gregg Rosen had showed up, so now everybody was looking for Keven. Rosen was her producer and also her boyfriend, if you paid attention to the gossip. Which Stan did. The glass in the booth was tinted and there was a lot of glare, but Stan could make out a Motley Crue T-shirt, purple jams, and glasses on a gold chain. Rosen's hair was crewcut on top and long enough at the sides to hit his shoulders.

They each gave Rosen some preliminary levels and then cooked for a couple of minutes. Rosen came out on the floor and moved a couple of microphones. Darryl got on the intercom from the control room and told them to shut up for a minute. He played back what he'd just taped and WhiteBread Walker, the albino keyboard player, started playing fills against the tape.

"Sounds okay," Rosen said.

"Uh, listen," Stan said. "I think the hi-hat's overmodulating."

Rosen stared at him for a good five seconds. The tape ran out and the studio got very quiet. Finally Rosen circled one finger in the air for a replay. The tape ran and then Darryl came on the speakers, "Uh, Gregg, I think the top end is, uh, breaking up a little on that hi-hat."

"Well, fix the fucking thing," Rosen said.

He walked out. As soon as the soundproof door closed there were a few low whistles and some applause. Stan leaned over until his cheek rested against the cool plastic skin of his riding tom. He could feel all the dents his sticks had left in it. Wonderful, he thought. We haven't even started and I've already pissed off the top producer in LA.

WHEN ROSEN CAME BACK, Keven was with him.

Jorge Martin, the 15-year-old boy wonder, fiddled with the tailpiece on his Kramer. WhiteBread pretended to hear something wrong with the high E on his electric piano. Art, the bass player, cleaned his glasses. Stan just went ahead and stared at her, but tried to make it a nice kind of stare.

She was small. He'd known that, but the fluorescent lights made her seem terribly fragile. She wore high heeled boots, jeans rolled up tight at the cuffs, a fringe jacket and a white ribbed tank top. She looked around at the setup, nodding, working on her lower lip with her teeth. Finally her eyes met Stan's, just for a second. The rest of the room went out of focus. Stan tried to smile back at her and ended up looking down at his snare. He had a folded-up piece of newspaper duct-taped off to one side of the head to kill overtones. The tape was coming loose. He smoothed the tape with his thumbnail until he was sure she wasn't looking at him anymore, and he could breathe again.

"THE SONG IS called 'Sticks,'" she said. She stood in front of WhiteBread's Fender Rhodes, her hands jammed nervously into her jacket pockets. "I don't have a demo or anything. Sorry. But it's pretty simple. Basically what I want is a real African sound, lots of drums, lots of backing vocals, chanting, all like that. Okay. Well, this is what it sounds like."

She started playing. Stan was disarmed by her shyness. On the other hand, she was not kidding around with the piano. She had both hands on the keys, and she pumped out a driving rhythm with a solid hook. She started singing. Suddenly she wasn't a skinny, shy little blonde any more. She was Keven Stacey. Everybody in the room knew it.

Stan's stomach hurt. It felt like ice had formed in there. The cold went out through his chest and down his arms and legs.

One by one they started to fall in. Stan played a roll on the hi-hat and punched accents on the kick drum. It sounded too disco but he couldn't think of anything else to play. It helped just to move his hands. After one verse Keven backed off and let WhiteBread take over the piano. She walked around and nodded and pointed, talking into people's ears.

She walked up to the drum riser and put her forearms on the railing. Stan could see the fine golden hair on her wrists. "Hi," she said. "You're Stan, right?"

"Right," he said. Somehow he kept his hands and feet moving.

"Hi, Stan. Do you think you could give me something a little more ... I don't know. More primitive, or something?"

"More toms, maybe?"

"Yeah. More of a 'Not Fade Away' kind of feel."

Buddy Holly was only Stan's all-time favorite. He nodded. He couldn't seem to look away from her. His hands moved over to the toms, right crossing over left as he switched from the riding tom to the floor toms. It was a bit of flash left over from the solos he'd played back when he was a kid. He mixed it up with a half-beat of press roll here and there and let the accents float around.

"That's nice," Keven said. She was watching his eyes and not his hands. He stared back, and she didn't look away.

"Thanks," he said.

"I like that a lot," she said, and flicked the side of the high tom with her fingernail. "A whole lot." She smiled again and walked away.

THE BASIC TRACK of drums, bass, and guitar went down in two takes. It was Stan's pride that they never had to put a click track on him to keep him steady. Keven and Rosen listened to the playback and nodded. Then they emptied the percussion closet. Stan put down a second drum track, just fills and punctuation, and the rest of the band loaded up another track with timbales, shakers, bongos and congas. Keven stood on top of a chair, clapping her hands over her head and moving with the music.

The tape ran out. Everybody kept playing and Rosen finally came down out of the booth to break it up, tapping on the diamond face of his Rolex. Keven got down off her chair, and everything went quiet. Stan took the wing-nuts off his cymbal stands and started to pack his brass away.

"Do you sing?"

Stan looked up. Keven was leaning on the rail again, watching him.

"Yeah, a little bit. Harmonies and stuff."

"Yeah? If you're not doing anything, you could stick around for a while. I could maybe use you later on."

"Sure," Stan said. "Why not?"

•

ROSEN WRAPPED THE SESSION at ten that night. Stan had spent five hours on hard plastic folding chairs, reading *Entertainment Weekly* and *Guitar for the Practicing Musician,* listening to WhiteBread and Jorge lay down their solos, waiting for Rosen and Keven to tinker with the mix. Keven found him there in the lounge.

"You're not doing the vocals tonight," he said.

She shook her head.

"You weren't even planning to."

"Probably not." She was smiling.

"So what am I doing here?"

"I just said I could maybe use you. I didn't say for what."

Her smile was on crooked and her jacket hung loose and open. Stan could see a small mole just below her collarbone. The skin around it was perfect, soft and golden. This isn't happening, he thought.

There was a second where he felt his life poised on a single balance point. Then he said, "You like Thai food?"

HE TOOK HER to the Siam on Ventura Boulevard. They left her car at the studio and took Stan's white CRX. The night air was cool and sweet and ZZ Top was on KLOS. The pumping, pedal-point bass and Billy Gibbon's pinched harmonics were like musk and hot sauce. Stan looked over at Keven, her hair blown back, her eyes closed, into the music. There was a stillness in the very center of Stan's being. Time had stopped.

Over dinner he told her about the sensitive singer-songwriter who'd gotten his start in junk food commercials. The guy always used pick-up musicians and then complained because they didn't know his songs. The only thing he actually took along on tour with him was his oversized white Baldwin grand piano.

The gig was in a hotel ballroom. Stan and the lead trumpet player were set up next to the piano and got to listen to his complaints through the entire first set. During the break they collected 16 place settings of silver and laid them across the piano strings. The second set was supposed to open with "Claire de Lune" on solo piano. After the first chord the famous singer-songwriter walked offstage and just kept walking. Stan would have lost his union card over that one, only nobody would testify against him.

Keven had done the same sort of time. After high school she'd been so broke she'd played piano in one of those red-jacket, soft-pop bands at the Hyatt Edgewater in Long Beach. When she wouldn't put out for the lead player, he kept upstaging her and sticking his guitar neck in her face. One night she reached over and detuned his strings, one at a time, in the middle of his solo on "Blue Moon." The stage was so small he couldn't get away from her without falling into the first row of tables. It was the last song of the night, and the audience loved it. The manager of the Hyatt wanted them to keep it in the act. Instead Keven got fired, and the guitarist found another blonde piano player from LA's nearly infinite supply.

Halfway through dinner Stan felt the calf of her leg press gently against his. He returned the pressure, ever so slightly. She didn't move away.

The chopsticks fit in Stan's hands like Regal Tip 5Bs. He found himself nervously playing his empty plate and water glass. Keven put the dinner on her American Express and told him Warner's would end up paying for it eventually.

In the parking lot Stan walked her to the passenger side of his car and stopped with his hand on the door. His throat was suddenly dry and his heart had lost the beat. "Well," he said. "Where to?"

She shrugged, watched his face.

"I have a place just over on Sunshine Terrace. If you want to, you know, have a drink. Or something."

"Sure," she said. "Why not?"

SOME OF THE HOUSES around him were multi-million dollar jobs, sprawling up and down the hillside, hidden behind trees and privacy fences. Stan had a one-bedroom apartment in a cluster of four, squeezed in between the mansions. Everything inside was wood—the paneling on the walls, the cabinets, the louvered doors and shutters. Through the open windows the cool summer wind rattled the leaves like tambourines.

Keven walked slowly around the living room, touching the shelves along the one wall that wasn't filled with windows, finally settling in an armchair and pulling her jacket around her shoulders. "I guess you're tired of people telling you how they expected to find your clothes all over the place and junk food boxes in the corners."

"People have said that, yeah."

"I'm a slob. My place looks like somebody played Tilt-A-Whirl with the rooms. And all those goddamn stuffed animals." Word had gotten out that Keven loved stuffed animals so her fans now handed them up to her by the dozen at Foolsgold concerts. "What's that?"

"It was my grandfather's," Stan said. It was the trunk of a sapling, six feet long, maybe an inch and a half in diameter at its thickest, the bark peeled away, feathers hanging off the end. Stan took it down from the wall and handed it to her. "It's a coup stick."

"Acoustic? Like a guitar?"

"Coup with a P. The Indians used it to help exterminate themselves. They thought there was more honor in touching an enemy with one of these than killing him. So they'd ride into a bunch of cavalry and poke them with their coup sticks and the cavalry would blow their heads off."

"Is that what happened to your grandfather?"

"No, he burned out his liver drinking Sterno. He was supposed to have whacked a cop with it once. All it got him was a beating and a night in jail."

"Why'd he do it?"

"Life in the big city, I guess. He had to put up with whatever people did to him, and he couldn't fight back or they'd kill him. He didn't have any options under the white man's rules, so he went back to the old rules. My old man said Grandpa was laughing when the cop dragged him away. You want a beer?"

She nodded and Stan brought two cans of Oly out of the kitchen. Keven was rummaging through her purse. "You want a little coke with that?" she asked.

"No thanks. You go ahead."

She cut two lines and snorted them through a short piece of plastic straw. "You're a funny kind of guy, you know that?"

"What do you mean?"

"You seem like you're just waiting for other people to catch up to you. Like you're just waiting for somebody to come up and ask you what you want. And you're ready to lay it all out for them."

"I guess maybe that's so."

"So what do you want, Stan? What you do want, right this second?"

"You really want to know? I'd like to take a shower. I really sweated it up in the studio."

"Go ahead," she said. "No, really. I'm not going anywhere. We took your car, remember?"

THE HEAT FROM the water went right into his muscles, and he started to relax for the first time since Darryl's call the day before. And he wasn't completely surprised when he heard a tapping on the glass.

She was leaning on the sink, posed for him, when he opened the sliding door. Her hair stuck out to one side where she'd pulled her tank top over her head. Her small, soft breasts seemed to sway just a little. One smooth hip was turned toward him in a kind of unconscious modesty, not quite hiding the dark tangle of her pubic hair.

"I guess you're tired of people telling you how beautiful you are."

"Try me," she said, and got in next to him.

Her mouth was soft and enveloping. He could feel the pressure of her breasts and the small, exquisite muscles of her back as he held her. Her small hands moved over him, and he thought he might pass out.

Later, in bed, she showed him what she liked, how to touch her and where. It seemed to Stan as if she'd offered him a present. She had condoms in her purse. He used his fingers and his tongue and later came inside her. She was high from the cocaine and not ready to sleep. Stan was half crazy from the touch and scent of her and never wanted to sleep again. Sometime around dawn she told him she was cold and he brought her a blanket. She curled up inside his arm, building an elaborate nest out of the pillows and covers.

They made love again in the morning. She whispered his name in his ear. Later they showered again, and he made her coffee and toast.

Stan offered her one of his T-shirts but she shook her head and dressed in yesterday's clothes. Time seemed to pick up speed as she dressed. She looked at the clock and said, "Christ, it's almost noon. Gregg is going to be waiting on us."

HE STOOD IN a circle with the other singers, blending his voice on an African chant that Keven had played them from a tape. He knew the gossip had started the minute he and Keven came in together. Rosen was curt and irritable and everybody seemed to watch Stan out of the corners of their eyes.

Stan couldn't have cared less.

When the backing tracks were down, Keven disappeared into the vocal booth. Jackson packed up his horn and sat down next to Stan. "Got to make a thing over at Sunset. You working this evening?"

"I don't know yet."

"Yeah," he said. "Be cool."

Rosen put the playback over the speakers. The song was about break-ups and betrayals:

> *...broke down all my fences*
> *And left me here alone*
> *Picking up sticks...*

As she stretched out the last word the percussion came up in the mix, drowning her in jungle rhythm. The weight of the drums was a perfect balance for the shallow sentiment. Together they sounded to Stan like number one with a bullet.

She nailed the vocal on the third try. When she came out of the booth she walked up to him and said, "Hey."

"Hey yourself. It's going to be a monster, you know. It's really great."

"You think so? Really?"

"Really," he said. She brushed his cheek with her hand.

"Listen," he said.

"No. I can't. I've got a dinner date with Warner's tonight. Gregg's dubbing down a cassette and we're going to play it for them. So I'm tied up until late."

"Okay," he said.

She started to walk away and then came back.

"Do you sleep with your door locked?"

HE MANAGED TO fall asleep. It was an effort of will that surprised even him. When he heard the door open, it was three AM. The door closed again and he heard a slightly drunken laugh and a gentle bumping of furniture. He saw a darker shadow in the doorway of the bedroom. There was a rustle of clothing. It seemed to Stan to be the single most erotic moment of his life.

She pulled back the covers and slid on top of him. Her skin was soft and cool and rich with perfume. When she kissed him, he tasted expensive alcohol on her breath.

"How were the Warner Brothers?" he whispered.

"They loved me. I'm going to be a star."

"You're already a star."

"Shhhhhh," she said.

HE OPENED HIS EYES in the morning and saw her fully dressed. "I've got to go," she said. It was only nine o'clock. "I'll call you."

It was only later that he realized the session was over. He'd never been to her place, he didn't even have a phone number where he could find her.

IT WAS LIKE he'd never had empty time to fill before. He spent most of the afternoon on the concrete stoop in front of his apartment, listening to Buddy Holly on his boombox. A mist had blown in from the Pacific and not burned off. His hands were nervous and spun his drumsticks through his fingers, over and over.

She called late that night. He should have been asleep but wasn't. There was a lot of traffic noise in the background and he had trouble hearing her. "I'll be by tomorrow night," she said. "We can go to a movie or something."

"Keven..."

"I have to go. See you tomorrow, okay?"

"Okay," Stan said.

•

SHE WAS SITTING on the stoop when he came home from a session the next afternoon. She was wrapped in a shawl and the clouds overhead all seemed to be in a hurry to get somewhere.

She let him kiss her, but her lips were awkward. "I can't make tonight," she said.

"Okay."

"Something came up. We'll try it another night, okay?"

"Sure," Stan said. "Why don't you give me your number?"

She stood up, took his hands as if to keep him from touching her. "I'll call you." She stopped at the gate. "I'm crazy, you know." She wouldn't look at him.

"I don't care."

"I'll call you," she said again, and ran across the street to her bright red MG. Stan held up one hand as she drove away, but she didn't look back.

AFTER TWO DAYS he started to look for her. Darryl reluctantly gave him Gregg Rosen's unlisted number. Stan asked Rosen for Keven's phone number and he just laughed. "Are you crazy, or what?"

"She won't care if you give it to me. I'm the guy from the CSR session—"

"I know who you are," Rosen said, and hung up.

He left a call for her at the Warner offices in Burbank and with Foolsgold's agent. He tried all the K. Staceys in all the LA area codes.

He called Rosen again. "Look," Rosen said. "Are you stupid, or what? Do you think you're the only kid in town that's had a piece of Keven Stacey's ass? End to end you guys would probably stretch to Tucson. Do you think she doesn't know you've been calling? Now are you going to quit hassling me or are you going to fuck over what little career you may have left?"

THE CHECK FOR Keven's session came in the mail. It was on CSR's account and Darryl had signed it, but there was no note in the envelope with it. On the phone Darryl said, "Face it, bud, you've been an asshole. Gregg Rosen is way pissed off. You're going to have to kick back for a while, pay some dues. Give it a couple months, maybe you can cruise back."

"Fuck you too, Darryl."

LA dried up. Stan hit the music stores and the musicians' classifieds. Most of the ads were drummers looking for work. The union offered him a six-month tour of the southern states with a revival of *Bye Bye Birdie*.

Jesus, Stan thought. Show tunes. Rednecks. Every night another Motel 6. I'm too old for this.

The phone rang.

Stan snatched it up.

"Stan. This is Dave Harris. Remember me?"

Harris was another session drummer, nothing special. He'd filled in for Stan a couple of times.

"Yeah, Dave. What's up?"

"I was, uh, I was just listening to a cassette of that Keven Stacey song? I was just wondering, like, what the hell were you doing there? I can't follow that part at all."

"What are you doing with a cassette of that song?"

"Uh oh."

"C'mon, Dave, spill it."

"They didn't tell you? Warner's going to use it as the first single from the album. So they're getting ready to shoot the video. They didn't even tell you? Oh man, that really sucks."

"Yeah, it sucks all right."

"Really, Stan, I didn't know, man. I swear. They told me you couldn't make the gig."

"Yeah, okay, Dave, hang on, all right? I'm trying to figure something out, here."

STAN SHOWED UP at the Universal lot at six in the morning. He cranked down his window and smelled the dampness in the air. Birds were chattering somewhere in the distance. Stan had the pass he'd gotten from Dave Harris. He showed it to the guard and the guard gave him directions to the Jungle Lot.

A Port-A-Sign on the edge of the road marked his turnoff. Stan parked behind the other cars and vans under the palm trees. A crew in matching blue T-shirts and caps was positioning the VTRs and laying down an Astro-turf carpet for the band.

He started setting up his drums. This was as far as his imagination had been able to take him. From here on he'd have to wing it. His nerves had tunneled his vision down to the wood and plastic and chrome under his hands and he jumped when a voice behind him said, "They gonna fry your ass, boy."

Stan turned to face a six-foot-six apparition in a feathered hat, leopard scarf, chains, purple silk shirt, green leather pants, and lizard boots.

"Jackson?" Stan asked carefully.

"Something wrong?"

"Jesus Christ, man, where did you get those clothes?"

Jackson stared at him without expression. "I'm a star now. Not trash like you, boy, a *star*. Do you know who I was talking to yesterday? Bruce. That's Bruce *Springsteen*. He says he might need me for his next tour."

"That's great, Jackson. I hope it works out."

"You laugh, boy, but when Rosen see you, he gonna shit a picket fence."

Rosen, Keven, and some blond kid pulled up in a Jeep. Stan slipped deeper into the shade of a palm tree to watch. Keven and the blond kid were holding hands. The kid was dressed in a white bush jacket and Bermuda shorts. Keven was in a matching outfit that had been artfully torn and smudged by the costume crew. The blond kid said something to Keven, and she laughed softly in his face. The director called places and the rest of the band settled in behind their instruments.

"Where the fuck is the drummer?" Rosen shouted.

Stan stepped out from behind the trees.

"Oh Christ," Rosen said. "Okay, take ten everybody. You, Stan Shithead. Off the set."

Stan was looking at Keven. Say the word, he thought. Tell him I can stay.

Keven glanced at him with mild irritation and walked away. She had hold of the blond kid's hand.

Stan looked back at Rosen. A couple of grips, ex-bikers by the size of them, were headed toward him. Stan held up his hands. "Okay," he said. He put his sticks in his back pocket and pointed at his drums. "Just let me..."

"No way," Rosen said. "Leave them here. We'll get them back to you. Right now you're trespassing, and I want your ass *out* of here."

On the other side of the road was a tall, grassy hill. Stan could see Keven and the blond kid halfway up it. "Okay," he said. He walked past Rosen and got in his car, started it, and got back onto the road.

Past the first switchback he pulled over and started up the other side of the hill on foot. He was still a hundred yards away from Keven when she spotted him and sent the blond kid down to cut him off.

"Don't even think about it," Stan said. The blond kid looked at Stan's face and swerved downhill toward the jungle set at a run.

"Keven!" She stopped at the top of the hill and turned back to look at him. The blond kid would be back with the bikers any minute. Stan didn't know what to say. "You're killing me," he said. "Rosen won't let me work. Did you know that?"

"Go away, Stan," she said.

"Goddammit," he said. "How was I supposed to *not* fall in love with you? What the hell did you expect? Do you ever listen to the words of all those songs you sing?"

A hand appeared on his shoulder, spinning him around. Stan tried to duck and ended up on his back as Rosen's fist cut the air above him. No bikers, then, Stan thought giddily. Not yet. He rolled a few feet, off balance. One of his drumsticks fell out of his pocket, and he grabbed for it.

Rosen's looked more annoyed than anything else. "You stupid piece of shit," he said. Stan scuttled around the hillside on his palms and his ass and his feet, dodging two more wild punches. The slope made it tricky. Finally he was up again. He kept moving, letting Rosen come after him. He outweighed Rosen by at least 40 pounds and had the reach on him besides. And if he actually hit Rosen he might as well throw his drums into the Pacific. On the other hand, if he waited around long enough, the bikers might just beat him to death.

It was what his grandfather would have called a classic no-win situation.

Kill me then, Stan thought, and to hell with you. He stepped inside Rosen's next swing and tapped him, very lightly, on the chest with his drumstick. Then he stepped back, smiling, into Rosen's roundhouse left.

"Hey, sitting bull," a voice said. It was Keven, kneeling next to him. "I think Custer just kicked your ass."

Stan propped himself up on his elbows. He could see Rosen walking down the hill, rubbing his knuckles. "Who'd have thought the little bastard could hit so hard? Did you call him off?"

"I wasn't going to let him kill you. Even if you did deserve it." She took his face in both her hands. "Stan. What am I going to do with you?"

Stan didn't have an answer for that one.

"This doesn't change anything," she said. "It's over. It's going to stay over."

"You never called me."

She sat back, arms wrapped around herself. "Okay. I should have called. But you're a scary guy, Stan. You're just so … intense, you know? You've got so much hunger in you that it's … it's hard to be around."

Stan looked at his hands.

"I wasn't, like, just playing with you, okay? What there was, what happened, it was real. I just, I changed my mind. That's all. I'm just a person, you know. Just like anybody else."

She believed that, Stan thought, but it wasn't true. She wasn't like other people. She didn't have that fist in her stomach, pushing her, tearing up her insides. Not any more. That was what made her different, but there wasn't any point trying to tell her that.

She stood up and walked away from him, breaking into a run as she moved downhill. Rosen was there at the bottom. She took him by the arm and talked to him, but Stan couldn't hear any of it. He watched the clouds for a while then headed down.

Rosen walked over, holding out his hand. "Sorry I lost my temper." Keven was back at the jungle set.

Stan took his hand. "No hard feelings."

"Keven says she wants you to do the video." Rosen clearly didn't like the idea. "She says nobody else can really do that drum part. She says there won't be any more trouble."

"No," Stan said. "No more trouble."

THE WORST PART was hearing her voice on the radio, but in time Stan even got used to that.

Her album was out just before Thanksgiving and that week they premiered the video on MTV. It opened with Keven and her boyfriend in their jungle suits, then cut back and forth between a sort of stylized Tarzan plot and the synched-up footage of the band playing under the palm trees.

The phone rang. "Dude, you watching?"

"Yeah, Darryl. I'm watching."

"Totally crucial video, bud. I'm serious."

"Good drummer," Stan said.

"The best. This is going to make your career. You are on the map."

"I could live with that. Listen, Darryl, I'll see you tomorrow, okay? I want to catch the rest of this."

Stan squatted in front of the TV. Keven sang hard into the camera. Stan could read the words of the song on her face. She turned and looked over her shoulder and the camera followed, panning past her to the drummer, a good-looking, muscular guy in his middle thirties, with black hair that hung straight to his collar. The drummer smiled at Keven and then bent back to his work.

The clear, insistent power of his drumming echoed through the jungle afternoon.

THE TALE OF MARK
THE BUNNY

ONE SPRING IT STOPPED raining in early March and didn't start again. There was one very well-off bunny in the village who had a large burrow and lots of food saved up. He wasn't worried about the drought at all. The other bunnies, though, looked at the purple-red nettles withering in the fields and the mayweed that hadn't even flowered and wondered if they were going to have enough food to get them through the next winter.

The very well-off bunny was named Albertus, but everybody called him Big Al—at least they called him that when they were sure he couldn't hear them. Big Al was in fact a very large bunny with long, white, silky fur. He had lots of land that his parents had left to him, and he never let any of the other bunnies gather food there. The story was that Big Al had sat on the one bunny who tried to make off with some of his carrots until the small bunny begged for mercy. After Big Al let him up, the small bunny moved to another village.

ONE MORNING A DOZEN or more bunnies sat around the village square, licking the dew off the dried and wrinkled clover to quench their thirsts, and talking about the drought. There was still a bit of a cool breeze from Possum Creek, a mile or so away. Sophie Bunny, who was large and sleek, with a black circle around one eye, was there with her husband Lenny and their youngest, Ralph, who still lived at home with them.

"I don't mind telling you," Lenny said, "I'm getting a little scared by all this." Lenny was a small, tan bunny with buck teeth and big cheeks like a chipmunk.

"No need to be afraid," said the short, overweight Reverend Billy Bunny, the village's spiritual leader. "The Easter Bunny will provide." He sat, as he usually did, by the thick green hawthorn bush in the middle of the square—although the bush was neither as thick nor as green as it had once been.

"Easter was two weeks ago," said Maria Bunny. "And there's not a cloud in the sky."

"I thought the Easter Bunny just did eggs," little Ralph said.

"Actually," Lenny said, "so did I."

"I never really understood what a bunny was doing with eggs in the first place," Sophie said, "if you want to know the truth."

"We could ask Big Al for help," Annie Bunny suggested. "He's got enough food for everybody."

It was well known that Big Al provided the Reverend Billy's food. He'd discovered Billy preaching in the village square a few years before and liked the fact that most of Billy's sermons were about keeping things the way they already were. Since then word had gone around that Big Al thought the other bunnies should pay attention when the Reverend Billy had something to say, and that he would frown on anyone who made fun of him in public. If anybody could talk to Big Al, it had to be the Reverend Billy.

"Well, ah, ahem," Billy said. Ever since he became official, he'd started to talk like a much older rabbit. "I think we should remember that the Easter Bunny helps those who help themselves." This was exactly the sort of thinking that had impressed Big Al.

"I agree," Annie said. "Let's help ourselves to some of Big Al's food."

Annie's husband Jonathan said, "I don't think that's what he meant."

Suddenly a bunny no one had ever seen before hopped out from behind a tree. He was very thin, with black fur and dark, intense eyes. "I know one thing you could do," he said. "You could stop eating all that clover while you're worrying about starving to death."

"Darn it!" Lenny said. "I *am* eating again."

"Who are you?" the Reverend Billy asked the stranger.

"My name is Mark."

Billy narrowed his eyes. "Are you the same Mark Bunny that used to live down by Clearwater Pond? The one that got kicked out of the village for being a troublemaker?"

"I guess I am," Mark said.

"Uh oh," somebody said. For a few seconds all the bunnies hopped around nervously, and when everyone quieted down again Mark had lots of space around him in all directions.

Billy continued to stare at Mark from his high position. "You keep moving along," he said. "We don't want your kind around here."

Mark looked at the other bunnies to see if anyone else wanted to speak up. When no one did he said, "Okay," and hopped slowly away.

LATE THAT AFTERNOON, as Sophie, Lenny, and Ralph headed home to their burrow, they saw Mark in the grass by the side of the path ahead of them.

"Oh dear," Lenny said. "It's that Mark bunny."

"I don't think he'd actually hurt us, do you?" Ralph said. "He just looks kind of sad."

"I don't know," Lenny said. "I'm afraid."

"I'm afraid too," Sophie said. "We're bunnies. We're always afraid. But sometimes we have to do the right thing, even when it's scary."

"And what exactly are you saying, in this case, the right thing might be?" Lenny asked.

"There's wolves around this time of year. We can't let him wander around all night without a burrow to stay in."

"Actually we could, if we wanted to..."

"Lenny..."

"Okay, okay, I'll go ask him."

Lenny hopped carefully over toward Mark. "Um, hi," Lenny said.

Mark nodded.

"My wife," Lenny said, "er, that is, *we,* wanted to know if maybe you needed a place to stay tonight? Of course if you have someplace else, that would be perfectly fine, and we wouldn't feel in the least insulted if you turned us down."

"No," Mark said, "I don't have a place. That's very kind of you."

"We've got some strawberries we've been saving," little Ralph said, bounding up. "They're kind of small, but you could have one."

"I do love strawberries," Mark said. "But you'll have to let me do something for you in return."

"How come?" Ralph said.

"That's just my philosophy."

"What's a philosophy?"

"Well," Mark said, "I guess it's just some ideas about life."

"Oh. Why don't you just say 'ideas about life,' then?"

"Ralph," Sophie said, "you're being rude."

"Sorry," Ralph said.

That evening, after sharing the strawberries, the four bunnies lay happily on the floor of the burrow. "Tell me some more about this philosophy of yours," Sophie said. Sophie was always interested in new things.

"You mean my ideas about life?" Mark asked. Ralph laughed at that and Mark wiggled his whiskers and went on. "Really I just have this one idea. I've thought about it a lot and got it down to the simplest words I could."

"So what is it?" Lenny asked.

Mark sat up and spoke in a deep voice, clearly liking the sound of the words as they came out. "'Give what you can. Take what you need.'"

"Is that what got you in trouble at Clearwater Pond?" Sophie asked.

"Actually most people seemed to like my idea, once they thought about it. There was just this one very well-off bunny named Sophocles who got upset, and told everybody I was dangerous."

"Are all rich bunnies mean?" Ralph asked.

"I've traveled around quite a bit," Mark said, "and I've seen rich bunnies who were very kind and generous. I've also seen quite a few who did tend to be a bit selfish."

"So are you saying," Sophie asked, "that if we get hungry enough it's okay to take some of Big Al's food?"

"Only if Big Al had already given up what he could for you to take from. Everybody has to agree. That's the hard part, of course, for those that have more than enough to give some of it up."

"It's hard to think about," Lenny said. "It scares me."

"Bunnies are always afraid," Sophie said. "But sometimes..."

"I know," Lenny said. "I know." He thought for a while. "Do you think if all of us put all our food together—except for Big Al, of course—we'd have enough to get us through the drought?"

"I don't think so," Sophie said.

Mark shrugged his shoulders and lay down again. "That's where the luck part comes in."

MARK LEFT BEFORE the others got up the next morning. When little Ralph went outside he found something very strange and called for his parents to come look. It seemed Mark had chewed some of the leaves off a nearby hawthorn bush and stuck some new branches where there hadn't been any before. Sophie, Lenny, and Ralph all looked at it for a while.

"You know," Lenny said, "it almost looks like ... nah. Couldn't be."

"Looks like what?" Sophie said. She was finishing her morning grooming, licking her front paws and then rubbing them over her big, silky ears.

"Well, except for being green and everything, don't you think it looks a bit like Ralph?"

"I think it looks a lot like Ralph," Sophie said.

"Why would somebody make a tree look like a bunny?" Lenny asked.

"I think it's called 'art,'" Sophie said.

"'Art,'" Lenny said. "No doubt about it. That was one weird bunny."

"I liked him," Ralph said.

"Me, too," said Sophie."

"I don't know," Lenny said. "I lay awake for a long time last night thinking about his—" He looked at Ralph. "—ideas about life, and this morning my head hurts. Now I look at this 'art' thing, and it makes my head hurt too." Slowly he reached up with his rear leg to scratch under his chin. "Okay," he said, "maybe it hurts in a nice kind of way."

•

T HEY ALL WENT BACK to the village that morning to talk some more about the drought. Everyone seemed a little crankier and a little thirstier than the day before.

"Everyone should just eat less," the Reverend Billy said.

"Some of us aren't eating much at all right *now,*" Maria said. She was in fact a very thin bunny, going gray in many places.

There was a long silence.

"What if we…" Lenny swallowed hard. "What if everybody gave all they could and only took what they needed?"

All the other bunnies turned to look at him. "What?" Jonathan asked.

The Reverend Billy hopped over from the high place in the middle of the square and stared right into Lenny's eyes. "What are you?" he said, squinting. "Some kind of Markist?"

Lenny took a short hop backwards without really meaning to.

"That's not very nice," Sophie said.

"That sounds like name-calling," said little Ralphie.

"I'm only speaking the truth," said the Reverend.

"It might be only speaking the truth to say somebody was short and fat," said Sophie, "but it still wouldn't be very nice to say it in that tone of voice."

The Reverend Billy, who was in fact rather short and fat, wrinkled up his nose and said, "Hmmph."

"Look," Sophie said. "The problem is water, right? But there's all the water we would ever need over in Possum Creek."

"What are you saying, that we should move the village?" Jonathan asked. "I don't like it by the creek, with all those holly bushes. Besides, wolves live there. And it would take forever to make new burrows."

"No," Sophie said, "I wasn't thinking about moving the village. I was thinking—what if we made the water come to us?"

A PPARENTLY S OPHIE HAD BEEN awake much of the night thinking, too. She knew that Possum Creek had once flowed right by the village, many, many years before Sophie's mother had been born. It had filled up with sand and after that the river had flowed away to other places.

But if there was one thing bunnies were good at, besides eating and having big families, it was digging. What if they dug out the old river bed and made part of Possum Creek—just a small part, not enough to hurt anyone down-stream—come through their village again? Then after it came through the village, it could go back and join back up with the main river.

After Sophie finished talking about her plan, the other bunnies found that their heads hurt just as much as Lenny's did. They all started to talk at once and it was almost an hour before it got quiet enough for Lenny to speak up.

"I've heard what everybody has to say," he said, "which mostly seems to be that they're afraid. Well, I can understand that. But we have to do something, or we won't have any food. I think everybody who wants to give what they can to this plan should meet us tomorrow down at Possum Creek."

LENNY AND SOPHIE and Ralph all slept badly that night, but as soon as the first rays of sunshine trickled into their burrow, they got up and went to Possum Creek. By the time the sun was fully up there were only five other bunnies there.

"Thank you all for coming," Lenny said, and looked up at the sky. "Boy, it looks like it's going to be another really hot day."

It looked like he shouldn't have said that, because as soon as he did, Jonathan made a little hop like he was going to try to sneak away.

"Good thing we're here by the *river*, then, isn't it?" said Sophie in a funny voice. "Where it's so *cool* and *nice?*"

"Uh, yeah!" Lenny said. "Sure is!"

"Right, Jonathan?" Sophie said.

Jonathan saw that all the bunnies were now looking at him. "I guess so," he said.

Sophie showed them what she'd been thinking, which was to start digging inland a little way from the river bank. That would leave a wall of dirt between the river and the ditch they were going to dig, so no water would get in the hole. Then, when they were all done, they could dig through the wall and let the water in.

"I figure we should start digging about here," Sophie said, scratching a line in the dirt with one paw.

"Well," Lenny said, "what are we waiting for? Let's make a river!"

They dug all day, and when they were done their paws were sore and their legs were tired, but they had a wide, deep channel about fifty feet long. In the last of the daylight they stood looking at it.

"This isn't going to work," Sophie said, very quietly, so nobody but Lenny could hear her. "It's just too much work and there aren't enough of us."

"It was a good idea, though," Lenny said.

"And you did your best," Sophie said. "You worked harder than anyone."

"So what happens now?"

"I don't know," Sophie said. "I'm all out of ideas."

Just then Jonathan started to hop slowly along the edges of the hole, looking at what they'd done. He seemed to be thinking very hard.

"This is it," Sophie whispered. "When Jonathan gives up, the others will, too."

Jonathan stopped and turned to face the other bunnies. He sat up on his hind legs and said, "Look! Look what we did!"

"It's not so bad," Lenny said.

"Not so bad?" Jonathan said. "Not so bad? It's *wonderful*. We're only bunnies, and we did this. We made this great big hole, which isn't just a hole, it's the start of a new river. Instead of just sitting around and being scared and hungry, we did something about it! I'm going to tell *everybody!*"

THE NEXT MORNING there were forty eager bunnies at the trench, and still more showed up as the day went on. Sophie and Lenny had to stop frequently to answer questions and explain Sophie's idea over and over. But with forty bunnies digging and laughing and having fun, the work went much faster than it had the day before.

In the afternoon Jane Bunny came to the edge of the ditch and asked if she could talk to Sophie. Sophie hopped out and said, "What can I do for you?"

"No, it's me," Jane said. "I want to do something for *you*. But I can't dig." She held up her left front leg, which had never worked right, even when she was a baby.

"There is something you can do," Sophie said. "If you really want to."

Sophie explained her ideas to Jane, who actually had some ideas of her own. For instance, she thought of making trees that had grown up in the old riverbed into islands, so the bunnies wouldn't have to dig them up or move to higher ground to get around them. Jane was able to hop up and down along the trench and answer questions and carry messages back and forth between the other workers.

On the third day, even more bunnies showed up. One of them was Albertus, though he hadn't come to work. He sat on a hill and watched for long enough that everyone could see him, and see that he was unhappy, before he hopped slowly away.

THAT EVENING THE REVEREND Billy Bunny called a meeting in the village square. "What you're doing," he said, "just isn't natural."

"Bunnies dig," Maria said. "What's unnatural about that?"

"You're changing things," the Reverend Billy said.

"We're just putting the river back where it used to be," Jane said. "We're not hurting any other animals."

"Only the Easter Bunny," the Reverend Billy said, "is supposed to change the shape of the land."

This was a very difficult idea and everyone got very quiet to think about it.

It was a hot night, with stars almost as bright as the moon, and crickets sang all around them.

Suddenly a voice spoke up from the back of the crowd.

"Eggs," little Ralph said.

The Reverend Billy seemed startled. "What did you say?"

"I said, 'eggs,'" Ralph told him. "I thought the Easter Bunny was just in charge of Easter eggs."

"Well, er, um..."

"Yeah," said Lenny, who seemed to be much less afraid than he used to be. "Who said the Easter bunny was in charge of rivers?"

"Yeah," said Annie. "You're always telling us the Easter Bunny helps those who help themselves. If this isn't helping ourselves, what is?"

"But, er, well..."

The bunnies, one and two at a time, began to slowly hop away from the square. "We're tired," Jonathan said as he left. "Let's do this some other time."

"If you want to help us dig," Maria said, "we'd be happy to see you tomorrow."

THE REVEREND BILLY BUNNY didn't show up to dig the next day, or any of the days after. However, he didn't call any more meetings either, which many of the bunnies thought almost made up for his not working.

Soon the hole went right up to the edge of the village. Some of the bunnies wanted to quit right then and there and let the water into the ditch, but Jane spoke up. "You've seen how water gets bad if it doesn't keep moving. We need to finish the job, just like Sophie said."

Other bunnies had ideas, too. Little Ralph surprised even himself when he figured out that they needed to tunnel under a big tree that had fallen across the old riverbed instead of going around it or trying to move it. "That way," he said, "when the water goes under it, we can use it to get to the other side."

Three weeks from the day they first broke ground, the ditch was almost finished. Sophie and Lenny together broke through at the downstream end, where the little river would eventually join back with the big one. All that was left was to break through the wall at the upstream end and let the water in.

THE ENTIRE VILLAGE gathered at the river, ready to celebrate, including old Albertus, who had found another hill where he could look down on them. Even the Reverend Billy was there, trying to look stern and disapproving.

Though there still hadn't been any rain in the bunnies' village, it had been raining upstream. The river was full of water and running very, very fast.

"You know," Sophie said, "We could have a problem here."

"What do you mean?" Lenny asked. "C'mon, c'mon, we've been working on this forever. Bunnies aren't very patient, you know. Let's finish this!"

"I'm afraid—"

"Bunnies are always afraid," Lenny said. "But sometimes—"

"No," Sophie said. "This is different. When we dig through that last wall of dirt, the whole river is going to rush right into our new hole. Whoever does it could get really, really hurt."

"Oh," Lenny said. "Do you think?"

They all stood and looked at the river, which no longer seemed peaceful, but seemed a little angry. Then they looked at Sophie's ditch. Then they looked at the river again.

"I'll do it," Lenny said.

"Lenny, no," Sophie said. "I won't let you."

"Somebody's got to do it," Lenny said. "It might as well be me."

"No," said a deep voice behind them. "It has to be me."

They all turned. "You?" Lenny said.

"Me," Albertus said.

"But ... but ... that doesn't make any sense," Sophie said. "You're *rich*."

"I used to be," Albertus said.

The others gathered around to listen. "What happened?" Maria asked.

"Back in February, when I went down to look at all my lovely food, it was gone."

"Gone?" Jonathan said.

"Mice," Albertus said. "They tunneled into my vault, between the big rocks, and they took everything. And because my land is so high up, the drought hurt me worse than anyone else."

"Why didn't you tell us?" Sophie asked.

"Why didn't you tell *me*?" Reverend Billy asked. He seemed more upset than Albertus was.

"I know you don't like me," Albertus said. "I know what you all call me behind my back. 'Albert Doo-Doo head.'"

"Um, actually, nobody's ever called you that," Ralph said.

"Really?"

"Really. 'Big Al,' that's what everybody calls you."

"'Big Al' isn't so bad," Albertus said thoughtfully. "Anyway, I've been hearing all these ideas going around, all this, 'give what you can, take what you can get away with—'"

"'Take what you *need*,'" Lenny said. "There's a difference."

"Whatever. At first I thought I would come sit on one of you until you gave me some food. But none of you has any food either. That was when it hit me: I'm the same as anybody else now."

"Wow," Maria said.

"I'm not exactly happy about it," Albertus said. "I stayed in my burrow and sulked for a long time. But after a while I would come out here and watch all of you digging. It looked like fun, but I didn't know how to, well, to ask to join in."

"I guess you just did," Sophie said. "Frankly, I think you have a lot to make up for, but if I understand what Mark taught us, once you're willing to give what you can, you're in."

"Thank you," Albertus said. "I mean that."

"I hope you meant what you said about digging through to the river," Lenny said.

"I did," Albertus said, "and I do."

With that he hopped into the hole and began to dig. Soon his paws were damp and muddy, and very slowly water began to seep into the ditch.

"Oh my," Sophie said. "Oh my. This might actually work."

"Are you just now figuring that out?" Lenny said.

Albertus kept digging. Dirty water splashed his beautiful white coat until he was almost as brown as Lenny, and his powerful forepaws sent mud and rocks flying out of the hole.

Jonathan began to hop up and down in one place. "Look out!" he said. "Look out! It's coming!"

With a roar the water broke through the wall, and it swept Albertus away with it. The last they saw of him before he disappeared around a bend in the brand new river was one massive paw raised in farewell.

"OH NO!" SOPHIE CRIED, and she began to run after Albertus. So did all the other bunnies, but the new river was much, much faster than they were and they couldn't begin to catch up.

The bunnies, all of whom had been working very hard for many days, simply ran out of strength before they even got to the village. Sophie dropped to the ground panting, and Lenny fell down beside her.

"I didn't want this to happen," she said. "I was mad at him because he never wanted to share his food, but I didn't want this. It's all my fault."

"What's all your fault?" asked a deep voice.

All the bunnies looked up from where they were sprawled on the dry grass.

"Albertus!" Sophie said. "Are you all right?"

"Apparently someone left a tree across the new river," Albertus said. "I was able to hold on and pull myself out."

"That was little Ralph," Lenny said proudly.

Albertus nodded at him grandly. "Thank you, young bunny," he said. "If you wish, you may call me 'Big Al.'"

THE BUNNIES WANTED to call it "Sophie's River," but Sophie said they should name it after Mark. They all nodded and pretended to agree with her, but went on calling it Sophie's River anyway.

The grass and the clover and the nettles began to bloom again almost immediately, and even the old hawthorn bush in the middle of the village square started to perk up. As soon as it did, though, a very strange thing happened. One night someone nibbled and worked at the bush until it came to look exactly like Mark the Bunny, whose ideas had inspired Sophie to save the village.

For several days afterwards Lenny had a bad stomach ache, and when anyone asked him if he'd made the art in the village square, he would only say that the question made his head hurt.

THE KILLING SEASON

O VERNIGHT THE CLOUDS had rolled in and the summer was dead. I sat at my office window and drank coffee, looking out on a dirty brown Saturday that smelled like rain.

Somebody knocked at the door and I swiveled around to see Pete McGreggor from down the hall. "Busy?" he asked.

I shook my head, and he came in, closing the door behind him. He poured a cup of coffee and sat down across from me.

"Big shakeup last night," he said. "I just got a call to defend one of the Preacher's errand boys."

"So they finally got to him," I said, remembering the furor that had raged in the newspapers a few months before. The law had never been able to break up the Preacher's drug operation, even though it was notorious as the biggest in Texas. "How'd they do it?"

"It's very hush-hush," he said, steam from his coffee making his hair seem to ripple. "They squelched the story at the papers, hoping to pull in a couple more fish, I guess. But what I gather is that the thing was pulled off from the inside, from somebody high up in the organization. But nobody knows exactly who it was that sold out."

"It'll all come clean at the trial, I suppose."

He nodded. "Sooner than that, I expect. The DA told me confidentially that they'll have everything they need by five o'clock tonight. You'll see it all on the evening news."

A sharp rapping came at the door, and Pete stood up.

"You've got business. I'll leave you to it."

"It's probably bill collectors," I said. "I'll yell if they get rough."

He opened the door and pushed past the two policemen that were waiting outside.

They were both in uniform, but I only knew one of them. That was Brady, the tall, curly headed one that looked like an Irish middleweight. His partner was dark and nondescript, sporting a Police Academy moustache.

"Hello, Sloane," Brady said. "How's the private cop business?" He was a bit of a hard case, not yet thirty, with the sense of humor of a caged animal.

"It's a living," I said. "What can I do for you?" I didn't bother to get up.

"This is Sgt. Dawson," Brady told me. "He thinks he wants to ask you some questions."

"Sit down," I said, waving at the chairs. Dawson sat, but Brady continued to pace the floor.

"Sorry to bother you like this," Dawson said.

"No problem. Coffee?" Dawson nodded, and I poured another cup. When I glanced at Brady, he just shook his head. I knew the game, and I wished they'd get on with it. Brady was going to play tough so Dawson could stick up for me and I'd talk to him. I couldn't think of anything they could possibly want from me. "Mind telling me what this is all about?"

"We're trying to find Elizabeth Canton. Known as Liz," Dawson said.

"Good luck. I can give you her address, but it won't do you much good. I find if I'm patient, she comes around to see me every once in a while."

Dawson looked down at his coffee with an absent expression. "How long have you known her?"

I turned my chair around and refilled my cup. "About six months, I guess. We've been going around together for the last couple of those. Is she in some sort of trouble?"

"I'd rather not say. How would you describe your ... relationship with her?"

"Oh lay off him, will you?" Brady said. "Get to the point." That was a switch. Dawson was supposed to be the one taking my side. I shrugged it off. I never would understand police, or their ideas of drama.

Dawson seemed subtly afraid of Brady, or perhaps just not willing to go through a showdown. "All right. When was the last time you saw her, Mr. Sloane?" His courtesy was stretching, and I was beginning to see the thinness of the veneer.

"Night before last, I guess, after she got home from work. Have you tried the hospital, by the way? She works at Brackenridge."

"We tried it. Have you heard from her since? Any idea where she could be?"

I shook my head. "You don't know Liz. She runs her own life. I don't even try to keep up with it. I see her when she wants to see me. I wish I could be more help, but I really can't."

"Satisfied?" Brady asked him in an ugly voice. "He doesn't know anything. Let's roll."

Dawson set down his unfinished coffee, and paused at the door. "We just want her for questioning at this point. But if she doesn't turn up by five o'clock, a warrant goes out for her arrest. So if you see her, let us know."

I went into the hall after him and saw the look that Brady gave him. It was full of suppressed anger and frustration. They walked to the elevators, and Brady slapped the button a little harder than necessary.

I stood for a second, scratching my head. Maybe it was a coincidence that the hour of five o'clock had come up twice that morning, but detectives don't believe in coincidence. I turned on my heel and marched right over to Pete's office. His door was open, and his secretary let me walk in.

"One question, Pete. Who was the arresting officer in the Preacher case?"

He twisted his eyebrows, then got a manila folder out of a stack. "A Sgt. Brady," he said, and then, "was that the—"

I rapped a knuckle on his desk. "Thanks, Pete," I said, and left him there.

So the cops want me to do their dirty work, I thought, sitting down at the phone. The hints had been plain enough. If I brought her in before five o'clock everything would be hunky-dory. If not, well, it would be my own fault. I resented being manipulated, and I didn't want to get involved in something that was none of my business. It was eleven AM, leaving only six hours until the police deadline. So I grumbled and made excuses to myself a while longer, and then I reached for the phone.

I CALLED LIZ'S HOUSE, less because I thought it would do any good than because I had to try it. If the police couldn't find her, it didn't seem very likely that I could. Her roommate answered the phone.

"Hello, Cathy, this is Dan. Have the police been there?"

"Yes, Dan, just a little while ago. I'm sorry they bothered you. I didn't realize they would ... I mean, I'm sorry I gave them your name." She sounded flustered and confused, just the way I would have expected her to after a run-in with the law. She was one of the world's innocents, and sometimes she was just too blushing and vulnerable to be true. Even though she and Liz were the same age, she had none of Liz's sensuality, only an awkward, child-like prettiness.

"Don't worry about it. Do you have any idea what's going on?"

"I was going to ask you that. I just thought she was at the hospital."

"I don't suppose she left a message for me or anything?"

"No, I..." There was a long pause and I waited it out. "I can't think of anything to tell you."

"What were you about to say?"

"Nothing."

"Cathy, this is important. I've got to find her before the police do. What is it you were going to say?"

"Nothing, I told you. I don't know anything." The last was almost a sob, and the receiver clicked in my ear. I hung up, dissatisfied and irritable. I didn't owe Liz anything. From a rational point of view I had no business even knowing her. I kept telling myself that as I put on my jacket to go look for her, a knot of worry in my stomach. She had kept me off balance so long that I suppose I was just off balance without her.

She was not my type, not my style. She lived too fast, and let nobody inside her defenses. But she'd come along at a bad time for me, and I'd been too weak to pass her by. She had a ripe body, with long legs and full breasts and swirls of slate colored hair. And if she was part of the lost generations of Austin, she was still a beautiful woman, and at the time that had been enough.

There was no good place to begin, so I drove home, hoping for a note or message of some sort. I left the windows rolled up, expecting rain at any minute. It never came.

I parked on the curb and checked the porch mailbox. It was empty, as usual. I unlocked the front door and went to the hall phone where I kept a pad and pencil, the place Liz would have been most likely to leave something.

I felt jumpy all of a sudden. Nothing was wrong that I could put my finger on, but I had the feeling that a noise had just stopped, or something had moved soundlessly in another room. I tiptoed into the kitchen and checked the back door. It was unlocked but closed, just as I'd left it. That should have satisfied me, but it didn't. I crept back to my bedroom and opened a drawer of the dresser to see if anything had been disturbed.

A small shaving mirror sat in front of me, just at eye level. A motion in it caught my attention and I looked up to see the closet door behind me slowly swing open.

I whirled around, but pulled up short when I saw the gun in his hand.

He was short and thin, with long black hair and a drooping moustache. The gun he held was a long barrel .38, accurate and deadly. Unless he got too close, I would have no chance to take it away from him.

"Put your hands away from your sides, Mr. Sloane, and back out into the hall, please." His voice had a slight Mexican accent and he held the pistol with care and authority. I backed up slowly, keeping my eyes on the gun. There was a smooth place on the sight that looked as if he'd started to file it down and changed his mind.

"You know my name, so I don't guess this is a stickup," I said. "What do you want?"

"On into the living room, please, and sit in that armchair. Slowly." I backed across the room, looking for an opening and not finding one. The kid knew his business and was not going to give me a chance. I sat down. "Put your arms on the chair and hold them still. That's fine."

He was by the door, and he had it open and was gone in the time it took me to realize what he was doing. I went to the window and watched him jog away down the block.

Going after him on foot would have been a waste of time. He was armed and I didn't think he'd balk at shooting me if I forced him to. So I let him get around the corner then sprinted out to my car and threw it into gear. By the time I made the turn he had disappeared. There were a hundred places he could have gone—over fences, down alleys, into empty houses. Just for my own peace of mind I got out and checked the parked cars on the street. Then I went back home.

Things were starting to get interesting. The fact that someone had sent a gunman to my house meant the stakes were higher than I'd expected. A quick look around showed me that the place had been searched, but nothing taken.

It was a neat, professional job, and they probably hadn't wanted me to know it had been done. There was no point in calling the police—I was willing to give even money that the kid had been working for them. And even if he hadn't, there wasn't much the police could do. Professional thugs meant a big operation, one the size of, say, the Preacher's.

That thought bothered me. After a big bust word traveled fast, and things got very quiet for a while. If the Preacher had no operation any more, there was no reason one of his gunmen should have been going through my house. Or the police either, for that matter.

I went back out to my car and drove to Liz's duplex. The temperature was falling, and the sky seemed even darker than before. I put my lights on and zipped the front of my jacket.

The house was empty, which saved my having to tell Cathy a complicated lie. I let myself in with a piece of plastic and went to work. It was time for answers, and I was going to get them if I had to tear the place apart.

It took me an hour and a half. It was not lying around waiting for me, and she obviously didn't want it to be stumbled over by accident. It was too well hidden to have been a plant. I went through the drawers, insides and undersides, tapped along shower curtain and closet rods, felt mattresses and shook boxes. I shifted furniture, and when I got to her stereo I noticed something wrong. The speaker cabinets weighed too much for the flimsy portable they had come off of, so I opened one up. Behind the cloth grille was a wad of Kleenex, and behind that was a big manila envelope. It was wedged into the enclosure behind the speaker and I didn't want to disturb it. I coaxed the flap open with my pocket knife, enough to see inside. It was crammed full of little white packets of sleep and death. The other speaker held more of the same, but in pill form, packaged in small plastic vials.

I felt something change inside of me. I went through the room again, looking for an address book, old letters, a match folder, anything. The longer I looked, the stranger it got, and the more disoriented I began to feel. There was nothing there, no trace of her past, of her friends, of her personality at all. She could have been no more than a cardboard cut-out, the merest shell of a human being.

It was 12:30. I had a sense of time running out. At first I had wanted to help Liz, maybe even protect her. Now I wanted answers from her. I suppose I should have been more shocked at finding the heroin, but I'd almost expected that.

Being with Liz was like following a ticking bomb, and when I looked back it seemed like I'd been waiting for the explosion all along. I'd never pressed her, never used my professional skills to find out about her. Probably because of what I'd been afraid I'd find.

I locked up behind myself and sat in my car, feeling the conditioned response to start it up and get moving, whether I had a destination or not. The car waited with eager obedience, ready to substitute its horsepower for my thinking. It was desperation made me feel that way, but I wasn't doing any good getting desperate all by myself, parked in a car.

BRACKENRIDGE HOSPITAL WAS just south of the campus, close to both the football stadium and Interstate 35. I parked in the lot and went in through the double front doors. There was the same sort of expectant smell inside that the weather had outside. I found the first floor nurses station and asked for Liz.

"She certainly seems popular today," said the head nurse, a heavy, crinkly-eyed woman of about forty. "The police were here looking for her this morning." She sounded as if she had mixed feelings about the whole situation.

"What do you suppose they wanted?" I asked her.

"Oh, I don't know. But they worried me, coming around like that." She was a professional mother, the very best kind of nurse. I envied Liz for having earned her protection.

"You couldn't give them any help, then."

"Not really—" she began, but a voice behind me interrupted her.

"She told them the same thing I'm going to tell you. Nobody's seen her for a couple of days. So get lost." The voice was harsh, with Texan overtones, and didn't fit his small Indian body.

"A little touchy, aren't we?" I asked.

"This is a hospital, mister, not a referral agency. We've got patients to take care of, and we don't need a lot of people tromping around and getting in the way."

"Maybe I should come back with a cast on," I offered.

"Don't tempt me." The tag on his intern's smock said his name was Dakhar something, but I missed the last name as he scowled and walked away. I didn't like to be threatened by people half my size, but I didn't see anything I could do about it. The nurse had gone back to filing her charts and didn't look up again. Doctors ran the show, and nurses took what they could get. I didn't particularly like that, either.

I walked up and down the halls restlessly. The big clocks hanging from the ceiling kept reminding me that it was after one. At five o'clock the dam was going to break. Police with warrants would find the goods in Liz's apartment, and things would really start getting tough. For everybody.

I finally caught sight of Dakhar again, and tagged along behind him. I didn't bother being subtle about it, and the set of his shoulders told me he was aware of me. He ducked into a small tiled room and I went in after him.

We were in a small kitchen with a sink, an icebox, and a coke machine. I closed the door behind me and put my weight against it.

"All right, what do you want?" he asked. Surliness and anger alternated behind his face.

"Answers," I said. "What makes Liz such a hot topic? What is it you want quiet?"

He started cursing me, and I reached out for him. His right hand made a sudden blur and I drew back, but not quickly enough. There was a knife in his fist and a thin red line behind my knuckles.

It happened like it always does, suddenly, without warning. My defense mechanisms took over, and all I could do was let it happen. I feinted with my eyes and snatched his wrist, hard. This time I was faster, and I felt the bones of his arm grind together in my grip. The knife clattered to the floor and I opened his lip with two quick slaps.

He had no tolerance for pain. He weakened instantly, but I had to force myself to ease off on his wrist. It was the legacy of my days in Vietnam, and I was not proud of it. "Talk," I said, as gently as I could.

"Prescriptions. I wrote her some prescriptions." His throat sounded knotted up, and he was taking in a lot of air. "That's all."

"For what?"

"You know. Downers. Seconal, Valium, Quaaludes."

"How much?"

"Just a few, not often."

"Did she pay you to do it?"

"Christ no, man. Everybody does it. You think it's a big deal?"

"If it's no big deal, what are you so scared of?"

"The heat's on."

"How do you know the heat's on? It wasn't in the papers. The cops know better than to spread it around. So who tipped you off?"

His face told me he'd said too much, and that he was through talking. I was convinced he'd be dead before I'd get it out of him. It was late, and I was wasting time.

I scooped the knife off the floor and dropped it down the sink. He could fish it out, but it would take him a couple of minutes. Then I let go of his wrist and closed the door on him.

The cut on my hand was starting to hurt. I tied a handkerchief over it and flexed the fingers, relieved that it was only a scratch, angry that I'd let it happen at all.

SOMEBODY HAD BEEN to my office before me. It was subtle, but I could sense the difference instantly. They were one step ahead of me, whoever they were, whatever they wanted. They had the organization to know when I'd left for the office in the morning, and when I'd gone back home. I felt the delicate touch of fear on my neck.

My thoughts spinning, I sat down at the desk. The phone rang and I stared at it for half a minute before the message got through to me. Then I jumped at it and snatched it off the hook.

"Sloane speaking."

"Hello, Sloane." I recognized the voice and my pulse picked up again.

"Go on," I said.

"A couple hours after I left your place this morning," the Chicano said, "somebody took a shot at me. Does that give you any ideas?"

"No. Should it?" I cradled the phone in my shoulder and reached for the office bottle. Splashing a little bourbon on my handkerchief, I dabbed at the cut wrist.

"Somebody's hot because I spilled the goods on his girlfriend. Are you reading me yet?"

"If you're talking about me, you're crazy. If you're not, I'm lost." I took a sip out of the bottle and felt better instantly.

"Sounds like you're way behind the times. Maybe we should get together."

"Let's. We had so little time this morning."

"There used to be a co-op dorm across from Harris Park. Big building, empty now. You know where that is?"

I said that I did.

"I'll be there in forty-five minutes. Bring a hundred dollars in ten dollar bills."

"That's a lot of money."

"Mexico's not that close, either, if you follow me."

"I think I'm beginning to," I said.

"Forty-five minutes," he said, and hung up.

I put the phone down and looked at my watch. It was getting to be a bad habit. I drove to my bank, cashing a check and sealing the money in the little envelope they gave me. Then I headed back north toward the campus, trying to put together what I had.

I had no doubts that Liz was involved. All that was left was the question of how deeply, and I wanted to believe it wasn't very far. At the same time my pride was telling me that I'd been a sucker long enough, and I ought to leave her to the wolves. But only after I learned the whole truth.

I passed through the tree-lined streets north of the university. A long dry spell had left the city withered and yellow, and the threatening but impotent clouds overhead were no help. It was a burned out, jaded, and pale world, and I was a part of it. What hurt the most was that I belonged there. The faded people sat on their porches, long-haired, easygoing, used up.

I swung past the old dorm once at cruising speed, just to make sure there weren't any machine guns hanging out the windows. It was built up the side of a low hill, with a good view of both sides and the park in front of it. I left my car out of sight on the edge of the park and took the long way around the house.

I came in from the back side, through a yard overgrown with weeds, wondering if I should have brought a gun after all, despite my dislike of them. The back of the house had only one window, a big single sheet of glass, but the sun was directly on it and I couldn't see through the accumulated dust. I was trying to decide whether I should go straight in or circle back to the front when I heard the shot.

I charged up to the door, then hesitated. There was no more gunfire so I opened the door and went in.

Inside was a single long room. I ducked out of the lighted doorway and waited for someone to shoot me. Finally my eyes adjusted and the feeling of vulnerability began to pass. I could see bare walls and a long, empty wooden floor. There was an interruption in the middle of it, and as I got closer I could make out the body of the Chicano who had called me. He was leaking blood onto the shiny waxed woodwork. He wouldn't be needing his hundred dollars.

Something moved in the shadows. I looked around for cover, but there wasn't any. A silhouette detached itself and moved toward me with familiar grace. In one hand was a pistol, and I could practically see smoke leaking out of the barrel.

"Hello, Liz," I said.

AT FIRST I THOUGHT she was drugged, but then I decided it was just detachment, almost shock—a withdrawal from the harsh fact of death. Her face was slack, and what might have otherwise passed for beauty seemed coarse. She was wearing old jeans and a dirty tee-shirt, and probably had been for a while. She half turned from me in the dim light and raised one arm in a vague gesture of despair. It was the one with the gun in it, held by the tips of her fingers like an ashtray. I took it away from her and put it in my pocket. It was a .38 Police Special; the barrel was warm and stank of cordite.

"Did you shoot him, Liz?" It was a stupid question, I suppose, but I had to ask it.

"Hello, Danny," she said dreamily.

"Answer me, Liz. Did you shoot him?"

"What are you doing here, Danny? You shouldn't have come. It's dangerous here." I might have been talking in Siamese, or not at all.

I left her and bent over the body. He was face down, so I didn't have to look at the messy side, where the bullet had come out. I fished the wallet out of his back pocket and pawed through the cards. The first one said his name was Carlos Quintana. The second one said that he was a police officer for the City of Austin.

I tucked the rest of the cards away, wiped the wallet, and stuck it back in the pocket. "I'm over my head, Liz. I can't cover this up. It's murder now, and everything's different. I have to call the police."

She pirouetted slowly away from me. I didn't know what else to do. I started for the door.

Police Sgt. Brady stepped into my path and the refracted sunlight glinted off his gun. "You don't need to call the cops, Sloane. The cops are here."

"Where did you come from?" I asked.

"Side door. I heard the shot and came to check it out. Now let's have that gun out of your pocket. Set it on the floor real nice and kick it away." I did so. "Fine. You want to tell me why you shot him? If it was to clear your girlfriend, you just made a big mistake. They're not going to get anything on Liz." Something about the way he wasn't really looking at her seemed odd, but it was a fleeting thought and was soon gone. "Okay, outside. We're taking your car."

That was the last straw. It was bad enough having the police show up without being called. When things stopped making sense altogether, it was time for me to get out. I started slowly for the front door, and Brady made the mistake of letting Liz get between us. It was all I needed. I hit the door hard and slammed it behind me. I heard a slug tear through the wood as I started running.

My mind was working as soon as I hit the pavement. So far there was one solid piece of evidence in the whole case. It was at Liz's house. Brady had said they weren't going to get anything on Liz. That suddenly made the evidence more important than I'd thought. But I didn't have time for the possibilities. Unless I got there first, it wasn't going to make any difference.

I was into the trees before he got the door open and his sights on me. I think I heard him yell "halt" but I could have been wrong. Another bullet ripped open a tree to the left of me and I dodged for deeper cover. He was clearly shooting to kill; at least I knew I'd done the right thing to get away. That left me with the one small problem of staying alive to explain it.

My keys were already out, and I didn't shut the car door until I was rolling. I figured I had no more than a couple of minutes' head start, and I needed every bit of it. I didn't have the time or concentration for any complicated thinking. I worked at keeping the car on the road and nothing else. Liz's house was only a few blocks away, and I could hear a siren not far behind me. My old Mustang was taking the curves well, but they could probably follow me just from the noise of the tires.

I swerved left to avoid a bicycle and screamed to a stop in front of the duplex. Cathy's car was in the driveway. I took the walk at a hard run and slammed both fists into the door. Cathy finally opened it, looking mildly annoyed, but I didn't give her a chance to say anything.

My breath was coming hard and I had to fight to make sense. "The cop that was here this morning," I gasped, "Brady—you'd seen him before, hadn't you?"

She got a trapped look in her eyes and didn't answer.

"You'd seen him all the time, hadn't you? *Hadn't you?*" I must have been yelling because she burst into tears.

"I can't! I can't tell you!" She might as well have just said yes.

"Get out of the house, fast," I said. "There's about to be a lot of trouble. Go to a neighbor, call the police, and then stay there." I must have hit some sort of parental tone that got through to her. She left the house without a word.

I could hear the siren again, not far off. Brady had known, obviously, where I was going. I didn't worry about the mess this time, but threw shredded Kleenex in a pile on the floor. My hand closed on stiff paper and pulled it into the light.

Brady was too late. I'd seen the rubber stamp on the front of the envelope.

It said PROPERTY OF AUSTIN POLICE DEPARTMENT.

I must have expected it, but my mind had shut out the consequences. Now that it was in front of me, everything snapped into place. I'd been on the heels of the police all day, and everywhere I went people were shifty-eyed and evasive, afraid to talk and ready to lash out at anything.

There was a noise outside. I stuffed the envelope down the back of my pants and tucked my shirt in over it. I threw the speaker and Kleenex in the trash and pretended to still be searching when Brady came in with Dawson behind him. I looked down the dark tunnel of Brady's gun again, with no more corners left to turn.

"Where is it?" Brady demanded, gesturing with the gun barrel. There was a smooth place on the gun sight that I had seen before.

I suddenly realized that my chances were about slim and none. All my clever detective work had just earned me a metal tag around the toe. If I had a chance at all, it hung on the fact that Brady had been alone when he'd found me with Liz. If he'd ditched his partner, it could mean that Dawson didn't know the score. If I was right, I had to make Dawson want to keep me alive. It didn't sound like much of a chance at all.

"Shoot me, Brady," I said. "It's the only way. Otherwise I'm going to talk."

I'd cut it fine, and for a moment I thought I'd gone too far. Then he added things up and his eyes shifted, just barely, toward Dawson. He was going to try to talk his way out of it.

"Stop trying to scare me," he said. "It's harder than you think."

"Maybe not. I've got three things to say, and I don't think you'll like any of them."

"Go ahead." This time it was Dawson talking. He was suddenly interested.

I had to buy time. If I sprang the envelope right off, I wouldn't live to see the reaction. "The first is not so much in itself. It's just funny. Funny that there should be so much activity today when there was a big bust last night. People getting shot, and shot at. It almost seems like the big dope racket wasn't cleaned up at all. Maybe it just changed hands."

"Feelings aren't worth a damn," Brady said.

Dawson said: "Lets hear the other two."

"Number two. I don't think Dawson can give you an alibi for the half hour or so before Carlos was shot. I think you were in the house the whole time. I think you left Dawson cooling his heels down the block, and only went back to him because you needed a car to chase me. I think it was your gun that killed Carlos. I think you pulled the trigger."

"You're crazy." His voice wasn't as steady as it should have been. A drop of sweat started at the edge of his curly hairline. "This gun hasn't been fired in days."

"That's not your gun. It's Carlos'. I saw him with it this morning when you sent him to search my place. Just before you decided he wasn't worth the risk and put the word out on him.

"You didn't think you'd have to kill him yourself, but when he showed up at Liz's hideout, you lost your head a little. It was a smart idea to change guns with him, but you won't get away with it. The ballistics people have samples from your gun downtown, and they'll connect you up with the killing sooner or later. Unless you pull a fix."

"So we got our guns mixed up," Brady snarled. "Why should I kill my own man?"

"Because he knew too much about the setup. He knew you'd staged the whole bust just to take over the organization. You were the man at the top that tipped off the police—tipped off yourself! Carlos was the only one who knew you in both roles, on both sides of the fence, because he was working both sides too. Carlos—and Liz."

Now I had scared him. He looked more like a fighter than ever, but this time he was on the way down. The sneer was gone off his face and instead I saw what Carlos couldn't have seen before he died. There was nothing human in his look. It was not a happy sight to end your life with.

"Number three," I said. My mouth was dry and it was hard to talk. I'd come to the place where I was probably going to get shot. "Dawson, there's an envelope under my shirt. I want you to come get it out."

Brady's jaw went white. "It's a trick." He seemed to be talking through clenched teeth. It was obvious he was afraid, why couldn't Dawson see it? What was he waiting for? "It's a trick, goddammit. Stay away from him, Dawson!"

We might have stood there all afternoon, but Brady's hand started shaking. He used his left hand to steady it, and the gesture must have touched a nerve in Dawson.

It happened in a blur. Dawson reached for his holster, but he moved too fast. Brady swung on him, startled, and I could see the pistol rising to cover him. I could see Brady's finger on the trigger, and I could see the finger start to tighten, and then I moved.

I kicked as hard as I could and Brady's gun roared angrily at the ceiling. Then I was on top of him. I hit him twice before I knew what I was doing or where the impulse had even come from. I might have kept on, but the feel of cold metal in my neck made me stop.

"Get up," Dawson said. "That's enough."

"Not yet." I was breathing hard and my hands were like ice. I didn't care about guns anymore. "Shoot if you want." Brady had a dull look in his eyes, but he was conscious. I grabbed the edges of his shirt and held them tight. "I want to know why," I said to him. "I want to know why Liz was going to take the rap for you."

He choked on his laugh. "They couldn't have made it stick. A paraffin test would clear her and give the trail time to get cold. And once they found out the murder was a frame-up they'd believe the drugs were too. They only had Carlos' word, and he's dead."

He still hadn't told me why, but by then I already knew. Sometimes it takes me a long time to see the most obvious things. Carlos had tried to tell me, and it was on Brady's face every time he'd looked at her.

I stood up and let Dawson put me against a wall and search me. When he got to the envelope, his eyes narrowed and he looked at me as if he was almost sorry to have to go through with the rest of it. He read me my rights, slapped the bracelets on, and took me outside.

Liz was handcuffed to the back seat of the prowl car. They put me in next to her. I couldn't think of anything to say. I could have asked her what she saw in a man like Brady, what he gave her that I couldn't, bur that was all high school stuff. I was too old and had seen too much of it before.

"So Cathy spilled it all," Liz said bitterly. "I should have known I couldn't trust her." It was a childish remark, and it brought me back to reality. I thought of Cathy and her despairing refusal to talk.

"No," I said. "It wasn't Cathy."

Another carload of cops pulled up, and a moment later they came out of the house with Brady in tow. He was in handcuffs, too.

"I suppose you hate me now," Liz said. "I guess I can't blame you."

"Shut up," I said. "Just shut up. Please."

Dawson started the car and we pulled away from the curb. It was over for me, but a long night still lay ahead. I wondered if Pete was going to be able to get me out of this one.

The sky overhead was the color of watery mud. It stared back at me in shifting silence and refused to rain.

SCALES

THERE'S A STANDARD rat behavior they call the Coolidge Effect. Back when I was a psych major, before I met Richard, before we got married, long before I had Emily, I worked in the lab 15 hours a week. I cleaned rat cages and typed data into the computer. The Coolidge Effect was one of those experiments that everybody had heard of but nobody had actually performed.

It seems if you put a new female in a male's cage, they mate a few times and go on with their business. If you keep replacing the female, though, it's a different story. The male will literally screw himself to death.

Someone supposedly told all this to Mrs. Calvin Coolidge. She said, "Sounds just like my husband."

IT STARTED IN JUNE, a few days after Emily's first birthday. I remember it was a Sunday night; Richard had to teach in the morning. I woke up to Richard moaning. It was a kind of humming sound, up and down the scale. It was a noise he made during sex.

I sat up in bed. As usual all the blankets were piled on my side. Richard was naked under a single sheet, despite the air conditioning. We'd fought about something that afternoon. I was still angry enough that I could find satisfaction in watching his nightmare.

He moved his hips up and down. I could see the little tent his penis made in the sheet. Clearly he was not squirming from fear. Just as I realized what was happening he arched his back and the sheet turned translucent. I'd never watched it before, not clinically like that. It wasn't especially interesting and certainly not erotic. All I could think of was the mess. I could smell it now, like water left standing in an orange juice jar.

I lay down, facing away from him. The bed jolted as he woke up. "Jesus," he whispered. I pretended to be asleep while he mopped up the bed with some Kleenex. In a minute or two he was asleep again.

I got up to check on Emily. She was face down in her crib, arms and legs stretched out like a tiny pink bearskin rug. I touched her hair, bent over to smell her neck. One tiny, perfect hand clutched at the blanket under her.

"You missed it, Tater," I whispered. "You could have seen what you've got to look forward to."

•

I MIGHT HAVE forgotten about it if Sally Keeler hadn't called that Friday. Her husband had the office next to Richard's in the English department.

"Listen," Sally said. "It's probably nothing at all."

"Pardon?"

"I thought somebody should let you know."

"Know what?"

"Has Richard been, I don't know, acting a little weird lately?"

For some reason I remembered his wet dream. "What do you mean weird?"

Sally sighed dramatically. "It's just something Tony said last night. Now Ann, I know you and Richard are having a few problems—that's okay, you don't have to say anything—and I thought, well, a real friend would come to you with this."

Sally was not a friend. Sally was someone who had been over to dinner two or three times. I hadn't realized my marital problems were such common knowledge. "Sally, will you get to the point?"

"Richard's been talking to Tony about this new grad student. She's supposed to be from Israel or something."

"So?"

"So Richard was apparently just drooling over this girl. That doesn't sound like him. I mean Richard doesn't even *flirt*."

"Is that all?"

"Well, no. Tony asked him what was the big deal and *Richard* said, 'Tony, you wouldn't believe it. You wouldn't believe it if I told you.' Those are like his exact words."

"Does this mystery woman have a name?"

"Lili, I think he said it was."

I tried to picture Richard, with his thinning hair and stubby little mustache, with his glasses and pot belly, sweeping some foreign sexpot off her feet.

Sally said, "It may not be anything at all."

One new associate professorship would open up next year. Richard and Tony were both in the running. Richard was generally thought to have the edge. "I'm sure you're right," I said. "I'm sure it's nothing at all."

"Hey, I wouldn't want to cause any problems."

"No," I said, "I'm sure you wouldn't."

THE NEXT WEDNESDAY Richard called to say he'd be home late. There was a visiting poet on campus for a reading. I looked it up in the paper. The reading was scheduled for eight.

At eight-thirty I put Emily in the station wagon and we drove over to the Fine Arts Center. We didn't find his car.

"Well, Tater," I said. "What do you think? Do we go across Central and check the hot sheet motels?"

She stared at me with huge, colorless eyes.

"You're right," I said. "We have too much pride for that. We'll just go home."

THERE WAS A COOKOUT that weekend at Dr. Taylor's. He was department chairman largely on the strength of having edited a Major American Writer in his youth. Now he had a drinking problem. His wife had learned that having parties at home meant keeping him off the roads.

The morning of the party, I told Richard I wanted to go. By now he was used to my staying home from these things. I watched for signs of disappointment. He only shrugged.

"You'd better start trying to find a sitter," he said.

After dinner we began the slow, seemingly random movements which would inevitably end with the women in one part of the house and the men in another. Already most of the wives were downstairs, clearing up the soggy paper plates and empty beer bottles. I was upstairs with Jane Lang, the medievalist, and most of the husbands. Taylor had made a pejorative remark about women writers and everyone had jumped on him for it. Then Tony said, "Okay, I want to see everybody come up with a sexist remark they believe is true."

Taylor said, a little drunkenly, "Men have bigger penises than women."

Jane said, "Usually." Everyone laughed.

Robbie Shappard, who was believed to sleep with his students, said, "I read something the other day. There's this lizard in South America that's extinct now. What happened was another species of lizard came along that could perform the mating rituals better than the real females. The males all fucked the impostors. The chromosomes didn't match, of course, so no baby lizards. The whole species went toes up."

"Is that true?"

"I read it in the *Weekly World News,*" Robbie said. "It has to be true. What I want to know is, what does it mean?"

"That's easy," Jane said. "When it comes to sex, men don't know what's good for them."

"I think men and women are different species," Tony said.

"Too easy," Robbie said. "They've just got conflicting programs. When we were living in caves we had these drives designed to produce the maximum number of kids from the widest range of partners. The problem is we've still got those drives and they're not useful any more. That's what did those poor lizards in."

Tony said, "Okay, Ann. Your turn. Be serious, now."

"I don't know," I said. "I guess I subscribe to the old business about how women are more emotional."

"Emotional how?" Tony said. "Be specific."

"Right," Robbie said. "Be brief and specific. It's fifty percent of your grade riding on this."

I looked at Richard. He seemed distracted rather than contentious. "Well, men always seem concerned with exactitude, being able to measure things." There was some laughter, and I blushed. "You know. Like they don't want to say 'I'll love you forever.' They want to say, 'at current rates our relationship could reasonably be expected to continue at least another six months.' Whereas I would appreciate the gesture. Of saying 'forever.'"

Tony nodded. "Good one. Rich?"

"You want one? Okay. Here's what Robbie was trying to say earlier, only without the bullshit. Men want women and women want babies."

Everyone went quiet; it wasn't just me overreacting. The first thing I thought of was Emily. What did Richard mean? Did he not want her anymore? Had he never wanted her? I'd heard that people felt this way when they were shot. No pain, only a sense of shock and loss, the knowledge that pain would surely follow.

"Speaking of babies," I said into the silence, "I should call home. Excuse me." I walked out of the room, looking for a phone, wanting most of all to be away from Richard.

I found a bathroom instead. I washed my face, put on fresh lipstick, and wandered downstairs. Sally found me there and raised an eyebrow. "Well?"

"Well what?"

"I assume you're here for a look at her."

"Who?"

"Lili. The mystery woman. All the men in the department are in love with her. Haven't you heard?"

"Is she here?"

Sally glanced around the room. As usual, the party had gradually segregated itself, husbands in one room, wives in another. I knew most of the women in the den with us. "I don't see her now. She was here a minute ago."

"What does she look like?"

"Oh, short, dark ... sexy, I suppose. If you like eyeliner and armpit hair."

"What's she wearing?"

"Is that more than idle curiosity I hear in your voice? A tank top, a red tank top. And blue jeans. Very tight."

"Excuse me," I said, finally seeing the phone. "I have to call home."

The sitter answered on the second ring. Emily was asleep. There were no problems. "Okay," I said. I wanted to be home with her, to blow raspberries on her belly and feel her fingers in my hair. The silence had gone on too long. I said thank you and hung up.

I couldn't face going back upstairs. It would be a boy's club up there by now anyway. Fart jokes and cigars. A sliding glass door opened up to the back yard. I walked into the darkness, smelling summer in the cut grass and the lingering smoke from the grill.

Richard found me there when the party broke up. I was sitting in a lawn chair, watching the Dallas sky, which glows red all summer long. Something about all the lights and the polluted air.

"Nice move," Richard said. "Just walk right out on me, let the entire fucking party know our marriage is on the rocks."

"Is it?"

"What?"

"On the rocks. Our marriage. Are we splitting up?"

"Hell, I don't know. This isn't the time to ask, that's for sure. Oh no. Don't start. How are we supposed to walk out with you crying like that?"

"We'll go around the side of the house. Taylor's too drunk to know if we said goodnight or not. Answer my question."

"I said I don't know."

"Maybe we ought to find out."

"What does *that* mean?"

"Let's do whatever it is people do. See a counselor or something."

"Okay."

"Okay? That's all? Just 'okay'?"

"You're the one pushing for this, not me."

"Fine," I said, suddenly giddy. It was like standing on the edge of a cliff. Would I actually do something irreversible? Only Emily held me back. Then I looked at Richard again and thought, do I really want this man as her father?

"Fine," I said again. "Let's get out of here."

MY BEST FRIEND Darla had been divorced twice. She recommended a Mrs. McNabb.

"Oh God," I said. "It's going to be so expensive. Is it really going to help?"

"What do you care about help?" Darla said. "This is step one in getting rid of the creep. The rest gets easier. Believe me, it gets easier. My second divorce was no worse than, oh, say, being in a body cast for six months."

I sat in front of the phone for a long time Monday. I was weighing the good and bad in our marriage, and I was throwing anything I could find onto the scales. Everything on the good side had to do with money—the house, Richard's insurance, financial security. It wasn't enough.

I got us an appointment for the next morning. When I told Richard about it Monday night he looked surprised, as if he'd forgotten the whole wretched scene. Then he shrugged and said, "Okay, whatever."

We left Emily at the sitter's house. It was hard to let go of her. Richard kept looking at his watch. Finally we got away and drove downtown, to a remodeled prairie-style house off of East Grand.

Mrs. McNabb was five-eleven, heavy in the chest and hips, fifty years old with short hair in various shades of gray. No makeup, natural fiber clothes, neutral-colored furniture. A single, ominous box of Kleenex on the table by the couch.

When we were both settled she said, "Now. Are either of you involved with anyone outside the marriage."

I said, "You mean, like, romantically?"

Richard was already shaking his head.

"That's right," Mrs. McNabb said.

"No," Richard said.

"No," I said.

She looked at Richard for a long time, as if she didn't believe him. I didn't believe him either. "What?" he said. His arms had been folded across his chest from the moment he sat down. "I said *no*, there's nobody else."

After a few minutes she split us up. Richard waited in reception while she asked me questions. Whenever I said anything about Richard, she made me preface it with "I think" or "it seems to me." I didn't mention Lili or my suspicions. Then I sat outside for half an hour, reading the same page of *Newsweek* over and over again, not able to make any sense of it.

Finally Richard came out. He was pale. "We're done," he said. "I paid her and everything."

We got in the car. Richard sat behind the wheel without starting the engine. "She asked about my parents," he said. He looked out the windshield, not at me. "I told her about how my father always made my mother bring him the mail, and then he would open it up and throw what he didn't want on the floor. And then my mother would have to get down on her knees and pick it up."

He looked so lost and childlike. I suddenly realized that the only other person who could understood what we were both going through was Richard. It was hard not to reach out for him.

"She asked me were they happy," he said. "I said no. And then the weirdest thing happened. I found myself explaining all this stuff to her. Stuff I didn't know I knew. How I'd always believed it would be so easy for my father to make my mother happy. That a marriage should work if you just didn't throw your trash on the floor for the other person to pick up. I don't remember Mrs. McNabb saying anything, it was just suddenly I had this flash of understanding. How I'd spent my life looking for an unhappy woman like my mother, to prove how easily I could make her happy. Only I was wrong. I couldn't make you happy after all."

That wonderful, brief moment of intimacy was gone. I was now an "unhappy woman." I didn't much like it.

"I feel all wrung out," he said, and started to cry. I couldn't remember the last time I'd seen him cry. "I don't know if I can go through this again."

"This was just the start," I said. "We haven't gotten *anywhere* yet."

He shook his head and started the car. "I don't know," he said. "I don't know if I can go on."

AND THAT WAS the end of counseling. The next time I brought it up Richard shook his head and refused to talk about it.

By that point he "worked late" at least two nights a week. It embarrassed me to hear the shopworn excuse. I pictured him in his office, his corduroys around his ankles, some exotic olive-skinned wanton sprawled on her back across his desk, her ankles locked behind his waist, her mouth open in an ecstatic scream, the rest of the department shaking their heads in shame as they passed his door.

I couldn't stop thinking about it. I lay awake at night and tortured myself. One morning in August I was so far out of my head I called Sally. "This woman Richard is supposed to be seeing. Lili or whatever her name is. Describe her."

"Can you spell slut, dear? What more do you need to know?"

"I want the details. Like you were doing it for the police."

"Oh, five-six I guess. Wavy brown hair, just to her shoulders. Deep tan. Make-up, of course. *Lots* of makeup. Did I mention armpit hair?"

"Yes," I said, "you did."

During summer sessions Richard taught a two-hour class, from one to three every afternoon. Assuming he was not so far gone that he'd given up teaching entirely. At one-fifteen I climbed the marble stairs to the second floor of Dallas Hall, looking for the woman Sally had described.

There was nobody in the common room. I got a cup of coffee and found Robbie in his office. "Hi," I said awkwardly. "I'm looking for one of Richard's students? Her name is Lili something? He had this paper he needed to give her, and he forgot it this morning."

He didn't buy my story for a second, of course. "Ah, yes. The redoubtable Lili. She was around a while ago. I could give it to her if you wanted."

"No, that's okay. I should try to find her myself."

"Well, you can't miss her. She's only about five one, with olive skin, blonde hair to her waist, and ... well, you know."

"And great tits," I said. "Right?"

Robbie shrugged, embarrassed. "You said it. Not me."

The descriptions didn't exactly match. I suspected Robbie was not seeing her with much objectivity. For that matter, neither was Sally.

The offices faced out into a central room which was divided into a maze of cubicles. I wandered through them for a while with no luck. On my way out I stopped at Taylor's secretary's office. "I'm looking for a student named Lili? She's short, with..."

"I know, the most gorgeous black hair in the world. I would hardly call her short, though—oh. There she goes right now."

I turned, hearing heels click on the polished floor. "Thanks," I said, and ran into the hall.

And froze.

She looked at me for no more than a second or two. Afterwards I couldn't say how tall she was, or describe the color of her hair. All I saw were her eyes, huge and black, like the eyes of a snake. It must have been some chemical in her sweat or her breath that I reacted to on such a blind, instinctive level. I could do nothing but stare at her with loathing and horror. When her eyes finally let me go I turned and ran all the way back to my car.

I picked Emily up at the sitter's and took her home and held her for the rest of the afternoon, until Richard arrived, rocking silently on the edge of the couch, remembering the blackness of those eyes, thinking, *not one of us. She's not one of us.*

THAT FRIDAY RICHARD came home at four. He was a half-hour late, no more than that. Emily was crawling furiously around the living room and I watched her with all the attention I could manage. The rest of my mind was simply numb.

Richard nodded at us and walked toward the back of the house. I heard the bathroom door close. I put Emily in her playpen and followed him. I could hear water running behind the bathroom door. Some wild bravado pushed me past my fear. I opened the door and walked in.

He stood at the sink. He had his penis in one hand and a bar of soap in the other. I could smell the sex he'd had with her, still clinging to him. The smell brought back the same revulsion I'd felt at the sight of her.

We looked at each other a long time. Finally he turned off the water and zipped himself up again. "Wash your hands," I said. "For God's sake. I don't want you touching anything in this house until you at least wash your hands."

He washed his hands and then his face. He dried himself on a hand towel and carefully put it back on the rack. He sat on the closed lid of the toilet, looked up at me, then back at the floor.

"She was lonely," he said. "I just ... I couldn't help myself. I can't explain it to you any better than that."

"Lili," I said. "Why don't you say her name? Do you think I don't know?"

"Lili," he said. He got too much pleasure out of the sound of it. "At least it's out in the open now. It's almost a relief. I can talk to you about it."

"Talk to me? You *bastard!* What gives you the idea that I want to hear anything ... *anything* about your cheap little slut?"

It was like he hadn't heard me. "Every time I see her she's different. She seduces me all over again. And there's this loneliness, this need in her—"

"Shut up! I don't want to hear it! Don't you care what you've done? Doesn't this marriage mean anything to you? Are you just a penis with legs? Maybe you're sick of me, but don't you care about Emily? At all?"

"I can't ... I'm helpless..."

He wouldn't even offer me the dignity of putting it in past tense. "You're not helpless. You're just selfish. A selfish, irresponsible little prick." I saw myself standing there, shouting at him. It wasn't like me. It was like a fever dream. I felt weightless and terribly cold. I slammed the bathroom door on my way out. I packed a suitcase and put Emily in her carseat and carried her outside. It wasn't until we were actually moving that she started to cry.

For me it took even longer.

DARLA KNEW EVERYTHING to do. She told me to finish the story while she drove me to my bank. I took all but a hundred dollars out of the checking account, and half the savings. Then she called her lawyer and set up an appointment for Monday morning. By midnight I had a one-bedroom apartment around the corner from hers. She even loaned me some Valium so I could sleep.

Even with the Valium, the first few days were hard. I would wake up every morning at five and lie there for an hour or more while my brain wandered in circles. Richard had said "Every time I see her she's different." And everyone I asked about her had a different description.

Helpless. He said he was helpless.

After a week of this, I saw it wasn't going to go away. I left Emily with Darla and spent the evening at the library.

Back when I was a lab assistant, back when I first met Richard, I took English courses too. Richard was a first year teaching assistant and I was a lovestruck senior. We read Yeats and Milton and Blake and Tennyson together. And Keats, Richard's favorite.

I found the quote from Burton's *Anatomy of Melancholy* in Keats' *Selected Poetry.* "Apollonius ... by some probable conjectures, found her out to be a serpent, a lamia; and that all her furniture was, like Tantalus' gold ... no substance, but mere illusions." The lamia had the head and breasts of a woman and the body of a snake. She could change her appearance at will to charm any man. Like Lilith, her spiritual ancestor, she fed off the men she ensnared.

> *I saw pale kings and princes too,*
> *Pale warriors, death pale were they all;*
> *They cried—"La Belle Dame sans Merci*
> *Hath thee in thrall!"*

I drove back toward my apartment. The night was hot and still. Suppose, I thought. Suppose it's true. Suppose there *are* lamias out there. And one of them has hold of Richard.

Then, I thought, she's welcome to him.

I brought Emily home and went to bed.

BY THE SECOND WEEK it was time to look for work. With luck, and child support, I hoped to get by with a part-time job. I hated the idea of Emily in day care even half-days, but there was no alternative.

I left her at the sitter's at nine o'clock. I came back a few minutes after noon. The sitter met me at the door. She was red-faced, had been crying.

"Oh God," she said. "I didn't know where to find you."

I would stay calm, I told myself, until I found out what was wrong. "What happened?"

"I only left her alone for five minutes. We were out here in the yard. The phone rang and I went inside, and—"

"Is she hurt?" I said. I had grabbed the sitter's arms. "Is she alive? What *happened?*"

"I don't know."

"Where *is* she?"

"I don't know!" she wailed. "She just ... disappeared!"

"How long ago?"

"Half an hour? Maybe less."

I turned away.

"Wait!" she said. "I called the police. They're on their way. They have to ask you some questions..."

I was already running for the car.

Subconsciously I must have made the connection. Lamia. Lilith. The legends of stolen children, bled dry, turned into vampires.

I knew exactly where Emily was.

MY TIRES SCREAMED as I came around the corner and again as I hit the brakes. I slammed the car door as I ran for the house. A fragment of my consciousness noticed how dead and dry the lawn looked, saw the yellowing newspapers still in their plastic wrappers. The rest of my mind could only say Emily's name over and over again.

I didn't bother with the doorbell. Richard hadn't changed the locks, and the chain wasn't on the door. There were no lights inside. I smelled the faint odor of spoiled milk.

I went straight to the bedroom. The door was open.

All three of them were in there. None of them had any clothes on. Richard lay on his back. Lili crouched over him, holding Emily. The smell of spoiled milk was stronger, and the smell of sperm, and the alien sex smell, Lili's smell. There was something else, something my eyes couldn't quite make out in the darkness, something like cobwebs over the three of them.

Lili turned her head toward me. I saw the black eyes again, staring at me without fear or regret. I couldn't help but notice her body—the thick waist, the small drooping breasts.

I said, "Let go of my baby."

She pulled Emily toward her. Emily looked at me and whimpered.

I was shaking with rage. There was a gooseneck table lamp by the bed and I grabbed it, knocking over the end table and spilling books across the floor. I swung it at Lili's head and screamed, "Let her go! Let her go!"

Lili put her arms up to protect herself, dropping Emily. I swung the lamp again, and she scrambled off the bed, crouched like an animal, making no effort to cover herself.

Emily had started to cry. I snatched her up and brushed the dust or whatever it was away from her face.

"Take the child," Lili said. I had never heard her voice before. It was hoarse and whispery, but musical, like pan pipes. "But Richard is mine."

I looked at him. He seemed drugged, barely aware of what was going on around him. He hadn't shaved in days, and his eyes seemed to have sunken deep into his head. "You can have him," I said.

I backed out of the room and then turned and ran. I drove to my apartment with Emily in my arms, made myself slow down, watch the road, stop for red lights. No one followed us. "You're safe now, Tater," I told her. "Everything's going to be okay."

I bathed her and fed her and wrapped her in her blanket and held her. Eventually her crying stopped.

THE POLICE FOUND no sign of Richard at the house. The place was deserted. I changed the locks and put it up for sale. Lili was gone too, of course. The police shook their heads when her descriptions failed to add up. Untrained observers, they said. It happened all the time. Richard and Lili would turn up, they assured me, probably at some resort hotel in Mexico. I shouldn't worry.

One night last week the phone woke me up. There was breathing on the other end. It sounded like someone fighting for air. I told myself it wasn't Richard. It was only breathing. Only a stranger, only a run-of-the-mill obscene phone call.

Some days I still wake up at five in the morning. If lamias are serpents, they can't interbreed with humans. Like vampires, they must somehow turn human children into their successors. I have no doubt that was what Lili was doing with Emily when I found her.

I can't say anything, not even to Darla. They would tell me about the stress I've been under. They would put me in a hospital somewhere. They would take Emily away from me.

She seems happy enough, most of the time. The only changes in her appearance are the normal ones for a healthy, growing baby girl. She's going to be beautiful when she grows up, a real heartbreaker. But puberty is a long way away. And I won't know until then whether or not she is still my daughter.

Time is already moving much too fast.

SNOWBIRDS

ONE MINUTE SHE'D been moving down Central Expressway at 40 miles an hour and the next she was stopped, closed in by cars on all sides. I should have known better, she thought, than to take Central. No matter how late it is.

It was cold, of course, bitterly cold. The sky was clear blue in the last light of the sun. A voice on the radio went on and on about the weather crisis, comparing temperatures from April of last year, reciting endless statistics. He had no answers, and Marge turned him off.

In the next car up, a little girl in a red party dress leaned halfway out her window. She pointed at the sky and shouted something at her mother. Just ahead another car door opened, and a man in a sheepskin jacket and cowboy hat got out to stare at the sky as well.

Marge put the car in neutral and set the hand brake. She rolled her window down, wincing as the icy wind hit her eyes, and looked up. She saw an old-fashioned biplane move across the sky in broad loops and swirls. Skywriting, she realized. She didn't think they did that anymore.

BEWARE, it said.

I don't like this, she thought. With the weird shit she'd learned at the bank today, and the cold, and the traffic, this put her over her limit.

The plane finished a second word: INVADERS.

People up and down the stalled expressway got out of their cars to watch, collars turned against the wind. The plane started a new line with FROM and followed it with THE. Marge smelled the exhaust coming up through the floorboards. She turned her engine off and drummed her fingers on the dash. Finally the party broke up, people rubbing their arms, nodding to each other, getting back into their cars. Marge saw the plane fly off, leaving a completed message behind.

BEWARE INVADERS FROM THE FUTURE.

Probably, she thought, a publicity stunt for some stupid science fiction movie. She failed to convince herself. She wanted to be home, nestled in the couch with a drink in her hand.

It was another fifteen minutes before traffic moved again. Two of the three lanes were stalled, and as Marge finally began to inch forward she could see the reason. Nearly a dozen cars sat motionless in their lanes as the rest of the traffic wound slowly around them.

Accidents? she wondered. Out of gas? Then she saw that several of the cars were still running, thin plumes of smoke trickling from their exhaust pipes. There were no piles of broken glass, no raised hoods, no dented bumpers.

The cars were simply deserted.

ON THE FOURTH TRY, Louis got through. He'd been calling every fifteen minutes since 6:00, telling himself he wasn't worried, but still vastly relieved when Marge answered the phone.

"Have you been calling?" she asked.

"A couple times," he lied.

"There was a humongous traffic jam on Central. Listen, you want to have dinner or something?"

"I thought that might be nice."

"Why don't you just come over? We can do something here."

"Fine. I'll be right there."

Before he left the apartment, he turned off the gas space heater and stood in front of it for a second or two, soaking up the last of its heat. About six-thirty he'd felt something hit him, a feeling of uneasiness that had left him weak and nauseated. Even now, knowing Marge was all right, the feeling still knotted up his stomach.

He drove to Marge's with the car heater on full blast. She answered the door in a terrycloth robe, her hair wrapped in a towel. "Why don't you get us some drinks?" she said. "Jesus, what a day."

By the time Louis had the whiskey poured she'd put on jeans and a sweater and sprawled back in her recliner. She wanted to be left alone, Louis knew, or she would have sat on the couch. He set a drink next to her hand and sat down across the room.

"So tell me about it," he said.

"I don't know if I want to. It sounds crazy."

"Try me."

"Well ... you know the bank has had me running credit checks. Mostly on snowbirds like you."

"Snowbirds?"

"You know. Northerners who move down here because of the supposedly warmer weather. Anyway. This morning I had a whole batch to process and suddenly I notice, hey, there's only about four or five different banks listed as credit references here."

Louis's stomach clenched hard enough to bring a taste of bile to his throat.

"So far," Marge went on, "all I've been doing is pulling reports off the net. I mean, there's not really a problem or anything, all the credit ratings are fine, but this business with the banks is bothering me. So I call one of the banks, where I know they've still got handwritten records in the basement. And guess what?"

"What?"

"Nothing there. I mean there's records, but not on any of these folks. Nothing to back up the data on the net."·

"Maybe they got rid of them?"

"Uh uh. No way. So I go to the boss with this and he just tells me to drop it. If the net says their credit's good, that's all he cares about."

"Sounds reasonable."

"Is it? What if somebody is ripping off the net? Shouldn't I like try to do something about it?"

"Hey. Relax. All you're going to do is piss your boss off and get yourself fired."

"Yeah, maybe." She finished off her drink and said, "You want to eat?"

"I..." A fist of nausea hit him. He blinked, and for a fraction of a second the apartment was gone. He had a fleeting impression of desolation, of cold, of rolling yellow-gray clouds. Then he was back in Marge's apartment, doubled up and gasping for breath.

"Louis?" Marge was out of her chair. "Are you okay?"

"Yeah," he said. "Must have been those tacos at lunch."

The couch was solid under his hand again, and his body felt all right. No tingling in the extremities, no signs of heart attack or stroke.

Then what was it? his mind screamed. What the hell just happened to me?

HE LAY AWAKE long after Marge had curled into sleep.

The episode, whatever it was, had left him off balance, wide awake. What he'd been able to choke down of Marge's meat loaf lay in a cold lump in his stomach.

They hadn't made love. Marge cared for him, he knew, but there wasn't much physical to it. I must seem old to her, he thought, though to himself 49 seemed barely middle age. He had a bit of a paunch, his hair was gray at the sides and thin on top. Then again, Marge at 34 was hard and thin from years of dieting and Texas sun, her voice and her temper both a bit brittle. Nothing that special about either one of us, he thought, each of us hanging on because there's nowhere else to go.

It was just the weather that had him down, he told himself. The weather and the heartburn, or whatever it had been. He put an arm around Marge's waist and listened to the comforting rhythm of her breathing.

MARGE COASTED THROUGH the morning on autopilot. Something dark and formless had lurked in all her dreams. She'd woken up three or four times frightened and out of breath, unable to get back to sleep for as long as an hour at a time. Outside the office it was gray and bitterly cold, with more snow threatened by afternoon. April blizzards bring May ... what? Mastodons, maybe, for a new ice age.

She was about to break for lunch when the phone rang, jarring her nerves so badly that she banged her knee under her desk. "Marge? This is Cathy, at First Bank in Albany. I talked to you yesterday? Well listen. I did some calling on my own. Trying to run down some of those addresses you gave me yesterday, from the net?"

"Yes?" Marge said, rubbing her knee.

"Well, none of the real estate agents listed have ever heard of those people. They aren't in any of the old phone books, either. It's like they never existed at all."

"That's weird," Marge said.

"Isn't it? I think it's kind of exciting. I bet it's the Mafia or something, you know? What do you think?"

"I don't know what to think," Marge said.

"I'm going to keep checking. If I find anything else I'll let you know."

"Okay," Marge said. "But listen ... be careful, will you?"

"Sure. Gotta go. 'Bye."

Marge put the phone down. So, she thought. Somebody was tampering with the net. It happened—they caught one or two every year, usually siphoning money. This was different. Who was doing it? And why? Who were these people with no pasts? Where were they coming from?

From the future, her mind answered her. Beware.

She shook her head. Whoa. Don't go off the deep end, here.

But, she thought. What if the skywriting hadn't been a publicity stunt? What if somebody else was onto the same thing? She started again to leave for lunch, and then sat down again. A couple of phone calls. It couldn't hurt.

She picked an aircraft charter company out of the Yellow Pages, and they gave her the names of two companies that did skywriting in the Dallas area. She called the first one and got a tired female voice.

"Yes," the woman said, "we did it. No, I can't tell you what it means. We just did a job, you know?"

Marge panicked and forgot the cover story she'd made up. "Look, this is really important. I have to talk to whoever paid for that message. It's important. It's ... life or death."

The tone of the woman's voice changed. "Then maybe you better talk to the police, hon."

"Why?"

"The guy that bought the ad was killed last night. The cops have been hanging around here all day. What did you say your name was?"

Marge hung up and reached for her terminal. Suppose, she thought. Suppose *everything* ties together?

ENTER SOCIAL SECURITY NUMBER.

She had seen Louis's number one day and memorized it, cursing herself as a nasty, prying bitch all the while. Let me be wrong, she thought, as she typed in the number and hit NEWLINE.

Louis's name appeared. CORRECT? (Y/N)

She hit the plus bar. The screen displayed fifteen lines of information. It was all there. First Bank of Albany, the lists of realtors, employers, and credit cards.

He was one of them.

LOUIS'S PHONE RANG at 4:17. "Louis?"

"That's right."

The voice began to recite a short poem of nonsense syllables. Louis wanted to hang up, but he felt oddly compelled to listen. Then the voice stopped and the world melted away.

It was like the night before, but stronger. His stomach lurched. He dropped to his knees, still clutching the phone. The snow under him was stained with oil slicks and foaming puddles; a freezing wind went right through his clothes and skin.

"Are you still there, Louis?"

"Yes," he gasped.

"Do·you know who you are, now?"

"Yes."

"Then you know what you have to do." There was a silence, then the buzz of a dial tone.

WHEN SHE GOT HOME, Louis was waiting for her. He sat in an armchair, holding a .22 target pistol. The barrel was lined up with her stomach. Marge felt a sick, scared bravado come over her.

"So it's real," she said.

"Yes. I didn't know about it myself until this afternoon. Somebody called and said some kind of code phrase that brought my memories back."

"And told you to kill me, because I know too much."

"I'm supposed to do that, yes."

He was pale, sweaty, and Marge could see the terror in his eyes. Otherwise he hadn't changed. He was the same ordinary man she'd slept with, and felt sorry for, and wished she could fall in love with, and hadn't been able to.

"Are you going to? Kill me?" It surprised her that she could say it.

"No," he said. He looked down at the gun, as if he didn't remember where it had come from. "I think it's too late, in any case." He tossed the gun onto the sofa.

"You shouldn't throw guns around," Marge said, wanting to scream with relief. "It's dangerous."

"Dangerous," he said. "We're being sucked back, you know. One at a time. The strain is too much."

"What strain? Back where? Am I supposed to have this all figured out or something?" She sat down heavily on the couch.

"We come from ... about a hundred years from now. I guess there's about a hundred thousand of us. We picked this time because it was the earliest when the net was in operation, so we wouldn't have to waste a lot of time building cover stories. And there's still another lifetime or so before things get bad."

"Bad?"

"There's no energy left. No heat, no cars. The oceans are dead, the rain forests are gone, the ozone layer is shot. I don't know exactly how it happened, but the weather got stranger and stranger and then just ... shifted. A hundred years from now most of North America is under six to a hundred feet of snow, and the glaciers are moving south.

"You think you can imagine it? Try to imagine not being able to bathe because there's no clean water, and if there was water you wouldn't be able to heat it, and if you could there wouldn't be anyplace warm enough to use it."

"Am I supposed to feel sorry for you?" She shrugged. "I guess I do, in spite of myself."

"It doesn't make any difference. I've held on this long, but I don't have much time left. Maybe an hour or two."

"And then?"

"It's like inertia. If you don't change anything, it's not too hard to stay here. But the more improbable your being here becomes, the more likely you'll just—snap back."

"And when people find out what you really are—or even suspect—that makes it worse, right? Like the skywriting yesterday. It snapped some of your people right out of their cars."

Louis nodded. "I saw it in the paper this morning."

"And the weather. Is that your fault too?"

"Yes. It's kind of ironic. The disturbance we made coming back here loused up your own climate. You know, people used to blame the migrating birds for bringing cold weather with them when they flew south. What was it you called us? Snowbirds?"

He stood up. "I'm going now. I can't fight it off much longer. I don't want to be here when it happens."

"Louis…" She reached for him, stopped with her hand on his sleeve.

"You're not even going to remember me, you know. It may take you a day or two to forget, but you will. People who don't really know me, they'll forget right away."

She felt bitter, used, betrayed. "Go on," she said. "Get out of here."

The door closed quietly and she heard his car pull out of the driveway.

"I won't forget," she said.

HE EASED INTO the street, sharp points of pain dancing up and down his ribs. Goddammit! he thought. Goddammit to hell!

The road in front of him flickered, and the houses to either side strobed in and out. It was like watching a film that wasn't framed in the projector. The car ran smoothly enough but his stomach felt like he was on a Tilt-A-Whirl.

He saw a set of abandoned metal furniture on the lawn ahead of him, left out through the long winter and the endless freezing spring. Lawn furniture, he thought. Sweet Jesus!

He didn't want to go back. Damn that man and his skywriting, damn Marge and her nosiness, damn them all to a cold and airless hell. He wrenched the wheel and the car shot over the curb, skidding on the patches of snow and the damp yellow grass. He crashed through the metal table and chairs. Something tore loose under the car as he jammed the accelerator down. He swerved into a mailbox and clipped a white picket fence, then wrestled the car back onto the street, his anger spent.

By the time the car coasted to a stop at the end of the street, the driver's seat was empty.

WANTING LIGHTS AND CROWDS and loud colors, Marge drove through the snow to Northpark. She window-shopped for a while, then stopped to rest at the fountain outside Neiman's, watching three grade-school kids slide down the tile sculpture.

"Hey," she said. "Come here a minute." They stopped and stared at her.

"It's okay," she said. "I just want to show you something."

One of them, a little older looking than the others, sauntered over.

"You want to see something neat?" she said. "See that man over there?" She pointed to a middle-aged man who reminded her of Louis (Louis who? What was his last name?), well-dressed, bundled in an overcoat and scarf. "Go up to him and ask him something for me."

"Ask him what?"

"Ask him, 'Are you from the future?' Then see what happens."

"You're crazy."

"Think so? Try it and see."

The boy laughed and ran away. She watched him tell his friends what she'd said. They argued back and forth, then the smallest of them went up to the man in the overcoat.

Marge found herself holding her breath.

The boy tugged at the man's trouser leg. He had to bend over to listen. The boy pointed to Marge and asked him something, and for a moment the man's eyes seemed to glow with a fierce hostility.

Marge blinked.

Hadn't that little boy just been talking to an older man?

She shook her head. I've been working too hard, she thought. I need to forget all this nonsense I've been worrying about (what nonsense?) and get some rest.

As she got up, three little boys, laughing wildly, ran past her, asking a question of everyone they saw.

Marge pushed open the heavy glass door of the mall and stepped out into a warm April mist.

MATCH

IT WAS A GOOD summer for tennis, hot and clear. I was newly divorced and working at home and had my mornings free. My partner was a radiologist from St. David's on the second shift. We played two sets a day, three if we could take the heat.

Afternoons I cranked up the headphones and sat down at the drawing table. I had discovered heavy metal. The louder the better—it kept my mind on my work instead of my marriage. This week work was one of those new fruit-juice-and-fizzy-water drinks called Tropical Blizzards. I started sketching a layout with a sweating tennis player. Right arm straight overhead, wrist cocked, body lunging forward. Face knotted in concentration. I worked on the face until I could see the heat in it. Brutal heat, murderous heat.

Suddenly it was my father's face.

I saw him clutch his chest and go down. My hand started to shake and the pencil lead snapped off.

I DIDN'T SLEEP much that night. In the morning I called my parents in Houston and my father answered.

"It's me," I said.

"Me who?"

"It's the Easter bunny, who do you think it is?"

"My only begotten son. Big deal." From his tone of voice I was supposed to figure he was kidding.

"I'm driving up for a meeting on Saturday. Thought I'd stay through the weekend if that's okay."

"I don't care. Talk to your mother." The phone clunked on the table. Distantly I heard him say, "It's your son."

"Hi darling," my mother said. "How are you?"

"I'm fine, Mom. Just thought I'd come up for the weekend."

"Of course. Your room's made up and ready."

I was 36. I hadn't lived with my parents in 19 years. "I'll be in Friday afternoon. I don't know what time, so don't panic if I'm not there for dinner, okay?"

"Yes, dear," my mother said.

•

Dinner at my parents' house was 5:00 pm sharp, in time for the evening news. I walked in as my mother set the tv tray in front of my father. Leftover pot roast, potatoes and gravy, canned green beans boiled for hours with hunks of bacon fat. I had a gray canvas bag in my left hand, with the handle of my racket sticking out.

My mother hugged me and said, "So, you're just going to let your hair grow now, is that it?" She was short, with a small pot belly and short hair dyed an odd sandy color. I got my gray hair from her. I already had more of it than my father did at 68.

"Nice to see you too, Mom."

My father squinted at me from his recliner. He wore a napkin tucked in over his shirt when he ate. He would have been six foot one, half an inch taller than me, if he ever stood up straight. He seemed to be devolving into some prototypical Texan ancestor, with long sideburns and hair combed straight back off his forehead. It made his nose seem to reach out toward his chin.

"Can you believe this crap? Thirty-two stations and not a goddamn thing worth watching."

"Great to see you too," I said.

"There's the same shitty stations you get without cable. Then there's three stations of niggers shouting at each other. Two stations of messkins. Two movie channels showing the same three movies over and over again. Rock and roll and country western on the rest. If it wasn't for sports I don't know why anybody would bother."

"Try some crack," I said. "That's how the rest of us manage."

He looked at the bag. My left hand clenched reflexively. "What's that? You're not trying to play tennis again, are you?"

"I've got a client here who plays."

"I wouldn't think it was good business to look like a jerk in front of somebody wants to give you money."

"Maybe I've been practicing."

"There's not enough practice in the world." He took a dainty bit of meat, then held the remote control out at arm's length. He switched through the channels, giving them no more than a couple of seconds each. His entire attention was on the screen.

"Is that all you brought?" my mother said, finally noticing the bag.

"I'm just staying the weekend."

"Could you two keep it down to a dull roar?" my father said. "I'm trying to watch a program here."

•

I MAY NOT have given much of a presentation the next morning, but I was hell on the tennis court. My client took me out to River Oaks and I slaughtered him 6-1, 6-0. As a career move, it was not exactly brilliant. I didn't care. I kept hearing my father say there wasn't enough practice in the world.

I came back to my parents' house drenched in sweat and flushed from the sun. "How'd it go?" my mother asked, meaning the presentation, of course.

I pretended to misunderstand. "Okay. My serve's a little off and I can't seem to get enough power out of my backhand."

"You're probably not swinging through," my father said, not looking up from the TV. "You always did chop your backhand."

My father had his first heart attack the summer after my junior year in high school. He was playing tennis with one of his students in 100-degree heat. My father won the first and third sets, and then he lit up a Roi Tan cigarillo and sucked in a big lungful of smoke. He said he felt something then, like a hunger pain, so he went home and had a banana and a glass of milk. Finally he went to bed and my mother called the doctor. I remember him lying there, white and shaking. Scared, I guess. Another half hour, the doctor said, and he would have died. I used to think about that a lot.

I looked at my father and said, "Maybe I need a lesson."

"Maybe you do."

My mother said to him, "You can't go on a tennis court. It would kill you."

"Says who?"

"Says Dr. Clarendon."

"It's not going to kill me to go out and look at his backhand."

My mother turned to me. The look said don't let him do this. If you let him do this, I'll never forgive you.

I thought about the time I ran away from home. It was the year after his heart attack. My mother promised we'd get counseling, talked me into coming back. The counselor turned out to be Dr. Clarendon. Mom took my father's side, and lied to protect him. Funny how things like that can still jerk your emotions around, even after twenty years.

I looked at my father. "Great," I said. "We'll go out tomorrow morning."

I LAY AWAKE past midnight in the tiny twin bed. Finally I told myself I wouldn't go through with it. I'd let the old man coach me a little and we'd come home. It bought me a few hours' sleep.

My father looked ten years younger Sunday morning. He wore his plain white tennis shorts and T-shirt to the breakfast table. Only queers, of course, wore all those bright colored outfits. He leaned forward and slurped loudly at his Shredded Wheat. "You're not dressed yet," he said.

"My stuff is in the wash." I'd brought blue shorts and a red T-shirt, just to stimulate his blood pressure.

"I thought we were playing this *morning.*" My father had been compulsively early all his life. If I said nine o'clock, he was impatient and angry by 8:30.

"Let your breakfast settle," I said. I couldn't eat. I choked down some orange juice and felt it eat through my stomach lining.

I kept him waiting until ten. The temperature was already in the 80s, and the air was like wet cotton. I drove us out to the courts we'd used when I was at Rice. They had fabric nets and a good composite surface, green inside the base-lines and brick red outside. Pine trees grew right up to the fence and dropped their needles on the backcourt. I could smell pine sap baking in the heat.

I got a bucket of tennis balls out of the trunk. "Haven't you got anything but those goddamn green balls?" My father was headed for the far court, working his arm in a circle. He had an ancient Jack Kramer wood racket, still in the press.

I carried the bucket to the other baseline. "They don't make white balls anymore. They haven't for ten years. You might as well forget about it."

"TV made them do that. You can't see a green ball as well as a white one." He threw the racket press aside, slashed the air with the racket. "You've got no depth perception on it. All it does is show up better on a TV screen."

"The players like them better. The human eye sees green better than any other color. Scientific fact."

"Bullshit. Don't tell me about science. What do you know about science?"

My father was a structural engineer. He worked on survey teams all through high school in the 1930s. He laid the course for I-35 all the way from Dilley, where his mother grew up, to the Mexican border. He joined the corps to get free tuition at A&M's engineering school, and when the beatings and hazing got too bad he convinced a maiden aunt to send him to UCLA. He was a self-made man, the son of dirt-poor Texas farmers, and he'd fought his way up to a tenured professorship at Rice University. He tended to not let anyone forget it.

I rubbed sunscreen on my arms and legs, then put sweatbands on my head and wrists. My father wolf-whistled. "Hey, bathing beauty. Any time you want to play some tennis."

I took two balls out of the bucket. I shoved one in my left pocket and squinted across the court. I was so pissed off I could feel it like something sharp stuck in my throat. I served at my father as hard as I could.

He stepped out of the way and said, "You still serve like a girl. Get that toss higher."

•

I REMEMBERED PLAYING Canasta with my father as a child, his smearing the cards together on the table because I was beating him, the cards bending and tearing, me starting to cry in helpless rage.

I tried to serve like a precision robot, hating myself because I didn't just walk away. My father crouched inside his baseline, leaning theatrically from side to side, swatting my serves long or into the net, not trying for the ones that were out of reach. After every serve he would point out what I did wrong, over and over, in a bored voice.

The bucket was empty. I started to gather up the balls. My father could have helped, but instead he watched, smiling sarcastically. I was painfully aware of my ass sticking out as I bent over. We traded sides and I picked up the rest of the balls. I stood on the baseline with the bucket next to my feet.

We'd played doubles with his students here, every playable Sunday, no matter how tired or hung over I was. I'd learned to pray for rain. My father had recovered from the heart attack and promised my mother he wouldn't overdo. I remembered the way he gloated over every point we won, and rode home in brooding silence if we lost.

"Waiting for something?" my father asked.

I bounced the ball with my left hand. It was the same motion as the toss, except the opposite direction. The idea was to focus on it. I couldn't focus. All I could hear was my heart, beating like crazy. I want it, I thought. I want it now.

"How about a game?" I said.

"Don't make me laugh. I can still kick your ass, on or off the court."

Twenty years ago, just out of the hospital, he'd said the same thing. He hadn't even made it into the house yet. He stood wobbling in the driveway, weak, gray-skinned, barely able to walk, threatening to kick my ass. Just the memory of it made my breath come fast.

"Prove it, old man."

I'd never said anything like it before, not to anybody. I felt the racket shiver in my hand.

"Serve 'em up," my father said. The look in his eyes was final. I'd done something that couldn't be undone. I felt like I was on a deserted stretch of interstate with the pedal all the way to the floor.

I picked out three balls and carried the bucket to the side of the court. I rolled one ball back to the chain link fence, put one in my left hand pocket. I leaned forward, bouncing the third in front of me.

I tossed the ball for the serve. My hand shook and the ball curved back over my head. I swung at it anyway and hit it into the net.

My father took one step closer.

I tried to get my breathing to even out. I couldn't get my breath at all. I took the second ball out of my pocket and bounced it, thinking, relax, relax. I pressed the ball into the racket head as I started my backswing. It felt all wrong. The toss was too low and I hit into the net again.

Double fault. My father straightened up and walked over to the ad court. I went to the net and picked the balls up, slapping the second with the racket so I could snag it out of the air. It got away from me. I chased after it, feeling my father's eyes on me the whole time.

"Love fifteen," I said. I pictured the serve in my mind and took a practice swing. I tossed the ball and hit it long.

"Back," my father said.

I was a little kid again, ugly, clumsy, with patches on my jeans and silver caps on my front teeth. I hated that little kid with everything I had. I got out the second ball and made a perfect, unselfconscious swing. The ball hit inside the line on my father's backhand. He jumped at it, took a stiff swing, and knocked it into the fence behind me.

I collected the balls and moved to the deuce court. "Fifteen all," I said. The first serve went in and my father hit it sharply down the backhand line. I got to and hit it crosscourt, thinking, run, you bastard, run. He stretched to make it, his shoes squealing as he turned. The ball floated back to me like a wounded bird. I hit it deep to his forehand. He chased it and didn't get there in time.

The knot in my guts loosened and the piney air tasted sweet and cool. I aced the next point and on the next my father hit into the net. It was my game. We changed sides, and I put the balls on my father's outstretched racket.

The sun started to bear down. There were only a couple of dry places on my father's shirt, high on his chest. "Think you can serve?" I asked. The doctors took a lump out of his lung five years ago, and he still complained about the pain in his shoulder muscles.

"Good enough for you," he said.

He took a few practices. His backswing had a hitch in it, and he couldn't get any height or power. The few balls that got over had no pace. My father saw where the serves hit and got a look in his eyes that I'd only seen once before. It was after his second heart attack, when they brought him into the ICU. He had an oxygen tube up one nostril and a catheter coming out from under the sheet. My mother said, "Well, dear, you're just going to have to take it a little easier." My father looked like a dying shark, hanging from the scales, eyes bitter and black and empty.

"Listen," I said. "We don't need to do this." It hurt me to look at him. All I could think of was my mother, what she would say. "C'mon. Let's go home, get something to drink."

"No. You've got this coming to you." He served, and I saw him wince from the pain. The ball came in soft, and I moved up on it automatically, driving it hard and deep to his backhand. He ran for it, missed, and went down on all fours.

I started for him. He got up into a crouch and froze me with a look. "Get away," he said. He picked up the ball and got ready to serve again. "Love fifteen," he said.

HE LASTED FIVE GAMES, and lost every one. I gave up trying to stop it. He was clearly exhausted, could hardly chase the ball. But he would not quit.

He started the sixth game with a junk serve, the ball flipped head-high and cut with exaggerated spin. I couldn't do anything with it. I hit it into the net, and the one after it into the fence. The third I couldn't even reach.

I moved up to the service line. "Forty love," my father said. "Set point."

I stared at him. Was he crazy? If he took this point he would win his first game of the day. If I'd been ahead forty love, *then* it would have been set point, set point for *me*. Did he not even know the difference?

He started to toss the ball. It dropped at his feet and rolled away. Then the racket came out of his hand and clattered on the court. His face was the color of wet cement. He put his hands on his hips and stood there, looking down, fighting for breath.

"Dad?" I said. But I already knew what had happened. Here it is, I thought. You did it. You killed him. Just like you always wanted. I took two steps toward him.

"Get away," my father said. He picked up the racket. I could hear his scratchy breathing all the way across the court. "Get away, goddamn you." He picked up a ball and hit it into the empty court before I could get to him. "Game," he said. "Set, match, and tournament."

He staggered to the fence and started to put the brace on his racket.

"Dad! Dad, goddammit!"

He looked at me. "What?"

"You're having a heart attack. Will you get in the goddamn car? I'm taking you to the hospital."

"Shit. Heart attack. What do you know about heart attacks?" He picked up the bucket and waited by the trunk until I unlocked it for him. He put the bucket and the rackets inside and slammed it closed. I watched him walk around the car and open his door and get in. He could barely move his feet, barely shut the door.

I got in and said, "I'm taking you to the hospital."

"You're taking me home. If you even start toward the hospital I'll open this door and get out, no matter how fast you're going. You hear me?"

He was sitting up straight, calm, one arm stuck out the window, the other on the back of the seat. Except for the fact that there was no color in his face he looked completely normal.

I knew what I'd seen. His heart had gone into fibrillation and he'd choked it down and ridden it out.

I drove him home.

When we got there, he went straight to the bedroom. I heard the shower start up.

"Is he all right?" my mother asked.

"No. I think he had a heart attack."

My mother squeezed her mouth into a hard, straight line. "You couldn't stop him."

"No. This isn't ... I didn't want this to happen."

"If he dies—he dies. I guess." It was the kind of thing she always said, to convince herself she didn't care.

I went to my room and packed my bag. When I came out my father was sitting in front of the TV, shouting at my mother. "I'm not going to the fucking hospital. Now go away and leave me alone."

My mother walked me out to the car. She was crying. I put my arms around her. I wished I could cry too. I wished it were that simple. "I'll call you," I said, and got in the car.

IT WAS A THREE-HOUR drive to Austin. After a while I couldn't think about my father anymore, and then I was thinking about my ex-wife. Counseling hadn't been able to save the marriage. We found ways to blame each other for everything—bounced checks, bad sex, spoiled food in the refrigerator.

When I was in grade school my smart mouth was my only defense. I was no good at sports and worthless in a fight, but I could hurt people with words. I never learned to stop. Even when the thing that had saved me in grade school began to kill my marriage.

I thought of the strength it would take to fight off a heart attack. It was the same kind of strength it took to pull yourself off a shit-poor Texas farm and become a professor at a major university, with two cars and a big house and a cabinet full of French wines. A strength that didn't know when to stop.

THE FIRST THING I saw when I got home was the sketch of the tennis player. His face was intent, unforgiving. I tore it up and threw it away.

When I got out of the shower, the pain was still there, knotted up in my stomach. I taped a sheet of clean, white Bristol board to the drafting table. I looked at it for a long time, trying to see what was inside it, waiting for me. After a while I started to draw.

It was a young woman in a sundress, someone I'd never seen before. She walked barefoot down a beach. She was thirsty. She licked her lips. She saw something in the distance and smiled. Maybe it was a bottle of my client's fruit drink. Seagulls drifted overhead, riding the updraft in the hot afternoon.

RELAY

STEVENS REWOUND the tape, pretending to concentrate on the hum of the machine. "What is it I'm supposed to be hearing?" he asked. "Voices?"

Across the desk from him, Blair was pale and sweaty. "It's Weston, the other man I was ... traveling with."

"Into the future," Stevens said, not bothering to make it a question, no longer believing that Blair would deny it.

"I know what you're thinking. With the tape that way and all. I don't know what happened to it. But if you concentrate, you can still hear it. You can hear him saying my name."

Blair's mother sat next to him, her face stiff as papier-mache. How old she looks all of a sudden, Stevens thought. Just since last week.

"Here," Blair said. "Let me play it again."

He leaned over the desk and pushed PLAY. As the weird humming and crackling began again, Stevens let his attention wander to the open window of his office. In the long twilight he could see miles of Kansas prairie rolling away from him, the glint of Fall River in the distance, beyond that the vivid pinks and purples of sunset. A warm breeze puffed at the white lace curtains and the smell of cut grass sent his mind back twenty years, to the day he'd first met Blair's mother.

She'd brought the boy in with chicken pox. Stevens had been drawn to her immediately: strong, thin, handsome, with an educated accent from the Eastern seaboard. He'd hoped at first she was widowed or divorced. She hadn't been, of course, so they'd become friends instead, and Stevens had no real regrets.

Though it broke his heart to see her now. She had so much grief locked up inside her, and no way for him to help her with it. Whatever was wrong with her boy would take a psychiatrist to figure out, maybe a team of them.

Stevens shut off the tape in mid-yowl.

"Look," Blair said. "You told me you'd heard of the Project."

"Heard of it, yes. I heard there was some kind of space station they were using for time research, or some such nonsense."

"A relay station. In geosynchronous orbit. With matter transporters and a Schwartzchild simulator that can produce nearly infinite acceleration. That's why they had to put it up there in space."

Stevens spread his hands out on the desk. "You've obviously read up on it. I'm not going to debate this with you. I don't even know what half those words mean. The simple fact is that they closed the project down five years ago. And you were never part of it."

Stevens pushed the EJECT button and handed Blair the cassette. "Until two days ago you were in California, in graduate school. Your mother has letters to prove it. Then you suddenly showed up on the train from Wichita, babbling a lot of nonsense about government projects and time machines. There's nothing else I can say."

Blair nodded, looking resigned. "I knew there wasn't any point in coming to you. But Mom insisted."

"Go on home. Get some sleep. If you still feel ... disoriented tomorrow, maybe I can prescribe something."

"Yeah, right," Blair said, getting heavily to his feet. Stevens wondered if he would ever get used to the sight of the adults he remembered as children. "I'll go wait in the car, Mom."

When the office door closed, Stevens said, "I'm sorry. I just don't think there's anything I can do."

Tears started in her eyes, then refused to fall. "I know. I just ... couldn't keep it to myself any longer." She stood and reached one hand across the desk to him.

Stevens took the hand and held it, but she wouldn't meet his eyes.

BLAIR LAY IN the darkness of his parents' house and lived through it all again. He and Weston, suiting up in the relay station. Stepping into the transport chamber, the energy field making his hair crackle and his stomach churn. The feeling of falling, a small impact against the bottoms of his feet. Then his first sight of the future.

They stood on an endless plain of concrete, rough textured, unpainted, broken only by a network of hairline cracks. The sky was clouded over, and a relentless wind sent sand and grit pinging against their helmets.

"Blair?" Weston said. "Do you feel something...?"

Blair turned to look at him. Through the distorted glass of the face plate he saw Weston's mouth tighten in pain. Blair was reaching for him when Weston began to scream.

Weston's suit seemed to shrivel and contract. In an instant he was gone.

Then Blair felt it himself, his entire body flexing and distorting like a reflection in a piece of foil. Something popped in the cooling system of his suit and he was suddenly flooded with freezing air. His stomach heaved. He took one step forward, groping blindly, and then the whole world shot away from him, in all directions. He blacked out.

He came to on the floor of the relay station, his skin covered with chill bumps inside the suit, his teeth rattling and his arms instinctively wrapped around his legs for warmth that wouldn't come.

He crawled to the control console and read the instruments. Power but no air, no heat. He was trapped in the malfunctioning suit.

A red light blinked next to the cassette recorder. Blair reached out with a shaking hand and played the tape through his suit radio.

"Blair ... I've waited here two hours and I can't see waiting any longer. I don't know what's happened, but the transporter seems to be working. I'm going to try it.

"Blair ... this is not the station we left from. Something's gone wrong. In this world, the station has been shut down for years. If you end up here, use the transporter. I'll try to find you somehow."

Blair had the tape in his hand as he staggered down the hall to the transporter. The room was empty. He could feel the blast of escaping air when he opened the hatch. Once inside, the room began to repressurize automatically. He got out of the freezing suit as soon as there was air to breathe.

His clothes weren't in the locker where he'd left them. Instead there was a suit of coveralls with someone else's name on the chest. He got into them and checked the transport controls. Everything seemed to be functioning. The destination coordinates were set for NASA in Houston.

He started to power up the machine with a hand that still shook—he wondered if he would ever be warm again—and then hesitated. If Weston was right, and this world wasn't the same one they'd left, he could transport himself into the middle of a concrete wall.

His mind suddenly flashed on Neodesha, the flat empty land where he'd grown up. It hadn't changed in hundreds of years, and he remembered the latitude and longitude from his school days. He reset the coordinates, and as he pushed the TRANSMIT button, he was thinking of home.

His mind skipped over the rest: the lurch of the transporter, falling into the field outside of town, catching a ride on the Wichita train. He concentrated on the earthly, visible reality in front of him, the cool breeze coming in the window, the sound of crickets and wind.

It's all right, he thought. I'm back. I'm safe. It's 1990 and this is Kansas, and I'm back again.

He found his old red and gray flannel bathrobe in the closet and put it on, hugging it against himself for warmth. He didn't want to go back to sleep, didn't want to let the fragile illusion of reality slip away.

He walked barefoot into the living room, stepping around the loose board that had creaked all his life. He sat on the blue floral sofa with his legs tucked under him, wanting a cup of coffee but unwilling to risk waking his father, who still got up at six every morning for his job at the lumber yard. He remembered the awkward silence when he'd tried to talk to his father about the project, the haunted look in his mother's eyes.

He picked up the newspaper from the coffee table and glanced at it by the moonlight coming in through the front window. The small town trivia of retirements and flower shows was comforting, had him on the verge of sleep.

Then he noticed the date at the top of the page.

April 23. 1997.

He clutched his stomach to keep from screaming.

Through the window he could see the spindly heads of the rye grass in the uncut lawn, the asphalt street, the lightning-split oak in the neighbor's yard. He'd grown up with that sight, but now it was terrifyingly alien.

When the voice spoke his name, he nearly jumped out of his skin.

"Blair..."

He turned to see Weston in the doorway.

"Had to warn you," Weston said. He was dressed in jeans and a sport shirt, reaching out with one hand. "It's not holding ... I wound up back on the station again ... couldn't tell if it was the same one or not ... used the transporter again but something's wrong..."

Weston reached for the wall and his hand passed through the paneling. "I don't know how much longer I've got. Listen, Blair, you have to..."

Clear streaks of lightning shot through Weston's image. His voice turned to static. In a second he was gone. Blair was left with the memory of his face, distorted in unbearable pain.

Blair ran to the spot where Weston had stood. Nothing remained, no smell of ozone, no stains on the wooden floor, nothing to show it had been anything but a dream.

THE MORNING CAME UP sunny, with a slight chill that had burned off by the time the coffee was done.

She hadn't wanted to wake her son yet, but he'd always been a light sleeper. He couldn't possibly have slept through the noise she'd already made. She put sugar in a cup of coffee and took it to his room.

She stopped outside his door. A wave of feeling, of loss, came over her for no reason. She had to swallow, hard, and brush her hair back to regain control. Then she knocked softly with one knuckle and eased the door open.

It was as if she'd known he would be gone.

She sat on the rumpled bed, touching the cool sheets, and let silent tears run down her face.

CASTLES MADE OF
SAND

J IM WORKED FOR a rental company—jackhammers, barricades, portable signs. He met Karla when he hired some temporaries from the agency she managed. There was just something about her. A sense that if anybody ever sprung her loose she might be capable of almost anything.

They got off to a slow start. She phoned just as he was leaving to pick her up for their first date. She was still at the office and would be there at least another hour. Could she come by and get him instead, late, maybe around nine?

Jim said okay. They had a slightly out-of-kilter dinner during which Karla drank too much wine and Jim too much coffee. When they got back to Jim's apartment, Jim asked her in, little more than a formality. She begged off because of an early meeting the next day. This is going nowhere, Jim thought. But when he leaned over to kiss her goodnight, she met him with her mouth already open.

She was a little overweight, with permed hair somewhere between blonde and brown, almost no color at all. Jim's hair was black and thinning, and some mornings he felt like a toy whose stuffing was migrating out of the arms and legs and into the middle. He was in the final stages of his second divorce. Karla had been married once, briefly, right out of high school. That was now a while ago.

It wasn't like they were laughing all the time. Mostly they talked about things that happened at their jobs. None of that seemed important to Jim. What counted was that, from the first, he could see they needed something in each other.

Karla was in no particular rush to have sex. Still, after a few weeks, it was clearly only a matter of time. Jim carefully raised the subject one night as they lay on his couch, watching old sitcoms on Nickelodeon. Karla thought they should make a big deal out of it, go away for the weekend. Maybe down to Galveston.

The next day she called him at work. She'd just seen a thing in the paper about a sand castle contest at Surfside Beach that coming Saturday. "Sure," Jim said. "Why not?"

•

IT WAS A two-hour drive to Surfside. Jim had been in a fender-bender midweek so they were in a rented Escort, courtesy of his insurance company. They got there around noon. They had to buy a beach parking permit, a little red sticker that cost six dollars and was good through the end of the year.

Jim was uncomfortable in baggy swim shorts and a T-shirt with a hole under one arm. He didn't want to put the sticker on a rent car and not get the rest of the use out of it.

"Maybe you can peel it off when you get home," Karla said.

"Maybe I can't."

"I'll pay for the sticker, how's that?"

"It's not the money, it's the principle."

Karla sighed and folded her arms and leaned back into the farthest corner of the front seat.

"Okay," Jim said. "Okay, for Christ's sake, I'm putting it on."

They turned left and drove down the beach. It was the first of June, indisputable summer. The sun blazed down on big cylinders of brown water that crashed and foamed right up to the edge of the road. The sand was a damp tan color and Jim worried about the car getting stuck, even though there was no sign of anyone else having trouble.

They drove for ten minutes with no sign of a sand castle. The beach was packed with red cars and little kids, college boys with coozie cups and white gimme caps, divorced mothers on green and yellow lawn chairs. Portable stereos played dance music cranked so high it sounded like no more than bursts of static. They drove under a pier with a sign that said, "Order Food Here," only there was no sign of food or anybody to give the order to. The air smelled of creosote and decay and hot sunlight.

Finally Jim saw a two-story blue frame building. A van from a soft-rock radio station was playing oldies at deafening volume and there were colored pennants on strings. It was not the mob scene Jim expected. He parked the Escort on a hard-packed stretch of sand and they got out. The sea air felt like a hot cotton compress. A drop of sweat broke loose and rolled down Jim's left side. He didn't know if he should reach for Karla's hand or not.

There were half a dozen sand sculptures inside the staked-out area. Jim looked up the beach and didn't see anything but more cars and coolers and lawn chairs. "I guess this is it?" he said. Karla shrugged.

At the far end was a life-size shark with a diver's head in its mouth. It had been spray painted in black and gray and flesh tones, with a splatter of red around the shark's mouth. Next to it a guy and three women were digging a moat. They all had long hair and skimpy bathing suits.

Jim stepped over the rope that separated them. "Is this it?" he said to the guy, half-shouting over the noise from the van.

"There's the big contest over on Galveston. They got architects, you know. Kind of like the professionals, and we're just the amateurs."

"I thought there would be, I don't know. More."

"The Galveston contest is big. They got, like this giant ice cream cone with the earth spilling out of it, they got animals, they got a giant dollar bill made of sand. I mean, perfect."

Jim looked back at Karla, still on the other side of the rope, and then said, "You do this every year?"

"Nah, this is my first time. I thought, what the hey. It's free, anybody can do it. You should enter, you and the lady. They got buckets and shovels and stuff over to the van. Hell, they got twelve trophies and not near that many people. You're sure to win something. There's a good spot right here next to us." He pointed to a stake with an entry number on it, stuck in a flat piece of ground.

"I don't know."

"You should at least go look at the trophies."

Jim nodded and the guy went back to work. It was too early to tell what his was going to look like. Jim stepped back over the rope and he and Karla looked at the other entries. There was only one real castle, pretty nice, looking like it had grown out of the top of a low hill. There was a sea serpent with a long tail. The other two both seemed to be some kind of humanoid figures, slowly emerging from the sand.

"This is kind of a letdown," Jim said.

"I wonder what they do with them after," Karla said. Jim could barely hear her over the music.

"What do you mean?"

"They're too high up for the tide to wash them out. That's what's supposed to happen, right? Digging moats and everybody running around, trying to delay the inevitable?"

Jim shook his head. "Want a Coke or something?"

"I don't know. Do you want to enter? Get a trophy?"

"I don't think so."

"Come on. It might be fun."

Jim looked at the flat patch of sand, the stake. He couldn't see it. "I'm going back to the car for a Coke. You want one or not?"

"I guess."

He took his time, trying to shake his mood. Nothing was ever easy. Everything was a struggle, and usually an argument besides. He unlocked the trunk and got two Cokes out of the ice, which was mostly melted already. He popped one and took a long drink, then started back.

He couldn't find Karla at first. He wandered around for a minute or so, then found her down near the water line. She'd taken a bucket and a garden trowel from the contest and built herself an elevated square of sand. On top of that she was dribbling watery mud from a bucket, making little twisty upside-down icicles. He watched her make five or six before she looked up.

She seemed to be blushing. "I used to do this when I was a kid," she said. "I called it the Enchanted Forest."

He squatted on his heels beside her.

She said, "You think this is really stupid, don't you." She took another handful of mud, made another tree.

"No," he said. He looked from the Enchanted Forest to the Gulf and back again. Close to shore the water was brown and foaming, farther out it was a deep shade of blue. He felt something inside him melt and collapse and wash away.

"No," he said. "It's beautiful."

PRODIGAL SON

HE WORE THE KIND of cheap Nike knock-offs that you see at Target, faded jeans, and a Lone Star Beer T-shirt that was last year's size. I made him to be about twelve years old, might even have guessed younger if his eyes hadn't been so hard. He was tan and fit, and his hair was the shade of blond that women in Dallas and Houston begged their hairdressers for.

"I want you to find my parents," he said.

I pointed to a chair and watched him sit in it, carefully, like it might move under him. "Now that's a new one," I said. "Don't tell me they ran away from home?"

"It's not a joke, Mr. Sloane. I got money."

"I'm sorry," I said. I got rid of my smile and straightened up in my chair. "Why don't you go back to the beginning and tell me about it?"

"Not much to tell, I don't guess. Just that I don't know who my parents are, and I want you to find them for me."

"You're adopted, is that it?"

"No sir," he said. "Kidnapped."

Either the kid had the world's best deadpan delivery or else he was serious. "Kidnapped?"

"That's right." He was looking at me like I'd left my mouth open, and I probably had.

"Go on," I said, waving a hand at him. "Talk to me."

"It was about ten years ago, here in Austin. Took me right out of a ... mister, are you sure you're okay?"

"Fine," I said. "Jesus Christ. This kind of thing happens to me every day. Shouldn't we be calling the cops?"

The kid shook his head. "I don't want to make trouble for nobody. Andy—that's the guy that took me—he's been real good to me. I know what he done was wrong, but I don't want nothing to happen to him. Okay? Me taking off like I did is going to hurt him bad enough."

"Ten years ago, you said?" Suddenly I could hear a buzzing in my head, and it wasn't just the AquaFest speedboats a few blocks away on Town Lake.

"Yeah. He always called me Buddy. I don't know if that was my real name or something he just came up with. He took me right out of a shopping cart outside some grocery store. It was raining, and..."

"Jesus Christ!" I said, and jumped out of my chair so hard that it slammed into the wall behind me. Buddy came out of his chair at the noise and put out one hand to make sure he knew where the door was.

I banged open the file cabinet and walked my fingers across the folders. "Burlenbach," I said, and yanked one out.

The kid stared at the folder, started to reach out a hand toward it and then snapped it back. "Just like that?" he said.

"Man," I told him, "if you knew how famous you were, you wouldn't have to ask that. Now, maybe I'm getting ahead of myself, and maybe it was some other shopping cart, but about ten years ago a guy named Burlenbach lost his son just that way. He was Councilman Burlenbach then, but he's a state senator now."

"State senator?" It was the kid's turn to look stunned, and I couldn't blame him. I had a feeling it was going to be a hell of a step up for him.

"He must have had half the PIs in this town scrounging for something the cops had missed. Me included. I even got my name in the paper over it."

"No shit," he said, and then glanced up quickly. "Pardon me."

"That's okay," I said. "Listen, have you got anything that might identify you? A baby ring, or a locket or something?"

"There's this," he said, pulling a bag out of his back pocket. It was the kind of little paper sack that they put single beers in at a 7-Eleven. "I was supposed to be wearing this when he found me."

Inside the bag was an infant's T-shirt. It had blue and yellow stripes, and Mrs. Burlenbach's description of it was on page 2 of the file.

THE SECRETARY DIDN'T want to put me through so I said, "Tell him it's about his son."

"Senator Burlenbach doesn't have a—"

"Just tell him that, will you?"

A moment later a deep voice said, "This is Frank Burlenbach. Now what the hell is this bull crap about my son?" The voice had a lot more authority than it used to, but I recognized it just the same.

"This is Daniel Sloane," I said. "I was one of the investigators looking into your son's kidnapping ten years ago. Um, to be blunt, sir, he just turned up."

"Now?" he said.

It wasn't what I was expecting to hear. "Pardon?"

"After ten years?" he asked. "He shows up now?"

"He's just fine, sir," I said to the phone, conscious of Buddy watching me from across the room. "Healthy, in good shape, a good-looking kid."

"If this is some kind of stunt..."

"I'd like to bring him out to you, sir, if that would be possible."

I seemed to have outlasted the bluster. "What did you say your name was?" he asked in a quieter voice.

"Sloane," I said. "Daniel Sloane."

"I remember you," he said, as if such a thing were a minor miracle. "Are you sure about this? I mean really sure? Because I am not going to put Georgia through this all over again and have it be for nothing. Do you understand me?"

I remembered Georgia, his tall, stylish wife, alternately hysterical and hideously uncomfortable during the few hours I'd spent with her. "It's no joke," I said. "Believe me."

He gave me his new address. It was in West Lake Hills, a big jump in equity from the one listed in the file. I told him we were on our way and hung up.

"Well?" the kid asked.

"We're going over," I said, not wanting to meet his eyes.

"He didn't even care, did he?"

I felt ashamed for Burlenbach, ashamed even of my own tawdry little profit-oriented part in the exchange. "Look," I said. "He went through a lot of pain over this ten years ago. He just wants to be sure, that's all."

"Yeah," the kid said. "Sure he does." He shifted his feet and made a face. "Before we go, I need to use the, uh, donniker."

I hadn't heard the expression before, but the meaning was obvious enough. I pointed him down the hall, and while he was gone I folded the tiny blue-and-yellow T-shirt into thirds and put it back in the paper bag.

THE AUGUST HEAT didn't seem to bother the kid much as we drove through downtown and crossed the river just below the Tom Miller Dam. He'd pulled back into himself after the phone call and I guessed he was working out the contingencies for himself.

The radio in my ancient Mustang told us that tonight was Czech night at AquaFest and there would be plenty of kolaches and bratwurst and cold Lone Star Beer on the Auditorium Shores. Not to mention the Golden State Carnival and a concert by Rusty Weir. I turned off on West Lake Drive and told Buddy to keep an eye out for the address.

The houses were almost invisible from the narrow, twisting road, most of them set well back and screened by mesquite and cedars. The odd glimpses, though, were enough to make the kid look back at me in disbelief. I found the driveway and eased down the graveled slope, steering around the BMW and the little sport Mercedes parked casually in the open.

It looked like the Burlenbachs had done pretty well for themselves in the last ten years, which was more than I could say for myself. When I came to think of it, the five weeks I'd put in for them back then had been about the last steady work I'd had.

Frank Burlenbach answered the door himself, wearing pleated khaki pants and a white shirt that had obviously been hand-pressed with a lot of starch. His hair had gone completely white since the last time I'd seen him, giving him the worldly air of a talk-show host. His handshake left heavy cologne on my palm and I resisted the impulse to wipe it off on my pants.

"This is Buddy," I said, having to reach back and pull him forward by his shoulder.

The two of them looked each other over like prizefighters, and then Burlenbach stepped aside to let us in. He didn't offer to shake with the boy.

He led us into a living room done in red tile, wicker and bentwood. Lots of plants stood around in terracotta pots that matched the floor, and ceiling fans kept the air moving briskly. I couldn't help but wonder if they laid down carpet and rolled in overstuffed chairs every winter.

Georgia Burlenbach huddled at one end of a long, low couch with white cushions. Her hair was short and not quite blonde, her clothes wrinkled the way only expensive linen wrinkles. She looked broken, somehow, as if carrying the weight of that abandoned shopping cart around with her had finally been too much. She wanted to stand up, but her eyes flashed first to her husband, and she read something there that made her stay put.

"You might remember Mr. Sloane," Burlenbach said, and she nodded. Her smile flickered on and off like it wasn't hooked up properly.

I took Buddy's shirt out of the paper bag and laid it on the coffee table in front of her. "He had this with him when he showed up at my office."

The woman gasped, and Burlenbach took half a step toward her. "Oh God," she said. "Oh God, it's Tommy." She picked up the shirt and hugged it against her, as if she hadn't yet connected it with the grown boy just across the room.

Buddy walked slowly over to her and held out his hands. "Mother?" he said.

That was all she needed to go over the edge. She jumped up and hugged him, sobbing loudly, the tears spilling onto the back of the boy's T-shirt.

"I'd better be going," I said to Burlenbach.

"What do we owe you?" He seemed abstracted, barely aware of me.

"Half a day's pay," I said, knowing I could have pushed for a lot more. "I'll send you a bill."

He barely heard me. "The boy—Tommy, or Buddy, or whatever—did he say anything to you?"

"Say anything?"

He licked his lips. "About us."

"I'm afraid I don't know what you're talking about." I looked over at his wife, but she was oblivious.

"Nothing," Burlenbach said. "Forget it. This is all just such a shock ... We'd gotten used to the idea that we'd never see Tommy again, and now ... well, I hardly know what to say." His brain was spinning like a roulette wheel, and I saw where the ball needed to drop.

"If nothing else," I said, "I imagine this will make for one hell of a newspaper story. Father and son reunited after all these years?"

"Hmmm? Yes, yes, I suppose it does at that." He shook my hand again and for the first time he actually managed a smile.

BY FOUR O'CLOCK the reporters tracked me to my house and I posed for a round of pictures and told them what I knew. After that I unplugged the phone and let my service take over. I needed the publicity badly enough, but I was starting to feel a little cheap. I'd really liked the kid, and it bothered me to make a profit off of something I should have wanted to do for free.

All night long my mind kept coming back to him. I wondered what it would be like for him, coming out of a world of dime stores and bad grammar and moving into that carefully manicured house, no longer even sure he'd done the right thing. What would Georgia Burlenbach think when the kid didn't know which fork to use or when she found him whizzing into the hedges?

I plugged the phone in before I went to bed and it woke me at six the next morning.

"Sloane?" Burlenbach sounded like the phone was cracking in his fist. "You've got thirty seconds to convince me not to call the police."

"Go ahead and call them," I said. "If you want to tell me why you're calling them, that's okay too."

"Don't get cute with me, Sloane. What's the price tag? Let's get that over with first and then we'll take it from there."

I yawned. "It's six in the morning, Senator, and I just woke up, and I don't have the foggiest notion what you're talking about."

"I'm talking about the boy, as you goddamned well know. Buddy, as you call him. He's gone."

I lay back down on the bed. "Oh Jesus."

"I called your goddamn reporters and now you know perfectly goddamn well how stupid this is going to make me look if I don't get him back. So what's it going to cost me?"

I spent five minutes convincing him that I didn't have anything to do with it. Finally I said, "Give it a while. Maybe he just went out for a walk or something. If you don't hear anything by noon, call the cops. They can be discreet when they have to be."

By the time I got him off the phone my sleep was shot to hell so I made a pot of coffee and read the morning *Statesman*. The kid's picture was all over the front page, and I even had a sidebar to myself on page 8. The longer I thought about it the more likely it seemed that Buddy had simply changed his mind, decided that his new home wasn't cutting it, and gone back to Andy.

I drove to the office, under the huge net banner for the AquaFest, and spent ten minutes finding a place to park. They were rebuilding Congress Avenue with trees and walks instead of a third lane each way, the first case I'd ever heard of a major city narrowing its streets. It had seemed like a good idea once, but we'd all gotten a little tired of the dust and the noise and the parking squeeze.

My service told me that the publicity had already brought in five missing pets, three divorces, and a short list of what might turn out to be real jobs. I was still sorting through them when Burlenbach called again.

"It's a kidnapping," he said.

"What happened?"

"Somebody called. Said his name was Andy, said he had the boy. He wants fifty thousand."

It sounded about right. Cheap enough that Burlenbach could put it together on his own, but enough of a payoff to justify the risk. "How long have you got?"

"Until eight tonight. Listen, Sloane, I'm sorry about this morning." He went quiet for a second, and I thought he was finished, then he started again in a voice thick with emotion. "I loved that boy. When we lost him, it almost killed me. We never tried to have another child. We just never got over it. And when you found him again, I couldn't trust it." Another pause. "And it looks like I was right not to." He took a breath and plowed on. "Anyway. I hope you'll accept my apology. And help us find him."

"Okay," I said. "But I haven't got much to go on."

"You've got as much as anybody. You spent time with him. Maybe you can come up with something."

"I'll do what I can," I said, and made him go over everything with me, what the kid had said and done, the kidnapper's voice, everything I could think of By then the cops were at his house, and he turned me over to a Lieutenant Rogers, who I vaguely knew. I got Rogers' okay to work on the case, and then I hung up the phone.

I put my head down on my folded arms. By now I had a long list of things I didn't like about this case, and at the top was the fact that Andy had set me up. It was obvious now that he'd sent the kid to me because of my publicized work on the kidnapping ten years ago, which meant I wouldn't miss the connection with the Burlenbachs. So much, I thought, for getting my name in the paper.

Then there were the nagging questions. Why wouldn't a two-and-a-half year old kid know his own name? Why did Andy wait so long to make his move? What was he doing with the kid in the meantime? Child porn? Some other kind of hustle?

Finally I sat up and went through it again, from the moment the kid had walked in the office. I took it slow and careful, and after about fifteen minutes I said, "Donniker."

I took my dictionary of American slang off the shelf and looked it up. The book said donniker was circus or carnival usage for "a restroom, esp. a public facility." I threw the book on the desk and looked up the date of the original kidnapping in Burlenbach's file. It was the first week in August, AquaFest week. Carnival week.

I was on a roll. I called my poker buddy Dutch at the cops and told him I needed a favor.

"So what else is new?"

"A couple years ago you said something about the carnivals that play here. You said what a pain in the ass it was to get a list of all the booths in the show, but you had to because of some kind of goddamned red tape."

"The language sounds familiar."

"Do you think you could maybe find the list from ten years ago and maybe a copy of this year's list?"

"Jesus, Danny, I'm supposed to be working for the City of Austin."

"I knew you could. I'll be over in half an hour."

When I saw the size of the lists, with over two hundred names on the old one and over three hundred on the new, a little of my enthusiasm wilted. What if he's not with the carnival anymore, I thought. What if he never was, and it's all a coincidence?

But detectives don't believe in coincidence, and the list, thank God, was alphabetical. In under an hour I had an index card with twenty names that had been on both lists.

It was 12 noon. The carnival was open.

I FELT DIRTY the minute I walked onto the midway. It wasn't just the heat, not just the pressure of all those booths crammed into the asphalt lot behind the Coliseum. It was the smell of greasy pots full of melted cheese to pour over nacho chips, the sticky puddles of dried coke under my feet, the recorded calliope and disco blaring out of metal horns, the lurking carnies in baseball shirts and gimme hats that sized me up as I walked by.

"Hey, gotta girlfriend? She'd love this Snoopy doll! Hey, where ya going? No girlfriend? Got a boyfriend, then?"

The big rides, the Merry-Go-Round and the Tilt-A-Whirl and the Ferris Wheel and something called a Dragon's Lair, were in the center of the lot. Around the edges were the shooting galleries and fortune wheels, concessions and fortune tellers, cooch dancers and freak shows, all the booths trying to look like anything but what they really were, the back ends of custom tractor-trailers.

One by one I crossed the booths off my list, the ones run by old couples or twenty-year-old kids. I marked off the grab joints because my instincts told me Andy was a hustler, not a food salesman. Finally there were three names left and A. Gresham looked like the best bet.

At the moment A. Gresham's balloon-breaking concession was being run by a thirty-year old woman with dark hair and prominent breasts, wearing a stained tan tank top. She could have been Andy's girlfriend, or she could have been A. Gresham herself. In any case it was time to move. I'd been there over an hour, and I was starting to draw a kind of attention I didn't like.

I settled down at the booth next to Gresham's and watched a scrawny man in his seventies hustle a pair of soldiers. He was running a big board laid out like a roulette wheel, with silver dollar sized holes by each of the numbers. When the bets were down the old man dropped a white mouse into the middle of the board. It walked around with its nose in the air while the soldiers shouted at it, and then it suddenly darted into one of the holes.

"Well," the old man said, "better luck next time, fellas. I could see he was close to feeling your number—did you see how he was sniffing for it? So I'll tell you what I'm gonna do..." But it was too late. The soldiers had wandered off. "How about you, young man? Fifty cents to win any prize on the second shelf."

I moved in, catching a quick whiff of ammonia. I'd read somewhere that a mouse would follow that smell, thinking it was the urine of other mice. An easy way to rig whatever hole you wanted.

"No thanks," I said. "I was kind of hoping to see Andy, next door, but he doesn't seem to be in."

The old man looked me over and I had about decided I'd blown it when he said, "Yeah, he's had Melissa in there all day. So you know Andy, do you?"

I nodded, trying to keep it casual. "Met him a few years back. Him and his boy..."

"Tommy?"

"Yeah, that's the one." My heart was thudding so hard I was afraid the old man would see the front of my shirt shaking. Tommy, was it? Then Andy did know the kid's real name. "Blond, good-looking kid."

"Yeah," the old man said. "A goddamned shame."

"How do you mean?"

"I guess you wouldn't know. Poor kid died about two years ago, while we was wintering in Florida. Pneumonia. Like to broke ol' Andy's heart."

BY THE TIME I got away from the old man I had it complete in my mind. I used a pay phone to call Burlenbach and told him to bring some cops and meet me at the main gate. "He's here," I said. "I'm sure of it. The kidnapper's named Andy Gresham and he runs a pop-the-balloon joint on the midway."

I stopped then and wondered if I should tell him the rest of it. No, I thought. Not over the phone. "The kid is one of them," I said. "It's not going to be easy to get to him."

"Maybe he'd be better off staying there," Burlenbach said, and then stopped himself. "Forget I said that, okay? I've been under a lot of strain."

It was hard to hear him over the noise. "Sure," I said. "But get those cops here. This could get ugly."

"We're on the way," he said.

I hung up the phone and started for the front gate, detouring for a last glance at Andy's booth. It was a mistake. The curtains were parted, and somebody was watching me from the darkness.

I looked away and started walking faster. When I turned my head again, Buddy was standing next to the woman, staring at me. As he watched he shook his head slowly, twice. And then he screamed, "Andy!"

I started to run. I could see them in my peripheral vision, vaulting their counters and coming after me. I made it almost halfway to the gates before the carny running the Tilt-A-Whirl saw me and saw who I was running from. He was young and tough-looking, with ragged hair and a Fu Manchu moustache, and as the ride slowed to a stop, he stepped out to block my way.

I tried to shift around him, but he was ready for me and a fist came out of nowhere and caught me in the stomach. My momentum took me past him and down, ripping the knees out of my pants. Before I could get back on my feet, they had me.

There were about ten of them, and they made a ring so that the townies couldn't see what they were about to do. There should have been cops on the midway, but I couldn't see them, and now they couldn't see me either.

The line broke for a second and one man stepped through. He was short, with the hard stringy muscles of an athlete, sandy hair and long sideburns.

"Sloane," he said.

"Hello, Andy."

He fired a kick at my head and I dropped out of the way, swinging both feet at him as I went over. One of them caught him in the thigh and he yelled "Shit!" and wobbled for a second.

I was struggling onto my stomach when a foot came from behind and caught me in the ribs. The air flashed white in front of me, and I couldn't find anything to breathe. Another boot landed and another, and I could tell, just barely, that I was moving with the blows and that the circle of men was following.

I rolled up against something metal and found myself in the clear. It took me a second or two to see that I'd hit the blue-painted barricade around the Tilt-A-Whirl. I twisted under it and got up into an unsteady crouch.

Somewhere in my mind I knew I only had to hold out a few minutes longer, that Burlenbach was on his way with the cops. So I got all the way up, swaying a little, wondering why they weren't coming at me anymore.

Then an engine fired noisily and I knew the answer.

I turned and saw Andy at the controls of the Tilt-A-Whirl, and as my eyes took it in, the first metal car sailed up toward my face.

I ducked, lost my balance, went down on my knees again. Somebody behind me let out a gasp, and I almost turned to look. If I had, the next car would have killed me, but instead I threw myself over the top of it as it went by.

The machine was picking up speed now and I didn't have time to get clear, even if the crowd and the barricades hadn't been in the way. The next car shot past high above me while I was still lying on my face, fighting for breath.

The next one would be low. I pushed myself flat onto the asphalt of the lot and felt the bottom of the car slap my back as it passed, hard enough to stun me and let me know I couldn't take much more.

I got to my knees. If I just lay there I was going to be dead anyway. The next one went high and gave me time to get my legs under me and say about half a prayer. Then the red blur of another car rushed at my knees and I jumped across it, my fingers scrabbling at the metal for a hold. One hand caught the safety bar and I felt myself being lifted up and away.

I rolled into the seat of the car, arms and legs all twisted wrong, but with breathing space for a few seconds. The wind roared past my face as the machine kept picking up speed. My lunch tried to crawl out my throat, but I held it down, crouching next to the seat, trying to see what was happening.

Andy still worked the controls from the hub of the ride. I was moving too fast to see him clearly, but the expression on his face was not pretty. It had just occurred to me that I wasn't as safe as I'd thought, that he could still probably push the speed up high enough to throw me loose, when I heard a voice.

It carried even over the noise of the wind, and it said, *"Stop it! Leave him alone!"*

It was the kid, and suddenly he was fighting Andy for the controls. The metal seat under me lurched, and the spinning began to slow.

I could still hear the kid's voice as I crawled back onto solid ground, my eyes closed, telling myself I wasn't going to throw up. "Give it over, Andy," the kid said. "It's finished."

Burlenbach helped me to my feet and kept hold of one arm while I looked around. The cops had cleared everyone away from the ride except Andy, and two of them were holding him by the shoulders. Georgia Burlenbach handed me a clean handkerchief. I didn't really know what to do with it so I just clenched it hard in my fist.

"Thank God Tommy is safe," she said. "Thank God he's all right."

"He's..." I wasn't getting the air I needed and I had to start again. "He's not Tommy," I said.

"What!" Frank Burlenbach shouted. "What do you mean?"

"Your boy is dead," I told him. "I'm sorry. But I don't think Andy would ever have given your real son back to you. This one, Buddy, is a substitute. Something he came up with later on."

"Dead?" Burlenbach said. He looked stunned. His wife reached out and took his hand, but he didn't seem to notice.

"What happened?" she asked. "How—"

"Pneumonia," I said. "He'd been living with Andy, grew up here in the carnival. It happened a couple of years ago. I'm sorry."

"Sorry," she said, and nodded. She didn't seem able to make sense out of what I was saying.

Frank Burlenbach turned to the boy. "Is all that true?"

Buddy nodded.

"Who are you? What are you doing here?"

Buddy looked at me and I said, " Go ahead. Tell him."

"I ... I don't really come from anywhere, I guess." He looked to me for help again, but there was nothing I could say. "An orphanage in Tampa," he said. "I been in and out of it all my life. Until I ran away to Gibtown, you know, Gibsonton, where all the carnies live. I heard they help kids our sometimes. That's where I met up with Andy, and when he saw me he got his idea."

Burlenbach walked over to where they were putting the cuffs on Andy and reading him his rights. Georgia Burlenbach's hand stayed in mid-air, where she'd left it, for just a second. Then it slowly dropped to her side.

"Clever," Burlenbach said. "We hadn't seem him since he was two. We had no idea what he would look like now. And with the shirt, and a few details he couldn't possibly have faked, why should we doubt him?"

The set of his shoulders changed, and I could see him digging his feet in

for balance, Clarence Darrow going after the jury. "And what difference does
it make to you if you opened up wounds that had taken years to heal? What
if you brought back all the doubts and nightmares and guilt that almost tore
my wife and I apart ten years ago? What do you care? We're just marks, right?
Yokels. What difference does it make to you?"

He had worked himself up to where he was almost shouting, and
Lieutenant Rogers took him by one arm. "Easy there, Frank."

But Andy had come back to life. He was staring at Burlenbach, and I could
see the little muscles working at the tops of his cheeks. "You didn't deserve
that boy, mister. You had no right to him, no matter what your laws say."

Suddenly something was wrong with Burlenbach. He obviously hadn't
expected Andy to talk back to him, and now he had gone pale and was
backing away.

"You know what I'm talking about," Andy sneered, and Burlenbach did. I
looked over at his wife and she was standing with one fist at her mouth, biting
down hard on the knuckle.

"You want me to tell your cop friends?" Andy said, leaning forward against
the two patrolmen that held him. "You want me to tell them about—"

"Shut up!" Burlenbach yelled. *"Shut up!"*

"—about the bruises that were all over that little boy's face when I found
him? About that cut over his eye that took two months to heal up?"

Burlenbach had covered his face with his hands and fallen onto his knees.

"Shit," Andy said. "When I saw that poor kid in that shopping basket, all
beat up, the rain coming down like that, I just couldn't let him go back to
somebody who was going to treat him that way. So I took him. I took him,
and I cared for him, and I brought him up. And I buried him. That was never
your boy. You lost the right to call him that before I ever came along."

The cops were pulling at Andy's arms now, and after one last look at
Burlenbach, he let them take him away.

I GAVE Georgia Burlenbach a lift downtown. She didn't look as though she
could drive, and I didn't think she wanted to be with her husband just then.

On the way I asked her if she was all right.

"I don't know," she said. "I don't know what I feel like. Things keep turning
around. First Tommy was back, then he was gone again, and now he's dead … I
don't know.

"When he first disappeared, ten years ago, I was so afraid it would all
come out. Then I was sort of relieved. I couldn't stand what was happening
to Frank, the violence … he'd always been so gentle, but after Tommy was
born he'd just go crazy. I just couldn't believe that it was really Frank doing it,

somehow. It just wasn't real. You know?" She finally turned and looked at me. "You know?"

Around midnight they told me I could go, and I went out through one of the side offices. Buddy and Andy were sitting there, with a couple of cops standing guard. I waited in the shadows for a minute or two, where they couldn't see me.

"...put me away for a while," Andy was saying, "but I don't see how they could do anything to you. Stick you back in that orphanage, maybe."

"They can't keep me there," Buddy said. "I'll be out in a week, under that fence again."

Andy smiled. "You just get yourself back to Gibtown, then. The folks'll take care of you."

"I will," he said. Then he saw me standing in the corner and his face changed. The smile stayed on, but the life went out of it. "Hello, Mr. Sloane."

Andy looked at me; and his face smoothed into a mask just like the boy's. He nodded pleasantly, and it nearly made me shiver. I hadn't touched him, nothing that had happened had touched him. I was still a mark and he was still a carny.

"Goodbye," I said to both of them. "Good luck."

FOR REASONS I didn't entirely understand I drove over to Lamar and swung off onto First Street, parking across the river from the carnival. The lights from the Ferris wheel reflected back to me from the surface of the lake, looking like a toy carnival in a paperweight.

From that distance it was easy to forget that the carnival was a message, a message to people like Frank Burlenbach, reminding him that there were people who didn't subscribe, who didn't care about his church and his Senate and his table manners, people who would take his kid away from him just because they thought they could do a better job of bringing it up. They were out there, and that was the message in Andy's frozen smile. Look out, it said. Look out.

I waited until all the lights went out, until the Ferris wheel stopped turning and went dark, and then I got back in my car and drove away.

MOZART IN
MIRRORSHADES
W I T H   B R U C E   S T E R L I N G

From the hill north of the city, Rice saw eighteenth-century Salzburg spread out below him like a half-eaten lunch.

Huge cracking towers and swollen, bulbous storage tanks dwarfed the ruins of the St. Rupert Cathedral. Thick white smoke billowed from the refinery's stacks. Rice could taste the familiar petrochemical tang from where he sat, under the leaves of a wilting oak.

The sheer spectacle of it delighted him. You didn't sign up for a time-travel project, he thought, unless you had a taste for incongruity. Like the phallic pumping station lurking in the central square of the convent, or the ruler-straight elevated pipelines ripping through Salzburg's maze of cobbled streets. A bit tough on the city, maybe, but that was hardly Rice's fault. The temporal beam had focused randomly in the bedrock below Salzburg, forming an expandable bubble connecting this world to Rice's own time.

This was the first time he'd seen the complex from outside its high chain-link fences. For two years, he'd been up to his neck getting the refinery operational. He'd directed teams all over the planet, as they caulked up Nantucket whalers to serve as tankers, or trained local pipefitters to lay down line as far away as the Sinai and the Gulf of Mexico.

Now, finally, he was outside. Sutherland, the company's political liaison, had warned him against going into the city. But Rice had no patience with her attitude. The smallest thing seemed to set Sutherland off. She lost sleep over the most trivial local complaints. She spent hours haranguing the "gate people," the locals who waited day and night outside the square-mile complex, begging for radios, nylons, a jab of penicillin.

To hell with her, Rice thought. The plant was up and breaking design records, and Rice was due for a little R and R. The way he saw it, anyone who couldn't find some action in the Year of Our Lord 1775 had to be dead between the ears. He stood up, dusting windblown soot from his hands with a cambric handkerchief.

A moped sputtered up the hill toward him, wobbling crazily. The rider couldn't seem to keep his high-heeled, buckled pumps on the pedals while carrying a huge portable stereo in the crook of his right arm. The moped lurched to a stop at a respectful distance, and Rice recognized the music from the tape player: Symphony No. 40 in G Minor.

The boy turned the volume down as Rice walked toward him. "Good evening, Mr. Plant Manager, sir. I am not interrupting?"

"No, that's okay." Rice glanced at the bristling hedgehog cut that had replaced the boy's outmoded wig. He'd seen the kid around the gates; he was one of the regulars. But the music had made something else fall into place. "You're Mozart, aren't you?"

"Wolfgang Amadeus Mozart, your servant."

"I'll be goddamned. Do you know what that tape is?"

"It has my name on it."

"Yeah. You wrote it. Or would have, I guess I should say. About fifteen years from now."

Mozart nodded. "It is so beautiful. I have not the English to say how it is to hear it."

By this time most of the other gate people would have been well into some kind of pitch. Rice was impressed by the boy's tact, not to mention his command of English. The standard native vocabulary didn't go much beyond *radio, drugs,* and *fuck.* "Are you headed back toward town?" Rice asked.

"Yes, Mr. Plant Manager, sir."

Something about the kid appealed to Rice. The enthusiasm, the gleam in the eyes. And, of course, he did happen to be one of the greatest composers of all time.

"Forget the titles," Rice said. "Where does a guy go for some fun around here?"

AT FIRST SUTHERLAND hadn't wanted Rice at the meeting with Jefferson. But Rice knew a little temporal physics, and Jefferson had been pestering the American personnel with questions about time holes and parallel worlds.

Rice, for his part, was thrilled at the chance to meet Thomas Jefferson, the first President of the United States. He'd never liked George Washington, was glad the man's Masonic connections had made him refuse to join the company's "godless" American government.

Rice squirmed in his Dacron double knits as he and Sutherland waited in the newly air-conditioned boardroom of the Hohensalzburg Castle. "I forgot how greasy these suits feel," he said.

"At least," Sutherland said, "you didn't wear that goddamned hat today." The VTOL jet from America was late, and she kept looking at her watch.

"My tricorne?" Rice said. "You don't like it?"

"It's a Masonista hat, for Christ's sake. It's a symbol of anti-modern reaction." The Freemason Liberation Front was another of Sutherland's nightmares, a local politico-religious group that had made a few pathetic attacks on the pipeline.

"Oh, loosen up, will you, Sutherland? Some groupie of Mozart's gave me the hat. Theresa Maria Angela something-or-other, some broken-down aristocrat. They all hang out together in this music dive downtown. I just liked the way it looked."

"Mozart? You've been fraternizing with him? Don't you think we should just let him be? After everything we've done to him?"

"Bullshit," Rice said. "I'm entitled. I spent two years on startup while you were playing touch football with Robespierre and Thomas Paine. I make a few night spots with Wolfgang and you're all over me. What about Parker? I don't hear you bitching about him playing rock and roll on his late show every night. You can hear it blasting out of every cheap transistor in town."

"He's propaganda officer. Believe me, if I could stop him I would, but Parker's a special case. He's got connections all over the place back in Realtime." She rubbed her cheek. "Let's drop it, okay? Just try to be polite to President Jefferson. He's had a hard time of it lately."

Sutherland's secretary, a former Hapsburg lady-in-waiting, stepped in to announce the plane's arrival. Jefferson pushed angrily past her. He was tall for a local, with a mane of blazing red hair and the shiftiest eyes Rice had ever seen. "Sit down, Mr. President." Sutherland waved at the far side of the table. "Would you like some coffee or tea?"

Jefferson scowled. "Perhaps some Madeira," he said. "If you have it."

Sutherland nodded to her secretary, who stared for a moment in incomprehension, then hurried off. "How was the flight?" Sutherland asked.

"Your engines are most impressive," Jefferson said, "as you well know." Rice saw the subtle trembling of the man's hands; he hadn't taken well to jet flight. "I only wish your political sensitivities were as advanced."

"You know I can't speak for my employers," Sutherland said. "For myself, I deeply regret the darker aspects of our operations. Florida will be missed."

Irritated, Rice leaned forward. "You're not really here to discuss sensibilities, are you?"

"Freedom, sir," Jefferson said. "Freedom is the issue." The secretary returned with a dust-caked bottle of sherry and a stack of clear plastic cups. Jefferson, his hands visibly shaking now, poured a glass and tossed it back. Color returned to his face. He said, "You made certain promises when we joined forces. You guaranteed us liberty and equality and the freedom to pursue our own happiness. Instead we find your machinery on all sides, your cheap manufactured goods seducing the people of our great country, our minerals and works of art disappearing into your fortresses, never to reappear!" The last line brought Jefferson to his feet.

Sutherland shrank back into her chair. "The common good requires a certain period of, uh, adjustment—"

"Oh, come on, Tom," Rice broke in. "We didn't 'join forces,' that's a lot of crap. We kicked the Brits out and you in, and you had damn-all to do with it. Second, if we drill for oil and carry off a few paintings, it doesn't have a god-damned thing to do with your liberty. We don't care. Do whatever you like, just stay out of our way. Right? If we wanted a lot of backtalk we could have left the damn British in power."

Jefferson sat down. Sutherland meekly poured him another glass, which he drank off at once. "I cannot understand you," he said. "You claim you come from the future, yet you seem bent on destroying your own past."

"But we're not," Rice said. "It's this way. History is like a tree, okay? When you go back and mess with the past, another branch of history splits off from the main trunk. Well, this world is just one of those branches."

"So," Jefferson said. "This world—my world—does not lead to your future."

"Right," Rice said.

"Leaving you free to rape and pillage here at will! While your own world is untouched and secure!" Jefferson was on his feet again. "I find the idea monstrous beyond belief, intolerable! Howcan you be party to such despotism? Have you no human feelings?"

"Oh, for God's sake," Rice said. "Of course we do. What about the radios and the magazines and the medicine we hand out? Personally I think you've got a lot of nerve, coming in here with your smallpox scars and your unwashed shirt and all those slaves of yours back home, lecturing us on humanity."

"Rice?" Sutherland said.

Rice locked eyes with Jefferson. Slowly, Jefferson sat down. "Look," Rice said, relenting. "We don't mean to be unreasonable. Maybe things aren't working out just the way you pictured them, but hey, that's life, you know? What do you want, *really?* Cars? Movies? Telephones? Birth control? Just say the word and they're yours."

Jefferson pressed his thumbs into the corners of his eyes. "Your words mean nothing to me, sir. I only want ... I want only to return to my home. To Monticello. And as soon as possible."

"Is it one of your migraines, Mr. President?" Sutherland asked. "I had these made up for you." She pushed a vial of pills across the table toward him.

"What are these?"

Sutherland shrugged. "You'll feel better."

After Jefferson left, Rice half expected a reprimand. Instead, Sutherland said, "You seem to have a tremendous faith in the project."

"Oh, cheer up," Rice said. "You've been spending too much time with these politicals. Believe me, this is a simple time, with simple people. Sure, Jefferson was a little ticked off, but he'll come around. Relax!"

RICE FOUND MOZART clearing tables in the main dining hall of the Hohensalzburg Castle. In his faded jeans, camo jacket, and mirrored sunglasses, he might almost have passed for a teenager from Rice's time.

"Wolfgang!" Rice called to him. "How's the new job?"

Mozart set a stack of dishes aside and ran his hands over his short-cropped hair. "Wolf," he said. "Call me Wolf, okay? Sounds more ... modern, you know? But yes, I really want to thank you for everything you have done for me. The tapes, the history books, this job—it is so wonderful just to be around here."

His English, Rice noticed, had improved remarkably in the last three weeks. "You still living in the city?"

"Yes, but I have my own place now. You are coming to the gig tonight?"

"Sure," Rice said. "Why don't you finish up around here, I'll go change, and then we can go out for some sachertorte, okay? We'll make a night of it."

Rice dressed carefully, wearing mesh body armor under his velvet coat and knee britches. He crammed his pockets with giveaway consumer goods, then met Mozart by a rear door.

Security had been stepped up around the castle, and floodlights swept the sky. Rice sensed a new tension in the festive abandon of the crowds downtown.

Like everyone else from his time, he towered over the locals; even incognito he felt dangerously conspicuous.

Within the club Rice faded into the darkness and relaxed. The place had been converted from the lower half of some young aristo's town house; protruding bricks still marked the lines of the old walls. The patrons were locals, mostly, dressed in any Realtime garments they could scavenge. Rice even saw one kid wearing a pair of beige silk panties on his head.

Mozart took the stage. Minuet-like guitar arpeggios screamed over sequenced choral motifs. Stacks of amps blasted synthesizer riffs lifted from a tape of K-Tel pop hits. The howling audience showered Mozart with confetti stripped from the club's hand-painted wallpaper.

Afterward Mozart smoked a joint of Turkish hash and asked Rice about the future.

"Mine, you mean?" Rice said. "You wouldn't believe it. Six billion people, and nobody has to work if they don't want to. Five-hundred-channel TV in every house. Cars, helicopters, clothes that would knock your eyes out. Plenty of easy sex. You want music? You could have your own recording studio. It'd make your gear on stage look like a goddamned clavichord."

"Really? I would give anything to see that. I can't understand why you would leave."

Rice shrugged. "So I'm giving up maybe fifteen years. When I get back, it's the best of everything. Anything I want."

"Fifteen years?"

"Yeah. You got to understand how the portal works. Right now it's as big around as you are tall, just big enough for a phone cable and a pipeline full of oil, maybe the odd bag of mail, heading for Realtime. To make it any bigger, like to move people or equipment through, is expensive as hell. So expensive they only do it twice, at the beginning and the end of the project. So, yeah, I guess we're stuck here."

Rice coughed harshly and drank off his glass. That Ottoman Empire hash had untied his mental shoelaces. Here he was opening up to Mozart, making the kid want to emigrate, and there was no way in hell Rice could get him a Green Card. Not with all the millions that wanted a free ride into the future—billions, if you counted the other projects, like the Roman Empire or New Kingdom Egypt.

"But I'm really *glad* to be here," Rice said. "It's like ... like shuffling the deck of history. You never know what'll come up next." Rice passed the joint to one of Mozart's groupies, Antonia something-or-other. "This is a great time to be alive. Look at you. You're doing okay, aren't you?" He leaned across the table, in the grip of a sudden sincerity. "I mean, it's okay, right? It's not like you hate all of us for fucking up your world or anything?"

"Are you making a joke? You are looking at the hero of Salzburg. In fact, your Mr. Parker is supposed to make a tape of my last set tonight. Soon all of Europe will know of me!" Someone shouted at Mozart, in German, from across the club. Mozart glanced up and gestured cryptically. "Be cool, man." He turned back to Rice. "You can see that I am doing fine."

"Sutherland, she worries about stuff like all those symphonies you're never going to write."

"Bullshit! I don't want to write symphonies. I can listen to them any time I want! Who is this Sutherland? Is she your girlfriend?"

"No. She goes for the locals. Danton, Robespierre, like that. How about you? You got anybody?"

"Nobody special. Not since I was a kid."

"Oh, yeah?"

"Well, when I was about six I was at Maria Theresa's court. I used to play with her daughter—Maria Antonia. Marie Antoinette she calls herself now. The most beautiful girl of the age. We used to play duets. We made a joke that we would be married, but she went off to France with that swine, Louis."

"Goddamn," Rice said. "This is really amazing. You know, she's practically a legend where I come from. They cut her head off in the French Revolution for throwing too many parties."

"No they didn't...."

"That was *our* French Revolution," Rice said. "Yours was a lot less messy."

"You should go see her, if you're that interested. Surely she owes you a favor for saving her life."

Before Rice could answer, Parker arrived at their table, surrounded by ex-ladies-in-waiting in spandex capris and sequined tube tops. "Hey, Rice," Parker shouted, serenely anachronistic in a glitter T-shirt and black leather jeans. "Where did you get those unhip threads? Come on, let's party!"

Rice watched as the girls crowded around the table and gnawed the corks out of a crate of champagne. As short, fat, and repulsive as Parker might be, they would gladly knife one another for a chance to sleep in his clean sheets and raid his medicine cabinet.

"No, thanks," Rice said, untangling himself from the miles of wire connected to Parker's recording gear.

The image of Marie Antoinette had seized him and would not let go.

RICE SAT NAKED on the edge of the canopied bed, shivering a little in the air conditioning. Past the jutting window unit, through clouded panes of eighteenth-century glass, he saw a lush, green landscape sprinkled with tiny waterfalls.

At ground level, a garden crew of former aristos in blue denim overalls trimmed weeds under the bored supervision of a peasant guard. The guard, clothed head to foot in camouflage except for a tricolor cockade on his fatigue cap, chewed gum and toyed with the strap of his cheap plastic machine gun. The gardens of Petit Trianon, like Versailles itself, were treasures deserving the best of care. They belonged to the Nation, since they were too large to be crammed through a time portal.

Marie Antoinette sprawled across the bed's expanse of pink satin, wearing a scrap of black-lace underwear and leafing through an issue of *Vogue*. The bedroom's walls were crowded with Boucher canvases: acres of pert silky rumps, pink haunches, knowingly pursed lips. Rice looked dazedly from the portrait of Louise O'Morphy, kittenishly sprawled on a divan, to the sleek, creamy expanse of Toinette's back and thighs. He took a deep, exhausted breath. "Man," he said, "that guy could really paint."

Toinette cracked off a square of Hershey's chocolate and pointed to the magazine. "I want the leather bikini," she said. "Always, when I am a girl, my goddamn mother, she keep me in the goddamn corsets. She think my what-you-call, my shoulder blade sticks out too much. "

Rice leaned back across her solid thighs and patted her bottom reassuringly. He felt wonderfully stupid; a week and a half of obsessive carnality had reduced him to a euphoric animal "Forget your mother, baby. You're with me now. You want ze goddamn leather bikini, I get it for you."

Toinette licked chocolate from her fingertips. "Tomorrow we go out to the cottage, okay, man? We dress up like the peasants and make love in the hedges like noble savages."

Rice hesitated. His weekend furlough to Paris had stretched into a week and a half; by now security would be looking for him. To hell with them, he thought. "Great," he said. "I'll phone us up a picnic lunch. Foie gras and truffles, maybe some terrapin—"

Toinette pouted. "I want the modem food. The pizza and burritos and the chicken fried." When Rice shrugged, she threw her arms around his neck. "You love me, Rice?"

"Love you? Baby, I love the very *idea* of you." He was drunk on history out of control, careening under him like some great black motorcycle of the imagination. When he thought of Paris, take-out quiche-to-go stores springing up where guillotines might have been, a six-year-old Napoleon munching Dubble Bubble in Corsica, he felt like the archangel Michael on speed.

Megalomania, he knew, was an occupational hazard. But he'd get back to work soon enough, in just a few more days....

The phone rang. Rice burrowed into a plush house robe formerly owned by Louis XVI. Louis wouldn't mind; he was now a happily divorced locksmith in Nice.

Mozart's face appeared on the phone's tiny screen. "Hey, man, where are you?"

"France," Rice said vaguely. "What's up?"

"Trouble, man. Sutherland flipped out, and they've got her sedated. At least six key people have gone over the hill, counting you." Mozart's voice had only the faintest trace of accent left.

"Hey, I'm not over the hill. I'll be back in just a couple days. We've got, what, thirty other people in Northern Europe? If you're worried about the quotas—"

"Fuck the quotas. This is serious. There's uprisings. Comanches raising hell on the rigs in Texas. Labor strikes in London and Vienna. Realtime is pissed. They're talking about pulling us out."

"What?" Now he was alarmed.

"Yeah. Word came down the line today. They say you guys let this whole operation get sloppy. Too much contamination, too much fraternization. Sutherland made a lot of trouble with the locals before she got found out. She was organizing the Masonistas for some kind of passive resistance and God knows what else."

"Shit." The fucking politicals had screwed it up again. It wasn't enough that he'd busted ass getting the plant up and on line; now he had to clean up after Sutherland. He glared at Mozart. "Speaking of fraternization, what's all this *we* stuff? What the hell are you doing calling me?"

Mozart paled. "Just trying to help. I got a job in communications now."

"That takes a Green Card. Where the hell did you get that?"

"Uh, listen, man, I got to go. Get back here, will you? We need you." Mozart's eyes flickered, looking past Rice's shoulder. "You can bring your little time-bunny along if you want. But hurry."

"I ... oh, shit, okay," Rice said.

RICE'S HOVERCAR huffed along at a steady 80 KPH, blasting clouds of dust from the deeply rutted highway. They were near the Bavarian border. Ragged Alps jutted into the sky over radiant green meadows, tiny picturesque farm-houses, and clear, vivid streams of melted snow.

They'd just had their first argument. Toinette had asked for a Green Card, and Rice had told her he couldn't do it. He offered her a Gray Card instead, that would get her from one branch of time to another without letting her visit Realtime. He knew he'd be reassigned if the project pulled out, and he wanted to take her with him. He wanted to do the decent thing, not leave her behind in a world without Hersheys and *Vogues*.

But she wasn't having any of it. After a few kilometers of weighty silence she started to squirm. "I have to pee," she said finally. "Pull over by the god-damn trees."

"Okay," Rice said. "Okay."

He cut the fans and whirred to a stop. A herd of brindled cattle spooked off with a clank of cowbells. The road was deserted.

Rice got out and stretched, watching Toinette climb a wooden stile and walk toward a stand of trees.

"What's the deal?" Rice yelled. "There's nobody around. Get on with it!"

A dozen men burst up from the cover of a ditch and rushed him. In an in-stant they'd surrounded him, leveling flintlock pistols. They wore tricornes and wigs and lace-cuffed highwayman's coats; black domino masks hid their faces. "What the fuck is this?" Rice asked, amazed. "Mardi Gras?"

The leader ripped off his mask and bowed ironically. His handsome Teutonic features were powdered, his lips rouged. "I am Count Axel Ferson. Servant, sir."

Rice knew the name; Ferson had been Toinette's lover before the Revolution. "Look, Count, maybe you're a little upset about Toinette, but I'm sure we can make a deal. Wouldn't you really rather have a color TV?"

"Spare us your satanic blandishments, sir!" Ferson roared. "I would not soil my hands on the collaborationist cow. We are the Freemason Liberation Front!"

"Christ," Rice said. "You can't possibly be serious. Are you taking on the project with these popguns?"

"We are aware of your advantage in armaments, sir. This is why we have made you our hostage." He spoke to the others in German. They tied Rice's hands and hustled him into the back of a horse-drawn wagon that had clopped out of the woods.

"Can't we at least take the car?" Rice asked. Glancing back, he saw Toinette sitting dejectedly in the road by the hovercraft.

"We reject your machines," Ferson said. "They are one more facet of your godlessness. Soon we will drive you back to hell, from whence you came!"

"With what? Broomsticks?" Rice sat up in the back of the wagon, ignoring the stink of manure and rotting hay. "Don't mistake our kindness for weakness. If they send the Gray Card Army through that portal, there won't be enough left of you to fill an ashtray."

"We are prepared to sacrifice! Each day thousands flock to our worldwide movement, under the banner of the All-Seeing Eye! We shall reclaim our destiny! The destiny you have stolen from us!"

"Your *destiny*?" Rice was aghast. "Listen, Count, you ever hear of guillotines?"

"I wish to hear no more of your machines." Ferson gestured to a subordinate. "Gag him."

THEY HAULED RICE to a farmhouse outside Salzburg. During fifteen bone-jarring hours in the wagon he thought of nothing but Toinette's betrayal. If he'd promised her the Green Card, would she still have led him into the ambush? That card was the only thing she wanted, but how could the Masonistas get her one?

Rice's guards paced restlessly in front of the windows, their boots squeaking on the loosely pegged floorboards. From their constant references to Salzburg he gathered that some kind of siege was in progress.

Nobody had shown up to negotiate Rice's release, and the Masonistas were getting nervous. If he could just gnaw through his gag, Rice was sure he'd be able to talk some sense into them.

He heard a distant drone, building slowly to a roar. Four of the men ran outside, leaving a single guard at the open door. Rice squirmed in his bonds and tried to sit up.

Suddenly the clapboards above his head were blasted to splinters by heavy machine-gun fire. Grenades whumped in front of the house, and the windows exploded in a gush of black smoke. A choking Masonista lifted his flintlock at Rice. Before he could pull the trigger a burst of gunfire threw the terrorist against the wall.

A short, heavyset man in flak jacket and leather pants stalked into the room. He stripped goggles from his smoke-blackened face, revealing Oriental eyes. A pair of greased braids hung down his back. He cradled an assault rifle in the crook of one arm and wore two bandoliers of grenades. "Good," he grunted. "The last of them." He tore the gag from Rice's mouth. He smelled of sweat and smoke and badly cured leather. "You are Rice?"

Rice could only nod and gasp for breath.

His rescuer hauled him to his feet and cut his ropes with a bayonet. "I am Jebe Noyon. Trans-Temporal Army." He forced a leather flask of rancid mare's milk into Rice's hands. The smell made Rice want to vomit. "Drink!" Jebe insisted. "Is *koumiss,* is good for you! Drink, Jebe Noyon tells you!"

Rice took a sip, which curdled his tongue and brought bile to his throat. "You're the Gray Cards, right?" he said weakly.

"Gray Card Army, yes," Jebe said. "Baddest-ass warriors of all times and places! Only five guards here, I kill them all! I, Jebe Noyon, was chief general to Genghis Khan, terror of the earth, okay, man?" He stared at Rice with great, sad eyes. "You have not heard of me."

"Sorry, Jebe, no."

"The earth turned black in the footprints of my horse."

"I'm sure it did, man."

"You will mount up behind me," he said, dragging Rice toward the door. "You will watch the earth turn black in the tireprints of my Harley, man, okay?"

FROM THE HILLS above Salzburg they looked down on anachronism gone wild.

Local soldiers in waistcoats and gaiters lay in bloody heaps by the gates of the refinery. Another battalion marched forward in formation, muskets at the ready. A handful of Huns and Mongols, deployed at the gates, cut them up with orange tracer fire and watched the survivors scatter.

Jebe Noyon laughed hugely. "Is like siege of Cambaluc! Only no stacking up heads or even taking ears any more, man, now we are civilized, okay? Later maybe we call in, like, grunts, choppers from 'Nam, napalm the son-of-a-bitches, far out, man."

"You can't do that, Jebe," Rice said sternly. "The poor bastards don't have a chance. No point in exterminating them."

Jebe shrugged. "I forget sometimes, okay? Always thinking to conquer the world." He revved the cycle and scowled. Rice grabbed the Mongol's stinking flak jacket as they roared downhill. Jebe took his disappointment out on the enemy, tearing through the streets in high gear, deliberately running down a group of Brunswick grenadiers. Only panic strength saved Rice from falling off as legs and torsos thumped and crunched beneath their tires.

Jebe skidded to a stop inside the gates of the complex. A jabbering horde of Mongols in ammo belts and combat fatigues surrounded them at once. Rice pushed through them, his kidneys aching.

Ionizing radiation smeared the evening sky around the Hohensalzburg Castle. They were kicking the portal up to the high-energy maximum, running cars full of Gray Cards in and sending the same cars back loaded to the ceiling with art and jewelry.

Over the rattling of gunfire Rice could hear the whine of VTOL jets bringing in the evacuees from the US and Africa. Roman centurions, wrapped in mesh body armor and carrying shoulder-launched rockets, herded Realtime personnel into the tunnels that led to the portal.

Mozart was in the crowd, waving enthusiastically to Rice. "We're pulling out, man! Fantastic, huh? Back to Realtime!"

Rice looked at the clustered towers of pumps, coolers, and catalytic cracking units. "It's a goddamned shame," he said. "All that work, shot to hell."

"We were losing too many people, man. Forget it. There's plenty of eighteenth centuries."

The guards, sniping at the crowds outside, suddenly leaped aside as Rice's hovercar burst through the gates. Half a dozen Masonic fanatics still clung to the doors and pounded on the windscreen. Jebe's Mongols yanked the invaders free and axed them while a Roman flamethrower unit gushed fire across the gates.

Marie Antoinette leaped out of the hovercar. Jebe grabbed for her, but her sleeve came off in his hand. She spotted Mozart and ran for him, Jebe only a few steps behind.

"Wolf, you bastard!" she shouted. "You leave me behind! What about your promises, you *merde,* you pig-dog!"

Mozart whipped off his mirrorshades. He turned to Rice. "Who is this woman?"

"The Green Card, Wolf! You say I sell Rice to the Masonistas, you get me the card!" She stopped for breath and Jebe caught her by one arm. When she whirled on him, he cracked her across the jaw, and she dropped to the tarmac.

The Mongol focused his smoldering eyes on Mozart. "Was you, eh? You, the traitor?" With the speed of a striking cobra he pulled his machine pistol and jammed the muzzle against Mozart's nose. "I put my gun on rock and roll, there nothing left of you but ears, man."

A single shot echoed across the courtyard. Jebe's head rocked back, and he fell in a heap.

Rice spun to his right. Parker, the DJ, stood in the doorway of an equipment shed. He held a Walther PPK. "Take it easy, Rice," Parker said, walking toward him. "He's just a grunt, expendable."

"You *killed* him!"

"So what?" Parker said, throwing one arm around Mozart's frail shoulders. "This here's my boy! I transmitted a couple of his new tunes up the line a month ago. You know what? The kid's number five on the *Billboard* charts! Number five!" Parker shoved the gun into his belt. "With a bullet!"

"You gave him the Green Card, Parker?"

"No," Mozart said. "It was Sutherland."

"What did you do to her?"

"Nothing! I swear to you, man! Well, maybe I kind of lived up to what she wanted to see. A broken man, you know, his music stolen from him, his very soul?" Mozart rolled his eyes upward. "She gave me the Green Card, but that still wasn't enough. She couldn't handle the guilt. You know the rest."

"And when she got caught, you were afraid we wouldn't pull out. So you decided to drag *me* into it! You got Toinette to turn me over to the Masons. That was *your* doing!"

As if hearing her name, Toinette moaned softly from the tarmac. Rice didn't care about the bruises, the dirt, the rips in her leopard-skin jeans. She was still the most gorgeous creature he'd ever seen.

Mozart shrugged. "I was a Freemason once. Look, man, they're very uncool. I mean, all I did was drop a few hints, and look what happened." He waved casually at the carnage all around them. "I knew you'd get away from them somehow."

"You can't just *use* people like that!"

"Bullshit, Rice! You do it all the time! I *needed* this seige so Realtime would haul us out! For Christ's sake, I can't wait fifteen years to go up the line. History says I'm going to be *dead* in fifteen years! I don't want to die in this dump! I want that car and that recording studio!"

"Forget it, pal," Rice said. "When they hear back in Realtime how you screwed things up here—"

Parker laughed. "Shove off, Rice. We're talking Top of the Pops, here. Not some penny-ante refinery." He took Mozart's arm protectively. "Listen, Wolf, baby, let's get into those tunnels. I got some papers for you to sign as soon as we hit the future."

The sun had set, but muzzle-loading cannon lit the night, pumping shells into the city. For a moment Rice stood stunned as cannonballs clanged harmlessly off the storage tanks. Then, finally, he shook his head. Salzburg's time had run out.

Hoisting Toinette over one shoulder, he ran toward the safety of the tunnels.

KIDDING AROUND

MOM PULLED OUT the fake vomit again yesterday. It's been almost a year and I thought maybe she was over all that. Guess not, huh? We were in the doctor's office. I'd just had a checkup so I could stay on the Pill. I'm not on it because of *that,* it's because my periods are messed up. Like there's somebody whose periods are normal? Could I see a show of hands, please? Mom is paying the bill. She waits until the nurse looks away for something and plop, drops it right there on the linoleum. Then she goes into her act. "Oh, Miss?" holding a handkerchief to her nose. "Miss? Don't you think you should do something about this? I mean, this is a doctor's office, and how healthy can it be," and on and on. I have to admit it's a little hard not to crack up when I see the nurse's face. The nurse has her hands up and fluttering around and runs out front, turning green like she's going to lose it herself. Mom gets That Look and says, "Well, if you won't do anything about it, I guess I'll have to take care of it myself," and sweeps it up with her handkerchief. She says, "Come along dear," and we're out the door.

This is pretty typical. It can go on for weeks. One time last year she drove me and my little brother Ricky to Houston for a speech tournament. Everybody was there, my best friend Gail, even this guy Ryan who I'm not really interested in, but is as close to cute as they get in Tomball, Texas. So my Mom dresses up in a clown costume. I'm *not* kidding. Purple wig, red ball nose, big net collar, the works. And in case there isn't anybody in the entire city who hasn't already noticed that I came with her, she pulls out this three-foot bicycle horn and honks goodbye to me with it.

My Dad's not any better. He doesn't carry around itching powder and Chinese finger traps, but he's never serious either. What kills me is he won't ever admit to anything. He'll like leave a *Playboy* centerfold around and there'll be something really gross written to him on it, like it was from the girl in the picture. Mom yells at him and he just shrugs and says, "Well, *somebody* did it."

Gail has been my best friend since I was three years old. She lives on the other side of the highway from me. We're totally different people. I'm kind of big-boned but I have a pretty okay face, just wear a little eye shadow and lipstick. Gail is short and blond and dresses to the max every day. All she really wants out of life is to marry some cute guy in Houston with a lot of money and a fast car. But that's okay. She'll be my best friend until I die. How can I make new friends when I don't dare bring them home? Gail is at least used to whoopie cushions and plastic ice cubes in her drink with flies or cockroaches inside.

When I sat down to eat with Gail today I found a note in my lunch that said, "I fixed your favorite, peanut butter and maggots. Love, Mom." I peel my banana and it falls apart in sections. Gail's seen it a hundred times but it still makes her laugh.

"Your Mom is so weird," she says.

"No kidding."

"At least you've got your hearing left." Gail's Mom plays this sixties music at unbelievable volume all day and night. Gail's absolutely most shameful secret is that she was originally named Magic Mountain. I'm *not* kidding. Her first day at school she told everybody she was named Gail. Only she didn't know how to spell it, and wrote it G-A-L. I had to take her aside and explain. Anyway, she kept on her Mom about it until her Mom finally made it legal. Nobody else remembers all that, but I do.

Everybody's parents seem to think the sixties were this unbelievably wonderful time. They even have TV shows and everything about it now. What I can't understand is, if it was so wonderful, why did they stop? Why don't they still wear long hair and bell-bottoms and madras or whatever it was? I don't think it was the sixties. I think they just liked being young.

Which is more than I can say. "Mom's into the plastic vomit again," I tell Gail.

"Oh God. Geez, you know, I can't come over this afternoon after all. I just remembered this really important stuff I have to do."

"Thanks, Gail. Thanks a lot. That means I'll be stuck at home alone with her."

"What about Ricky?"

"He'll spend the night at the Jameson's. At the first sight of novelty items he's out the door, and Dad with him."

"I saw him this morning, did I tell you?"

"Ricky?"

"Your dad."

"No. Where was this?"

She looked sorry she brought it up. "Oh, it wasn't anything. I just saw him when Mom drove me to school."

I wanted to say, if it wasn't anything, then why did you bring it up, dork-brain? But she looked embarrassed and a little scared, so I let it drop.

When I got home, Mom was already in the kitchen. You can imagine my nervousness. Among the delights she's cooked when she's in a mood like this are: lemon meringue enchiladas, steak a la mode, chili con cookies, and

banana pizza. The pizza was actually not too bad, but you understand what
I'm saying.

We all sit down at the table. Mom brings out this big aluminum tray with a
cover over it, like in the movies. She takes the cover off with a big flourish and
goes, "Ta da!"

It's a casserole dish with what looks like overcooked brownies inside. We all
stare at it.

"Eat," Mom says. "Come on, eat!"

No one wants to go first. Finally Ricky breaks down and pokes at it with
a fork. It makes this nasty grinding sound. "Oh gross," he says. He looks
more tired than really disgusted. Not like the time Mom walked around
with the plastic dog mess on a Pamper, eating a piece of fudge. I lean over
for a look myself.

"Mom," I say, "this is a mud pie." I sniff at it. It really *is* mud. Dried, baked
mud now. "This is like not funny."

"If you don't eat every bite, you don't get dessert."

"You're slipping, Mom," Ricky says. "You're losing it. This is not even
remotely funny. I'm going to the Jamesons'. If I hurry, maybe I'll be in time
for supper."

Dad is just staring off into the corner, holding onto his chin. It's like he's
not really there at all.

I went into the den and put on MTV. If there was a God it would have
been AL TV, but it wasn't. I think Weird Al Yankovic is the greatest thing in
the world. He plays the accordion and does goofed-up versions of songs, in
case you've never heard of him. I saw him in concert in Houston and broke
through his bodyguards so I could hug him.

I watched TV for a while and then Mom came in dressed in a maid's
costume and started dusting. She has this huge feather duster, a joke feather
duster, so big she can hardly move it around without knocking things over.
Dad comes in and says, "Let's go for a burger."

I was glad to get away. That mud pie business was just *too* weird. We got
in his pickup and headed for the Wendy's just down the highway. Outside
the pickup is Tomball, Texas in all its glory. Flat, except for the gullies, brown
except for the trash. In a little over a year I go to college, and I won't ever
look back.

"Gail said she saw you this morning," I tell him.

"She could have, I suppose."

"She was real weird about it. She acted like she shouldn't have told me. Do
you know why that is?"

He rolls his window down with one hand, and makes a big deal out of scratching his head, real casual, you know, with the other. He's pretending not to pay any attention to the road, only he's really steering with his knee.

"Were you doing something you weren't supposed to do, Dad? Were you *with* somebody? Is that why Mom's acting weird? Because it's really hard to be in this family, you know? I mean, at any minute it could hit me. I could get this irresistible craving for an exploding cigar. It could be like diabetes. One minute I'm fine, the next I'm filling up my pockets with plastic ants. So I want you to tell me. Did you do something?"

He cranes his head out the window and drives for a while that way, then settles back into his seat. He shrugs. "*Somebody* did."

MYSTERY TRAIN

A S H E C L I M B E D the stairs, Elvis popped the cap off the pill bottle
and shook a couple more Dexedrines into his palm. They looked like
pink candy hearts, lying there. He tossed them into the back of his throat and
swallowed them dry.

"Hey, Elvis, man, are you sure you want to keep taking those things?"
Charlie was half a flight behind, drunk and out of breath. "I mean, you been
flying on that shit all weekend."

"I can handle it, man. Don't sweat it." Actually the last round of pills
hadn't affected him at all, and now his muscles burned and his head felt like
a bowling ball. He collapsed in an armchair in the third floor bedroom, as
far as possible from the noise of the reporters and the kids and the girls who
always stood outside the house. "In three weeks we're out of here, man. Out
of Germany, out of the Army, out of these goddamn uniforms." He untied his
shoes and kicked them off.

"Amen, brother."

"Charlie, turn on the goddamn TV, will you?"

"Come on, man, that thing's got a remote control, and I ain't it."

"Okay, okay." Elvis lunged for the remote control box and switched on the
brand-new RCA color console. It was the best money could buy, the height of
American technology, even if Germany didn't have any color transmissions to
pick up with it.

Charlie had collapsed across the bed. "Hey, Elvis. When you get home, man,
you ought to get yourself three different TVs. I mean, you're the king, right?
That way, not only can you fuck more girls than anybody and make more
money than anybody and take more pills than anybody, you can watch more
TV than anybody, too. You can have a different goddamn TV for every channel.
One for ABC..." He yawned. "One for NBC..." He was asleep.

"Charlie?" Elvis said. "Charlie, you lightweight." He looked around the edge
of the chair and saw Charlie's feet hanging off the end of the bed, heels up and
perfectly still.

To hell with it, Elvis thought, flipping through the channels. Let him sleep.
They'd had a rough weekend, driving into Frankfurt in the BMW and picking
up some girls, skating on the icy roads all across the north end of Germany,
hitting the booze and pills. In the old days it had annoyed Elvis mightily that

his body couldn't tolerate alcohol, but ever since one of his sergeants had given him his first Dexedrine he hadn't missed booze at all. Charlie still liked the bottle, but for Elvis there was nothing like that rush of power he got from the pills.

Well, there was one thing, of course, and that was being on stage. It was not quite two years now since he'd been inducted—since Monday, March 24, 1958, and he'd been counting the days. The Colonel had said no USO shows, no nothing until he was out. Nobody got Elvis for free.

The Colonel had come to take the place of his mother, who had died while Elvis was still in basic, and his father, who had betrayed Gladys's memory by seeing other women. There was no one else that Elvis could respect, that he could look to for advice. If the Colonel said no shows then that was it.

Something flashed on the TV screen. Elvis backed through the dead channels to find it again, ending up with a screen full of electronic snow. He got up and played with the fine tuning ring to see if he could sharpen it any.

Memories of his early years haunted him. Those had been the best times, hitting the small towns with just Scotty and Bill, the equipment strapped to the top of Scotty's brand-new, red-and-white '56 Chevy. Warming the audience up with something slow, like "Old Shep," then laying them out, ripping the joint with "Good Rockin' Tonight." Getting out of control, his legs shaking like he had epilepsy, forgetting to play the guitar, his long hair sticking out in front like the bill of a cap, taking that mike stand all the way to the floor and making love to it, shaking and sweating and feeling the force and power of the music hit those kids in the guts like cannon fire.

He gave up on the TV picture and paced the room, feeling the first pricklings of the drug. His eyelids had started to vibrate and he could feel each of the individual hairs on his arms.

When he sat down again, there was something on the screen.

It looked like a parade, with crowds on both sides of the street and a line of cars approaching. They were black limousines, convertibles, with people waving from the back seats. Elvis thought he recognized one of the faces, a Senator from up north, the one everybody said was going to run for President.

He tried the sound. It was in German and he couldn't make any sense of it. The only German words he'd learned had been in bed, and they weren't the kind that would show up on television.

The amphetamine hit him just as the senator's head blew apart.

Elvis watched the chunks of brain and blood fly through the air in slow motion. For a second he couldn't believe what he was seeing, then he jumped up and grabbed Charlie by the shoulder.

"Charlie, wake up! C'mon man, this is serious!" Charlie rolled onto his back, eyes firmly shut, a soft snore buzzing in his throat. No amount of shaking could wake him up.

On the television, men in dark suits swarmed over the car as it picked up speed and disappeared down the road. The piece of film ran out, hanging in the projector for a moment, then the screen turned white.

He went back to the chair and stood with his hands resting on its high, curved back. Had he really seen what he thought he saw? Or was it just the drugs? He dug his fingers into the dingy gray-green fabric of the chair, the same fabric that he'd seen by the mile all through Europe. He was tired of old things: old chairs, old wood-floored houses, Frau Gross, the old woman who lived with them, the old buildings and cobbled streets of Bad Nauheim.

America, he thought, here I come. Clean your glass and polish your chrome and wax your linoleum tile.

The TV flickered and showed a hotel room with an unmade bed and clothes all around. On the nightstand was an overflowing ashtray and an empty bottle. Elvis recognized the Southern Comfort label even in the grainy picture. A woman sat on the floor with her back against the bed. She had ratty hair and a flabby, pinched sort of face. The nipples of her small breasts showed through her T-shirt, which looked like somebody had spilled paint and bleach all over it.

Elvis thought she must be some kind of down-and-out hooker. He was a little disgusted by the sight of her. Still he couldn't look away as she brought a loaded hypodermic up to her arm and found a vein.

Static shot across the screen and the image broke up. Diagonal lines scrolled past a field of fuzzy gray. Elvis felt the Dexedrine bounce his heart against the conga drum of his chest. He sat down to steady himself, his fingers rattling lightly against the arm of the chair.

"Man," Elvis said to the room, "I am really fucked up."

A new voice came out of the TV. It must have originally belonged to some German girl, breathy and sexual, but bad recording had turned it into a mechanical whisper. Another room took shape, another rumpled bed, this one with a black man lying in it, long frizzy hair pressed against the pillow, a trickle of vomit running out of his mouth. He bucked twice, his long, muscular fingers clawing at the air, and lay still.

Elvis pushed the heels of his hands into his burning eyes. It's the drugs, he thought. The drugs and not sleeping and knowing I'm going home in a couple of weeks...

He wandered into the hall, one hand on the crumbling plaster wall to steady himself. He tried the handle on the room next to his but the door refused to open.

"Red? Hey, Red, get your ass up and answer this door." He slapped the wood a couple of times and then gave up, afraid to deal with Frau Gross when he was so far gone. He went into the bathroom instead and splashed cold water on his face, letting it soak the collar of his shirt. He wouldn't miss this screwy European plumbing, either.

"I feel so good," he sang to himself, "I'm living in the USA..." He looked like shit. With his green fatigues and sallow skin he looked like a fucking Christmas tree, with two red ornaments where his eyes were supposed to be.

He went back to the bedroom and sat down again. He needed sleep. He'd find something boring, like *Bonanza* in German, and maybe he could doze off in the chair.

As he reached for the remote, another film started. It was scratched and grainy and not quite in focus. Some fat guy in a white suit was hanging on to a mike stand and mumbling. It was impossible to understand what he said, especially with the nasal German narration that ran on top. Elvis made out a lot of "you knows" and "well, wells."

The camera moved in and Elvis went cold. Despite his age and his blubber and his long, girlish hair, the guy was trying to do an Elvis imitation. A band started up in the background and the fat man began to sing.

The Colonel had warned him this might happen. You don't drop out for two years and not expect somebody to try and cut you. Bobby Darin with all his finger-popping and that simpering Ricky Nelson had been bad enough, but this was really the end. Elvis had never heard the song that the fat guy was trying to sing. He was obviously being carried by the size of the orchestra behind him. Pathetic, Elvis thought. A joke. The fat guy curled his lip, threw a couple karate punches, and let one leg begin to shake.

Dear God, Elvis thought.

It wasn't possible.

Elvis lurched out of the chair and yanked Charlie out of bed by the ankles. "Wha...?" Charlie moaned.

"Get up. Get up and look at this shit."

Charlie struggled to a sitting position and scrubbed his eyes with his hands. "I don't see nothing."

"On the TV, man. You got eyes in your head?"

"There's nothing there, man. Nothing."

Elvis turned, saw snowy interference blocking out the signal again. "Get a chair," Elvis said.

"Aw, man, I'm really whacked..."

"Get the goddamn chair."

Elvis sat back in front of the TV, his heels pounding jump time against the hardwood floor. He heard Charlie dragging a chair up the stairs as the screen cleared and a caption flashed below the singer's face.

Rapid City, South Dakota, it said.

June, 1977.

Elvis didn't know he was on his feet, didn't know he had the service automatic in his hand until his finger went tight on the trigger.

Huge white letters filled the screen.

ELVIS, they said.

He fired. The roar of the gun seemed make the entire building jump. The picture tube blew in with a sharp crack and a shower of glass. Sparks hissed out on the floor and a single breath of sour smoke wafted out of the ruined set.

Elvis felt the room buzz with hostile forces. He had to get out. Charlie stood in the doorway, staring open-mouthed at the ruins of the set as Elvis shoved past him, letting the gun drop from his nerveless fingers and clatter across the floor. It wasn't until he was downstairs and the cold air hit him that he realized he'd left his shoes and coat inside. The sidewalk was slick with ice and a mixture of sleet and rain fell as he stood there, eyes jerking back and forth, fingers twitching, legs tensed to run and go on running.

It had to be a mistake, he thought. Something from a burlesque show over in Frankfurt, maybe. Somebody had just screwed up the titles, gotten the date wrong.

Yeah, and the name wrong too.

The silence closed in on him. For the first time since they'd moved into the house on Goethestrasse there weren't any people on the street. In the distance, whining high and faint like a mosquito's wings, he heard a motorcycle approaching. It was the only sound in the night.

He started to feel the cold. Still it wasn't bad enough to make him go back inside, to face the empty, staring socket of the TV set. He shivered, lifted one foot off the icy pavement.

A light winked at him from the end of the street. The motorcycle, coming toward him, rattled like machine gun fire and echoed off the wet streets and flat brick walls. It was moving too fast for the icy roads and the driver seemed barely in control. He slid in and out of the streetlamps' circles of light, shadowy in leather and denim.

Something like a premonition made Elvis start to turn and run back inside. The cold had numbed him and he couldn't seem to get the message through to his legs.

The bike skidded to a stop in front of the house and its engine died.

For a second Elvis and the rider started at each other in the silent moonlight. The rider had no helmet or goggles, just a pair of round, tortoise-shell glasses. Frost and bits of ice had clumped in his hair and the creases of his jacket. A cigarette hung out of the corner of his mouth, and Elvis was sure that if he could have seen the man's face he would have recognized him.

But the man's face was gone. Scars flowed and branched like rivers across the dead white skin of his cheeks. He had no eyebrows, and patches of hair were missing from his temples and forehead. One eye was permanently half-closed and the other was low enough to throw the ruined face off balance. The nose was little more than a flat place and the mouth smiled on one side and frowned on the other.

"Hey," the rider said.

"What?" Elvis was startled by the man's American accent.

"Hey, man. What happened to your shoes?"

The voice was maddeningly familiar. "Who are you?"

"You look shook, man." The scarred mouth stretched in what might have been a grin. "Like, 'All Shook Up,' right?"

"Dean," Elvis said, stunned. "Jimmy Dean, the actor."

The rider shrugged.

"You're dead," Elvis said. "I saw the pictures in the paper. That car was torn to pieces, man."

Dean, if that was truly who it was, touched the underside of his mutilated eye and rubbed it softly, as if remembering pain that Elvis could not even imagine.

"What are you doing here?"

Dean shrugged again. "They just, like, wanted me to come by and check up on you. It looks like you already got the message." He rose up on the bike, about to kick the starter, and Elvis moved toward him.

"Wait! Who's 'they?' What do you know about..." He stopped himself. Dean couldn't possibly know anything about what Elvis had seen on TV.

"Hey, be cool, man. If *they* wanted you to know who *they* were, then *they* would tell you, dig? I mean, they didn't even tell *me* shit, you know?" Dean looked him over. "But I can take a guess, man. I can take a real good guess what they want with you. I seen you on TV, the way you shake your legs and all that. The way you dress like a spade and sing all those raunchy songs. You scare people, man. People think you want to fuck all their daughters and turn their sons into hoods. *They* don't like that, man."

"I never tried to scare nobody," Elvis said.

Dean giggled. Coming out of that scarred mouth, it was terrifying. "Yeah, right. That's what I used to say."

"What do you mean? Are you threatening me?"

"No threats, man. You're the King. You know? You're the fucking King of America. King of all the cheeseburgers and pink Cadillacs and prescription drugs and handguns in the greatest country in the world. Shit, you *are* America. They don't have to threaten you. They don't have to hurt you. Just a little nudge here and a nudge there, and you'll fall right in line."

A door slammed and Charlie came staggering down the sidewalk. "Elvis? What the fuck, man?"

Dean looked like he wanted to say something else, then changed his mind. He started the bike, hunched his shoulders, and sped away.

"Jesus Christ," Charlie said. "You know who that was?"

"It was nobody," Elvis said. He put his hand in the middle of Charlie's chest and shoved him back toward the house. "Understand? It was nobody."

"THERE'S GOING TO BE a new Elvis, brand new. I don't think he will go back to sideburns or ducktails. He's twenty-five now, and he has genuine adult appeal. I think he's going to surprise everyone..."

—*Colonel Tom Parker on Elvis's return from Germany*

DURING REHEARSALS ELVIS kept the windows of his hotel room covered with aluminum foil. It kept out the light and there was something comforting about having it there. It might even keep his TV set from picking up weird, lying broadcasts that would mess with his head. Just in case, he kept a loaded .45 on the bedside table, ready to blow the whole thing away. When forced to go out of the hotel, he kept his bodyguards with him at all times, the ones the papers had started to call his "Memphis Mafia."

He stayed inside as much as he could. The Florida air was hot and dead, seemed to pull the life right out of him. It had been the same in California and Las Vegas, everywhere he'd been since he came home from Germany. Everything was dry and hot and still. He was starting to believe it would be dry and hot and still forever.

As they taped the opening of the show he fought, without much success, to control his unease. They had him in his Army uniform again, walking out onstage to shake hands with Sinatra and his entire Rat Pack, all of them in tuxedos, mugging the camera, slapping each other on the back.

Over and over he caught himself thinking: What am I doing here?

He worked his way through the crowd, the faces blurring together into single entity with Bishop's mocking smile, Davis's processed hair and hideous rings, Lawford's limp handshake and Martin's whiskey breath. He had to learn to be comfortable with them. The Colonel had told him how it was going to be, and it was far too late to argue with the Colonel.

It happened while they were taping his duet with Sinatra, Sinatra who had called rock and roll "phony" and the singers "goons" just a couple of years before. Now they were trading verses, Elvis singing "Witchcraft" and Sinatra doing "Love Me Tender."

The scream came from somewhere toward the front of the audience. "That's not him!" It was a girl's voice, and it sounded at least as frightened as it was angry. The stage lights were blinding and Elvis couldn't see her face. "That's not Elvis!" she screamed. "What did you do with him?" The orchestra stopped and the girl's voice carried on unaccompanied. "Where is he? *Where's Elvis?*"

Elvis saw Sinatra make a gesture toward the wings. A moment later there were muffled noises from the audience and then a vast and empty silence.

"Don't worry," Sinatra said. "You're one of us now. We'll take good care of you."

"Yes, sir." Elvis nodded and closed his eyes. "Yes, sir," he said.

SECRETS

THEY'D BEEN MARRIED 16 days.

Michael spent a lot of time in the bathroom, as some of her other boyfriends had. So maybe it wasn't entirely an accident when Teresa walked in that night without knocking.

"Sorry," she smiled. "I didn't know—"

Michael was leaning over the lavatory, fully dressed. He had an index finger under each eyelid, pulling it down. A stream of blood poured out of the underside of each eye into the sink.

"Michael?" she whispered.

He turned to look at her. His eyes were rolled back in his head and blood flowed down his cheeks like dark red tears. "GET OUT!" he roared.

In panic she reverted to Spanish: "*Lo siento, lo siento!* I'm sorry!"

When he came to bed it was like nothing had happened. He kissed her forehead and went back to reading his trial transcript. He didn't ask why she shivered at the sight of him.

It was a week before she let him make love to her again. He was so gentle and insistent that she finally gave in. Afterwards, while he slept, she stared at him in the moonlight, searching for strangeness, for some kind of explanation.

She never walked in on him unexpectedly again. As the years went by and she failed to get pregnant, she wondered, sometimes, if that was meaningful, if it was related to what she'd seen. The thing that was never mentioned, the thing she tried to tell herself she'd only imagined. The thing she could never forget.

In the end it was Michael who left her. In the ten years they'd been together, he didn't seem to have aged a day. He left her for a younger woman, of course. Theresa thought about calling the woman, trying to warn her, but what could she say?

The feeling eventually passed. Theresa remarried, an older man, a man with few demands or expectations. They had a lovely home, gave many parties, and slept in separate beds.

GOLFING VIETNAM

S HE HADN'T SEEN Brian in five years, not since they both graduated from
UNC Wilmington. His phone call caught her at a perfect time: between
relationships, bored, a little nostalgic. When he mentioned Ashley and Dylan's
wedding she was blindsided by a powerful longing to see everyone again.

"I'd been thinking about going," she said, "but then I had to pay for a new
engine in the Honda."

"Why don't you go with me? I'll fly you to Wilmington, we could stay at a
bed and breakfast or something, go to the wedding together." When she hesitated he said, "No obligation or anything. I mean in terms of … you know."

On two separate occasions in college they'd tried and failed to sustain a
serious romance. It seemed to her that the sex, while fun, had not been profound for either one of them. On the other hand, she was not above a little
fun at this point in her life.

"Can you afford to do that?" she asked. "Is your father paying you
that much?"

"I'm not working for the old man anymore," he said with a note of satisfaction. "Just wait. I'll tell you all about it when I see you."

AND SO SHAWN found herself in the passenger seat of Brian's rented Sentra,
headed south toward downtown from the airport. It was the first Saturday in
June, unseasonably cool enough that Brian had asked to leave the windows
down. Half a mile to their right she could see a solid green wall of trees on the
far side of the Cape Fear River. The Atlantic was close enough that she could
taste its salt in the air, bringing back memories of pelicans gliding in front of
pink and purple clouds, of waking up without an alarm clock, of Brian's boy-
ish, nearly hairless body.

"So tell me this big secret," she said, turning toward him and noticing again,
as she had at the airport, how dramatically his short, reddish-blond hair had
receded from his forehead. "When did you quit the oil business?"

"Two years ago. It kind of took me by surprise, really. I'd been playing at the
club every weekend, and before I knew it I was doing really great."

He'd lost her. "What club? Are you in a band?"

"The Dallas Country Club. I'm playing golf."

"Golf? *Golf*? You're a *golfer* now, is that what you're trying to tell me?"

379

"I did a year as a club pro, and then last year a bunch of the guys there put a stake together for me and I went out on the Australian tour. I was out for nine months and I've already paid everybody back." He glanced at her for a reaction.

"You never said anything to me about golf."

"I was on the team in high school. I kind of kept a low profile about it in college, I guess because I was afraid it wouldn't sound cool or something, but I still went out every once in a while. Wilmington has some outstanding courses. With the Spanish moss and everything, first thing in the morning, with the mist over the water hazards..."

"Well, you were right about it not sounding cool," she said. "I can't believe you mutated into a golfer when I wasn't looking. Do they make you wear plaid pants and those awful polyester caps?"

He was staring straight ahead, the smile frozen on his face. He'd paid for her trip, and not thirty minutes into it she'd trounced on his feelings. She really did hate herself sometimes. "I'm sorry, Brian. I didn't mean to tease you."

"When I was thinking about you, about us, I never thought about what a smart mouth you have. I'd completely forgotten that whole side of your character."

"I said I was sorry." She leaned over and kissed his cheek. "Come on, Bri, forgive me. Even if I don't deserve it. Tell me about this tour you're on."

She had to coax a little more, but by the time they crossed Market Street, she had him talking again. He parked on Third in front of a two-story Victorian with turrets and a wraparound porch.

The sight of the place warmed her like a glass of champagne. The house was beautiful and romantic and just slightly decadent. The magnolia tree in the front yard was in full bloom, drenching the air with heavy, sensuous perfume. Brian rang the bell and a middle-aged woman answered the door. She gave them a short tour and then left them alone in the Hibiscus Room.

Brian went to the window and opened it. "You like it?" he asked.

"It's great," she said. He stood awkwardly with his hands in his pockets, and Shawn knew he was waiting to take his cue from her. The minor skirmish in the car had somehow put her off and now she couldn't seem to find an intimate mood. The queen-sized bed loomed large in her mind. "Um," she said, "I've got a lot of getting ready to do before six."

"Sure," Brian said, with only a hint of disappointment.

THE SERVICE TOOK forty minutes, counting processional and recessional, hymns, prayers, vows, and some sort of contemporary Christian love song that one of Dylan's fraternity brothers delivered in a prissy tenor that made Shawn cringe. Ashley was radiant in a low-cut, arctic-white gown, her blonde hair piled Gibson-girl style with long wisps curling free on both sides, her veil suspended from a pearl headband. Dylan and his groomsmen, all in white dinner jackets, looked like waiters at an exclusive resort: tanned, muscular, poised on the balls of their feet.

Drawn-out as it was, Shawn appreciated the ritual, the sense that nothing was being left out, nothing hurried over. Ashley and Dylan would have to come out of this, she thought, feeling well and truly married.

The congregation was up and down a half-dozen times for one reason or another, and each time she sat Shawn found Brian's arm stretched out on the pew behind her. Brian himself did not even seem to be looking at her, seemed more impersonally possessive than overtly sexual, though she knew in Brian's dream world they would have made love before she got dressed. What she needed, she thought, was to feel desired instead of merely obligated.

In the reception line, Ashley seemed genuinely thrilled to see her. "I was so afraid you weren't going to make it!"

"I had a mysterious benefactor," Shawn said.

Ashley glanced at Brian, who'd just kissed her and was now pumping Dylan's hand. "You'll have to tell me everything later."

"Nothing to tell," she said, but Ashley had already turned to the next in line.

Dylan grabbed her and kissed her. "You look so hot. What's Brian got that I don't?"

It was impossible to set him straight in the milliseconds available. "It's what he doesn't have. Like a brand-new wife, remember?"

"Oh yeah," Dylan said. "Her." Shawn assumed he was kidding but still didn't know how to react, other than to smile and keep moving.

Dylan's father pretended to remember her while also pretending not to look down the front of her dress. The effort left him somewhat frazzled and left Shawn feeling better about herself than she had in a while. It was in fact a major statement of a dress, strapless and short, the perfect shade of taupe to set off her shoulder-length brown hair. There were plenty of disadvantages to living in DC, but a lack of shopping was not one of them.

The video crew kept them waiting for nearly half an hour while they shot close-ups at the altar, then, unhappy with the camera placement on the church steps, handed out fresh packets of birdseed for a second take of the exit.

"Did you ever think," Shawn asked, "that we work so hard to immortalize all the big events of our lives that we're forgetting to have any emotions to come back and revisit?"

"You're never going to have any fun if you keep thinking so much," Brian said. He took her arm. "Let's go find the bar."

•

DURING THE CIVIL WAR, Wilmington had been the last refuge of the Confederate blockade runners. After the war there'd been money in textiles and shipping. In the 1890s, a mob of white citizens had burned down the offices of the city's black-owned newspaper and run its black mayor out of town in one of the bloodiest race riots of the century. Now the city catered to supertankers, tourists, and the film industry. It was an easygoing city, for the most part, willing to do whatever it took to get by.

In the eighties, when Shawn had first come to Wilmington with her parents, the entire downtown area had been a slum. Fifteen years and millions of dollars had brought the tourists back to cobbled streets and restored Victorian houses, historical plaques and a boardwalk along the river.

Ashley's parents had rented the Ice House, a downtown bar, for the reception. There was air-conditioning inside and an R&B band out on the patio, with bouncers at the back gate to keep Riverwalk tourists from wandering in.

There was no champagne, only white wine, beer, and well liquor. Shawn, not yet ready to commit to serious drinking, settled for a Coke. The bride and groom made their entrance and Shawn stayed well away from the bouquet toss. Dylan threw a garter and there were photo opportunities galore as they cut and posed with their cakes.

She and Brian ended up at a big table outside under the floodlights with a dozen old friends. "You know me," Brian said. "I'm not going to be indoors if there's an alternative." It got very drunk very quickly. Between the band and the shouting back and forth across the table, Shawn found it hard to keep up an individual conversation.

It was evidently getting drunk inside as well. On her way to the bathroom Shawn heard somebody's father say, "I'm sort of the junior partner in a one-partner firm." Across the room a red-faced man in his thirties waved his hands and said, "This goddamn mild weather is putting my utility shares in the toilet. If we don't get some serious ice storms this winter I'm fucked." Standing at the mirror in the ladies' room one of the bridesmaids said, to no one in particular, "I just think a lot more people would have liked Ashley if she hadn't been so popular."

At the buffet Shawn ran into one of her roommates from freshman year. "So," Kirsten said, "are you still painting?" Kirsten's hair was an expensive shade of blonde and her makeup was impeccable.

"Not for a while," Shawn said. "There just doesn't seem to be any time."

"You're working?"

Shawn nodded. "I was in Greensboro for a year, living with my parents, and I wanted to just get away from everything and everybody, so I took a job with this ad agency in DC. I mean, I still get to draw, just..."

"Just not what you want."

The men she worked with all had the right haircuts and suits and worked twelve hours a day. It made her feel nearly human again to get a little sympathy. "One of the accounts they gave me is a tobacco company, I guess because of my being from North Carolina and all. I hate it, but I'm afraid they'll fire me if I say anything."

"It's a bitch," Kirsten said. "Come sit down?"

They found two places at a table full of parents. "So what's happening with you?" Shawn asked.

"Well, you know I married Stephen, right? I'm still teaching second grade, but we're hoping I can quit in a couple more years?" Shawn nodded, thinking how she'd missed the upward-turning cadence of Kirsten's speech, its simple need for acknowledgment. "So Stephen's in the Law Library twenty-four hours a day, wondering how he's going to bring in any new business if he can't even get to the golf course."

"Golf," Shawn said. "You'd think it would have died out, except for maybe a few decrepit old guys. With real estate brokers circling them like vultures, waiting to put condos on all the fairways."

"Honey, where have you been? You can't do business if you can't break ninety. Especially if you're dealing with the Japanese? And of course every big corporation in the world is buying themselves a PGA tournament." She glanced up. "Uh oh, we've been found out. Hey, Brian."

"Hey, Kirsten." He offered Shawn an unconvincing smile. "I was wondering where you got off to."

"We were just talking about golf," Shawn said.

"Very funny."

"No, really."

"Stephen's been playing the Carolina Country Club?" Kirsten said. "And I've been taking lessons."

"Brian's turned pro," Shawn said. It gave Brian obvious pleasure to hear her say it, and she thought it might make up for the grief she'd given him earlier. "He's on the Australian Tour now."

Kirsten seemed puzzled. "Right now?"

"It's winter there now," Brian explained patiently. "We start up again in August."

"I wouldn't think there'd be enough golf courses there for a whole tour?" Kirsten said.

"We play all over the place. Australia, New Zealand, Southeast Asia. I love the travel, I love getting to play in all these exotic places. We're even playing Vietnam this year."

"Excuse me," said a guy in his fifties from the other side of the table. "Did I hear you say you're playing *golf* in *Vietnam?*"

"Yes sir, that's right."

The guy was short and barrel-chested and had on an ugly yellow suit. "Jesus Christ," he said, collapsing back in his chair. "Jesus Christ. I did three tours over there, and now they're playing fucking golf."

The woman next to him put her hand on his arm. "Now, Ray."

Another old guy at the end of the table said, "What the hell you want to go over there for, son?"

"I played in Bangkok last year," Brian said, looking like he didn't know whether to get self-righteous or apologize. "It was great. Everybody seemed really excited to see us."

"To see your money," the guy in the yellow suit said.

"Probably," Brian agreed. Shawn liked him for that; five years ago he wouldn't have bothered to be polite to a cranky old drunk. "It's kind of primitive over there. You have to step over the rats if you get up in the night, the power goes on and off all the time. They told us all to carry pocket flashlights everywhere. But it was crazy, just wide open. With a little money over there you can do just about anything you can imagine."

"So this year it's Vietnam," the guy in the yellow suit said. "They still got some of our boys prisoner over there, you know that?"

"He's one of those X-Generation people, Ray," said the old guy at the end of the table. "He doesn't give a damn."

"Actually," Shawn said, "Gen X is all in their thirties now." She kept talking, wondering if she could keep Ashley and Dylan's wedding from breaking down into open warfare. "We're the Un Generation. Kirst-UN, Bri-UN, Dyl-UN, half the people I know have UN names. No wonder we're so depressed."

Brian was looking at her like she was retarded when one of the groomsmen came up and whispered in his ear. "Excuse me," Brian said. "Duty calls." He smiled briefly and walked away.

"Go ahead," said the guy in the yellow suit, not quite loud enough, Shawn thought, for Brian to hear. "Have a great fucking time."

Shawn stood up too. "Sorry, gentlemen," she said. "Peace with honor, okay?"

SHE FOLLOWED BRIAN outside where he, Dylan, and another seven fraternity brothers formed a circle, arms around each other's shoulders, in front of the stage. They rocked back and forth and sang, in maudlin *a cappella* detail, about lying on their death beds with the name of their beloved fraternity on their lips.

The band—with the waiters and busboys, the only black faces at the reception—looked on with mild amusement, and when it was over launched a medley of disco hits including "Brick House" and the inevitable "YMCA." Shawn got Brian briefly onto the dance floor where she asked, "Are you having a good time?"

He'd shed his coat and tie and undone a couple of buttons on his white shirt. "Yeah. I forgot how good it is to see all those guys. You?"

She was no more able to explain her sense of dislocation than she was willing to seem ungrateful. She wished she hadn't brought it up. "Me too. It's been a long time." Actual years, she thought, might not entirely express how long it felt.

After two songs, someone called Brian's name, and he excused himself with a smile. Shawn got a glass of bourbon and found a chair off to herself. She was close to the wall that separated the club from the cool, humid darkness of the Riverwalk a few yards away. She sniffed at the drink, which suddenly smelled medicinal and unappealing. One of the waiters, wearing a white dinner jacket like the groomsmen, was leaning against the wall and smoking a cigarette. He looked to be about Shawn's age, clean-shaven, with his hair trimmed to a short stubble. His skin looked purplish-black in the harsh floodlights.

"You want this?" she asked, offering the drink. "I haven't touched it."

"No, thank you. It'd be worth my job, they saw me drinking that."

"Sorry," she said. "I guess I wasn't thinking."

"That's okay. You not supposed to be thinking, you supposed to be having a good time."

"You work for the caterer?"

"Yes, ma'am."

"I wish you wouldn't call me ma'am. My name's Shawn." She held out her hand.

"Franklin," he said, and shook it warily. Then he dropped his cigarette in the gravel and crushed it with his shoe. "I better get back to work."

Stephen, Kirsten's husband, grabbed at Franklin's sleeve as he walked by. "Say, man," Stephen said, "you wouldn't happen to have change for a twenty, would you?"

"Think so," Franklin said, reaching into his pants pocket. Shawn abandoned her drink and went to find a chair at the table.

THE GENDERS HAD POLARIZED, with Brian and the other males all at one end. Brian was telling a story in a hushed voice as Shawn came up behind him. Apparently it was something she was not supposed to hear, because even as she reached out to rest her hand on his shoulder, Dylan looked up and saw her and said, "Yo, Brian, cool it, dude."

"What's the deal, Dylan?" she said.

"Nothing," Dylan said.

"Golf stories," Brian said, and the men all laughed.

Kirsten, from the far side of the table and just over the border into the women's zone, said, "They were talking about hookers."

Shawn felt ill. She clutched her purse with both hands behind her back, hearing her mother's voice in her head saying, "Sooner or later, you have to pay the piper."

"Hey," Stephen said. "Guy's ten thousand miles from home, not going to see any woman he knows for another two or three months, what's he supposed to do? Terrorize the sheep?"

"Australians," Brian said, "are very protective of their sheep."

More laughter. There was no way, Shawn thought, she could sit down at that table now. As she walked away she heard Dylan say, "You're in deep shit now, man."

She sat for half an hour with Ashley's parents, then decided she was being childish. Why should Brian keep her from the rest of her friends? Back on the patio, Brian had found a broomstick and was giving golf lessons at the back fence. "So," Brian said, "the old boy asks, 'Aren't there *any* Democrats at this club?' and Billy says, 'Not on *my* watch.'"

In the laughter one of the groomsmen bent over and came up with a crumpled piece of paper. "I'll be damned," he said. "Look! Twenty bucks!"

"That's the only way *you're* gonna get lucky tonight, Jason," somebody yelled.

"Found money," Brian said, straightening from where he'd been bent over his improvised club. Shawn heard a focused quality in his voice that was new to her. "Want to double it?"

Jason squinted drunkenly at Brian. "Double it how?"

"I'll bet you I can take this rock, hit a tee shot with this broomstick right here, and knock it over the fence and all the way into the river."

"No way. This is some kind of trick, right?"

"No tricks, just pure golfing ability. Twenty bucks says I can do it."

"You're on."

The thing Shawn had found most appealing about Brian in college was the very thing that eventually broke them up, both times. He'd been laid back, always willing to go with the flow, able to take his own pleasure out of nearly any situation he might find himself in. Long-term, his lack of direction dragged her own ambitions down, but in the short term it had always made him fun for a weekend at the beach.

Somewhere Brian had found his direction, and Shawn didn't care much for the way it sat on him. His posture was still nonchalant, but there was a light in his eyes as he took a golf tee out of his pocket and set the rock on it. He adjusted his grip, took a practice swing, and then stepped up to the tee.

There were twenty or more people around him now in a loose gallery. A few of the more drunken fraternity brothers were laughing and calling out comments but Shawn could see, even from her obstructed view, that Brian was inside a zone of silence and perfect concentration. He brought the broomstick back smoothly and turned his whole body into his swing, hitting the rock with a solid *crack*.

He turned away just before the rock splashed into the river, and with a polished gesture, he plucked the twenty dollar bill from Jason's fingers. His friends surrounded him, slapping his back and lifting both his arms in victory. Someone handed him a fresh beer.

Of course he's different, Shawn thought. He has this now.

Someone brushed past her. "Hey, Franklin," she said.

Franklin nodded, distracted, and headed for the group that surrounded Brian. "Excuse me," he said when he got there. "Sorry to interrupt, but did any of y'all maybe see a twenty dollar bill out here? Thought maybe I might have dropped it when I was giving that man some change."

Franklin's posture was awkward, defensive, and Shawn thought of Brian with the Vietnamese vet earlier, unsure whether to flatter or attack. Life, she thought suddenly, was full of Vietnams. She seemed to be having one now.

Nobody answered at first. Two or three faces in the crowd turned briefly toward Brian, then looked away again. "Don't think so," Brian said. "We'll keep an eye out for it, though."

More than anything, Shawn was embarrassed by the transparency of the lie. She stepped up and asked, "Did you say you lost something?"

Franklin held her eyes for a second. She wasn't sure what he was looking for. "It wasn't nothing," he said. "Forget I asked."

"Because I found this a few minutes ago," she said, fumbling in her purse, finding a twenty, and crumpling it as she pulled it out.

Franklin took it from her, nodded stiffly, and walked away. He was barely out of earshot when Brian said, "What the hell did you do that for? You made us all look like we were trying to rip that guy off."

"Weren't you?"

"I *earned* that money."

"You won it. It's not the same thing."

"Shit," Jason said. "I wouldn't have bet him if I hadn't just found that money. No way I was going to cough up another twenty."

"Earned and won is exactly the same to me," Brian said. He moved in toward her, turning his back on his friends and dropping his voice. This was the new, intense Brian. "Where do you think half my money comes from? Gambling and hustling."

"You and me both," she said, thinking at first of work, then realizing how it must sound to Brian in the context of the weekend. Then she thought, that's okay. Let it stand.

"Look," Brian said. "Here's the twenty bucks, okay? I don't want you covering for me. I can take care of myself."

"Keep it. Consider it a down payment on my plane ticket. I'll send you the rest when I get home."

"What's that supposed to mean? You've had a chip on your shoulder since you got off that plane. I don't want anything from you. I just want to have a good time and see my friends. I don't want your money."

The crack about the chip on her shoulder hurt. It was something her mother always said to her, and she worried that it might be true. In the flame of Brian's self-righteousness the hurt flared into anger. "Why not? What's so special about my money? You seem to want everybody else's. You could always use it to buy yourself a hooker while you're in Vietnam."

"Is that what all this is about? Sex?"

"A little. Some of it's about money. And I think some of it's about golf. About black men carrying white men's clubs. You know? About all you guys living in this pretty green fantasy world and getting paid millions of dollars for it. And then you walk right past the napalm victims on your way to the clubhouse."

"Vietnam again. You don't get it, do you? You just don't get it."

"Get what?"

"What an asshole that vet inside was. Me playing golf in Vietnam means we won. No bombs, no helicopters, just good old-fashioned American hustle. The way we won the Cold War, the way we're about to win in China. We *won*."

The band had finished and there was a chill blowing in off the river. The voices around her had begun to sound strident and artificial.

Time to go, she thought. She smiled at Brian, touched his cheek, and went to find a taxi.

STOMPIN' AT THE SAVOY

What I really need, Guy thought, is to duck into a Porta-Santa and blow off some of these bad vibes.

WLCD, "the easy-watching channel," blared at him from a video store across the street. He'd sweated clear through his collarless pink shirt, and burglar alarms were going off in his brain. One of the familiar red-and-green booths stood open and inviting at the next corner. Guy lurched inside and slammed the door.

"Hello, Guy," said Santa, scanning Guy's ID bracelet. The white-bearded face smiled down from the CRT on the back wall and winked. "How are you?"

"Pretty shitty, Santa. I'm really paranoid at the moment."

"I see. What are your feelings about being paranoid?"

Guy wrestled with that for a few seconds. "I think that's the stupidest question I ever heard."

"I see. Why do you feel it's the stupidest question you ever heard?"

"Look, Santa, there's three guys back there been following me all afternoon. Business suits, mirror glasses, pointy shoes, the whole bit, you know?" He rubbed nervously at a scrape on his plasteel jacket. Guy loved that jacket and he really cared about the way he looked, not like those other assles at work who'd wear anything they saw on WLCD. "I think I lost them, but I don't even understand what's going down, you know? First the computer goes apeshit at work. Then—"

"One moment please," Santa said. The chubby face on the screen seemed to think something over, and then the voice came back. "Okay, you're Guy Zendales, right?"

"Right," Guy said. Santa's voice suddenly had a lot more personality than a moment before.

"You said something about a computer?"

"Yeah. I like, work at Modern Sounds, you know? And I was ringing up this sale when all of a sudden some wires must have got crossed. All this data just starts pouring out all over the screen, you know? Filled up a whole floppy that was supposed to have our daily sales records on it."

"You got it with you? Can I look at it?"

"Sure," Guy said. He stuck the diskette in the slot next to the screen.

"Hmmm," Santa said. "This is very interesting. Do you know what this is?"

Suddenly Guy twigged bad vibes again. He trusted Santa, of course. Just like that deal with priests and confessionals, only Santa was for everybody. The ads on TV told you it was okay. "Get it off your chest ... tell Santa."

But Guy didn't like the way Santa's voice had changed. Why should Santa want to look at a bunch of receipts from a music store?

"Uh, listen, Santa, man, I don't know *what* the fuck this is about, okay? I really think I better split now."

"Oh, no, Guy, wait just a second. I've got something I want to ... uh ... show you..."

Guy heard footsteps running toward the booth. "Just stay where you are," Santa said.

Guy snatched the diskette and stuck it back inside his jacket, just as the pounding started on the door of the booth.

Guy's vision blurred as the adrenaline hit him. "Holy shit!" he yelled. He lashed out instinctively with his reinforced shoes and the side of the booth split from floor to ceiling. Hunching his shoulders, he dove through the opening and knocked a man in a suit and sunglasses to the astroturf sidewalk.

Still shouting, Guy ran into the middle of the street.

HONDAS ZIPPED AROUND HIM on either side, the drivers squeezing their brakes and shouting at him. Guy flinched and stood paralyzed for a second, then felt himself lifted by the elbows and carried across the street.

"Shit!" cried a voice behind him that had to belong to a suit and sunglasses. "Muties! Hey you assles! Come back here with him!"

Guy remained unnaturally rigid, afraid to even turn his head. He watched numbly as he was swept into a deserted building and down a flight of concrete stairs. Finally his terror began to subside and he risked a quick glance to his left.

Shit, he thought, snapping his eyes away. Muties, all right. Guy had heard stories about the so-called Law of Genetic Conservation, that for every genetically engineered "improvement" something else would go hideously wrong. The mutie on Guy's left could have been Exhibit A in the trial that had outlawed the whole field of genetic research.

The near side of its head was as swollen and lumpy as an organlegger's sack of cut-rate eyeballs. The muties' own eyes were about two inches out of line, the right one protruding a good half inch or so. The rest of its body was fairly normal, except for the hunched back and the enormous hands and feet.

At the bottom of the steps they began running through a tiled hallway, then down a wooden ramp and into a rough-cut tunnel that was black from years of soot. Guy listened almost hopefully for footsteps following them.

There weren't any.

Guy had never smelled rat urine before, but he was sure he was smelling it now. It's the subway, Guy thought. As if it wasn't bad enough to be chased by assles in mirror sunglasses and kidnapped by muties, they had to bring him here.

He began to really get frightened.

The muties slowed and turned into a side tunnel. Guy could see the nose of the mutie on his right in his peripheral vision. It was the size and color of an unripe cucumber. What next? he wondered.

One more turn and they were in a long, narrow room, done in white tile on all the surfaces. Greasy daylight filtered in through a reticulated plastic skylight. From the rusted pipes that still protruded at waist height, Guy could tell that the place had been a rest room once, long enough ago to have accumulated a thick layer of dust and cobwebs, but not long enough to have lost the acrid odor.

Finally he had to stop looking at the walls and face the other inhabitants of the room.

At least ten muties lounged against the walls in a range of shapes and sizes, but in the center of them was the Bull Goose Mutie, the ugliest thing Guy had ever seen. Empty breasts dangled from its enormous, Buddha-like chest. Faceted, insectile eyes stared out of a skull shaped like a rotting pumpkin. Its matchstick arms ended in waxy, serrated fingers, and its legs folded too many times under its huge weight. The final, ghastly touch was provided by a smoldering Dr. Graybow pipe in the raw wound of its mouth.

"Guy Zendales," the Big Mutie said in a squeaky cartoon voice. "We have decided to render you our assistance."

"Terrific," Guy said. "Thanks a lot. Why don't you, like, give me a phone number, and I'll get back to you?"

"Give him Slack," the Big Mutie said, and Guy was set on the floor to brush ineffectually at the wrinkles in his jacket. "The govt agents," the squeaking voice went on, "were going to kill you, you know."

"Kill?" Guy said. "Me?" One of the muties correctly diagnosed his expression and brought him a folding chair. Guy sat in it and massaged the muscle spasms in the back of his legs.

"They must destroy the information on that diskette of yours. Because you've seen that information, they must destroy you as well."

"But ... but ... I've never done anything to the govt..."

The Big Mutie, Guy realized, was attempting a bitter smile. "Neither have we. Yet they have systematically attempted to exterminate us for years, despite the fact that it was their experiments that produced us."

"Why me? What did I do?"

"There was a glitch in the govt computer and it accidentally dumped 297 sectors of classified information into your store's system. I believe the file was called BLOOPERS."

"Bloopers," Guy echoed. None of this seemed to fit together. He remembered a video he'd seen once, about a patient in a mental hospital. It showed a woman sitting at a gray metal table, setting out lines and patterns with paper clips and pencils and scraps of paper. Tears ran slowly out of the woman's eyes. At the time he'd wanted to cry himself, without really knowing why. Now he thought he was beginning to understand.

"Perhaps we should explain," the Big Mutie said. "The govt agents would have destroyed all of us long ago if it weren't for our special genetic programming. Bob005, for example—" it pointed to the one with the gigantic nose, "is especially strong and fast. Bob667—" here it pointed to the one with the lopsided head, "was adapted for increased intuitive and precognitive powers. He anticipated your problem and enabled us to rescue you."

"It's not that I'm not grateful or anything," Guy said, "but what's in it for you?"

"We will never be free until the govt falls. We are always on the lookout for a weapon to use against them, and that diskette may be the one we need." When it moved its head, dozens of identical reflections darted across its faceted eyes, making Guy's stomach turn precariously.

"Look, I'd love to help, but I have to have the other data that's on here. I need to get this thing unfucked and sent in to the main office, or I'll lose my job."

The Big Mutie sighed. "All right. Suppose we get you safely to a computer. Will you at least let us look at the BLOOPERS file?"

"Sure," Guy said. "Anything you want. Just get me out of here, okay?"

The Big Mutie seemed hurt. "Are we that ugly? Can you not stand to be around us even long enough for us to help you?"

Guy started to lift his hands in denial, then let them drop. "Well, yeah," he said. "I guess that about sums it up."

They refused to let him go home. "It's too dangerous," the Big Mutie said, "and that's that."

Finally Guy suggested the apt of some friends, Sam and Janet Evening. He had a moment of compunction at involving them, but didn't see any other choice. They had a computer and their apt wasn't too far away. Bob667 went with them, leading the way through the twisting subway tunnels.

"Are you all named Bob?" Guy asked.

"That's right. It's in honor of our first prophet. He was a twentieth century salesman named J. R. 'Bob' Dobbs. He was the First Mutie."

"Oh," Guy said. He didn't hold much with religions, even inherently bogus ones. Still, the idea that the muties had a hero made them seem more, well, human. He regretted what he'd said to the Big Mutie about how ugly they were. Actually, they weren't so bad as long as you didn't really look right at them or anything.

Once they got to street level Guy took Bob667 to Sam and Janet's apartment. Night had fallen and Guy felt strangely lonely and uncomfortable. I'm on the lamb, he told himself, trying out the hopelessly antiquated words.

Janet answered the door. "Hi, Guy," she said, "This is a pleasant—look out! Behind you!"

Guy ducked, then remembered. "Oh, yeah. This is, uh, Bob667. We were wondering ... can we borrow your computer for a minute?"

"You mean you want me to let that mutie in my house? Yuck."

"It's really important, Janet."

"Well if you say so. Sam! Guy's here! Wait till you see what he brought over..."

Sam glanced up from the pornographic home video he was watching. A couple of the performers looked familiar to Guy—probably neighbors of Sam and Janet's. "Make yourself at home," Sam said, and went back to the TV.

Guy slipped his diskette into the computer and punched up a printout of BLOOPERS. Bob667 stood behind him as the printer zinged out the lines of data. Sam and Janet stayed in the other room, talking quietly to each other and pointing occasionally at the mutie.

"Do these names mean what I think they mean?" Guy asked.

"I'm afraid I really don't know what they are."

Guy showed the printout to Sam and Janet. "It's a list of the worst TV shows of all time, right?" Sam offered.

"Not all of them, though," Janet said. "Just the successful ones. What do those dollar amounts beside the titles mean?"

"I think," Guy said, "they mean I'm in a shitload of trouble."

"So what you and the mutie here are trying to tell me," Sam said, "is that the govt has been subsidizing bad TV?"

Janet looked from Guy to Bob667 and back again. "Isn't that a little ... well ... silly?"

"If you'd told me about all this yesterday," Guy said, "I would probably have agreed with you. Today I'm not so sure."

"It's not just the shows," Bob667 said. He slurred his Ss even more than usual when he got excited. "They were fixing the ratings, too, which means they were more or less forcing the competition to produce shows just as bad. You get a vicious circle going, and after a while it's not just TV anymore. People are getting trained not to think, not to make decisions, not to take anything seriously. What we have to do now is decide what we're going to do about it."

"I don't really see what the big deal is anyway," Janet complained. "Who cares about all this stuff? Why are they hunting Guy down? Who are we going to blab to, anyway?"

"You don't understand the govt," Bob667 explained. "There's hardly anybody working there anymore, just a lot of paranoid programmers and a lot of interconnected computers."

"What about all those people we elect?" Sam asked. "What do they do?"

"Sit at home, mostly, and watch TV. There's nothing left *for* them to do. The computers do it all."

"Well fuck it, then," Guy said. "I'll just clean up the floppy and send it in, like I was going to, and—"

"Just a second," Bob667 interrupted, holding up a decayed-looking finger. "The govt agents are closing in."

A fist hammered on the door.

Janet switched the TV to hall monitor and glanced quickly away. "Yuck," she said. "It's another one of *them.*"

Guy opened the door for Bob005. "The govt agents are closing in," it said. "The High Bob sent me to warn you. If you don't come with us and let us hide you, they're going to catch you. We can't stop them."

"Didn't we go through all that this afternoon?"

"Look," said Bob667. "If you won't let us hide you, can we at least try something else? Nobody's ever had a chance to get on the govt's computer before. They may just burn that diskette of yours, but there's a chance they'll want to look at it first. To at least make sure they have the right one. Let me copy a virus on there."

"A virus?"

It took a diskette out of a fold in its toga—or a fold in its chest, Guy wasn't sure which. "It is our sacred bulldada in program form—a self-concatenating string loop. We've spent a long time working this up, for just such an opportunity."

Guy hesitated. "How much more trouble would this get me in?" he asked, but Bob667 apparently misunderstood.

"A good attitude," it said, popping the second diskette into a drive and typing a command. "Are you sure you won't come with us?" it asked again as it took out Guy's diskette and handed it back to him.

"I'm sure."

"Ahem," Sam said. "Did someone say they were 'closing in?'"

"Uh, yeah," Guy said. "Apparently."

Janet yawned widely. "Gee. Really sleepy all of a sudden."

"Gosh," Sam said. "Look at the time."

"I'll just walk you downstairs," Guy said to the muties.

"Don't mean to rush you," Janet said. "But..."

THE THREE OF THEM stopped on a street corner near the subway entrance. "I don't really understand why you won't come with us," Bob667 said.

"It's like this. If I came with you, that would mean I believe all this shit you told me. I'd have to be crazy to believe that. So I'd rather just go to work and pretend that everything's okay."

"Well, all right then."

Guy felt strangely reluctant to let them go. He was certain he would never see either of them again, less certain why that idea should bother him. "So," he asked. "If they do catch this virus, thing, what happens then?"

"I don't know. Maybe the end of the govt. If so, that takes a lot of pressure off of us. I'm not sure anybody else would notice."

"I would," Guy said.

"Yes, well, good luck then," said Bob667. The two muties walked away. Between one streetlight and the next they were gone.

THE GOVT AGENTS picked Guy up a block later. He was wandering aimlessly, trying to make up his mind where to go. The agents, Guy noticed, wore their mirror glasses even in the dark, even as they tossed him lightly in the back of their Honda.

During the trip, one of them lifted the diskette out of Guy's jacket. "Hey," Guy said. "You can't—"

"Shut up, assle," the agent said.

Guy shut up.

He kept expecting them to stop the Honda and throw him off a bridge, or take him into an alley and shoot him, but instead they led him to the basement of the midtown govt complex and handed him a stack of change. "Machines there, bathroom there," the agent said, and left.

The place looked and smelled abandoned. Pipes gridded the ceiling, oily water stained the floor, and plastic crates lay scattered everywhere. At one end of the room stood a big-screen TV, a ratty couch, and a wheelchair containing an old woman.

"You ever watch this channel?" she asked. "I watch it sometimes. It's not too bad."

Guy walked over to her. "Who are you?"

"Sit down, sit down," she said. "Or if you're going to talk, do it in the other room."

Guy went to the door and pushed against it. Its surface was devoid of handles to shake or locks to pick; some kind of electronic seal held it in place. Guy bought himself a Coke and went back to sit on the couch.

The woman was watching WLCD, "the browsing station." A lot of football players chased a slippery ball to the accompaniment of synthesized bassoons. The station cut to the WLCD logo, then ran two-and-a-half minutes of pie fight scenes from old black-and-white comedies. Then back to the logo, a big dance number, the logo, and a man in a white coat talking very seriously for a minute and a half about hemorrhoids.

After a short piece on crippled orphans, the old lady said, "Makes you sad, don't it?"

Guy thought about the floppy with the BLOOPERS file on it. Was this what the govt had been shooting for? He wondered how much money they'd quietly put into superstation WLCD. How perfect it was for them—a station you never had to turn off, because if you didn't like what was on you only had to wait a minute or two. No complicated plots to follow, no characters to get mixed up, no difficult shadings of emotion.

Guy tried to lure the old woman into conversation, but she refused to talk in more than three- or four-second bursts. He learned that her name was Mildred, but nothing else about her, or the reason he was being kept with her in the basement.

Trying to ignore the TV proved beyond Guy's will. He had nothing else to do in that basement but drink Cokes and eat candy bars, and in that suffocating grayness the splash of big screen color drew his eyes irresistibly.

He was able to doze off for a few minutes at a time, but a sudden fanfare from the set would wake him up. The old woman never seemed to sleep.

Finally he decided to risk the old woman's wrath and tried to switch the thing off. "Hey!" she shouted at him. "Whatcha doing there? Get away!" The power knob was frozen, as was the channel selector.

"Nothing," Guy said. "Never mind."

"This is a good program," she said. "I like this one."

"Okay," Guy said. "Okay."

He soon lost his sense of time. His watch was still running, but he didn't know if the numbers were AM or PM. He'd told that new girl at the store, the one with the soft, mobile lower lip, that he would call her this weekend. He didn't know if the weekend had come or gone.

He began to stay asleep longer, wake up less fully. He wished he had clean clothes and a razor. He wondered about Bob667's virus program and decided that it had failed because nobody had come to rescue him.

Then one day he couldn't remember the last time the old woman had said anything. He struggled up from the couch and waved a hand in front of her inert face. No response. He felt her arm for a pulse, and though he couldn't find one he noticed the flesh was still warm and soft. As he let go of her hand it knocked the afghan off her lap, revealing a mass of circuitry.

An andie, he thought. No wonder.

He ran to the door and began pounding on it. "Hey! Hey, somebody, let me out of here!"

The door drifted open under his hands.

The building was deserted. Chairs lay haphazardly around the offices and glass was broken out of the doors. Guy tapped on one of the CRTs, but it was dead as the old woman downstairs.

The programmers had obviously panicked when the computer went down. So, Guy thought, no more govt.

He compared his watch to the bright sunlight out, side and decided it was eleven in the morning. He went home, took a long shower, and walked to work.

ISABEL NECESSARY, his district manager, wanted to fire him at first. She couldn't believe that Guy could have lost the diskette *and* missed five days' work without phoning in.

"I was in an accident," Guy lied cheerfully. "I lost my memory."

"I'll bet," Isabel sneered. "You were probably just lying around watching TV."

But in the end she let him stay. Probably, Guy thought, because she couldn't find anybody else for the money who'd wear decent clothes.

He stopped at Sam and Janet's place after work, but they'd moved away, with no forwarding address. The new tenant, a middle-aged man in a bathrobe, had WLCD running in the background when he answered the door.

"Sorry I can't help you," he told Guy. He had one eye still on the TV as Guy thanked him and left.

Standing in the street, Guy realized it was the first time he'd been outside in recent memory without something terrible happening to him. The astroturf sidewalk felt firm and springy beneath his feet; he was clean and nicely dressed again. He should have been happy, but somehow he felt like he'd missed out on something, as if he'd woken up and found himself inexplicably old and frail.

He decided he really ought to talk it over with Santa. He crossed the street and went into the booth on the comer.

The Porta-Santa was dead.

Santa's face was frozen on the screen, half, way into a wink. One eye was almost closed and his mouth was twisted in what looked like a grimace of pain.

Guy stood there for half an hour, watching the distorted face, waiting for some kind of message. It's not coming, he realized at last. It's like the mutie said. The revolution happened, but nobody noticed. They were all home watching TV.

"So long, Santa," Guy said.

He shut the door of the booth and shuffled away down the green plastic lawn of the sidewalk.

GOLD

PIRATE GOLD. Coins, rings, ingots. Necklaces of emeralds and opals and sapphires. Chalices, bracelets, daggers inlaid with diamonds and lapis and ivory.

Malone rolled over in the soft hotel bed.

Not just gold but the things it would buy. A two-story house of brick and wrought iron. Greek columns in front and coaches parked in the drive. Built high on the center of Galveston Island, away from the deadly storms of the Gulf, away from the noise and stink of the port. White servants and negro slaves. Fair-haired women to sit at the piano in his parlor. Dark-skinned women to open their legs to him in the secrecy of the night...

He sat up in a sweat. I will think no evil thoughts, he told himself.

Outside, the sun rose over New Orleans. Horse-drawn carts creaked and rattled through the streets, and chickens complained about the light. The smell of the Mississippi, damp and sexual, floated through the open window.

Malone got up and put a robe on over his nightshirt, despite the heat. He turned up the gas lamp over the desk, took out pen, ink and paper, and began to write.

"My dearest Becky..."

HE SMELLED the French Market before he saw it, a mixture of decayed fruit, coffee, and leather. He crossed Decatur Street to avoid a side of beef hung over the sidewalk, swarming with flies. Voices shouted in a dozen different languages. All manner of decrepit wooden carts stood on the street, their contents passed from hand to hand until they disappeared under the yellow canvas awnings of the market. Beyond the levee, Malone could see the tops of the masts of the tall ships that moved toward Governor Nicholl's Street Wharf.

The market was crowded with cooks from the town's better families, most of them Negro or Creole. The women wore calico dresses and aprons and kerchiefs, in all shades of reds and yellows and blues. The men wore second-hand suits in ruby or deep green, with no collars or neckties. Like their suits, their hats were battered and several years out of style. They carried shopping baskets on their shoulders or heads because there was no room to carry them at their sides.

Malone let himself be drawn in. He moved slowly past makeshift stands

built of crates and loose boards, past heaps of tomatoes and peppers and
bananas and field peas, searching the faces of the vendors. His concern turned
out to be groundless; he recognized Chighizola immediately.

Nez Coupe, Lafitte had called him. With the end of his nose gone, he looked
like a rat that stood on hind legs, sniffing at something foul. The rest of his
ancient face was covered with scars as well. One of them, just under his right
eye, looked pink and newly healed. He was tiny, well over eighty years old now,
his frock coat hanging loose on his shoulders. Still, his eyes had a fierce look,
and he moved with no sign of stiffness. His hands were large and energetic,
seeming to carry his arms unwillingly behind them wherever they went.

"Louis Chighizola," Malone called out. The old man turned to look at him.
Chighizola's eyes were glittering black. He seemed ready to laugh or fly into a
rage at a moment's notice. Malone pushed closer. "I need a word with you."

"What you want, you?"

"I have a proposition. A business proposition."

"This not some damn trash about Lafitte again?" The black eyes had
narrowed. Malone took a half step back, colliding with an enormous Negro
woman. He no longer doubted that some of Chighizola's scars were fresh.

"This is different, I assure you."

"How you mean different?"

"I have seen him. Alive and well, not two weeks ago."

"I got no time for ghosts. You buy some fruit, or you move along."

"He gave me this," Malone said. He took a flintlock pistol from his coat,
holding it by the barrel, and passed it to the old man.

Chighizola looked behind him, took one reluctant step toward Malone. He
took the pistol and held it away from him, into the sunlight. "Fucking hell,"
Chighizola said. He turned back to Malone. "We talk."

CHIGHIZOLA LED HIM east on Chartres Street, then turned into an alley. It
opened on a square full of potted palms and flowers and sheets hung out to
dry. They climbed a wrought-iron spiral staircase to a balcony cluttered with
pots, old newspapers, empty barrels. Chighizola knocked at the third door and
a young woman opened it.

She was an octoroon with skin the color of Lafitte's buried gold. She wore
a white cotton shift with nothing under it. The cotton had turned translucent
where it had drunk the sweat from her skin. Smells of fruit and flowers and
musk drifted from the room behind her.

Malone followed the old man into an aging parlor. Dark flowered wallpaper
showed stains and loose threads at the seams. A sofa with a splinted leg sat
along one wall and a few unmatched chairs stood nearby. An engraving of a

sailing ship, unframed, was tacked to one wall. Half a dozen children played on the threadbare carpet, aged from a few months to six or seven years. Chighizola pointed to a chair, and Malone sat down.

"So. Where you get this damn pistol?"

"From Lafitte himself."

"Lafitte is dead. He disappears thirty years ago. The Indians down in Yucatan, they cook him and eat him, I think."

"Is the pistol Lafitte's, or is it not?"

"You are not Lafitte, yet *you* have his pistol. Any man could."

Malone closed his eyes, fatigue taking the heart out of him. "Perhaps you are right. Perhaps I have only deceived myself." A small child, no more than two years old, crawled into Malone's lap. She had the features of the woman who answered the door, in miniature. Her dress was clean, if too small, and her black hair had been pulled back and neatly tied in red and blue ribbons. She rubbed the wool of Malone's coat, then stuck two fingers in her mouth.

"I do not understand," Chighizola said. "You come to me with this story. Do you not believe it yourself?"

"I wish I knew," Malone said.

MALONE WAS BORN poor in Ohio. His parents moved to the Republic of Texas in 1837 to get a new start. Some perverse symbolism made them choose the island of Galveston, recently swept clean by a hurricane. There they helped with the rebuilding, and Malone's father got work as a carpenter. Malone was 10 years old at the time, and the memories of the disaster would stay with him the rest of his life. Block-long heaps of shattered lumber, shuffled like cards, the ruin of one house indistinguishable from the next. Stacks of bodies towed out to sea, and those same bodies washing in again days and weeks later. Scuff marks six feet up inside one of the few houses left standing, where floating furniture had knocked against the walls. The poor, Malone saw, would always be victims. For the rich there were options.

One of the richest men on Galveston Island was Samuel May Williams. On New Year's Day of 1848 he had opened the doors of the Commercial and Agricultural Bank of Texas, his lifetime dream. It sat on a choice piece of land just two blocks off the Strand Avenue, "the Wall Street of Texas." Williams' fellow Texans hated him for his shrewd land speculation, his introduction of paper money to the state, his participation in the corrupt Monclova legislature of '35. Malone thought them naive. Williams was a survivor, that was all.

Not like his father, who found that a new start did not necessarily mean a new life. Malone's mother died, along with a quarter of Galveston's population, in the yellow fever epidemic of '39. Soon his father was drinking again.

Between the liquor and his son's education, there was barely money for food. Malone swore that he would see his father in a fine house in the Silk Stocking district. He never got the chance. He returned from Baylor University in the spring of '48 in time to carry one corner of his father's coffin.

Malone's classes in accounting were enough to land him a position as a clerk in Sam Williams' new bank. Within a year he had married the daughter of one of its board members. His father-in-law made Malone a junior officer and an acceptable member of society. A long, slow climb lay ahead of him, leading to a comfortable income at best. It did not seem enough, somehow.

He had been in Austin on the bank's business. It was a foreclosure, the least pleasant of Malone's duties. The parcel of land was one that Williams had acquired in his early days in Texas, "going halves" with immigrants brought in by the Mexican government.

That night he had stood at the Crystal Saloon on Austin's notorious Congress Avenue, drinking away the sight of the sheriff examining Malone's papers, saying, "Sam Williams, eh?" and spitting in the dirt, the sight of the Mexican family disappearing on a mule cart that held every battered thing they owned.

A tall man in a bright yellow suit had stood at Malone's table, nodded at his satchel, and said, "On the road, are you?" The man spat tobacco onto the floor, the reason Malone had kept his satchel safely out of the way. The habit was so pervasive that Malone took precautions now by instinct. "I travel myself," the man said. "I am in ladies' garments. By trade, that is."

Malone saw that it was meant to be a joke. The drummer's name was O'Roarke, but he constantly referred to himself in the third person as Brimstone Jack, "on account of this head of hair." He lifted his hat to demonstrate. The hair that was visible was somewhere between yellow and red, matching his mustache and extravagant side-whiskers. There was, however, not much of it.

Malone mentioned Galveston. The talk soon turned to Jean Lafitte, the world's last pirate and the first white settler of Galveston Island. That was when O'Roarke offered to produce the genuine article.

Four glasses of bourbon whiskey had raised Malone's credulity to new heights. He followed O'Roarke to a house on West Avenue, the limits of civilization, and there stepped into a world he had never seen before. Chinese, colored, and white men sat in the same room together, most of them on folding cots along the walls. Heavy, sour smoke hung in the air. The aroma left Malone both nervous and oddly euphoric. "Sir," he said to O'Roarke, "this is an opium den."

A man in the far corner began to laugh. The laugh went on and on, rich, comfortable, full of real pleasure. Malone, his good manners finally giving way to curiosity, turned and stared.

The laughing man had fair skin, a hatchet nose, and piercing black eyes. His black hair fell in curls to the middle of his back. He was in shirt sleeves, leather trousers, and Mexican sandals. There was a power about him. Malone felt a sudden, strong desire for the man's good opinion.

"May I present," O'Roarke said with a small bow, "the pirate Jean Lafitte?" Malone stared in open disbelief.

"Privateer," the dark-haired man said, still smiling. "Never a pirate."

"Tell him," O'Roarke said to the dark-haired man. "Tell him who you are."

"My name is John Lafflin," the man said.

"Your real name," O'Roarke said, "damn you."

"I have been known by others. You may call me Jean Lafitte, if it pleases you."

"Lafitte's son, perhaps," Malone said. "Lafitte himself would be, what, nearly seventy years old now. If he lived."

The hatchet-faced man laughed again. "You may believe me or not. It makes no difference to me."

SITTING THERE IN Chighizola's apartment, watching dust motes in the morning sunlight, Malone found his own story more difficult to believe than ever. From the shadows the woman watched him in silence. He wondered how foolish he must look to her.

"And yet," Chighizola said, "you *did* believe him."

"It was something in his bearing," Malone said. "That and the fact that he wanted nothing from me. Not even my belief. I found myself unable to sleep that night. I returned to the house before dawn and searched his belongings for evidence."

"Which is when you stole the pistol. He did not give it to you."

"No. He had no desire to convince me."

"So why does this matter so much to you?"

Malone sighed. Sooner or later it had to come out. "Because of the treasure. If he is truly Lafitte—or even if he is merely Lafitte's son—he could lead us to the treasure."

"Always to the treasure it comes."

"I grew up on Galveston Island. We all live in the shadow of Jean Lafitte. As children we would steal away into the bayous and search for his treasure. Once there, we found grown men doing the same. And if I feel so personally connected, how can you not feel even more so? It is your treasure as much as Lafitte's. You sailed with him, risked your life for him. And yet look at yourself. In poverty, living by the labor of your hands."

"I have not much time left."

"All the more reason you should want what is yours. You should want the money for your family, for your daughter here, and her children."

Chighizola looked at the woman. "He thinks you are my daughter, him." She came over to kiss his scarred and twisted face. Malone felt his own face go red. "Here is a boy who knows nothing of life."

"I am young," Malone said. "It is true. But so is this nation. Like this nation I am also ambitious. I want more than my own enrichment. I know that it takes money to bring about change, to create the growth that will bring prosperity to everyone."

"You sound like a politician."

"With enough money, I would become one. Perhaps a good one. But without your help it will never happen."

"Why am I so important? This man, Lafitte or not, what does it matter if he can lead you to the treasure?"

"If he is Lafitte, he will listen to you. He cares nothing for me. He will lead me nowhere. I need you to make him care."

"I will think on this."

"I am stopping at the French Market Inn. My ship leaves tomorrow afternoon for Galveston. I must know your answer by then."

"Tell me, you who are in such a hurry. What of ghosts?"

"I do not understand."

"Ghosts. The spirits of the dead."

"Lafitte is alive. That is all that concerns me."

"Ah, but you seek his gold. And where there is gold, there are ghosts. Always."

"Then I leave them to you, old man. I will take my chances with the living."

MALONE HAD ALREADY packed his trunk and sent for his bill when the woman arrived. He mistook her knock for the bellman and was shocked into silence when he opened the door. Finally he backed away and stammered an apology.

"I bring a message from Chighizola," she said. She pushed the door closed and leaned her weight against it. "We will go with you to see this Lafitte."

"'We?'" Malone could not take his eyes away from her.

"He says we are to divide the treasure four ways, equal shares, you, me, Louis, Lafitte."

"Which leaves the two of you with half the treasure. I thought he did not care for money."

"Perhaps not. Perhaps you care too much for it."

"I am not a schoolboy. I have no desire to be taught humility at Chighizola's hands."

"Those are his terms. If they are agreeable, we leave today."

Malone took a step closer to her. Curls of black hair had stuck to the damp flesh of her throat. It was difficult for him to speak. "I do not know your name."

"Fabienne."

"And what is your interest in this?"

"Louis," she said. "He is my only interest." She stepped to one side and pulled the door open. "We will meet you at the wharf in one hour." She closed the door behind her.

THE VOYAGE TO GALVESTON took a day and a half aboard the S.S. Columbia, now-aging stalwart of the Morgan line. Malone saw Chighizola and his woman only once, when the three of them shared a table for dinner. Otherwise Malone remained in his cabin, catching up on accounts and correspondence.

Malone stood on the bow as the ship steamed into Galveston Bay. Even now Sam Williams might have his eye on him. Legend had it that Williams watched incoming ships with a telescope from the cupola of his house, deducing their cargoes from their semaphored messages. He would then hurry into town to corner the market on the incoming merchandise. It did not increase his popularity. Then again, Williams had never seen public opinion as a necessary condition for money and power.

Williams had proven what a man of ambition could do. He had arrived in Texas under an assumed name in May of 1822, fleeing debts as so many others had. He had created himself from scratch. Malone knew that he could do the same. It was not proper that a man should live on his wife's fortune and social position. He needed to increase and acquire, to shape the world around him.

Chighizola joined him as they swung in toward the harbor. "Do you never miss the sea?" Malone asked him.

"I had enough of her," Chighizola said. "She care for nobody. You spend your life on top of her, she love you no more than she did the first day. A woman is better." He squinted at the island. The harbor was crowded with sailboats and steamers, and beyond it the two-story frame buildings of the Strand were clearly visible. "Hard to believe that is the same Campeachy." He looked at Malone. "Galveston, you call it now. Are there still the snakes?"

"Not like there used to be."

"Progress. Well, I will be glad to see it. Every new thing, it always is such a surprise for me."

"You will have to see it another time. We must catch a steamer for the mainland this morning, then a coach to Austin."

"Yes, I forget the hurry you are in."

"I have to know. I have to know if it is Lafitte or not."

"It is him."

"How can you be certain without even seeing him? I tell you he looks no more than forty years old."

"And I tell you we buried Lafitte twice, once at the Barataria, once at Campeachy."

"Buried him?"

"For being dead. Lafitte, he eats the blowfish, him. You understand? Poison fish. In Haiti he learns this. Sometimes he eats it, nothing happens. Sometimes he loses the feeling in his tongue, his mouth. Twice he gets stiff all over and looks dead. Twice we bury him, twice the Haitian spirit man watch the grave and dig him up again. Ten years he eats the blowfish, that I know him. In all that time, he gets no older. But it makes him different, in his head. Money is nothing to him after. Then the second time, he cares about nothing at all. Sets fire to Campeachy, sails off to Yucatan with his brother Pierre."

"I have read the accounts," Malone said. "Lt. Kearny and the *Enterprise* drove him away."

"You think one man, one ship, stand against Lafitte if he wants to fight? He sees the future that night. He sees more and more Lt. Kearnys in their uniforms, with their laws and courts and papers. More civilization, like in Louisiana. More government telling you what you can do. No more room for privateers. No place left in this country where a man stands alone. So he goes to Mexico. But first, before he goes, we burn the whole town to the ground. So Lt. Kearny does not get Lafitte's nice red house."

Malone knew that Lafitte's pirate camp had numbered two thousand souls by the time Kearny arrived in 1821. Lafitte himself ruled from a two-story red house near the port, surrounded by a moat, guarded by his most loyal men. Campeachy had been a den of vice and iniquity: gaming, whores, liquor, gun-fights and duels. There were those in Galveston still who wondered if the island would ever recover from the evil that had been done there.

Malone shook his head. Chighizola had got him thinking of ghosts and now he could not rid himself of them.

"You did not go with him," Malone said. "To Mexico. Why not?"

"I do not like the odds. I think, a man looks at Death so many times, then one day Death looks back. Life always seems good to me. I am not like Lafitte, *moi*. I do not have these ideas and beliefs to keep me awake all night. You are still young, I give you advice. To sleep good at night, this is not such a bad thing."

•

THE COACH TOOK them from Houston to San Felipe along the Lower
Road, then overland to Columbus. From there along the Colorado River to
La Grange and Bastrop and Austin. Chighizola was exhausted by the trip, and
the woman Fabienne blamed Malone for it. Malone was tired and irritable
himself. Still he forced himself out of the hotel that night to search for Lafitte.

The opium house was deserted, with no sign left of its former use. He
stopped in two or three saloons and left word for O'Roarke, then gave up and
retired to the comparative luxury of the Avenue Hotel.

Malone searched all the next day, asking for both O'Roarke and Lafitte
by name. The first name met with shrugs, the second with laughter. Malone
ordered a cold supper sent to his room, where he ate in silence with
Chighizola and the woman.

"It would seem," the woman said, "that we have come a long, painful
distance for nothing." She was dressed somewhat more formally than Malone
had seen her before, in a low-cut yellow frock and a lace cap. The dangling
strings of the cap and her dark, flashing eyes made her seem as wanton as ever.

"I do not believe that," Malone said. "Men have destinies, just as nations do.
I cannot believe that my opportunity has passed me by."

There was a knock and Malone stood up. "That may be destiny even now."

It was in fact O'Roarke, with Lafitte in tow. "I heard," O'Roarke said, "you
sought for Brimstone Jack. He has answered your summons." He noticed
Fabienne, removed his hat, and directed his gobbet of tobacco juice at the
cuspidor rather than the floor.

Malone turned back to the room. Chighizola was on his feet, one hand to
his throat. "Holy Christ," he said, and crossed himself.

Lafitte sank into an armchair. He seemed intoxicated, unable to focus his
eyes. "Nez Coupe? Is it really you?"

"Me, I look how I should. You are the one that is not to be believed.
Lafitte's son, you could be."

Malone said, "I warned you."

"A test," Chighizola said. "That is what you want, no?"

Malone shrugged. "I feel certain it would reassure us all."

Chighizola rubbed a thick scar that ran along the edge of his jaw. "There is
a business with a golden thimble I could ask him about."

Lafitte waved his hand, bored. "Yes, yes, of course I remember the thimble.
But I suppose I must tell the story, to satisfy your friends." He shifted in the
chair and picked at something on his shirt. "It happened in the Barataria.
We had made the division of the spoils from a galleon taken out in the Gulf.
There were three gold coins left over. I tried to give them to your wife." His

eyes moved to Fabienne, then back. "Your wife of the time, of course. But you were greedy and wanted them for yourself. So I had the smith make them into a thimble for her. I think it ended up in a chest full of things that we buried somewhere."

"It is Lafitte," Chighizola said to Malone. "If you doubted it."

"No," Malone said, "I had no doubt." He turned to O'Roarke. "How can we reward you for bringing him to us?"

"You can cut me in on the treasure," O'Roarke said. Lafitte put back his head and laughed.

"I do not know what you mean," Malone said.

O'Roarke's face became red. "Do not take Brimstone Jack for an idiot. What you want is obvious. You are not the first to try. If you succeed I would ask for only a modest amount. Say, a hundredth share. It would be simpler to cut me in than to do the things you would have to do to lose me."

Malone looked at Chighizola. Chighizola said, "It comes from your share, not from ours." Fabienne smiled her agreement.

"All right, damn it," Malone said. "Done."

Lafitte leaned forward. "You seem to have matters well in hand. Perhaps I should be on my way."

Malone stared at him for a second in shock. "Please. Wait."

"You, sir, though I know your face, I do not know your name. I seem to remember you in connection with the disappearance of my pistol."

Malone handed the pistol to Lafitte, butt first. With some embarrassment he said, "The name is Malone."

"Mr. Malone, now that you have divided up my treasure, may I ask a question or two? How do you know the treasure even exists? If it does exist, that I have not long ago spent it? If I have not spent it, that I even recall where it was buried?" Unspoken was the final question: if he recalled it, why should he share?

"Is there a treasure?" Malone asked at last.

Lafitte took out a clay pipe shaped like some Mexican deity and stuffed it with brittle green leaves. He did not offer the odd tobacco to anyone else. When he lit it the fumes were sour and spicy. Lafitte held the smoke in his lungs for several long seconds then exhaled loudly. "Yes, I suppose there is."

"And you could find it again?"

Lafitte shrugged again. "Perhaps."

"You make sport of us, sir. You know our interests, and you seem to take pleasure in encouraging them. But you give us no satisfaction. What are your motives in this? Has money in fact lost all appeal for you?"

"I never cared for it," Lafitte said. "You may believe that or not. I cared for justice and freedom. Spain stood against those principles, and so I carried letters of marque to make war upon her. The riches were incidental, necessary merely to prolong that war. But time has moved on. Justice and freedom are antique concepts, of no importance to our modern world. The world, in the person of Lt. Kearny, made it clear that it had no use for me or my kind. I have learned to return the sentiment. I have no use for the things of this world."

He relighted his pipe and took another lungfull of smoke. "You ask about my appearance. I met a Brahman from the Indian continent a few years ago. He explained that it is our connection to worldly things that ages us. *Karma,* he called it. I believe I am living proof of the Brahman's beliefs."

"What of those of us still in the world?" Malone said. "I see in you the signs of a former idealist, now disillusioned. I still have ideals. There are still wars to be fought, against ignorance and disease and natural disaster. Wars your treasure could fight. And what of Chighizola, your shipmate? Is he not entitled to his share?" For some reason the fumes from Lafitte's pipe had left Malone terribly hungry. He cast a sideways glance toward the remains of supper.

"If you sailed with him," O'Roarke said to Chighizola, "you must persuade him."

"I think," Chighizola said, "people try that for years now."

"You never answered my question," Malone said to Lafitte. "Money does not motivate you. Neither, it seems, does idealism. At least not any longer. So what is it you care for? What can we offer you?"

"A trip to Galveston," Lafitte said. "I would like to see my island again. To see how things have changed in thirty years. Then we will talk some more." He set his pipe down. "And for the moment, you could hand me the remains of that loaf of bread. I find myself suddenly famished."

THEY OCCUPIED an entire coach on the return trip. Between O'Roarke's spitting and Lafitte's pipe, it was even less pleasant than the outbound journey. They got off the steamer in Galveston late in the evening of a Sunday. The wharf was crowded nonetheless. Several freighters were being filled with cotton, the bales crammed into place with mechanical jackscrews to allow larger loads. The screwmen were the kings of the dock and shouldered their way contemptuously through the newly-arrived passengers, carrying huge bales of cotton on their backs.

Malone led his party, now including a couple of Negro porters, past Water Street to the Strand. It felt good to have the familiar sand and crushed shells under his feet again. "The Tremont Hotel is just over there, on 23rd Street," he said. "If there's any problem with your rooms, just mention the Commercial and Agricultural Bank. Mr. Williams, my employer, is part owner of the hotel."

"And where do *you* live?" Lafitte asked. He had not ceased to smile in the entire time Malone had known him.

"About a mile from here. On 22nd Street. With my wife and her family."

"Do they not have guest rooms?"

"Yes, of course, but it would be awkward..."

"In other words, since this is a purely business venture, you would prefer to put us up like strangers, well away from the sanctity of your home."

"That was never my intent. My wife, you see, is ... highly strung. I try not to impose on her, if at all possible."

"We are an imposition, then," Lafitte said. "I see."

"Very well! Enough! You will stop at our house then. We shall manage somehow."

"That is gracious of you," Lafitte said. "I should be delighted."

THERE WAS NO TIME, of course, to warn Becky. Thus Malone arrived on his wife's doorstep with four strangers. He had the porters bring the luggage up the long flight of steps to the porch; like most Galveston houses, it was supported by eight-foot columns of brick.

Jefferson, the Negro butler, answered the door. "Please get the guest room ready," Malone told him. "I shall put a pair of cots in the study as well, I suppose. And tell Mrs. Malone that I have returned."

"Sir."

Chighizola and his woman left with Jefferson. Malone paid the porters and took Lafitte and O'Roarke into the study.

"Nice place," O'Roarke said.

"Thank you," Malone said, painfully pinching a finger as he set up the cots. "Use the cuspidor while in the house, if you do not mind."

Becky appeared in the doorway. "How nice to see you again," she said to Malone, without sincerity. "It would appear your expedition was more successful than you expected."

"This is Mr. O'Roarke and Mr. ... Lafflin," he said. Lafitte smiled at the name. "This is my wife, Becky."

She sketched a curtsy. "How do you do."

"They are business associates of mine. I regret not letting you know they would be stopping here. It came up rather suddenly."

"I trust you will find a way to explain this to my father. I know it is hopeless to expect you to offer any explanation to me." She turned and disappeared.

"When I lived on the island," Lafitte said, "we had a whorehouse on this very spot."

"Thank you for that bit of history," Malone said. "My night is now complete."

"Is there anything to eat?" O'Roarke asked.

"If you cannot wait until morning, you are welcome to go down to the kitchen and see what you can find. Please do not disturb Jefferson unless you have to." Malone felt sorry for the old Negro. In keeping with current abolitionist sentiment in Texas, he had been freed, but his wages consisted of his room and board only. "And now, if you have no objections, I shall withdraw. It is late, and we can resume our business in the morning."

THE HOUSE WAS brutally hot, even with the doors and windows open. There had been a southeast breeze when it was first built; the city's growth had long since diverted it. Malone put on his nightshirt and crawled under the mosquito net. He arranged the big square pillow under his shoulders so that night-borne fevers would not settle in his lungs. Becky lay under the covers, arms pressed against her sides, feigning sleep.

"Good night," he said. She made no answer. He knew that he would be within his rights to pull the covers off and take her, willing or not. She had made it clear she would not resist him. No, she would lie there, eyes closed, soundless, like a corpse. He was almost tempted. The days of confinement with Fabienne had taken their toll.

He could recall the flush of Fabienne's golden skin, her scent, her cascading hair. She would not receive a man so passively, he thought. She could, he imagined, break a man's ribs with the heat of her passion.

Malone got up and drank a small glass of whisky. Imagination had always been his curse. Lately it kept him from sleep and interfered with his accounts. Enough gold, he thought, would cure that. The rich needed no imagination.

MALONE ROSE BEFORE his guests, eyes bloodshot and head aching. He scrubbed his face at the basin, dressed, and went downstairs. He found his father-in-law in the breakfast room and quickly put his lies in order. He explained Lafitte and the others as investors, wealthy but eccentric, here to look at the possibility of a railroad causeway to the mainland. Becky's father was mad for progress, in love with the idea of the railroad. He smiled and shook Malone's hand.

"Good work, son," he said. "I knew you would make your mark. Eventually."

Chighizola and Fabienne came down for breakfast at eight. Becky had left word for Cook and there were chafing dishes on the sideboard filled with poached eggs, liver, flounder, sausage, broiled tomatoes, and steak. There was a toast rack, a coffee service, a jug of orange juice, a tray of biscuits, and a large selection of jams in small porcelain pots. O'Roarke joined them shortly before nine. He seemed rather sullen, though he consumed two large plates full of food. He ate in silence, tugging on his orange side whiskers with his left hand.

Lafitte, in contrast, was cheerful when he finally arrived. He was unshaven, without collar, braces, or waistcoat, and his long hair was in disarray. He ate only fish and vegetables and refused Malone's offer of coffee.

When Jefferson came to clear away the dishes Malone asked, "Where is Mrs. Malone this morning?"

"In her room, sir. She said to tell you she had letter writing to see to."

She might come down for supper, then. Unless, of course, she suddenly felt unwell, a condition he could predict with some confidence. "If she asks, you may tell her I have taken our visitors for a walk."

First he showed them St. Mary's cathedral, at 21st Street and Avenue F, with its twin Gothic towers on either side of the arched entranceway. It was barely two years old, the first church on the island and the first cathedral in Texas. To Malone it was a symbol. Virtually the entire city had been rebuilt since 1837 and structures like St. Mary's showed a fresh determination, a resolution to stay no matter what the odds.

He pointed out the purple blossoms of the oleanders that now grew wild all over the city, brought originally from Jamaica in wooden tubs. He led them west to 23rd Street, past Sam Williams' bank. Then he brought them down the Strand, with its commission houses and government offices.

"The similarities to Manhattan Island are clear," Malone said. "Galveston stands as the gateway to Texas, a perfect natural harbor, ideally situated on the Gulf."

"Except for the storms," Lafitte said.

"Man's ingenuity will find a way to rob them of their power. Look around you. This is already the largest city in Texas. And everything you see was brought about by human industry. Nature withheld her hand from this place."

"You need hardly remind me," Lafitte said. "When we first came here there were salt cedars and scrub oaks, poisonous snakes, and man-eating Indians. And nothing else. Am I right, Nez Coupe?"

Chighizola said, "You leave out the malaria and the infernal gulls."

"You can see that things have greatly improved," Malone said.

"Improved? Hardly. I see churches and banks, custom houses and shops, all the fetters and irons of civilization."

"Shops?" O'Roarke said. "Against shops as well, are you? What would you have?"

"No one owned the land when we lived here. Everything was held in common. The prizes we took were divided according to agreed-upon shares. No one went hungry for lack of money."

"Communism," Malone said. "I have heard of it. That German, Karl Marx, has written about it."

"He was hardly the first," Lafitte said. "Bonaparte urged many of the same reforms. As did Rousseau, for that matter."

They had turned east on Water Avenue. At 14th Street Lafitte stopped. He turned back, with one hand shading his eyes, then smiled. "Here," he said.

"Pardon?" Malone asked.

"La Maison Rouge. This is where my house was. Look, you can see where the ground is sunken. This is where I had my moat. Inland stood the gallows. Rebels and mutineers, those who raided any but Spanish ships, died there."

Now there was only an abandoned shack, with wide spaces between the boards where the green wood had shrunk. Malone stepped into its shade for a moment to escape the relentless sun. "Truly?" he said. "Truly, you never attacked an American ship?"

"Truly," Chighizola said. "The Spanish only. He was obsessed."

"Why?"

Chighizola shook his head.

"A private matter," Lafitte said. "I was angry then. Angry enough to burn La Maison Rouge and all the rest of it when I left, burn the entire city to the ground."

"Your anger," Malone said, "is legendary."

"No more," Lafitte said. "To have that much anger, you have to care deeply. To be attached to the world."

"And you care for nothing?" O'Roarke said. "Nothing at all?"

Lafitte shrugged. "Nothing comes to mind."

DINNER WAS LONG and arduous. Lafitte seemed willing enough to play along with Malone's railroad charade. However his lack of seriousness, bordering on contempt, left Becky's father deeply suspicious. O'Roarke's crude speech and spitting would have maddened Becky had she not been upstairs, "feeling poorly," in the words of her maid. As for Chighizola and Fabienne, they were simply ignored.

Afterwards O'Roarke stopped him in the hall. "How much longer? By thunder, Brimstone Jack is not one for waiting around. We should be after the treasure."

"If it is any consolation," Malone said, "I am enjoying this no more than you."

Malone retired, but was unable to sleep. Exhausted, yet with his nerves wound tight, he lay propped up in bed and listened to the clock on the dresser loudly tick away the seconds. He finally reached the verge of sleep, only to come awake again at the sound of someone moving in the hallway.

He dressed hastily and went downstairs. He found Lafitte in the porch glider, smoking his hemp tobacco.

"Might I join you?" Malone asked.

"It is your house."

"No," Malone said, sitting on the porch rail. "It is my wife's house. It is a difference that has plagued me for some time. I crave my independence."

"And you think my treasure will buy that for you."

"That and more. Political power. The ability to change things. To bring real civilization to Galveston, and all of Texas."

"I am no admirer of civilization."

"Yet you fought for this country against the British. You were the hero of New Orleans."

"Yes, I fought for your Union. I was young and foolish, not much older than you. I believed the Union would mean freedom for me and all my men. Instead they pardoned us for crimes we had not committed, then refused to let us make a living. When we removed ourselves to this island of snakes, your Lt. Kearney found us. He came with his laws based on wealth and social position, to tell us we were not to live equally, as brothers. Is this civilization?"

"You cannot judge a country by its frontier. It is always the worst of the old and the new."

"Perhaps. But I have seen New York and Washington, and there the poor are more oppressed than anywhere else. But I shall not convince you of this. You shall have to see it for yourself."

They sat for a few moments in silence. A ship's horn sounded faintly in the distance. "What of your wife?" Lafitte asked. "Do you not love her?"

"Certainly," Malone said. "Why do you ask that?"

"You seem to blame her for your lack of independence."

"Rather she seems to blame me, for my lack of a fortune. It is the same fortune I lacked when she married me."

"She is a lovely woman. I wish there were more happiness between you."

"What of you? Did you ever marry?"

"Once. Long ago."

"Was this in France?"

"I never lived in France. I was born and raised in Santo Domingo. My parents were French." He stopped to relight his pipe. Malone could see him consider whether he would go on or not. At last he said, "They came to the New World to avoid the guillotine. Trouble always found them, just the same. Haiti and Santo Domingo have been fighting since Columbus, two little countries on one island, back and forth, the French against the Spanish, the peasants against the aristocracy."

"And your wife?"

"She was fourteen when we married. I was twenty. She was pledged to a Spanish aristocrat. We eloped. He took her from me by force. She killed herself."

"I—"

Lafitte waved away his apologies. "It was long ago. I took my revenge against Spain, many times over. It proved nothing. I always hoped I would find him on one of the ships we captured. Of course I never did. But as I have said, that was long ago. When my anger, as you say, was legend."

"I do not believe you," Malone said.

Lafitte raised one eyebrow.

"You have told me again and again how you care nothing for things of this world. Yet you nearly destroyed Spanish shipping in the gulf for the sake of a woman, and that pain eats at you still. As does your hatred of Lt. Kearny and everything he stood for. As does your belief in liberty, equality, fraternity. Perhaps I am young, but I have seen men like you, men who numb themselves with alcohol or other substances to convince themselves they have no feelings. My father was one of them. It is not your lack of feeling that has preserved you. It is your passion and commitment that has kept you young. Whether you have the courage to admit that or not."

Lafitte sat for at least a minute without moving. Then, slowly, he tapped the ash out of his clay pipe and put it in his coat pocket. He stood up. "Perhaps you are right, perhaps not. But I find myself too weary for argument." He began to descend the stairs to the street.

"Where are you going?"

"Mexico, perhaps. I should thank you for your hospitality."

"What, you mean to simply walk away? With no farewell to Chighizola or the others? All this simply to prove to yourself how unfeeling you are?"

Lafitte shrugged.

"Wait," Malone said. "You are the only hope I have."

"Then you have no hope," Lafitte said, but he paused at the bottom of the steps. Finally he said, "Suppose I took you to the treasure. Tonight. Right now. Would that satisfy you?"

"Are you serious?"

"I do not know. Perhaps."

"Yes, then. Yes, it would satisfy me."

He took another half dozen paces, then turned back. "Well?"

"Am I not to wake the others? To fetch tools? To tell anyone where I am bound?"

"If we are meant to succeed, fate will provide. That is my whim. Come now or lose your chance."

Malone stood, looked uncertainly toward the house. "I will share it with the others," he said. "Just as we agreed. I swear."

"That is your concern, not mine. If you are coming, then come now."

LAFITTE LED HIM to the harbor at a pace too rapid for conversation. The docks still swarmed with activity. With no attempt at stealth Lafitte stepped into a small sailboat. He motioned Malone to silence and gestured for him to get aboard. Malone saw a shovel, a machete, and several gunny sacks on the floor of the boat.

"But..." he said.

Lafitte held a finger to his lips and then pointed it angrily at Malone. Malone untied the stern line and got in. Lafitte rowed them out into the channel. Once they were well away from land Malone whispered, "This is not your boat!"

Lafitte smiled. There was little humor in it. "Do you accuse me of piracy, sir? I warn you I am not fond of the term."

"Is this not theft, at least?"

"Reparations. Owed me by the Republic of Texas and the United States of America. Besides which, you shall have it back before dawn."

Once into Galveston Bay the wind picked up. A chill came off the water and Malone was glad for his coat. In the moonlight the Texas coast was clearly visible, a gray expanse dotted with darker patches of brush. Malone counted at least another dozen sails on the water. Shrimpers, probably, though smuggling was still common. As they passed Jones Point the mainland receded again.

Lafitte was a mediocre sailor at best. He steered them inside South Deer Island, barely avoiding the sandbars. At one point they had to wait for a swell to lift them free. Then, a few minutes later, they rounded a spit of land and headed into Gang's Bayou. It was little better than a swamp, full of marsh grass and sucking mud. Mesquite bushes, with their thorns and spindly branches, grew along the banks around an occasional salt cedar or dwarf willow. It seemed unlikely that Lafitte could hope to find anything in this shifting landscape. Malone began to fear for his life. He should not, he thought, have challenged Lafitte on his lack of feeling.

Lafitte passed one paddle to Malone and kept the other for himself. He lowered the sail and together they pulled the boat into the bayou. The inlet turned quickly around a U-shaped intrusion of land. At the base of it, out of sight of the bay, Lafitte tied up to a squat, massive old oak.

"Bring the shovel," Lafitte said. Malone gathered it up with the gunny sacks. He brought the machete as well, though the thought of violence appalled him. Lafitte took his bearings from the low, marshy ground around them, then drew an X with his boot near the base of the tree. "Dig here," he said.

"How far?"

"Until you strike the chest."

Malone removed his coat and waistcoat and began to dig. He soon lost his chill. Sweat ran into his eyes and his hands began to blister. Lafitte sat a few yards away, uphill on a hummock of grass, smoking his pipe again. The swamp dirt was fine-grained and damp and had a cloying smell of decay. Malone managed a hole three feet around and at least that deep before giving out. It was as if the evil air that came up from the earth had robbed him of his strength.

"I must rest," he said. He laid the shovel by the hole and then crawled over to the trunk of the tree.

"Rest, then," Lafitte said. "I will take a turn."

MALONE FELL INTO a trance between waking and sleep. He knew he was on Gangs Bayou, on the north shore of Galveston Island. He had lost track of the year. From where he sat it seemed he could see the entire city of Galveston. The streets of the city began to pulse and swell, like an animate creature. Bricks and blocks of quarried stone floated in the air overhead, then alighted on the ground. They formed themselves into towering heaps, not in the shape of houses and churches and schools, but rather in chaotic columns that swayed to impossible heights, blocking the sun. They filled nearly every inch of the island.

Then Malone noticed bits of paper floating in the air between the towers. They seemed to guide the shape of the buildings as they grew. There was printing on the bits of paper and Malone suddenly recognized them. They were paper notes from Sam Williams' C & A Bank. As he watched, they folded themselves into halves and quarters and diagonals. He had once seen a Japanese sailor fold paper that way. They made themselves into people and dogs and birds, and they crawled over the crevices between the bricks, as if looking for shelter. Then, slowly, their edges turned brittle and brown. They began to burn. As they burned, the wind carried them toward Malone, who huddled in terror as they began to fall on him.

"Wake up," Lafitte said. "I need your help."

Malone lurched forward, grabbing at nothing. It took him a moment to remember himself. "Forgive me," he said. "I have had the strangest dream. Less a dream than some sort of vision." His head hurt from it, a dull ache that went all the way down his neck.

"Ghosts, most likely," Lafitte said. "They favor treasure. Now come help me get it out of the hole."

"The gold?" Malone said. "You have found it?" It seemed beyond belief.

"See for yourself."

Malone got up and peered into the hole. There did seem to be a sort of trunk there, though mud obscured its details. The top of it was more than four feet down, one end higher than the other. The hole around it, seeping water, was another two feet deep. The thing seemed to have fetched up against the roots of the tree, else it might have sunk to the center of the earth. Malone climbed into the hole and found a handle on one end. Lafitte joined him at the other and together they wrestled the box up onto solid ground.

"Have you the key?" Malone asked, his voice unsteady.

"It is not locked."

Malone used the machete to pry open the lid. Inside he found a greasy bundle of oilcloth. He tugged at it until it unfolded before him.

Even in the moonlight its contents glowed. Gold, silver, precious gems. Malone knelt before it. He took out a golden demitasse and rubbed it against a clean spot on his sleeve. It gleamed like a lantern.

A voice behind him said, "So. This is what you made off to do."

It was O'Roarke. Malone got up to face him. Behind O'Roarke stood Chighizola and the woman. O'Roarke kept walking, right up to Malone. He took the demitasse from Malone's left hand, looked it over, then threw it in the chest. "We thought as long as you were determined to cross us, we would let you do the work. I see now what your promises are worth. You never intended me to gain from all my efforts on your behalf. You merely waited for me to turn my back."

"I swore I would share this with you," Malone stammered, knowing how weak it sounded. "Lafitte witnessed my vow."

"Liar," O'Roarke said. He turned to Lafitte, looming half a foot over him. "And as for you. I should have expected no less from your kind. Once a pirate, always a pirate."

Lafitte slapped him, hard enough to send O'Roarke staggering backward. Malone was suddenly aware of the machete, still in his hand. He wished he were rid of it but was afraid to let it go, afraid to do anything to call attention to himself.

O'Roarke's hand went to his waist. It came up with a pistol, a two-shot derringer. "Die here, then," he said to Lafitte. "Treacherous bastard."

Malone knew he had to act. This was neither dream nor vision, and in a second Lafitte would die. He took a single step forward and swung the machete blindly at O'Roarke's head. O'Roarke's eyes moved to follow the blade and Malone realized, too late, how terribly slow it moved. But O'Roarke turned into the blow and the machete buried itself two inches into his neck.

O'Roarke dropped to his knees. The blade came free, bringing a geyser of blood from the wound. O'Roarke's eyes lost focus and his arms began to jerk. A stain appeared on his trousers and Malone smelled feces, almost indistinguishable from the odor of the swamp. O'Roarke slowly tumbled onto his back, arms and legs quivering like a dreaming dog's.

"Christ," Fabienne said, turning away.

"Finish him, for God's sake," Lafitte said.

Malone was unable to move, unable to look away. He had witnessed violence all his life: the drowned, the mangled, the amputated. But never before had he been the cause.

Chighizola grabbed Malone's arm. "Kill him, you stinking coward, eh? Or I do it myself." The old man jerked the machete from Malone's hand and brought it down swiftly on O'Roarke's neck. It made the same noise as the shovel going into the mud. The head rolled sideways, connected only by a thin strip of skin and muscle, and the hideous tremors stopped.

"So, Lafitte, what you up to here, eh? What tricks you pull now?"

"Whim," Lafitte said. "I thought you did not care for this treasure."

"I do not care to play the fool." He threw the machete toward the hillock and it buried itself in the ground. The man's scars were monstrous, inhuman, in the moonlight. Malone could barely stand to look at them, barely get breath into his lungs. "It makes no difference now," Chighizola said. "The deed is done. Help me put this dead one in the ground."

They dragged O'Roarke's corpse to the hole and threw it in. The head came loose in the process and Chighizola sent it tumbling after the body with a short kick. "So much," he said, "for Brimstone Jack." Malone shoveled mud onto the corpse, eager to see it disappear, to give his shaking hands something to do.

"You have your own boat, I trust," Lafitte said.

Chighizola nodded, then was taken with a bout of coughing. "By Christ, this air is foul. Yes, we ... borrowed a felucca from the dock." Chighizola seemed exhausted. Fabienne took him by the arm. When she looked away from him, at either Lafitte or Malone, her face filled with contempt.

"The three of you can take the treasure back in your boat then," Lafitte said. "I shall keep this one for myself."

"You will take none of the gold?" Malone asked.

Lafitte shook his head. "It would only be extra weight."

Fabienne said, "I will help Louis back to the boat. The two of you can manage the trunk."

Malone watched her help Chighizola up the hillock. "This is the end, then. You will simply disappear again into Mexico. To hide in a drunken stupor from a world you have not the courage to change."

Lafitte smiled. "Courage is certainly not something you lack. Not for you to speak to me this way."

"I have come to respect you," Malone said. "I had hoped for better from you."

"Would it please you to know that I have given much thought to your words? All that thought, and now the sight of your gold and the things it has already brought you. Quarrels and deceit and death. For one who is wrong in so many, many ways, you are right in at least one small one. Perhaps it is time to take the lessons of Campeachy to the world. To Europe. Perhaps to this German, Marx. I think we might have much in common."

Malone held out his hand. "I wish you luck."

Lafitte took it. "And I you. I fear you will need it far more than I."

Lafitte got in the boat. "How will you get to Europe without gold?" Malone asked. "What will you have to offer this Marx?"

Lafitte took up the oars, then looked back at Malone. "Life is simpler than you believe it. I hope some day you will see that." He raised one hand and then pushed away from the bank, into darkness.

MALONE DIVIDED the treasure between the two gunny sacks and carried them to the other boat. The sacks must have weighed thirty pounds each. That much gold alone was worth a fortune, even before including the value of the jewels.

Chighizola did not look well. He lay with his head in Fabienne's lap, pale and sweating. Malone rowed them out into the bay, then Fabienne raised the sail. She was far more skillful than Lafitte had been. She took them through the Deer Island sandbars without incident, the water hissing smoothly past the hull.

There was no sign of Lafitte or his boat. He had utterly disappeared.

As the lights of the harbor grew close, Fabienne said, "We shall not return to your house, I think. Louis is very sick. We shall find the first boat headed for New Orleans and be gone this morning."

"I will not argue with you," Malone said. "No more than I would with Lafitte. The agreement was equal shares. You must help me divide it."

She looked at the two sacks. "We will take this one," she said. "You keep the rest."

"As you wish. I shall forward your luggage to you in New Orleans." She had picked, Malone was sure, the smaller of the sacks. His heart filled with joy.

HE TOOK THE BURLAP sack to the carriage house. There he transferred the treasure to a steamer trunk, piece by piece. At the bottom of the sack was a golden thimble. Malone held it up to the lantern. The words CHARITY & HUMILITY were engraved around the inner lip. He placed the thimble in his waistcoat pocket, locked the trunk, and put it safely away.

He was clean, with his muddy pants and shirt hidden away, by sunrise.

•

DISCREET INQUIRIES PROVIDED Malone with a man in San Felipe willing to dispose of "antiquities" with no questions asked. Malone began to carefully convert the treasure to gold specie, a piece at a time, whenever he travelled north on bank business.

In the fall of 1851 he arranged an invitation to dinner at Sam Williams' house, set on a 20-acre tract west of the city. Williams was in his mid-fifties now, his hair completely white and parted high on the left side. He was short and heavyset, with a broad forehead and deep lines at the corners of his mouth. He took Malone up to his cupola, where they stood on the narrow walkway and watched for ships in the Gulf. They could hear Williams' daughter Caddy, aged 9, as she played the piano downstairs.

"I understand you have come into some money," Williams said.

"Yes, sir. An inheritance from a long-lost uncle."

"And you are interested in politics."

"Yes, sir."

"There is a good deal an able politician could accomplish these days. I regret I had no knack for it. People found me cold. I do not know why that is." After a moment he said, "You know they are determined to destroy my bank."

"There is a faction, of course, sir, but..."

"Make no mistake, they are out to finish me. They consider me a criminal because I made a profit while I worked for the public good. Why, profit is the heart of this country. It is the very thing that makes us grow. And paper money is essential to that growth. Paper money and venture capitalism. Mark my words. That is where the future lies. You're married to—"

"Becky Kinkaid, sir. John Kinkaid's daughter."

"Yes, a good man. And an important connection. You will want to hold on to her, son, believe me. That name can take you a long way."

"Yes, sir."

"Well, let us see. We can start you out on the city council. It will not be cheap, of course, but then you understand that already."

"Yes, sir."

"Good lad. Nothing like a realistic attitude. You will have need of that."

THERE WAS NEARLY a run on the C&A the following January when a rival bank folded. But Galveston merchants exchanged Robert Mills' paper at par and disaster was narrowly averted. In March the Supreme Court upheld Sam Williams' charter. The anti-bank faction replied with yet another suit, this one based on the illegality of paper money. In April, Malone took his seat on

the city council and bought his first block of shares in the Commercial and
Agricultural Bank.

He found himself with many new friends. They wore tight-fitting suits and
brightly colored waistcoats and smoked Cuban cigars. Their opinions became
Malone's own by a process he did not entirely understand. But he learned
how things were done. A divorce, for example, or even a separation, was not to
be considered. Instead he kept a succession of mulatto girls in apartments on
the Gulf side of the island, girls with long, curling black hair and unguessable
thoughts behind their dark eyes. In time he found that he and Becky could
live together with a certain affection and consideration, and it was quite nearly
enough. Except for certain hot, muggy nights in the summer when his dreams
were haunted by Fabienne.

Still, they were preferable to the nights when he dreamed of towers of stone
and folded bank notes and Brimstone Jack O'Roarke with a machete buried
in his neck. On those nights he awoke with his hands clutched in the air, on
the verge of a scream.

In the next five years he moved from the city council to the Railroad
Commission. The next step was the state legislature, via the election in
February of 1857. Malone had thought himself a Democrat, but Williams'
power lay with the Whigs. The Whigs were traditionally the money party in
Texas, and so Malone became a Whig. The campaign was expensive, and took
a firm pro-banking stance. On January 19th, banker Robert Mills was fined
$100,000 for issuing paper money. Two days later Williams settled out of court
on similar charges, paying a token $2000 fine. Editorials condemning banks
and paper money appeared throughout the state.

The Democrats carried the election. The week after his defeat, Malone
accepted a position on the board of directors of the C & A.

In August the Panic of '57 brought the closure of one bank after another, all
across the country. Tales of bank failures in New Orleans arrived via steamer
on October 16. There was a run on the C & A. Williams exchanged specie for
his own notes, but refused to cash depositor checks. Malone sat through the
night with him, drinking brandy, waiting to see if the bank would open the
next day. They did open, and Malone brought in the last of the gold coins
from his safe deposit boxes to make sure there would be enough.

That afternoon the bank closed early. Malone stopped for a whiskey on the
way home and found the bartender honoring paper money at 75 cents on the
dollar. Malone saw only fear and resignation in his eyes. "I got kids, mister," he
said. "What can I do? Blame the bankers."

Williams continued to pay gold the next day. The police came to keep lines
orderly. By noon the fear had gone out of the customers' eyes. By the end of

the month the crisis had passed, only to make way for a new one: counterfeit C & A notes.

The weeks began to blur. In December, Sam Williams' eldest son died. In January the Supreme Court postponed another anti-banking suit, and Williams' lawyers fought delaying actions through the spring and summer. In the first days of September the yellow fever came again.

Malone watched the fever take Becky, watched her skin jaundice and her flesh melt away. Williams' wife Sarah, ever thoughtful, sent servants with ice to soothe Becky's fever. It was no more use than Jefferson's herbs. She died on September 7, a Tuesday.

That Friday Samuel May Williams succumbed to old age and general debility. He was 62.

It was the end of an era. Malone moved out of Becky's parents' house and took a suite of rooms on Water Street. The building was not far from where Lafitte's Maison Rouge had stood. Nothing remained of the treasure but the golden thimble, which Malone still carried in the watch pocket of his waistcoat. He sat at his window and studied the workmen as they built the trestle for the first train from Houston, due to arrive in a little over a year.

He still attended board meetings, though there was little hope the bank could survive. Malone watched with detachment. He saw now how money had a life of its own. For a while he had lived the life of his money, but that life was drawing to a close. The money would go on without him. It was money that had brought the future to Galveston, not Malone. The future would have come without him, in spite of anything he might have done to stop it, had he wanted to. Lafitte had learned that lesson long ago.

He gave up the last of his string of mistresses. The sight of her parents, living on fish heads and stale bread, was more than he could bear. He mounted one final campaign for mayor. His platform advocated better schools, better medicine, a better standard of living. But he was unable to explain where the money would come from. He lost by a landslide.

In March of 1859, the Texas Supreme Court ruled that the Commercial and Agricultural Bank of Texas was illegal. Its doors were closed, its assets liquidated. The last of Malone's money was gone.

HE ARRIVED IN New Orleans early in the morning. The city had grown as much as Galveston had. The changes were even more obvious to his stranger's eye. The old quarter was bordered now by a new business district, with bigger buildings growing up every day.

They still knew Chighizola's name at the market. Many of them had been at his funeral, years before. They knew his children and they remembered the beautiful octoroon with the French name. Malone followed their directions through crowded streets and stopped at an iron gate set into a brick wall. Through the arch he could see a shaded patio, broadleafed plants, small children.

Fabienne answered the bell herself. She was older, her skin a dusty tan instead of gold. Strands of gray showed in her hair. "I know you," she said. "Malone. The hunter of treasure. What do you want here?"

"To give you this," Malone said. He handed her the golden thimble.

She took it and turned it over in her hands. "Why?"

"I am not sure. Perhaps as an apology."

She held it out to him. "I do not care for your apology. I do not want anything of yours."

"It is not mine," Malone said. He closed her hand over it and pushed it back toward her. "It never was."

He turned away. A sudden movement in the crowd caught his attention and, for a moment, he thought he looked into the sparkling black eyes of Jean Lafitte, unchanged, despite the years. Malone blinked, and the man was gone. It was merely, he thought, another ghost. He took a step, then another, toward the river and the ships. He had enough left for a passage somewhere. He had only to decide where to go.

"Wait," Fabienne said.

Malone paused.

"You have come this far," she said. "The least I can do is offer you a cup of coffee."

"Thank you," Malone said. "I should like a cup of coffee very much."

DIRTY WORK

T HE OFFICE SMELLED like money. Brand new carpet, somebody's
expensive perfume still hanging in the air. The chairs in the waiting
room are leather and the copy machine has a million attachments and there's
pictures on the wall that I don't know what they're supposed to be. Made me
ashamed of the shirt I was wearing, the cuffs all frayed and some of the buttons
don't match.

The secretary is a knockout and I figure Dennis has got to be getting in her
pants. Red hair and freckles and shiny skin that looks like she just got out of a
hot shower. A smile like she really means it. My name was in the book and she
showed me right on in.

Dennis shook my hand and put me in a chair that was slings and tube steel.
The calendar next to his desk had a ski scene on it. Behind him was solid books,
law books all in the same binding, also some biographies and political stuff.

"Too bad you couldn't make the reunion," Dennis said. "It was a hoot."

"I just felt weird about it," I said. I still did. It looked like he wanted me to
go on, so I said, "I knew there'd be a bunch of y'all there that had really made
good, and I guess I ... I don't know. Didn't want to have to make excuses."

"Hard to believe it's been twenty years. You look good. I still wouldn't want
to run into you in a dark alley, but you look fit. In shape."

"I got weights in the garage, I try to work out. When you're my size you
can go to hell pretty quick. You look like you're doing pretty good yourself."
Charlene is always pointing to people on TV and talking about the way they
dress. With Dennis I could see for the first time what she's talking about. The
gray suit he had on looked like part of him, like it was alive. When I think
about him in grungy sweats back at Thomas Jefferson High School, bent
double from trying to run laps, it doesn't seem like the same guy.

"Can't complain," Dennis said.

"Is that your Mercedes downstairs? What do they call those, SLS?"

"My pride and joy. Can't afford it, of course, but that's what bankers are for,
right? You were what, doing something in oil?"

"Rig foreman. You know what that means. 'I'm not saying business is bad,
but they're telling jokes about it in Ethiopia.'"

Dennis showed me this smile that's all teeth and no eyes. "Like I told you on
the phone. I can't offer you much. The technical name for what you'll be is a

425

paralegal. Usually that means research and that kind of thing, but in your case it'll be legwork."

Beggars can't be choosers. What Dennis pays for his haircut would feed Charlene and the kids for close to a week. I must look ten years older than him. All those years in the sun put the lines in your face and the ache in your bones. He was 18 when we graduated, I was only 17, now I'm the one that's middle aged. He was tennis, I was football. Even in high school he was putting it to girls that looked like that secretary of his. Whereas me and Charlene went steady from sophomore year, got married two weeks after graduation. I guess I've been to a couple of topless bars, but I've never been with anybody else, not that way.

It was hard for me to call Dennis up. What it was, I got the invitation for the class reunion, and they had addresses for other people in the class. Seemed like fate or something, him being right here in Austin and doing so good. I knew he'd remember me. Junior year a couple of guys on the team were waiting for him in the parking lot to hand him his ass, and I talked them out of it. That was over a girl too, now that I think about it.

Dennis said, "I got a case right now I could use some help with." He slid a file over from the corner of the desk and opened it up. "It's a rape case. You don't have a problem with that, do you?"

"What do you mean?"

Dennis sat back, kind of studying me, playing with the gold band on his watch. "I mean my client is the defendant. The thing is—and I'm not saying it's this way all the time or anything—but a lot of these cases aren't what you'd think. You got an underage girl, or married maybe, gets caught with the wrong jockey in her saddle, she hollers 'rape' and some guy goes to the slammer for nothing. Nothing you and I haven't ever done, anyway."

"So is this one of those cases?"

"It's a little fishy. The girl is at UT, blonde, good family, the guy is the wrong color for Mom and Dad. Maybe she wanted a little rough fun and then got cold feet. The point is, the guy gets a fair trial, no matter what he did." He took a form out of the file. "I'll get you a xerox of this. All I want is for you to follow this broad around for a couple of days, just kind of check her out."

"How do you mean?"

"Just get an idea of what kind of person she is. Is she some little ice princess, like she wants the DA to believe? Or is she showing her panties to anybody with a wallet and a dick?"

"Geez, Dennis, I really don't know..."

"There's nothing to it. This is absolutely standard procedure in a case like this. She knows she's going to have people watching her, it's just part of the legal bullshit game." When I didn't say anything, he said, "It's ten bucks an hour, time-and-a-half if you go over forty hours a week, which I don't see this doing. We pay you cash, you're responsible for your own taxes and like that, and if you forget to declare it, that's your lookout. Hint hint. If this works out, we can probably find some other things for you."

Here's the carrot, was what he was saying, and here's the stick. Good money, tax free, if you do it. Turn this case down because it sounds a little hinky and you're back on the street.

"What's this woman's name?"

"Some horrible yuppie name..." He looked at the file. "Lane, that's it. Lane Rochelle. Isn't that a hoot?"

I didn't like the way her name made me feel. Like I was standing outside the window of one of those big Highland Park mansions back in Dallas, wearing last week's clothes, watching guys in tuxedos and women in strapless dresses eat little sandwiches with the crusts cut off. I blamed her for it. "I don't know anything about this kind of work," I said. "I mean, if she sees me I'm liable to scare her off. I don't exactly blend into a crowd."

"Let her see you. It's not a problem."

I still wasn't sure. "When would you want me to start?"

He slapped me on the shoulder as he came around the desk. "There you go," he said. He walked out of the office and I heard the hum of his big new copy machine.

SO I DROVE over to campus in my good corduroy jacket and my frayed cuffs and my black knit tie. I parked my pickup in the Dobie garage and walked down 21st Street to the Perry Casteñeda Library, where Lane Rochelle works. The piece of paper Dennis gave me shows her address and her job history and her criminal record (NONE). Also a xerox of a photo of her from the society page of the *Statesman*.

She's older than Dennis let on, 28, she's working on her master's degree in History. She's paying her own way with her job at the library, not living off her rich parents back in Virginia, which makes me like her more too. The photo doesn't tell me much. Blonde hair, nice smile, wears her clothes the way Dennis wears his.

I went past the security guard and the turnstiles and looked around. I mean, I don't spend a lot of time in libraries. The place is big and there's this smell of old paper that makes me a little sick to my stomach. The Circulation desk is off to my left and across from it there are some shelves with new books and a yellow Naugahyde couch. I found a book that looked interesting, a true-crime thing about this guy that kept a woman in a box. I sat down and every so often looked up and finally I caught sight of Lane moving around behind the counter.

She's not an ice princess, and she's not some kind of sexpot either. She's just a real person, maybe a little prettier than most. Right then she looked like somebody that didn't get a lot of sleep the night before and is having a tough day. The second time she caught me looking at her I saw it hit home—some big guy lurking around her job. I hated to see the look on her face, which was mostly fear.

A little before eleven o'clock, she came out a door to one side of the counter with her purse and a book bag. I let her get out the front door and then followed. It was nice out, warmer than you could ask February to be. The trees had their first buds, which would all die if it froze again. There were even birds and everything. She headed up 21st Street and turned at the Littlefield fountain, the one with the horses, and climbed the steps toward the two rows of buildings on top of the hill. Once she looked back and I turned away, crouched down to pretend to tie my shoe, not fooling anybody.

I watched her go in the first building on the left, the one with the word MUSIC over the door. I followed her inside. The halls were full of students and I watched her push through them and go in one of the classrooms. Just before she went in she turned and gave me this look of pure hatred.

Made me feel pretty low. I stood there for ten minutes just the same, after the hall cleared and the bell rang, to make sure she stayed put. Then I went outside and walked around the side of the building. The classrooms all had full-length windows. The top halves were opened out to let in the warm air. I found Lane's room and sat in the grass, watching a woman teacher write on the board. She had heavy legs and glasses and dark hair in a pony tail. Charlene always talks about going back to college, but I can't see it, not for me. I had a semester of junior college, working construction all day and sleeping through class at night. They didn't have football scholarships and I wasn't good enough for the four-year colleges that did. So I went with what I knew and took a job on my daddy's drilling crew.

By eleven-thirty I was starving to death. There was a Vietnamese woman with a pushcart down by the fountain selling eggrolls. I walked down there and got me a couple and a Coke and took them back up the hill to eat. It would have been okay, really, eating eggrolls outside on a pretty spring day and getting paid for it. Only Lane knew I was there watching and I could see what it was doing to her.

At noon we went back to the library. Lane sat off to herself in the shelves behind the counter. She had brought her lunch in her bookbag, a carton of yogurt and a Diet Coke. She didn't seem to be able to eat much. After a couple of bites she threw it away and went to the rest room.

She got off work at two in the afternoon. I watched her climb on a shuttlebus and then I drove out to her apartment and waited for her. She has a one-bedroom on 53rd Street near Airport, what they call a mixed neighborhood—black, white, brown, all low-income. This is where the rape happened. There's a swimming pool that doesn't look too clean and a couple of seventies muscle cars up on blocks. A lot like my neighborhood, over on the far side of Manor Road.

She walked right past me on her way to her apartment. I was sitting in my truck, watching the shuttlebus pull away. She went right past me. I could tell by the set of her shoulders that she knew I was there. She went in her apartment, toward the near end of the second floor, and I could hear the locks click shut from where I sat. She pulled the blinds and that was it.

I did what Dennis told me. I got out and made a log of all the cars parked along the street there, make and model and license number, and then I went on home.

I WAS IN TIME to give the kids a ride back from the bus stop. Ricky is 15 and going through this phase where he doesn't talk except to say yes or no to direct questions. Mostly he shrugs and shakes his head in amazement at how stupid adults are. So naturally he didn't say anything about me wearing a tie. Judy, who is 17, wouldn't let it alone. "What's it for, Dad? You look way cool. You messing around? Got a girlfriend?" She doesn't mean anything by it, she's just kidding.

I had TV dinners in the oven by the time Charlene got home. Salisbury steak, mashed potatoes, and that apple cobbler dessert she loves. Her new issue of *Vogue* was there and she took it into the bathroom with her for a while. When she came out she was showered and in her blue-gray bathrobe and fuzzy slippers, with her hair in a towel. She loves *Vogue* magazine. I guess it takes her to some other world, where she isn't pushing forty and she still weighs what she did in high school and she doesn't spend all her days answering phones for a heating and air conditioning company.

"How'd it go?" she said. We had *Wheel of Fortune* on, the kids on the floor with their dinners between us and the TV.

"I got four hours in today, ten bucks an hour. I should make at least that tomorrow."

"That wasn't what I asked."

One reason I never ran around on Charlene is I don't think I could fool her for a second. "I don't like it," I said. "I think he's using me to scare somebody, because I'm big and ugly."

Charlene grabbed the back of my neck and shook me like a cat. "You're big all right. But I always thought you was handsome." Then she leaned back and picked up her magazine again and she was gone.

EVERYBODY WAS ASLEEP by eleven. I went out real quiet and drove over to Lane's apartment. There were a lot more cars out front this time and I wrote down all the new ones on my log sheet. The light was still on in her apartment. I was about to head home when the blinds moved and she looked out and saw my truck.

I wanted out of there bad enough that I made the tires on that pickup squeal.

I SLEPT AWHILE and then laid awake awhile and then it was morning. I had a lot of coffee and not too much to eat, which made my stomach hurt.

I was already at the library when Lane came in. She saw me and went straight through the STAFF door and stayed out of sight. A few minutes later a campus cop knocked on the door and she stood in the doorway with him and pointed me out.

I felt like high school again, like I'd been caught with a *Playboy* in the toilet. The campus cop walked over and asked me if I had any ID. I showed him my driver's license.

"What you up to here?"

I gave him one of Dennis's cards, like Dennis said I should. "I'm doing research for a law office. Call this number, they'll back me up."

"Don't look like you're doing research to me. Maybe you should move along."

"Fine," I said. I put my book back on the shelf, which was too bad because it had gotten interesting. Only I couldn't check it out because I wasn't a student. I went outside and sat on a wall.

It was a nice day for something. Warm again, a few clouds, the birds getting ready for spring. College girls all around. I never saw so many good-looking girls in one place. Young and healthy, in tight jeans and running shoes, clean soft hair blowing around, sweet smells trailing along behind them. It hurts to see so much that you want, that you can never have, to be so close you could reach out and touch it.

About a half hour later Lane came out of the library and headed down Speedway, right through the middle of campus. I didn't think she saw me. I found myself noticing the way she walked, the way her young, firm ass strained against her jeans. Don't even think about it. I waited until she had a good lead on me before I started after her.

She turned left on 24th Street, by the Experimental Science building, and I lost sight of her. When I turned the corner she was gone. I hesitated for a second, kids shouldering by me on both sides and then I went up to the first door I came to and looked inside. Not there.

When I turned around she was right in front of me. "What do you want?" she said. She was shaking and her voice was too loud.

"I'm working for a lawyer—"

"That defense lawyer? That fuck? Did he hire you to follow me around? What the fuck does he want from me? Is this Gestapo bullshit supposed to make me drop the case?"

"I don't think he—"

"What kind of slimebag are you, anyhow? Haven't I had enough shit already? How can you stand to go around and humiliate people this way?" Crying now, people stopping to stare at us. "Do you know what happened this morning? My boss called me in and wanted to know why I was being followed. Like it was my fault! I had to tell him everything. Everything! Can you imagine how humiliating that was? No. Of course you can't. If you could imagine it you would go shoot yourself."

A boy walked up and put his hand on her arm. She shook it off and shouted at him, too. "Leave me the fuck *alone*!" She turned back to me, her mascara running all over her face, and spit on my left shoe. Then she shoved her way through the crowd and started running back down Speedway, back the way she came.

I STARTED SHAKING too, as soon as I got in the truck. I shook all the way to Dennis's office.

He was with "one of his people" when I came in. After a few minutes his door opened and this good-looking Chicano came out. He was in his twenties, with longish hair and a mustache and an expensive black leather coat that hung down to his knees. He smiled at the red haired receptionist and pointed at her and said, "You be good, now."

"You too, Javier."

"No chance," he said, and rubbed his mustache and sniffed. The receptionist laughed. I couldn't help but think that Dennis was paying him more than ten bucks an hour for whatever it was he did.

Dennis was standing in the doorway of his office. "Come on in," he said.

I sat on the edge of the armchair. It wasn't really built for that and it made me feel off-balance. There was a dusty-looking mirror and a soda straw on his desk.

"You want a little toot?"

I shook my head. "It's about this case. This is really nasty. I don't know if I can go on with it."

"Okay," he said. He put the mirror and the straw in the top center drawer and then got a bank bag out of another one. It was one of those rubberized deals with the zipper and the little lock, except it wasn't zipped or locked. "How many hours did you have?"

I guess I expected him to argue with me at least, maybe even offer me something else. "Call it seven," I said. "And two parking receipts." I put my log sheet with the license numbers on it and the receipts on the corner of his desk. I felt small sitting there, just waiting for him to pay me.

"So what happened?" he said.

"She turned on me, started screaming. Said I was trying to scare her off."

"Gave you the old not-a-moment's-peace bit, right?" He counted out four twenties and put them in front of me. "Haven't got any singles, you can keep the change."

"Something like that, yeah."

"Well, I understand. If you can't hack it..."

"It's not that I can't hack it, I just don't see why I should want to."

Dennis sat back in his chair. Today he was wearing his casual outfit. I'd never seen a silk jacket before, but Charlene had showed me pictures and I was pretty sure that's what it was. The pants were khaki, the shirt was pale blue, the shoes had little tassels on them. "Let me explain something to you. This business isn't about who makes the most noise or who sheds the most tears. At least it's not supposed to be. It's about the *truth*. And the truth is not always what it seems. Ever have some asshole nearly run you off the road, and then he gives *you* the finger? A guilty conscience can make for a lot of righteous-sounding anger. This Rochelle bimbo has been going to one of those dyke counselling centers, and who knows what kind of crap they've been feeding her."

"But what if she's telling the truth?"

"If she is, my client goes to jail, probably does ten years of hard time. If she's lying, she could go up herself for perjury. These are not matchsticks we're play-ing for, here." He leaned forward again. Every time he moved he did some-thing different with his voice and I felt my emotions getting yanked around in another direction. "Look, I understand where you're coming from. It takes a while to build up your calluses. Just like working on an oil rig, right? You get a lot of blisters at first and it hurts like hell. Then you toughen up and you can really get the job done." He put the bank bag in the drawer. "Take the after-noon off, think it over. If you still want out, call me tonight, I'll put somebody else on the case. I'll be here in the office, I'm working late all week. Okay?"

"Okay," I said. I took the small stack of bills and folded it and put it in my front pants pocket. I wondered when was the last time Dennis got a blister on his hands.

As I got up he said, "Just one thing you want to keep in mind. Everybody's got something to hide."

I CAN'T REMEMBER the last time I had that much cash in my pocket. It made me a little drunk. I drove to the Victoria's Secret store at Highland Mall and spent $58 on a crepe de chine sarong-wrap chemise in mango, size L. I took it home and hid it in the bedroom, and all through supper I was goofy as a little kid, just thinking about it.

I gave it to Charlene after we went to bed. She started crying. She said, "I'll get back on my diet tomorrow. It's so beautiful. I can't wear it the way I look now." She put it in the back of her drawer. She didn't even try it on.

She kissed me on the cheek and lay down with her back to me. I sat there, my hands all knotted up into fists. After a while she went to sleep.

I just sat there. I hadn't called Dennis. I was supposed to call him if I wasn't going back on the job. If I didn't do it he would just get somebody else. Somebody with all those calluses I don't have. Finally I got up and put my clothes back on and went out driving.

I guess I was supposed to be thinking things over, but what I did was drive to Lane Rochelle's apartment. It was a quarter to twelve. I wrote the time down on a new log sheet and walked around and wrote down all the cars and license numbers. Lane's window was dark. I got back in the truck and tried to find a comfortable way to sit. I wondered what she wore to bed. Maybe it was a crepe de chine sarong-wrap chemise in mango, size S. Maybe it was nothing at all.

A car door slammed and woke me up. The digital clock on my dash said one AM. I saw a guy walking away from a black Trans Am, two slots down on the right. It was the guy I saw in Dennis's office that afternoon. I slid a little lower in the seat.

I wondered what he was doing there. Did Dennis give him my job? He went through the gate by the pool, headed for the far set of stairs.

The apartments are kind of L-shaped, with the long part parallel to the street and the short part coming toward where I was. There was another set of stairs on the end of the building closest to me. I got out of the truck as quiet as I could and went up the stairs. I got to the corner just as the guy knocked on Lane's door.

I could hear my heart. It sounded like it was in my neck. The guy knocked again, louder this time. I heard the door open and catch on its chain.

"Javier," Lane said. She sounded only a little surprised.

"I got your message," the guy, Javier, said.

"It's late. What time is it?"

"Not that late. You gonna let me in or what?"

"Not tonight. Come back tomorrow, okay?"

"Listen, I went to a lot of trouble to drive over here. How about a beer or something, anyway?"

"Fuck off." I wondered where she learned to talk like that. "Come back tomorrow night."

The door slammed and two or three locks turned. I didn't hear any footsteps. Javier was still standing there. Then he said, *"Chingate, puta!"* and walked away.

I moved away from the corner and pushed my back flat against the wall. I was in the shadows, I didn't think he could see me. He took one last look at Lane's apartment and then spit in the swimming pool and got in his Trans Am and drove away.

I WAS COVERED in sweat when I got home. I had to sponge myself off with a wet washcloth before I could get back into bed. Charlene was still asleep, snoring away.

I wondered if I should call Dennis. What if he already knew Javier was hanging around? What if it was his idea? I thought about the smooth way he handled me that afternoon in his office and decided it wasn't any of my business. If Dennis wanted to ask me a question I would answer it. Otherwise I was on my own.

Being on my own is okay. I've been that way most of my life. It makes some things a lot easier. Like taking Dennis's money.

I GOT TO the library about ten o'clock and went right up to the circulation desk. Lane was there and when she saw me she turned and walked away. This older woman came over and asked if she could help me.

"I need to talk to Lane for a second."

"What is this in reference to?"

"It's in reference to I would like to apologize to her."

The old lady went to talk to Lane. They went back and forth a little and at one point the old lady put her arms around Lane and gave her a hug. It made me feel lonely to look at them like that. Then Lane came up to the counter. She took hold of the edge with both hands and waited for me to talk.

"Look," I said. "I'm sorry I scared you. I've been out of work for two years. This is just a job to me." She stared, no expression. "I thought about the things you said, and maybe I don't trust this lawyer very much either. What I'm trying to say is, you don't have anything to be afraid of from me. If you're ... I mean, if things are the way you say they are, I would maybe like to help a little if I could."

She stared a while longer, and then she said, very quiet, "If you want to help, just go away. Just get the fuck away from me and stay out of my life."

"I can't do that right now," I said. "I have this job to do and it's the only thing I've got. All I want is to try to make the best of it."

Her eyes teared up. "Make the best of it. Oh God. What do you know about anything?"

She walked away and there was no use calling her back. I got my true crime book again and took it over by the card catalog, where I could see her if she left the building but she wouldn't have to watch me hang around all day. At eleven I followed her to her class at the Music building and back again after. I had an eggroll lunch while I waited and if she noticed me she didn't let on.

It was another nice day. I sat outside until she left at two, watching the clouds move around in the sky. She got on her shuttlebus and I sat there a little longer, wishing things were different but not knowing what exactly I would change. Just a mood, I guess. Then I started the long uphill walk back to the Dobie Garage.

Dobie is the only place a non-student can park anywhere near the library. It's across from Dobie Mall, which is this combination shopping center and dormitory. Kids can eat, shop, sleep, go to movies, have sex, live and die there without ever going outside. The garage is always full so I had to park on the fourth level, one down from the roof. Homeless guys, what we used to call winos, what the kids call Drag worms, sleep in the stairwells, which smell of them peeing and throwing up there. I can't stand to see those guys, I want to knock them down to get away from them. If it wasn't for Charlene that could be me. No work, no future.

I got up to level four and even from the end of the row I could tell something was wrong. The truck was not sitting right. I felt sick. It goes back to my days on the rigs. Your wheels are your livelihood. If you can't get around you can't work, if you can't work you can't feed yourself, if you can't do that you're not a man anymore.

I wanted to run over and see what was wrong and at the same time I wanted it not to be happening and the two things were pulling me in opposite directions. By the time I got to the truck my heart was pounding and my eyes were blurry.

It was all four tires flat. They weren't cut, not that I could see. The valve stem covers were off and they'd let the air out with a Bic pen or something. In addition they had taken their car keys or something and put long, ugly scratches down both sides of the body. I walked all the way around and then I started kicking one of the tires, which was stupid. It wasn't the tire that had done it.

It wasn't Lane that had done it either. She wasn't out of my sight all morning.

There was a note under the windshield wiper. It was in block capitals on lined yellow legal paper. It said GO AWAY.

I CALLED THE TRIPLE A and they sent a truck. The driver said something about those fucking college kids and I nodded along. While he was doing the tires I looked under the frame and inside the hood to make sure there wasn't a bomb or anything. Then I had the guy wait to make sure it started, which it did.

I stopped off at Airport Auto Supply and got some white primer and sprayed it on the scratches and it didn't look quite so bad. Then I went home. I wasn't shaking this time, not outside. It was all inside. It's like the constant vibration from the rotary table out on the drilling platform. It goes right through you. The kids were already there so I went out in the back yard and looked at the dead yellow grass. There were patches of green coming through and every one was a weed.

Call Dennis. He can get the note fingerprinted.

Sure. Students use legal pads, but so do lawyers. Maybe it was his cocaine buddy Javier did my tires. I can handle him one on one, but I know he's the kind of guy carries a gun.

The house needs a paint job, the lawn needs a gardener. The kids are nearly old enough for college and I got no money to send them. I wish I had a Mercedes SL instead of a Pinto wagon and a Ford pickup truck. I need a drink but I don't dare start. When was the last time I thought about who I am, instead of what I have? When did it start being the same thing?

In the bedroom, on the bottom of my undershirt drawer, was my daddy's gun. A Colt Woodsman .22 target pistol, loaded, because my daddy taught me an unloaded gun is worse than no gun at all. I went in the bedroom and locked the door and got it out. It smelled of oil and a little bit like cedar from the drawer. It felt great in my hand. I made sure the safety was on and stuck it in my pants. No, that was stupid. It would fall out or I would shoot myself in the foot. I folded it up in an old Dallas Cowboys nylon jacket.

Charlene was home. I heard her try the bedroom door, then knock quietly. I opened it. "I need to use the wagon," I said.

We never ask each other a lot of questions. It's like we don't really know how to go about it. I could see her try to make up her mind if she wanted to ask now. She must have decided not because she gave me the keys and got out of my way.

Judy said, "I need the wagon tonight, Dad, I got choir."

"Take the truck."

"I hate the truck. I don't like that stick shift."

"Just take the truck, all right?"

Now Judy was ready to start crying. I put the truck keys on the little table by the door and went out.

I was starving to death. I hadn't eaten anything since those two eggrolls before noon. I bought a hamburger and fries and a chocolate shake at Gaylord's there on Airport and ate them in the car. Then I got worried about Lane recognizing me, even in a different car. I looked around and found a bandanna in the back seat. I took off my tie and rolled up my shirt sleeves and put on my sunglasses. Then I tied the bandanna over my head, pirate style, the way I'd seen some biker guys do. Looked stupid as hell in the rear view mirror, but at least it didn't look much like me.

I made a pass all the way around the apartments and then parked out of sight of Lane's window. No sign of the Trans Am. The lights had been on behind her mini-blinds when I drove by. It was seven-thirty and full dark. A little after eight my bladder started to kill me. I got out and peed against the back of the apartments, which didn't have any windows. From the smell there I wasn't the first.

A little after nine it started to rain.

By ten I thought maybe I'd made a mistake. That old Pinto wagon is too small for me and the springs in the seats are shot. I hurt like hell after ten minutes, let alone two and a half hours. I could have been in bed asleep. Worse yet, Javier could have showed up without me seeing him, or in another car.

I got out and walked up and down the parking lot. No Trans Ams. Lights still on in Lane's apartment. The rain soaked my bandanna and got in my shoes. Half an hour, I thought. Then I either go home or I go upstairs for a look. I was about to get back in the wagon when a black Trans Am pulled into the lot.

I ducked down and listened. The engine revved, then stopped. I could hear the hot metal tick and the rain make a softer tick against the hood. The door opened, the springs groaned, feet scraped against the asphalt. The door shut again. Silence. What if he can see me? My gun was still inside the Pinto.

I heard his footsteps move away. I could see his black leather coat as he went in the gate, Javier for sure, headed for the stairs. I waited until he was blocked by the corner of the apartment and then I crawled in the wagon head first. I stuck the little Colt in the back of my pants and jogged over to the other set of stairs, putting the jacket on as I ran.

By the time I got to the corner of the building, Lane had her door open. I heard her say, "There you are."

"You look nervous." Javier's voice. "Something wrong?"

"What do you think, you fucking prick? I'm going to welcome you with open arms?" I couldn't get used to the language she used. It just didn't fit with the way she looked.

"It's like raining out here, okay? Are you going to let me in, or what?"

"Yeah, I'm going to let you in."

A second later I heard the door close. The locks went again and then there was a crash and a muffled shout and then silence.

I COULDN'T JUST stand there. Even if it was none of my business, even if I was carrying a gun I had no permit for, even if somebody in that apartment had trashed my truck and left me threatening notes.

I turned the corner and tried to see through the blinds. Nothing. I heard voices but I couldn't tell male or female, let alone what they were saying.

Christ Jesus. It's happening right now, and I can't let it go on.

I knocked on the door. It went so quiet in there I could hear the raindrops ping on the railing behind me. I stepped back and kept my hands away from my sides, away from the gun stuck down the back of my pants. I don't know how long I waited but it felt like at least a minute.

Something moved behind the peephole and the door opened on the chain. It was Lane, fully dressed, not a mark on her. I suddenly realized I was still wearing the bandanna and sunglasses. She laughed and it sounded more nervous than anything. I wadded up the glasses and bandanna in my left hand.

"Just go away," she said. "Don't pull any knight-in-shining-armor numbers, don't give me any shit, just go away. Tell your lawyer friend it's over. I'm dropping the charges. The law sucks, you can tell him that too. Happy now? Go fuck yourself and stay away."

She started to close the door. I stuck my foot in, I don't know why. I couldn't let it end that way.

"Look," I said, "I just want to say—"

"I don't want to hear it." She leaned on the door, and it hurt.

To hell with it. "Let me get my foot out and I'm gone," I said.

She eased off on the door and right then something crashed in the back of the apartment and I heard Javier's voice, muffled, yelling.

"Oh shit," Lane said. She took a step back.

A woman's voice from off to the side said, "Bring him in."

All of a sudden Lane's apartment didn't seem like such a good idea. The door slammed and I heard the chain come off and I turned around and ran for the stairs. Something hit me in the back of the knees and I skidded into the railing at the edge of the walkway. Then something metal poked me in the ear and a woman's voice said, "Get up and go inside."

My knees hurt where I'd slid. I got up real slow and the woman got behind me where I still couldn't see her. I walked back to the apartment. I was so scared that everything looked tilted and the light hurt my eyes. Then I was inside and she pushed me and I went down on my knees again, next to the far wall of the living room.

"Put your hands on your head," the woman said, "and turn around and sit against the wall." I did what she said. There was the gun still stuck down the back of my pants. All I wanted was out of there. If I could get the gun out without getting shot in the process, maybe I could walk away.

Lane was there, and two women I didn't know. The one with the gun was close to six feet tall, heavy, with crewcut blonde hair. She wore jeans and a plain white sweatshirt and a green flannel shirt over that. The sleeves of the flannel shirt were rolled up to show the sweatshirt underneath. The gun was some kind of little automatic and there was a silencer screwed on to the end of the barrel. That was when I realized for the first time that I was probably going to die.

The other woman was closer to my age. She had on jeans and a bulky orange sweater. Most of her hair had gone white. She had a pair of pliers which she was taking apart a plain wire coat hanger with. I could see a wad of paper on the breakfast bar that she'd torn off the hanger.

Against the wall across from me, behind the door, was Javier. They'd done something to his hair, cut a lot of it off the front, and it gave him a startled look. His hands were behind his back. One of his shoes was off and the sock was gone. His mouth was taped shut with silver duct tape. It looked like there was something in his mouth behind the tape. They'd run the tape all the way around his head a couple of times. I figured out where the missing sock was and decided I would be quiet.

"You know him?" the one with the gun said to Lane.

"He works for Asshole's lawyer. He's the one with the truck you fixed this afternoon. He's nobody, just hired meat."

"Scum," she said sadly. "What would make somebody take a job like that?"

"Money," the woman with the coat hanger said. "It's all about money. Even Asshole there, women are just property to him. Right, Asshole? Like cattle or something. You can do anything you want to them."

That was when I finally got it. "He's the one," I said.

The woman with the gun gave me a funny look. "I think Dr. Watson over here just figured something out."

"Javier," I said. "He's the one that..."

"Raped me," Lane said. "That's right. He raped me. Do you mean to sit there and tell me you didn't know?"

"I didn't know. But ... I saw him here the other night. You called him by name..."

"Jesus," said the woman with the coat hanger. She sounded disgusted.

"Yeah, I know his name," Lane said. "I knew him before he raped me. So what? Because I know who he is, does that give him the right? I bought some coke from him, okay? And now my lawyer says he'll probably get off because of it. Even though he raped me. You want to hear about it? He pulled a knife, and he cut my clothes off, and he made me lie on my stomach, and he fucked me up the ass." She took two steps and kicked Javier in the face. She was wearing boots and she caught him on the cheekbone.

The woman with the coat hanger said, "Careful. Break his nose and he'll suffocate."

The woman with the gun said, "That'd be a real pity."

"Kind of misses the point, doesn't it? If we just *kill* him?" She had the hanger straightened out now and she was twisting one end into loops. It looked like a letter at the end of the straight piece of wire. It was a letter. It was the letter R.

"What are you going to do?" I said. Nobody paid any attention to me.

The woman with the coat hanger took it into the kitchen. I could see her through the breakfast bar. She took an ice bucket out of the freezer and set it on the counter. Then she bent the long end of the hanger double to make a handle. Then she got down a potholder, it was a red potholder, quilted in little diamond shapes, it fit over her hand like a mitten. Then she turned on a gas burner, turned it up to high. The flames were blue and the potholder was red.

Suddenly Javier started to spasm and make choking noises. There was a sour smell and he snorted a fine spray of vomit onto his clothes.

The woman with the coat hanger put it down on the stove and hurried over to take his gag off. The woman with the gun knelt on his legs and shoved the silencer into his crotch. "Don't make a sound," she told him. "Or you'll never fuck anybody again."

They were all looking at Javier. I got the Colt out. I was shaking again. It seemed like it was a million degrees below zero in that apartment. Javier spit puke on the floor and Lane ran into the kitchen for paper towels. She ran right past me and didn't even see the gun in my hand.

I stood up and the woman with the gun turned around. "What do you think you're—" She saw the Colt. Her face didn't change hardly at all. "So you want to play cowboy."

"I just want out of here. Let me walk out the door and you'll never see me again."

"I'd rather kill you," she said. I could tell she meant it. "I don't do anything with a gun pointed at me. So you can either use it or you can put it away."

We stayed like that, just looking at each other, pointing our guns at each other, Javier on his side, gasping, Lane with a handful of wet paper towels, the woman in the orange sweater standing to one side with a look on her face like she was only mildly interested. I tried to imagine myself pulling the trigger and knew I couldn't do it. It was the first rule my daddy taught me, that you don't pull a gun unless you're willing to use it, and here I'd gotten it wrong. I wondered how much noise her gun would make, with the silencer and all. I wondered if it would hurt.

"That's better," the woman with the gun said. I looked at my hand, saw my daddy's Colt now pointed down at the floor. My legs had gone weak and I eased down onto my knees and put the Colt on the cheap brown carpet between us.

I said, "Now what?"

The woman with the gun said, "Good question."

The woman in the sweater taped Javier's mouth shut again and went back in the kitchen. Lane went over to Javier and wiped up the mess on the floor. Then she got up and opened the front door.

The woman with the gun said, "Are you crazy?"

Lane looked at me, crooked her finger toward the door. "Get out of here."

The woman with the gun said, "Lane—"

"Let him go," Lane said. "Maybe he learned something."

I stood up. It didn't look like the woman with the gun was going to stop me. I took one careful step toward the door, and looked back. The woman with the coat hanger was holding it over the burner. A bright yellow flame was coming off it and the metal was turning red hot. I took another step and then I was walking, fast, and then I was outside and the door slammed shut behind me. I ran for the stairs and I was just to the corner of the building when I heard Javier, right through the tape, let out one long, muffled scream.

I JUST WANTED to finish it. I stopped at the Diamond Shamrock on Airport and called Dennis's house. The rain was still falling, slower now, and I turned up the collar of my jacket while I listened to the phone ring. His wife answered and told me he was at the office. I remembered he'd told me that.

I parked next to his Mercedes in the lot. I had to knock on the glass door of his office for him to come unlock it. He was working at the copier and there was a big stack of what looked like tax forms on the table next to it.

"What's up?" he said. He fed another form into the machine.

"Lane Rochelle's dropping the case," I said.

"You're kidding."

"That's what you wanted, isn't it? I mean, that's why you'd hire a big, stupid guy like me in the first place, right?"

"Maybe you're not so dumb as you look."

"Maybe not."

"I think this calls for a bonus. I expect my client could afford a couple hundred on top of your hourlies."

I expected it was worth a lot more than that to Dennis, not to have to put Javier on the stand, not to have him talk about his cocaine customers. But all I said was, "Why don't I get that bank bag for you?"

"Sure. It's in the desk there."

I went into Dennis's office and got the bank bag out of the side drawer. I guess I was just looking for something. I didn't know what it was going to be until I found it. I looked back into the waiting room and Dennis still had his back to me, feeding papers into the machine. I eased open the top drawer and there it was, a fat plastic bag full of cocaine. I figured it must have been about a quarter of a pound. I flattened it out and put it down the front of my pants and tucked my shirt back in around it.

I took the bank bag in to Dennis and he counted out three brand new hundred dollar bills. "Not bad for a day's work, eh?" he said. I couldn't do anything but nod. "You did good," he said. "There's plenty more where this came from. Just let me know, okay?"

I even shook his hand.

I went downstairs and jimmied the lock on the gas tank of his Mercedes. Then I took off the gas cap and poured the entire baggie of cocaine inside. When I closed it all back up I could hardly tell the difference. Then I threw the baggie in the dumpster. I don't really know what cocaine does to an engine, but I figure there's at least a lot of sugar in whatever it's cut with. Any way you look at it, it's just bound to be expensive.

I was still kind of pumped up when I got in the Pinto, but it wasn't like I thought it would be. I didn't feel any better. In fact I felt worse, I felt like hell. Lane said maybe I learned something, but if I did then maybe I learned the wrong thing. I got turned around and headed north on the I-35 access road, and I must not have been paying attention, because when I went to get on the freeway there was suddenly this car behind me that I never saw, his tires screaming on the wet road. I kept waiting for the thump as he hit me and it didn't happen, there was just his horn as he whipped around, leaning over in his seat to shake his fist at me. And there was nothing I could do except sit there and hold onto the wheel. Because there are all these millions of gestures for being pissed off and not one to say I'm sorry.

LIZARD MEN OF LOS ANGELES

T HE BEAUTIFUL black-haired woman suddenly turned, raised the gleaming revolver, and fired six resounding shots. Five .38 caliber slugs ripped into the wooden packing crate that Johnny Cairo had crawled into only moments before. The sixth bullet exploded a vase of red carnations that stood next to the crate.

Something slumped against the inside of the wooden box. A thread of bright crimson oozed between the pine boards and slowly trickled downwards.

The woman lowered the pistol, shock and horror spreading across her elegant features. The empty revolver clattered to her feet and she took one tentative step, then another, toward the crate.

"Stop!" cried a man's voice from the back of the theater. "Don't touch that box!"

The audience turned, gasped, and broke into applause as they saw that the speaker was none other than Johnny Cairo himself, changed from his dark suit and cape to evening clothes and sporting a bright, blood-red cummerbund.

BACKSTAGE, THE ENTIRE vaudeville troupe mingled with journalists and well-wishers, though in this Depression year of 1934 the crowds were smaller than they'd ever been. When the rest had departed, one lone man remained behind. He was heavy set, with elaborate side-whiskers and thinning hair. He carried a cashmere topcoat and scarf that had attracted some notice from those exiting past him.

He approached the magician and spoke in a deep and resonant voice. "I'm sorry, but I missed the evening's ... entertainment. You are Johnny Cairo? The man the press refers to as 'Mr. Impossible?'"

Cairo nodded, and gestured to the black-haired woman beside him. "This is Myra Lockhart, my associate." She had covered her revealing stage costume with a black velvet dressing gown. From a distance she had appeared to be in her twenties, but fine lines around her eyes and mouth made her true age much harder to determine. Those eyes, set in a complexion as white as cream, flashed a keen intelligence.

"Miss Lockhart," the man said with a short bow.

"Mrs.," she replied coolly.

"Errr, yes." He paused, then inquired, "Mr. Cairo, are you entirely well?"

Cairo had closed his eyes. He too seemed much older than he had from the stage. Beneath his heavy pancake makeup he was perspiring and his complexion had taken on a yellowish hue. "It's nothing," he said. "A legacy of my travels—dengue fever, a persistent amoebae, a trace of jaundice. How may I assist you, sir?"

"My name is Emil Rosenberg. I understand that you, under certain circumstances, have been known to undertake confidential investigations."

Mrs. Lockhart interrupted. "Certain very specific circumstances."

"I seek knowledge, Mr. Rosenberg," Cairo elaborated. "My investigations are always directed toward the great Mystery."

Rosenberg shook his head. "I fear you've lost me, sir."

"Some believe life to be full of mysteries. My studies in the East—and elsewhere—have convinced me there is but One, a single web of relationships that binds everything in the universe together. It's the principle by which magic works."

"I am not a magician, sir. And my concern is with what seems to be a single mystery, the disappearance of my daughter, Vera. The police are stymied and I'm afraid something drastic may have befallen her."

"I'm sympathetic, of course, Mr. Rosenberg," Cairo offered, "but surely this is a matter for a conventional private investigator, not someone of my particular talents."

"There are ... other factors involved. Factors that I believe you might ... Good Lord!" The color drained from Rosenberg's face as he pointed a shaking finger toward the hallway outside the dressing room. "There's one of them now!"

Cairo spun around to look. A sinister figure, heavily muffled in a wide-brimmed hat, raincoat, and baggy trousers, had just turned from the doorway and scuttled toward the stage door exit.

CAIRO LEAPED to his feet, his previous semblance of weariness gone. He bolted down the corridor in feverish pursuit of the mysterious onlooker. The heavily muffled man—if man it was—slammed open the bright red stage door and banged down the metal steps outside. As Cairo emerged into the warm darkness of the Los Angeles night, he saw the figure moving rapidly down the sidewalk, its body strangely contorted. It was bent at the waist, its short arms jerking convulsively, as if fighting the impulse to drop to all fours.

Only a dozen yards separated Cairo from the creature as it turned the corner onto a side street. When Cairo rounded the same corner seconds later, it had disappeared.

Mrs. Lockhart found Cairo there, staring at a scarf, hat, coat, and pants lying in the gutter. A damp, fetid smell rose from the clothing. "Methane," Cairo said. "Swamp gas."

"I suppose," Mrs. Lockhart said, "this means we'll be taking the case."

"HAVE YOU EVER," Rosenberg asked, "heard the name Aleister Crowley?"

They sat the parlor of Rosenberg's house in the community of Silver Lake, located to the north and west of Los Angeles proper. Rosenberg was fortifying himself with brandy while Cairo drank strong tea. Mrs. Lockhart, who had changed into a low-cut black evening dress, had declined refreshment.

"The Great Beast?" Cairo asked, startled. "He's involved in this?"

"I'm afraid he may have corrupted my daughter. And I believe the creatures that have been following me—you saw one of them tonight—may be his minions. So you do know of him?"

"We have had ... encounters," Mrs. Lockhart said. "He's here in Los Angeles?"

"He's staying in Pasadena, in the home of a businessman rumored to have Satanic allegiances. From there Crowley is able to make acquaintances in the film industry. Or rather, to speak frankly, to prey upon members of that profession. Spending their money on drugs and liquor, using their homes for unspeakable acts—I hope my candor doesn't offend you, sir."

"No," Cairo said. "I rely on it. And this man Crowley is worse than you imagine. How did your daughter come in contact with him?"

"She's a film actress. She uses a stage name, Veronica Fleming. Perhaps you've heard of her?" The last was said with unmistakable pride. He offered Cairo a framed color photograph from the mantle that showed a beautiful woman with luminous eyes and lustrous dark red hair falling past her shoulders.

"She was a child actress," Cairo said. "Now playing ingénue roles."

Rosenberg nodded. "She first met Crowley through her producer. I believe it's been less than a month. She began to attend parties at the mansion where Crowley's staying. Then, three days ago, she disappeared. I fear that even if she hasn't been physically harmed, her reputation may have been so damaged by her association with this ... Great Beast, as you call him, that her ingénue days may be finished."

"You were right to come to us," Cairo said. "Crowley is reputed to be past his prime, but he is still one of the most dangerous men alive. As he becomes more debauched and decadent, in fact, it becomes ever more dangerous to trifle with him." He got to his feet and adjusted the cuffs of his jacket. "If you have an address for him, in fact, we'll be on our way."

"My chauffeur will drive you," Rosenberg said. "Make whatever use of him you require." He looked at his pocket watch. "However, it's nearly midnight. Surely..."

"Crowley will be awake," Cairo assured him. "Hesitation at this point could be fatal."

"Besides," Mrs. Lockhart added, "our vaudeville troupe has an engagement in San Diego in less than twenty-four hours."

THE HOUSE HAD been designed by Frank Lloyd Wright, its long, shingled walls blending almost invisibly with the heavily landscaped grounds, its roof beams extending beyond the structure like a draftsman's energetic pencil lines. Every light in the mansion burned brightly, and the driveway was filled with cars.

"Such physical beauty," Cairo remarked, "so full of corruption."

"I trust you're not waxing metaphorical," Mrs. Lockhart said. "You know how I feel about that."

They walked up the curving driveway together and Cairo tried the massive teak door. It was securely locked and bolted. Cairo paused momentarily to pick the locks, then led them through a long entry hall into a scene of utter debauchery.

Perhaps two dozen men, women, and children sprawled in various postures throughout the large, oak-paneled room. None of them was Victoria Fleming. Few were fully dressed; some were bound with scarves or leather. They were grouped, for the most part, in twos and threes, with most of the possible combinations of gender represented. A blazing fire kept the room uncomfortably warm. On low tables throughout lay syringes, liquor bottles, and untidy heaps of white powders.

A low divan in the center of the room held a tall, sturdily-built man in his fifties, his head shaved, his thick jowls sagging with mindless pleasure. He was completely naked.

"Crowley!" Cairo shouted.

The bald man's eyes slowly opened and focused upon Cairo. "You!" he cried. His stare exuded malevolence. "How dare you confront me here?"

Mrs. Lockhart turned to Cairo. "If everything is under control here, I'll just have a look at the rest of the house."

Without looking away from Crowley, Cairo nodded. "Excellent suggestion."

"What are you doing here, Cairo?" Crowley bellowed, slowly rising to a sitting position, but making no attempt to cover himself. "You and that bloodless imitation of a woman? What do you want from me?"

"Information, merely," Cairo said. "I'm looking for a woman named

Veronica Fleming. She might also call herself Vera Rosenberg. We have reason to believe you might know her."

"Or have knowledge of her?" Crowley smiled. "In the so-called Biblical sense, perhaps? Do not waste my time, Cairo. There are so many women. Sometimes they are masked or blindfolded, and I never even see their faces, let alone learn their names. They are all one to me. Merely vessels for the transmission of magickal power."

"It's not your childish blasphemy that I object to," Cairo observed evenly. "Nor your physical depravity, nor even your wretched verse. It is your lack of compassion. It renders you less than human, and beneath contempt."

Crowley colored at the mention of his poetry, but quickly regained control. "You are so sanctimonious, Cairo." He waved one massive, long-fingered hand dismissively. "Yet you and I are two sides of the same coin. I debauch young women to feed my self-esteem, you rescue them to the same end. You focus your will through your 'craft' and your petty conjurings, I focus mine through ritual and tantric practice, but both of us know that will is the key. 'Do what thou wilt—'"

"'—shall be the whole of the Law,'" Cairo intoned. "So you have told us, again and again."

"You weary me, Cairo. Begone."

Mrs. Lockhart had not yet returned. Cairo glanced at his watch. "I dispute your comparisons," he said. "We are separate coins, and yours is made of base metal, counterfeit."

Crowley, in a show of indifference, put a pinch of white powder on the web of his left thumb and inhaled it briskly. From one of the darkened corners of the room came a sharp cry, though whether of pain or pleasure was not immediately obvious.

"And whatever else may be true of me," Cairo persisted, "I can at least console myself that I am not the author of poetry so wretched that it is universally reviled in my lifetime and will be forgotten promptly thereafter."

This, at last, reduced Crowley to rage. "Hassan!" he screamed in a high-pitched voice. A young Arab in an embroidered galabeya and turban appeared, carrying a scimitar.

Crowley pointed to Cairo. "Kill him!"

CAIRO, WITH AN EXPRESSION of distaste, let his gaze wander around the room. He took three strides to the fireplace where he hefted the brass poker. "Mmmm," he said with some dissatisfaction, and extended the implement from a practiced fencer's stance.

Suddenly wary, Hassan, who had raised his scimitar and seemed to be on the point of charging, glanced nervously at Crowley. "Kill him!" Crowley shrieked again, and the young Arab inched forward, twirling the blade with a circular motion of his wrist. Cairo gave way before it, passing behind a sofa from which two scantily-clad women regarded him with mild interest.

Hassan lunged and swung the curved blade in a murderous arc. Cairo somehow stepped out of its path, letting it carry on unimpeded into a priceless white Chinese vase, which shattered into a hundred fragments. Glancing behind him, Cairo's eyes fell upon a heavily-laden coffee table, and he reached back with his left foot to kick it aside. Powders, liquids, and candles flew across the room in a graceful arc and a teenage boy, who'd been reaching for one of the bowls, let out a sigh of regret.

Another furious scimitar slash failed to connect, reducing Hassan to blind fury. He became a windmill of flashing steel and yet Cairo remained untouched as the young Arab hurtled past him, colliding with a love seat and sending himself and its occupants sprawling across the deep red Oriental carpet of the adjacent dining room.

Stumbling to his feet, Hassan hurled a massive chair at Cairo, who ducked it easily. "Damn you," Crowley shouted at the boy. "Can you not finish him?"

Hassan moved in with the sword again, backing Cairo toward a corner. The boy's confidence was gone and he fought with the desperate intensity of the hopeless. His blade clashed with Cairo's poker once, twice, a third time, and then Cairo said, "Ah. There you are."

With a fluid motion he sent the scimitar spinning out of Hassan's grip, leaving the boy with a purpling bruise across the back of his hand.

Mrs. Lockhart, who had reappeared from the back of the house, stood in the center of the room, staring at the upturned furniture and the shattered vase and bowls. "Shall we?" she asked Cairo.

"Indeed," Cairo replied, and he saluted Crowley with the poker before tossing it into the fireplace. "If you'll forgive us, we'll take our leave."

"I will curse you, Cairo," Crowley muttered. "Carefully, elaborately, and inescapably. You will regret this. Briefly, in the time that remains to you."

"Do what thou wilt," Cairo said, and extended his arm to Mrs. Lockhart.

As they walked down the driveway Mrs. Lockhart said, "No sign of Veronica Fleming, but I did find an acquaintance of hers. She claims that her name is Blanche. I assisted her escape through a window, and she's now waiting for us in the car."

Mrs. Lockhart walked around to the front passenger seat while Cairo got in back next to a thin, pale woman with limp ash-blonde hair. She wore a low-cut evening dress of white satin. "Blanche, indeed," Cairo smiled. "What's your real name?"

After a long pause the woman lifted her pale eyes and said, "Mildred. Mildred Davis. Of Hillsboro, Missouri."

"Drive," Mrs. Lockhart said to the chauffeur. "Back toward Los Angeles."

"You know Veronica Fleming?" Cairo asked the girl.

"I should think I know her. She stole my boyfriend." In contrast to her fashionable appearance, her voice was uneducated and somewhat shrill.

Cairo raised one eyebrow and the girl continued. "The first time she come to the house, I couldn't even believe it, her being in pictures and all. I used to watch her back in Hillsboro when she was just a little girl. She's one of the reasons I come out here to Hollywood. Brother Perdurabo was going to make me a star just like her." Cairo frowned at the name Perdurabo, one of Crowley's many aliases. "Then," the girl went on, "she went and moved in on my Bruno."

"Bruno?" Cairo asked.

"Bruno Galt. He's a geologist. Works for one of those big mining companies. He's got piles of money. Brother Perdurabo was going to teach Bruno the Art, so he give me to Bruno for his, you know, those tantrum rituals?"

"Tantric," Cairo said.

"That's the ones. Then three days ago Veronica, she puts the moves on Bruno, and he leaves the mansion with her. That was the last time I seen either one of them."

"Do you know where Galt lives?"

"I should think I do. He's got a place downtown." She gave the driver an address on Grand Avenue.

"As quickly as you can," Cairo told him. The driver nodded, made a right turn, and accelerated into the eastbound traffic on Huntington Drive. Cairo turned back to the girl. "What makes a geologist so interested in the occult?"

"It's this guy he works with. Warren Shufelt. He's a mining engineer."

"Another of Crowley's benefactors?"

"As far as I know, Mr. Shufelt don't got nothing to do with Brother Perdurabo. He's only interested in his tunnels."

"Tunnels?"

"Yeah, the tunnels that—"

She broke off as a police siren suddenly split the night. Red lights flashed through the rear windscreen. The chauffeur slowed the car and steered toward the side of the road. Cairo leaned forward. "I'll handle this."

A policeman ran up to the car as Cairo wound down the rear window. "Your name Cairo?" the patrolman asked.

Cairo nodded.

"Follow us," the man called, already running back to his own vehicle. "There's trouble at Mr. Rosenberg's."

WHEN THEY ARRIVED at Rosenberg's house three police cars already sat in the driveway, red lights flashing. Cairo sprang out of the limousine and one of the policemen led him toward the house, with Mildred and Mrs. Lockhart following closely behind.

"There was a break-in," the policeman said. "Mr. Rosenberg asked us to put out an all-points for you. He said he needed to talk to you right away, and when Mr. Rosenberg needs something, well, we try to oblige him."

"I'm sure," Cairo said.

Rosenberg awaited them in his sun room, wearing a heavy terrycloth robe and drinking coffee. He was pacing back and forth in front of the sliding glass doors that led to his swimming pool. His hair was damp, and he seemed feverish.

Cairo sat in a wicker chair. As soon as Mildred and Mrs. Lockhart had settled themselves on the divan he said, "Tell us what happened."

"I was fast asleep," Rosenberg explained. "I awoke when I felt the covers pulled away from me, and I sat up in bed. I caught just a glimpse of one of those creatures standing over me, and then it doused me in some kind of liquid."

"Can you describe the liquid?" Mrs. Lockhart asked, leaning forward.

"It was greenish and slightly oily to the touch. Thicker than water, somehow. And it had a faint, fetid smell, like a marsh."

Cairo and Mrs. Lockhart exchanged a significant look.

"I sprang out of bed," Rosenberg continued, "and caught only a glimpse of my attacker. He was small, heavily swathed—in short, almost identical to the intruder at the theater this evening. The way he moved, I tell you, sir, I'm not entirely sure he..." Rosenberg shook his head, then dabbed at his forehead with a handkerchief. "Is it unnaturally hot in here?"

"Quite the contrary," Cairo said. "Tell me what it is you were unsure of."

Rosenberg's voice dropped to a whisper. "I am not entirely sure he was ... human."

Cairo nodded. "I see. What happened next?"

"The creature disappeared into the night. I called the police immediately, of course, and then I took a hot bath and scrubbed my skin nearly raw. It had begun to itch most fearsomely. In fact," he confided, mopping his brow again, "it still does."

Suddenly Rosenberg stood stock still. "My God—" he said.

Cairo got to his feet. "Rosenberg? Is something wrong?"

Rosenberg's only reply was a high-pitched moan that seemed to escape involuntarily from his lips.

Cairo looked at Mrs. Lockhart. "What's wrong with him? Do you see anything?"

Mrs. Lockhart shook her head but Mildred suddenly gasped and put her hand to her mouth. "L-look!"

Cairo turned back. Faint wisps of smoke had begun to rise from Rosenberg's robe.

"What's going on?" Mildred cried.

"Open those glass doors, Mrs. Lockhart, if you please," Cairo said with icy calm.

"Hellllllp ... meeeeeeee..." Rosenberg howled, as the first tiny flames began to flicker at the back of his head, like an infernal halo. The very air around him had begun to warp from the intense heat that poured off his body.

Cairo reached one hand toward Rosenberg, then snatched it back. There now seemed to be a fire deep inside Rosenberg's chest, like the glow inside a piece of charcoal whose surface has turned to ash. In fact, Rosenberg's skin had begun to flutter away in small, gray sheets.

Mrs. Lockhart wrestled open one of the massive glass doors and stood aside as Cairo snatched a Navajo rug from the tile floor and, using it as a shield, attempted to wrap it around Rosenberg's body. At that instant Rosenberg burst into flames as hot as those in a crematorium. The blanket was consumed instantly and Cairo fell back with his hands before his face.

When he got to his feet, nothing remained of Emil Rosenberg but a pile of ashes and one charred gray foot.

A POLICEMAN BURST through the door with a revolver in his hand. "What's going on here?" He glanced nervously around the room. "Where's Mr. Rosenberg? And what's that smell?"

Cairo faced him, his eyes intent. He held up his right hand, middle finger bent and held by the thumb, the remaining fingers extended. "Listen to my voice," Cairo intoned. "There is nothing wrong here. You will give us the keys to your patrol car. You will walk us to the car and explain to the others that I am a high-ranking member of the Los Angeles police department."

The policeman's eyes clouded over and his brow furrowed as if he were studying a complex mathematical formula. "Nothing's wrong here. You can put your badge away, sir. My car is right outside."

Mildred looked at Mrs. Lockhart in amazement. "How did he do that?"

"A very great deal of self-confidence," Mrs. Lockhart replied. "Don't dawdle."

The officer escorted them to his car and waved to them from the driveway as Mrs. Lockhart expertly backed the long, black automobile, lights still flashing, into the street. Cairo turned to Mildred, who sat wide-eyed in the back. "First we need directions to Galt's apartment," he said. "Then I want you to finish telling me about the tunnels."

The night was dark and cool and the stars burned fiercely overhead as Mrs. Lockhart drove toward the city. Mildred's face, in the starlight, showed a mixture of fear and excitement, innocence and cupidity. "Mr. Shufelt, see, he had this idea about a lost city under Los Angeles. He thought there was gold down there, big tablets of it—I guess like Moses had, only gold. He said he had maps that he made with what he called his Radio X-Ray. It just looked like a fancy dowsing rod to me, but what do I know? He drilled a big hole on Fort Moore Hill this spring trying to find it."

"I assume he was unsuccessful," Cairo said. "Otherwise it would have been in every newspaper in the civilized world."

"Bruno says he *did* find it."

"Then perhaps we should be talking to this Shufelt instead of Galt."

"I don't think even Brother Perdurabo could talk to Mr. Shufelt now."

"Are you saying he's dead?"

"The city gave up drilling, see, on account of being scared the hole was going to cave in, even though Mr. Shufelt said they were almost through. So Bruno and Mr. Shufelt went out there one night and Bruno lowered him into the hole with his Radio X-Ray machine and a pickax. Bruno stayed up top to watch for cops and all, and after three or four hours Mr. Shufelt said he found something. Then Bruno heard Mr. Shufelt say something like, 'Oh my God, they're alive!' Then there was this awful noise that Bruno said was like bones going through a grinder and the bottom part of the tunnel fell in. By the time Bruno could get down there, there was a hundred tons of rock where Mr. Shufelt had been."

"Did Bruno go to the police?"

The girl nodded. "He says they didn't believe him. They thought it was just a trick so they'd let Bruno and Mr. Shufelt start drilling again."

"Do you have any idea what Mr. Shufelt might have meant when he said, 'They're alive?'"

"Bruno thought he knew. He thought—"

"Yes?"

She looked out the window, then back into Cairo's eyes. "He thought it was the lizard men."

•

"SEE," MILDRED EXPLAINED, the words rushing out now in a torrent, "the tunnels are all supposed to connect together in the shape of this giant lizard. The head is up by Chinatown and the tail is down by the Central Library. There's some kind of Indian legend about it. It was supposed to be built by lizard people five thousand years ago."

"The lizard people are real," Cairo said. "We saw one of them at the theater this evening, and it was one of them that attacked Rosenberg at his house. But what was Veronica's part in all of this?"

"She was real interested in those gold tablets. See, Bruno, he was sure there was another way into the tunnels. He was telling me about it at the mansion, about how he had all of Mr. Shufelt's maps and everything, and about how he thought Brother Perdurabo could help him find the entrance. That's when Veronica made her move. I bet she convinced Bruno she'd be better at that tantric stuff than me."

"The maps are at Galt's apartment?"

"He used to show them to me. I tell you, I don't understand half the things he'd say to me, and those maps ain't like any maps I ever saw." She leaned forward and said to Mrs. Lockhart, "Turn right on Grand Avenue, and go slow. We're almost there."

Mrs. Lockhart parked the police cruiser on the nearly deserted street and killed the lights. Downtown Los Angeles was a gray place, nothing like the outlying cities with their palm trees and ocean views. Cairo hunched his shoulders slightly as Mildred led them into a Spanish-style apartment building that had seen more prosperous days. No one answered the buzzer labeled "B. Galt," so they climbed the stairs to the third floor, where Cairo opened the door as easily as if it hadn't been locked.

The apartment consisted of a living room, a bedroom, and a kitchen: red tile floors, arched doorways, white plaster walls, and ceiling fans. The Spartan furnishings included no paintings, plants, or knickknacks. Two glasses sat in the kitchen sink, one of them showing lipstick traces, and a handbag lay on the rug beside the couch. Mrs. Lockhart made a quick inspection of its contents. "It's Veronica's," she said.

A drafting table stood against the far wall of the bedroom. Cairo shuffled through the neat stacks of paper and said, "Come look at this."

A map of downtown Los Angeles was taped to the surface of the table, onto which three vellum overlays had been added. Several hundred short lines crisscrossed the top layer. The second layer showed several longer, more complex lines, one of them winding through El Pueblo de Los Angeles State Historic Park downtown.

The third overlay contained the outlines of a lizard, resembling the Gila monster of Arizona. Its head stretched north of Chinatown and its straight, stubby tail terminated at the Los Angeles Central Library, only a few blocks from where they stood.

"That's the map," Mildred said. "Crazy, ain't it?"

"The lizard I understand—more or less," Mrs. Lockhart said. "The other two diagrams baffle me."

Cairo shook his head. "Mildred, did Bruno ever say anything that might make sense of all this?"

She shook her head. "I don't think he understood it so much himself. That's why he was going to Brother Perdurabo."

"We'll search all the rooms," Cairo said. "There must be something else here to—"

At that moment the front door of the apartment flew open with a crash. A dark figure stood in the hallway, silhouetted by the hall light.

"Bruno?" Mildred said.

The figure groaned and toppled face-first onto the floor.

CAIRO ROLLED THE MAN onto his back. He had an athletic build, short blond hair, and wire-rimmed glasses. One lens had shattered and his khaki work clothes were bloodied and torn. "Is this Bruno?" Cairo asked Mildred.

Mildred nodded, wide-eyed. "Is he...?"

"Alive at the moment," Cairo said. "But not at all well."

"Lizard men..." Bruno whispered.

"Easy," Cairo warned. "We have to get you to a hospital."

"No time," Bruno whispered. "I'm ... a walking dead man ... have to warn ... lizard men ... on the move ... kill us all ... take back their city..." His eyes suddenly opened wide. "Lizard queen! Must stop ... the lizard queen!"

"Where are they?" Cairo asked intently. "These lizard men, how do we find them?"

"To ... the tunnels ... from ... the tunnels..."

Cairo looked to Mrs. Lockhart. "He's making no sense. If you'd be so kind as to get his feet, perhaps we—" He broke off as waves of heat began to pour off of Bruno's body.

"Lizard!" Bruno screamed. "Queeeeeeeeeeeeen!"

"Oh no," Cairo sighed. "Not again."

Flames leaped out of Bruno's clothing and the glass of his spectacles melted and ran like tears. The skull inside Bruno's head seemed to glow as if made of molten lava.

"Your hands," Mrs. Lockhart said sharply. "Where you touched him."

Cairo looked down. Smoke was already rising from his skin.

"I'll get ice," Mrs. Lockhart said, moving swiftly to the icebox in the kitchen. Cairo ignored her. He backed away from Bruno's furiously burning body and lowered himself into a cross-legged posture on the floor. He closed his eyes. Flames flickered between his fingers and then, just as suddenly, died out. A moment later Cairo opened his eyes and inspected the hands he held out in front of him, unharmed.

"There's no ice," Mrs. Lockhart said, returning. "Are you all right?"

"Perfectly," Cairo assured her.

"How ... how..." Mildred stammered.

"It was no worse than the hot coals I used to walk upon in India. Any *fakir* could have done the same."

"You ... you were faking it?" She burst into sudden tears. "I don't understand any of this! This is all so horrible! Poor Bruno, and poor Mr. Rosenberg! And that monster, Crowley, who wanted to have relations with anything that moved! I wish I never came to California! I wish none of this had ever happened!"

"Listen to my voice," Cairo said. He held up his hand, palm first, with the middle finger bent again. "I will not command you to forget, because if you forget you will only make the same mistakes again. And I cannot undo the things that happened tonight. I can, however, make you able to remember them without much pain, or fear, or curiosity, so that you can go back to Missouri and be Mildred Davis once again. Do you understand?"

Mildred nodded and Cairo lowered his hand. "Do you have any money?" he asked her. She shook her head. Cairo reached into the limp blonde hair behind her ear and produced a small, tightly folded piece of paper. He carefully unfolded it to reveal a twenty-dollar bill. "That should get you home," he said.

Mildred wiped her nose with the back of her hand. "How can I ever thank you?"

"Help me search for another map," Cairo said, "before we take you to the train station."

DAWN WAS A PALE gray promise in the eastern sky when they pulled up in front of Union Station on Alameda Street. Even at this hour, the sidewalks teemed with well-dressed travelers, while children sold newspapers and fresh fruit. The smell of oranges blended with the scent of orange blossoms in the air.

They had searched Bruno's apartment top to bottom and found no other maps than the ones on the drafting table. Cairo had appropriated those, along with a massive battery-powered miner's lamp they'd found in Bruno's closet.

They got out of the police car. "Thank you so much, Mr. Cairo, Mrs.

Lockhart," Mildred said. "I don't know how I could ever pay you back."

"Just take care of yourself," Cairo said. He reached into thin air and pulled back a business card. "This is the address of our manager. Write us a letter when you're safely back in Missouri."

"I will."

"A moment," Mrs. Lockhart said suddenly. "Mildred, what's that?"

She was pointing to a ramp, paved with cobblestones, that led down into the ground.

"That?" Mildred said. "Why, that's just a walkway, for people and horses to cross the street."

"Are there many of them in the city?"

"Maybe a couple of hundred."

"As many," Mrs. Lockhart pressed on, "as there were little marks on the top sheet of Bruno's map? Cairo, would you be so kind?" He nodded, reached back into the police car for the map, and unrolled it on the sidewalk.

"You're right," Cairo said. "It's a map of the pedestrian tunnels. Very astute, Mrs. Lockhart."

"There's more," Mrs. Lockhart said. "Note how these pedestrian tunnels connect with a longer tunnel that goes under the park? That park right behind us?"

"By heaven," Cairo said. "I think you're on to it." He rolled up the maps and exchanged them for the miner's lamp. "What did Bruno say when I asked him how to find the lizard men? Could it have been that he meant us to get 'to the tunnels'—meaning the tunnels of the lizard men—'from the tunnels'—meaning from the pedestrian tunnels?"

"Let us find out," Mrs. Lockhart said. "Mildred, can you make your way to your train on your own?"

"Compared to a lot of things I done since I came out here," Mildred said, "it'll be a piece of cake."

She blew a kiss, and Cairo managed a short bow, then he and Mrs. Lockhart turned and hurried down the ramp that led to the tunnels beneath Los Angeles.

THE SHORT TUNNEL crossed beneath Alameda and emerged again at the end of Olvera Street in the park. Cairo walked the length of it, then returned, searching the walls and floor. "I don't see any way this can join the other tunnel."

"That's because," Mrs. Lockhart said, "you're using your eyes."

Cairo stopped. "You're right, of course." He produced a long, red handkerchief from his sleeve and tied it over his eyes. Once again he slowly walked the length of the tunnel, arms raised slightly from his sides, turning his head every few seconds to listen or to sniff the air. An elderly Mexican woman, muffled in a black dress and shawl, passed him with a frightened look, crossing herself and muttering under her breath.

Once she had climbed the ramp to the park Cairo asked, "Are we alone?"

"Quite," Mrs. Lockhart replied.

Cairo nodded, walked to the middle of the south wall of the tunnel, and ran his fingers carefully over the massive stone blocks. "Ah," he said, and a section of the wall pivoted backward into darkness. He removed the blindfold and switched on Bruno's mining lamp. Sniffing the air of the passage he commented, "Methane. Volatile stuff. Don't light up one of your cigars in here, Mrs. Lockhart."

"Very droll, Cairo. If you don't wish to lead, I'll be happy to oblige."

Cairo handed her the lamp and followed her into the passage. The tunnel was ten feet high and nearly that wide, paved with large, uniform stones. The scars of pickaxes were visible in the rock of the ceiling. Cairo and Mrs. Lockhart had advanced no more than a few paces when the section of wall that had pivoted to admit them rumbled slowly back into place.

Mrs. Lockhart looked at Cairo. "I trust you'll be able to get us out again."

"I hope so too," Cairo smiled. "Lead on."

The passage ran straight and unencumbered for several hundred yards, angling slightly downward. Suddenly Cairo halted. "Mrs. Lockhart. Shut the lamp off, if you would."

She did so, and for a moment they were plunged into what seemed to be absolute, stygian darkness. Then, after a few agonizing seconds, a faint, yellowish-green outline emerged from the general gloom of the floor. Cairo knelt and lifted away a stone trap-door, revealing a drop of ten feet or so, with handholds in the rock, and a stone staircase below it that led deep into the bowels of the earth. The green glow rose from the stairs.

Mrs. Lockhart handed the lamp to Cairo and began to descend. "Be careful," she said. "It's a bit slippery."

Cairo passed down the lamp and joined her on the first platform. "Are you prepared to go on?" Cairo asked. "I have no idea where this may lead."

A narrow smile barely registered on Mrs. Lockhart's agelessly beautiful features. "That lack has never stopped me before."

The stairs seemed to have been carved from living rock, untold generations before. The risers were over a foot in height, and the uncomfortably narrow treads were well worn. The passage curved gently to the right as it descended. After the initial turning, Cairo and Mrs. Lockhart continued straight downward in a northwesterly direction for hundreds of feet before abruptly emerging into a chamber the size of a banquet hall with a smooth, level floor. The mysterious green glow came from a single sphere, somewhat larger than a man's head, in the center of the ceiling. It provided enough light to easily read the carvings in the walls of the cave. Interspersed with vaguely humanoid figures were rows of hieroglyphs. Cairo took the lamp and studied them.

"Remind you of anything?" Mrs. Lockhart asked.

"The Temple of Ramses the Second at Abu Simbel," Cairo returned, awe in his voice.

Mrs. Lockhart nodded. "And...?"

"And Chichen Itza in the Yucatan."

"Exactly."

"But if there is a single civilization that bridges those two cultures, it must mean—"

"Correct," Mrs. Lockhart said. "These tunnels can only have been built by the survivors of Atlantis."

CAIRO STOOD for a moment, as if trying to fathom all the implications of the idea. "Are you saying that the Atlanteans were not human? That they were some sort of ... lizard race?" Cairo turned slowly, taking in the carvings, the alien technology of the light sphere. "It could explain so much..."

He froze. "Did you hear something?"

Mrs. Lockhart shook her head once, a curt gesture that barely disturbed her jet-black hair.

Another tunnel led from the far end of the chamber. Cairo glided silently toward the opening and looked into the darkness. "I don't think—"

This time the noise was clearly audible, a sort of wet thump. It was quickly followed by another. Cairo backed into the center of the room and held the lamp high. Mrs. Lockhart moved behind him, crouching slightly, her arms raised in the posture of an oriental science of self-defense.

A panel of hieroglyphs suddenly slid open to reveal a small passageway, followed almost instantly by a second panel and then a third. A fourth opened in the opposite wall, then two more. For a moment silence fell on the underground chamber, an absence more terrifying than the sounds that had preceded it.

And then the openings poured forth lizard men.

There were at least a hundred of them, all about four feet in height, their skins gray-green in the eerie luminescence. Their loins were wrapped in some sort of bindings that left room for the massive tails that dragged the ground behind them. They had almost no necks, and their lipless mouths extended more than an inch beyond where their noses should have been. Their bulbous eyes stared unblinkingly as they shambled forward on massive lower legs that bent nearly double. Had they straightened those legs, they would have been the height of a man.

They formed a great circle around Cairo and Mrs. Lockhart. The odor of methane in the air was almost unbearable. Cairo shifted the lamp to his left hand and gestured with his right. "We are looking for a human woman, Veronica Fleming. We have no desire to harm you."

"Speak for yourself, Cairo," Mrs. Lockhart said. "In any case, I don't believe they're listening."

The lizard men had begun to move forward. "I will protect myself," Cairo warned them, waving the lamp in an arc in front of him. "Have a care."

The lizard men charged.

Cairo swung the lamp once, grazing one of them and tracing a line of dark green across its chest. He had no further opportunity. In the next moment the weight of the creatures bore him and Mrs. Lockhart to the floor of the cave, and consciousness fled from them both.

CAIRO RECOVERED to find himself leaning back against one face of a steep, ten-foot tall pyramid, his wrists and ankles secured by golden chains. He winced in pain as soon as he opened his eyes, and it took him a moment to try again.

"Are you all right, Cairo?" Mrs. Lockhart asked. She was chained to a second pyramid a few yards away.

"Somewhat the worse for beating," he said, "but I hope to survive." He blinked, raised his head, and gasped in astonishment as he looked around.

They'd been brought to a huge underground chamber, larger than any cathedral in Europe. A massive green globe seemed to hang well below the vaulted ceiling, where it blazed with a light to rival the noonday sun. Pyramids, altars, and figurines rose from the smooth stone floor at irregular intervals. Surrounding them swarmed hundreds, perhaps thousands, of the lizard creatures. Many of them carried spears that appeared to be tipped with gold. And on a dais in front of Cairo and Mrs. Lockhart stood a woman in long, flowing white robes and a golden mask.

Cairo smiled. "Veronica Fleming, I presume?"

The woman moved to the edge of the dais. She was but a few paces away from Cairo, had he been able to move, her waist on a level with his eyes. "No," she said, and removed the mask. "I was never Veronica Fleming."

Rosenberg's daughter stood revealed before them, her haunted eyes and shining red hair appearing almost black in the mysterious light. "Veronica Fleming was a creation of my father's, the invention of a status-seeking, fame-obsessed immigrant ashamed of his own heritage. It was Veronica Fleming who was sold into the child slavery of the studio system, Veronica Fleming who was given drugs and liquor before she even became physically a woman, Veronica Fleming who was used by producers and directors and has-been actors. Not me. Never me."

She spread her arms wide above her head, fingers extended. "I am Vera Rosenberg, and I have found my true destiny ... as a queen." Her subjects answered her with percussive sounds from their throats, horrid gulping barks that resounded the length and breadth of the chamber and built to a deafening crescendo.

"What do you mean to do with us?" Cairo demanded, his voice raised to be heard above the hideous cacophony.

"You will be sacrificed, of course," Vera said. "In due time."

"Three days ago," Mrs. Lockhart said, "you stood in the same relation to Aleister Crowley, the Great Beast 666, that Veronica Fleming stood to her Hollywood masters. How did your situation change so utterly in so short a time?"

"The span of time is not three days," Vera said, "but rather five thousand years. I am the fulfillment of ancient prophecy." She beckoned to four of the nearest lizard creatures. "Leave them chained, but release them to walk about."

"So your subjects speak English?" Cairo asked, as his manacles were unfastened from the pyramid, the loose ends of the chains held by shambling lizard guards.

"English, Latin, Hebrew—all of your warm-blood languages are descended from those of my people."

"Your people, then," Mrs. Lockhart commented, "would be the cold-bloods?"

"Your reputation has preceded you, Mrs. Lockhart," Vera said. "You are hardly one to cast aspersions on cold-bloodedness." She smiled without humor. "But I will give you some few answers before your deaths. The rituals are more effective if the victims have some understanding of their purpose."

She walked gracefully down the steps of the dais and swept her arm toward a monumental sculpture which had the same Gila-monster form as the underground complex itself on Shufelt's map. It stretched a hundred yards in length, some thirty feet in height, and its surface was formed of beaten gold. At Vera Rosenberg's gesture, an opening appeared in the side of the giant reptile.

"Clearly," Cairo murmured to Mrs. Lockhart, "she may have shed her former identity, but she hasn't lost her flair for the dramatic." One of the lizard men responded by jabbing him in the kidneys with the blunt end of a spear.

"In this chamber," Vera said, "are thirty-seven golden tablets." She snapped her fingers and two of the lizard men scuttled into the chamber then reappeared, awkwardly carrying one of the tablets between them. The tablet had the rudimentary form of a lizard, with abbreviated head, tail, and legs breaking the otherwise oblong form. It appeared to be a slab of solid gold four feet in length, a little more than a foot wide, and perhaps half an inch thick. The upper surface was covered in hieroglyphs similar to those in the outer chamber.

"If the information inscribed on these tablets became public knowledge," Vera said, "it would destroy your civilization. Together they contain the entire history of the world since its creation, and believe me, its creation is nothing at all like you imagine it to be. They tell of the origin of warm-blooded life as an experiment gone awry. They even predict the coming of a warm-blooded, red-haired woman in the fifth millennium of exile to lead them back to domination of the surface world."

"You've read them all in three days?" Mrs. Lockhart remarked. "You've been busy."

"Your sarcasm is wasted," Vera replied imperiously. "Fragments of this knowledge have escaped over the centuries. Hopi legends tell of the great lost cities of the Lizard Clan. Bruno Galt heard of the Lizard Queen from a Hopi medicine man that they'd hired to help with their research. When Bruno and I met, we were two ambitious people who quickly saw how we could benefit from one another."

"Bruno's dead," Cairo said.

"Yes. He could never see past the gold. He didn't realize that gold was meaningless once you had the power to rule an entire city—perhaps an entire continent. The power to repay anyone who had ever hurt you."

"Then you must know your father is dead as well."

"I ordered it."

"We watched both of them die," Cairo told her, "terrifying and painful deaths. Both were incinerated before our eyes."

Vera nodded again. "It is our preferred means of execution: the Blood of the Green Lion."

Cairo's eyes widened at the name. "The universal solvent," he murmured, "that the alchemists have always spoken of. It dissolves the seven metals and gold. How can you transport it?"

"Your warm-blood alchemists were wrong. Gold contains it, if the gold is pure enough. Our scientists developed it in the days when we ruled the surface world. Simply douse any object and gradually, in the space of half an hour or so, the energy within the molecules of that object releases itself as heat. We used the Blood of the Green Lion to melt these tunnels. Because gold can resist this chemical process, it became sacred to our people. As you can see, we've accumulated a good deal of it."

She seemed to drift into a kind of reverie. "The race has fallen off greatly since then. Rapid evolution is both a blessing and a curse. But in a few generations—mere decades in human terms—I know we can rise again."

She turned to back to Cairo and Mrs. Lockhart. Her smile at last appeared more genuine. "I realize you've only scratched the surface of the knowledge we have to offer you, but I fear we must break off. It's time for you to die."

LIZARD SOLDIERS STRETCHED Cairo and Mrs. Lockhart on two adjacent altars, securing their chains to the stone. On a third altar lay the heavy mining lamp. Two further lizard disciples staggered into view carrying a massive golden urn between them. They set it at the foot of the altars and stepped away.

"That would be the Blood of the Green Lion?" Cairo asked. "You mean, then, to burn us to death?"

"That is correct, Mr. Cairo. But your deaths will inspire my people to their conquest of the surface world, so you will not die completely in vain."

"I take it," Mrs. Lockhart ventured, "that no one has actually used this chemical here, underground, in quite some time?"

"Why do you say that?"

"Because," Cairo explained, "these tunnels are full of methane. The ground under Los Angeles is notoriously unstable, and clearly a fissure has opened some deposit of the gas. There may be other natural gases present as well which are not so easily recognizable, and even more flammable. In any event, an open flame in this chamber will result in an explosion of epic proportions."

Vera's face registered her concern. One of the lizard men tugged at her robe, and she bent over to listen to his hoarse, croaking voice.

Cairo raised his right hand as far as the chains would allow and pinned his middle finger with his thumb. "You must believe me," he said intently. "We are all in danger. You must release us now and let us return to the surface."

Vera dismissed him with a shake of her magnificent red hair. "Before poor Bruno showed me my destiny, I had planned to achieve my independence by means of Brother Perdurabo's techniques. I learned enough from him to resist such feeble parlor tricks as yours, Cairo." She clapped her hands. "Cover them with the Blood! When you have finished, we will begin the rite of war. As they burn, they will light our charge to the surface world and the restoration of our empire!"

Two lizard men carefully raised the urn onto a pedestal. A third held a golden bowl to a tap at the bottom of the urn and filled it with a viscous liquid. Vera mounted a second pedestal near the urn from which she could look down upon the sacrificial altars. The creature carrying the golden bowl held it high overhead and the chamber resounded again to the yelping cries of the lizard men, as bone-chilling a sound as ever heard by human ears.

Cairo shrank from the creature as it mounted the steps of the altar, still carrying the bowl held high. Cairo's two hands were clasped together, his knees drawn up as far as his chains would permit. From the lizard's bulbous throat came a high-pitched warbling moan. A dozen more lizards took up the sound, then a hundred, then a thousand, until the very bedrock seemed to quiver and shake.

"Now!" Vera screamed. "Cover him now!"

Cairo seemed frozen. The lizard began to lower the bowl. The cries of the lizard army reached a feverish climax. And suddenly Cairo moved.

His hands flew free of the golden manacles as he caught the golden bowl from underneath and sent its contents arcing backward through the air. The thick liquid seemed to cohere and hang suspended as a single transparent mass in the bright green light for an eternity. Then it fell, covering Vera Rosenberg from head to foot.

"No!" Vera shrieked. "No! This cannot be! I have a destiny!"

Cairo froze momentarily, shocked by what he had inadvertently done. Then he shook himself and began to move again. In a second he released his feet, and in another he freed Mrs. Lockhart. In another he wrenched a spear from the hands of one of the stunned lizard soldiers and scrambled onto the altar that held the mining lamp.

"Kill them!" Vera demanded as Cairo drew back his arm. "Cairo, you're a fool. You're outnumbered thousands to one. My servants will tear you limb from limb for what you've done to me!"

"There is no antidote, then?" Cairo asked softly.

"None!"

"Then I am sorry," Cairo said. "It was not my intent that the fluid fall on you. As to your subjects ... they will have to find us before they can kill us."

With that he turned and hurled the spear upward with all his strength.

It sailed straight and true toward the small green sun overhead, and when it struck, the sphere imploded with a crack, a brief flash of green fog, and a rain of glass fragments.

The huge cavern was plunged into night. For a moment the beam of the miner's lamp revealed Mrs. Lockhart extending her hand toward Cairo and then the darkness closed again over the panic and chaos that reigned in the tunnels of the lizard men.

GASPING FOR BREATH, Mrs. Lockhart sank to the floor of the tunnel, then reached down and pulled Cairo up the last of the stairs they had descended only hours before. Cairo collapsed beside her, panting heavily.

"That," Mrs. Lockhart said between breaths, "was a horrific risk you took, exploding that lamp. It could have ignited the gasses and finished us then and there."

"We would have been no more dead," Cairo returned, equally exhausted, "than we would have been otherwise. I could only hope they couldn't track us by smell."

"A safe wager. If their senses were so acute, they would have known about the methane."

Cairo turned on the miner's lamp and examined his wrist-watch. "I fear that I may have underestimated the danger of that methane. It's been more than half an hour since Vera Rosenberg was doused in the Blood of the Green Lion and—"

As if in answer, a muffled explosion shook the floor underneath them. Instead of dying out, the noise seemed to grow. "Cairo," Mrs. Lockhart said, pointing down the stairs they had just climbed. The green glow was gone, replaced by the hellish orange of an inferno. "Run!"

They lunged to their feet and sprinted for the entrance to the tunnel. The walls were shaking now, and dirt and small rocks clattered around them and filled the air with dust.

"How much farther?" Mrs. Lockhart gasped. "I can feel the heat..."

"There!" Cairo exclaimed, as a wall materialized out of the fog of dirt and rubble. He flung himself at it, fumbling for a catch. "It must be here!"

"Patience," Mrs. Lockhart said with forced calm. Her voice was barely audible above the roar as one chamber after another ignited below them. "Let it find you..."

More quietly still she said, "And let it be soon..."

"I have it!" Cairo cried, and the wall opened to reveal the pedestrian tunnel beneath Alameda Street. He pulled Mrs. Lockhart through the opening, went to the mechanism on the outer side with sure fingers, and the wall slid closed as the very air behind it exploded into a blinding yellow fireball.

IN THE BRIGHT Los Angeles sunshine they sat on a park bench and watched the ordinary citizens of Los Angeles buying lunch from the vendors on Olvera Street. Cairo's shirt and trousers were in shreds, and the skin beneath was a mass of bruises and lacerations. Mrs. Lockhart had fared little better; her black hair was caked with dust and she wore the remains of Cairo's jacket to cover the damage to her gown.

"The thing that most frightens me," Cairo said, "is the knowledge that some of those lizard creatures doubtless escaped. If what Vera Rosenberg said is true, their rapid evolution could allow them to become more humanoid in the space of a few generations. In our lifetimes there could be lizard men walking among us undetected."

"What is it that you're afraid of?" Mrs. Lockhart asked. "That cold-blooded, repugnant creatures might gain control of the film industry? How would we know the difference?"

"You make light of it, but the knowledge that was lost today—for good or ill—can never be recovered."

"Knowledge is not always the highest good," Mrs. Lockhart said, turning to follow the progress of an early summer breeze through the trees in the park.

"Really? If Rosenberg were alive, what would you have told him about his daughter?"

"I would merely have said that she died in an unfortunate accident, while exploring the tunnels under the city."

"After the way he exploited her throughout her childhood?"

"His cruelty would not justify lack of compassion on my part." Her eyes seemed to lose their focus. "It would be ... less than human, somehow."

A small green lizard, no longer than Cairo's hand, had crawled out onto the sidewalk to sun itself. As Cairo watched, it darted toward the busy street, hesitating a few inches from Cairo's right shoe.

"I suppose you're right, as always, Mrs. Lockhart."

She blinked, brushed at the front of her borrowed jacket, and instantly recovered her composure. "Of course I am," she said. "And as it's already past one o'clock in the afternoon, may I suggest we be on our way? We have an engagement in San Diego this evening."

"Indeed," Cairo answered. As he rose, he nudged the lizard gently with his foot and sent it scampering back into the safety of the bushes. "Indeed, Mrs. Lockhart," he laughed, "lead on."

AUTHOR'S NOTES

THIS BOOK is the brainchild of Bill Schafer, publisher of Subterranean Press. In keeping with our plan to reissue my novels in definitive editions, he urged me to do a definitive collection of my short fiction—everything I wanted to preserve (plus a few). Bill is a writer's dream, because he loves books and he publishes from his heart. I am more grateful than I can say for his support.

While I'm at it, I'd like to thank Karen Joy Fowler, one of the best writers in the world, for writing the most perfect introduction I could ever have. Big thanks to all the editors who first published these pieces, especially my friend Joe R. Lansdale, who in his guise as anthology editor nagged and pestered and annoyed me into writing my favorite stories in this book. Richard Butner read most of these stories from 1987 on in draft form and offered great insight and suggestions. Arthur Hoffman was there from before the beginning, with unflagging enthusiasm, friendship, and great bass playing. And my partner, Orla Swift, has helped nurture this book as she has nurtured me.

I WENT BACK and forth on the idea of writing notes for the individual stories, and finally decided to do it because I like reading them in other people's collections. Be warned that I cribbed from the notes I'd written for previous collections, from my autobiographical essay, and from notes on my Fiction Liberation Front website (www.fictionliberationfront.net).

PERFIDIA

I was hugely flattered when Steve Erickson asked me to write something for his literary magazine, *Black Clock,* in the fall of 2003. He was doing a theme issue on Lost Music, and he thought of me because of *Glimpses.* Off the top of my head I pitched him a story about the mystery of Glenn Miller's death. I had a book called *Millergate* by David Graham Wright that I had skimmed years before, and I returned to it for most of my background information. Then I went to Paris with Orla for research (our first trip together), with no real idea of what the story was going to look like. Orla's love for flea markets provided the key.

I threw in a reference to Dachau at the beginning of the first draft, not knowing where I was going with it. It was a bit of background I had appropriated from a friend's father who would talk at length about everything he did in the war except his part in liberating Dachau. Then Orla told me about hearing Paul Fussell on NPR, and his World War II history, *The Boys' Crusade,* provided the final puzzle piece.

It's an amazing feeling to watch a series of coincidences come to feel like the hand of the inevitable.

STUFF OF DREAMS

I wrote this in late 1979, shortly after moving to Austin. It's really a collaboration with John Swann, who'd been a few years behind me in high school, and was living at the time in the big house in front of my garage apartment. He was in pharmacy school, and he provided me with all the background color on med school, the slang, the routines, and, of course, the drugs. It was his idea that the drug would be a virus—all the cool reverse transcriptase stuff is his. Later he would provide invaluable support on my novel *Deserted Cities of the Heart,* which features a peculiar psychotropic mushroom. And a few years after that, John was diagnosed with a brain aneurysm that killed him after a long and painful struggle. I miss his friendship, his creativity, and his great generosity.

When I nervously showed the story to Lisa Tuttle, a fellow Austin writer whose work still dazzles me, she said, "Ed Ferman will buy this." I didn't believe her; Ferman was the editor of *The Magazine of Fantasy and Science Fiction,* the most literary of the SF magazines, and I had thus far failed to impress him. But Lisa was right, and this became my first major SF sale.

My only real regret about the piece is the names of the characters: Matheson after Richard Matheson, a hero of mine since childhood, and Blake after the poet. I suppose I thought I was being clever.

This is one of the few stories of mine that my father ever read. His one comment was, "No medical student would *ever* take drugs!"

THE WAR AT HOME

Shawna McCarthy, then editor of *Asimov's,* said something to me in 1983 about the need for a reimagined SF short-short story, getting away from the contrived twist endings of the pulp days. In fact, Gardner Dozois and Jack Dann had already done it in a beautiful piece of weirdness called "Slow Dancing with Jesus." That story was somewhere in the back of my mind when I put a nightmare I had about Vietnam together with the 1984 San Ysidro McDonald's massacre and came up with what would be my most anthologized story, and the one that got me into the *Norton Book of SF.*

•

STRAWS
I hate the fact that I have to support my writing habit with a day job, and every once in a while I let out a *cri du coeur* like this one.

NINE HARD QUESTIONS ABOUT THE NATURE OF THE UNIVERSE
This started with the idea that aliens in SF stories so often turn out to be disappointingly human. I wondered if I could write some aliens that were both incomprehensible and yet weirdly consistent.

I had the crazy idea that this was going to be the story to break me into the best-of-the-year anthologies and win me award nominations. What was I thinking? SF fans and flying saucer nuts are mortal enemies. And this is hardly a feel-good tale. It did, however, get me a great postcard from John Kessel, whom I'd met the year before at the Chicago World SF Convention, and whose work I admired greatly (and continue to admire, now that we live in the same town and have dinner together as often as we can manage).

WHITE CITY
One of the great injustices in this country is that when people think "inventor," they think "Thomas Edison," even though Edison stole more than he invented and was dead wrong about electricity. He staked his reputation on direct current, and it was Nikola Tesla's alternating current that won the day. But Edison was the better self-publicist, and Tesla was a strange and distant man, whose most amazing experiments only worked when he performed them, making him too much akin to a magician for science to be comfortable with him. The details of this story come from Margaret Cheney's biography, *Tesla: Man Out of Time,* including the invention at the center of it, one that the real Tesla never quite got around to finishing.

PRIMES
Like many of my stories, this started with me stuck in traffic. It seemed like twice as many cars as I had ever seen on I-40 before, and I started to wonder what it would mean if that were literally true. About that time (5:44), the truck with the number 544 painted on the side passed me, and I figured it had to be a sign—though I still don't know of what.

I thought this was going to be a story about overpopulation, but once I started writing it, it turned out to be about racism. I dug deep into some of my worst fears here, and it is still painful for me to read it.

THE LONG RIDE OUT
I wrote the first version of this in 1976. As there was only one market for

Western short fiction at the time, I threw in a mystery element to increase my odds of finding a home for it. The mystery magazines passed, and *Far West* magazine sent it back completely copy-edited for publication (in green felt tip pen), with a form rejection slip that said it "duplicated" material already in their files. This was before the days of decent photocopies, so it was the original that they callously ruined. It's a wonder writers survive this kind of constant, pig-headed abuse. Actually a lot of us don't.

As an exercise, I spent a few weeks in the early 1980s expanding it into a full-length "adult western" novel. This was when I was still trying to sell a novel, any novel, to anybody. This proved not to be that sale.

I wasn't willing to give up on it, though, and I did some minor clean-up on the short story version in 1993 and sent it around again, still with no luck. That's the version that appears here.

My initial idea was to do a twist on the innocent homesteader vs. greedy rancher scenario, and I turned up some loopholes in the Homestead Act to drive the plot. The name "Marlin" was meant to suggest "Marlowe" as much as it possibly could, and Wallace was named for Bill Wallace, one of the best writers in Austin in the 1980s. Bill is one of the ones who gave up trying to get published rather than put up with the insults, and it's a loss to us all. We'll see Bill again later in "The Circle."

SITCOM

If you didn't immediately know that this story was about *The Brady Bunch,* you may be as old as I am. It all started when one of my students at the Clarion West writer's workshop in Seattle in the summer of 1990 turned in an extended *Brady Bunch* inside joke that went completely over my head. I'd heard the name but never seen the show. In the ensuing discussion everyone agreed the show was awful, but they also admitted they had all watched it and that it had powerful iconic status in their memories. When I started toying with the idea of writing about it, I was amazed to discover that I couldn't actually see the show anywhere—it was not in syndication at that point, and these were the dark days before everything in the world was on DVD. The harder I looked, the less there was visible, yet everyone somehow knew everything about it. I started to get a really creepy feeling. Once I combined that with my less than charitable feelings toward US network TV in the first place (see "Stompin' at the Savoy"), I was ready to write.

THE DEATH OF CHE GUEVARA

Bill Schafer asked me to write an original story for the book that he could premiere in his *Subterranean* on-line magazine. I had nothing whatsoever in mind at the time, but within a week this idea showed up at the door, suitcase in hand.

I've been doing research for a couple of years now on the "Dirty War" in Argentina, an era of savage repression by the military dictatorship that ruled between 1976 and 1983. That had led me to an amazing book of interviews with the people who were actually involved with many of the key events in Argentine history between 1955 and 1983, *Lo Pasado Pensado* (roughly, "Considering the Past"), put together by the immensely popular historian Felix Pigna. One section of the book contains interviews with people who were there in 1967 when Che was captured and executed by the Bolivian army (with lots of help from the CIA). That was where I first heard of Che's dreams of returning to his homeland of Argentina to lead a revolution there.

I had always been troubled by Che's image—on the one hand a doctor and a humanitarian, on the other a violent revolutionary and a ruthless killer. I smelled a story, and it took me to Jon Lee Anderson's massive biography, *Che Guevara: A Revolutionary Life,* among other sources. I came away even more ambivalent.

My story departs from historical reality when Tania avoids the ambush that killed her in our reality, and thus is able to save Che. All the characters, names, places, and revolutionary movements I mention are real and historical, with the exception of Veronique—and she is based on a woman Orla and I saw on Calle Defensa in Buenos Aires. (Orla figured out, after I'd decided to use the character in the story, exactly what she was playing and singing.) Che's last words in the story are those attributed to him in Bolivia, though of course the context is different (and the translation my own).

Special thanks to Heather Craige for the insight on Che's executions, and to Carol Stevens for the discussions on capital punishment. The interview format is an homage to Pigna's wonderful book.

HIS GIRLFRIEND'S DOG

This story was inspired by the spare, reverberating fictions of Lydia Davis in her collection *Break It Down,* and by Lisa Tuttle's dog, Quilla June. It was first published as a postcard insert in the independent magazine *New Pathways.* It makes me happy to think that someone might have torn it out and mailed it to a friend somewhere.

DEEP WITHOUT PITY

I've recounted the background to this story at length in the introduction I wrote for the small press book *Private Eye Action As You Like It,* which collected hardboiled detective stories by Joe R. Lansdale and myself. I called the piece

"The Short, Unhappy Career of Lew Shiner, Tough-Guy Writer," and I'll just hit the high points here. When I finished the story in the summer of 1976, I dreamed of being a private eye writer in the mold of Robert B. Parker, Timothy Harris, Arthur Lyons, and other young(ish) turks of the genre. It was not to be. Every time I sold a story featuring Dan Sloane, the magazine died. After poisoning three periodicals (*Mystery Monthly, Mystery,* and *The Saint Mystery Magazine*), I tried a novel, *The Slow Surrender,* which never found a publisher. Shortly after that, William Gibson's "Burning Chrome" showed me how SF could accommodate the kind of writing I wanted to do, and my career went in a different direction.

I still love a good mystery, though my tastes have drifted more to the police procedural and writers like Jess Walter, Barry Maitland, and Mo Hayder.

THE CIRCLE

This is not one of my favorites of my own stories, though it seems to have its fans. It's been in a couple of Halloween anthologies, I had a request to post it on Fiction Liberation Front, and it even got filmed (though never broadcast) for the NBC horror anthology *Fear Itself.*

I did in fact write it for a Halloween gathering like the one described in the story, and all the characters are loosely based on friends who were who were regulars at the readings: Bill and Sally Wallace ("Walter and Susan"), Bruce Sterling ("Brian"), Walton "Bud" Simons and Gilda Ginsel ("Guy and Dana"), and Lisa Tuttle ("Lesley"). It got genuinely creepy once everybody figured out what was going on, and right before the Brian character said that they should burn the manuscript, Bruce (who has never been comfortable with horror fiction) cried out, "Burn the damned thing!"

TWILIGHT TIME

My father was an archeologist for the National Park Service, and I moved constantly as a kid. Until high school, the longest I'd been in any one place was the small town of Globe, Arizona, where I spent third through sixth grade. I loved Arizona—the dry air that smelled of creosote bushes and cottonwood leaves, the big artificial lakes, the rolling hills behind our subdivision. I first started listening to rock and roll on a transistor radio in sixth grade, and went to my first dance at the end of that school year. My father was a rockhound, and we spent a lot of time on the nearby Apache reservation, the biggest source of peridot gemstones on the planet.

Given all that, it's not surprising that I continued to dream about Globe well into adulthood. The image of the two kids standing beside the road came in an unusually vivid dream. When I realized that the setting was Globe in the early

1960s, and stirred in some contemporary music, a flying saucer or two, and my powerful nostalgia for the comics rack at the National Newsstand and the sci-fi movies that I'd watched on Sunday afternoons, I felt I really had something. I refused to give up even when the first version of the story was rejected by every editor in the business. I rewrote it and sent it around again, and this time Shawna McCarthy, the new editor at *Asimov's*, went for it. It made the preliminary Nebula ballot and was my first story to be picked for a best of the year anthology (Gardner Dozois's *Year's Best SF #2*).

This story also features the Xirconian conspiracy that my friend Mike Minzer developed in the early 1970s. Among the hallmarks of this theory are: control of the TV networks by aliens since the 1950s, leisure suits as Xirconian military uniforms, and the substitution of empty form for content as the goal of the invasion. It's a recurring motif in my work (along with the opposition organization YASK, the Youth Awaiting Saucer Kidnap, another Minzer brainstorm) that you can see in "Kings of the Afternoon," "Stompin' at the Savoy," and my novel *Slam*.

JEFF BECK

If there's such a thing as a typical Shiner story, this is it: a magic wish that doesn't work out; a troubled marriage; rock and roll; and a big dose of working-class angst. I don't think there's anything pro forma about it, though, because I pulled all of it either out of my own experience or my own obsessive longing.

My friend Anson Long had the thousand home-recorded cassettes. I'd known him since high school, and we hung out again during my early days in Austin, during which he turned me on to Doug and the Slugs, Jo Jo Zep and the Falcons, and other great bands. And it was Tommy Cox, lead singer of my sixties revival band The Dinosaurs, who worked the Amada punch press.

In the first draft, Felix finds an actual magic lamp in a junk store. Somebody (Bud Simons? My then wife, Edie?) talked me into dropping that in favor of the magic drug. Whatever. I wish I could have dispensed with having to create a wish delivery mechanism over and over (Converse All-Stars in "Tommy and the Talking Dog," the time machine in "Twilight Time") and been able to go straight to the good stuff. Why isn't there a *Magic Wish Comics?* Every month Aladdin's Lamp shows up in a new place and time. Now there's an idea...

WILD FOR YOU

Another traffic story. I used to have to travel between Dallas and Austin—200 miles of the flattest, most boring scenery this side of Death Valley—several times a year. My home and my friends were in Austin, but my parents and my computer job were in Dallas.

This story happened pretty much like I tell it. A red convertible with WILD4U plates passed me as I was leaving Dallas, and I caught up to it in Waco where I swear a different, older woman was behind the wheel, now with a male companion. That was all my allegory engine needed, with nothing better to do for the rest of the drive, to crank out the story.

Let me take this opportunity to say thanks to Robert and Nancy Squyres, who managed to find work for me year after year, even when they could barely feed themselves. They were my personal art patrons, and I will always be grateful.

TILL HUMAN VOICES WAKE US

In the early 1980s I was getting encouraging letters from the fiction editors of both *Playboy* and *Penthouse* (though I've still never sold to either). I tried to think of an idea for a fantasy story that would be sexy enough to go to a men's magazine. Mermaids, I thought. How about a scientifically plausible mermaid? Given that ontogeny recapitulates phylogeny, that is, that a developing fetus basically goes through the history of evolution, she could have gotten hung up in the fish stage.

The rest fell into place by itself. I set the story on Roatan, one of the Bay Islands in Honduras, where I'd been scuba diving with my father. As it turned out, both Lucius Shepard ("Black Coral") and Pat Murphy ("In the Islands") had also set stories on Roatan. I don't know how we avoided being dubbed a "movement."

To make it an even smaller world, Lisa Tuttle had already published a mermaid story called "Till Human Voices Wake Us," which I remembered after I'd already started submitting mine. I would have changed the title to "Between the Windows of the Sea" (quoting Dylan's "Desolation Row") if I'd sent it out again--but *F&SF* bought it before I had the chance.

It's too late to change the title now, as this ended up being one of my most visible stories. As well as appearing in Dozois and Dann's *Mermaids!*, it's in Sterling's much-translated and reprinted *Mirrorshades* and Pat Cadigan's *Ultimate Cyberpunk*.

FLAGSTAFF

The Sunday paper here in Raleigh actually prints short-short fiction by area writers. Because of the 1000-word limit, they frequently use excerpts from longer works, but when editor Peder Zane asked me for a contribution, I wanted to write something specific for him. Failing any other ideas, I did what

I usually do and followed my obsessions. At the time I was being haunted by a memory of an overnight trip we made to Flagstaff one summer. I don't remember the actual reason for the trip—something to do with the Park Service, I'm sure, as we spent our summers at one Indian ruin or another in New Mexico where my father was working. However, the motel, the whiffle ball and bat, the Jules Verne novel, and the Yahtzee dice are all part of that strangely emotional recollection.

TOMMY AND THE TALKING DOG

By 1981 I had entered the most productive phase of my career. I was publishing in *F&SF* regularly, and I'd started selling to a brand new magazine that was absolutely perfect for my sensibility—*The Twilight Zone*. This was a "bedsheet" sized magazine (like *Omni* or *Thrasher*), but printed on pulp paper, like the digests. Under the editorial hand of the fine horror writer T.E.D. "Ted" Klein, the magazine published some really great stories—it was the only magazine I sold to that I read cover to cover every month. Ted liked my work, as he did that of my fellow Texan Joe Lansdale, and both of us got to be regulars—boosting both our careers.

Ted was the best editor I ever worked for. He always asked for changes, and I can't remember any of them I didn't agree with. And in the case of "Tommy and the Talking Dog," he actually wrote the best line in the story. Toward the end, the dog pees on an expensive car—this after much discussion of a treasure that Tommy can't seem to find—and Ted suggested that the drops spatter "like little gold coins." He not only completely understood the story, he gave it a depth and richness it didn't have before.

I should also credit the influence of my bedtime reading from this period, the "Coloured" *Fairy Books* of Andrew Lang.

This story includes the real names of two kids from, and the teacher of, my sixth-grade class in Globe, Arizona. As I was setting type for this project, I got an email from Bobby—now Robert—Cubitto, who'd been tipped off that his name was on Fiction Liberation Front. He also put me in touch with Dickie—now Richard—Benney, my best friend from those days. It was a completely unexpected benefit to get to catch up with both of them. For more about Globe, see "Twilight Time."

OZ

I don't know why I decided one day to conflate Ozzy Osbourne with Lee Harvey Oswald. A trivial idea, and not worth much, except that it provoked my dear friend and mentor Neal Barrett to send me an even shorter alternate universe Kennedy assassination story that featured Jackie Kennedy and flying saucers. We went back and forth a couple of times, each story shorter than the last, then I sent him "The World's Shortest Alternate Universe Kennedy Assassination Story," which consisted of the single word "Missed!" Neal screamed foul—"It means nothing without the title!"—but of course he had to, because otherwise he would have had to admit I had totally kicked his ass.

LOVE IN VAIN

In Austin in the summer of 1987 I read a long and extremely well-written article about the serial killer Henry Lee Lucas (unfortunately I don't remember the name of the magazine or the reporter, though I can remember the look of the pages vividly). Lucas achieved a peculiar fame for his very vocal conversion to Christianity after his arrest, as well as his eagerness to confess to murders he'd never committed. Something about Lucas so repelled me that I couldn't look away.

Once I started writing I couldn't stop, and in a matter of days I had gone through several drafts and had a finished story. I read it at midnight at the North American SF Convention in Phoenix that September, and got a gratifying reaction from the audience.

Gardner Dozois was willing to buy it for *Asimov's*, but convinced me to sell it instead to an original anthology he and his wife, Susan Casper, were putting together about Jack the Ripper. I added one line to make it fit that theme, but after publication decided the story was really better off without it.

It was reprinted in both the *Year's Best SF* and *Year's Best Fantasy* anthologies, and I nearly pulled a hat trick when I sold it to a *Year's Best Mystery and Suspense* book as well—but the story got dropped at the last minute.

During my years in Austin, Bud Simons (see "The Circle") was not just a close friend but a trusted sounding board for my work. His insights into Jack's character were essential to this story.

STEAM ENGINE TIME

This was the first story Joe Lansdale hounded me into writing for him. My concept was simple: What if Elvis had been born 50 years earlier?

Once I'd decided to set a rock and roll story in 1890s Austin, the great stuff started to turn up thick and fast: O. Henry was actually publishing a newspaper there at the time called *The Rolling Stone*. If I wanted a punk haircut for my character, well, they don't call them "Mohawks" for nothing. I found a great book of old photos in the library that provided a wealth of detail, from the Tom Moore cigars and the Crystal Bar to the web of streetcar wires overhead. I even found an old map with the original street names, predating the numbers used on east-west streets today.

Joe and I did go around a bit on the word "fuck." Did people actually say that then? If not, then what? The slang dictionaries said it was around, so we went with it. Whether the Western Writers of America, for whom Joe was editing the anthology, were as sanguine about it, we never heard.

KINGS OF THE AFTERNOON

This comes from 1976, when I was living on Rankin Street in Dallas and holding down a variety of odd jobs. I was pushing hard on the writing, and I had just bought myself a present: a reconditioned IBM Selectric, one of the most beautiful machines ever made. This is the first story I wrote on that new typewriter.

The title is so good I was convinced for days after I came up with it—I was washing dishes at the time, as I remember—that I had stolen it from somewhere, but I couldn't find it. My best guess now is that I had Cordwainer Smith's "The Queen of the Afternoon" somewhere in my subconscious.

On one level it was an answer story to a post-apocalyptic Western by a fellow Dallas writer named Glenn Gillette. Rather than tying up their horses to broken parking meters, I wanted to see cowboys riding motorcycles and big 1950s sedans through the desert.

On another level it was the first of what I think of as "alternate biography" stories (later to include "Jeff Beck" and "Mystery Train"). As well as James Dean in the featured role as Byron (Byron was of course Dean's middle name), I pictured Humphrey Bogart and Marlene Dietrich as co-stars. With Dean's fragile personality at the center, the story forced me to take some emotional risks I never had before.

STICKS

In case it's not obvious enough who inspired this story, her name is coded into the title—something I didn't notice until I'd finished the first draft. I was watching the video for "Stop Draggin' My Heart Around" and thinking what it would have been like if the backing band was not the Heartbreakers, but a bunch of studio musicians who'd gotten lucky.

The emotional core of the story, which is one reason it still means a lot to me, comes from a very short relationship I once had. No, not with a famous LA singer; I changed all the inessential details like characters, setting, and professions.

Stan's Studio City apartment actually belonged to my good friend George R.R. Martin when he was doing a lot of work in Hollywood. He loaned it to me for a week when I was in LA researching *Glimpses* and promoting *Slam*. It later turns up as Laurie Moss's apartment in *Say Goodbye*.

I wrote the first draft of this in the summer of 1982. I sent it everywhere, with no luck, but I couldn't let it go. I rewrote it in 1988 and sent it out, again to no interest. Finally my friend Paul McCauley asked me to contribute to an anthology of SF and fantasy stories with rock music themes that he was editing with Kim Newman. They agreed to take "Sticks," even though it wasn't a genre piece, because they understood the fundamental fantasy that drove it.

THE TALE OF MARK THE BUNNY

I don't have kids of my own, but I like children's stories, especially the brilliant work of Daniel M. Pinkwater (*Lizard Music, The Worms of Kukumlima*). I also like being around animals, whom I tend to anthropomorphize shamelessly.

I was further inspired by Thomas M. Disch, whose "Brave Little Toaster" first appeared in *F&SF*, then was later published as a children's book. I hoped for the same trajectory, but I think the socialist subtext (e.g., Mark and Lenny) was not as subtle as it needed to be.

THE KILLING SEASON

See "Deep Without Pity" for the history of Dan Sloane. I will mention here a story called "Rip Tide," which, if memory serves, I started shortly after this one, though I never wrote more than a few pages of it.

"Rip Tide" was going to be one of those clever problem stories, in this case a kind of "locked pouch" mystery. A guy steals some diamonds, goes into hiding, then surfaces in Sloane's office. He hires Sloane to drive him to Galveston, where he wades into the ocean, carrying the diamonds in a pouch, in front of a hundred witnesses. When the cops fish him out, there's nothing in the sealed pouch but salt water. No evidence—the guy gets off. The diamonds are assumed lost. Months later, the guy shows up trying to steal Sloane's unabridged dictionary. Turns out that after the robbery he traded the diamonds for stamps and had the envelope of stamps laminated. He hid that in the spine of Sloane's dictionary, then took salt crystals into the ocean—where they dissolved into the water.

The problem with problem stories, and the reason I suspect I never finished "Rip Tide," is the lack of an emotional hook. The work of mine that I continue to care about comes from the dark recesses of the right brain, not from the intellectual left.

SCALES

I wrote a paper my senior year at SMU (the unnamed university at which "Scales" is set) on Lilith and the way Philip Jose Farmer had used elements of the myth in his novel *The Lovers*. Given all the research I'd already done, I was bound to write a Lilith story eventually, but Ellen Datlow pushed me to it when she asked me for an original story for her *Alien Sex* anthology.

I had a hard time finding a title, and I was really pleased when I came up with "Scales"—until I realized that I'd stolen it from a brilliant (though unpublished) mermaid story by Nancy Sterling. (See "Till Human Voices Wake Us"—apparently I have a penchant for stealing the titles of mermaid stories by female Austin fantasy writers.) Nancy was kind enough to let me keep it.

SNOWBIRDS

This is a blatant homage to one of my favorite writers, Philip K. Dick. It was also my only sale to *Analog,* the venerable hard SF magazine whose glory days had been overseen by the great John W. Campbell. Managing editor Betsy Mitchell, who later bought my first novel, *Frontera,* had urged me to send her something. She wanted to expand the range of fiction that the magazine published, but it turned out to be a vicious circle. *Analog* readers didn't much care for what I was doing, and I felt I'd squandered one of my best stories where it failed to get any attention. So I went back to *Asimov's* and *F&SF,* and *Analog* went back to what it did best.

It's worth noting that global climate change was already a source of worry when I published this in 1982. Now, more than 25 years later, we still haven't done anything to try to slow it down.

MATCH

I mentioned earlier that I don't have kids. This is why.

RELAY

Many of my stories come from dreams, but this is one of the few that came to me complete, beginning to end. The Philip K. Dick influence is obvious again, both in the cramming of multiple viewpoints into such a short story, and in the concern for the emotions of the characters over the logic of the plot.

CASTLES MADE OF SAND

One of the consolations of art is that when you end up at the wrong sand castle contest, you can turn it into a short story. Surfside was a favorite destination of mine when I lived in Texas, and the setting for my novel *Slam.*

This is one of the more hopeful of my stories, with things turning sweet rather than sour at the end.

PRODIGAL SON

The third and last of the Dan Sloane stories. See "Deep Without Pity" for the history of the series. I used *Carnival* by Arthur H. Lewis, a wonderful book full of slang and tricks of the trade, for background on this one. I was still not over my annoying habit of naming characters for writers; Andy Gresham's last name comes from William Lindsay Gresham, author of the carny novel *Nightmare Alley*.

MOZART IN MIRRORSHADES
In the mid-1980s Bruce Sterling was making a point of collaborating with several other "movement" writers, including Bill Gibson, Rudy Rucker, and me. He approached me with the core idea of the story, using time travel to mine the past as a metaphor for exploitation of the third world. I remember his saying something about cracking towers in eighteenth century Salzburg. I never got around to asking him if he had Mozart in mind when he picked the time and place.

Bruce left me to get things rolling, including the details of viewpoint, characters, and plot. I wrote the opening few pages and showed them to him, and he just shook his head. "No, no, this is all wrong. If these people sit around feeling guilty and sorry for themselves, this will never work. This has to be full throttle all the way."

He was clearly right. With that course correction, I wrote approximately the first half of the story, and Bruce finished it. Then I rewrote the whole thing and then he rewrote it (all on typewriters, of course), and then the real arguments began.

It's always educational to learn that other writers really do write that way on purpose, and that merely showing them the right way is not always enough. Bruce and I each discovered this about the other. We hammered out the final draft on the phone one afternoon and night, pretty much word by word, and once we were speaking to each other again, our friendship seemed hardly damaged by the experience.

KIDDING AROUND
Joe Lansdale and I—among many others—taught at a writing workshop for high school students at Texas A & M in the late 1980s. One of our students was a young woman from Tomball, Texas (a Houston suburb), named Kimberly Rector. Kim was smart, outspoken, and hilarious, and once she started talking about her family, I started taking notes. With her permission, I turned the stuff she told me into this story, though please note that the motivations and "plot" are entirely my own invention.

MYSTERY TRAIN
I love Elvis—the real Elvis, the early Elvis, the needy, jumped-up, rebellious-

but-polite young man who was just beginning to feel the power of his charisma, backed up by standup bass and rockabilly guitar. But something happened between 1958 and 1960: Elvis went into the Army, Chuck Berry got busted under the Mann Act, Buddy Holly crashed into a snow-covered cornfield, and guys like Fabian and Frankie Avalon took over the charts. Coincidence or conspiracy? Well, I answer that question with another: *Quo bono?*

I was still trying to break into the men's slicks, and I sort of did with this one. I sold it to *Oui*, which at one time had been a European-style spinoff from *Playboy*. Unfortunately the name had been sold to a much sleazier outfit in the meantime. The upside was that they didn't ask me to back off on using the names of real—and powerful—men in the entertainment industry.

As I remember, it was Bruce Sterling who suggested the Fisher King imagery at the end. For that and much more, this story is dedicated to him.

SECRETS

I started with the image of someone releasing blood from their eyes into the bathroom sink, and it seemed a very pure moment of otherness. The Russians call it *ostranyenye*—the moment when the familiar becomes strange. I wasn't interested in the mechanism or what sort of creature Michael was, which is why I suppose I'm not really a science fiction writer.

GOLFING VIETNAM

I was staying at a bed and breakfast in Wilmington, North Carolina, and there were a bunch of kids in their 20s there for a wedding. I ended up talking to one of them, who told me about the Australian tour and a whole world of second-tier professional golf that I knew nothing about. A few months later I ended up at another wedding of 20-somethings, this time in Dallas.

That was enough to start me writing, but I still didn't have an ending. Then, one afternoon, as I was jogging through a park near my house, I found a $20 bill. The moral dilemma hit me immediately. If I put up a sign that said FOUND $20 BILL there would be no way to be sure that the real owner claimed it. And almost immediately I saw that I had discovered not only free money, but the ending to my story.

STOMPIN' AT THE SAVOY

This is a classic clean-out-the-notebook story—all the weird little notions that had accumulated over a period of months or years, dumped into a blender. In this case, I also threw in my favorite knock-knock jokes and a big dollop of Subgenius mythos (www.subgenius.com). I went to high school with the founder of the cult and had been a card-carrying member for years when I wrote the story.

I wrote it for the Turkey City Workshop in Austin, and I confess that it was mostly aimed at Bruce Sterling. Bruce tended to work me over pretty thoroughly and wanted to see if just once I could deliberately push his buttons. It worked, and I had a good time doing it.

The title is hard to explain. It's from a favorite swing era song, and it seemed to me to conjure the ultimate night of fun on the town. Used here ironically, of course. I might have been willing to change it, but no one seemed to notice that it didn't make much sense.

GOLD

I'd already written a "punk western" story for one of his anthologies (see "Steam Engine Time"), but Joe Lansdale wasn't satisfied, and he almost immediately came back wanting another. I told him I didn't have one, but that trick doesn't work with Joe.

My friend Tim Powers had just published a terrific pirate novel, *On Stranger Tides,* and that clicked with the fact that the infamous Jean Lafitte had once had his base of operations on Galveston Island, one of my favorite day-trips from Austin. I'd taken a tour of the historical homes on the island and picked up some tidbits about how people had lived in the nineteenth century. Put the two together, and what you get is not exactly gunfights and outlaws, but it is Texas and the right time period.

The blowfish business came from Wade Davis's *The Serpent and the Rainbow,* and I got the financial history from *Samuel May Williams: Early Texas Entrepreneur* by Margaret Swett Henson. Gary Cartwright's excellent *Galveston: A History of the Island* was another invaluable reference. I cobbled together the Lafitte lore, including the golden thimble, from multiple sources that I found at the library.

DIRTY WORK

During the time I was writing the Dan Sloane stories (see "Deep Without Pity"), I had it in the back of my mind to write something I thought of as "The Last Dan Sloane story." It would have shown Sloane becoming so disillusioned during the investigation of a rape case that he gave up and got another job.

When Joe Lansdale refused to take "maybe" or "later" for an answer on his *Dark at Heart* anthology in 1990, that last Dan Sloane story was the only suspense idea that spoke to me. I didn't want to write about Sloane anymore, but when I rethought it in terms of another protagonist, I came up with "Dirty Work," which turned out to be one of my favorites of my own stories.

Some of the details in this story came from a friend who was raped, then stalked by a thug working for the rapist's lawyer. My thanks to her for her courage in speaking up about it.

LIZARD MEN OF LOS ANGELES

I had somehow grown to an advanced age without ever hearing the word *chupacabra* ("goat sucker"), a vampiric creature of Southwestern folk tales. In looking up *chupacabra* on the Internet, I stumbled upon the whole world of cryptids: creatures of myth and folklore including *yeti*, the Loch Ness monster, and lizard men.

Alarm bells went off in my head, and I printed a number of Web pages that talked about the giant lizard-shaped cavern under the city of LA, the associated Native American legends, and the mysterious death of Warren Shufelt. It was still fermenting there when Joe Lansdale called again, this time wanting something for an anthology of pulp stories.

I carefully explained that I didn't write pulp stories, and Joe said "fine" and called the next week and asked again. And the week after. Then every couple of days.

The truth is, there are a number of pulp writers whose work I love, from H. P. Lovecraft to Robert E. Howard to Edgar Rice Burroughs. And the lizard men were perfect for a pulp story, as Shufelt's search for their tunnels took place during the height of the pulp era.

I've loved the idea of caves since reading the Hardy Boys novels and Cave Carson comics as a kid. I've been fascinated by stage magic and magicians like Houdini for at least as long. Once I realized that Joe had hooked me again, I started reaching for more recent obsessions, like spontaneous human combustion (SHC to its students) and Aleister Crowley.

I tried to find a style that would suggest pulp without drifting too far into actual bad writing. And I wanted to bring a modern, compassionate sensibility to the story that would not be anachronistic. Once I came up with Johnny Cairo and Mrs. Lockhart, the story began writing itself.

A few inside jokes: Crowley is staying at the Gamble House in Pasadena, a place Jim Blaylock had taken me to visit. Gamble (of Proctor and Gamble fame) was rumored to be an occultist because of the crescent and star P&G logo. Hassan was inspired by the Chuck Jones cartoon "Ali Baba Bunny" ("Hassan chop!"). At one point a policeman comes through the door with a gun in his hand, deliberately echoing Chandler's advice on how to pick up a dragging story line.

Ironically, after I had sent the story to Joe, he ended up cancelling the contract for the book. I took it back and sold it to *F&SF,* where it was the cover story (my first ever in an anthology or magazine), though the artist inexplicably ignored all the fabulous pulp tribute possibilities and instead showed Cairo (dressed as Indiana Jones) and Mrs. Lockhart merely walking down the street.

A few months later, Joe called again. The pulp anthology was back on. Yes, he understood I'd already sold "Lizard Men" elsewhere. How about writing him a new one?

I can't tell you exactly why, but this is my favorite of all the stories I've ever written.

COPYRIGHTS

"Twilight Time" is © 1984 by Davis Publications, Inc. First published in *Isaac Asimov's SF Magazine,* April, 1984.

"Jeff Beck" is © 1986 by Davis Publications, Inc. First published in *Isaac Asimov's SF Magazine,* January 1986.

"Wild for You" is © 1990 by Lewis Shiner. First published in *Isaac Asimov's SF Magazine,* December, 1990.

"Till Human Voices Wake Us" is © 1984 by Mercury Press, Inc. First published in *The Magazine of Fantasy and Science Fiction,* May, 1984.

"Flagstaff" is © 1998 by The News and Observer. First published in *The Raleigh News and Observer,* December 27, 1998.

"Tommy and the Talking Dog" is © 1982 by TZ Publications, Inc. First published in *The Twilight Zone,* July, 1982.

"Oz" is © 1988 by Lewis Shiner. First published in *Full Spectrum,* 1988.

"Love in Vain" is © 1988 by Gardner Dozois and Susan Casper. First published in *Jack the Ripper,* September, 1988.

"Steam Engine Time" is © 1989 by The Western Writers of America. First published in *Best of the West 2,* May, 1989.

"Kings of the Afternoon" is © 1980 by Flight Unlimited, Inc. First published in *Shayol,* Winter, 1980.

"Sticks" is © 1992 by Lewis Shiner. First published in *In Dreams,* Spring, 1992.

"The Tale of Mark the Bunny" is © 1999 by Lewis Shiner. First published on Lewis-Shiner.com, September, 1999.

"The Killing Season" is © 1998 by Lewis Shiner. First published in *Private Eye Action As You Like It,* July, 1998.

"Scales" is © 1990 by Lewis Shiner. First published in *Alien Sex,* May, 1990.

"Snowbirds" is © 1982 by Davis Publications, Inc. First published in *Analog,* November, 1982.

"Match" is © 1990 by Stephen F. Austin State University. First published in *RE:AL,* Fall, 1990.

"Relay" is © 1991 by Lewis Shiner. First published in *The Edges of Things,* 1991.